A PENGUIN MYSTERY

THE CORNELL WOOLRICH OMNIBUS

Cornell Woolrich was born in 1903. He began writing fiction while at Columbia University in the 1920s, and went on in the '30s and '40s to become, along with Raymond Chandler and James M. Cain, one of the creators of the *noir* genre, producing such classics as *Rear Window*, *I Married a Dead Man*, and the so-called Black Series of suspense novels. Woolrich died a recluse in 1968.

THE CORNELL WOOLRICH OMNIBUS

Rear Window and Other Stories
I Married a Dead Man
Waltz into Darkness

PENGUIN BOOKS

PENGUIN BOOKS
Published by the Penguin Group
Penguin Books USA Inc., 375 Hudson Street,
New York, New York 10014, U.S.A.
Penguin Books Ltd, 27 Wrights Lane,
London W8 5TZ, England
Penguin Books Australia Ltd, Ringwood,
Victoria, Australia
Penguin Books Canada Ltd, 10 Alcorn Avenue,
Toronto, Ontario, Canada M4V 3B2
Penguin Books (N.Z.) Ltd, 182–190 Wairau Road,
Auckland 10, New Zealand

Penguin Books Ltd, Registered Offices:
Harmondsworth, Middlesex, England

This volume first published in Penguin Books 1998

3   5   7   9   10   8   6   4   2

Rear Window and Other Stories first published in
the United States of America by Ballantine Books 1984
Published in Penguin Books 1994
Copyright © Sheldon Abend D/B/A Authors Research Company, 1984
All rights reserved

I Married a Dead Man first published in
the United States of America by J. B. Lippincott Company 1948
Published in Penguin Books 1994
Copyright William Irish, 1948
Copyright assigned to Sheldon Abend D/B/A Authors Research Company, 1982
All rights reserved

Waltz into Darkness first published in
the United States of America by J. P. Lippincott Company 1947
Published in Penguin Books 1995
Copyright William Irish, 1947
Copyright renewed Chase Manhattan Bank as Executor, 1974
Copyright thereafter assigned to
Sheldon Abend D/B/A Authors Research Company
All rights reserved

LIBRARY OF CONGRESS CATALOGING IN PUBLICATION DATA
Woolrich, Cornell, 1903–1968.
The Cornell Woolrich omnibus.
p.   cm.
Contents: Rear window and other stories—I married a dead man—
Waltz into darkness.
ISBN 0 14 02.6977 0
1. Detective and mystery stories, American.   I. Title.
PS3515.06455A6   1998
813'.52—dc21   97–18114

Printed in the United States of America
Set in Old Style 7
Designed by Sabrina Bowers

Contents

REAR WINDOW AND OTHER STORIES
1

Rear Window
5

Post-Mortem
37

Three O'Clock
65

Change of Murder
93

Momentum
113

I MARRIED A DEAD MAN
143

WALTZ INTO DARKNESS
319

REAR WINDOW

AND OTHER STORIES

This book is dedicated to Peter J. Anderson, Esq. of Santa Monica, California who picked up the baton involuntarily dropped by Mel Nimmer, Esq. (due to his untimely death), my original attorney in the landmark copyright case that commenced in 1983 and culminated on April 24, 1990 with the United States Supreme Court decision of six-to-three in favor of Sheldon Abend. This decision affected, to their benefit, tens of thousands of widows and heirs throughout the world. Peter proved himself to be another David, as the opponents were MCA, Universal Studios, the Estate of Alfred Hitchcock, Jimmy Stewart, et al. and the Amicus briefs filed by every major motion picture studio except Walt Disney, who apparently thought otherwise. Our hat's off to Irwin Karp, Esq., Herbert Jacoby, Esq., Barbara Ringer, Esq., Ralph Oman, Esq., present Register of Copyrights of the U.S. Copyright Office, and the Songwriters Guild of America, all of whom filed Amicus briefs in support of Sheldon Abend's position in the *Rear Window* case; and Robert E. Ossanna; and Zsuzsa Molnar and her late mother Margit Molnar.

—Sheldon Abend a/k/a Buffalo Bill

Rear Window

I DIDN'T know their names. I'd never heard their voices. I didn't even know them by sight, strictly speaking, for their faces were too small to fill in with identifiable features at that distance. Yet I could have constructed a timetable of their comings and goings, their daily habits and activities. They were the rear-window dwellers around me.

Sure, I suppose it *was* a little bit like prying, could even have been mistaken for the fevered concentration of a Peeping Tom. That wasn't my fault, that wasn't the idea. The idea was, my movements were strictly limited just around this time. I could get from the window to the bed, and from the bed to the window, and that was all. The bay window was about the best feature my rear bedroom had in the warm weather. It was unscreened, so I had to sit with the light out or I would have had every insect in the vicinity in on me. I couldn't sleep, because I was used to getting plenty of exercise. I'd never acquired the habit of reading books to ward off boredom, so I hadn't that to turn to. Well, what should I do, sit there with my eyes tightly shuttered?

Just to pick a few at random: Straight over, and the windows square, there was a young jitter-couple, kids in their teens, only just married. It would have killed them to stay home one night. They were always in such a hurry to go, wherever it was they went, they never remembered to turn out the lights. I don't think it missed once in all the time I was watching. But they never forgot altogether, either. I was to learn to call this delayed action, as you will see. He'd always come skittering madly back in about five minutes, probably from all the way down in the street, and rush around killing the switches. Then fall over something in the dark on his way out. They gave me an inward chuckle, those two.

The next house down, the windows already narrowed a little with perspective. There was a certain light in that one that always went out each night too. Something about it, it used to make me a little sad. There was a woman living there with her child, a young widow

I suppose. I'd see her put the child to bed, and then bend over and kiss her in a wistful sort of way. She'd shade the light off her and sit there painting her eyes and mouth. Then she'd go out. She'd never come back till the night was nearly spent. Once I was still up, and I looked and she was sitting there motionless with her head buried in her arms. Something about it, it used to make me a little sad.

The third one down no longer offered any insight, the windows were just slits like in a medieval battlement, due to foreshortening. That brings us around to the one on the end. In that one, frontal vision came back full-depth again, since it stood at right angles to the rest, my own included, sealing up the inner hollow all these houses backed on. I could see into it, from the rounded projection of my bay window, as freely as into a doll house with its rear wall sliced away. And scaled down to about the same size.

It was a flat building. Unlike all the rest it had been constructed originally as such, not just cut up into furnished rooms. It topped them by two stories and had rear fire escapes, to show for this distinction. But it was old, evidently hadn't shown a profit. It was in the process of being modernized. Instead of clearing the entire building while the work was going on, they were doing it a flat at a time, in order to lose as little rental income as possible. Of the six rearward flats it offered to view, the topmost one had already been completed, but not yet rented. They were working on the fifth-floor one now, disturbing the peace of everyone all up and down the "inside" of the block with their hammering and sawing.

I felt sorry for the couple in the flat below. I used to wonder how they stood it with that bedlam going on above their heads. To make it worse the wife was in chronic poor health, too; I could tell that even at a distance by the listless way she moved about over there, and remained in her bathrobe without dressing. Sometimes I'd see her sitting by the window, holding her head. I used to wonder why he didn't have a doctor in to look her over, but maybe they couldn't afford it. He seemed to be out of work. Often their bedroom light was on late at night behind the drawn shade, as though she were unwell and he was sitting up with her. And one night in particular he must have had to sit up with her all night, it remained on until nearly daybreak. Not that I sat watching all that time. But the light was still burning at three in the morning, when I finally transferred from chair to bed to see if I could get a little sleep myself. And when

I failed to, and hopscotched back again around dawn, it was still peering wanly out behind the tan shade.

Moments later, with the first brightening of day, it suddenly dimmed around the edges of the shade, and then shortly afterward, not that one, but a shade in one of the other rooms—for all of them alike had been down—went up, and I saw him standing there looking out.

He was holding a cigarette in his hand. I couldn't see it, but I could tell it was that by the quick, nervous little jerks with which he kept putting his hand to his mouth, and the haze I saw rising around his head. Worried about her, I guess. I didn't blame him for that. Any husband would have been. She must have only just dropped off to sleep, after night-long suffering. And then in another hour or so, at the most, that sawing of wood and clattering of buckets was going to start in over them again. Well, it wasn't any of my business, I said to myself, but he really ought to get her out of there. If I had an ill wife on my hands. . . .

He was leaning slightly out, maybe an inch past the window frame, carefully scanning the back faces of all the houses abutting on the hollow square that lay before him. You can tell, even at a distance, when a person is looking fixedly. There's something about the way the head is held. And yet his scrutiny wasn't held fixedly to any one point, it was a slow, sweeping one, moving along the houses on the opposite side from me first. When it got to the end of them, I knew it would cross over to my side and come back along there. Before it did, I withdrew several yards inside my room, to let it go safely by. I didn't want him to think I was sitting there prying into his affairs. There was still enough blue night-shade in my room to keep my slight withdrawal from catching his eye.

When I returned to my original position a moment or two later, he was gone. He had raised two more of the shades. The bedroom one was still down. I wondered vaguely why he had given that peculiar, comprehensive, semicircular stare at all the rear windows around him. There wasn't anyone at any of them, at such an hour. It wasn't important, of course. It was just a little oddity, it failed to blend in with his being worried or disturbed about his wife. When you're worried or disturbed, that's an internal preoccupation, you stare vacantly at nothing at all. When you stare around you in a great sweeping arc at windows, that betrays external preoccupation, outward interest. One doesn't quite jibe with the other. To call such a discrepancy trifling is to add to its importance. Only someone like me, stewing in a vacuum of total idleness, would have noticed it at all.

The flat remained lifeless after that, as far as could be judged by its windows. He must have either gone out or gone to bed himself. Three of the shades remained at normal height, the one masking the bedroom remained down. Sam, my day houseman, came in not long after with my eggs and morning paper, and I had that to kill time with for awhile. I stopped thinking about other people's windows and staring at them.

The sun slanted down on one side of the hollow oblong all morning long, then it shifted over to the other side for the afternoon. Then it started to slip off both alike, and it was evening again—another day gone.

The lights started to come on around the quadrangle. Here and there a wall played back, like a sounding board, a snatch of radio program that was coming in too loud. If you listened carefully you could hear an occasional click of dishes mixed in, faint, far off. The chain of little habits that were their lives unreeled themselves. They were all bound in them tighter than the tightest straitjacket any jailer ever devised, though they all thought themselves free. The jitterbugs made their nightly dash for the great open spaces, forgot their lights, he came careening back, thumbed them out, and their place was dark until the early morning hours. The woman put her child to bed, leaned mournfully over its cot, then sat down with heavy despair to redden her mouth.

In the fourth-floor flat at right angles to the long, interior "street" the three shades had remained up, and the fourth shade had remained at full length, all day long. I hadn't been conscious of that because I hadn't particularly been looking at it, or thinking of it, until now. My eyes may have rested on those windows at times, during the day, but my thoughts had been elsewhere. It was only when a light suddenly went up in the end room behind one of the raised shades, which was their kitchen, that I realized that the shades had been untouched like that all day. That also brought something else to my mind that hadn't been in it until now: I hadn't seen the woman all day. I hadn't seen any sign of life within those windows until now.

He'd come in from outside. The entrance was at the opposite side of their kitchen, away from the window. He'd left his hat on, so I knew he'd just come in from the outside.

He didn't remove his hat. As though there was no one there to remove it for any more. Instead, he pushed it farther to the back of his head by pronging a hand to the roots of his hair. That gesture didn't denote removal of perspiration, I knew. To do that a person makes a sidewise sweep—this was up over his forehead. It indicated some sort of harassment or uncertainty. Besides, if he'd been suffering from excess warmth, the first thing he would have done would be to take off his hat altogether.

She didn't come out to greet him. The first link, of the so-strong chain of habits, of custom, that binds us all, had snapped wide open.

She must be so ill she had remained in bed, in the room behind the lowered shade, all day. I watched. He remained where he was, two rooms away from there. Expectancy became surprise, surprise incomprehension. Funny, I thought, that he doesn't go in to her. Or at least go as far as the doorway, look in to see how she is.

Maybe she was asleep, and he didn't want to disturb her. Then immediately: but how can he know for sure that she's asleep, without at least looking in at her? He just came in himself.

He came forward and stood there by the window, as he had at dawn. Sam had carried out my tray quite some time before, and my lights were out. I held my ground, I knew he couldn't see me within the darkness of the bay window. He stood there motionless for several minutes. And now his attitude was the proper one for inner preoccupation. He stood there looking downward at nothing, lost in thought.

He's worried about her, I said to myself, as any man would be. It's the most natural thing in the world. Funny, though, he should leave her in the dark like that, without going near her. If he's worried, then why didn't he at least look in on her on returning? Here was another of those trivial discrepancies, between inward motivation and outward indication. And just as I was thinking that, the original one, that I had noted at daybreak, repeated itself. His head went up with renewed alertness, and I could see it start to give that slow circular sweep of interrogation around the panorama of rearward windows again. True, the light was behind him this time, but there was enough of it falling on him to show me the microscopic but continuous shift of direction his head made in the process. I remained carefully immobile until the distant glance had passed me safely by. Motion attracts.

Why is he so interested in other people's windows, I wondered detachedly. And of course an effective brake to dwell on that thought too lingeringly clamped down almost at once: Look who's talking. What about you yourself?

An important difference escaped me. I wasn't worried about anything. He, presumably, was.

Down came the shades again. The lights stayed on behind their beige opaqueness. But behind the one that had remained down all along, the room remained dark.

Time went by. Hard to say how much—a quarter of an hour, twenty minutes. A cricket chirped in one of the back yards. Sam came in to see if I wanted anything before he went home for the night. I told him no, I didn't—it was all right, run along. He stood there for a minute, head down. Then I saw him shake it slightly, as if at something he didn't like. "What's the matter?" I asked.

"You know what that means? My old mammy told it to me, and she never told me a lie in her life. I never once seen it to miss, either."

"What, the cricket?"

"Any time you hear one of them things, that's a sign of death—someplace close around."

I swept the back of my hand at him. "Well, it isn't in here, so don't let it worry you."

He went out, muttering stubbornly: "It's somewhere close by, though. Somewhere not very far off. Got to be."

The door closed after him, and I stayed there alone in the dark.

It was a stifling night, much closer than the one before. I could hardly get a breath of air even by the open window at which I sat. I wondered how he—that unknown over there—could stand it behind those drawn shades.

Then suddenly, just as idle speculation about this whole matter was about to alight on some fixed point in my mind, crystallize into something like suspicion, up came the shades again, and off it flitted, as formless as ever and without having had a chance to come to rest on anything.

He was in the middle windows, the living room. He'd taken off his coat and shirt, was bare-armed in his undershirt. He hadn't been able to stand it himself, I guess—the sultriness.

I couldn't make out what he was doing at first. He seemed to be busy in a perpendicular, up-and-down way rather than lengthwise. He remained in one place, but he kept dipping down out of sight and then straightening up into view again, at irregular intervals. It was almost like some sort of calisthenic exercise, except that the dips and rises weren't evenly timed enough for that. Sometimes he'd stay down a long time, sometimes he'd bob right up again, sometimes he'd go down two or three times in rapid succession. There was some sort of a widespread black V railing him off from the window. Whatever it was, there was just a sliver of it showing above the upward inclination to which the window still deflected my line of vision. All it did was strike off the bottom of his undershirt, to the extent of a sixteenth of an inch maybe. But I haven't seen it there at other times, and I couldn't tell what it was.

Suddenly he left it for the first time since the shades had gone up, came out around it to the outside, stooped down into another part of the room, and straightened again with an armful of what looked like varicolored pennants at the distance at which I was. He went back behind the V and allowed them to fall across the top of it for a moment, and stay that way. He made one of his dips down out of sight and stayed that way a good while.

The "pennants" slung across the V kept changing color right in front of my eyes. I have very good sight. One moment they were white, the next red, the next blue.

Then I got it. They were a woman's dresses, and he was pulling them down to him one by one, taking the topmost one each time. Suddenly they were all gone, the V was black and bare again, and his torso had reappeared. I knew what it was now, and what he was doing. The dresses had told me. He confirmed it for me. He spread his arms to the ends of the V, I could see him heave and hitch, as if exerting pressure, and suddenly the V had folded up, become a cubed wedge. Then he made rolling motions with his whole upper body, and the wedge disappeared off to one side.

He'd been packing a trunk, packing his wife's things into a large upright trunk.

He reappeared at the kitchen window presently, stood still for a moment. I saw him draw his arm across his forehead, not once but several times, and then whip the end of it off into space. Sure, it was hot work for such a night. Then he reached up along the wall and took something down. Since it was the kitchen he was in, my imagination had to supply a cabinet and a bottle.

I could see the two or three quick passes his hand made to his mouth after that. I said to myself tolerantly: That's what nine men out of ten would do after packing a trunk—take a good stiff drink. And if the tenth didn't, it would only be because he didn't have any liquor at hand.

Then he came closer to the window again, and standing edgewise to the side of it, so that only a thin paring of his head and shoulder showed, peered watchfully out into the dark quadrilateral, along the line of windows, most of them unlighted by now, once more. He always started on the left-hand side, the side opposite mine, and made his circuit of inspection from there on around.

That was the second time in one evening I'd seen him do that. And once at daybreak, made three times altogether. I smiled mentally. You'd almost think he felt guilty about something. It was probably nothing, just an odd little habit, a quirk, that he didn't know he had himself. I had them myself, everyone does.

He withdrew into the room, and it blacked out. His figure passed into the one that was still lighted next to it, the living room. That blacked next. It didn't surprise me that the third room, the bedroom with the drawn shade, didn't light up on his entering there. He wouldn't want to disturb her, of course—particularly if she was going away tomorrow for her health, as his packing of her trunk showed. She needed all the rest she could get, before making the trip. Simple enough for him to slip into bed in the dark.

It did surprise me, though, when a match-flare winked some time later, to have it still come from the darkened living room. He must be lying down in there, trying to sleep on a sofa or something for the night. He hadn't gone near the bedroom at all, was staying out of it altogether. That puzzled me, frankly. That was carrying solicitude almost too far.

Ten minutes or so later, there was another matchwink, still from that same living room window. He couldn't sleep.

The night brooded down on both of us alike, the curiosity-monger in the bay window, the chain-smoker in the fourth-floor flat, without giving any answer. The only sound was that interminable cricket.

I was back at the window again with the first sun of morning. Not because of him. My mattress was like a bed of hot coals. Sam found me there when he came in to get things ready for me. "You're going to be a wreck, Mr. Jeff," was all he said.

First, for awhile, there was no sign of life over there. Then suddenly I saw his head bob up from somewhere down out of sight in the living room, so I knew I'd been right; he'd spent the night on a sofa or easy chair in there. Now, of course, he'd look in at her, to see how she was, find out if she felt any better. That was only common ordinary humanity. He hadn't been near her, so far as I could make out, since two nights before.

He didn't. He dressed, and he went in the opposite direction, into the kitchen, and wolfed something in there, standing up and using both hands. Then he suddenly turned and moved off side, in the direction in which I knew the flat-entrance to be, as if he had just heard some summons, like the doorbell.

Sure enough, in a moment he came back, and there were two men with him in leather aprons. Expressmen. I saw him standing by while they laboriously maneuvered that cubed black wedge out between them, in the direction they'd just come from. He did more than just stand by. He practically hovered over them, kept shifting from side to side, he was so anxious to see that it was done right.

Then he came back alone, and I saw him swipe his arm across his head, as though it was he, not they, who was all heated up from the effort.

So he was forwarding her trunk, to wherever it was she was going. That was all.

He reached up along the wall again and took something down. He was taking another drink. Two. Three. I said to myself, a little at a loss: Yes, but he hasn't just packed a trunk this time. That trunk has been standing packed and ready since last night. Where does the hard work come in? The sweat and the need for a bracer?

Now, at last, after all those hours, he finally did go in to her. I saw his form pass through the living room and go beyond, into the bedroom. Up went the shade, that had been down all this time. Then he turned his head and looked around behind him. In a certain way, a way that was unmistakable, even from where I was. Not in one certain direction, as one looks at a person. But from side to side, and up and down, and all around, as one looks at—*an empty room*.

He stepped back, bent a little, gave a fling of his arms, and an unoccupied mattress and bedding upended over the foot of a bed, stayed that way, emptily curved. A second one followed a moment later.

She wasn't in there.

They use the expression "delayed action." I found out then what it meant. For two days a sort of formless uneasiness, a disembodied suspicion, I don't know what to call it, had been flitting and vol-planing around in my mind, like an insect looking for a landing place. More than once, just as it had been ready to settle, some slight thing, some slight reassuring thing, such as the raising of the shades after they had been down unnaturally long, had been enough to keep it winging aimlessly, prevent it from staying still long enough for me to recognize it. The point of contact had been there all along, waiting to receive it. Now, for some reason, within a split second after he tossed over the empty mattresses, it landed—*zoom!* And the point of contact expanded—or exploded, whatever you care to call it—into a certainty of murder.

In other words, the rational part of my mind was far behind the instinctive, subconscious part. Delayed action. Now the one had caught up to the other. The thought-message that sparked from the synchronization was: He's done something to her!

I looked down and my hand was bunching the goods over my kneecap, it was knotted so tight. I forced it to open. I said to myself, steadyingly: Now wait a minute, be careful, go slow. You've seen nothing. You know nothing. You only have the negative proof that you don't see her any more.

Sam was standing there looking over at me from the pantryway. He said accusingly: "You ain't touched a thing. And your face looks like a sheet."

It felt like one. It had that needling feeling, when the blood has left it involuntarily. It was more to get him out of the way and give myself some elbow room for undisturbed thinking, than anything else, that I said: "Sam, what's the street address of that building down there? Don't stick your head too far out and gape at it."

"Somep'n or other Benedict Avenue." He scratched his neck helpfully.

"I know that. Chase around the corner a minute and get me the exact number on it, will you?"

"Why you want to know that for?" he asked as he turned to go.

"None of your business," I said with the good-natured firmness that was all that was necessary to take care of that once and for all. I called after him just as he was closing the door: "And while you're about it, step into the entrance and see if you can tell from the mail-boxes who has the fourth-floor rear. Don't get me the wrong one now. And try not to let anyone catch you at it."

He went out mumbling something that sounded like, "When a man ain't got nothing to do but just sit all day, he sure can think up the blamest things——" The door closed and I settled down to some good constructive thinking.

I said to myself: What are you really building up this monstrous supposition on? Let's see what you've got. Only that there were several little things wrong with the mechanism, the chain-belt, of their recurrent daily habits over there. 1. The lights were on all night the first night. 2. He came in later than usual the second night. 3. He left his hat on. 4. She didn't come out to greet him—she hasn't appeared since the evening before the lights were on all night. 5. He took a drink after he finished packing her trunk. But he took three stiff drinks the next morning, immediately after her trunk went out. 6. He was inwardly disturbed and worried, yet superimposed upon this was an unnatural external concern about the surrounding rear windows that was off-key. 7. He slept in the living room, didn't go near the bedroom, during the night before the departure of the trunk.

Very well. If she had been ill that first night, and he had sent her away for her health, that automatically canceled out points 1, 2, 3, 4. It left points 5 and 6 totally unimportant and unincriminating. But when it came up against 7, I hit a stumbling block.

If she went away immediately after being ill that first night, why didn't he want to sleep in their bedroom *last night?* Sentiment? Hardly. Two perfectly good beds in one room, only a sofa or uncomfortable easy chair in the other. Why should he stay out of there if she was already gone? Just because he missed her, was lonely? A grown man doesn't act that way. All right, then she was still in there.

Sam came back parenthetically at this point and said: "That house is Number 525 Benedict Avenue. The fourth-floor rear, it got the name of Mr. and Mrs. Lars Thorwald up."

"Sh-h," I silenced, and motioned him backhand out of my ken.

"First he wants it, then he don't," he grumbled philosophically, and retired to his duties.

I went ahead digging at it. But if she was still in there, in that bedroom last night, then she couldn't have gone away to the country, because I never saw her leave today. She could have left without my seeing her in the early hours of yesterday morning. I'd missed a few hours, been asleep. But this morning I had been up before he was himself, I only saw his head rear up from the sofa after I'd been at the window for some time.

To go at all she would have had to go yesterday morning. Then why had he left the bedroom shade down, left the mattresses undisturbed, until today? Above all, why had he stayed out of that room last night? That was evidence that she hadn't gone, was still in there. Then today, immediately after the trunk had been dispatched, he went in, pulled up the shade, tossed over the mattresses, and showed that she hadn't been in there. The thing was like a crazy spiral.

No, it wasn't either. *Immediately after the trunk had been dispatched*——

The trunk.

That did it.

I looked around to make sure the door was safely closed between Sam and me. My hand hovered uncertainly over the telephone dial a minute. Boyne, he'd be the one to tell about it. He was on Homicide. He had been, anyway, when I'd last seen him. I didn't want to get a flock of strange dicks and cops into my hair. I didn't want to be involved any more than I had to. Or at all, if possible.

They switched my call to the right place after a couple of wrong tries, and I got him finally.

"Look, Boyne? This is Hal Jeffries——"

"Well, where've you been the last sixty-two years?" he started to enthuse.

"We can take that up later. What I want you to do now is take down a name and address. Ready? Lars Thorwald. Five twenty-five Benedict Avenue. Fourth-floor rear. Got it?"

"Fourth-floor rear. Got it. What's it for?"

"Investigation. I've got a firm belief you'll uncover a murder there if you start digging at it. Don't call on me for anything more than that—just a conviction. There's been a man and wife living there until now. Now there's just the man. Her trunk went out early this morning. If you can find someone who saw *her* leave herself——"

Marshaled aloud like that and conveyed to somebody else, a lieutenant of detectives above all, it did sound flimsy, even to me. He said hesitantly, "Well, but——" Then he accepted it as was. Because I was the source. I even left my window out of it completely. I could do that with him and get away with it because he'd known me years, he didn't question my reliability. I didn't want my room all cluttered up with dicks and cops taking turns nosing out of the window in this hot weather. Let them tackle it from the front.

"Well, we'll see what we see," he said. "I'll keep you posted."

I hung up and sat back to watch and wait events. I had a grandstand seat. Or rather a grandstand seat in reverse. I could only see from behind the scenes, but not from the front. I couldn't watch Boyne go to work. I could only see the results, when and if there were any.

Nothing happened for the next few hours. The police work that I knew must be going on was as invisible as police work should be. The figure in the fourth-floor windows over there remained in sight, alone and undisturbed. He didn't go out. He was restless, roamed from room to room without staying in one place very long, but he stayed in. Once I saw him eating again—sitting down this time— and once he shaved, and once he even tried to read the paper, but he didn't stay with it long.

Little unseen wheels were in motion around him. Small and harmless as yet, preliminaries. If he knew, I wondered to myself, would he remain there quiescent like that, or would he try to bolt out and flee? That mightn't depend so much upon his guilt as upon his sense of immunity, his feeling that he could outwit them. Of his guilt I myself was already convinced, or I wouldn't have taken the step I had.

At three my phone rang. Boyne calling back. "Jeffries? Well, I don't know. Can't you give me a little more than just a bald statement like that?"

"Why?" I fenced. "Why do I have to?"

"I've had a man over there making inquiries. I've just had his report. The building superintendent and several of the neighbors all agree she left for the country, to try and regain her health, early yesterday morning."

"Wait a minute. Did any of them *see* her leave, according to your man?"

"No."

"Then all you've gotten is a second-hand version of an unsupported statement by him. Not an eyewitness account."

"He was met returning from the depot, after he'd bought her ticket and seen her off on the train."

"That's still an unsupported statement, once removed."

"I've sent a man down there to the station to try and check with the ticket agent if possible. After all, he should have been fairly conspicuous at that early hour. And we're keeping him under observation, of course, in the meantime, watching all his movements. The first chance we get we're going to jump in and search the place."

I had a feeling that they wouldn't find anything, even if they did.

"Don't expect anything more from me. I've dropped it in your lap. I've given you all I have to give. A name, an address, and an opinion."

"Yes, and I've always valued your opinion highly before now, Jeff——"

"But now you don't, that it?"

"Not at all. The thing is, we haven't turned up anything that seems to bear out your impression so far."

"You haven't gotten very far along, so far."

He went back to his previous cliché. "Well, we'll see what we see. Let you know later."

Another hour or so went by, and sunset came on. I saw him start to get ready to go out, over there. He put on his hat, put his hand in his pocket and stood still looking at it for a minute. Counting change, I guess. It gave me a peculiar sense of suppressed excitement, knowing they were going to come in the minute he left. I thought grimly, as I saw him take a last look around: If you've got anything to hide, brother, now's the time to hide it.

He left. A breath-holding interval of misleading emptiness descended on the flat. A three-alarm fire couldn't have pulled my eyes off those windows. Suddenly the door by which he had just left parted slightly and two men insinuated themselves, one behind the other. There they were now. They closed it behind them, separated at once, and got busy. One took the bedroom, one the kitchen, and they started to work their way toward one another again from those extremes of the flat. They were thorough. I could see them going over everything from top to bottom. They took the living room together. One cased one side, the other man the other.

They'd already finished before the warning caught them. I could tell that by the way they straightened up and stood facing one another frustratedly for a minute. Then both their heads turned sharply, as at a tip-off by doorbell that he was coming back. They got out fast.

I wasn't unduly disheartened, I'd expected that. My own feeling all along had been that they wouldn't find anything incriminating around. The trunk had gone.

He came in with a mountainous brown-paper bag sitting in the curve of one arm. I watched him closely to see if he'd discover that someone had been there in his absence. Apparently he didn't. They'd been adroit about it.

He stayed in the rest of the night. Sat tight, safe and sound. He did some desultory drinking, I could see him sitting there by the window and his hand would hoist every once in awhile, but not to excess. Apparently everything was under control, the tension had eased, now that that—the trunk was out.

Watching him across the night, I speculated: Why doesn't he get out? If I'm right about him, and I am, why does he stick around—after it? That brought its own answer: Because he doesn't know anyone's on to him yet. He doesn't think there's any hurry. To go too soon, right after she has, would be more dangerous than to stay awhile.

The night wore on. I sat there waiting for Boyne's call. It came later than I thought it would. I picked the phone up in the dark. He was getting ready to go to bed, over there, now. He'd risen from where he'd been sitting drinking in the kitchen, and put the light out. He went into the living room, lit that. He started to pull his shirttail up out of his belt. Boyne's voice was in my ear as my eyes were on him, over there. Three-cornered arrangement.

"Hello, Jeff? Listen, absolutely nothing. We searched the place while he was out——"

I nearly said, "I know you did, I saw it," but checked myself in time.

"—and didn't turn up a thing. But——" He stopped as though this was going to be important. I waited impatiently for him to go ahead.

"Downstairs in his letter box we found a post card waiting for him. We fished it up out of the slot with bent pins——"

"And?"

"And it was from his wife, written only yesterday from some farm up-country. Here's the message we copied: 'Arrived O. K. Already feeling a little better. Love, Anna.' "

I said, faintly but stubbornly: "You say, written only yesterday. Have you proof of that? What was the postmark-date on it?"

He made a disgusted sound down in his tonsils. At me, not it. "The postmark was blurred. A corner of it got wet, and the ink smudged."

"All of it blurred?"

"The year-date," he admitted. "The hour and the month came out O. K. August. And seven thirty P.M., it was mailed at."

This time I made the disgusted sound, in my larynx. "August, seven thirty P.M.—1937 or 1939 or 1942. You have no proof how it got into that mail box, whether it came from a letter carrier's pouch or from the back of some bureau drawer!"

"Give up, Jeff," he said. "There's such a thing as going too far."

I don't know what I would have said. That is, if I hadn't happened to have my eyes on the Thorwald flat living room windows just then. Probably very little. The post card *had* shaken me, whether I admitted it or not. But I was looking over there. The light had gone out as soon as he'd taken his shirt off. But the bedroom didn't light up. A match-flare winked from the living room, low down, as from an easy chair or sofa. With two unused beds in the bedroom, he was *still staying out of there.*

"Boyne," I said in a glassy voice, "I don't care what post cards from the other world you've turned up, I say that man has done away with his wife! Trace that trunk he shipped out. Open it up when you've located it—and I think you'll find her!"

And I hung up without waiting to hear what he was going to do about it. He didn't ring back, so I suspected he was going to give my suggestion a spin after all, in spite of his loudly proclaimed skepticism.

I stayed there by the window all night, keeping a sort of death-watch. There were two more match-flares after the first, at about half-hour intervals. Nothing more after that. So possibly he was asleep over there. Possibly not. I had to sleep some myself, and I finally succumbed in the flaming light of the early sun. Anything that he was going to do, he would have done under cover of darkness and not waited for broad daylight. There wouldn't be anything much to watch, for a while now. And what was there that he needed to do any more, anyway? Nothing, just sit tight and let a little disarming time slip by.

It seemed like five minutes later that Sam came over and touched me, but it was already high noon. I said irritably: "Didn't you lamp that note I pinned up, for you to let me sleep?"

He said: "Yeah, but it's your old friend Inspector Boyne. I figured you'd sure want to——"

It was a personal visit this time. Boyne came into the room behind him without waiting, and without much cordiality.

I said to get rid of Sam: "Go inside and smack a couple of eggs together."

Boyne began in a galvanized-iron voice: "Jeff, what do you mean by doing anything like this to me? I've made a fool out of myself thanks to you. Sending my men out right and left on wild-goose chases. Thank God, I didn't put my foot in it any worse than I did, and have this guy picked up and brought in for questioning."

"Oh, then you don't think that's necessary?" I suggested, dryly.

The look he gave me took care of that. "I'm not alone in the department, you know. There are men over me I'm accountable to for my actions. That looks great, don't it, sending one of my fellows one-half-a-day's train ride up into the sticks to some God-forsaken whistle-stop or other at departmental expense——"

"Then you located the trunk?"

"We traced it through the express agency," he said flintily.

"And you opened it?"

"We did better than that. We got in touch with the various farm-houses in the immediate locality, and Mrs. Thornwald came down to the junction in a produce-truck from one of them and opened it for him herself, with her own keys!"

Very few men have ever gotten a look from an old friend such as I got from him. At the door he said, stiff as a rifle barrel: "Just let's forget all about it, shall we? That's about the kindest thing either one of us can do for the other. You're not yourself, and I'm out a little of my own pocket money, time and temper. Let's let it go at that. If you want to telephone me in future I'll be glad to give you my home number."

The door went *whopp!* behind him.

For about ten minutes after he stormed out my numbed mind was in a sort of straitjacket. Then it started to wriggle its way free. The hell with the police. I can't prove it to them, maybe, but I can prove it to myself, one way or the other, once and for all. Either I'm wrong or I'm right. He's got his armor on against them. But his back is naked and unprotected against me.

I called Sam in. "Whatever became of that spyglass we used to have, when we were bumming around on that cabin-cruiser that season?"

He found it some place downstairs and came in with it, blowing on it and rubbing it along his sleeve. I let it lie idle in my lap first. I took a piece of paper and a pencil and wrote six words on it: *What have you done with her?*

I sealed it in an envelope and left the envelope blank. I said to Sam: "Now here's what I want you to do, and I want you to be slick about it. You take this, go in that building 525, climb the stairs to the fourth-floor rear, and ease it under the door. You're fast, at least you used to be. Let's see if you're fast enough to keep from being caught at it. Then when you get safely down again, give the outside doorbell a little poke, to attract attention."

His mouth started to open.

"And don't ask me any questions, you understand? I'm not fooling."

He went, and I got the spyglass ready.

I got him in the right focus after a minute or two. A face leaped up, and I was really seeing him for the first time. Dark-haired, but unmistakable Scandinavian ancestry. Looked like a sinewy customer, although he didn't run to much bulk.

About five minutes went by. His head turned sharply, profile-wards. That was the bell-poke, right there. The note must be in already.

He gave me the back of his head as he went back toward the flat-door. The lens could follow him all the way to the rear, where my unaided eyes hadn't been able to before.

He opened the door first, missed seeing it, looked out on a level. He closed it. Then dipped, straightened up. He had it. I could see him turning it this way and that.

He shifted in, away from the door, nearer the window. He thought danger lay near the door, safety away from it. He didn't know it was the other way around, the deeper into his own rooms he retreated the greater the danger.

He'd torn it open, he was reading it. God, how I watched his expression. My eyes clung to it like leeches. There was a sudden widening, a pulling—the whole skin of his face seemed to stretch back behind the ears, narrowing his eyes to Mongoloids. Shock. Panic. His hand pushed out and found the wall, and he braced himself with it. Then he went back toward the door again slowly. I could see him creeping up on it, stalking it as though it were something alive. He opened it so slenderly you couldn't see it at all, peered fearfully through the crack. Then he closed it, and he came back, zigzag, off balance from sheer reflex dismay. He toppled into a chair and snatched up a drink. Out of the bottle neck itself this time. And even while he was holding it to his lips, his head was turned looking over his shoulder at the door that had suddenly thrown his secret in his face.

I put the glass down.

Guilty! Guilty as all hell, and the police be damned!

My hand started toward the phone, came back again. What was the use? They wouldn't listen now any more than they had before. "You should have seen his face, etc." And I could hear Boyne's answer: "Anyone gets a jolt from an anonymous letter, true or false. You would yourself." They had a real live Mrs. Thorwald to show me—or thought they had. I'd have to show them the dead one, to prove that they both weren't one and the same. I, from my window, had to show them a body.

Well, he'd have to show me first.

It took hours before I got it. I kept pegging away at it, pegging away at it, while the afternoon wore away. Meanwhile he was pacing back and forth there like a caged panther. Two minds with but one thought, turned inside-out in my case. How to keep it hidden, how to see that it wasn't kept hidden.

I was afraid he might try to light out, but if he intended doing that he was going to wait until after dark, apparently, so I had a little time yet. Possibly he didn't want to himself, unless he was driven to it—still felt that it was more dangerous than to stay.

The customary sights and sounds around me went on unnoticed, while the main stream of my thoughts pounded like a torrent against that one obstacle stubbornly damming them up: how to get him to give the location away to me, so that I could give it away in turn to the police.

I was dimly conscious, I remember, of the landlord or somebody bringing in a prospective tenant to look at the sixth-floor apartment, the one that had already been finished. This was two over Thorwald's; they were still at work on the in-between one. At one point an odd little bit of synchronization, completely accidental of course, cropped up. Landlord and tenant both happened to be near the living room windows on the sixth at the same moment that Thorwald was near those on the fourth. Both parties moved onward simultaneously into the kitchen from there, and, passing the blind spot of the wall, appeared next at the kitchen windows. It was uncanny, they were almost like precision-strollers or puppets manipulated on one and the same string. It probably wouldn't have happened again just like that in another fifty years. Immediately afterwards they digressed, never to repeat themselves like that again.

The thing was, something about it had disturbed me. There had been some slight flaw or hitch to mar its smoothness. I tried for a moment or two to figure out what it had been, and couldn't. The landlord and tenant had gone now, and only Thorwald was in sight. My unaided memory wasn't enough to recapture it for me. My eyesight might have if it had been repeated, but it wasn't.

It sank into my subconscious, to ferment there like yeast, while I went back to the main problem at hand.

I got it finally. It was well after dark, but I finally hit on a way. It mightn't work, it was cumbersome and roundabout, but it was the only way I could think of. An alarmed turn of the head, a quick precautionary step in one certain direction, was all I needed. And to get this brief, flickering, transitory give-away, I needed two phone calls and an absence of about half an hour on his part between them.

I leafed a directory by matchlight until I'd found what I wanted: *Thorwald, Lars. 525 Bndct. . . . SWansea 5-2114.*

I blew out the match, picked up the phone in the dark. It was like television. I could see to the other end of my call, only not along the wire but by a direct channel of vision from window to window.

He said "Hullo?" gruffly.

I thought: How strange this is. I've been accusing him of murder for three days straight, and only now I'm hearing his voice for the first time.

I didn't try to disguise my own voice. After all, he'd never see me and I'd never see him. I said: "You got my note?"

He said guardedly: "Who is this?"

"Just somebody who happens to know."

He said craftily: "Know what?"

"Know what you know. You and I, we're the only ones."

He controlled himself well. I didn't hear a sound. But he didn't know he was open another way too. I had the glass balanced there at proper height on two large books on the sill. Through the window I saw him pull open the collar of his shirt as though its stricture was intolerable. Then he backed his hand over his eyes like you do when there's a light blinding you.

His voice came back firmly. "I don't know what you're talking about."

"Business, that's what I'm talking about. It should be worth something to me, shouldn't it? To keep it from going any further." I wanted to keep him from catching on that it was the windows. I still needed them, I needed them now more than ever. "You weren't very careful about your door the other night. Or maybe the draft swung it open a little."

That hit him where he lived. Even the stomach-heave reached me over the wire. "You didn't see anything. There wasn't anything to see."

"That's up to you. Why should I go to the police?" I coughed a little. "If it would pay me not to."

"Oh," he said. And there was relief of a sort in it. "D'you want to—see me? Is that it?"

"That would be the best way, wouldn't it? How much can you bring with you for now?"

"I've only got about seventy dollars around here."

"All right, then we can arrange the rest for later. Do you know where Lakeside Park is? I'm near there now. Suppose we make it there." That was about thirty minutes away. Fifteen there and fifteen back. "There's a little pavilion as you go in."

"How many of you are there?" he asked cautiously.

"Just me. It pays to keep things to yourself. That way you don't have to divvy up."

He seemed to like that too. "I'll take a run out," he said, "just to see what it's all about."

I watched him more closely than ever, after he'd hung up. He flitted straight through to the end room, the bedroom, that he didn't go near any more. He disappeared into a clothes-closet in there, stayed a minute, came out again. He must have taken something out of a hidden cranny or niche in there that even the dicks had missed. I could tell by the piston-like motion of his hand, just before it disappeared inside his coat, what it was. A gun.

It's a good thing, I thought, I'm not out there in Lakeside Park waiting for my seventy dollars.

The place blacked and he was on his way.

I called Sam in. "I want you to do something for me that's a little risky. In fact, damn risky. You might break a leg, or you might get shot, or you might even get pinched. We've been together ten years, and I wouldn't ask you anything like that if I could do it myself. But I can't, and it's got to be done." Then I told him. "Go out the back way, cross the back yard fences, and see if you can get into that fourth-floor flat up the fire escape. He's left one of the windows down a little from the top."

"What do you want me to look for?"

"Nothing." The police had been there already, so what was the good of that? "There are three rooms over there. I want you to disturb everything just a little bit, in all three, to show someone's been in there. Turn up the edge of each rug a little, shift every chair and table around a little, leave the closet doors standing out. Don't pass up a thing. Here, keep your eyes on this." I took off my own wrist watch, strapped it on him. "You've got twenty-five minutes, starting from now. If you stay within those twenty-five minutes, nothing will happen to you. When you see they're up, don't wait any longer, get out and get out fast."

"Climb back down?"

"No." He wouldn't remember, in his excitement, if he'd left the windows up or not. And I didn't want him to connect danger with the back of his place, but with the front. I wanted to keep my own window out of it. "Latch the window down tight, let yourself out the door, and beat it out of the building the front way, for your life!"

"I'm just an easy mark for you," he said ruefully, but he went.

He came out through our own basement door below me, and scrambled over the fences. If anyone had challenged him from one of the surrounding windows, I was going to backstop for him, explain I'd sent him down to look for something. But no one did. He made it pretty good for anyone his age. He isn't so young any more. Even the fire escape backing the flat, which was drawn up short, he managed to contact by standing up on something. He got in, lit the light, looked over at me. I motioned him to go ahead, not weaken.

I watched him at it. There wasn't any way I could protect him, now that he was in there. Even Thorwald would be within his rights in shooting him down—this was break and entry. I had to stay in back behind the scenes, like I had been all along. I couldn't get out in front of him as a lookout and shield him. Even the dicks had had a lookout posted.

He must have been tense, doing it. I was twice as tense, watching him do it. The twenty-five minutes took fifty to go by. Finally he came over to the window, latched it fast. The lights went, and he was out. He'd made it. I blew out a bellyful of breath that was twenty-five minutes old.

I heard him keying the street door, and when he came up I said warningly: "Leave the light out in here. Go and build yourself a great big two-story whisky punch; you're as close to white as you'll ever be."

Thorwald came back twenty-nine minutes after he'd left for Lakeside Park. A pretty slim margin to hang a man's life on. So now for the finale of the long-winded business, and here was hoping. I got my second phone call in before he had time to notice anything amiss. It was tricky timing but I'd been sitting there with the receiver ready in my hand, dialing the number over and over, then killing it each time. He came in on the 2 of 5-2114, and I saved that much time. The ring started before his hand came away from the light switch.

This was the one that was going to tell the story.

"You were supposed to bring money, not a gun; that's why I didn't show up." I saw the jolt that threw him. The window still had to stay out of it. "I saw you tap the inside of your coat, where you had it, as you came out on the street." Maybe he hadn't, but he wouldn't remember by now whether he had or not. You usually do when you're packing a gun and aren't an habitual carrier.

"Too bad you had your trip out and back for nothing. I didn't waste my time while you were gone, though. I know more now than I knew before." This was the important part. I had the glass up and I was practically fluoroscoping him. "I've found out where—it is. You know what I mean. I know now where you've got—it. I was there while you were out."

Not a word. Just quick breathing.

"Don't you believe me? Look around. Put the receiver down and take a look for yourself. I found it."

He put it down, moved as far as the living room entrance, and touched off the lights. He just looked around him once, in a sweeping, all-embracing stare, that didn't come to a head on any one fixed point, didn't center at all.

He was smiling grimly when he came back to the phone. All he said, softly and with malignant satisfaction, was: "You're a liar."

Then I saw him lay the receiver down and take his hand off it. I hung up at my end.

The test had failed. And yet it hadn't. He hadn't given the location away as I'd hoped he would. And yet that "You're a liar" was a tacit admission that it was there to be found, somewhere around him, somewhere on those premises. In such a good place that he didn't have to worry about it, didn't even have to look to make sure.

So there was a kind of sterile victory in my defeat. But it wasn't worth a damn to me.

He was standing there with his back to me, and I couldn't see what he was doing. I knew the phone was somewhere in front of him, but I thought he was just standing there pensive behind it. His head was slightly lowered, that was all. I'd hung up at my end. I didn't even see his elbow move. And if his index finger did, I couldn't see it.

He stood like that a moment or two, then finally he moved aside. The lights went out over there; I lost him. He was careful not even to strike matches, like he sometimes did in the dark.

My mind no longer distracted by having him to look at, I turned to trying to recapture something else—that troublesome little hitch in synchronization that had occurred this afternoon, when the renting agent and he both moved simultaneously from one window to the next. The closest I could get was this: it was like when you're looking at someone through a pane of imperfect glass, and a flaw in the glass distorts the symmetry of the reflected image for a second, until it has gone on past that point. Yet that wouldn't do, that was not it. The windows had been open and there had been no glass between. And I hadn't been using the lens at the time.

My phone rang. Boyne, I supposed. It wouldn't be anyone else at this hour. Maybe, after reflecting on the way he'd jumped all over me—I said "Hello" unguardedly, in my own normal voice.

There wasn't any answer.

I said: "Hello? Hello? Hello?" I kept giving away samples of my voice.

There wasn't a sound from first to last.

I hung up finally. It was still dark over there, I noticed.

Sam looked in to check out. He was a bit thick-tongued from his restorative drink. He said something about "Awri' if I go now?" I half heard him. I was trying to figure out another way of trapping *him* over there into giving away the right spot. I motioned my consent absently.

He went a little unsteadily down the stairs to the ground floor and after a delaying moment or two I heard the street door close after him. Poor Sam, he wasn't much used to liquor.

I was left alone in the house, one chair the limit of my freedom of movement.

Suddenly a light went on over there again, just momentarily, to go right out again afterwards. He must have needed it for something, to locate something that he had already been looking for and found he wasn't able to put his hands on readily without it. He found it, whatever it was, almost immediately, and moved back at once to put the lights out again. As he turned to do so, I saw him give a glance out the window. He didn't come to the window to do it, he just shot it out in passing.

Something about it struck me as different from any of the others I'd seen him give in all the time I'd been watching him. If you can qualify such an elusive thing as a glance, I would have termed it a glance with a purpose. It was certainly anything but vacant or random, it had a bright spark of fixity in it. It wasn't one of those precautionary sweeps I'd seen him give, either. It hadn't started over on the other side and worked its way around to my side, the right. It had hit dead-center at my bay window, for just a split second while it lasted, and then was gone again. And the lights were gone, and he was gone.

Sometimes your senses take things in without your mind translating them into their proper meaning. My eyes saw that look. My mind refused to smelter it properly. "It was meaningless," I thought. "An unintentional bull's-eye, that just happened to hit square over here, as he went toward the lights on his way out."

Delayed action. A wordless ring of the phone. To test a voice? A period of bated darkness following that, in which two could have played at the same game—stalking one another's window-squares, unseen. A last-moment flicker of the lights, that was bad strategy but unavoidable. A parting glance, radioactive with malignant intention. All these things sank in without fusing. My eyes did their job, it was my mind that didn't—or at least took its time about it.

Seconds went by in packages of sixty. It was very still around the familiar quadrangle formed by the back of the houses. Sort of a breathless stillness. And then a sound came into it, starting up from nowhere, nothing. The unmistakable, spaced clicking a cricket makes in the silence of the night. I thought of Sam's superstition about them, that he claimed had never failed to fulfill itself yet. If that was the case, it looked bad for somebody in one of these slumbering houses around here——

Sam had been gone only about ten minutes. And now he was back again, he must have forgotten something. That drink was responsible. Maybe his hat, or maybe even the key to his own quarters uptown. He knew I couldn't come down and let him in, and he was trying to be quiet about it, thinking perhaps I'd dozed off. All I could hear was this faint jiggling down at the lock of the front door. It was one of those old-fashioned stoop houses, with an outer pair of storm doors that were allowed to swing free all night, and then a small vestibule, and then the inner door, worked by a simple iron key. The liquor had made his hand a little unreliable, although he'd had this difficulty once or twice before, even without it. A match would have helped him find the keyhole quicker, but then, Sam doesn't smoke. I knew he wasn't likely to have one on him.

The sound had stopped now. He must have given up, gone away again, decided to let whatever it was go until tomorrow. He hadn't gotten in, because I knew his noisy way of letting doors coast shut by themselves too well, and there hadn't been any sound of that sort, that loose slap he always made.

Then suddenly it exploded. Why at this particular moment, I don't know. That was some mystery of the inner workings of my own mind. It flashed like waiting gunpowder which a spark has finally reached along a slow train. Drove all thoughts of Sam, and the front door, and this and that completely out of my head. It had been waiting there since midafternoon today, and only now——More of that delayed action. Damn that delayed action.

The renting agent and Thorwald had both started even from the living room window. An intervening gap of blind wall, and both had reappeared at the kitchen window, still one above the other. But some sort of a hitch or flaw or jump had taken place, right there, that bothered me. The eye is a reliable surveyor. There wasn't anything the matter with their timing, it was with their parallel-ness, or whatever the word is. The hitch had been vertical, not horizontal. There had been an upward "jump."

Now I had it, now I knew. And it couldn't wait. It was too good. They wanted a body? Now I had one for them.

Sore or not, Boyne would *have* to listen to me now. I didn't waste any time, I dialed his precinct-house then and there in the dark, working the slots in my lap by memory alone. They didn't make much noise going around, just a light click. Not even as distinct as that cricket out there——

"He went home long ago," the desk sergeant said.

This couldn't wait. "All right, give me his home phone number."

He took a minute, came back again. "Trafalgar," he said. Then nothing more.

"Well? Trafalgar what?" Not a sound.

"Hello? Hello?" I tapped it. "Operator, I've been cut off. Give me that party again." I couldn't get her either.

I hadn't been cut off. My wire had been cut. That had been too sudden, right in the middle of——And to be cut like that it would have to be done somewhere right here inside the house with me. Outside it went underground.

Delayed action. This time final, fatal, altogether too late. A voiceless ring of the phone. A direction-finder of a look from over there. "Sam" seemingly trying to get back in a while ago.

Suddenly, death was somewhere inside the house here with me.
And I couldn't move, I couldn't get up out of this chair. Even if I
had gotten through to Boyne just now, that would have been too
late. There wasn't time enough now for one of those camera-finishes
in this. I could have shouted out the window to that gallery of sleeping rear-window neighbors around me, I supposed. It would have
brought them to the windows. It couldn't have brought them over
here in time. By the time they had even figured which particular
house it was coming from, it would stop again, be over with. I didn't
open my mouth. Not because I was brave, but because it was so
obviously useless.

He'd be up in a minute. He must be on the stairs now, although
I couldn't hear him. Not even a creak. A creak would have been a relief, would have placed him. This was like being shut up in the dark
with the silence of a gliding, coiling cobra somewhere around you.

There wasn't a weapon in the place with me. There were books
there on the wall, in the dark, within reach. Me, who never read.
The former owner's books. There was a bust of Rousseau or Mon-
tesquieu, I'd never been able to decide which, one of those gents with
flowing manes, topping them. It was a monstrosity, bisque clay, but
it too dated from before my occupancy.

I arched my middle upward from the chair seat and clawed desperately up at it. Twice my fingertips slipped off it, then at the third
raking I got it to teeter, and the fourth brought it down into my lap,
pushing me down into the chair. There was a steamer rug under me.
I didn't need it around me in this weather, I'd been using it to soften
the seat of the chair. I tugged it out from under and mantled it
around me like an Indian brave's blanket. Then I squirmed far down
in the chair, let my head and one shoulder dangle out over the arm,
on the side next to the wall. I hoisted the bust to my other, upward
shoulder, balanced it there precariously for a second head, blanket
tucked around its ears. From the back, in the dark, it would look—
I hoped——

I proceeded to breathe adenoidally, like someone in heavy upright
sleep. It wasn't hard. My own breath was coming nearly that labored
anyway, from tension.

He was good with knobs and hinges and things. I never heard the
door open, and this one, unlike the one downstairs, was right behind
me. A little eddy of air puffed through the dark at me. I could feel

it because my scalp, the real one, was all wet at the roots of the hair right then.

If it was going to be a knife or head-blow, the dodge might give me a second chance, that was the most I could hope for, I knew. My arms and shoulders are hefty. I'd bring him down on me in a bear-hug after the first slash or drive, and break his neck or collarbone against me. If it was going to be a gun, he'd get me anyway in the end. A difference of a few seconds. He had a gun, I knew, that he was going to use on me in the open, over at Lakeside Park. I was hoping that here, indoors, in order to make his own escape more practicable——

Time was up.

The flash of the shot lit up the room for a second, it was so dark. Or at least the corners of it, like flickering, weak lightning. The bust bounced on my shoulder and disintegrated into chunks.

I thought he was jumping up and down on the floor for a minute with frustrated rage. Then when I saw him dart by me and lean over the window sill to look for a way out, the sound transferred itself rearwards and downwards, became a pummeling with hoof and hip at the street door. The camera-finish after all. But he still could have killed me five times.

I flung my body down into the narrow crevice between chair arm and wall, but my legs were still up, and so was my head and that one shoulder.

He whirled, fired at me so close that it was like looking at sunrise in the face. I didn't feel it, so—it hadn't hit.

"You——" I heard him grunt to himself. I think it was the last thing he said. The rest of his life was all action, not verbal.

He flung over the sill on one arm and dropped into the yard. Two-story drop. He made it because he missed the cement, landed on the sod-strip in the middle. I jacked myself up over the chair arm and flung myself bodily forward at the window, neatly hitting it chin first.

He went all right. When life depends on it, you go. He took the first fence, rolled over that bellywards. He went over the second like a cat, hands and feet pointed together in a spring. Then he was back in the rear yard of his own building. He got up on something, just about like Sam had——The rest was all footwork, with quick little corkscrew twists at each landing stage. Sam had latched his windows down when he was over there, but he'd reopened one of them for ventilation on his return. His whole life depended now on that casual, unthinking little act——

Second, third. He was up to his own windows. He'd made it. Something went wrong. He veered out away from them in another pretzel-twist, flashed up toward the fifth, the one above. Something sparked in the darkness of one of his own windows where he'd been just now, and a shot thudded heavily out around the quadrangle-enclosure like a big bass drum.

He passed the fifth, the sixth, got to the roof. He'd made it a second time. Gee, he loved life! The guys in his own windows couldn't get him, he was over them in a straight line and there was too much fire escape interlacing in the way.

I was too busy watching him to watch what was going on around me. Suddenly Boyne was next to me, sighting. I heard him mutter: "I almost hate to do this, he's got to fall so far."

He was balanced on the roof parapet up there, with a star right over his head. An unlucky star. He stayed a minute too long, trying to kill before he was killed. Or maybe he was killed, and knew it.

A shot cracked, high up against the sky, the window pane flew apart all over the two of us, and one of the books snapped right behind me.

Boyne didn't say anything more about hating to do it. My face was pressing outward against his arm. The recoil of his elbow jarred my teeth. I blew a clearing through the smoke to watch him go.

It was pretty horrible. He took a minute to show anything, standing up there on the parapet. Then he let his gun go, as if to say: "I won't need this any more." Then he went after it. He missed the fire escape entirely, came all the way down on the outside. He landed so far out he hit one of the projecting planks, down there out of sight. It bounced his body up, like a springboard. Then it landed again—for good. And that was all.

I said to Boyne: "I got it. I got it finally. The fifth-floor flat, the one over his, that they're still working on. The cement kitchen floor, raised above the level of the other rooms. They wanted to comply with the fire laws and also obtain a dropped living room effect, as cheaply as possible. Dig it up——"

He went right over then and there, down through the basement and over the fences, to save time. The electricity wasn't turned on yet in that one, they had to use their torches. It didn't take them long at that, once they'd got started. In about half an hour he came to the window and wigwagged over for my benefit. It meant yes.

He didn't come over until nearly eight in the morning; after they'd tidied up and taken them away. Both away, the hot dead and the cold dead. He said: "Jeff, I take it all back. That damn fool that I sent up there about the trunk—well, it wasn't his fault, in a way. I'm to blame. He didn't have orders to check on the woman's description, only on the contents of the trunk. He came back and touched on it in a general way. I go home and I'm in bed already, and suddenly pop! into my brain—one of the tenants I questioned two whole days ago had given us a few details and they didn't tally with his on several important points. Talk about being slow to catch on!"

"I've had that all the way through this damn thing," I admitted ruefully. "I called it delayed action. It nearly killed me."

"I'm a police officer and you're not."

"That how you happened to shine at the right time?"

"Sure. We came over to pick him up for questioning. I left them planted there when we saw he wasn't in, and came on over here by myself to square it up with you while we were waiting. How did you happen to hit on that cement floor?"

I told him about the freak synchronization. "The renting agent showed up taller at the kitchen window in proportion to Thorwald, than he had been a moment before when both were at the living room windows together. It was no secret that they were putting in cement floors, topped by a cork composition, and raising them considerably. But it took on new meaning. Since the top floor one has been finished for some time, it had to be the fifth. Here's the way I have it lined up, just in theory. She's been in ill health for years, and he's been out of work, and he got sick of that and of her both. Met this other——"

"She'll be here later today, they're bringing her down under arrest."

"He probably insured her for all he could get, and then started to poison her slowly, trying not to leave any trace. I imagine—and remember, this is pure conjecture—she caught him at it that night the light was on all night. Caught on in some way, or caught him in the act. He lost his head, and did the very thing he had wanted all along to avoid doing. Killed her by violence—strangulation or a blow. The rest had to be hastily improvised. He got a better break than he deserved at that. He thought of the apartment upstairs, went up and looked around. They'd just finished laying the floor, the cement hadn't hardened yet, and the materials were still around. He gouged a trough out of it just wide enough to take her body, put her in it, mixed fresh cement and recemented over her, possibly raising the general level of the floor an inch or two so that she'd be safely covered. A permanent, odorless coffin. Next day the workmen came back, laid down the cork surfacing on top of it without noticing anything, I suppose he'd used one of their own trowels to smooth it. Then he sent his accessory upstate fast, near where his wife had been several summers before, but to a different farmhouse where she wouldn't be recognized, along with the trunk keys. Sent the trunk up after her, and dropped himself an already used post card into his mailbox, with the year-date blurred. In a week or two she would have probably committed 'suicide' up there as Mrs. Anna Thorwald. Despondency due to ill health. Written him a farewell note and left her clothes beside some body of deep water. It was risky, but they might have succeeded in collecting the insurance at that."

By nine Boyne and the rest had gone. I was still sitting there in the chair, too keyed up to sleep. Sam came in and said: "Here's Doc Preston."

He showed up rubbing his hands, in that way he has. "Guess we can take that cast off your leg now. You must be tired of sitting there all day doing nothing."

Post-Mortem

THE WOMAN wondered who they were and what they wanted out there at this time of the day. She knew they couldn't be salesmen, because salesmen don't travel around in threes. She put down her mop, wiped her hands nervously on her apron, started for the door.

What could be wrong? Nothing had happened to Stephen, had it? She was trembling with agitation and her face was pale under its light golden tan by the time she had opened the door and stood confronting them. They all had white cards stuck in their hat bands, she noticed.

They crowded eagerly forward, each one trying to edge the others aside. "Mrs. Mead?" the foremost one said.

"Wha-what is it?" she quavered.

"Have you been listening to your radio?"

"No, one of the tubes burned out."

She saw them exchange zestful glances. "She hasn't heard yet!" Their spokesman went on: "We've got good news for you!"

She was still as frightened as ever. "Good news?" she repeated timidly.

"Yes. Can't you guess?"

"N-no."

They kept prolonging the suspense unendurably. "You know what day this is, don't you?"

She shook her head. She was wishing they'd go away, but she didn't have the sharp-tongued facility of some housewives for ridding themselves of unwelcome intruders.

"It's the day the Derby is run off!" They waited expectantly. Her face didn't show any enlightenment whatever. "Can't you guess why we're here, Mrs. Mead? *Your horse has come in first!*"

She still showed only bewilderment. Disappointment was acutely visible on all their faces. "My horse?" she said blankly. "I don't own any hor—"

"No, no, no, Mrs. Mead, don't you understand? We're newspaper men; word has just flashed to our offices from London that you're one of the three Americans to hold a ticket on Ravenal in the sweepstakes. The other two are in 'Frisco and in Boston."

They had forced her half-way down the short front hall by now, back toward the kitchen, simply by crowding in on her. "Don't you understand what we're trying to tell you? It means you've won a hundred and fifty thousand dollars!"

Luckily there happened to be a chair at hand, up against the wall. She dropped down on it limply. "Oh, no!"

They eyed her in baffled surprise. She wasn't taking this at all the way they'd expected. She kept shaking her head, mildly but obstinately. "No, gentlemen. There must be some mistake somewhere. It must be somebody else by the same name. You see, I haven't any ticket on Rav—What'd you say that horse's name was? I haven't any sweepstakes ticket at all."

The four of them regarded her reproachfully, as though they felt she was trying to put one over on them.

"Sure you have, you must have. Where'd they get your name and address from, otherwise? It was cabled to our offices from London, along with the names of the other winners. They didn't just make it up out of thin air. It must have been down on the slip that was dug up out of the drum in Dublin before the race. What're you trying to do, kid us, Mrs. Mead?"

She perked up her head alertly at that, as though something had occurred to her just then for the first time.

"Just a moment, I never stopped to think! You keep calling me Mead. Mead is no longer my name, since I remarried. My present name is Mrs. Archer. But I've been so used to hearing Mead for years, and the sight of so many of you at the door all at one time flustered me so, that I never noticed you were using it until now.

"If this winning ticket is in the name of Mrs. Mead, as you say, then Harry, my first husband, must have bought it in my name shortly before his death, and never told me about it. Yes, that must be it, particularly if this address was given in the cable report. You see, the house was in my name, and I stayed on here after I lost Harry, and even after my remarriage." She looked up at them helplessly. "But where is it, the counterfoil or whatever they call it? I haven't the faintest idea."

They stared in dismay. "You mean you don't know where it is, Mrs. Mea—Mrs. Archer?"

"I never even knew he'd bought one, until now. He never said a word to me about it. He may have wanted to surprise me, in case it won something." She gazed sadly down at the floor. "Poor dear, he died quite suddenly," she said softly.

Their consternation far surpassed her own. It was almost comical; you would have thought the money came out of their pockets instead of hers. They all began talking at once, showering questions and suggestions on her.

"Gee, you'd better look around good and see if you can't find it! You can't collect the money without it, you know, Mrs. Archer."

"Have you gotten rid of all his effects yet? It may still be among them."

"Did he have a desk where he kept old papers? Should we help you look, Mrs. Archer?"

The telephone began to ring. The poor woman put her hands distractedly to her head, lost a little of her equanimity, which wasn't to be wondered at. "Please go now, all of you," she urged impatiently. "You're upsetting me so that I really can't think straight!"

They went out jabbering about it among themselves. "This makes a better human-interest story than if she had it! I'm going to write it up this way."

Mrs. Archer was answering the phone by now. "Yes, Stephen, some reporters who were here just now told me about it. It must still be around some place; a thing like that wouldn't just *disappear*, would it? Good; I wish you would."

He'd said, "A hundred and fifty thousand dollars is too much money to let slip through our fingers that easily." He'd said, "I'm coming home to help you look for it."

FORTY-EIGHT HOURS later they'd reached the end of their ingenuity. Or rather, forty-eight hours later they finally were willing to admit defeat. They'd actually reached the end of their ingenuity long before then.

"Crying won't help any!" Stephen Archer remarked testily across the table to her. Their nerves were on edge, anyone's would have been by this time, so she didn't resent the sharpness of his tone.

She smothered a sob, dabbed at her eyes. "I know, but—it's agonizing. So near and yet so far! Coming into all that money would have been a turning point in both our lives. It would have been the difference between living and merely existing. All the things we've wanted so, done without. . . . And to have to sit helplessly by and watch it dance away like a will o' the wisp! I almost wish they'd never come here and told me about it."

The table between them was littered with scrawled-over scraps of paper. On them was a curious sort of inventory. An inventory of the belongings of the late Harry Mead. One list was headed: "Bags, suitcases, etc." Another: "Desk, office desk, drawers, etc." A third: "Suits." And so on. Most of these things were hopelessly scattered and lost track of by now, a few were still in their possession. They had wanted to reconstruct his entire accumulation of physical properties, as it stood at or just before his death, in order to trace the ticket through all possible channels of disappearance. A hopeless task.

Some were checked. Others had question marks beside them. Still others had crosses after them, marking their elimination as possibilities. Stephen Archer had been methodical about it to say the least; anyone would have been, for one hundred and fifty thousand dollars.

They'd gone over them item by item, ten, twenty, fifty times, adding, discarding, revising, as the physical search kept pace with the inventory. Slowly the checks and crosses had overtaken and outnumbered the question marks. They'd even got in touch with people, former friends, business acquaintances of the dead man, his barber, his favorite bartender, the youth who had shined his shoes once a week, as many of them as they could think of and reach, to find out if maybe casually one day he hadn't mentioned buying such a ticket, and more to the point, happened to mention where he'd put it. He hadn't. If he hadn't thought it important enough to mention to his own wife, why would he mention it to an outsider?

Archer broke off tapping his nails on the table edge, shoved his chair back exasperatedly, squeezed his eyelids. "It's driving me nuts! I'm going out for a walk. Maybe something'll come to me while I'm by myself." He picked up his hat, called back from the front door: "*Try,* will you, Josie? Keep trying!" That was all he'd been saying for the past two days and they were still no further. "And don't let anyone in while I'm gone," he added. That was another thing. They'd been pestered to within an inch of their lives, as might have been expected. Reporters, strangers, curiosity mongers.

He'd hardly turned off at the end of the front walk than the doorbell rang. In fact it was such a short time after, that she was sure it was he, come back for his latchkey, or to tell her some new possibility that had just occurred to him. Every time he'd left the house the last two days he'd come back again two or three times to tell her some new idea that had just struck him—of where it could be. But none of them were ever any good.

But when she opened it she saw her mistake: it was one of those three reporters from the other day. Alone, this time.

"Any luck yet, Mrs. Archer? I saw your husband just leaving the house, so I thought I'd find out from you. He's been hanging up the phone every time I tried to call."

"No, we haven't found it. And he told me not to talk to anyone."

"I know, but why don't you let me see if I can help you? I'm not here as a reporter now; my paper ran the story long ago. It's the human angle of the thing has got me. I'd like to do what I can to help you."

"How can you?" she said doubtfully. "We've gotten nowhere ourselves, so how could an outsider possibly succeed?"

"Three heads are better than two."

She stood aside reluctantly, let him pass. "You'll have to go before he comes back, I know he won't like it if he finds you here. But I *would* like to talk it over with someone; we are at our wits' end."

He took off his hat as he came in. "Thank you, Mrs. Archer. My name's Westcott."

They sat down on opposite sides of the paper-littered round table, he in the same chair Archer had been in before. She crossed her wrists dejectedly on the table top. "Well, we've tried everything," she said helplessly. "What can you suggest?"

"He didn't sell it, because a thing like that is not transferable; your name was down on the stub that went to Dublin, and you would still remain the payee. He may possibly have lost it, though."

She shook her head firmly. "My husband suggested that too, but I know better. Not Harry; he never lost a pin in his whole lifetime! Besides if he had, I know he would have told me about it, even if he didn't tell me about buying it in the first place. He was a thrifty type of man; it would have upset him too much to lose two-and-a-half dollars' worth of anything to be able to keep still about it."

"Then we're safe in saying he still had it when he died. But *where,* that's the thing. Because wherever it was *then*, it still is *now,* most likely."

He was riffling through the scraps of paper while he spoke, reading the headings to himself. "What about wallets or billfolds? I don't see any list of them."

"He didn't have one to his name, never used them. He was the sort who preferred to carry things loose in his pockets. I remember I tried to give him one once, and he exchanged it right after the holidays."

"How about books? People use funny things for bookmarks, sometimes, and then the objects stay in between the pages and have a habit of getting lost."

"We've covered that. Harry and I were never great readers, we didn't belong to any public or circulating libraries, so the one or two books that were in the house didn't leave it again afterwards. And the same one or two that were here in Harry's day are still here now. I've turned them upside-down, shaken them out thoroughly, examined them page by page."

He picked up another slip. "He only owned three suits?"

"It was hard to get him to buy a new one; he wasn't much given to dress."

"Did you dispose of them after he died?"

"Only one of them, the brown. The gray is still up there in the storeroom. It was so old and threadbare I was ashamed to even show it to the old clothes dealer who took the other one, to tell the truth. Harry had lived in it for years; I wouldn't let him be seen out in it, toward the end. He just used it around the house."

"Well, what about the one you did give away, or sell? Did you go through the pockets before you disposed of it? It may have remained in one of them."

"No, I'm absolutely sure it didn't. The woman never lived, Mr. Westcott, I don't care who she is, who didn't probe through pockets, turn the linings inside out, before she got rid of any of her husband's old clothes. It's as much an instinctive feminine gesture as primping the hair. I recall distinctly doing that—it wasn't very long ago, after all—and there was nothing in those pockets."

"I see." He stroked his chin reflectively. "And what about this third one you have down—dark blue doublebreasted? What became of that?"

She lowered her eyes deprecatingly. "That was practically brand new; he'd only worn it once before he died. Well, when he died, money wasn't any too plentiful, so instead of buying a new outfit, I gave it to them and had them . . . put him in it."

"He was buried in it, in other words."

"Yes. It wouldn't be in that, naturally."

He looked at her a minute before answering. Finally he said, "Why not?" Before she could answer that, except by a startled look, he went on: "Well, do you mind if we talk about it for a minute, anyway."

"No, but what——"

"Would you have approved of his buying a thing like this sweepstakes ticket, if you had known about it at the time?"

"No," she admitted. "I used to scold him about things like that, buying chances on Thanksgiving turkeys and drawing numbers out of punch boards. I considered it money thrown out. He went ahead doing it, though."

"He wouldn't want you to know he had this ticket then—unless it paid off—as, in fact, it did. So he'd put it in the place you were least likely to come upon it. That's logical, isn't it?"

"I suppose so."

"Another question: I suppose you brushed off his clothes from time to time, the way most wives do, especially when he had so few suits?"

"Yes, the brown, the one he wore daily to work."

"Not the dark blue?"

"It was new, he'd only had it on his back once, there was no need to yet."

"He probably knew that. He'd also know, therefore, that the safest place for him to put a sweepstakes ticket—in case he didn't want you to come across it in the course of one of your daily brushings—would be in one of the pockets of that unworn dark blue suit."

Her face was starting to pale dreadfully.

He looked at her solemnly. "I think we've found that elusive counterfoil at last. I'm very much afraid it's still with your late husband."

She stared at him with a mixture of dawning hope and horror.

Dawning hope that the exhausting mystery was at last solved. Horror at what was implied if the solution were to be carried through to its logical conclusion. "What can I do about it?" she breathed fearfully.

"There's only one thing you can do. Get a permit to exhume the coffin."

She shuddered. "How can I contemplate such a thing? Suppose we're mistaken?"

"I'm sure we're not, or I wouldn't suggest your doing it."

And he could tell by looking at her that she was sure too, by now. Her objections died lingeringly, but they died one by one. "But wouldn't they, the men who prepared him, have found it themselves just before they put the suit on him, and returned it to me, if it was in that suit?"

"In the case of anything bulky, such as a thick envelope or a note-book, they probably would have. But a tissue-thin ticket like that, you know how flimsy they are, could easily have been overlooked, in the depths of one of the vest pockets, for instance."

She was growing used to the idea, repellent as it had seemed at first glance. "I really think that's what must have happened, and I want to thank you for helping us out. I'll talk it over with Mr. Archer when he comes back, hear what he says."

Westcott cleared his throat deprecatingly as he moved toward the front door. "Maybe you'd better let him think the idea was your own, not mention me at all. He might consider it butting in on the part of an outsider, and resent it. You know how it is. I'll drop by tomorrow and you can let me know what you've decided to do about it. You see, if you go ahead with the disinterment, I'd like an exclusive on it for my paper." He touched the press card stuck in his hat band, on which was written "*Bulletin.*"

"I'll see that you get one," she promised him. "Good night."

When Archer had returned from his walk, she let him hang up his hat and slump frustratedly back into the chair he'd been in earlier, before coming out with it.

"Stephen, I know where it is now!" she blurted out with positive assurance.

He stopped raking fingers through his hair, jerked his face toward her. "You sure this time, or is it just another false alarm?"

"No, this time I'm sure!" Without mentioning Westcott or his visit, she rapidly outlined his theory and also the steps by which he had built it up. "So I'm certain it's in the—casket with him. The one and only time he wore that suit before his death was one Sunday afternoon when he went out for a stroll and stopped in at a taproom for a couple of beers. What more likely place than that for him to have bought it? And then he simply left it in the suit, knowing I wouldn't be apt to find it."

She had expected him to be overjoyed, not even to feel her own preliminary qualms—which she'd overcome by now anyway. It wasn't that her line of reasoning hadn't convinced him. She could see at a glance that it had, by the way his face first lit up; but then it grew strangely pale immediately afterwards.

"We can kiss it good-bye, then!" he said huskily.

"But why, Stephen? All we need to do is to get permission to——"

There was no mistaking his pallor. He was ashen with some emotion or other. She took it to be repugnance. "I won't stand for it! If it's there, it'll have to stay there!"

"But, Stephen, I don't understand. Harry really meant nothing to you, why should you feel that way about it? If I don't object, why should you?"

"Because it's—it's like sacrilege! It gives me the creeps! If we've got to disturb the dead to come into that money, I'd rather let it go." He was on his feet now, one clenched fist on the table-top. The wrist that stemmed from it was visibly tremulous. "Anyway, I'm superstitious; I say no good can come of it."

"But that's the one thing you're not, Stephen," she contradicted gently but firmly. "You've always made a point of walking under ladders every time you see one, simply to prove you aren't superstitious. Now you say you are!"

Instead of calming him, her persistence seemed to have an adverse effect, nearly drove him frantic. His voice shook. "As your husband, I forbid you to disturb that man's remains!"

She gazed at him uncomprehendingly. "But why are you so jumpy about it? Why is your face so white? I never saw you like this before."

He wrenched at his collar as though it were choking him. "Shut up about it! Forget there ever was such a sweepstakes ticket! Forget all about the hundred and fifty thousand!" And he poured himself a double drink, but he only got half of it in the glass, his hand trembled so.

LITTLE MRS. ARCHER followed Westcott out of the taxi with a visible effort. Despite her tan, her face was deathly white under the bleaching scrutiny of the arc lights at the cemetery entrance. A night watchman, advised beforehand of their arrival and its purpose, opened a small pedestrian wicket for them in the massive grilled gates, closed since sunset.

"Don't take it that way," the newspaper man tried to reassure her. "We're not guilty of any crime by coming here and doing this. We have a court order all properly signed and perfectly legal. Your consent is all that's necessary, and you signed the application. Archer's isn't. You're the deceased's wife; he's no kin to him."

"I know, but when he finds out . . ." She cast a look behind her into the surrounding dark, almost as though fearful Archer had followed them out here. "I wonder why he was so opposed——"

Westcott gave her a look as much as to say, "So do I," but didn't answer.

"Will it take very long?" she quavered as they followed the watchman toward a little gatekeeper's lodge just within the entrance.

"They've been at work already for half an hour. I phoned ahead as soon as the permit was okayed, to save time. They ought to be about ready for us by now."

She stiffened spasmodically against his arm, which was linked protectively to hers. "You won't have to look," he calmed her. "I know it makes it seem twice as bad, to come here at night like this, after the place is already closed for the day, but I figured this way we could do it without attracting a lot of annoying publicity and attention. Just look at it this way: With part of the money you can build him a classy mausoleum if you want to, to make up for it. Now just sit here in this little cubbyhole and try to keep your mind off it. I'll be back just as soon as—it's been done."

She gave him a wan smile under the dim electric light of the gatekeeper's lodge. "Make sure he's—it's put back properly afterwards." She was trying to be brave about it, but then it would have been a trying experience for any woman.

Westcott followed the watchman along the main graveled walk

that seemed to bisect the place, the white pill of his guide's torch rolling along the ground in front of them. They turned aside at a particular little lane, and trod Indian-file until they had come to a group of motionless figures eerily waiting for them by the light of a couple of lanterns placed on the ground.

The plot had been converted into an open trough now, hillocks of displaced fill ringing it around. A withered wreath that had topped it had been cast aside. Mead had died too recently for any headstone or marker to be erected yet.

The casket was up and straddling the hillock of excavated soil, waiting for Westcott to get there. The workmen were resting on their shovels, perfectly unconcerned.

"All right, go ahead," Westcott said curtly. "Here's the authorization."

They took a cold chisel to the lid, hammered it in for a wedge along the seam in various places, sprang the lid. Then they pried it with a crowbar. Just the way any crate or packing case is opened. The squealing and grating of the distorted nails was ghastly, though. Westcott kept taking short turns to and fro in the background while it was going on. He was glad now that he'd had sense enough to leave Mrs. Archer at the entrance to the grounds. It was no place for a woman.

Finally the sounds stopped and he knew they were ready for him. One of the workmen said with unintentional callousness: "It's all yours, mister."

Westcott threw his cigarette away, with a grimace as though it had tasted bad. He went over and squatted on his haunches beside the open coffin. Somebody was helpfully keeping the pill of white trained directly down before him. "Can you see?"

Westcott involuntarily turned his head aside, then turned it back again. "More than I care to. Keep it off the face, will you? I just want something in the pockets."

It fluctuated accommodatingly, giving an eery impression of motion to the contents of the coffin. The watchman silently handed him a pair of rubber gloves over his shoulder. Westcott drew them on with a faint snapping sound, audible in the intense stillness that hung over the little group.

It didn't take long. He reached down and unbuttoned the double-breasted jacket, laid it open. The men around him drew back a step.

His hand went unhesitatingly toward the upper-left vest-pocket. If it required mental effort to make it do so, it wasn't visible. Two fingers hooked searchingly, disappeared into blue serge. They came out again empty, shifted to the lower pocket on that same side, sheathed themselves again. They came up with a folded square of crepe-like paper, that rattled like a dry leaf.

"Got it," Westcott remarked tonelessly.

The men ringing him around, or at least the one wielding the torch, must have been over to peer at it. The pill of light shifted inadvertently upward again. Westcott blinked. "Keep it away from the face. I told——" It obediently corrected itself. He must have given a double-take-'em in the brief instant it had been up where it shouldn't. "Put it on the face!" he suddenly countermanded.

The sweepstakes ticket, the center of attraction until now, fell back on the vest, lay there unnoticed. Westcott only had eyes for that white light on the face. An abnormal silence hung suspended over the macabre scene. It was like a still-life, they were all so motionless.

Westcott broke it at last. He only said two things. "Um-hum," with a corroborative shake of his head. And then, "Autopsy." He said the latter after he'd finally straightened to his feet and retrieved the discarded ticket as an afterthought. . . .

Mrs. Archer was still standing beside him in the caretaker's lodge, salvaged ticket clutched in her hand, when men, carrying the coffin, went by in the gloom a few minutes later. The lantern leading the way revealed it to her.

She clutched at his sleeve. "What's that they're carrying out? That isn't *it*, is it? What's that closed car, like a small delivery truck, that just drove up outside the grounds?"

"That's from the morgue, Mrs. Archer."

"But why? What's happened?" For the second time that night the ticket fluttered, discarded, to the ground.

"Nothing, Mrs. Archer. Let's go now, shall we? I want to have a talk with you before you go home."

As she was about to re-enter the taxi they had kept waiting for them outside the grounds, she drew back. "Just a minute. I promised Stephen to bring an evening paper back with me when I came home. There's a newsstand over there on the other side of the roadway."

Westcott waited by the cab while she went over to it alone. It occurred to her it would be a good idea to see whether or not he had written up anything beforehand about the missing ticket's where-abouts. If it wasn't already too late, she wanted to prevail upon him not to, if possible. "Let me have the *Bulletin,* please."

The news vendor shook his head. "Never heard of it, lady. No such paper in this town."

"Are you sure?" she cried thunderstruck. She glanced across the street to the figure waiting for her by the taxi.

"I oughta be, lady. I handle every paper published in the city and I never yet come across one called the *Bulletin!*"

When she rejoined Westcott, she explained quietly, "I changed my mind." She glanced up at the press card sticking in his hat band. "*Bulletin*" was plainly to be seen, typed on it.

She was very quiet in the taxi riding homeward, seemed lost in thought. The only sign she gave was an occasional gnawing at the lining of her cheek.

"I've been assigned to do a feature article about you, Mrs. Archer," Westcott began when they were seated in the little cafeteria to which he had brought her. "Human-interest stuff, you know. That's why I'd like to ask you a few questions."

She looked at him without answering. She was still gnawing the lining of her cheek, lost in thought.

"Mead died quite suddenly, didn't he? Just what were the cir-cumstances?"

"He hadn't been feeling well for several days . . . indigestion. We'd finished dinner that night and I was doing the dishes. He complained of feeling ill and I suggested he go outside the house for a breath of fresh air. He went out in back, to putter around in the little truck-garden he was trying to raise."

"In the dark?"

"He took a pocket-light with him."

"Go ahead." He was taking notes in shorthand or something while she spoke—as newspapermen *don't* do.

"About half an hour went by. One time I heard a crash somewhere near at hand, but nothing else, so I didn't investigate. Then shortly after, Stephen—Mr. Archer—dropped around for a friendly visit. He'd been doing that those last few weeks; he and Harry would sit and chew the rag the way men do, over a couple of highballs.

"Well, I went to the back door to call Harry in. I could see his light lying out there on the ground, but he didn't answer. We found him lying there, writhing and unable to speak. His eyes were rolling and he seemed to be in convulsions. Stephen and I carried him in between us and I phoned for the doctor, but by the time he'd come, Harry was already dead. The doctor told us it was an attack of acute indigestion, plus a shock to his heart, perhaps brought on by the noise of that crash I told you about."

He lidded his eyes at her. "I am convinced that 'crash' had something to do with bringing it on. And you mean the coroner passed it off as acute indigestion, went on record in his official report to that effect? That's something for the municipal council to take up later."

"Why?" she gasped.

He went ahead as though he hadn't heard her. "You say Archer was the salesman who insured Mead? In your favor, of course?"

"Yes."

"Was it for a large amount?"

"Is it necessary to know all this for a newspaper article? You're no reporter, Mr. Westcott, and never were; there's no such paper as the *Bulletin*. You're a detective." Her voice frayed with hysteria. "What are you questioning me like this for?"

He said, "I'll answer that when I come back. Will you excuse me a minute, I want to make a phone call. Stay right where you are, Mrs. Archer."

He kept his eye on her while he was standing beside the wall phone across the room, dialing, and then asking a brief question or two. She sat there in a state of dazed apprehension, occasionally moistening her lips with the tip of her tongue.

She repeated her question when he had seated himself again. "What do you want with me? Why are you questioning me about Harry's death?"

"Because I found the skin was broken as if from a blow on your first husband's skull when I had the remains disinterred earlier tonight. I phoned the morgue; they've just made a hasty examination and told me the skull was fractured!"

Her face paled to an unearthly gray. He hadn't realized until now that she was lightly tanned to an even, golden hue like a biscuit all over her face, neck and arms. Her paling beneath it revealed it. She had to grip the table edge with both hands. For a minute he thought she was going to topple over, chair and all. He spaded a hand out toward her to support her, but it wasn't necessary. He handed her a glass of water. She barely touched her lips to it, then took a deep breath.

"Then that was Harry's coffin that I saw them carry past us in the dark, out there?"

He nodded, riffled the scraps of paper he had been taking notes on. "Now let me get the story straight." But his eyes were boring into her tormented face like gimlets instead of consulting the "notes" while he spoke.

"Stephen Archer insured your first husband's life heavily, in your favor. He became his friend, fell into the habit of dropping over to the house of an evening and sitting and chatting with him.

"The night of his death Mead went out into the dark behind the house. You heard a sound like a crash. Then Archer came to the front door of the house not long after. When you went to call your husband, he was dying, and he died. A private physician and the municipal coroner both passed it off as acute indigestion. Both those gent's finances and ethics are going to be investigated—but I'm not concerned with that now, I'm only concerned with the part up to your husband's death. That's my job. Now, have I got the story straight?"

She took so long to answer that it almost seemed as if she wasn't going to, but still he waited. And finally she did. With the impassive, frozen face of a woman who has made a momentous decision and put all thought of the consequences behind her.

"No," she said, "you haven't got it straight. Shall we go over it a second time? First, would you mind tearing up those notes you made? They will have very little bearing on it by the time I'm through."

He tore them up into small pieces and dribbled them onto the floor, smiling as though he had intended doing that all along. "Now, Mrs. Archer."

She spoke like a person in their sleep, eyes centered high over his head, as if drawing her inspiration from the ceiling. "Stephen attracted me from the first time I saw him. He was not to blame in any way for what happened. He came over to see Harry, not me. But the more I saw him, the stronger the feeling grew on my part. Harry was heavily insured in my favor. I couldn't help thinking how opportune it would be if—anything took him from me. I would be comfortably well off, and since Stephen was unmarried, what was to prevent my eventual remarriage to him? From thinking it became day-dreaming, from day-dreaming it became action.

"That night when Harry went out in back of the house to get some air, I thought it out for the last time, while doing the dishes. Suddenly I found myself carrying it out. I went upstairs, got out an—an old flat-iron I no longer used. I came downstairs with it, hidden under my kitchen apron, and, in the dark, went out to him. I knew Stephen was coming over later, that was all I could think of. Harry was no longer my husband, someone I loved; to me he had become just an obstacle standing between Stephen and myself.

"I stood and chatted with him a moment, wondering how I was going to do it. I wasn't afraid of being heard or seen, our house stands by itself, 'way out. But I was afraid of the look there would be in his eyes at the last moment. Suddenly I saw a firefly behind him. I said, 'Look, dear, there's a firefly, in your radishes.'

"He turned his back to me, and I did it. I swung the flat-iron by its handle, squarely at the back of his head. He didn't die right away, but his brain was already paralyzed and he couldn't talk, so I saw it was all over. I went further out into the fields and buried the iron, using his garden hoe.

"Then I returned to the house, washed up. Just as I got through, Stephen came around. I went out to the back door with him, pretended to call Harry. Then we found him and carried him in. Stephen has never found out to this day that I did it."

"You mean he didn't notice the wound? Didn't it bleed?"

"It did a little, but I had washed it off. I took some pinkish face enamel that I used on myself to hide wrinkles, plastered the wound over with that, and even powdered it so that it would be less noticeable. He was slightly bald, you know. And I combed his hair to conceal it completely. I made a good job of it, after all I've been using the enamel stuff for years."

"Very interesting. And it evidently passed muster with the doctor you called, the coroner, and finally the undertaker who prepared him. That explains that. Now, did you hit him squarely in the back of the head—or a little to one side, say the left."

She paused. Then: "Yes, a little to the left."

"You can show me where it is you buried the weapon afterwards, I suppose?"

"No, I—I dug it up again afterwards, and then one time when I was crossing the river on the ferry to visit my sister-in-law, I dropped it in, out in the middle."

"But you *can* tell me how much it weighed? Was it large or——"

She shook her head. "I know I'm very stupid, but I couldn't say. Just a flat-iron."

"After you'd had it all those years?" He sighed ruefully. "But at least it *was* a flat-iron, you're sure of that?"

"Oh, yes."

"Well, that about covers everything." He stood up. "I know you're tired, and I won't keep you any longer. Thanks a lot, and good night, Mrs. Archer."

"*Good night?*" she echoed nonplused. "You mean you're not going to hold me, not going to arrest me, after what I've just told you?"

"Much as I'd like to accommodate you," he said drily, "there are one or two little loose threads; oh, nothing much to speak of, but just enough to impede a nice clean-cut arrest, such as you seem to have your loyal wifely heart set on. Taking them at random, there isn't a wrinkle on your entire face, so it shows a lot of mistaken diligence on your part if you actually do use any pinkish facial enamel as you say.

"And secondly, he wasn't hit on the back of the head, but high on the right temple. You wouldn't forget a thing like that! And there was no hair on his temple, Mrs. Archer."

Suddenly she crumpled, buried her face in her arms on the table. "Oh, I know what you're going to think now! Stephen didn't do it, I know he didn't! You're not going to——"

"I'm not going to do anything for the present. But on one condition only: I want your solemn promise not to mention this conversation to him. Nor about my having the remains sent down to the morgue, nor any of the rest of it. Otherwise, I'll arrest him as a precautionary measure and have him held. And he'll have a hard time getting out of it, even if not guilty."

She was almost abject in her gratitude. "Oh, I promise, I promise! I swear I won't say a word! But I'm sure you'll find out that he didn't! He's so kind and considerate of me, so thoughtful."

"You, in turn, are insured in his favor, I suppose?"

"Oh, yes, but there's nothing in that. Somebody has to be beneficiary, and I have no children nor close relatives. You're entirely mistaken if you suspect him of harboring such thoughts! Why, if I even catch the slightest cold, he's as worried as he can be! A week or so ago I had a slight chest cold, and he rushed me right to the doctor, all upset about it. He even brought home one of these sun lamps, has insisted on my taking treatments with it ever since, to build up my resistance. Of course it's sort of a nuisance to have around the place but——"

He was leading her outside while she jabbered, looking around and trying to find a taxi to send her off in. The conversation no longer seemed to hold much interest for him. "That so? In what way?"

"Well, the bathroom's tiny to begin with, and it's constantly falling over on top of me. He insists the best time to use it is while I'm in the tub, in that way I'm entirely uncovered and can get the best results."

He was still looking around for a taxi to get her off his hands. "They're rather heavy, aren't they?"

"No, long and spindly. But luckily he's been there each time, to right it again."

"*Each* time?" was all he said.

"Yes." She laughed deprecatingly, as if trying to build up a disarming picture of her devoted husband for him, turn this man's suspicions away from anyone so good-hearted and generous. "I always wait until after he's left the house in the mornings to take my bath. But then he almost always forgets something at the last minute after he's already at the station, and comes dashing back and blundering into the bathroom, and over it goes."

"What sort of things does he forget?" He'd found her a taxi, but now he was keeping it waiting.

"Oh, one day a clean handkerchief; the next certain papers, that he needs; the next, his fountain pen——"

"But does he keep those things in the bathroom?"

She laughed again. "No. But he never can find where they are, so he comes barging into the bathroom to ask me—and then over goes the lamp!"

"And this happens practically every time you have it turned on?"

"I don't think it's missed once."

It was now he who was looking up over her head, just as she had before. The last thing he said, as he took leave of her, was: "You'll keep your promise not to mention this interview to your husband?"

"I will," she assured him.

"Oh, and one other thing. Postpone your bath and sun lamp treatment for just a few minutes tomorrow morning. I may want to question you further, as soon as your husband leaves the house, and I wouldn't want to get you out of the tub once you're in it."

STEPHEN ARCHER shot up from his chair when she entered, as though a spring had been released under him. She couldn't identify the emotion that gripped him, save that whatever it was, it was strong. Some sort of anxiety. "You must have sat through the show twice!" he accused her.

"Stephen, I——" She fumbled in her purse. "I didn't go to a picture. I got it!" Suddenly it lay on the table between them. Just as it had come out of the vest pocket. "I did what you told me not to."

The way his eyes dilated she thought they would shoot out of his face. Suddenly he had her by the shoulders, gripping her like a vise. "Who was with you? Who saw it—done?"

"Nobody. I obtained a permit, and I took it out there and showed it to the man in charge of the grounds, and he got a couple of workmen——" Westcott's warning was in her mind, like a cautioning finger.

"Yes. Go on." His grip never relaxed.

"One of them got it out of the vest pocket, and then they put the lid on again and lowered it, and covered it up."

Breath slowly hissed from his knotted lips as from a safety valve. His hands left her shoulders.

"Look, Stephen—$150,000! Here, on the table before us! Wouldn't anyone have done the same thing, if they had to?"

He didn't seem interested in the ticket. His eyes kept boring into hers. "And you're sure it was put back again, just the way it was?"

She didn't say a word more.

He felt for the back of his neck. "I'd hate to think—he wasn't left just the way he was," he said lamely. He left her there and went upstairs.

It seemed as if she could see vague shadows all around her on the walls, that she knew weren't there at all. Had that detective done this to her—poisoned her mind with suspicion? Or. . . .

ARCHER REACHED for his hat the following morning, kissed her briefly, opened the door. " 'Bye. And don't forget to take your bath. I want to see you strong and husky, and the only way is to keep up those treatments daily."

"Sure you haven't overlooked anything this morning?" she called after him.

"Got everything this time. Just think, after we cash in on that ticket, I won't have to lug this brief-case and all these papers to work with me each morning. We'll celebrate tonight. And don't forget to take that bath."

Seconds after he had turned off their front walk, the doorbell rang. Westcott must have been watching for him to leave, came around the side of the house, to get there that soon.

All her fears came back at sight of him; they showed plainly on her face. She stood aside sullenly. "I suppose you want to come in and go ahead trying to find a murder where there hasn't been any."

"That's as good a way to put it as any," he agreed somberly. "I won't keep you long; I know you're anxious to take your bath. I can hear the water running into the tub upstairs. He left a little later than his usual time this morning, didn't he?"

She eyed him in undisguised awe. "He did—but how did you know that?"

"He took a little longer to shave this morning, that's why."

This time she couldn't even answer, just gaped bewilderedly.

"Yes, I've been watching the house. Not only this morning, but ever since you arrived home last night. And at the odd times I've been called away by other matters, I've left someone in my place. From where I was posted, I had a fairly good view into your bathroom window. I could tell he—took longer to shave this morning. Can I go up there and look?"

Again she mutely stood aside, followed him up the stairs. The tiny tiled bathroom was already steamy with the water threatening to overflow the tub. Beside it stood an ultra-violet sun lamp, plugged into a wall outlet. He eyed both without touching either. What he did touch was a rolled-up tape measure resting on the hamper. He picked it up without a word, handed it back to her.

"I guess one of us left it in here," she said blankly. "It belongs——"

He had already started down the stairs again without waiting to hear her out. She took the precaution of turning off the taps first, then followed him down. He had gone on down into the basement, without asking her permission. He came up from there again a moment later and rejoined her at the back of the hall.

"Just trying to locate the control box that supplies the current to the house," he answered her questioning look.

She retreated a precautionary step. She didn't say anything, but he translated the fleeting thought that had just passed through her mind aloud. "No, I'm not insane. Maybe I am just a little touched; maybe a good detective, like a good artist or a good writer, has to be a little touched. Now we haven't very much time. Mr. Archer's almost certainly going to forget something again at the depot and come back. Before he does, just let me ask you two or three brief questions. You say Archer began to drop in quite frequently of an evening, shortly before Mead's death. They got quite pally."

"Yes indeed. Called each other by their first names and were on the best of terms. They'd sit chatting and nursing their highballs. Why, Stephen even brought Harry a present of some expensive whiskey two or three days before his death. That's how much he thought of him."

"Was that before or after Mead had this siege of indigestion that, according to corner or physician, resulted in his death?"

"Why, just before."

"I see. And it was quite an expensive whiskey. So expensive that Archer insisted on Mead's drinking it alone, wouldn't even share it with him: kept him company with some of Mead's common, ordinary, every day domestic rye," Westcott said.

Her face paled with surprise. "How did you know that?"

"I didn't. I do now."

"It was such a small quantity, in a little stone flagon, and he'd already sampled it himself at home before he brought it." She broke off short at the unmistakable, knowing look on his face. "I know what you're driving at! You're thinking Stephen poisoned him with it, aren't you? Last night it was a rifle bullet, this morning it's poison whiskey! Well, Mr. Detective, for your information, not a drop of that ever reached Harry's lips. I dropped the jug and lost it all over the kitchen floor while I was fixing their drinks for them. And I was ashamed and afraid to tell either one of them about it, after the way Stephen had been singing its praises, so I sent out for a bottle of ordinary Scotch and mixed the drinks with that instead, and they never knew the difference!"

"How do I know you're telling the truth?"

"I had a witness to the accident, that's how! The delivery man that brought the new bottle over from the liquor store saw me picking up the pieces all over the kitchen floor. He even shook his head and remarked what a shame it was, and pointed out that some of the rounded pieces of the jug still held enough liquor in their hollows for a man to get the makings of one good drink out of them! And then he helped me pick them up. Go ask him!"

"I think I would like to check with him. What store did he work for?"

"The Ideal, it's only a few blocks from here. And then be sure you come back and persecute my husband some more!" she flared.

"No, ma'am, I don't intend making a move against your husband. Any move that's made will have to come from him. And now, that's all the questioning I'm going to do, or need to do. I have my case all complete. And here he comes back—for something that he overlooked!"

A shadow blurred the plate glass insert of the front door, a key began to titillate in the lock. A low-pitched bleat of alarm was wrung from her. "No, you're going to arrest him!" Her hands went out appealingly toward his shoulders, to ward him off.

"I don't arrest people for things they haven't done. I'm leaving by the back door as he comes in the front. You run up and get in that tub—and let nature take its course. Hurry up, and not a word to him!"

She fled up the stairs like one possessed, wrapper fluttering after her like a parachute. A stealthy click from the back door, as Westcott let himself out, was drowned out by the opening of the front one, and Archer came in, wrangling the key that had delayed him, to get it out of the lock. A faint rippling of displaced water reached him from above.

He closed the door after him, advanced as far as the foot of the stairs, called up with perfect naturalness: "Josie! Got any idea where my iron pills are? I went off without them."

"Stephen! Again?" Her voice came down rebukingly. "I asked you when you left—And now I bet you've missed your train, too."

"What's the difference, I'll take the 9:22."

"They're in the sideboard in the dining-room, you know perfectly well." Her voice came down to him with metronome-like clarity, backed by the tiling around her as a sounding board.

"Can't hear you." He was half-way up the stairs by now. "Wait a minute, I'll come up."

His shuffling ascent of the stairs blotted out a second faint click from the direction of the back door, as though it had been left with its latch free instead of closed entirely, and a moment later Westcott's figure darted around the turn at the back of the hall and dove in swift silence through the basement door. He hastily wedged something under it to keep it ajar, then went on down the cellar steps.

"I said they're in the sideboard," she was still calling out.

But Archer was in the bathroom with her by this time. She was in a reclining position in the tub, hidden up to the chin by blue-green water. Modesty had made her sink lower in it at his entrance. The lighted sun lamp, backed by its burnished oblong reflector, cast a vivid violet-white halo down over her.

"Are you sure they're not in the medicine cabinet?" He crossed the tiny tiled cubicle toward it before she could answer. As he came abreast of the lamp, his elbow almost unnoticeably hitched outward, by no more than a fraction of an inch.

The long-stemmed lamp teetered, started to go over toward the brimming tub with almost hypnotic slowness.

"Stephen, the lamp!" she screamed warningly.

He had his back to her, was fumbling in the medicine cabinet. He didn't seem to hear her.

"The lamp!" she screamed a second time, more piercingly. That was all there was time for.

The violet-white had already dulled to orange, however, as it arched through the air. The orange dimmed to red. Then the water quenched it with a viperish hiss. The current seemed to have died out in it even before it went in.

He finally turned, at the sound of the splash, and faced her with perfect composure. It was only when he saw that she had jumped to her feet in the tub, snatched a towel to swathe around herself, and was trying to step back from the hissing lamp, that surprise showed in his face.

His eyes shot angrily and questioningly to the wall outlet at the other end of it. The cord was still plugged in. He stepped forward, pulled out the plug, replugged it—as though to re-establish contact if it had broken. She was still standing in water up to her knees. She didn't topple. Stood there erect, eyes wide open, fumblingly trying to lift the lamp with her one free hand.

The surprise on his face hardened into a sullen, lowering look of decision. The fingers of his two hands hooked in toward one another, in grasping position. The hands themselves slowly came up and out. He took a step forward, to reach her across the rim of the tub.

A voice said:

"O. K., you had your chance and you muffed it. Now put your hands into these—instead of where they were heading—before I kick out a few of your front teeth."

Westcott was standing in the bath doorway, one hand worrying a pair of handcuffs the way a man fiddles with a key ring or watch chain, the other hand half withdrawing a right angle of welded metal from over his hip.

Archer made an uncontrollable start forward, quickly checked it in time, as the right angle expanded into a pugnacious snub nose. He retreated as far as the small space would allow, then when he couldn't retreat any more, slumped there with the back of his neck up against the medicine chest mirror.

Mrs. Archer's reaction, toward this man who had just saved her life, was a typically feminine one. "Don't you dare come in here like this! Can't you see how I am?" She snatched a shower curtain around her to add to the towel.

"Sorry, little lady," Westcott said soothingly, keeping his eyes away from her with gentlemanly tact, "but it couldn't be helped. That was your murder just then." The handcuffs snapped hungrily around Archer's wrist, then his own. He went to the bath window, signaled to someone outside somewhere in the immediate vicinity of the house to come in.

"My murder!" gasped Mrs. Archer, who was simply a pair of eyes above the shower curtain by now.

"Sure. If I hadn't shut off the current in the house a split second after I heard you give that first warning scream—by throwing the master switch in the control box down in the basement—he would have had you electrocuted by now. The water around you in the tub would have been a perfect conductor. That's what he's been trying to do to you every time he knocked over that lamp.

"Don't you know what happens when a thing like that lands in a tub of water, with you in the middle of it? The rim of the tub probably saved your life a couple of times, caught it too far up near the top and held it in a leaning position. Today he made sure it wouldn't by measuring off the distance between the lamp base and the tub rim, and setting it in close enough so that the filaments of the lamp would be bound to overreach the tub rim and go in the water. I watched him through the window. C'mon, you. Join us downstairs as soon as you're dressed, Mrs. Archer."

They were sitting there waiting for her in the livingroom when she came down the stairs some time later, walking as though her knees were weak, bathrobe tightly gathered about her as though she were cold, and a stony, disillusioned look on her face. There was another man with Westcott, probably the assistant who had helped him keep watch on the house all night long.

Archer was saying sullenly to his captor as she entered the room: "D'you think you'll ever be able to convince my wife of that rigmarole you handed out upstairs?"

"I have already," Westcott answered. "Just look at her face."

"He has, Stephen," she said in a lifeless voice, slumping into a chair, shading her eyes, and shivering uncontrollably. "It happened too many times to be just a coincidence. You must have been trying to do something to me. Why did you *always* forget something and come back for it, just when I was in the tub? Why did the lamp *always* go over? And what was the tape measure from my sewing kit doing in the bathroom this morning? *I* didn't take it there." But she didn't look at him while she spoke, stared sadly down at the floor.

Archer's face darkened, he curled his lip sneeringly at her. "So that's the kind you are, ready to believe the first tinhorn cop that walks in here!" He turned angrily toward Westcott. "All right, you've poisoned her against me, you've got her on your side," he snarled, "but what'll it get you? You can't get me on a crime that wasn't even committed at all!"

Westcott walked toward his assistant. "What'd you find about that—anything?"

The other man silently handed him something written on a sheet of paper. Westcott read it over, then looked up, smiling a little.

"I can't get you on the crime that you wanted to commit and were prevented from just now. But I *can* get you on a crime you don't even *know* you committed, but that went through just the same. And that's the one I'm going to hook you on!"

He waved the paper on him. "One Tim McRae, employed as a messenger by the Ideal Liquor Store, died in agony several hours after he quit work and went home, on December 21st, 1939, this report says. It was thought to be accidental, from poisonous liquor, 'smoke,' at the time, and nothing was made of it.

"But I'm going to prove, with the help of Mrs. Archer here, and also through a casual remark McRae let drop to his employer, and which the latter didn't pay much attention to until now, that he scooped out dregs of liquor left in a broken flagon, that you brought into this house, offered to Harry Mead, and refused to touch yourself. I'm going to have McRae exhumed, and I think I'll find all the evidence I need in his vital organs. And I can tell by the look on your face that you think so, too!"

"Here's the taxi come to take us in to Headquarters. Let's just sum the whole thing up before we get started, shall we?

"Mead actually *did* die a natural death, of acute indigestion, aggravated by the shock of hearing an unexpected crash—probably some kids playing somewhere. So that clears the coroner of any dereliction of duty. But you thought all along you'd murdered him, because you knew damn well you'd brought in a poisoned jug of whiskey, and you thought he'd had some.

"She, the innocent party, came into his insurance, and you married her. That meant that she was the next one slated to go. You weren't going to try any more poisoning, even though you thought you'd gotten away with it the first time. That was asking for trouble, you felt.

"The electrocution in the bath gag was absolutely foolproof—if it had worked; you wouldn't have needed to worry about it afterwards. So you took it slow, to make sure it couldn't be proven to be anything but an accident. Who was going to prove that you'd been in the room at the time it happened? Who was going to prove that you'd given the lamp that little hitch with your elbow that sent it over? You would have left her shocked to death in the tub at 9:15 in the morning, and only 'discovered' her that way when you got back from work at five.

"Then the sweepstakes business came up in the middle of all this. That didn't stop you; you were conditioned to murder by that time. You decided to go ahead anyway. If it had been good for an 'accident' before she stood to win $150,000, it was even better for an 'accident' afterwards.

"Meanwhile, Mead's old-maid sister, who suspected all along there was something suspicious about his death—probably only because his widow married you instead of wearing sackcloth and ashes the rest of her life—came to us at Headquarters demanding an investigation, and I was quietly assigned to it.

"You were scared stiff to have Mead exhumed, fearful that your 'crime' might come to light in some unforeseen way. Fearful, maybe, we could tell by the condition of his body if he'd been poisoned. Something entirely different came to light. I found a wound on his temple—the skin broken and a bone in his head cracked. I thought at first that was it. It turned out not to be so at all.

"It was only when I went downtown and examined the coffin more closely, that I noticed the dent in it where it had been dropped after he was already in it. The undertaker's assistant, just a kid, broke down and told us the coffin had dropped when he'd been loading it into the hearse. It had fallen on the head part from the loading side. The fall banged the dead man's head against the side hard enough to break the skin and crack his skull.

"I questioned Mrs. Archer and she flew to your defense, and only managed to acquit herself, better than any lawyer could have, with a cock and bull tale of a flat-iron. But, accidentally, while on the trail of one murder, that it turned out had never been committed, I uncovered another, in process of being built up. In other words, what seemed to be a murder, but wasn't, forestalled a murder that was coming up.

"I can't get you for either of them. But when I pile the weight of both of them on top of the murder you actually *did* commit, but didn't know about until now, that of this Tim McRae, I can get you put away long enough so that there won't be a murder left in your system by the time you get out.

"Sort of crazy, isn't it? But sort of neat. Our cab's waiting."

Three O'Clock

SHE HAD SIGNED her own death-warrant. He kept telling himself over and over that he was not to blame, she had brought it on herself. He had never seen the man. He knew there was one. He had known for six weeks now. Little things had told him. One day he came home and there was a cigar-butt in an ashtray, still moist at one end, still warm at the other. There were gasoline-drippings on the asphalt in front of their house, and they didn't own a car. And it wouldn't be a delivery-vehicle, because the drippings showed it had stood there a long time, an hour or more. And once he had actually glimpsed it, just rounding the far corner as he got off the bus two blocks down the other way. A second-hand Ford. She was often very flustered when he came home, hardly seemed to know what she was doing or saying at all.

He pretended not to see any of these things; he was that type of man, Stapp, he didn't bring his hates or grudges out into the open where they had a chance to heal. He nursed them in the darkness of his mind. That's a dangerous kind of a man.

If he had been honest with himself, he would have had to admit that this mysterious afternoon caller was just the excuse he gave himself, that he'd daydreamed of getting rid of her long before there was any reason to, that there had been something in him for years past now urging Kill, kill, kill. Maybe ever since that time he'd been treated at the hospital for a concussion.

He didn't have any of the usual excuses. She had no money of her own, he hadn't insured her, he stood to gain nothing by getting rid of her. There was no other woman he meant to replace her with. She didn't nag and quarrel with him. She was a docile, tractable sort of wife. But this thing in his brain kept whispering Kill, kill, kill. He'd fought it down until six weeks ago, more from fear and a sense of self-preservation than from compunction. The discovery that there was some stranger calling on her in the afternoons when he was away, was all that had been needed to unleash it in all its hydra-headed ferocity. And the thought that he would be killing two instead of just one, now, was an added incentive.

So every afternoon for six weeks now when he came home from his shop, he had brought little things with him. Very little things, that were so harmless, so inoffensive, in themselves that no one, even had they seen them, could have guessed—Fine little strands of copper wire such as he sometimes used in his watch-repairing. And each time a very little package containing a substance that—well, an explosives expert might have recognized, but no one else. There was just enough in each one of those packages, if ignited, to go Fffft! and flare up like flashlight-powder does. Loose like that it couldn't hurt you, only burn your skin of course if you got too near it. But wadded tightly into cells, in what had formerly been a soap-box down in the basement, compressed to within an inch of its life the way he had it, the whole accumulated thirty-six-days worth of it (for he hadn't brought any home on Sundays)—that would be a different story. They'd never know. There wouldn't be enough left of the flimsy house for them to go by. Sewer-gas they'd think, or a pocket of natural gas in the ground somewhere around under them. Something like that had happened over on the other side of town two years ago, only not as bad of course. That had given him the idea originally.

He'd brought home batteries too, the ordinary dry-cell kind. Just two of them, one at a time. As far as the substance itself was concerned, where he got it was his business. No one would ever know where he got it. That was the beauty of getting such a little at a time like that. It wasn't even missed where he got it from. She didn't ask him what was in these little packages, because she didn't even see them, he had them in his pocket each time. (And of course he didn't smoke coming home.) But even if she had seen them, she probably wouldn't have asked him. She wasn't the nosey kind that asked questions, she would have thought it was watch-parts, maybe, that he brought home to work over at night or something. And then too she was so rattled and flustered herself these days, trying to cover up the fact that she'd had a caller, that he could have brought in a grandfather-clock under his arm and she probably wouldn't have noticed it.

Well, so much the worse for her. Death was spinning its web beneath her busy feet as they bustled obliviously back and forth in those ground-floor rooms. He'd be in his shop tinkering with watch-parts and the phone would ring. "Mr. Stapp, Mr. Stapp, your house has just been demolished by a blast!"

A slight concussion of the brain simplifies matters so beautifully.

He knew she didn't intend running off with this unknown stranger, and at first he had wondered why not. But by now he thought he had arrived at a satisfactory answer. It was that he, Stapp, was working, and the other man evidently wasn't, wouldn't be able to provide for her if she left with him. That must be it, what other reason could there be? She wanted to have her cake and eat it too.

So that was all he was good for, was it, to keep a roof over her head? Well, he was going to lift that roof skyhigh, blow it to smithereens!

He didn't really want her to run off, anyway, that wouldn't have satisfied this thing within him that cried Kill, kill, kill. It wanted to *get* the two of them, and nothing short of that would do. And if he and she had had a five-year-old kid, say, he would have included the kid in the holocaust too, although a kid that age obviously couldn't be guilty of anything. A doctor would have known what to make of this, and would have phoned a hospital in a hurry. But unfortunately doctors aren't mind-readers and people don't go around with their thoughts placarded on sandwich-boards.

The last little package had been brought in two days ago. The box had all it could hold now. Twice as much as was necessary to blow up the house. Enough to break every window for a radius of blocks—only there were hardly any, they were in an isolated location. And that fact gave him a paradoxical feeling of virtue, as though he were doing a good deed; he was destroying his own but he wasn't endangering anybody else's home. The wires were in place, the batteries that would give off the necessary spark were attached. All that was necessary now was the final adjustment, the hook-up, and then—

Kill, kill, kill, the thing within him gloated.

Today was the day.

He had been working over the alarm-clock all morning to the exclusion of everything else. It was only a dollar-and-a-half alarm, but he'd given it more loving care than someone's Swiss-movement pocket-watch or platinum and diamond wristwatch. Taking it apart, cleaning it, oiling it, adjusting it, putting it together again, so that there was no slightest possibility of it failing him, of it not playing its part, of it stopping or jamming or anything else. That was one good thing about being your own boss, operating your own shop, there was no one over you to tell you what to do and what not to do. And he didn't have an apprentice or helper in the shop, either, to notice this peculiar absorption in a mere alarm-clock and tell someone about it later.

Other days he came home from work at five. This mysterious caller, this intruder, must be there from about two-thirty or three until shortly before she expected him. One afternoon it had started to drizzle at about a quarter to three, and when he turned in his doorway over two hours later there was still a large dry patch on the asphalt out before their house, just beginning to blacken over with the fine misty precipitation that was still falling. That was how he knew the time of her treachery so well.

He could, of course, if he'd wanted to bring the thing out into the open, simply have come an unexpected hour earlier any afternoon during those six weeks, and confronted them face to face. But he preferred the way of guile and murderous revenge; they might have had some explanation to offer that would weaken his purpose, rob him of his excuse to do the thing he craved. And he knew her so well, that in his secret heart he feared she would have if he once gave her a chance to offer it. Feared was the right word. He wanted to do this thing. He wasn't interested in a showdown, he was interested in a pay-off. This artificially-nurtured grievance had brought the poison in his system to a head, that was all. Without it it might have remained latent for another five years, but it would have erupted sooner or later anyway.

He knew the hours of her domestic routine so well that it was the simplest matter in the world for him to return to the house on his errand at a time when she would not be there. She did her cleaning in the morning. Then she had the impromptu morsel that she called lunch. Then she went out, in the early afternoon, and did her marketing for their evening meal. They had a phone in the house but she never ordered over it; she liked, she often told him, to see what she was getting, otherwise the tradespeople simply foisted whatever they chose on you, at their own prices. So from one until two was the time for him to do it, and be sure of getting away again unobserved afterwards.

At twelve-thirty sharp he wrapped up the alarm-clock in ordinary brown paper, tucked it under his arm, and left his shop. He left it every day at this same time to go to his own lunch. He would be a little longer getting back today, that was all. He locked the door carefully after him, of course; no use taking chances, he had too many valuable watches in there under repair and observation.

He boarded the bus at the corner below, just like he did every day when he was really going home for the night. There was no danger of being recognized or identified by any bus-driver or fellow-passenger or anything like that, this was too big a city. Hundreds of people used these busses night and day. The drivers didn't even glance up at you when you paid your fare, deftly made change for you backhand by their sense of touch on the coin you gave them alone. The bus was practically empty, no one was going out his way at this hour of the day.

He got off at his usual stop, three interminable suburban blocks way from where he lived, which was why his house had not been a particularly good investment when he bought it and no others had been put up around it afterwards. But it had its compensations on such a day as this. There were no neighbors to glimpse him returning to it at this unusual hour, from their windows, and remember that fact afterwards. The first of the three blocks he had to walk had a row of taxpayers on it, one-story store-fronts. The next two were absolutely vacant from corner to corner, just a panel of advertising billboards on both sides, with their gallery of friendly people that beamed on him each day twice a day. Incurable optimists these people were; even today when they were going to be shattered and splintered they continued to grin and smirk their counsel and messages of cheer. The perspiring bald-headed fat man about to quaff some non-alcoholic beverage. "The pause that refreshes!" The grinning colored laundress hanging up wash. "No ma'am, I just uses a little Oxydol." The farmwife at the rural telephone sniggering over her shoulder: "Still talking about their new Ford 8!" They'd be tatters and kindling in two hours from now, and they didn't have sense enough to get down off there and hurry away.

"You'll wish you had," he whispered darkly as he passed by beneath them, clock under arm.

But the point was, that if ever a man walked three "city" blocks in broad daylight unseen by the human eye, he did that now. He turned in the short cement walk when he came to his house at last, pulled back the screen door, put his latchkey into the wooden inner door and let himself in. She wasn't home, of course; he'd known she wouldn't be, or he wouldn't have come back like this.

He closed the door again after him, moved forward into the blue twilight-dimness of the inside of the house. It seemed like that at first after the glare of the street. She had the green shades down three-quarters of the way on all the windows to keep it cool until she came back. He didn't take his hat off or anything, he wasn't staying. Particularly after he once set this clock he was carrying in motion. In fact it was going to be a creepy feeling even walking back those three blocks to the bus-stop and standing waiting for the bus to take him downtown again, knowing all the time something was going *tick-tock, tick-tock* in the stillness back here, even though it wouldn't happen for a couple of hours yet.

He went directly to the door leading down to the basement. It was a good stout wooden door. He passed through it, closed it behind him, and went down the bare brick steps to the basement-floor. In the winter, of course, she'd had to come down here occasionally to regulate the oil-burner while he was away, but after the fifteenth of April no one but himself ever came down here at any time, and it was now long past the fifteenth of April.

She hadn't even known that he'd come down, at that. He'd slipped down each night for a few minutes while she was in the kitchen doing the dishes, and by the time she got through and came out, he was upstairs again behind his newspaper. It didn't take long to add the contents of each successive little package to what was already in the box. The wiring had taken more time, but he'd gotten that done one night when she'd gone out to the movies (so she'd said—and then had been very vague about what the picture was she'd seen, but he hadn't pressed her.)

The basement was provided with a light-bulb over the stairs, but it wasn't necessary to use it except at night; daylight was admitted through a horizontal slit of window that on the outside was flush with the ground, but on the inside was up directly under the basement-ceiling. The glass was wire-meshed for protection and so cloudy with lack of attention as to be nearly opaque.

The box, that was no longer merely a box now but an infernal machine, was standing over against the wall, to one side of the oil-

burner. He didn't dare shift it about any more now that it was wired
and the batteries inserted. He went over to it and squatted down on
his heels before it, and put his hand on it with a sort of loving gesture.
He was proud of it, prouder than of any fine watch he'd ever repaired
or reconstructed. A watch, after all, was inanimate. This was going
to become animate in a few more minutes, maybe diabolically so,
but animate just the same. It was like—giving birth.

He unwrapped the clock and spread out the few necessary small
implements he'd brought with him from the shop on the floor beside
him. Two fine copper wires were sticking stiffly out of a small hole
he'd bored in the box, in readiness, like the antennæ of some kind
of insect. Through them death would go in.

He wound the clock up first, for he couldn't safely do that once it
was connected. He wound it up to within an inch of its life, with a
professionally deft economy of wrist-motion. Not for nothing was he
a watch-repairer. It must have sounded ominous down in that
hushed basement, to hear that *crick-craaaack, crick-craaaack,* that
so-domestic sound that denotes going to bed, peace, slumber, security; that this time denoted approaching annihilation. It would have
if there'd been any listener. There wasn't any but himself. It didn't
sound ominous to him, it sounded delicious.

He set the alarm for three. But there was a difference now. Instead
of just setting off a harmless bell when the hour hand reached three
and the minute hand reached twelve, the wires attached to it leading
to the batteries would set off a spark. A single, tiny, evanescent
spark—that was all. And when that happened, all the way downtown where his shop was, the showcase would vibrate, and maybe
one or two of the more delicate watch-mechanisms would stop. And
people on the streets would stop and ask one another: "What was
that?"

They probably wouldn't even be able to tell definitely, afterwards,
that there'd been anyone else beside herself in the house at the time.
They'd know that she'd been there only by a process of elimination;
she wouldn't be anywhere else afterwards. They'd know that the
house had been there only by the hole in the ground and the litter
around.

He wondered why more people didn't do things like this; they
didn't know what they were missing. Probably not clever enough to
be able to make the things themselves, that was why.

When he'd set the clock itself by his own pocketwatch—1:15—he pried the back off it. He'd already bored a little hole through this at his shop. Carefully he guided the antenna-like wires through it, more carefully still he fastened them to the necessary parts of the mechanism without letting a tremor course along them. It was highly dangerous but his hands didn't play him false, they were too skilled at this sort of thing. It wasn't vital to reattach the back to the clock, the result would be the same if it stood open or closed, but he did that too, to give the sense of completion to the job that his craftsman's soul found necessary. When he had done with it, it stood there on the floor, as if placed there at random up against an innocent-looking copper-lidded soapbox, ticking away. Ten minutes had gone by since he had come down here. One hour and forty minutes were still to go by.

Death was on the wing.

He stood up and looked down at his work. He nodded. He retreated a step across the basement floor, still looking down, and nodded again, as if the slight perspective gained only enhanced it. He went over to the foot of the stairs leading up, and stopped once more and looked over. He had very good eyes. He could see the exact minute-notches on the dial all the way over where he now was. One had just gone by.

He smiled a little and went on up the stairs, not furtively or fearfully but like a man does in his own house, with an unhurried air of ownership, head up, shoulders back, tread firm.

He hadn't heard a sound over his head while he was down there, and you could hear sounds quite easily through the thin flooring, he knew that by experience. Even the opening and closing of doors above could be heard down here, certainly the footsteps of anyone walking about in the ground-floor rooms if they bore down with their normal weight. And when they stood above certain spots and spoke, the sound of the voices and even what was said came through clearly, due to some trick of acoustics. He'd heard Lowell Thomas clearly, on the radio, while he was down here several times.

That was why he was all the more unprepared, as he opened the basement door and stepped out into the ground-floor hall, to hear a soft tread somewhere up above, on the second floor. A single, solitary footfall, separate, disconnected, like Robinson Crusoe's footprint. He stood stockstill a moment, listening tensely, print. He stood stockstill a moment, listening tensely, thinking—hoping, rather, he'd been mistaken. But he hadn't. The slur of a bureau-drawer being drawn open or closed reached him, and then a faint tinkling sound as though something had lightly struck one of the glass toilet-articles on Fran's dresser.

Who else could it be but she? And yet there was a stealth to these vague disconnected noises that didn't sound like her. He would have heard her come in; her high heels usually exploded along the hardwood floors like little firecrackers.

Some sixth sense made him turn suddenly and look behind him, toward the dining-room, and he was just in time to see a man, half-crouched, shoulders bunched forward, creeping up on him. He was still a few yards away, beyond the dining-room threshold, but before Stapp could do more than drop open his mouth with reflex astonishment, he had closed in on him, caught him brutally by the throat with one hand, flung him back against the wall, and pinned him there.

"What are you doing here?" Stapp managed to gasp out.

"Hey, Bill, somebody *is* home!" the man called out guardedly. Then he struck out at him, hit him a stunning blow on the side of the head with his free hand. Stapp didn't reel because the wall was at the back of his head, that gave him back the blow doubly, and his senses dulled into a whirling flux for a minute.

Before they had cleared again, a second man had leaped down off the stairs from one of the rooms above, in the act of finishing cramming something into his pocket.

"You know what to do, hurry up!" the first one ordered. "Get me something to tie him with and let's get out of here!"

"For God's sake, don't tie—!" Stapp managed to articulate through the strangling grip on his windpipe. The rest of it was lost in a blur of frenzied struggle on his part, flailing out with his legs, clawing at his own throat to free it. He wasn't fighting the man off, he was only trying to tear that throttling impediment off long enough to get out what he had to tell them, but his assailant couldn't tell the difference. He struck him savagely a second and third time, and Stapp went limp there against the wall without altogether losing consciousness.

The second one had come back already with a rope, it looked like Fran's clothesline from the kitchen, that she used on Mondays.

Stapp, head falling forward dazedly upon the pinioning arm that still had him by the jugular, was dimly aware of this going around and around him, crisscross, in and out, legs and body and arms.

"Don't—" he panted. His mouth was suddenly nearly torn in two, and a large handkerchief or rag was thrust in, effectively silencing all further sound. Then they whipped something around outside of that, to keep it in, and fastened it behind his head. His senses were clearing again, now that it was too late.

"Fighter, huh?" one of them muttered grimly. "What's he protecting? The place is a lemon, there's nothing in it."

Stapp felt a hand spade into his vest-pocket, take his watch out. Then into his trouser-pocket and remove the little change he had on.

"Where'll we put him?"

"Leave him where he is."

"Naw. I did my last stretch just on account of leaving a guy in the open where he could put a squad-car on my tail too quick; they nabbed me a block away. Let's shove him back down in there where he was."

This brought on a new spasm, almost epileptic in its violence. He squirmed and writhed and shook his head back and forth. They had picked him up between them now, head and feet, kicked the basement door open, and were carrying him down the steps to the bottom. They still couldn't be made to understand that he wasn't resisting, that he wouldn't call the police, that he wouldn't lift a finger to have them apprehended—if they'd only let him get out of here, *with* them.

"This is more like it," one said, as they deposited him on the floor. "Whoever lives in the house with him won't find him so quick—"

Stapp started to roll his head back and forth on the floor like something demented, toward the clock, then toward them, toward the clock, toward them. But so fast that it finally lost all possible meaning, even if it would have had any for them in the first place, and it wouldn't have of course. They still thought he was trying to free himself in unconquerable opposition.

"Look at that!" one of them jeered. "Did you ever see anyone like him in your life?" He backed his arm threateningly at the wriggling form. "I'll give you one that'll hold you for good, if you don't cut it out!"

"Tie him up to that pipe over there in the corner," his companion suggested, "or he'll wear himself out rolling all over the place." They dragged him backwards along the floor and lashed him in a sitting position, legs out before him, with an added length of rope that had been coiled in the basement.

Then they brushed their hands ostentatiously and started up the basement stairs again, one behind the other, breathing hard from the struggle they'd had with him. "Pick up what we got and let's blow," one muttered. "We'll have to pull another one tonight—and this time you let *me* do the picking!"

"It looked like the berries," his mate alibied. "No one home, and standing way off by itself like it is."

A peculiar sound like the low simmering of a tea-kettle or the mewing of a newborn kitten left out in the rain to die came percolating thinly through the gag in Stapp's mouth. His vocal cords were strained to bursting with the effort it was costing him to make even that slight sound. His eyes were round and staring, fastened on them in horror and imploring.

They saw the look as they went on up, but couldn't read it. It might have been just the physical effort of trying to burst his bonds, it might have been rage and threatened retribution, for all they knew.

The first passed obliviously through the basement doorway and passed from sight. The second stopped halfway to the top of the stairs and glanced complacently back at him—the way he himself had looked back at his own handiwork just now, short minutes ago.

"Take it easy," he jeered, "relax. I used to be a sailor. You'll never get out of *them* knots, buddy."

Stapp swiveled his skull desperately, threw his eyes at the clock one last time. They almost started out of their sockets, he put such physical effort into the look.

This time the man got it finally, but got it wrong. He flung his arm at him derisively. "Trying to tell me you got a date? Oh no you haven't, you only think you have! Whadda you care what time it is, *you*'re not going any place!"

And then with the horrible slowness of a nightmare—though it only seemed that way, for he resumed his ascent fairly briskly—his head went out through the doorway, his shoulders followed, his waist next. Now even optical communication was cut off between them, and if only Stapp had had a minute more he might have made him understand! There was only one backthrust foot left in sight now, poised on the topmost basement step to take flight. Stapp's eyes were on it as though their burning plea could hold it back. The heel lifted up, it rose, trailed through after the rest of the man, was gone.

Stapp heaved himself so violently, as if to go after it by sheer will-power, that for a moment his whole body was a distended bow, clear of the floor from shoulders to heels. Then he fell flat again with a muffled thud, and a little dust came out from under him, and a half-dozen little separate skeins of sweat started down his face at one time, crossing and intercrossing as they coursed. The basement door ebbed back into its frame and the latch dropped into its socket with a minor click that to him was like the crack of doom.

In the silence now, above the surge of his own tidal breathing that came and went like surf upon a shoreline, was the counterpoint of the clock. Tick-tick, tick-tick, tick-tick, tick-tick.

For a moment or two longer he drew what consolation he could from the knowledge of their continued presence above him. An occasional stealthy footfall here and there, never more than one in succession, for they moved with marvelous dexterity, they must have had a lot of practice in breaking and entering. They were very cautious walkers from long habit even when there was no further need for it. A single remark filtered through, from somewhere near the back door. "All set? Let's take it this way." The creak of a hinge, and then the horrid finality of a door closing after them, the back door, which Fran may have forgotten to lock and by which they had presumably entered in the first place; and then they were gone.

And with them went his only link with the outside world. They were the only two people in the whole city who knew where he was at this moment. No one else, not a living soul, knew where to find him. Nor what would happen to him if he wasn't found and gotten out of here by three o'clock. It was twenty-five to two now. His discovery of their presence, the fight, their trussing him up with the rope, and their final unhurried departure, had all taken place within fifteen minutes.

It went tick-tick, tick-tock; tick-tick, tick-tock, so rhythmically, so remorselessly, so *fast*.

An hour and twenty-five minutes left. Eighty-five minutes left. How long that could seem if you were waiting for someone on a corner, under an umbrella, in the rain—like he had once waited for Fran outside the office where she worked before they were married, only to find that she'd been taken ill and gone home early that day.

How long that could seem if you were stretched out on a hospital-bed with knife-pains in your head and nothing to look at but white walls, until they brought your next tray—as he had been that time of the concussion. How long that could seem when you'd finished the paper, and one of the tubes had burned out in the radio, and it was too early to go to bed yet. How short, how fleeting, how instantaneous, that could seem when it was all the time there was left for you to live in and you were going to die at the end of it!

No clock had ever gone this fast, of all the hundreds that he'd looked at and set right. This was a demon-clock, its quarter-hours were minutes and its minutes seconds. Its lesser hand didn't even pause at all on those notches the way it should have, passed on from one to the next in perpetual motion. It was cheating him, it wasn't keeping the right time, somebody slow it down at least if nothing else! It was twirling like a pinwheel, that secondary hand.

Tick-tock-tick-tock-tick-tock. He broke it up into "Here I go, here I go, here I go."

There was a long period of silence that seemed to go on forever after the two of them had left. The clock told him it was only twenty-one minutes. Then at four to two a door opened above without warning—oh blessed sound, oh lovely sound!—the front door this time (over above *that* side of the basement), and high-heeled shoes clacked over his head like castanets.

"Fran!" he shouted. "Fran!" he yelled. "Fran!" he screamed. But all that got past the gag was a low whimper that didn't even reach across the basement. His face was dark with the effort it cost him, and a cord stood out at each side of his palpitating neck like a splint.

The tap-tap-tap went into the kitchen, stopped a minute (she was putting down her parcels; she didn't have things delivered because then you were expected to tip the errand-boys ten cents), came back again. If only there was something he could kick at with his interlocked feet, make a clatter with. The cellar-flooring was bare from wall to wall. He tried hoisting his lashed legs clear of the floor and pounding them down again with all his might; maybe the sound of the impact would carry up to her. All he got was a soft, cushioned sound, with twice the pain of striking a stone surface with your bare palm, and not even as much distinctness. His shoes were rubber-heeled, and he could not tilt them up and around far enough to bring them down on the leather part above the lifts. An electrical discharge of pain shot up the backs of his legs, coursed up his spine, and exploded at the back of his head, like a brilliant rocket.

Meanwhile her steps had halted about where the hall closet was (she must be hanging up her coat), then went on toward the stairs that led to the upper floor, faded out upon them, going up. She was out of earshot now, temporarily. But she was in the house with him at least! That awful aloneness was gone. He felt such gratitude for her nearness, he felt such love and need for her, he wondered how he could ever have thought of doing away with her—only one short hour ago. He saw now that he must have been insane to contemplate such a thing. Well if he had been, he was sane now, he was rational now, this ordeal had brought him to his senses. Only release him, only rescue him from his jeopardy, and he'd never again . . .

Five-after. She'd been back nine minutes now. There, it was ten. At first slowly, then faster and faster, terror, which had momentarily been quelled by her return, began to fasten upon him again. Why did she stay up there on the second floor like that? Why didn't she come down here to the basement, to look for something? Wasn't there anything down here that she might suddenly be in need of? He looked around, and there wasn't. There wasn't a possible thing that might bring her down here. They kept their basement so clean, so empty. Why wasn't it piled up with all sorts of junk like other people's! That might have saved him now.

She might intend to stay up there all afternoon! She might lie down and take a nap, she might shampoo her hair, she might do over an old dress. Any one of those trivial harmless occupations of a woman during her husband's absence could prove so fatal now! She might count on staying up there until it was time to begin getting his supper ready, and if she did—no supper, no she, no he.

Then a measure of relief came again. The man. The man whom he had intended destroying along with her, *he* would save him. He would be the means of his salvation. He came other days, didn't he, in the afternoon, while Stapp was away? Then, oh God, let him come today, make this one of the days they had a rendezvous (and yet maybe it just wasn't!). For if he came, that would bring her down to the lower floor, if only to admit him. And how infinitely greater his chances would be, with two pairs of ears in the house to overhear some wisp of sound he might make, than just with one.

And so he found himself in the anomalous position of a husband praying, pleading with every ounce of fervency he can muster, for the arrival, the materialization, of a rival whose existence he had only suspected until now, never been positive of.

Eleven past two. Forty-nine minutes left. Less than the time it took to sit through the "A"-part of a pictureshow. Less than the time it took to get a haircut, if you had to wait your turn. Less than the time it took to sit through a Sunday meal, or listen to an hour program on the radio, or ride on the bus from here to the beach for a dip. Less than all those things—to live. No, no, he had been meant to live thirty more years, forty! What had become of those years, those months, those weeks? No, not just *minutes* left, it wasn't fair!

"Fran!" he shrieked. "Fran, come down here! Can't you hear me?" The gag drank it up like a sponge.

The phone trilled out suddenly in the lower hallway, midway between him and her. He'd never heard such a beautiful sound before. "Thank God!" he sobbed, and a tear stood out in each eye. That must be the man now. That would bring her down.

Then fear again. Suppose it was only to tell her that he wasn't coming? Or worse still, suppose it was to ask her instead to come out and meet him somewhere else? Leave him alone down here, once again, with this horror ticking away opposite him. No child was ever so terrified of being left alone in the dark, of its parents putting out the light and leaving it to the mercy of the boogy-man as this grown man was at the thought of her going out of the house and leaving him behind.

It kept on ringing a moment longer, and then he heard her quick step descending the stairs to answer it. He could hear every word she said down there where he was. These cheap matchwood houses.

"Hello? Yes, Dave. I just got in now."

Then, "Oh Dave, I'm all upset. I had seventeen dollars upstairs in my bureau-drawer and it's gone, and the wrist-watch that Paul gave me is gone too. Nothing else is missing, but it looks to me as if someone broke in here while I was out and robbed us."

Stapp almost writhed with delight down there where he was. She knew they'd been robbed! She'd get the police now! Surely they'd search the whole place, surely they'd look down here and find him!

The man she was talking to must have asked her if she was sure. "Well, I'll look again, but I know it's gone. I know just where I left it, and it isn't there. Paul will have a fit."

No Paul wouldn't either; if she'd only come down here and free him he'd forgive her anything, even the cardinal sin of being robbed of his hard-earned money.

Then she said, "No, I haven't reported it yet. I suppose I should, but I don't like the idea—on your account, you know. I'm going to call up Paul at the shop. There's just a chance that he took the money and the watch both with him when he left this morning. I remember telling him the other night that it was losing time; he may have wanted to look it over. Well, all right, Dave, come on out then."

So he was coming, so Stapp wasn't to be left alone in the place; hot breaths of relief pushed against the sodden gag at the back of his palate.

There was a pause while she broke the connection. Then he heard her call his shop-number, "Trevelyan 4512," and wait while they were ringing, and of course no one answered.

Tick-tick, tick-tick, tick-tick.

The operator must have told her finally that they couldn't get the number. "Well, keep ringing," he heard her say, "it's my husband's store, he's always there at this hour."

He screamed in terrible silence: "I'm right here under your feet! Don't waste time! For God's sake, come away from the phone, come down here!"

Finally, when failure was reported a second time, she hung up. Even the hollow, cupping sound of that detail reached him. Oh, everything reached him—but help. This was a torture that a Grand Inquisitor would have envied.

He heard her steps move away from where the phone was. Wouldn't she guess by his absence from where he was supposed to be that something was wrong? Wouldn't she come down here now and look? (Oh, where was this woman's intuition they spoke about?!) No, how could she be expected to. What connection could the basement of their house possibly have in her mind with the fact that he wasn't in his shop? She wasn't even alarmed, so far, by his absence most likely. If it had been evening; but at this hour of the day—He might have gone out later than other days to his lunch, he might have had some errand to do.

He heard her going up the stairs again, probably to resume her search for the missing money and watch. He whimpered disappointedly. He was as cut off from her, while she remained up there, as if she'd been miles away, instead of being vertically over him in a straight line.

Tick, tock, tick, tock. It was twenty-one past two now. One half-hour and nine scant minutes more left. And they ticked away with the prodigality of tropical raindrops on a corrugated tin roof.

He kept straining and pulling away from the pipe that held him fast, then falling back exhausted, to rest awhile, to struggle and to strain some more. There was as recurrent a rhythm to it as there was to the ticking of the clock itself, only more widely spaced. How could ropes hold that unyieldingly? Each time he fell back weaker, less able to contend with them than the time before. For he wasn't little strands of hemp, he was layers of thin skin that broke one by one and gave forth burning pain and finally blood.

The doorbell rang out sharply. The man had come. In less than ten minutes after their phone talk he had reached the house. Stapp's chest started rising and falling with renewed hope. Now his chances were good again. Twice as good as before, with two people in the house instead of only one. Four ears instead of two, to hear whatever slight sound he might manage to make. And he must, he must find a way of making one. He gave the stranger his benediction while he stood there waiting to be admitted. Thank God for this admirer or whatever he was, thank God for their rendezvous. He'd give them his blessing if they wanted it, all his worldly goods; anything, anything, if they'd only find him, free him.

She came quickly down the stairs a second time and her footfalls hurried down the hall. The front door opened. "Hello, Dave," she said, and he heard the sound of a kiss quite clearly. One of those loud unabashed ones that bespeak cordiality rather than intrigue.

A man's voice, deep, resonant, asked: "Well, did it turn up yet?"

"No, and I've looked high and low," he heard her say. "I tried to get Paul after I spoke to you, and he was out to lunch."

"Well, you can't just let seventeen dollars walk out the door without lifting your finger."

For seventeen dollars they were standing there frittering his life away—and their own too, for that matter, the fools!

"They'll think I did it, I suppose," he heard the man say with a note of bitterness.

"Don't say things like that," she reproved. "Come in the kitchen and I'll make you a cup of coffee."

Her quick brittle step went first, and his heavier, slower one followed. There was the sound of a couple of chairs being drawn out, and the man's footfalls died out entirely. Hers continued busily back and forth for a while, on a short orbit between stove and table.

What were they going to do, *sit* up there for the next half-hour? Couldn't he *make* them hear in some way? He tried clearing his throat, coughing. It hurt furiously, because the lining of it was all raw from long strain. But the gag muffled even the cough to a blurred purring sort of sound.

Twenty-six to three. Only minutes left now, minutes; not even a full half-hour any more.

Her footsteps stopped finally and one chair shifted slightly as she joined him at the table. There was linoleum around the stove and sink that deadened sounds, but the middle part of the room where the table stood was ordinary pine-board flooring. It let things through with crystalline accuracy.

He heard her say, "Don't you think we ought to tell Paul about—us?"

The man didn't answer for a moment. Maybe he was spooning sugar, or thinking about what she'd said. Finally he asked, "What kind of a guy is he?"

"Paul's not narrow-minded," she said. "He's very fair and broad."

Even in his agony, Stapp was dimly aware of one thing: that didn't sound a bit like her. Not her speaking well of him, but that she could calmly, detachedly contemplate broaching such a topic to him. She had always seemed so proper and slightly prudish. This argued a sophistication that he hadn't known she'd had.

The man was evidently dubious about taking Paul into their confidence, at least he had nothing further to say. She went on, as though trying to convince him: "You have nothing to be afraid of on Paul's account, Dave, I know him too well. And don't you see, we can't keep on like this? It's better to go to him ourselves and tell him about you, than wait until he finds out. He's liable to think something else entirely, and keep it to himself, brood, hold it against me, unless we explain. I know that he didn't believe me that night when I helped you find a furnished room, and told him I'd been to a movie. And I'm so nervous and upset each time he comes home in the evening, it's a wonder he hasn't noticed it before now. Why I feel as guilty as if—as if I were one of these disloyal wives or something." She laughed embarrassedly, as if apologizing to him for even bringing such a comparison up.

What did she mean by that?

"Didn't you ever tell him about me at all?"

"You mean in the beginning? Oh, I told him you'd been in one or two scrapes, but like a little fool I let him think I'd lost track of you, didn't know where you were any more."

Why, that was her brother she'd said that about!

The man sitting up there with her confirmed it right as the thought burst in his mind. "I know it's tough on you, Sis. You're happily married and all that. I've got no right to come around and gum things up for you. No one's proud of a jailbird, an escaped convict, for a brother—"

"David," he heard her say, and even through the flooring there was such a ring of earnestness in her voice Stapp could almost visualize her reaching across the table and putting her hand reassuringly on his, "there isn't anything I wouldn't do for you, and you should know that by now. Circumstances have been against you, that's all. You shouldn't have done what you did, but that's spilt milk and there's no use going back over it now."

"I suppose I'll have to go back and finish it out. Seven years, though, Fran, seven years out of a man's life—"

"But this way you have no life at all—"

Were they going to keep on talking his life away? Nineteen to three. One quarter of an hour, and four minutes over!

"Before you do anything, let's go downtown and talk it over with Paul, hear what he says." One chair jarred back, then the other. He could hear dishes clatter, as though they'd all been lumped together in one stack. "I'll do these when I come back," she remarked.

Were they going to leave again? Were they going to leave him behind here, alone, with only minutes to spare?

Their footsteps had come out into the hall now, halted a moment undecidedly. "I don't like the idea of you being seen with me on the streets in broad daylight, you could get in trouble yourself, you know. Why don't you phone him to come out here instead?"

Yes, yes, Stapp wailed. Stay with me! Stay!

"I'm not afraid," she said gallantly. "I don't like to ask him to leave his work at this hour, and I can't tell him over the phone. Wait a minute, I'll get my hat." Her footsteps diverged momentarily from his, rejoined them again.

Panic-stricken, Stapp did the only thing he could think of. Struck the back of his head violently against the thick pipe he was attached to.

A sheet of blue flame darted before his eyes. He must have hit one of the welts where he had already been struck once by the burglars. The pain was so excruciating he knew he couldn't repeat the attempt. But they must have heard something, some dull thud or reverberation must have carried up along the pipe. He heard her stop short for a minute and say, "What was that?"

And the man, duller-sensed than she and killing him all unknowingly, "What? I didn't hear anything."

She took his word for it, went on again, to the hall-closet to get her coat. Then her footsteps retraced themselves all the way back through the dining-room to the kitchen. "Wait a minute, I want to make sure this back door's shut tight. Locking the stable after the horse is gone!"

She came forward again through the house for the last time, there was the sound of the front door opening, she passed through it, the man passed through it, it closed, and they were gone. There was the faint whirr of a car starting up outside in the open.

And now he was left alone with his self-fashioned doom a second time, and the first seemed a paradise in retrospect compared to this, for then he had a full hour to spare, he had been rich in time, and now he only had fifteen minutes, one miserly quarter-hour.

There wasn't any use struggling any more. He'd found that out long ago. He couldn't anyway, even if he'd wanted to. Flames seemed to be licking lazily around his wrists and ankles.

He'd found a sort of palliative now, the only way there was left. He'd keep his eyes down and pretend the hands were moving slower than they were, it was better than watching them constantly, it blunted a little of the terror at least. The ticking he couldn't hide from. Of course every once in a while when he couldn't resist looking up and verifying his own calculations, there'd be a renewed burst of anguish, but in-between-times it made it more bearable to say, "It's only gained a half-minute since the last time I looked." Then he'd hold out as long as he could with his eyes down, but when he couldn't stand it any more and would have to raise them to see if he was right, it had gained *two* minutes. Then he'd have a bad fit of hysterics, in which he called on God, and even on his long-dead mother, to help him, and couldn't see straight through the tears. Then he'd pull himself together again, in a measure, and start the self-deception over again. "It's only about thirty seconds now since I last looked. . . . Now it's about a minute . . ." (But was it? But was it?) And so on, mounting slowly to another climax of terror and abysmal collapse.

Then suddenly the outside world intruded again, that world that he was so cut off from that it already seemed as far-away, as unreal, as if he were already dead. The doorbell rang out.

He took no hope from the summons at first. Maybe some peddler—no, that had been too aggressive to be a peddler's ring. It was the sort of ring that claimed admission as its right, not as a favor. It came again. Whoever was ringing was truculently impatient at being kept waiting. A third ring was given the bell, this time a veritable blast that kept on for nearly half-a-minute. The party must have kept his finger pressed to the bell-button the whole time. Then as the peal finally stopped, a voice called out forcefully: "Anybody home in there? Gas Company!" And suddenly Stapp was quivering all over, almost whinnying in his anxiety.

This was the one call, the one incident in all the day's domestic routine, from earliest morning until latest night, that could have possibly brought anyone down into the basement! The meter was up there on the wall, beside the stairs, staring him in the face! And her brother had had to take her out of the house at just this particular time! There was no one to let the man in.

There was the impatient shuffle of a pair of feet on the cement walk. The man must have come down off the porch to gain perspective with which to look inquiringly up at the second-floor windows. And for a fleeting moment, as he chafed and shifted about out there before the house, on the walk and off, Stapp actually glimpsed the blurred shanks of his legs standing before the grimy transom that let light into the basement at ground-level. All the potential savior had to do was crouch down and peer in through it, and he'd see him tied up down there. And the rest would be so easy!

Why didn't he, why didn't he? But evidently he didn't expect anyone to be in the basement of a house in which his triple ring went unanswered. The tantalizing trouserleg shifted out of range again, the transom became blank. A little saliva filtered through the mass of rag in Stapp's distended mouth, trickled across his silently vibrating lower lip.

The gas inspector gave the bell one more try, as if venting his disappointment at being balked rather than in any expectation of being admitted this late in the proceedings. He gave it innumerable short jabs, like a telegraph-key. Bip-bip-bip-bip-bip. Then he called out disgustedly, evidently for the benefit of some unseen assistant waiting in a truck out at the curb, "They're never in when you want 'em to be!" There was a single quick tread on the cement, away from the house. Then the slur of a light truck being driven off.

Stapp died a little. Not metaphorically, literally. His arms and legs got cold up to the elbows and knees, his heart seemed to beat slower, and he had trouble getting a full breath; more saliva escaped and ran down his chin, and his head drooped forward and lay on his chest for awhile, inert.

Tick-tick, tick-tick, tick-tick. It brought him to after awhile, as though it were something beneficent, smelling salts or ammonia, instead of being the malevolent thing it was.

He noticed that his mind was starting to wander. Not much, as yet, but every once in awhile he'd get strange fancies. One time he thought that his *face* was the clock-dial, and that thing he kept staring at over there was his face. The pivot in the middle that held the two hands became his nose, and the 10 and the 2, up near the top, became his eyes, and he had a red-tin beard and head of hair and a little round bell on the exact top of his crown for a hat. "Gee, I look funny," he sobbed drowsily. And he caught himself twitching the muscles of his face, as if trying to stop those two hands that were clasped on it before they progressed any further and killed that man over there, who was breathing so metallically: tick, tock, tick, tock.

Then he drove the weird notion away again, and he saw that it had been just another escape-mechanism. Since he couldn't control the clock over there, he had attempted to change it into something else. Another vagary was that this ordeal had been brought on him as punishment for what he had intended doing to Fran, that he was being held fast there not by the inanimate ropes but by some active, punitive agency, and that if he exhibited remorse, pledged contrition to a proper degree, he could automatically effect his release at its hands. Thus over and over he whined in the silence of his throttled throat, "I'm sorry. I won't do it again. Just let me go this one time, I've learned my lesson, I'll never do it again."

The outer world returned again. This time it was the phone. It must be Fran and her brother, trying to find out if he'd come back here in their absence. They'd found the shop closed, must have waited outside of it for a while, and then when he still didn't come, didn't know what to make of it. Now they were calling the house from a booth down there, to see if he had been taken ill, had returned here in the meantime. When no one answered, that would tell them, surely, that something was wrong. Wouldn't they come back now to find out what had happened to him?

But why should they think he was here in the house if he didn't answer the phone? How could they dream he was in the basement the whole time? They'd hang around outside the shop some more waiting for him, until as time went on, and Fran became real worried, maybe they'd go to the police. (But that would be hours from now, what good would it do?) They'd look everywhere but here for him. When a man is reported missing the last place they'd look for him would be in his own home.

It stopped ringing finally, and its last vibration seemed to hang tenuously on the lifeless air long after it had ceased, humming outward in a spreading circle like a pebble dropped into a stagnant pool. *Mmmmmmmmm,* until it was gone, and silence came rolling back in its wake.

She would be outside the pay-booth or wherever it was she had called from, by this time. Rejoining her brother, where he had waited. Reporting, "He's not out at the house either." Adding the mild, still unworried comment, "Isn't that strange? Where on earth can he have gone?" Then they'd go back and wait outside the locked shop, at ease, secure, unendangered. She'd tap her foot occasionally in slight impatience, look up and down the street while they chatted.

And now *they* would be two of those casuals who would stop short and say to one another at three o'clock: "What was that?" And Fran might add, "It sounded as though it came from out our way." That would be the sum-total of their comment on his passing.

Tick, tock, tick, tock, tick, tock. Nine minutes to three. Oh, what a lovely number was nine. Let it be nine forever, not eight or seven, nine for all eternity. Make time stand still, that he might breathe though all the world around him stagnated, rotted away. But no, it was already eight. The hand had bridged the white gap between the two black notches. Oh, what a precious number was eight, so rounded, so symmetrical. Let it be eight forever—

A woman's voice called out in sharp reprimand, somewhere outside in the open: "Be careful what you're doing, Bobby, you'll break a window!" She was some distance away, but the ringing dictatorial tones carried clearly.

Stapp saw the blurred shape of a ball strike the basement-transom, he was looking up at it, for her voice had come in to him through there. It must have been just a tennis-ball, but for an instant it was outlined black against the soiled pane, like a small cannonball; it seemed to hang there suspended, to adhere to the glass, then it dropped back to the ground. If it had been ordinary glass it might have broken it, but the wire-mesh had prevented that.

The child came close up against the transom to get its ball back. It was such a small child that Stapp could see its entire body within the height of the pane, only the head was cut off. It bent over to pick up the ball, and then its head came into range too. It had short golden ringlets all over it. Its profile was turned toward him, looking down at the ball. It was the first human face he'd seen since he'd been left where he was. It looked like an angel. But an inattentive, unconcerned angel.

It saw something else while it was still bent forward close to the ground, a stone or something that attracted it, and picked that up too and looked at it, still crouched over, then finally threw it recklessly away over its shoulder, whatever it was.

The woman's voice was nearer at hand now, she must be strolling along the sidewalk directly in front of the house. "Bobby, stop throwing things like that, you'll hit somebody!"

If it would only turn its head over this way, it could look right in, it could see him. The glass wasn't too smeary for that. He started to weave his head violently from side to side, hoping the flurry of motion would attract it, catch its eye. It may have, or its own natural curiosity may have prompted it to look in without that. Suddenly it had turned its head and was looking directly in through the transom. Blankly at first, he could tell by the vacant expression of its eyes.

Faster and faster he swiveled his head. It raised the heel of one chubby, fumbling hand and scoured a little clear spot to squint through. Now it could see him, now surely! It still didn't for a second. It must be much darker in here than outside, and the light was behind it.

The woman's voice came in sharp reproof: "Bobby, what are you doing there?!"

And then suddenly it saw him. The pupils of its eyes shifted over a little, came to rest directly on him. Interest replaced blankness. Nothing is strange to children—not a man tied up in a cellar any more than anything else—yet everything is. Everything creates wonder, calls for comment, demands explanation. Wouldn't it say anything to her? Couldn't it talk? It must be old enough to; she, its mother, was talking to it incessantly. "Bobby, come away from there!"

"Mommy, look!" it said gleefully.

Stapp couldn't see it clearly any more, he was shaking his head so fast. He was dizzy, like you are when you've just gotten off a carousel; the transom and the child it framed kept swinging about him in a half-circle, first too far over on one side, then too far over on the other.

But wouldn't it understand, wouldn't it understand that weaving of the head meant he wanted to be free? Even if ropes about the wrists and ankles had no meaning to it, if it couldn't tell what a bandage around the mouth was, it must know that when anyone writhed like that they wanted to be let loose. Oh God, if it had only been two years older, three at the most! A child of eight, these days, would have understood and given warning.

"Bobby, are you coming? I'm waiting!"

If he could only hold its attention, keep it rooted there long enough in disobedience to her, surely she'd come over and get it, see him herself as she irritably sought to ascertain the reason for its fascination.

He rolled his eyes at it in desperate comicality, winked them, blinked them, crossed them. An elfin grin peered out on its face at this last; already it found humor in a physical defect, or the assumption of one, young as it was.

An adult hand suddenly darted downward from the upper right-hand corner of the transom, caught its wrist, bore its arm upward out of sight. "Mommy, look!" it said again, and pointed with its other hand. "Funny man, tied up."

The adult voice, reasonable, logical, dispassionate—inattentive to a child's fibs and fancies—answered: "Why that wouldn't look nice, Mommy can't peep into other people's houses like you can."

The child was tugged erect at the end of its arm, its head disappeared above the transom. Its body was pivoted around, away from him; he could see the hollows at the back of its knees for an instant longer, then its outline on the glass blurred in withdrawal, it was gone. Only the little clear spot it had scoured remained to mock him in his crucifixion.

The will to live is an unconquerable thing. He was more dead than alive by now, yet presently he started to crawl back again out of the depths of his despair, a slower longer crawl each time, like that of some indefatigable insect buried repeatedly in sand, that each time manages to burrow its way out.

He rolled his head away from the window back toward the clock finally. He hadn't been able to spare a look at it during the whole time the child was in sight. And now to his horror it stood at three to three. There was a fresh, a final blotting-out of the burrowing insect that was his hopes, as if by a cruel idler lounging on a beach.

He couldn't *feel* any more, terror or hope or anything else. A sort of numbness had set in, with a core of gleaming awareness remaining that was his mind. *That* would be all that the detonation would be able to blot out by the time it came. It was like having a tooth extracted with the aid of novocaine. There remained of him now only this single pulsing nerve of premonition; all the tissue around it was frozen. So protracted foreknowledge of death was in itself its own anaesthetic.

Now it would be too late even to attempt to free him first, before stopping the thing. Just time enough, if someone came down those stairs this very minute, sharp-edged knife with which to sever his bonds already in hand, for him to throw himself over toward it, reverse it. And now—now it was too late even for that, too late for anything but to die.

He was making animal-noises deep in his throat as the minute hand slowly blended with the notch of twelve. Guttural sounds like a dog worrying a bone, though the gag prevented their emerging in full volume. He puckered the flesh around his eyes apprehensively, creased them into slits—as though the closing of his eyes could ward off, lessen, the terrific force of what was to come! Something deep within him, what it was he had no leisure nor skill to recognize, seemed to retreat down long dim corridors away from the doom that impeded. He hadn't known he had those convenient corridors of evasion in him, with their protective turns and angles by which to put distance between himself and menace. Oh clever architect of the Mind, oh merciful blueprints that made such emergency exits available. Toward them this something, that was he and yet not he, rushed; toward sanctuary, security, toward waiting brightness, sunshine, laughter.

The hand on the dial stayed there, upright, perpendicular, a perfect right-angle to its corollary, while the swift seconds that were all there were left of existence ticked by and were gone. It wasn't so straight now any more, but he didn't know it, he was in a state of death already. White reappeared between it and the twelve-notch, *behind* it now. It was one minute after three. He was shaking all over from head to foot—not with fear, with laughter.

IT BROKE into sound as they plucked the dampened, bloodied gag out, as though they were drawing the laughter out after it, by suction or osmosis.

"No, don't take those ropes off him yet!" the man in the white coat warned the policeman sharply. "Wait'll they get here with the straitjacket first, or you'll have your hands full."

Fran said through her tears, cupping her hands to her ears, "Can't you stop him from laughing like that? I can't stand it. Why does he keep laughing like that?"

"He's out of his mind, lady," explained the intern patiently.

The clock said five past seven. "What's in this box?" the cop asked, kicking at it idly with his foot. It shifted lightly along the wall a little, and took the clock with it.

"Nothing," Stapp's wife answered, through her sobs and above his incessant laughter. "Just an empty box. It used to have some kind of fertilizer in it, but I took it out and used it on the flowers I—I've been trying to raise out in back of the house."

Change of Murder

He who hesitates is caught

BRAINS DONLEAVY, early one Chicago evening, set out to call upon his friend Fade Williams. He was dressed for the occasion in a dark blue hourglass overcoat, eyebrow-level derby, and armpit-cuddling .38. It being a windy evening he would have caught cold without any one of the three, particularly the last.

He and Fade had known each other for years. They had so much on each other they were of necessity the best of friends; the .38 therefore was just habit and not precaution. Fade, to be accurate, was not the given name of the gent. Although he had been known to vanish, disappear into thin air, for long stretches at a time, his nickname didn't derive from that trait either. It was borrowed from a game of chance, the lowly pastime of shooting craps, in which the expression "fade" means one player is willing to match the other's stake—put up an equal amount—in other words, back the hazard.

Not that Fade ever played craps; there were bigger and better ways of earning money. He was a semi-professional alibi doctor, a backstop, a set-up arranger. Although good stiff fees figured in his adroit juggling of times, places and circumstances, his amateur standing must be granted; he wasn't listed in the telephone red book and he had no shingle out advertising his services. He had to know you; you couldn't just walk in off the street, plank down a retainer and walk out with an alibi all neatly done up in brown paper. A too-frequent appearance in the witness chair, helping to clear persons "mistakenly" accused of committing crime, might have caused Justice to squint suspiciously at Fade after awhile.

But Fade's batting-average was consistently good, that arranging a deal with him was almost like buying immunity at the outset. Which was why Brains Donleavy was on his way to him right then, having a murder in mind.

Brains would have been indignant to hear it called that. With him it was just "getting squared up." Murder was the name for other people's killings, not his. Not one of the half-a-dozen he already had to his credit had lacked cause or justice as he saw it. He never killed simply for the sake of killing, nor even for profit; it was just that he had an almost elephantine faculty for holding grudges.

Yet relentless as he could be about wiping out old scores, there was also a wide streak of sentimentality in his make-up. "Mother Machree" could bring tears to his eyes if his beer had been needled enough. He had been known to pitch rocks through butcher-shop windows in the dead of night simply to release the imprisoned kittens locked behind them. Anyway, he found his way into one of the lesser honky-tonks that infest the Loop district, the designation "The Oasis" flaming above it in red tube-letters. It was not a club or cabaret, simply a beer-garden used by Fade as a front. A radio provided what entertainment there was. The bartender tilted his head to inquire "Waddle it be?"

"It'll be the boss," said Brains. "Tell him Donleavy."

The bartender didn't move from the spot, just bent over as if to take a look at what stock he had lined up below the bar. His lips moved soundlessly, he straightened up, and a thumb popped out of his balled fist.

"Straight through the back," he said. "See that door there?"

Brains did and went toward it. Before he quite made it, it opened and Fade was standing there to welcome him.

"How's the boy?" he said hospitably.

"I got something I gotta talk over with you," said Brains.

"Sure," said Fade, "come right in." He guided him through with an affectionate arm about his shoulder, looked back to scan the outside of the establishment once more, then closed the door after them.

There was a short passageway with a telephone-booth on each side of it, ending at the open door of Fade's office. The booth on the left-hand side had a sign dangling from it, "Out of order." In brushing by, Brains dislodged it and it fell down. Fade carefully picked it up and replaced it before following him in. Then he closed the office door after them.

"Well," he said, "how d'ye like my new place? Nifty, ain't it?"

Brains looked around. On the desk that Fade had recently been sitting at lay a .38, broken open. Near it was a scrap of soiled chamois rag, and a little pile of the bullets that had come out of the gun.

Brains smiled humorlessly. "Weren't expecting trouble, were you?" he asked.

"I always do that, like to fiddle around with 'em, keep 'em clean," explained Fade. "Helps me pass the time away, sitting in here by the hour like I do. I've got quite a few hanging around, sometimes I take 'em out and look 'em over—makes me think of the old days." He sat down, scooped up the bullets in the hollow of his hand, and began to replace them in the gun one by one. "What's on your mind?" he said, poring over his task.

Brains abruptly sat down opposite him. "Listen, I got a little squaring-up set for tomorrow night," he began confidentially. "You be the doctor, will ya? Set me up good and foolproof—"

"A rub-out?" asked Fade without even looking up at him. "What, again?"

"Why, I haven't raised a rod to no one in eighteen months," protested Brains virtuously.

"Maybe so, but you was in stir the first twelve, or so they tell me. Why don't you lay off once in awhile, give it a rest?"

"I wasn't up for no rub-out," contradicted Brains, "you oughta know that; you squared my last one for me. They got me for knocking down an old lady one time I was practising learning to drive a pal's car."

Fade clicked the reloaded gun shut and put it down.

"Which reminds me," he remarked, getting up and going over to a small wall-safe, "I think I got something coming to me on that Cincinnati cover-up I done for you."

"Sure," agreed Brains placidly, tapping an inner pocket. "I got the do-re-mi with me right now."

Fade apparently wasn't taking his word for it unsupported; he opened the little built-in strongbox, drew out a cluttered handful of papers, and scanned them one by one.

"Yeah, here it is," he said. "One-fifty, made out to look like a gambling debt. You gave me the other one-fifty the night before, remember?" He thrust the rest back into the safe, brought it over to the desk with him—without, however, taking his hand off it.

Brains was laboriously counting out ten-spots, moistening his thumb. He pushed the heap across the desk when he was through. "There y'go—"

"Want me to tear this up for you?" offered Fade, edging the I.O.U.

forward with one hand, pulling the money toward him with the other.

"I'll tear it up myself," remarked Brains. He looked at it, folded it, and carefully put it away. "It might slip your mind." Neither one showed any animosity. "Now, how about it?" he went on. "Will you cover me for tomorrow night?"

Fade picked up the .38 and the rag once more, went back to cleaning it.

"You're getting to be a bad risk, Brains," he murmured between puffs of breath on the metal. "Once or twice it's a pushover, but you're starting to go in for it too often. If I keep popping up in front of you each time, it starts to look bad for me; they were already smelling a rat in Cincinnati that time, kept coming around questioning me for weeks afterwards." He went on scouring lovingly for awhile. "It's gonna take five hundred this time, if I do it for you," he let his client know. "It keeps getting tougher to make it look right all the time."

"Five hundred!" exclaimed Brains heatedly. "You must be screwy! For five hundred I could go out and get half-a-dozen guys paid off, without having to do it myself!"

Fade jerked his head impassively toward the door. "Then go ahead, why come to me?" Brains made no move to get up and leave, however. "You know as well as me," Fade told him, "whoever you hired would loosen up in the first station-house back room they brought him to. And another thing," he added shrewdly, "it's the satisfaction of doing it yourself you're after."

Brains nodded vigorously. "Sure. Who the hell wants to git squared up by remote control? I like t'see their eyes when they lamp the slug with their name on it coming outa the gat. I like t'see them fall and turn over, kinda slow the way they do—" He shuffled through the remainder of the money he was holding. "Give ya a century now," he offered, "that's all I got left on me. I guarantee ya the other four hundred the minute the heat goes down. You couldn't expect the full amount beforehand anyway; nobody does business that way."

He slithered the money enticingly under Fade's downturned palm. "What d'ya say?" he urged. "It's a pushover, a natural—you can fix me up with one hand tied behind your back." And by way of professional flattery, "I coulda got him in Gary last week already, but I kept my hands down. I wouldn't pull it without one of your outs to back me."

Fade put down his cleaning-rag, snapped the wad of bills back and forth a couple of times under his thumb-nail, finally wacked them against the edge of the desk by way of consent.

"Gimme a little dope on it," he said gruffly. "And make it your last for a while, will ya? I'm no Houdini."

Brains hitched his chair forward eagerly. "What my reason is, is poisonal. This guy has stomped all over my pet corns. You don't needa know who he is and I ain't telling ya. I followed him there from Gary early in the week, like I said, and I been keeping close tabs on him ever since. He ain't even expecting nothing to happen to him, which is what's so beautiful about it." He clasped his hands, spit between them, and rubbed them together, eyes beaming. "He's at a rat-hole on the North Side, and the way the layout is, he's practically begging for it. I been drawing diagrams all week and I got it by heart." He took out pencil and paper and began to scratch away. Fade leaned forward interestedly, cautioning, "Keep your voice down."

"It's seven stories high and he's got a room on the top floor. Now I don't even have to go in and out or pass anybody to get at him, see? The winder of his room looks out on an air shaft that dents in the side wall. There's no fire-escape—nothing—just a drain-pipe running up and down the shaft. Now across the shaft is a six-story tenement-flat smack up against the hotel. It's such a cheesy place they don't even keep the roof door locked, you can walk right up from the street. I been up there all week, lying flat on my belly looking into his room. I got a plank hidden away up there right now, waiting for me to use it to get across on. I even measured it across to his window ledge while he was out of his room, and it reaches with lots of room left over. He's on the seventh floor, the flat's six stories high, so the roof is only about a yard above the top of his winder, there ain't even enough incline to the plank to make it hard getting back across again—" He spread his hands triumphantly. "I plug him through one of these big Idaho potatoes, and they won't even hear it happen in the next room, much less out on the street!"

Fade dug at his nose judiciously. "It's got points in its favor and it's got points against it," he submitted. "Watch yourself on that plank business, remember what happened that time at Hopewell."

"I didn't even bring it in the house with me," gloated Brains. "It was half off and I yanked it outa the backyard fence."

"Suppose he sees you coming across on it; won't he duck outa the room?"

"I'm getting in while he's out, I'll be laying for him in the closet when he comes back. He leaves his winder open from the bottom each time to get air in the room."

"How about other windows on a line with his? Somebody might squint out and happen to get a look at you crossing over."

"There's no dent in the wall of the flat, so there's no winders on that side at all. On the hotel side there's just one winder to a floor on the shaft, all straight under his. The room under him's been vacant since day before yesterday—no one there to see. From the fifth floor down I don't think they could see the plank that far away against the night sky; it's painted dark green and the shaft is a buzzard for darkness. That's my end of it and it's a lulu. Now let's hear your end, showing how I wasn't even there at all to do it!"

"How much time you want?" Fade asked.

"I can be there and back and leave him lying stretched out cold behind me in thirty minutes," said Brains.

"I'll give you an hour, starting from here and coming back here," clipped Fade. "Now sign this I.O.U., and then pay close attention. If it goes wrong you've only got yourself to blame."

Brains read the slip of paper Fade had filled out. Like the last transaction of this kind between them, it was disguised as a simple gambling debt and had absolutely no legal value. It didn't have to have. Brains knew what the penalty for welshing on one of those haphazard little scraps of writing would have been. It had no time limit, but Fade was surer of collecting on it in the end than a creditor backed to the hilt by all the legal red tape ever devised.

Brains laboriously scrawled "Brains Donleavy" at the bottom of it, mouth open, and returned it. Fade put it in the safe along with the hundred cash, closed it without bothering to lock it.

"Now come outside the door with me a minute," he said. "I wanna show you something."

In the passageway between the two phone booths he said, "Get this and hang onto it; you're paying five hundred for it: There's no way in or out of my office except through the front, like you came in. No windows, nothing. Once you're in, you're in—until everyone outside there sees you come out again." He dug his elbow into Brains' ribs. "But here's how you leave—and here's how you come back in again when you're all squared-up over there."

He unhitched the "Out of Order" sign, tucked it under his arm, and folded back the glass slide of the booth. "Step in," he invited, "like you was gonna call up somebody—and shove hard against the back wall of the booth."

Brains did so—and nearly fell out into the open on his ear; the wall was hinged like a door. He took a quick look around him, saw that he was at the back of a dimly-lighted garage. The nearest light-bulb was yards away. The outside of the door was whitewashed to blend with the plaster of the walls; the battered hulk of an old car, with the wheels removed, was standing in such a way that it formed a screen for the peculiar exit.

Brains got back in again, the door swung to after him. He stepped out of the booth, Fade closed it and hung the sign back in place.

"I own the garage," he mentioned, "but just the same don't let the guy out there see you come through. He ain't hep to it; neither is the bartender on this side. The booth's a dummy I had built for myself."

"Kin it open from the outside for you to get back again?" Brains wanted to know.

"No, leave a little wedge of cardboard under it on your way out, like a shoehorn," Fade told him, "but not wide enough for any light to shine through. Now, what time you showing up here?"

"Ten," said Brains. "He always gets in the same time each night, round ten-thirty."

"Okay," said Fade briskly. "You ask for me out front, like tonight. I come out there and we slap each other on the back, toss off a couple together. Then we wander back here and somehow we get into a friendly little game of two-handed draw poker. I send out for more drinks and the barman brings 'em in and sees us both in here, in our shirtsleeves. We yell a lot at each other, so that everybody in the place can hear us—I'll see that the radio ain't going. Then we quiet down, and that's when you duck out. I'll raise a howl every once in awhile, like you was still in here with me. After you get back, we both stroll out again and I see you to the door. You won heavy, see, and to prove it you stand everyone in the place a drink before you go—they'll remember you by that alone, don't worry. There's your set-up."

Brains looked at him admiringly. "Kid," he said, "it's worth close to five hundred at that, the way you tell it!"

"Hell," said Fade lugubriously, "I ain't making enough profit on it you could sneeze at—installin' that fake booth alone come to near a hundred-fifty."

He sat down at the desk once more, took up the .38 and rag, and resumed his fancy work. "Another thing, if you're riding back, zig-zag and change cabs. Don't give 'em a chance to trace you in a straight line back to the garage. I own it, like I told you." He squinted down the bore of the gun toward the handle, blew his breath along it.

"Watch y'self, you reloaded that thing," Brains warned jumpily. "One of these days you're gonna blow your own head off monkeying around that way. Well, I'm gonna go home and get a good night's rest so I can enjoy myself t'morra night." He saluted from his eyebrow and departed.

"S'matta wit the radio, don't it work?" a barfly was asking the following evening when Brains walked in. An unusual silence hung over "The Oasis," although they were lined up two deep before the mirror.

"It's gotta go to the repair-shop," answered the bartender curtly. He saw Brains coming and ducked below the counter without waiting to be told, put his mouth to the speaking-tube Fade had rigged up between the bar and his office. The back door opened and Fade came out, booming cordial greetings. Every head turned that way.

Fade and Brains each slung an arm to the other's shoulder, made a place for themselves at the rail.

"Set 'em up for my pal Donleavy," ordered Fade. Brains tried to pay. "Naw, this is my house," protested Fade.

Several minutes of this at the top of their voices, and the bartender slung a pair of dice down before them. They clicked busily for awhile, idle eyes watching every move. Finally Fade cast them from him impatiently.

"Y'got my blood up now," he confessed. "I know a better way than this of getting back atcha! C'mon back in the office, I'll go you a few rounds with the cards." The door closed behind them.

"They'll be in there all night," said the bartender knowingly.

Once they were behind the door all their labored cordiality vanished. They went to work in cold-blooded silence. Fade stripped the stamp off a new deck of cards, strewed them across the table. He sluiced off coat and vest, hung them on a peg; Brains likewise, revealing his shoulder-holster. They each grabbed up five cards at random, sat down at opposite sides of the desk.

"Jack," muttered Fade, tapping the table. Brains hauled out a fistful of change and singles, flung it down between them. They both relaxed, scanned their hands.

"Play with what y'got," mouthed Fade, "he'll be in with the drinks in a minute."

The second door, between the office and the phone booths, had been left open. Brains flipped down two cards, reached for two more. The outside door suddenly opened and the barman came in with two glasses and a bottle on a tray. He left it open behind him, and they were in full sight of those at the bar for a few minutes. He put down the bottle and glasses, then paused to glance noisily over his employer's shoulder. His eyes widened; Fade was holding a royal flush, it had just happened that way.

"Scram," the latter remarked curtly, "and don't come back in again. I gotta concentrate!"

The man edged out with the empty tray, closed the outer door after him, and went back to tell the customers about the phenomenal luck his boss was having.

Fade instantly turned his hand around so Brains could see it.

"Raise a racket," he commanded, "and get going! Don't forget the wedge under the booth or you won't get in again."

Brains was busy shoveling on vest, coat, and topcoat and buttoning himself into them. He banged his fist down on the desk with enough force to shatter it and let loose a roar of startled profanity. Fade matched him bellow for bellow; both their faces were stonily impassive.

"I'll let out a howl every once in awhile like you was still in here with me," Fade promised.

Brains downed his drink, clasped his own hands together and shook them at him, pushed back the door of the booth with the "Out of Order" sign on it, and sandwiched himself into it. He closed it, tore the cover off a folder of matches and pleated it together, then pushed the hinged door ajar on the other side of him and slipped through. The wedge held it on a crack; there was just room enough to get a nail-hold.

The back of the garage was steeped in gloom. He edged forward around the derelict chassis and peered ahead. The single attendant was way out front at the entrance, standing talking to the owner of a car that had just driven in.

Brains skittered along toward them, but stayed close to the wall, screened by a long row of parked cars, bending double to bridge the gap between each one and the next. One had been run in too close to the wall; he had to climb the rear bumper and run along it like a monkey to get by. The last car in line, however, was still a good fifteen or twenty yards from the mouth of the garage, and there was a big, bare, gasoline-soaked stretch between him and the open street ahead. He skulked waiting where he was, in the shadow cast by the last car. In about a minute more the customer went away on foot, the mechanic got in the car and drove it past Brains' hiding-place to the back of the garage. It was an ideal chance to leave unseen, better than he'd thought he'd get. He straightened up, sprinted across the remaining stretch of concrete, turned from sight at the entrance, and went walking unhurriedly down the street.

AT THE second corner he came to, he got into a cab, and got out again half-way to his destination. He went into a store, asked the price of a fountain pen, came out again and got into another cab. This time he got out two blocks from where he was going, at right angles to it. The cab went one way and he went the other, around the corner. He headed straight for the dingy flat, as though he lived in it; didn't look around him going in and above all didn't make the mistake of passing it the first time and then doubling back.

There was no one out on the stoop to watch him go by. He pushed the unlocked door in and went trudging slowly up the stairs, just like anyone coming home tired. Everything was with him tonight, he didn't even meet anyone the whole six flights, although the place was a beehive of noise.

Someone came out and went down, but that was after he was two floors above. After the top landing, he put the soft pedal on his trudge and quickened it. The roof door, latched on the inside, didn't squeak any more; he'd oiled the hinges himself two nights before. He eased it shut behind him and found himself out in the dark, moving silently across graveled tar. The plank was still there where he'd left it, on

the opposite side from where he was going to use it, so no one seeing
it in the daytime would connect it with the hotel window across the
air shaft. He brought it over, set it down, flattened himself on his
stomach, and peered over the edge.

He treated himself to a one-cornered smile. The room behind the
window was dark, its occupant hadn't come in yet. The lower pane
was open a foot from the bottom, to get a little air in. Just the way
he'd told Fade it would be! The window below was blank; they
hadn't rented that room yet since last night. Even the second and
third ones down were dark; there wasn't a light above the third floor,
and this far up it showed no bigger than a postage stamp. The whole
layout was made to order.

He got up on his knees, hauled the plank across the low lead coping, and began to pay it out aimed at the window. He kept pressure
on it at his end with one foot so it wouldn't sink below the window-
ledge in midair with his own weight. It crossed the ledge without
touching it and pushing the curtains back under the open window.
Then he let it down very slowly and carefully and the gap was
bridged. He made sure it extended far back enough over the coping,
lest it slip off after he was on it; then he let go of it, brushed his
hands, stood up, and stepped up on it where it rested on the coping.
He balanced himself gingerly.

He wasn't worried about it snapping under his weight; he'd tested
it plenty before now on the roof itself. He bent down on it, grasped
one edge with each hand, and started across it on hands and knees.
The distance wasn't great, and he kept from looking down, fastened
his eyes on the window just ahead. There was a very slight incline,
but not enough to bother him. He saw to it that it didn't tip by
keeping his weight in the middle as much as possible. In fact, he had
everything down pat—couldn't miss. The window pane came to
meet him until it lay cold across the tip of his nose. He hooked his
hands onto the bottom of it, flung it the rest of the way up, and
corkscrewed down under it into the room. It had been as easy as all
that!

The first thing he did was lower it again behind him to its original
level. He shoved the board back a little so the dent it made wouldn't
be so noticeable against the curtains, but left it in place. He didn't
have to put the lights on; he'd memorized the exact position of every
article of furniture in the room from his vantage point on the roof

opposite. He opened the closet door, shoved the clothes on their hangers a little to one side to make room for himself. Then he took the .38 out from under his arm, went over to the room door, and stood listening. There wasn't a sound from outside. He reached in his topcoat pocket and pulled out a large raw potato with a small hole carefully bored through it. He jammed this onto the muzzle of his gun for a silencer, tight enough so it wouldn't fall off. Then he sat down for awhile on a chair in the dark, holding it in his hand and peering toward the door.

After about fifteen minutes an elevator-door clashed open somewhere in the distance. He got right up, stepped backwards into the closet, and swung the door to in front of him. He left it on a slight crack, a thread of visibility, just enough for one eye to see through. That one-cornered smile had come back on his face. A key jiggled in the room door. It opened, and someone's black outline showed against the lighted hall. It closed again and the lights went up in the room.

For a split second the face that turned was in a line with the crack of the closet door, and Brains nodded to himself; the right guy had come home to the right room, and the last possible, but unlikely, hitch to his plan was safely out of the way—he'd come home alone.

Then the face passed on out of focus. The key clashed down on the glass bureau top, an edge of a dark coat fell across the white bed, and there was a click and a midget radio started to warm up with a low whine. The guy yawned once out loud, moved around a little out of sight. Brains just stood there waiting, muffled gun in hand.

When it came it was quick as the flash of a camera shutter. The closet door was suddenly wide open and they were staring into each other's faces, not more than six inches apart. The guy's one hand was still on the doorknob, the other was holding up his coat ready to hang. He dropped that first of all. Brains didn't even bring the gun up, it was already in position. The guy's face went from pink to white to gray, and sort of slid loose like jelly ready to fall off his skull. He took a very slow step back to keep from falling, and Brains took a very slow step out after him. He kicked the guy's coat out of the way without looking at it.

"Well, Hitch," he said softly, "the first three out have your name on 'em. Close your eyes if you want to."

Hitch didn't; instead they got big and round as hard-boiled eggs with their shells off. His mouth and tongue moved for a whole minute without getting anything off. Finally three words formed. "What's it for?"

Brains only heard them because he was so close.

"Keep turning slowly around while I remind you," he said, "paws loose like a dog begging for a bone."

As the victim tottered around in one place like a top riding for a fall, hands dangling downward at shoulder level, Brains deftly slapped him in just the right number of places to make sure he was unarmed.

"All right," he acquiesced, "that was the last exercise you'll be taking."

The other man stopped rotating, buckled a little at the knees, then just hung there as if he was suspended from a cord.

The toy radio finally got through its warming up, the whine faded out of it, and a third voice entered the room, tinny and blurred. Brains' eyes flickered over that way for an instant, then back to the doughy face in front of him.

"I get out of stir six months ago," he snarled, "and the first thing I do is come back looking for my last year's frail—they call her Goldie—you used to see me with her, remember?"

Hitch's eyes began rolling around in his face like buckshot.

"No sign of Goldie anywhere," resumed Brains, "so I ask around, and what do I hear? That a rat named Hitch, who was supposed to be a friend of mine, had stepped up and walked off with Goldie while my back is turned. Now get me right"—he motioned the gun slightly—"it ain't the dame that's troubling me; they got no sense anyway and I wouldn't want her now even if I could have her—but no guy does that to me and gets way with it. Don't matter if it's business, or a dame, or just passing remarks about me I don't like, anyone that crowds me, this is how I git squared up."

The creases across the knuckle of his trigger-finger began to smooth out as it started bending back; Hitch's eyes were on them, dilated like magnifying glasses. "Don't I get a word in?" he said hoarsely.

"It won't do ya no good," Brains promised, "but go ahead, let's hear ya try to lie out of it—the same answer'll still be ready for ya behind this spud."

Hitch began to shake all over, in his anxiety to get the greatest number of words out of his system in the shortest possible length of time. "I ain't gonna lie, you've got me and what good would it do? She was starving," he yammered, "the cash you left with her run out on her—" Even in the midst of the panic that gripped him his eyes found time to gauge Brains' reaction to this. "I know you left her well-heeled but—but somebody lifted it, cleaned her out," he corrected. "She came to me, and she didn't have the price of a meal on her, didn't have a roof over her. I—I started looking after her, on account of you was my friend—"

Brains snorted disgustedly. Sweat was pouring down Hitch's face. The voice on the radio had been replaced by thin weepy strains of music now. Again Brains' eyes shifted to it, lingered for a minute, then came back again.

"Wouldn'tcha have done that for anyone yourself?" Hitch pleaded. "Wouldn'tcha have done that yourself? Then, without meaning to, I guess we kinda fell for each other—"

Brains didn't bat an eye, but the gun was pointed a little lower, at the victim's thigh now, not his chest; the weight of the potato may have done that. Hitch's head had followed it down, his eyes were on it; he seemed to be staring contritely at the floor.

"We knew we was wrong. We talked it over lots; we both said how swell you was—" A shade of color had returned to his face; it was still pale but no longer gray. He kept swallowing, it could have been either over-powering emotion or the need for keeping his throat well-lubricated. "Finally we give in—we just couldn't help it—we got married—" A slight sob thickened his voice.

For the first time Brains showed some surprise; his mouth opened a little and stayed that way. Hitch seemed to find inspiration in the pattern of the hotel rug that met his eyes.

"Not only that but—but Goldie has a kid now. We have a little baby—" He looked up ruefully. "We named it after you—" The gun was pointing straight down at the floor now; the opening between Brains' nose and chin had widened. His mouth softened.

"Wait, I got one of her letters right in the drawer here—you can read it for yourself. Open it," Hitch invited, "so you won't think I'm trying to get out a rod. I'll stand here by the wall."

Brains reached past him, yanked at the drawer, looked down into it.

"Get it out," he said uncertainly, "show it to me, if you got it."

Hitch's hand had rested idly on the radio for a moment; the volume went up. "Just a song at twilight," it lisped. He fumbled hurriedly in the drawer, brought out an envelope, stripped it away with eager fingers. He unfolded the letter, turned it toward Brains, showed him the signature. "See? It's from her—'Goldie.' "

"Show me about the kid," said Brains gruffly.

Hitch turned it around, pointed to the bottom of the first page. "There it is, read it—I'll hold it up for you."

Brains had good eyes, he didn't have to come any closer. It stood out in black and white. *"I am taking good care of your baby for you. I think of you every time I look at it—"*

Hitch let the letter drop. His jaw wobbled. "Now go ahead, buddy, do like you said you were gonta," he sighed.

Brains' narrow stretch of brow was furrowed with uncertainty. He kept looking from the radio to the letter on the floor, and back to the radio again. "Still to us at twilight," it drooled, "comes love's old sweet song—" He blinked a couple of times. No moisture actually appeared in his eyes, but they had a faraway, gluey look. Hitch didn't seem to be breathing any more, he was so quiet.

There was a *clop* and the potato dropped off the downturned gun and split on the floor. Brains came to with an effort.

"And yuh named it after me?" he said. "Donleavy Hitchcock?"

The other nodded wistfully.

Brains took a deep breath. "I dunno," he said doubtfully, "maybe I'm wrong about letting ya get away with this; maybe I hadn't oughta—I never changed me mind before." He gave him a disgusted look. "Somehow ya got me outa the mood now—" He tucked the gun back under his arm, took possession of the room key on the bureau-top. "Go stand outside the door and wait there," he ordered curtly. "I ain't going out the front way, I'm leaving like I come in, see, without nobody being the wiser. You can tell 'em you locked yourself out. I don't want you in the room back of me while I'm crossing over."

Hitch was halfway through the door before he had finished speaking.

"And don't try nothing funny, or I may change me mind yet," Brains warned him. He thrust one leg through the window, found the plank, then turned his head to ask, "What color eyes has it got, anyway?" But Hitch hadn't waited to discuss the matter any further, he was far down the hall by that time, mopping his face on his sleeve as he ran.

Brains, dragging his feet after him across the plank like a cripple, muttered glumly, "How could I plug him when he named his kid after me? Maybe Fade was right. I oughta let up oncet in awhile. I guess I've bumped off enough guys. It won't hurt to let one off; maybe it'll bring me good luck."

It was easier going back than it had been coming over. The tilt of the board helped. He vaulted down over the low parapet onto the roof of the flat. He hauled the board over after him. Then he took Hitch's room key out of his pocket and calmly dropped it down the shaft; brushed his hands with a strange new feeling of nobility, of having done a good deed, that none of the actual killings he'd committed had ever been able to give him. He gave his hat a jaunty upward hoist in back, went in through the roof door, and started down the stairs to the street. He didn't care if anyone saw him or not now, but again no one did, just as when he'd come in.

HE CAME out on the sidewalk and looked around for a taxi to take him back to Fade; he wanted his century back of course; he didn't need any alibi now. He hoped Fade wouldn't try to get petty-larceny about it, but he could show him his gun, fully loaded, to convince him he hadn't done it, if necessary. It wasn't exactly a taxi-using neighborhood; there weren't any in sight, so he started walking along, waiting to pick one up. He gave his hat another tilt from behind, he felt so good.

"Gee, it gives ya a funny feeling," he mumbled, "to have a kid named after ya."

By this time Hitch was back in his room again, having sent a bellboy in ahead of him with a passkey to make sure the coast was clear. He had the door closed, the window tightly latched, and the shade drawn, and just to be on the safe side he was checking out, going somewhere else to sleep, as soon as he could get his things together. But for the time being he was helpless, couldn't do a thing, just leaned there against the bureau shaking all over and with his head bobbing up and down. He wasn't shaking with fright, but with uncontrollable, splitting laughter. In his hand he held the letter from Brains' former ladylove, Goldie, that he'd picked up from the floor.

At the bottom of the first page it said, just as Brains had read, *"taking good care of your baby. Think of you every time I look at it."* But every time he turned the page to the other side he went into a fresh spasm of hilarity. It went on: *"—and I'm sure glad you left it with me, never can tell what might turn up while you're gone. There's nothing like having a .32 around when a gal is by herself. Don't forget to pick up another in Chi for yourself, in case you run across you-know-who—"* The proud parent had to hold his sides, if he laughed any harder he was going to bust a rib.

BRAINS GOT a cab about three blocks down from the tenement. He didn't bother changing half-way, but out of consideration for Fade, he didn't ride straight up to the garage with it. He got out a short walk away from his destination. He could have gone back in the front way through "The Oasis" just as well as not now, but after all that trick out was Fade's bread-and-butter, so why spoil it for him? Why give it away to everyone at the bar? They'd be bound to find out about it if he did that.

The garage entrance yawned as wide open as ever, but even the mechanic wasn't in sight this time; there didn't seem to be much business. He went in just like he'd come out, squeezing along between the wall and the line of parked cars, walking the bumper of the one that was pushed in too far, unseen by living eyes.

When he got a considerable distance past the open office door he could see the guy sitting in there, reading a paper. He circled around the wheelless chassis, found the slight ridge in the whitewashed wall that the out-thrust booth made, got a grip on it with his nails, eased the wedge out from under it, and got it open. He stayed in the booth until the wall had closed tight behind him, then looked out through the glass. The door to the front room was still closed, the door to Fade's office was still open waiting to welcome him. He stepped out of the booth, closed it behind him, sign and all, and then he stopped to listen. Gee, they were making a lot of noise out there—everyone's feet seemed to be running at once. Somebody was pounding on the door from the outside. They wanted Fade—he hadn't gotten back a minute too soon! He could hear the bartender hollering through, "Boss! Are ya'll right, boss? What's up, boss?" Brains twisted around and ducked into the office.

"I changed me mind," he gasped. "Just made it. They're callin' for ya—whadda they want out there? Wait'll I get my—!" His fingers went racing down the front of his topcoat, jacket; unbuttoning. He shrugged them both off his shoulders together and they slipped down his back. They caught at his elbows and stayed that way, half-on, half-off, while he blinked and stared across the table.

The set-up was the same—the cards, the drinks, the money—only Fade had dozed over it waiting for him to come back. His chin was down over his chest and his head kept going lower right while Brains was looking at him, sort of hitching a notch at a time. There was a funny bluish sort of haze in three horizontal lines hanging like a curtain right over Fade's head, and there wasn't any cigar around that he'd been smoking.,

Brains leaned across the table, gripped Fade by the shoulder, felt the warmth of his body through the shirt.

"Hey, wake up—!" Then he saw the gun in Fade's lap where it had dropped, and the tag-end of the haze was still lazily coming from it. The chamois rag was down below on the floor. He knew the answer even before he'd picked up the gun, tilted Fade's face and looked at it. Fade had cleaned one of those guns of his once too often. When his head came up he only had one eye, it had gone right through the other.

The door out there slammed back and they came pouring through, everyone in the place. The room was suddenly choked with them. They saw him like that, straightening up across the desk, the gun in his hand, coat half-on. He felt somebody take the gun away from him, and then his arms were being held at his sides and the bartender was saying "What'd you do to him?" and sending out for cops. The hell with keeping his secret now, the guy was dead! He struggled violently, tried to free himself, couldn't.

"I just got in!" he roared. "He did it himself—I tell ya I just got in!"

"You been rowing with him all evening!" the bartender shouted. "Just a minute before the shot I heard him bawling you out; so did everyone else in the place—how can you say you just got in?"

Brains recoiled as though an invisible sledge-hammer had hit him, and slowly began to freeze where he stood. He could feel unidentified hands fumbling around him, cops' hands now, and kept trying to think his way out; kept trying to think while they compared the

I.O.U. he'd taken back from Fade with the new one he'd given him afterwards. He shook his head as if he was groggy, trying to clear it.

"Wait, lemme show you," he heard himself saying, "there's a dummy telephone-booth right outside the door there; I came in through it right after it happened—lemme show you!"

He knew they'd let him all right, knew they'd go and look at it— but somehow he already knew what good it was going to do him. No one had seen him go and no one had seen him come. Only Hitch, and just try to get Hitch to help him!

As he led them outside toward it, body straining downward toward the floor in his eagerness to get there quick, he kept whimpering under his breath, "Six guys I killed and they never touch me for it; the seventh I let live, and they hook me for a killing I never even done at all!"

Momentum

PAINE HUNG AROUND outside the house waiting for old Ben Burroughs' caller to go, because he wanted to see him alone. You can't very well ask anyone for a loan of $250 in the presence of someone else, especially when you have a pretty strong hunch you're going to be turned down flat and told where to get off, into the bargain.

But he had a stronger reason for not wanting witnesses to his interview with the old skinflint. The large handkerchief in his back pocket, folded triangularly, had a special purpose, and that little instrument in another pocket—wasn't it to be used in prying open a window?

While he lurked in the shrubbery, watching the lighted window and Burroughs' seated form inside it, he kept rehearsing the plea he'd composed, as though he were still going to use it.

"Mr. Burroughs, I know it's late, and I know you'd rather not be reminded that I exist, but desperation can't wait; and I'm desperate." That sounded good. "Mr. Burroughs, I worked for your concern faithfully for ten long years, and the last six months of its existence, to help keep it going. I voluntarily worked at half-wages, on your given word that my defaulted pay would be made up as soon as things got better. Instead of that, you went into phony bankruptcy to cancel your obligations."

Then a little soft soap to take the sting out of it. "I haven't come near you all these years, and I haven't come to make trouble now. If I thought you really didn't have the money, I still wouldn't. But it's common knowledge by now that the bankruptcy was feigned; it's obvious by the way you continue to live that you salvaged your own investment; and I've lately heard rumors of your backing a dummy corporation under another name to take up where you left off. Mr. Burroughs, the exact amount of the six months' promissory half-wages due me is two hundred and fifty dollars."

Just the right amount of dignity and self-respect, Pauline had commented at this point; not wishy-washy or maudlin, just quiet and effective.

And then for a bang-up finish, and every word of it true. "Mr. Burroughs, I have to have help tonight; it can't wait another twenty-four hours. There's a hole the size of a fifty-cent piece in the sole of each of my shoes, I have a wedge of cardboard in the bottom of each one. We haven't had light or gas in a week now. There's a bailiff coming tomorrow morning to put out the little that's left of our furniture and seal the door.

"If I was alone in this, I'd still fight it through, without going to anyone. But, Mr. Burroughs, I have a wife at home to support. You may not remember her, a pretty little dark-haired girl who once worked as a stenographer in your office for a month or two. You surely wouldn't know her now, she's aged twenty years in the past two."

That was about all. That was about all anyone could have said. And yet Paine knew he was licked before he even uttered a word of it.

He couldn't see the old man's visitor. The caller was out of range of the window. Burroughs was seated in a line with it, profile toward Paine. Paine could see his mean, thin-lipped mouth moving. Once or twice he raised his hand in a desultory gesture. Then he seemed to be listening and finally he nodded slowly. He held his forefinger up and shook it, as if impressing some point on his auditor. After that he rose and moved deeper into the room, but without getting out of line with the window.

He stood against the far wall, hand out to a tapestry hanging there. Paine craned his neck, strained his eyes. There must be a wall safe behind there the old codger was about to open.

If he only had a pair of binoculars handy.

Paine saw the old miser pause, turn his head and make some request of the other person. A hand abruptly grasped the looped shade cord and drew the shade to the bottom.

Paine gritted his teeth. The old fossil wasn't taking any chances, was he? You'd think he was a mind-reader, knew there was someone out there. But a chink remained, slowing a line of light at the bottom. Paine sidled out of his hiding place and slipped up to the window. He put his eyes to it, focused on Burroughs' dialing hand, to the exclusion of everything else.

A three-quarters turn to the left, about to where the numeral 8 would be on the face of the clock. Then back to about where 3 would be. Then back the other way, this time to 10. Simple enough. He must remember that—8–3–10.

Burroughs was opening it now and bringing out a cash box. He set it down on the table and opened it. Paine's eyes hardened and his mouth twisted sullenly. Look at all that money! The old fossil's gnarled hand dipped into it, brought out a sheaf of bills, counted them. He put back a few, counted the remainder a second time and set them on the table top while he returned the cash box, closed the safe, straightened out the tapestry.

A blurred figure moved partly into the way at this point, too close to the shade gap to come clearly into focus; but without obliterating the little stack of bills on the table. Burroughs' claw-like hand picked them up, held them out. A second hand, smoother, reached for them. The two hands shook.

Paine prudently retreated to his former lookout point. He knew where the safe was now, that was all that mattered. He wasn't a moment too soon. The shade shot up an instant later, this time with Burroughs' hand guiding its cord. The other person had withdrawn offside again. Burroughs moved after him out of range, and the room abruptly darkened. A moment later a light flickered on in the porch ceiling.

Paine quickly shifted to the side of the house, in the moment's grace given him, in order to make sure his presence wasn't detected.

The door opened. Burroughs' voice croaked a curt "Night," to which the departing visitor made no answer. The interview had evidently not been an altogether cordial one. The door closed again, with quite a little force. A quick step crossed the porch, went along the cement walk to the street, away from where Paine stood pressed flat against the side of the house. He didn't bother trying to see who it was. It was too dark for that, and his primary purpose was to keep his own presence concealed.

When the anonymous tread had safely died away in the distance, Paine moved to where he could command the front of the house. Burroughs was alone in it now, he knew; he was too niggardly even to employ a full-time servant. A dim light showed for a moment or two through the fanlight over the door, coming from the back of the hall. Now was the time to ring the doorbell, if he expected to make his plea to the old duffer before he retired.

He knew that, and yet something seemed to be keeping him from stepping up onto the porch and ringing the doorbell. He knew what it was, too, but he wouldn't admit it to himself.

"He'll only say no point-blank and slam the door in my face" was the excuse he gave himself as he crouched back in the shrubbery, waiting. "And then once he's seen me out here, I'll be the first one he'll suspect afterwards when—"

The fanlight had gone dark now and Burroughs was on his way upstairs. A bedroom window on the floor above lighted up. There was still time; if he rang even now, Burroughs would come downstairs again and answer the door. But Paine didn't make the move, stayed there patiently waiting.

The bedroom window blacked out at last, and the house was now dark and lifeless. Paine stayed there, still fighting with himself. Not a battle, really, because that had been lost long ago; but still giving himself excuses for what he knew he was about to do. Excuses for not going off about his business and remaining what he had been until now—an honest man.

How could he face his wife, if he came back empty-handed tonight? Tomorrow their furniture would be piled on the sidewalk. Night after night he had promised to tackle Burroughs, and each time he'd put it off, walked past the house without summoning up nerve enough to go through with it. Why? For one thing, he didn't have the courage to stomach the sharp-tongued, sneering refusal that he was sure he'd get. But the more important thing had been the realization that once he made his plea, he automatically canceled this other, unlawful way of getting the money. Burroughs had probably forgotten his existence after all these years, but if he reminded him of it by interviewing him ahead of time—

He tightened his belt decisively. Well, he wasn't coming home to her empty-handed tonight, but he still wasn't going to tackle Burroughs for it either. She'd never need to find out just how he'd got it.

He straightened and looked all around him. No one in sight. The house was isolated. Most of the streets around it were only laid out and paved by courtesy; they bordered vacant lots. He moved in cautiously but determinedly toward the window of that room where he had seen the safe.

Cowardice can result in the taking of more risks than the most reckless courage. He was afraid of little things—afraid of going home and facing his wife empty-handed, afraid of asking an ill-tempered old reprobate for money because he knew he would be reviled and driven away—and so he was about to break into a house, become a burglar for the first time in his life.

It opened so easily. It was almost an invitation to unlawful entry. He stood up on the sill, and the cover of a paper book of matches, thrust into the intersection between the two window halves, pushed the tongue of the latch out of the way.

He dropped down to the ground, applied the little instrument he had brought to the lower frame, and it slid effortlessly up. A minute later he was in the room, had closed the window so it wouldn't look suspicious from the outside. He wondered why he'd always thought until now it took skill and patience to break into a house. There was nothing to it.

He took out the folded handkerchief and tied it around the lower part of his face. For a minute he wasn't going to bother with it, and later he was sorry he had, in one way. And then again, it probably would have happened anyway, even without it. It wouldn't keep him from being seen, only from being identified.

He knew enough not to light the room lights, but he had nothing so scientific as a pocket torch with him to take their place. He had to rely on ordinary matches, which meant he could only use one hand for the safe dial, after he had cleared the tapestry out of the way.

It was a toy thing, a gimcrack. He hadn't even the exact combination, just the approximate position—8-3-10. It wouldn't work the first time, so he varied it slightly, and then it clicked free.

He opened it, brought out the cash box, set it on the table. It was as though the act of setting it down threw a master electric switch. The room was suddenly drenched with light and Burroughs stood in the open doorway, bathrobe around his weazened frame, left hand out to the wall switch, right hand holding a gun trained on Paine.

Paine's knees knocked together, his windpipe constricted, and he died a little—the way only an amateur caught red-handed at his first attempt can, a professional never. His thumb stung unexpectedly, and he mechanically whipped out the live match he was holding.

"Just got down in time, didn't I?" the old man said with spiteful satisfaction. "It mayn't be much of a safe, but it sets off a buzzer up by my bed every time it swings open—see?"

He should have moved straight across to the phone, right there in the room with Paine, and called for help, but he had a vindictive streak in him, he couldn't resist standing and rubbing it in.

"Ye know what ye're going to get for this, don't ye?" he went on, licking his indrawn lips. "And I'll see that ye get it too, every last month of it that's coming to ye." He took a step forward. "Now get away from that. Get all the way back over there and don't ye make a move until I—"

A sudden dawning suspicion entered his glittering little eyes. "Wait a minute. Haven't I seen you somewhere before? There's something familiar about you." He moved closer. "Take off that mask," he ordered. "Let me see who the devil you are!"

Paine became panic-stricken at the thought of revealing his face. He didn't stop to think that as long as Burroughs had him at gun point anyway, and he couldn't get away, the old man was bound to find out who he was sooner or later.

He shook his head in unreasoning terror.

"No!" he panted hoarsely, billowing out the handkerchief over his mouth. He even tried to back away, but there was a chair or something in the way, and he couldn't.

That brought the old man in closer. "Then by golly I'll take it off for ye!" he snapped. He reached out for the lower triangular point of it. His right hand slanted out of line with Paine's body as he did so, was no longer exactly covering it with the gun. But the variation was nothing to take a chance on.

Cowardice. Cowardice that spurs you to a rashness the stoutest courage would quail from. Paine didn't stop to think of the gun. He suddenly hooked onto both the old man's arms, spread-eagled them. It was such a hare-brained chance to take that Burroughs wasn't expecting it, and accordingly it worked. The gun clicked futilely, pointed up toward the ceiling; it must have jammed, or else the first chamber was empty and Burroughs hadn't known it.

Paine kept warding that arm off at a wide angle. But his chief concern was the empty hand clawing toward the handkerchief. That he swiveled far downward the other way, out of reach. He twisted the scrawny skin around the old man's skinny right wrist until pain made the hand flop over open and drop the gun. It fell between them to the floor, and Paine scuffed it a foot or two out of reach with the side of his foot.

Then he locked that same foot behind one of Burroughs' and

pushed him over it. The old man went sprawling backwards on the floor, and the short, unequal struggle was over. Yet even as he went, he was victorious. His downflung left arm, as Paine released it to send him over, swept up in an arc, clawed, and took the handkerchief with it.

He sprawled there now, cradled on the point of one elbow, breathing malign recognition that was like a knife through Paine's heart. "You're Dick Paine, you dirty crook! I know ye now! You're Dick Paine, my old employee! You're going to pay for this—"

That was all he had time to say. That was his own death warrant. Paine was acting under such neuromuscular compulsion, brought on by the instinct of self-preservation, that he wasn't even conscious of stooping to retrieve the fallen gun. The next thing he knew it was in his hand, pointed toward the accusing mouth that was all he was afraid of.

He jerked the trigger. For the second time it clicked—either jammed or unloaded at that chamber. He was to have that on his conscience afterwards, that click—like a last chance given him to keep from doing what he was about to do. That made it something different, that took away the shadowy little excuse he would have had until now; that changed it from an impulsive act committed in the heat of combat to a deed of cold-blooded, deliberate murder, with plenty of time to think twice before it was committed. And conscience makes cowards of us all. And he was a coward to begin with.

Burroughs even had time to sputter the opening syllables of a desperate plea for mercy, a promise of immunity. True, he probably wouldn't have kept it.

"Don't! Paine—Dick, don't! I won't say anything. I won't tell 'em you were here—"

But Burroughs knew who he was. Paine tugged at the trigger, and the third chamber held death in it. This time the gun crashed, and Burroughs' whole face was veiled in a huff of smoke. By the time it had thinned he was already dead, head on the floor, a tenuous thread of red streaking from the corner of his mouth, as though he had no more than split his lip.

Paine was the amateur even to the bitter end. In the death hush that followed, his first half-audible remark was: "Mr. Burroughs, I didn't mean to—"

Then he just stared in white-faced consternation. "Now I've done it! I've killed a man—and they kill you for that! Now I'm in for it!"

He looked at the gun, appalled, as though it alone, and not he, was to blame for what had happened. He picked up the handkerchief, dazedly rubbed at the weapon, then desisted again. It seemed to him safer to take it with him, even though it was Burroughs' own. He had an amateur's mystic dread of fingerprints. He was sure he wouldn't be able to clean it thoroughly enough to remove all traces of his own handling; even in the very act of trying to clean it, he might leave others. He sheathed it in the inner pocket of his coat.

He looked this way and that. He'd better get out of here; he'd better get out of here. Already the drums of flight were beginning to beat in him, and he knew they'd never be silent again.

The cash box was still standing there on the table where he'd left it, and he went to it, flung the lid up. He didn't want this money any more, it had curdled for him, it had become bloody money. But he had to have some, at least; to make it easier to keep from getting caught. He didn't stop to count how much there was in it; there must have been at least a thousand, by the looks of it. Maybe even fifteen or eighteen hundred.

He wouldn't take a cent more than was coming to him. He'd only take the two hundred and fifty he'd come here to get. To his frightened mind that seemed to make his crime less heinous, if he contented himself with taking just what was rightfully his. That seemed to keep it from being outright murder and robbery, enabled him to maintain the fiction that it had been just a collection of a debt accompanied by a frightful and unforeseen accident. And one's conscience, after all, is the most dreaded policeman of the lot.

And furthermore, he realized as he hastily counted it out, thrust the sum into his back trouser pocket, buttoned the pocket down, he couldn't tell his wife that he'd been here—or she'd know what he'd done. He'd have to make her think that he'd got the money somewhere else. That shouldn't be hard. He'd put off coming here to see Burroughs night after night, he'd shown her plainly that he hadn't relished the idea of approaching his former boss; she'd been the one who had kept egging him on.

Only tonight she'd said, "I don't think you'll ever carry it out. I've about given up hope."

So what more natural than to let her think that in the end he hadn't? He'd think up some other explanation to account for the presence of the money; he'd have to. If not right tonight, then to-morrow. It would come to him after the shock of this had worn off a little and he could think more calmly.

Had he left anything around that would betray him, that they could trace to him? He'd better put the cash box back; there was just a chance that they wouldn't know exactly how much the old skinflint had had on hand. They often didn't, with his type. He wiped it off carefully with the handkerchief he'd had around his face, twisted the dial closed on it, dabbed at that. He didn't go near the window again; he put out the light and made his way out by the front door of the house.

He opened it with the handkerchief and closed it after him again, and after an exhaustive survey of the desolate street, came down off the porch, moved quickly along the front walk, turned left along the gray tape of sidewalk that threaded the gloom, toward the distant trolley line that he wasn't going to board at this particular stop, at this particular hour.

He looked up once or twice at the star-flecked sky as he trudged along. It was over. That was all there was to it. Just a jealously guarded secret now. A memory, that he daren't share with anyone else, not even Pauline. But deep within him he knew better. It wasn't over, it was just beginning. That had been just the curtain raiser, back there. Murder, like a snowball rolling down a slope, gathers momentum as it goes.

He had to have a drink. He had to try to drown the damn thing out of him. He couldn't go home dry with it on his mind. They stayed open until four, didn't they, places like that? He wasn't much of a drinker, he wasn't familiar with details like that. Yes, there was one over there, on the other side of the street. And this was far enough away, more than two-thirds of the way from Burroughs' to his own place.

It was empty. That might be better; then again it might not. He could be too easily remembered. Well, too late now, he was already at the bar. "A straight whiskey." The barman didn't even have time to turn away before he spoke again. "Another one."

He shouldn't have done that; that looked suspicious, to gulp it that quick.

"Turn that radio off," he said hurriedly. He shouldn't have said that, that sounded suspicious. The barman had looked at him when l e did. And the silence was worse, if anything. Unbearable. Those throbbing drums of danger. "Never mind, turn it on again."

"Make up your mind, mister," the barman said in mild reproof.

He seemed to be doing all the wrong things. He shouldn't have come in here at all, to begin with. Well, he'd get out, before he put his foot in it any worse. "How much?" He took out the half-dollar and the quarter that was all he had.

"Eighty cents."

His stomach dropped an inch. Not *that* money! He didn't want to have to bring that out, it would show too plainly on his face. "Most places they charge thirty-five a drink."

"Not this brand. You didn't specify." But the barman was on guard now, scenting a dead beat. He was leaning over the counter, right square in front of him, in a position to take in every move he made with his hands.

He shouldn't have ordered that second drink. Just for a nickel he was going to have to take that whole wad out right under this man's eyes. And maybe he wouldn't remember that tomorrow, after the jumpy way Paine had acted in here!

"Where's the washroom?"

"That door right back there behind the cigarette machine." But the barman was now plainly suspicious; Paine could tell that by the way he kept looking at him.

Paine closed it after him, sealed it with his shoulder-blades, unbuttoned his back pocket, riffled through the money, looking for the smallest possible denomination. A ten was the smallest, and there was only one of them; that would have to do. He cursed himself for getting into such a spot.

The door suddenly gave a heave behind him. Not a violent one, but he wasn't expecting it. It threw him forward off balance. The imperfectly grasped outspread fan of money in his hand went scattering all over the floor. The barman's head showed through the aperture. He started to say: "I don't like the way you're acting. Come on now, get out of my pla—" Then he saw the money.

Burroughs' gun had been an awkward bulk for his inside coat pocket all along. The grip was too big, it overspanned the lining. His abrupt lurch forward had shifted it. It felt as if it was about to fall out of its own weight. He clutched at it to keep it in.

The barman saw the gesture, closed in on him with a grunted "I thought so!" that might have meant nothing or everything.

He was no Burroughs to handle, he was an ox of a man. He pinned Paine back against the wall and held him there more or less helpless. Even so, if he'd only shut up, it probably wouldn't have happened. But he made a tunnel of his mouth and bayed: "Pol-eece! Holdup! Help!"

Paine lost the little presence of mind he had left, became a blurred pinwheel of hand motion, impossible to control or forestall. Something exploded against the barman's midriff, as though he'd had a firecracker tucked in under his belt.

He coughed his way down to the floor and out of the world.

Another one. Two now. Two in less than an hour. Paine didn't think the words, they seemed to glow out at him, emblazoned on the grimy washroom walls in characters of fire, like in that Biblical story.

He took a step across the prone, white-aproned form as stiffly as though he were high up on stilts. He looked out through the door crack. No one in the bar. And it probably hadn't been heard outside in the street; it had had two doors to go through.

He put the damned thing away, the thing that seemed to be spreading death around just by being in his possession. If he hadn't brought it with him from Burroughs' house, this man would have been alive now. But if he hadn't brought it with him, he would have been apprehended for the first murder by now. Why blame the weapon, why not just blame fate?

That money, all over the floor. He squatted, went for it bill by bill, counting it as he went. Twenty, forty, sixty, eighty. Some of them were on one side of the corpse, some on the other; he had to cross over, not once but several times, in the course of his grisly paper chase. One was even pinned partly under him, and when he'd wangled it out, there was a swirl of blood on the edge. He grimaced, thrust it out, blotted it off. Some of it stayed on, of course.

He had it all now, or thought he did. He couldn't stay in here another minute, he felt as if he were choking. He got it all into his pocket any old way, buttoned it down. Then he eased out, this time looking behind him at what he'd done, not before him. That was how he missed seeing the drunk, until it was too late and the drunk had already seen him.

The drunk was pretty drunk, but maybe not drunk enough to take a chance on. He must have weaved in quietly, while Paine was absorbed in retrieving the money. He was bending over reading the list of selections on the coin phonograph. He raised his head before Paine could get back in again, and to keep him from seeing what lay on the floor in there Paine quickly closed the door behind him.

"Say, itsh about time," the drunk complained. "How about a little servish here?"

Paine tried to shadow his face as much as he could with the brim of his hat. "I'm not in charge here," he mumbled, "I'm just a customer myself—"

The drunk was going to be sticky. He barnacled onto Paine's lapels as he tried to sidle by. "Don't gimme that. You just hung up your coat in there, you think you're quitting for the night. Well you ain't quitting until I've had my drink—"

Paine tried to shake him off without being too violent about it and bringing on another hand-to-hand set-to. He hung on like grim death. Or rather, he hung on *to* grim death—without knowing it.

Paine fought down the flux of panic, the ultimate result of which he'd already seen twice now. Any minute someone might come in from the street. Someone sober. "All right," he breathed heavily, "hurry up, what'll it be?"

"Thass more like it, now you're being reg'lar guy." The drunk released him and he went around behind the bar. "Never anything but good ole Four Roses for mine truly—"

Paine snatched down a bottle at random from the shelf, handed it over bodily. "Here, help yourself. You'll have to take it outside with you, I'm—we're closing up for the night now." He found a switch, threw it. It only made part of the lights go out. There was no time to bother with the rest. He hustled the bottle-nursing drunk out ahead of him, pulled the door to after the two of them, so that it would appear to be locked even if it wasn't.

The drunk started to make loud plaint, looping around on the sidewalk. "You're a fine guy, not even a glass to drink it out of!"

Paine gave him a slight push in one direction, wheeled and made off in the other.

The thing was, how drunk was he? Would he remember Paine, would he know him if he saw him again? He hurried on, spurred to a run by the night-filling hails and imprecations resounding behind him. He couldn't do it again. Three lives in an hour. He couldn't!

THE NIGHT was fading when he turned into the little courtyard that was his own. He staggered up the stairs, but not from the two drinks he'd had, from the two deaths.

He stood outside his own door at last—3-B. It seemed such a funny thing to do after killing people—fumble around in your pockets for your latchkey and fit it in, just like other nights. He'd been an honest man when he'd left here, and now he'd come back a murderer. A double one.

He hoped she was asleep. He couldn't face her right now, couldn't talk to her even if he tried. He was all in emotionally. She'd find out right away just by looking at his face, by looking in his eyes.

He eased the front door closed, tiptoed to the bedroom, looked in. She was lying there asleep. Poor thing, poor helpless thing, married to a murderer.

He went back, undressed in the outer room. Then he stayed in there. Not even stretched out on top of the sofa, but crouched beside it on the floor, head and arms pillowed against its seat. The drums of terror kept pounding. They kept saying, "What am I gonna do now?"

THE SUN seemed to shoot up in the sky, it got to the top so fast. He opened his eyes and it was all the way up. He went to the door and brought in the paper. It wasn't in the morning papers yet, they were made up too soon after midnight.

He turned around and Pauline had come out, was picking up his things. "All over the floor, never saw a man like you—"

He said, "Don't—" and stabbed his hand toward her, but it was already too late. He'd jammed the bills in so haphazardly the second time, in the bar, that they made a noticeable bulge there in his back pocket. She opened it and took them out, and some of them dribbled onto the floor.

She just stared. "Dick!" She was incredulous, overjoyed. "Not Burroughs? Don't tell me you finally—"

"No!" The name went through him like a red-hot skewer. "I didn't go anywhere near him. He had nothing to do with it!"

She nodded corroboratively. "I thought not, because—"

He wouldn't let her finish. He stepped close to her, took her by both shoulders. "Don't mention his name to me again. I don't want to hear his name again. I got it from someone else."

"Who?"

He knew he'd have to answer her, or she'd suspect something. He swallowed, groped blindly for a name. "Charlie Chalmers," he blurted out.

"But he refused you only last week!"

"Well, he changed his mind." He turned on her tormentedly. "Don't ask me any more questions, Pauline, I can't stand it! I haven't slept all night. There it is, that's all that matters." He took his trousers from her, went into the bathroom to dress. He'd hidden Burroughs' gun the night before in the built-in laundry hamper in there; he wished he'd hidden the money with it. He put the gun back in the pocket where he'd carried it last night. If she touched him there—

He combed his hair. The drums were a little quieter now, but he knew they'd come back again; this was just the lull before the storm.

He came out again, and she was putting cups on the table. She looked worried now. She sensed that something was wrong. She was afraid to ask him, he could see, maybe afraid of what she'd find out. He couldn't sit here eating, just as though this was any other day. Any minute someone might come here after him.

He passed by the window. Suddenly he stiffened, gripped the curtain. "What's that man doing down there?" She came up behind him. "Standing there talking to the janitor—"

"Why, Dick, what harm is there in that? A dozen people a day stop and chat with—"

He edged back a step behind the frame. "He's looking up at our windows! Did you see that? They both turned and looked up this way! Get back!" His arm swept her around behind him.

"Why should we? We haven't done anything."

"They're coming in the entrance to this wing! They're on their way up here—"

"Dick, why are you acting this way, what's happened?"

"Go in the bedroom and wait there." He was a coward, yes. But there are varieties. At least he wasn't a coward that hid behind a woman's skirts. He prodded her in there ahead of him. Then he gripped her shoulder a minute. "Don't ask any questions. If you love me, stay in here until they go away again."

He closed the door on her frightened face. He cracked the gun. Two left in it. "I can get them both," he thought, "if I'm careful. I've got to."

It was going to happen again.

The jangle of the doorbell battery steeled him. He moved with deadly slowness toward the door, feet flat and firm upon the floor. He picked up the newspaper from the table on his way by, rolled it into a funnel, thrust his hand and the gun down into it. The pressure of his arm against his side was sufficient to keep it furled. It was as though he had just been reading and had carelessly tucked the paper under his arm. It hid the gun effectively as long as he kept it slanting down.

He freed the latch and shifted slowly back with the door, bisected by its edge, the unarmed half of him all that showed. The janitor came into view first, as the gap widened. He was on the outside. The man next to him had a derby hat riding the back of his head, a bristly mustache, was rotating a cigar between his teeth. He looked like— one of those who come after you.

The janitor said with scarcely veiled insolence, "Paine, I've got a man here looking for a flat. I'm going to show him yours, seeing as how it'll be available from today on. Any objections?"

Paine swayed there limply against the door like a garment bag hanging on a hook, as they brushed by. "No," he whispered deflatedly. "No, go right ahead."

HE HELD the door open to make sure their descent continued all the way down to the bottom. As soon as he'd closed it, Pauline caught him anxiously by the arm. "Why wouldn't you let me tell them we're able to pay the arrears now and are staying? Why did you squeeze my arm like that?"

"Because we're not staying, and I don't want them to know we've got the money. I don't want anyone to know. We're getting out of here."

"Dick, what is it? Have you done something you shouldn't?"

"Don't ask me. Listen, if you love me, don't ask any questions. I'm—in a little trouble. I've got to get out of here. Never mind why. If you don't want to come with me, I'll go alone."

"Anywhere you go, I'll go." Her eyes misted. "But can't it be straightened out?"

Two men dead beyond recall. He gave a bitter smile. "No, it can't."

"Is it bad?"

He shut his eyes, took a minute to answer. "It's bad, Pauline. That's all you need to know. That's all I want you to know. I've got to get out of here as fast as I can. From one minute to the next it may be too late. Let's get started now. They'll be here to dispossess us sometime today anyway, that'll be a good excuse. We won't wait, we'll leave now."

She went in to get ready. She took so long doing it he nearly went crazy. She didn't seem to realize how urgent it was. She wasted as much time deciding what to take and what to leave behind as though they were going on a weekend jaunt to the country. He kept going to the bedroom door, urging, "Pauline, hurry! Faster, Pauline!"

She cried a great deal. She was an obedient wife; she didn't ask him any more questions about what the trouble was. She just cried about it without knowing what it was.

He was down on hands and knees beside the window, in the position of a man looking for a collar button under a dresser, when she finally came out with the small bag she'd packed. He turned a stricken face to her. "Too late—I can't leave with you. Someone's already watching the place."

She inclined herself to his level, edged up beside him.

"Look straight over to the other side of the street. See him? He hasn't moved for the past ten minutes. People don't just stand like that for no reason—"

"He may be waiting for someone."

"He is," he murmured somberly. "Me."

"But you can't be sure."

"No, but if I put it to the test by showing myself, it'll be too late by the time I find out. You go by yourself, ahead of me."

"No, if you stay, let me stay with you—"

"I'm not staying, I can't! I'll follow you and meet you somewhere. But it'll be easier for us to leave one at a time than both together. I can slip over the roof or go out the basement way. He won't stop you, they're not looking for you. You go now and wait for me. No, I have a better idea. Here's what you do. You get two tickets and get on the train at the downtown terminal without waiting for me—" He was separating some of the money, thrusting it into her reluctant hand while he spoke. "Now listen closely. Two tickets to Montreal—"

An added flicker of dismay showed in her eyes. "We're leaving the country?"

When you've committed murder, you have no country any more. "We have to, Pauline. Now there's an eight o'clock limited for there every night. It leaves the downtown terminal at eight sharp. It stops for five minutes at the station uptown at twenty after. That's where I'll get on. Make sure you're on it or we'll miss each other. Keep a seat for me next to you in the day coach—"

She clung to him despairingly. "No, no. I'm afraid you won't come. Something'll happen. You'll miss it. If I leave you now I may never see you again. I'll find myself making the trip up there alone, without you—"

He tried to reassure her, pressing her hands between his. "Pauline, I give you my word of honor—" That was no good, he was a murderer now. "Pauline, I swear to you—"

"Here—on this. Take a solemn oath on this, otherwise I won't go." She took out a small carnelian cross she carried in her handbag, attached to a little gold chain—one of the few things they hadn't pawned. She palmed it, pressed the flat of his right hand over it. They looked into each other's eyes with sacramental intensity.

His voice trembled. "I swear nothing will keep me from that train; I'll join you on it no matter what happens, no matter who tries to stop me. Rain or shine, *dead or alive*, I'll meet you aboard it at eight-twenty tonight!"

She put it away, their lips brushed briefly but fervently.

"Hurry up now," he urged. "He's still there. Don't look at him on your way past. If he should stop you and ask who you are, give another name—"

He went to the outside door with her, watched her start down the stairs. The last thing she whispered up was: "Dick, be careful for my sake. Don't let anything happen to you between now and tonight."

He went back to the window, crouched down, cheekbones to sill.

She came out under him in a minute or two. She knew enough not to look up at their windows, although the impulse must have been strong. The man was still standing over there. He didn't seem to notice her. He even looked off in another direction.

She passed from view behind the building line; their windows were set in on the court that indented it. Paine wondered if he'd ever see her again. Sure he would, he had to. He realized that it would be better for her if he didn't. It wasn't fair to enmesh her in his own doom. But he'd sworn an oath, and he meant to keep it.

Two, three minutes ticked by. The cat-and-mouse play continued. He crouched motionless by the window, the other man stood motionless across the street. She must be all the way down at the corner by now. She'd take the bus there, to go downtown. She might have to wait a few minutes for one to come along, she might still be in sight. But if the man was going to go after her, accost her, he would have started by now. He wouldn't keep standing there.

Then, as Paine watched, he did start. He looked down that way, threw away something he'd been smoking, began to move purposefully in that direction. There was no mistaking the fact that he was looking *at* or *after* someone, by the intent way he held his head. He passed from sight.

Paine began to breathe hot and fast. "I'll kill him. If he touches her, tries to stop her, I'll kill him right out in the open street in broad daylight." It was still fear, cowardice, that was at work, although it was almost unrecognizable as such by now.

He felt for the gun, left his hand on it, inside the breast of his coat, straightened to his feet, ran out of the flat and down the stairs. He cut across the little set-in paved courtyard at a sprint, flashed out past the sheltering building line, turned down in the direction they had both taken.

Then as the panorama before him registered, he staggered to an abrupt stop, stood taking it in. It offered three component but separate points of interest. He only noticed two at first. One was the bus down at the corner. The front-third of it protruded, door open. He caught a glimpse of Pauline's back as she was in the act of stepping in, unaccompanied and unmolested.

The door closed automatically, and it swept across the vista and disappeared at the other side. On the other side of the street, but nearer at hand, the man who had been keeping the long vigil had stopped a second time, was gesticulating angrily to a woman laden with parcels whom he had joined. Both voices were so raised they reached Paine without any trouble.

"A solid half-hour I've been standing there and no one home to let me in!"

"Well, is it my fault you went off without your key? Next time take it with you!"

Nearer at hand still, on Paine's own side of the street, a lounging figure detached itself from the building wall and impinged on his line of vision. The man had been only yards away the whole time, but Paine's eyes had been trained on the distance, he'd failed to notice him until now.

His face suddenly loomed out at Paine. His eyes bored into Paine's with unmistakable intent. He didn't look like one of those that come to get you. He acted like it. He thumbed his vest pocket for something, some credential or identification. He said in a soft, slurring voice that held an inflexible command in it, "Just a minute there, buddy. Your name's Paine, ain't it? I want to see you—"

Paine didn't have to give his muscular coordination any signal; it acted for him automatically. He felt his legs carry him back into the shelter of the courtyard in a sort of slithering jump. He was in at the foot of the public stairs before the other man had even rounded the building line. He was in behind his own door before the remorselessly slow but plainly audible tread had started up them.

The man seemed to be coming up after him alone. Didn't he know Paine had a gun? He'd find out. He was up on the landing now. He seemed to know which floor to stop at, which door to come to a halt before. Probably the janitor had told him. Then why hadn't he come sooner? Maybe he'd been waiting for someone to join him, and Paine had upset the plan by showing himself so soon.

Paine realized he'd trapped himself by returning here. He should have gone on up to the roof and over. But the natural instinct of the hunted, whether four-legged or two, is to find a hole, get in out of the open. It was too late now: he was right out there on the other side of the door. Paine tried to keep his harried breathing silent.

To his own ears it grated like sand sifted through a sieve.

He didn't ring the bell and he didn't knock; he tried the knob, in a half-furtive, half-badgering way. That swirl of panic began to churn in Paine again. He couldn't let him get in; he couldn't let him get away, either. He'd only go and bring others back with him.

Paine pointed the muzzle of the gun to the crack of the door, midway between the two hinges. With his other hand he reached out for the catch that controlled the latch, released it.

Now if he wanted to die, he should open this door.

The man had kept on trying the knob. Now the door slipped in past the frame. The crack at the other side widened in accompaniment as it swung around. Paine ran the gun bore up it even with the side of his head.

The crash was thunderous. He fell into the flat, with only his feet and ankles outside.

Paine came out from behind the door, dragged him the rest of the way in, closed it. He stopped, his hands probed here and there. He found a gun, a heftier, more businesslike one than his. He took that. He found a billfold heavy with cash. He took that, too. He fished for the badge.

There wasn't any in the vest pocket he'd seen him reach toward downstairs. There was only a block of cheaply printed cards. *Star Finance Company. Loans. Up to any amount without security.*

So he hadn't been one, after all; he'd evidently been some kind of a loan shark, drawn by the scent of Paine's difficulties.

Three times now in less than twenty-four hours.

Instinctively he knew he was doomed now, if he hadn't before. There wasn't any more of the consternation he had felt the first two times. He kept buying off time with bullets, that was all it was now. And the rate of interest kept going higher, the time limit kept shortening. There wasn't even any time to feel sorry.

Doors had begun opening outside in the hall, voices were calling back and forth. "What was that—a shot?"

"It sounded like in 3-B."

He'd have to get out now, right away, or he'd be trapped in here again. And this time for good. He shifted the body out of the line of vision from outside, buttoned up his jacket, took a deep breath; then he opened the door, stepped out, closed it after him. Each of the other doors was open with someone peering out from it. They hadn't ganged up yet in the middle of the hall. Most of them were women, anyway. One or two edged timidly back when they saw him emerge.

"It wasn't anything," he said. "I dropped a big clay jug in there just now."

He knew they didn't believe him.

He started down the stairs. At the third step he looked over the side, saw the cop coming up. Somebody had already phoned or sent out word. He reversed, flashed around his own landing, and on up from there.

The cop's voice said, "Stop where you are!" He was coming on fast now. But Paine was going just as fast.

The cop's voice said, "Get inside, all of you! I'm going to shoot!"

Doors began slapping shut like firecrackers. Paine switched over abruptly to the rail and shot first.

The cop jolted, but he grabbed the rail and stayed up. He didn't die as easy as the others. He fired four times before he lost his gun. He missed three times and hit Paine the fourth time.

It went in his chest on the right side, and knocked him across the width of the staircase. It flamed with pain, and then it didn't hurt so much. He found he could get up again. Maybe because he had to. He went back and looked down. The cop had folded over the railing and gone sliding down it as far as the next turn, the way a kid does on a banister. Only sidewise, on his stomach. Then he dropped off onto the landing, rolled over and lay still, looking up at Paine without seeing him.

Four.

PAINE WENT on up to the roof, but not fast, not easily any more. The steps were like an escalator going the other way, trying to carry him down with them. He went across to the roof of the next flat, and down through that, and came out on the street behind his own. The two buildings were twins, set back to back. The prowl car was already screeching to a stop, out of sight back there at his own doorway. He could hear it over the roofs, on this side.

He was wet across the hip. Then he was wet as far down as the knee. And he hadn't been hit in those places, so he must be bleeding a lot. He saw a taxi and he waved to it, and it backed up and got him. It hurt getting in. He couldn't answer for a minute when the driver asked him where to. His sock felt sticky under his shoe now, from the blood. He wished he could stop it until eight-twenty. He had to meet Pauline on the train, and that was a long time to stay alive.

The driver had taken him off the street and around the corner without waiting for him to be more explicit. He asked where to, a second time.

Paine said, "What time is it?"

"Quarter to six, cap."

Life was awfully short—and awfully sweet. He said, "Take me to the park and drive me around in it." That was the safest thing to do, that was the only place they wouldn't look for you.

He thought, "I've always wanted to drive around in the park. Not go anywhere, just drive around in it slow. I never had the money to do it before."

He had it now. More money than he had time left to spend it.

The bullet must still be in him. His back didn't hurt, so it hadn't come out. Something must have stopped it. The bleeding had let up. He could feel it drying on him. The pain kept trying to pull him over double though.

The driver noticed it, said: "Are you hurt?"

"No, I've got kind of a cramp, that's all."

"Want me to take you to a drug store?"

Paine smiled weakly. "No, I guess I'll let it ride."

Sundown in the park. So peaceful, so prosaic. Long shadows across the winding paths. A belated nursemaid or two pushing a perambulator homeward. A loiterer or two lingering on the benches in the dusk. A little lake, with a rowboat on it—a sailor on shore leave rowing his sweetheart around. A lemonade and popcorn man trundling his wagon home for the day.

Stars were coming out. At times the trees were outlined black against the copper western sky. At times the whole thing blurred and he felt as if he were being carried around in a maelstrom. Each time he fought through and cleared his senses again. He had to make that train.

"Let me know when it gets to be eight o'clock."

"Sure, cap. It's only quarter to seven now."

A groan was torn from Paine as they hit a lumpy spot in the driveway. He tried to keep it low, but the driver must have heard it.

"Still hurts you, huh?" he inquired sympathetically. "You oughta get it fixed up." He began to talk about his own indigestion. "Take me, for instance. I'm okay until I eat tamales and root beer. Any time that I eat tamales and root beer—"

He shut up abruptly. He was staring fixedly into the rear-sight mirror. Paine warily clutched his lapels together over his darkened shirt front. He knew it was too late to do any good.

The driver didn't say anything for a long time. He was thinking it over, and he was a slow thinker. Then finally he suggested off-handedly, "Care to listen to the radio?"

Paine knew what he was out for. He thought, "He wants to see if he can get anything on me over it."

"May as well," the driver urged. "It's thrown in with the fare, won't cost you nothing extra."

"Go ahead," Paine consented. He wanted to see if he could hear anything himself.

It made the pain a little easier to bear, like music always does. "I used to dance, too," Paine thought, listening to the tune, "before I started killing people."

IT DIDN'T come over for a long time.

"A city-wide alarm is out for Richard Paine. Paine, who was about to be dispossessed from his flat, shot and killed a finance company employee. Then when Officer Harold Carey answered the alarm, he met the same fate. However, before giving up his life in the perfor-mance of his duty, the patrolman succeeded in seriously wounding the desperado. A trail of blood left by the fugitive on the stairs lead-ing up to the roof over which he made good his escape seems to confirm this. He's still at large but probably won't be for long. Watch out for this man, he's dangerous."

"Not if you leave him alone, let him get to that train," Paine thought ruefully. He eyed the suddenly rigid silhouette in front of him. "I'll have to do something about him—now—I guess."

It had come through at a bad time for the driver. Some of the main driveways through the park were heavily trafficked and pretty well lighted. He could have got help from another car. But it hap-pened to come through while they were on a dark, lonely byway with not another machine in sight. Around the next turn the bypass rejoined one of the heavy-traffic arteries. You could hear the hum of traffic from where they were.

"Pull over here," Paine ordered. He'd had the gun out. He was only going to clip him with it, stun him and tie him up until after eight-twenty.

You could tell by the way the driver pulled his breath in short that he'd been wise to Paine ever since the news flash, had only been waiting until they got near one of the exits or got a red light. He braked. Then suddenly he bolted out, tried to duck into the underbrush.

Paine had to get him and get him fast, or he'd get word to the park division. They'd cork up the entrances on him. He knew he couldn't get out and go after him. He pointed low, tried to hit him in the foot or leg, just bring him down.

The driver had tripped over something, gone flat, a moment ahead of the trigger fall. The bullet must have ploughed into his back instead. He was inert when Paine got out to him, but still alive. Eyes open, as though his nerve centers had been paralyzed.

He could hardly stand up himself, but he managed to drag him over to the cab and somehow got him in. He took the cap and put it on his own head.

He could drive—or at least he'd been able to before he was dying. He got under the wheel and took the machine slowly on its way. The sound of the shot must have been lost out in the open, or else mistaken for a backfire; the stream of traffic was rolling obliviously by when he slipped into it unnoticed. He left it again at the earliest opportunity, turned off at the next dark, empty lane that offered itself.

He stopped once more, made his way to the back door, to see how the cabman was. He wanted to help him in some way if he could. Maybe leave him in front of a hospital.

It was too late. The driver's eyes were closed. He was already dead by this time.

Five.

It didn't have any meaning any more. After all, to the dying death is nothing. "I'll see you again in an hour or so," he said.

He got the driver's coat off him and shrouded him with it, to keep the pale gleam of his face from peering up through the gloom of the cab's interior, in case anyone got too close to the window. He was unequal to the task of getting him out again and leaving him behind in the park. The lights of some passing car might have picked him up too soon. And it seemed more fitting to let him rest in his own cab, anyway.

It was ten to eight now. He'd better start for the station. He might be held up by lights on the way, and the train only stopped a few minutes at the uptown station.

He had to rejoin the main stream of traffic to get out of the park. He hugged the outside of the driveway and trundled along. He went off the road several times. Not because he couldn't drive, but because his senses fogged. He pulled himself and the cab out of it each time. "Train, eight-twenty," he waved before his mind like a red lantern. But like a spend-thrift he was using up years of his life in minutes, and pretty soon he was going to run short.

Once an alarm car passed him, shrieking by, taking a short cut through the park from one side of the city to the other. He wondered if they were after him. He didn't wonder very hard. Nothing mattered much any more. Only eight-twenty—train—

He kept folding up slowly over the wheel and each time it touched his chest, the machine would swerve crazily as though it felt the pain, too. Twice, three times, his fenders were grazed, and he heard faint voices swearing at him from another world, the world he was leaving behind. He wondered if they'd call him names like that if they knew he was dying.

Another thing: he couldn't maintain a steady flow of pressure on the accelerator. The pressure would die out each time, as when current is failing, and the machine would begin drifting to a stop. This happened just as he was leaving the park, crossing the big circular exit plaza. It was controlled by lights and he stalled on a green out in the middle. There was a cop in control on a platform. The cop shot the whistle out of his own mouth blowing it so hard at him. He nearly flung himself off the platform waving him on.

Paine just sat there, helpless.

The cop was coming over to him, raging like a lion. Paine wasn't afraid because of what the back of his cab held; he was long past that kind of fear. But if this cop did anything to keep him from that eight-twenty train—

He reached down finally, gripped his own leg by the ankle, lifted it an inch or two clear of the floor, let it fall back again, and the cab started. It was ludicrous. But then some of the aspects of death often are.

The cop let him go, only because to have detained him longer would have created a worse traffic snarl than there was already.

He was nearly there now. Just a straight run crosstown, then a short one north. It was good he remembered this, because he couldn't see the street signs any more. Sometimes the buildings seemed to lean over above him as though they were about to topple down on him. Sometimes he seemed to be climbing a steep hill, where he knew there wasn't any. But he knew that was just because he was swaying around in the driver's seat.

The same thing happened again a few blocks farther on, directly in front of a large, swank apartment house, just as the doorman came flying out blowing a whistle. He'd caught hold of Paine's rear door and swung it wide before the latter could stop him, even though the cab was still rolling. Two women in evening dress came hurrying out of the entrance behind him, one in advance of the other.

"No—taken," Paine kept trying to say. He was too weak to make his voice heard, or else they ignored it. And he couldn't push his foot down for a moment.

The foremost one shrieked, "Hurry, Mother. Donald'll never forgive me. I promised him seven-thirty—"

She got one foot on the cab doorstep. Then she just stood there transfixed. She must have seen what was inside; it was better lighted here than in the park.

Paine tore the cab away from her, open door and all, left her standing there petrified, out in the middle of the street in her long white satin gown, staring after him. She was too stunned even to scream.

And then he got there at last. He got a momentary respite, too. Things cleared a little. Like the lights going up in a theater when the show is over, before the house darkens for the night.

The uptown station was built in under a viaduct that carried the overhead tracks across the city streets. He couldn't stop in front of it; no parking was allowed. And there were long lines of cabs on both sides of the no-parking zone. He turned the corner into the little deadend alley that separated the viaduct from the adjoining buildings. There was a side entrance to the station looking out on it.

Four minutes. It was due in another four minutes. It had already left downtown, was on its way, hurtling somewhere between the two points. He thought, "I better get started. I may have a hard time making it." He wondered if he could stand up at all.

He just wanted to stay where he was and let eternity wash over him.

Two minutes. It was coming in overhead, he could hear it rumbling and ticking along the steel viaduct, then sighing to a long-drawn-out stop.

That sidewalk looked awfully wide, from the cab door to the station entrance. He brought up the last dregs of vitality in him, broke away from the cab, started out, zigzagging and going down lower at the knees every minute. The station door helped pull him up straight again. He got into the waiting room, and it was so big he knew he'd never be able to cross it. One minute left. So near and yet so far.

The starter was calling it already. "Montreal express—eight-twenty!—Pittsfield, Burlington, Rouse's Point, Montreyall! Bo-o-ard!"

There were rows of lengthwise benches at hand and they helped him bridge the otherwise insuperable length of the waiting room. He dropped into the outside seat in the first row, pulled himself together a little, scrambled five seats over, toppled into that; repeated the process until he was within reach of the ticket barrier. But time was going, the train was going, life was going fast.

Forty-five seconds left. The last dilatory passengers had already gone up. There were two ways of getting up, a long flight of stairs and an escalator.

He wavered toward the escalator, made it. He wouldn't have been able to get by the ticket taker but for his hackman's cap—an eventuality he and Pauline hadn't foreseen.

"Just meeting a party," he mumbled almost unintelligibly, and the slow treadmill started to carry him up.

A whistle blew upstairs on the track platform. Axles and wheel-bases gave a preliminary creak of motion.

It was all he could do to keep his feet even on the escalator. There wasn't anyone in back of him, and if he once went over he was going to go plunging all the way down to the bottom of the long chute. He dug his nails into the ascending hand-belts at both sides, hung on like grim life.

There was a hubbub starting up outside on the street somewhere. He could hear a cop's whistle blowing frenziedly.

A voice shouted: "Which way'd he go?"

Another answered: "I seen him go in the station."

They'd at last found what was in the cab.

A moment after the descending waiting-room ceiling had cut off his view, he heard a spate of running feet come surging in down there from all directions. But he had no time to think of that now. He was out on the open platform upstairs at last. Cars were skimming silkily by. A vestibule door was coming, with a conductor just lifting himself into it. Paine went toward it, body low, one arm straight out like in a fascist salute.

He gave a wordless cry. The conductor turned, saw him. There was a tug, and he was suddenly sprawled inside on the vestibule floor. The conductor gave him a scathing look, pulled the folding steps in after him, slammed the door.

Too late, a cop, a couple of redcaps, a couple of taxi drivers, came spilling out of the escalator shed. He could hear them yelling a car-length back. The trainmen back there wouldn't open the doors. Suddenly the long, lighted platform snuffed out and the station was gone.

They probably didn't think they'd lost him, but they had. Sure, they'd phone ahead, they'd stop the train to have him taken off at Harmon, where it changed from electricity to coal power. But they wouldn't get him. He wouldn't be on it. Just his body.

Each man knows when he's going to die; he knew he wouldn't even live for five minutes.

He went staggering down a long, brightly lighted aisle. He could hardly see their faces any more. But she'd know him; it'd be all right. The aisle ended, and he had to cross another vestibule. He fell down on his knees, for lack of seat backs to support himself by.

He squirmed up again somehow, got into the next car.

Another long, lighted aisle, miles of it.

He was nearly at the end, he could see another vestibule coming. Or maybe that was the door to eternity. Suddenly, from the last seat of all, a hand darted out and claimed him, and there was Pauline's face looking anxiously up at him. He twisted like a wrung-out dish-cloth and dropped into the empty outside seat beside her.

"You were going to pass right by," she whispered.

"I couldn't see you clearly, the lights are flickering so."

She looked up at them in surprise, as though for her they were steady.

"I kept my word," he breathed. "I made the train. But oh, I'm tired—and now I'm going to sleep." He started to slip over sidewise toward her. His head dropped onto her lap.

She had been holding her handbag on it, and his fall displaced it. It dropped to the floor, opened, and everything in it spilled out around her feet.

His glazing eyes opened for one last time and centered feebly on the little packet of bills, with a rubber band around them, that had rolled out with everything else.

"Pauline, all that money—where'd you get that much? I only gave you enough to buy the train tickets—"

"Burroughs gave it to me. It's the two hundred and fifty we were talking about for so long. I knew in the end you'd never go near him and ask for it, so I went to him myself—last night right after you left the house. He handed it over willingly, without a word. I tried to tell you this morning, but you wouldn't let me mention his name. . . ."

I Married
a Dead Man

This book is dedicated to Zsuzsa Molnar and her late mother Margit Molnar; and to producer Dale Pollock who has been diligently at work making a new motion picture at TriStar based on this novel.

—Sheldon Abend a/k/a Buffalo Bill

THE SUMMER NIGHTS are so pleasant in Caulfield. They smell of heliotrope and jasmine, honeysuckle and clover. The stars are warm and friendly here, not cold and distant, as where I came from; they seem to hang lower over us, be closer to us. The breeze that stirs the curtains at the open windows is soft and gentle as a baby's kiss. And on it, if you listen, you can hear the rustling sound of the leafy trees turning over and going back to sleep again. The lamplight from within the houses falls upon the lawns outside and copperplates them in long swaths. There's the hush, the stillness of perfect peace and security. Oh, yes, the summer nights are pleasant in Caulfield.

But not for us.

The winter nights are too. The nights of fall, the nights of spring. Not for us, not for us.

The house we live in is so pleasant in Caulfield. The blue-green tint of its lawn, that always seems so freshly watered no matter what the time of day. The sparkling, aerated pinwheels of the sprinklers always turning, steadily turning; if you look at them closely enough they form rainbows before your eyes. The clean, sharp curve of the driveway. The dazzling whiteness of the porch-supports in the sun. Indoors, the curving white symmetry of the bannister, as gracious as the dark and glossy stair it accompanies down from above. The satin finish of the rich old floors, bearing a telltale scent of wax and of lemon-oil if you stop to sniff. The lushness of pile carpeting. In almost every room, some favorite chair waiting to greet you like an old friend when you come back to spend a little time with it. People who come and see it say, "What more can there be? This is a home, as a home should be." Yes, the house we live in is so pleasant in Caulfield.

But not for us.

Our little boy, our Hugh, his and mine, it's such a joy to watch him growing up in Caulfield. In the house that will some day be his, in the town that will some day be his. To watch him take the first tottering steps that mean—now he can walk. To catch and cherish each newly minted word that fumblingly issues from his lips—that means, now he's added another, now he can talk.

But even that is not for us, somehow. Even that seems thefted, stolen, in some vague way I cannot say. Something we're not entitled to, something that isn't rightfully ours.

I love him so. It's Bill I mean now, the man. And he loves me. I know I do, I know he does, I cannot doubt it. And yet I know just as surely that on some day to come, maybe this year, maybe next, suddenly he'll pack his things and go away and leave me. Though he won't want to. Though he'll love me still, as much as he does on the day that I say this.

Or if he doesn't, it will be I who will. I'll take up my valise and walk out through the door, never to come back. Though I won't want to. Though I'll love him still, as much as I do on the day that I say this. I'll leave my house behind. I'll leave my baby behind, in the house that will some day be his, and I'll leave my heart behind, with the man it belongs to (How could I take it with me?), but I'll go and I'll never come back.

We've fought this thing. How bitterly we've fought it, in every way that we know how. In every way there is. We've driven it away, a thousand times we've driven it away, and it comes back again in a look, a word, a thought. It's there.

No good for me to say to him, "You didn't do it. You've told me so once. Once was enough. No need to repeat it now again, this late. I *know* you didn't. Oh, my darling, my Bill, you don't lie. You don't lie, in money, or in honor, or in love—"

(But this isn't money, or honor, or love. This is a thing apart. This is murder.)

No good, when I don't believe him. At the moment that he speaks, I may. But a moment later, or an hour, or a day or week, again I don't. No good, for we don't live just within a single moment, we can't. The other moments come, the hours, weeks, and, oh God, the years.

For each time, as he speaks, I know it wasn't I. That's all I know. So well, too well, I know. And that leaves only—

And each time, as I speak, perhaps he knows that it wasn't he (but I cannot know that, I cannot; there is no way for him to reach me). So well he knows, so well. And that leaves only—

No good, no good at all.

One night six months ago I dropped upon my knees before him, with the boy there between us. Upon my bended knees. I put my hand on the little boy's head, and I swore it to him then and there. Speaking low, so the child wouldn't understand.

"By my child. Bill, I swear to you on the head of my child, that I didn't. Oh Bill, I didn't do it—"

He raised me up, and held me in his arms, and pressed me to him.

"I know you didn't. I know. What more can I say? In what other way can I tell you? Here, lie against my heart, Patrice. Perhaps that can tell you better than I—Listen to it, can't you tell that it believes you?"

And for a moment it does, that one moment of our love. But then the other moment comes, that one that always comes after. And he has already thought, "But I know it wasn't I. I know so well it wasn't I. And that leaves only—"

And even while his arms go tighter than ever about me, and his lips kiss the wetness from my eyes, he already doesn't again. He already doesn't.

There's no way out. We're caught, we're trapped. The circle viciously completes itself each time, and we're on the inside, can't break through. For if he's innocent, then it has to be me. And if I am, it has to be he. But I *know* I'm innocent. (Yet he may know he is too.) There's no way out.

Or, tired with trying to drive it away, we've rushed toward it with desperate abandon, tried to embrace it, to be done with it once and for all in that way.

One time, unable to endure its long-drawn, unseen, ghostly vigil over our shoulders any longer, he suddenly flung himself out of the chair he'd been in, though nothing had been said between us for an hour past. Flung the book he hadn't been reading, only pretending to, far from him like a brickbat. Flung himself up as wildly as though he were going to rush forward to grapple with something he saw there before him. And my heart flung itself wildly up with him.

He surged to the far end of the room and stopped there—at bay. And made a fist, and raised his arm, and swung it with a thundering crash against the door, so that only the panel's thickness kept it from shattering. Then turned in his helpless defiance and cried out:

"I don't care! It doesn't matter! Do you hear me? It doesn't matter! People have done it before. Lots of times. And lived out their happiness afterward. Why shouldn't we? He was no good. It was what he deserved. He wasn't worth a second thought. The whole world said so then, and they'd still say so now. He isn't worth a single minute of this hell we've gone through—"

And then he poured a drink for each of us, lavish, reckless, and came back toward me with them. And I, understanding, agreeing, one with him, rose and went to meet him halfway.

"Here, take this. Drink on it. Drown it. Drown it until it's gone. One of us *did* do it. It doesn't matter. It's done with. Now let's get on with living."

And striking himself on the chest, "All right, *I* did it. There. I was the one. Now it's settled. Now it's over at last—"

And then suddenly our eyes looked deep into one another's, our glasses faltered in mid-air, went down, and it was back again.

"But you don't believe that," I whispered, dismayed.

"And you do," he breathed, stricken.

Oh, it's everything, it's everywhere.

We've gone away, and it's where we go. It's in the blue depths of Lake Louise, and high up in the fleecy cloud formations above Biscayne Bay. It rolls restlessly in with the surf at Santa Barbara, and lurks amid the coral rocks of Bermuda, a darker flower than the rest.

We've come back, and it's where we've come back to.

It's between the printed lines on the pages of the books we read. But it peers forth dark, and they fade off to illegibility. "Is he thinking of it now, as I read? As I am? I will not look up at him, I will keep my eyes to this, but—is he thinking of it now?"

It's the hand that holds out its coffee-cup across the breakfast-table in the mornings, to have the urn tipped over it. Bloody-red for a moment in fancy, then back again to pale as it should be. Or maybe, to the other, it's that other hand opposite one, that does the tipping of the urn; depending upon which side of the table the beholder it sitting.

I saw his eyes rest on my hand one day, and I knew what he was thinking at that instant. Because I had looked at his hand much the same way on a previous day, and I had been thinking then what he was thinking now.

I saw him close his eyes briefly, to efface the sickly illusion; and I closed mine to dispel the knowledge of it that his had conveyed to me. Then we both opened them, and smiled at one another, to tell one another nothing had happened just then.

It's in the pictures that we see on the theatre-screen. "Let's get out of here, I'm—tired of it, aren't you?" (Somebody is going to kill somebody, up there, soon, and he knows it's coming.) But even though we do get up and leave, it's already too late, because he knows why we're leaving, and I know too. And even if I didn't know until then, this—the very fact of our leaving—has told me. So the precaution is wasted after all. *It's* back in our minds again.

Still, it's wiser to go than to stay.

I remember one night it came too quickly, more suddenly than we could have foretold, there was less warning given. We were not able to get all the way out in time. We were still only making our way up the aisle, our backs to the screen, when suddenly a shot rang out, and then a voice groaned in accusation, "You've—you've killed me."

It seemed to me it was *his* voice, and that he was speaking to us, to one of us. It seemed to me, in that moment, that every head in the audience turned, to look our way, to stare at us, with that detached curiosity of a great crowd when someone has been pointed out to them.

My legs for a moment seemed to refuse to carry me any further. I floundered there for a minute as though I were going to fall down helpless upon the carpeted aisle. I turned to look at him and I saw, unmisakably, that his head had cringed for a moment, was down defensively between his shoulders. And he always carried it so straight and erect. A moment later it *was* straight again, but just for that instant it hadn't been, it had been hunched.

Then, as though sensing that I needed him just then, because, perhaps, he needed me, he put his arm around my waist, and helped me the rest of the way up the aisle that way, steadying me, promising me support rather than actually giving it to me.

In the lobby, both our faces were like chalk. We didn't look at one another, it was the mirrors on the side told us that.

We never drink. We know enough not to. I think we sense that,

Cornell Woolrich

rather than close the door on awareness, that would only open it all the wider and let full horror in. But that particular night, I remember, as we came out, he said, "Do you want something?"

He didn't say a drink; just "something." But I understood what that "something" meant. "Yes," I shuddered quietly.

We didn't even wait until we got home; it would have taken us too long. We went in to a place next door to the theatre, and stood up to the bar for a moment, the two of us alike, and gulped down something on the run. In three minutes we were out of there again. Then we got in the car and drove home. And we never said a word the whole way.

It's in the very kiss we give each other. Somehow we trap it right between our lips, each time. (Did I kiss him too strongly? Will he think by that I forgave him, again, just then? Did I kiss him too weakly? Will he think by that I was thinking of it, again, just then?)

It's everywhere, it's all the time, it's *us*.

I don't know what the game was. I only know its name; they call it life.

I'm not sure how it should be played. No one ever told me. No one ever tells anybody. I only know we must have played it wrong. We broke some rule or other along the way, and never knew it at the time.

I don't know what the stakes are. I only know we've forfeited them, they're not for us.

We've lost. That's all I know. We've lost, we've lost.

1

THE DOOR WAS closed. It had a look of pitiless finality about it, as though it would always be closed like this from now on. As though nothing in the world could ever make it open again. Doors can express things. This one did. It was inert, it was lifeless; it didn't lead anywhere. It was not the beginning of anything, as a door should be. It was the ending of something.

Above the push-button there was a small oblong rack, of metal, affixed to the woodwork, intended to frame a namecard. It was empty. The card was gone.

The girl was standing still in front of the door. Perfectly still. The way you stand when you've been standing for a long time; so long, you've forgotten about moving, have grown used to not moving. Her finger was to the push-button, but it wasn't pushing any more. No pressure was being exerted; no sound came from the battery behind the door-frame. It was as though she had been holding it that way so long, she had forgotten to take that, too, away.

She was about nineteen. A dreary, hopeless nineteen, not a bright, shiny one. Her features were small and well turned, but there was something too pinched about her face, too wan about her coloring, too thin about her cheeks. Beauty was there, implicit, ready to reclaim her face if it was given the chance, but something had beaten it back, was keeping it hovering at a distance, unable to alight in its intended realization.

Her hair was hazel-colored, and limp and listless, as though no great heed had been paid to it for some time past. The heels of her shoes were a little run-down. A puckered darn in the heel of her stocking peered just over the top of one. Her clothing was functional, as though it were worn for the sake of covering, and not for the sake of fashion, or even of appeal. She was a good height for a girl, about five-six or seven. But she was too thin, except in one place.

Her head was down a little, as though she were tired of carrying it up straight. Or as though invisible blows had lowered it, one by one.

She moved at last. At long last. Her hand dropped from the push-button, as if of its own weight. It fell to her side, hung there, forlorn. One foot turned, as if to go away. There was a wait. Then the other turned too. Her back was to the door now. The door that wouldn't open. The door that was an epitaph, the door that was finality.

She took a slow step away. Then another. Her head was down now more than ever. She moved slowly away from there, and left the door behind. Her shadow was the last part of her to go. It trailed slowly after her, upright against the wall. Its head was down a little, too; it too was too thin, it too was unwanted. It stayed on a moment, after she herself was already gone. Then it slipped off the wall after her, and *it* was gone too.

Nothing was left there but the door. That remained silent, obdurate, closed.

2

IN THE TELEPHONE-booth she was motionless again. As motionless as before. A telephone pay-station, the door left shunted back in order to obtain air enough to breathe. When you are in one for more than just a few moments, they become stifling. And she had been in this one for more than just a few moments.

She was like a doll propped upright in its gift-box, and with one side of the box left off, to allow the contents to be seen. A worn doll. A leftover, marked-down doll, with no bright ribbons or tissue wrappings. A doll with no donor and no recipient. A doll no one bothered to claim.

She was silent there, though this was meant to be a place for talking. She was waiting to hear something, something that never came. She was holding the receiver pointed toward her ear, and it must have started out by being close to it, at right angles to it, as receivers should be. But that was a long time before. With the passage of long, disappointing minutes it had drooped lower and lower, until now it was all the way down at her shoulder, clinging there wilted, defeated, like some sort of ugly, black, hard-rubber orchid worn for corsage.

The anonymous silence became a voice at last. But not the one she wanted, not the one she was waiting for.

"I am sorry, but I have already told you. There is no use waiting on the line. That number has been discontinued, and there is no further information I can give you."

Her hand dropped off her shoulder, carrying the receiver with it, and fell into her lap, dead. As if to match something else within her that was dead, by the final way it fell and stirred no more.

But life won't grant a decent dignity even to its epitaphs, sometimes.

"May I have my nickel back?" she whispered. "*Please.* I didn't get my party, and it's—it's the last one I've got."

3

SHE CLIMBED THE rooming-house stairs like a puppet dangling from slack strings. A light bracketed against the wall, drooping upside-down like a withered tulip in its bell-shaped shade of scalloped glass, cast a smoky yellow glow. A carpet-strip ground to the semblance of decayed vegetable-matter, all pattern, all color, long erased, adhered to the middle of the stairs, like a form of pollen or fungus encrustation. The odor matched the visual imagery. She climbed three flights of them, and then turned off toward the back.

She stopped, at the last door there was, and took out a long-shanked iron key. Then she looked down at the bottom of the door. There was a triangle of white down by her foot, protruding from under the seam. It expanded into an envelope as the door swept back above it.

She reached into the darkness, and traced her hand along the wall beside the door, and a light went on. It had very little shine. It had very little to shine on.

She closed the door and then she picked up the envelope. It had been lying on its face. She turned it over. Her hand shook a little. Her heart did too.

It had on it, in hasty, heedless pencil, only this:

"Helen Georgesson."

No Miss, no Mrs., no other salutation whatever.

She seemed to come alive more fully. Some of the blank hopelessness left her eyes. Some of the pinched strain left her face. She grasped the envelope tight, until it pleated a little in her hold. She moved more briskly than she had until now. She took it over with her to the middle of the room, beside the bed, where the light shone more fully.

She stood still there and looked at it again, as though she were a little afraid of it. There was a sort of burning eagerness in her face; not joyous, but rather of desperate urgency.

She ripped hastily at the flap of it, with upward swoops of her hand, as though she were taking long stitches in it with invisible needle and thread.

Her hand plunged in, to pull out what it said, to read what it told her. For envelopes carry words that tell you things; that's what envelopes are for.

Her hand came out again empty, frustrated. She turned the envelope over and shook it out, to free what it must hold, what must have stubbornly resisted her fingers the first time.

No words came, no writing.

Two things fell out, onto the bed. Only two things.

One was a five-dollar bill. Just an impersonal, anonymous five-dollar bill, with Lincoln's picture on it. And over to the side of that, the neat little cachet they all bear, in small-size capitals: "This certificate is legal tender for all debts public and private." For all debts, public and *private*. How could the engraver guess that that might break somebody's heart, some day, somewhere?

And the second thing was a strip of railroad-tickets, running consecutively from starting-point to terminus, as railroad tickets do. Each coupon to be detached progressively en route. The first coupon was inscribed "New York"; here, where she was now. And the last was inscribed "San Francisco"; where she'd come from, a hundred years ago—last spring.

There was no return-ticket. It was for a one-way trip. There and—to stay.

So the envelope *had* spoken to her after all, though it had no words in it. Five dollars legal tender, for *all* debts, public and private. San Francisco—and no return.

The envelope plummeted to the floor.

She couldn't seem to understand for a long time. It was as though she'd never seen a five-dollar bill before. It was as though she'd never seen an accordion-pleated strip of railroad-tickets like that before. She kept staring down at them.

Then she started to shake a little. At first without sound. Her face kept twitching intermittently, up alongside the eyes and down around the corners of the mouth, as if her expression were struggling to burst forth into some kind of fulminating emotion. For a moment or two it seemed that when it did, it would be weeping. But it wasn't.

It was laughter.

Her eyes wreathed into oblique slits, and her lips slashed back, and harsh broken sounds came through. Like rusty laughter. Like laughter left in the rain too long, that has got all mildewed and spoiled.

She was still laughing when she brought out the battered valise, and placed it atop the bed, and threw the lid back. She was still laughing when she'd filled it and closed it again.

She never seemed to get through laughing. Her laughter never stopped. As at some long-drawn joke, that goes on and on, and is never done with in its telling.

But laughter should be merry, vibrant and alive.

This wasn't.

4

THE TRAIN HAD already ticked off fifteen minutes' solid, steady headway, and she hadn't yet found a seat. The seats were full with holiday crowds and the aisles were full and the very vestibules were full; she'd never seen a train like this before. She'd been too far behind at the dammed-up barrier, and too slow and awkward with her cumbersome valise, and too late getting on. Her ticket only allowed her to get aboard, it gave her no priority on any place to sit.

Flagging, wilting, exhausted, she struggled down car-aisle after car-aisle, walking backward against the train-pull, eddying, teetering from side to side, leaden valise pulling her down.

They were all packed with standees, and this was the last one now. No more cars after this. She'd been through them all. No one offered her a seat. This was a through train, no stops for whole States at a time, and an act of courtesy now would have come too high. This was no trolley or bus with a few moments' running time. Once you were gallant and stood, you stood for hundreds and hundreds of miles.

She stopped at last, and stayed where she'd stopped, for sheer inability to turn and go back again to where she'd come from. No use going any further. She could see to the end of the car, and there weren't any left.

She let her valise down parallel to the aisle, and tried to seat herself upon its upturned edge as she saw so many others doing. But she floundered badly for a moment, out of her own topheaviness, and almost tumbled in lowering herself. Then when she'd succeeded, she let her head settle back against the sideward edge of the seat she was adjacent to, and stayed that way. Too tired to know, too tired to care, too tired even to close her eyes.

What makes you stop, when you have stopped, just where you have stopped? What is it, what? Is it something, or is it nothing? Why not a yard short, why not a yard more? Why just there where you are, and nowhere else?

Some say: It's just blind chance, and if you hadn't stopped there, you would have stopped at the next place. Your story would have been different then. You weave your own story as you go along.

But others say: You could not have stopped any place else but this even if you had wanted to. It was decreed, it was ordered, you were meant to stop at this spot and no other. Your story is there waiting for you, it has been waiting for you there a hundred years, long before you were born, and you cannot change a comma of it. Everything you do, you have to do. You are the twig, and the water you float on swept you here. You are the leaf and the breeze you were borne on blew you here. This is your story, and you cannot escape it; you are only the player, not the stage manager. Or so some say.

On the floor before her downcast eyes, just over the rim of the seat-arm, she could see two pairs of shoes uptilted, side by side. On the inside, toward the window, a diminutive pair of pumps, pert, saucy, without backs, without sides, without toes, in fact with scarcely anything but dagger-like heels and a couple of straps. And on the outside, the nearer side to her, a pair of man's brogues, looking by comparison squat, bulky, and tremendously heavy. These hung one above the other, from legs coupled at the knee.

She did not see their faces and she did not want to. She did not want to see anyone's face. She did not want to see anything.

Nothing happened for a moment. Then one of the pumps edged slyly over toward one of the brogues, nudged gently into it, as if in a deft little effort to communicate something. The brogue remained oblivious; it didn't get the message. It got the feeling, but not the intent. A large hand came down, and scratched tentatively at the sock just above the brogue, then went up again.

The pump, as if impatient at such obtuseness, repeated the effort. Only this time it delivered a good sharp dig, with a bite to it, and on the unprotected ankle, above the armorlike brogue.

That got results. A newspaper rattled somewhere above, as if it had been lowered out of the way, to see what all this unpleasant nipping was about.

A whispered remark was voiced above, spoken too low to be distinguishable by any but the ear for which it was intended.

An interrogative grunt, in masculine timbre, answered it.

Both brogues came down even on the floor, as the legs above uncoupled. Then they swivelled slightly toward the aisle, as if their owner had turned his upper body to glance that way.

The girl on the valise closed her eyes wearily, to avoid the gaze that she knew must be on her.

When she opened them again, the brogues had come out through the seat-gap, and the wearer was standing full-height in the aisle, on the other side of her. A good height too, a six-foot height.

"Take my seat, miss," he invited. "Go ahead, take my place for awhile."

She tried to demur with a faint smile and a halfhearted shake of the head. But the velour back looked awfully good.

The girl who had remained in it added her insistence to his. "Go ahead, honey, take it," she urged. "He wants you to. We want you to. You can't stay out there like that, where you are."

The velour back looked awfully good. She couldn't take her eyes off it. But she was almost too tired to stand up and effect the change. He had to reach down and take her by the arm and help her rise from the valise and shift over.

Her eyes closed again for a moment, in ineffable bliss, as she sank back.

"There you are," he said heartily. "Isn't that better?"

And the girl beside her, her new seat-mate, said: "Why, you *are* tired. I never saw anyone so all-in."

She smiled her thanks, and still tried to protest a little, though the act had already been completed, but they both overrode her remonstrances.

She looked at the two of them. Now she at least wanted to see their two faces, if no others, though only a few moments ago she hadn't wanted to see any faces, anywhere, ever again. But kindness is a form of restorative.

They were both young. Well, she was too. But they were both happy, gay, basking in the world's blessings, that was the difference between them and her. It stood out all over them. There was some sort of gilded incandescence alight within both of them alike, something that was more than mere good spirits, more than mere good fortune, and for the first few moments she couldn't tell what it was. Then in no time at all, their eyes, and every turn of their heads, and every move they made, gave it away: they were supremely, brimmingly in love with one another. It glowed out all over them, almost like phosphorus.

Young love. New untarnished love. That first love that comes just once to everyone and never comes back again.

But, conversationally, it expressed itself inversely, at least on her part if not his; almost every remark she addressed to him was a friendly insult, a gentle slur, an amiable depreciation. Not so much as a word of tenderness, or even ordinary human consideration, did she seem to have for him. Though her eyes belied her. And he understood. He had that smile for all her outrageous insolences, that worshipped, that adored, that understood so well.

"Well, go on," she said with a peremptory flick of her hand. "Don't stand there like a dope, breathing down the backs of our necks. Go and find something to do."

"Oh, pardon me," he said, and pretended to turn the back of his collar up, as if frozen out. He looked vaguely up and down the aisle. "Guess I'll go out on the platform and smoke a cigarette."

"Smoke two," she said airily. "See if I care."

He turned and began to pick his way down the thronged aisle.

"That was nice of him," the newcomer said appreciatively, glancing after him.

"Oh, he's tolerable," her companion said. "He has his good points." She gave a shrug. But her eyes made a liar out of her.

She glanced around to make sure he'd gone out of earshot. Then she leaned slightly toward the other, dropped her voice confidentially. "I could tell right away," she said. "That's why I made him get up. About you, I mean."

The girl who'd been on the valise dropped her eyes for an instant, confused, deprecating. She didn't say anything.

"I am too. You're not the only one," her companion rushed on, with just a trace of vainglory, as if she couldn't wait to tell it quickly enough.

The girl said, "Oh." She didn't know what else to say. It sounded flat, superficial; the way you say "Is that so?" or "You don't say?" She tried to force a smile of sympathetic interest, but she wasn't very good at it. Out of practice at smiling, maybe.

"Seven months," the other added gratuitously.

The girl could feel her eyes on her, as though she expected some return in kind to be made, if only for the record.

"Eight," she said, half-audibly. She didn't want to, but she did.

"Wonderful," was her companion's praise for this arithmetical information. "Marvelous." As though there were some sort of a caste system involved in this, and she unexpectedly found herself speaking to one of the upper brackets of nobility: a duchess or a marquise, who outranked her by thirty days. And all around them, snobbishly ignored, the commonality of the female gender.

"Wonderful, marvelous," echoed the girl inwardly, and her heart gave a frightened, unheard sob.

"And your husband?" the other rushed on. "You going to meet him?"

"No," the girl said, looking steadily at the green velour of the seat-back in front of them. "No."

"Oh. D'd you leave him back in New York?"

"No," the girl said. "No." She seemed to see it written on the seat-back in transitory lettering, that faded again as soon as it was once read. "I've lost him."

"Oh, I'm sor—" Her vivacious companion seemed to know grief for the first time, other than just grief over a broken doll or a school-girl crush betrayed. It was like a new experience passing over her radiant face. And it was, even now, bound to be someone else's grief, not her own; that was the impression you had. That she'd never had any grief of her own, had none now, and never would have. One of those star-blessed rarities, glittering its way through the world's dark vale.

She bit off the rest of the ejaculation of sympathy, gnawed at her upper lip; reached out impulsively and placed her hand upon her companion's for a moment, then withdrew it again.

Then, tactfully, they didn't speak any more about such things. Such basic things as birth and death, that can give such joy and can give such pain.

She had corn-gold hair, this sun-kissed being. She wore it in a hazy aureole that fluffed out all over her head. She had freckles that were like little flecks of gold paint, spattered from some careless painter's brush all over her apricot cheeks, with a saddle across the bridge of her tiny, pert nose. It was her mouth that was the beautiful part of her. And if the rest of her face was not quite up to its matchless beauty, that mouth alone was sufficient to make her lovely-looking, unaided, drawing all notice to itself as it did. Just as a single light is enough to make a plain room bright; you don't have to have a whole chandelier. When it smiled, everything else smiled with it. Her nose crinkled, and her eyebrows arched, and her eyes creased, and dimples showed up where there hadn't been any a minute before. She looked as though she smiled a lot. She looked as though she had a lot to smile about.

She continually toyed with a wedding-band on her third finger. Caressed it, so to speak, fondled it. She was probably unconscious of doing so by this time; it must have become a fixed habit by now. But originally, months ago, when it was first there, when it was new there, she must have taken such a fierce pride in it that she'd felt the need for continually displaying it to all the world—as if to say, "Look at *me*! Look what I've got!"—must have held such an affection for it that she couldn't keep her hands off it for very long. And now, though pride and affection were in nowise less, this had formed itself into a winning little habit that persisted. No matter what move her hands made, no matter what gesture they expressed, it always managed to come uppermost, to be foremost in the beholder's eye.

It had a row of diamonds, and then a sapphire at each end for a stop. She caught her new seat-mate's glance resting upon it, so then she turned it around her way a little more, so she could see it all the better, gave it a pert little brush-off with her fingers, as if to dispel the last, lingering, hypothetical grain of dust. A brush-off that pretended she didn't care any more about it just then. Just as her attitude toward him pretended she didn't care anything about him either. A brush-off that lied like the very devil.

They were both chatting away absorbedly, as new-found friends do, by the time he reappeared some ten minutes later. He came up to them acting secretive and mysterious in a rather conspicuous way. He looked cautiously left and right first, as if bearing tidings of highest secrecy. Then screened the side of his mouth with the edge of one hand. Then leaned down and whispered, "Pat, one of the porters just tipped me off. They're going to open up the dining-car in a couple of minutes. Special, inside, advance information. You know what that'll mean in this mob. I think we better start moving up that way if we want to get in under the rope on the first shift. There'll be a stampede under way as soon as word gets around."

She jumped to her feet with alacrity.

He immediately soft-pedalled her with the flats of both hands, in comic intensity. "Sh! Don't give it away! What are you trying to do?

Act indifferent. Act as if you weren't going anywhere in particular, were just getting up to stretch your legs."

She smothered an impish chuckle. "When I'm going to the dining-car, I just *can't* act as if I weren't going anywhere in particular. It stands out all over me. You're lucky if you hold me down to a twenty-yard dash." But to oblige his ideas of Machiavellian duplicity, she exaggeratedly arched her feet and tiptoed out into the aisle, as though the amount of noise she made had any relation to what they were trying to do.

In passing, she pulled persuasively at the sleeve of the girl beside her. "Come on. You're coming with us, aren't you?" she whispered conspiratorially.

"What about the seats? We'll lose them, won't we?"

"Not if we put our baggage on them. Here, like this." She raised the other girl's valise, which had been standing there in the aisle until now, and between them they planked it lengthwise across the seat, effectively blocking it.

The girl was on her feet now, dislodged by the valise, but she still hung back, hesitant about going with them.

The young wife seemed to understand; she was quick that way. She sent him on ahead, out of earshot, to break trail for them. Then turned to her recent seat-mate in tactful reassurance. "Don't worry about—anything; *he'*ll look after everything." And then, making confidantes of the two of them about this, to minimize the other's embarrassment, she promised her: "I'll see that he does. That's what they're for, anyway."

The girl tried to falter an insincere denial, that only proved the surmise had been right. "No, it isn't that—I don't like to—"

But her new friend had already taken her acceptance for an accomplished fact, had no more time to waste on it. "Hurry up, we'll lose him," she urged. "They're closing in again behind him."

She urged her forward ahead of herself, a friendly hand lightly placed just over her outside hip.

"You can't neglect yourself now, of all times," she cautioned her in an undertone. "I *know.* They told me that myself."

The pioneering husband, meanwhile, was cutting a wide swath for them down the center of the clogged aisle, causing people to lean acutely in over the seats to give clearance. And yet with never a resentful look. He seemed to have that way about him; genial but firm.

"It's useful to have a husband who used to be on the football team," his bride commented complacently. "He can run your interference for you. Just look at the width of that back, would you?"

When they had overtaken him, she complained petulantly, "Wait for me, can't you? I have two to feed."

"So have I," was the totally unchivalrous remark over his shoulder. "And they're both me."

They were, by dint of his foresight, the first ones in the dining-car, which was inundated within moments after the doors had been thrown open. They secured a choice table for three, diagonal to a window. The unlucky ones had to wait on line in the aisle outside, the door inhospitably closed in their faces.

"Just so we won't sit down to the table still not knowing each other's names," the young wife said, cheerfully unfolding her napkin, "he's Hazzard, Hugh, and I'm Hazzard, Patrice." Her dimples showed up in depreciation. "Funny name, isn't it?"

"Be more respectful," her young spouse growled, without lifting his forehead from the bill of fare. "I'm just trying you out for it. I haven't decided yet whether I'll let you keep it or not."

"It's mine now," was the feminine logic he got. "I haven't decided whether I'll let *you* keep it or not."

"What's your name?" she asked their guest.

"Georgesson," the girl said. "Helen Georgesson."

She smiled hesitantly at the two of them. Gave him the outside edge of her smile, gave her the center of it. It wasn't a very broad smile, but it had depth and gratitude, the little there was of it.

"You've both been awfully friendly to me," she said.

She looked down at the menu card she held spread between her hands, so they wouldn't detect the flicker of emotion that made her lips tremble for a moment.

"It must be an awful lot of fun to be—you," she murmured wistfully.

5

By the time the overhead lights in their car had been put out, around ten, so that those who wanted to sleep could do so, they were already old and fast friends. They were already "Patrice" and "Helen" to one another; this, as might have been surmised, at Patrice's instigation. Friendship blooms quickly in the hothouse atmosphere of travel; within the space of hours, sometimes, it's already full-blown. Then just as suddenly is snapped off short, by the inevitable separation of the travelers. It seldom if ever survives that separation for long. That is why, on ships and trains, people have fewer reticences with one another, they exchange confidences more quickly, tell all about themselves; they will never have to see these same people again, and worry about what opinion they may have formed, whether good or bad.

The small, shaded, individual sidelights provided for each seat, that could be turned on or off at will, were still on for the most part, but the car was restfully dimmer and quieter, some of its occupants already dozing. Patrice's husband was in an inert, hat-shrouded state on the valise that again stood alongside his original seat, his crossed legs precariously slung upward to the top of the seat ahead. However, he seemed comfortable enough, judging by the sonorous sounds that escaped from inside his hat now and then. He had dropped out of their conversation fully an hour before, and, an unkind commentary this on the importance of men to women's conversations, to all appearances hadn't even been missed.

Patrice was acting the part of a look-out, her eyes watchfully and jealously fastened on a certain door, far down the aisle behind them, in the dim distance. To do this, she was kneeling erect on the seat, in reverse, staring vigilantly over the back of it. This somewhat unconventional position, however, did nothing whatever to inhibit her conversational flow, which proceeded as freely and blithely as ever. Only, owing to her elevated stance, the next seat back now shared the benefit of most of it, along with her own. Fortunately, however, its occupants were disqualified from any great amount of interest in it by two facts; they were both men, and they were both asleep.

A ripple of reflected light suddenly ran down the sleek chromium of the door that had her attention.

"She just came out," she hissed with an explosive sibilance, and executed an agitated series of twists, turns, and drops on the seat, as though this were something vital that had to be acted upon immediately. "Hurry up! *Now!* Now's our chance. Get a move on. Before somebody else gets there ahead of us. There's a fat woman three seats down been taking her things out little by little. If she ever gets in first, we're sunk!" Carried away by her own excitement (and everything in life, to her, seemed to be deliciously, titillatingly exciting), she even went so far as to give her seat-mate a little push and urge her: "Run! Hold the door for us. Maybe if she sees you there already, she'll change her mind."

She prodded her relaxed spouse cruelly and heartlessly in a great many places at once, to bring him back to awareness.

"Quick! Hugh! The overnight-case! We'll lose our chance. Up there, stupid. Up there on the rack—"

"All right, take it easy," the somnolent Hugh grunted, eyes still completely buried under his obliterating hat-brim. "Talk, talk, talk, Yattatta, yattatta, yattatta. Woman is born to exercise her jaw."

"Man is born to get a poke on his, if he doesn't get a move on."

He finally pushed his hat back out of the way. "What do you want from me now? You got it down yourself."

"Well, get your big legs out of the way and let us by! You're blocking the way—"

He executed a sort of drawbridge maneuver, folding his legs back to himself, hugging them, then stretching them out again after the passage had been accomplished.

"Where y'going, in such a hurry?" he asked innocently.

"Now, isn't that stupid?" commented Patrice to her companion.

The two of them went almost running down the aisle, without bothering to enlighten him further.

"He takes a thirty-six sleeve, and it doesn't do me a bit of good in an emergency," she complained en route, swinging the kit.

He had turned his head to watch them curiously, and in perfectly sincere incomprehension. Then he went, "Oh." Understanding their destination now, if not the turmoil attendant on it. Then he pulled his hat down to his nose again, to resume his fractured slumbers where they had been broken off by this feminine logistical upheaval.

Patrice had closed the chromium door after the two of them, meanwhile, and given its inside lock-control a little twist of defiant exclusion. Then she let out a deep breath. "There. We're in. And possession is nine-tenths of the law. I'm going to take as long as I want," she announced determinedly, setting down the overnight-case and unlatching its lid. "If anybody else wants to get in, they'll just have to wait. There's only room enough for two anyway. And even so, they have to be awfully good friends."

"We're nearly the last ones still up, anyway," Helen said.

"Here, have some?" Patrice was bringing up a fleecy fistful of facial tissues from the case; she divided them with her friend.

"I missed these an awful lot on the Other Side. Couldn't get them for love nor money. I used to ask and ask, and they didn't know what I meant—"

She stopped and eyed her companion. "Oh, you have nothing to rub off, have you? Well, here, rub some of this on; then you'll have that to rub off."

Helen laughed. "You make me feel so giddy," she said with a wistful sort of admiration.

Patrice hunched her shoulders and grimaced impishly. "It's my last fling, sort of. From tomorrow night on I may have to be on my best behavior. Sober and sedate." She made a long face, and steepled her hands against her stomach, in mimicry of a bluenosed clergyman.

"Oh, on account of meeting your in-laws," Helen remembered.

"Hugh says they're not like that at all; I have absolutely nothing to worry about. But of course he just may be slightly prejudiced in their favor. I wouldn't think much of him if he wasn't."

She was scouring a mystic white circle on each cheek, and then spreading them around, mouth open the whole while, though it played no part in the rite itself.

"Go ahead, help yourself," she invited. "Stick your finger in and dig out a gob. I'm not sure what it does for you, but it smells nice, so there's nothing to lose."

"Is that really true, what you told me?" Helen said, following suit. "That they've never even seen you until now? I can't believe it."

"Cross my heart and hope to die, they've never laid eyes on me in their lives. I met Hugh on the Other Side, like I told you this afternoon, and we were married over there, and we went on living over there until just now. My folks were dead, and I was on a scholarship, studying music, and he had a job with one of these government agencies; you know, one of these initialed outfits. They don't even know what I *look* like!"

"Didn't you even send them a picture of yourself? Not even after you were married?"

"We never even had a wedding-picture taken; you know how us kids are nowadays. Biff, bing, bang! and we're married. I started to send them one of myself several times, but I was never quite satisfied with the ones I had. Self-conscious, you know; I wanted to make *such* a good first impression. One time Hugh even arranged a sitting for me at a photographer, and when I saw the proofs I said, 'Over my dead body you'll send these!' Those French photographers! I knew I was going to meet them eventually, and snapshots are so— so—Anyway the ones *I* take. So finally I said to him, 'I've waited this long, I'm not going to send any to them at all now. I'll save it up for a surprise, let them see me in the flesh instead, when they finally do. That way, they won't build up any false hopes and then be disappointed.' I used to censor all his letters too, wouldn't let him describe me. You can imagine how he would have done it. 'Mona Lisa,' Venus on the half-shell. I'd say, 'No you don't!' when I'd catch him at it, and scratch it out. We'd have more tussles that way, chase each other around the room, trying to get the letter back or trying to get it away from me."

She became serious for a moment. Or at least, approached as closely to it as she seemed capable of.

"Y'know, now I wish I hadn't done that, sort of. Played hide and seek with them like this, I mean. Now I *have* got cold feet. Do you think they'll really like me? Suppose they don't? Suppose they have me built up in their expectations as someone entirely different, and—"

Like the little boy in the radio skit who prattles about a self-invented bugaboo until he ends up by frightening himself with it.

"How on earth do you make the water stay in this thing?" she interrupted herself. She pounded lightly on the plunger set into the washbasin. "Every time I get it to fill, it runs right out again."

"Twist it a little, and then push down on it, I think."

Patrice stripped off her wedding-band before plunging her hands in. "Hold this for me, I want to wash my hands. I have a horror of losing it. It slipped down a drain on the Other Side, once, and they had to take out a whole section of pipe before they could get it out for me."

"It's beautiful," Helen said wistfully.

"Isn't it, though?" Patrice agreed. "See? It has our names, together, around it on the inside. Isn't that a cute idea? Keep it on your finger for me a minute, that's the safest."

"Isn't it supposed to be bad luck to do that? I mean, for you to take it off, and for me to put it on?"

Patrice tossed her head vaingloriously. "I *couldn't* have bad luck," she proclaimed. It was almost a challenge.

"And I," thought Helen somberly, "couldn't have good."

She watched it curiously as it slowly descended the length of her finger, easily, without forcing. There was a curiously familiar feeling to it, as of something that should have been there long ago, that belonged there and had been strangely lacking until now.

"So this is what it feels like," she said to herself poignantly.

The train pounded on, its headlong roar deadened, in here where they were, to a muted jittering.

Patrice stepped back, her toilette at last completed. "Well, this is my last night," she sighed. "By this time tomorrow night we'll already be there, the worst'll be over." She clasped her own arms, in a sort of half-shiver of fright. "I hope they like what they're getting." She nervously stole a sidelong look at herself in the glass, primped at her hair.

"You'll be all right, Patrice," Helen reassured her quietly. "Nobody could help but like you."

Patrice crossed her fingers and held them up to show her. "Hugh says they're very well-off," she rambled on. "That makes it all the worse sometimes." She tittered in recollection. "I guess they must be. I know they even had to send us the money for the trip home. We were always on a shoestring, the whole time we were over there. We had an awful lot of fun, though. I think that's the only time you have fun, when you're on a shoestring, don't you?"

"Sometimes—you don't," remembered Helen, but she didn't answer.

"Anyway," her confidante babbled on, "as soon as they found out

I was Expecting, that did it! They wouldn't hear of my having my baby over there. I didn't much want to myself, as a matter of fact, and Hugh didn't want me to either. They should be born in the good old U.S.A., don't you think so? That's the least you can do for them."

"Sometimes that's *all* you can do for them," Helen thought wryly. "That—and seventeen cents."

She had finished now in turn.

Patrice urged, "Let's stay in here long enough to have a puff, now that we're here. We don't seem to be keeping anybody else out. And if we try to talk out there, they might shush us down; they're all trying to sleep." The little lighter-flame winked in coppery reflection against the mirrors and glistening chrome on all sides of them. She gave a sigh of heartfelt satisfaction. "I love these before-retiring talks with another girl. It's been ages since I last had one. Back in school, I guess. Hugh says I'm a woman's woman at heart." She stopped short and thought about it with a quizzical quirk of her head. "Is that good or bad? I must ask him."

Helen couldn't repress a smile. "Good, I guess. I wouldn't want to be a man's woman."

"I wouldn't either!" Patrice hastily concurred. "It always makes me think of someone who uses foul language and spits out of the corner of her mouth."

They both chuckled for a moment in unison. But Patrice's butterfly-mind had already fluttered on to the next topic, as she dropped ash into the waste-receptacle. "Wonder if I'll be able to smoke openly, once I'm home?" She shrugged. "Oh well, there's always the back of the barn."

And then suddenly she had reverted to their mutual condition again.

"Are you frightened? About *it*, you know?"

Helen made the admission with her eyes.

"I am too." She took a reflective puff. "I think everyone is, a little, don't you? Men don't think we are. All I have to do is look at Hugh—" she deepened the dimple-pits humorously—"and I can see he's frightened enough for the two of us, so then I don't let on that I'm frightened too. And *I* reassure *him*."

Helen wondered what it was like to have someone to talk to about it.

"Are *they* pleased about it?"

"Oh sure. They're tickled silly. First grandchild, you know. They didn't even ask us if we *wanted* to come back. 'You're coming back,' and that was that."

She pointed the remnant of her cigarette down toward one of the taps, quenched it with a sharp little jet of water.

"Ready? Shall we go back to our seats now?"

They were both doing little things. All life is that, the continuous doing of little things, all life long. And then suddenly a big thing strikes into their midst—and where are the little things, what became of them, what were they?

Her hand was to the door, reversing the little handlatch that Patrice had locked before, when they first came in. Patrice was somewhere behind her, replacing something in the uplidded dressing-kit, about to close it and bring it with her. She could see her vaguely in the chromium sheeting lining the wall before her. Little things. Little things that life is made up of. Little things that stop—

Her senses played a trick on her. There was no time for them to synchronize with the thing that happened. They played her false. She had a fleeting impression, at first, of having done something wrong to the door, dislodged it in its entirety. Simply by touching that little hand-latch. It was as though she were bringing the whole door-slab down inward on herself. As though it were falling bodily out of its frame, hinges and all. And yet it never did, it never detached itself, it never came apart from the entire wall-section it was imbedded in. So the second fleeting impression, equally false and equally a matter of seconds only, was that the entire wall of the compartment, door and all, was toppling, threatening to come down on her. And yet that never did either. Instead, the whole alcove seemed to upend, shift on a crazy axis, so that what had been the wall before her until now, had shifted to become the ceiling over her; so that what had been the floor she was standing on until now, had shifted to become the wall upright before her. The door was gone hopelessly out of reach; was a sealed trap overhead, impossible to attain.

The lights went. All light was gone, and yet so vividly explosive were the sensory images whirling through her mind that they glowed on of their own incandescence in the dark; it took her a comparatively long time to realize she was steeped in pitch-blackness, could no longer see physically. Only in afterglow of imaginative terror.

There was a nauseating sensation as if the tracks, instead of being rigid steel rods, had softened into rippling ribbons, with the train still trying to follow their buckling curvature. The car seemed to go up and down, like a scenic railway performing foreshortened dips and rises that followed one another quicker and quicker and quicker. There was a distant rending, grinding, coming nearer, swelling as it came. It reminded her of a coffee-mill they had had at home, when she was a little girl. But that one didn't draw you into its maw, crunching everything in sight, as this one was doing.

"Hugh!" the disembodied floor itself seemed to scream out behind her. Just once.

Then after that the floor fell silent.

There were minor impressions. Of seams opening, and of heavy metal partitions being bent together over her head, until the opening that held her was no longer foursquare, but tent-shaped. The darkness blanched momentarily in sudden ghostly pallor that was hot and puckery to breathe. Escaping steam. Then it thinned out again, and the darkness came back full-pitch. A little orange light flickered up somewhere, far off. Then that ebbed and dimmed again, and was gone, too.

There wasn't any sound now, there wasn't any motion. Everything was still, and dreamy, and forgotten. What was this? Sleep? Death? She didn't think so. But it wasn't life either. She remembered life; life had been only a few minutes ago. Life had had lots of light in it, and people, and motion, and sound.

This must be something else. Some transitional stage, some other condition she hadn't been told about until now. Neither life, nor death, but something in-between.

Whatever it was, it held pain in it; it was *all* pain, only pain. Pain that started small, and grew, and grew, and grew. She tried to move, and couldn't. A slim rounded thing, cold and sweating, down by her feet, was holding her down. It lay across her straight, like a water pipe sprung out of joint.

Pain that grew and grew. If she could have screamed, it might have eased it. But she couldn't seem to.

She put her hand to her mouth. On her third finger she encountered a little metal circlet, a ring that had been drawn over it. She bit on it. That helped, that eased it a little. The more the pain grew, the harder she bit.

She heard herself moan a little, and she shut her eyes. The pain went away. But it took everything else with it; thought, knowledge, awareness.

She opened her eyes again, reluctantly. Minutes? Hours? She didn't know. She only wanted to sleep, to sleep some more. Thought, knowledge, awareness, came back. But the pain didn't come back; that seemed to be gone for good. Instead there was just this lassitude. She heard herself whimpering softly, like a small kitten. Or was it she?

She only wanted to sleep, to sleep some more. And they were making so much noise they wouldn't let her. Clanging, and pounding on sheets of loose tin, and prying things away. She rolled her head aside a little, in protest.

An attenuated shaft of light peered through, from somewhere up over her head. It was like a long thin finger, a spoke, prodding for her, pointing at her, trying to find her in the dark.

It didn't actually hit her, but it kept probing for her in all the wrong places, all around her.

She only wanted to sleep. She mewed a little in protest—or was it she?—and there was a sudden frightened flurry of activity, the pounding became faster, the prying became more hectic.

Then all of it stopped at once, there was a complete cessation, and a man's voice sounded directly over her, strangely hollow and blurred as when you talk through a tube.

"Steady. We're coming to you. Just a minute longer, honey. Can you hold out? Are you hurt? Are you bad? Are you alone under there?"

"No," she said feebly. "I've—I've just had a baby down here."

6

RECOVERY WAS LIKE a progressive equalization of badly unbalanced solstices. At first time was all nights, unbroken polar nights, with tiny fractional days lasting a minute or two at a time. Nights were sleep and days were wakefulness. Then little by little the days expanded and the nights contracted. Presently, instead of many little days during the space of each twenty-four hours, there was just one long one in the middle of it each time, the way there should be. Soon this had even begun to overlap at one end, to continue beyond the setting of the sun and impinge into the first hour or two of evening. Now, instead of many little fragmentary days in the space of one night, there were many little fragmentary nights in the space of one day. Dozes or naps. The solstices had reversed themselves.

Recovery was on a second, concurrent plane as well. Dimension entered into it as well as duration. The physical size of her surroundings expanded along with the extension of her days. First there was just a small area around her that entered into awareness each time; the pillows behind her head, the upper third of the bed, a dim face just offside to her, bending down toward her, going away, coming back again. And over and above everything else, a small form allowed to nestle in her arms for a few moments at a time. Something that was alive and warm and hers. She came more alive then than at any other time. It was food and drink and sunlight; it was her lifeline back to life. The rest remained unfocussed, lost in misty gray distances stretching out and around her.

But this core of visibility, this too expanded. Presently it had reached the foot of the bed. Then it had jumped over that, to the wide moat of the room beyond, its bottom hidden from sight. Then it had reached the walls of the room, on all three sides, and could go no further for the present; they stopped it. But that wasn't a limitation of inadequate awareness any more, that was a limitation of physical equipment. Even well eyes were not made to go through walls.

It was a pleasant room. An infinitely pleasant room. This could not have been a haphazard effect achieved at random. It was too immediate, too all-pervading; every chord it struck was the right one: whether of color, proportion, acoustics, bodily tranquility and well-being, and above all, of personal security and sanctuary, of belonging somewhere at last, of having found a haven, a harbor, of being let be. The height of scientific skill and knowledge, therefore, must have entered into it, to achieve that cumulative effect that her mind could only label pleasant.

The over-all effect was a warm glowing ivory shade, not a chill, clinical white. There was a window over to her right, with a Venetian blind. And when this was furled, the sun came through in a solid slab-like shaft, like a chunk of copper-gold ore. And when it was unfurled, the dismembered beams blurred and formed a hazy mist flecked with copper-gold motes that clung to the whole window like a halo. And still at other times they brought the slats sharply together, and formed a cool blue dusk in the room, and even that was grateful, made you close your eyes without effort and take a nap.

There were always flowers standing there, too, over to her right near the head of the bed. Never the same color twice. They must have been changed each day. They repeated themselves, but never in immediate succession. Yellow, and then the next day pink, and then the next day violet and white, and then the next day back to yellow again. She got so she looked for them. It made her want to open her eyes and see what color they would be this time. Maybe that was why they were there. The Face would bring them over and hold them closer for her to see, and then put them back again.

The first words she spoke each day were: "Let me see my little boy." But the second, or not far behind, were always: "Let me see my flowers."

And after awhile there was fruit. Not right at first, but a little later on when she first began to enjoy appetite again. That was in a different place, not quite so close, over by the window. In a basket, with a big-eared satin bow standing up straight above its handle. Never the same fruit twice, that is to say, never the same arrangement or ratio of the various species, and never any slightest mark of spoilage, so she knew it must be new fruit each day. The satin bow was never the same twice, either, so presumably the basket was a different one too. A new basketful of fresh fruit each day.

And if it could never mean quite as much to her as the flowers that is because flowers are flowers and fruit is fruit. It was still good to look at in its way. Blue grapes and green, and purple ones, with the sunlight shining through them and giving them a cathedral-window lustre; bartlett pears, with a rosy flush that almost belonged to apples on their yellow cheeks; plushy yellow peaches; pert little tangerines; apples that were almost purple in their apoplectic full-bloodedness.

Every day, nestled in cool, crisp, dark-green tissue.

She hadn't known that hospitals were so attentive. She hadn't known they provided such things for their patients; even patients who only had seventeen cents in their purses—or would have, had they had purses—when they were admitted.

She thought about the past sometimes, remembered it, reviewed it, the little there was of it. But it brought shadows into the room, dimmed its bright corners, it thinned even the thick girder-like shafts of sunlight coming through the window, it made her want the covers closer up around her shoulders, so she learned to avoid thinking of it, summoning it up.

She thought:

I was on a train. I was closeted in the washroom with another girl. She could remember the metallic sheen of the fixtures and the mirrors. She could see the other girl's face; three dimples in triangular arrangement, one on each cheek, one at the chin. She could even feel the shaking and vibration, the slight unsteadiness of footing, again, if she tried hard enough. But it made her slightly nauseated to do so, because she knew what was coming next, in a very few seconds. She knew now, but she hadn't known then. She usually snapped off the sensory image, as if it were a lightswitch, in a hurry at this point, to forestall what was surely coming next.

She remembered New York. She remembered the door that wouldn't open. She remembered the strip of one-way tickets falling out of an envelope. That was when the shadows really formed around, good and heavy. That was when the temperature of the room really went down. When she went back behind the train-trip, to remember New York, on the other side of it.

She quickly shut her eyes and turned her head aside on the pillow, and shut the past out.

The present was kinder by far. And you could have it so easy, any given moment of the day. You could have it without trying at all. Stay in the present, let the present do. The present was safe. Don't stray out of it—not in either direction, forward or backward. Because there was only darkness, way out there all around it, and you didn't know what you'd find. Sit tight; lie tight, right where you were.

She opened her eyes and warmed to it again. The sunlight coming in, thick and warm and strong enough to carry the weight of a toboggan from the window-sill to the floor. The technicolored burst of flowers, the beribboned basket of fruit. The soothing quiet all around. They'd bring the little form in pretty soon, and let it nestle against her, and she'd know that happiness that was something new, that made you want to circle your arms and never let go.

Let the present do. Let the present last. Don't ask, don't seek, don't question, don't quarrel with it. Hang onto it for all you were worth.

7

IT WAS REALLY the flowers that were her undoing, that brought the present to an end.

She wanted one of them one day. Wanted to separate one from the rest, and hold it in her hand, and smell its sweetness directly under her nose; it wasn't enough any longer just to enjoy them visually, to look at them in the abstract, in group-formation.

They'd been moved nearer by this time. And she herself could move now more freely. She'd been lying quietly on her side admiring them for some time when the impulse formed.

There was a small one, dangling low, arching over in her direction, and she thought she'd get that. She turned more fully, so that she was completely sideward, and reached out toward it.

Her hand closed on its stalk, and it quivered delicately with the pressure. She knew she wouldn't have been able to break the stalk off short just with one hand alone, and she didn't want to do that anyway; didn't want to damage the flower, just borrow it for awhile. So she started to withdraw the stalk vertically from the receptacle, and as it paid off and seemed never to come to an end, this swept her hand high upward and at last back over her own head.

It struck the bed-back, that part that was so close to her that she could never have seen it without making a complete head-turn, and something up there jiggled and quivered a little, as if threatening to detach itself and come down.

She made the complete head-turn, and even withdrew out from it a little, into a half-sitting position, something she had never attempted before, to bring it into focus.

It was a featherweight metal frame, a rectangle, clasped to the top bar of the bed, loose on its other three sides. Within was held a smooth mat of paper, with fine neat writing on it that blurred until it had stopped the slight swaying that her impact had set in motion.

It had been inches from her head, just over her head, all this time, but she'd never seen it until now.

Her chart.

She peered at it intently.

Suddenly the present and all its safety exploded into fragments, and the flower fell from her extended hand onto the floor.

There were three lines at the top, in neat symmetry. The first part of each was printed and left incomplete; the rest was finished out in typescript.

It said at the top: "Section—"
And then it said: "Maternity."
It said below that: "Room—"
And then it said: "25."
It said at the bottom: "Patient's Name—"
And then it said: "Hazzard, Patrice (Mrs.)."

8

THE NURSE OPENED the door, and her face changed. The smile died off on it. You could detect the change in her face from all the way over there, even before she'd come any closer to the bed.

She came over and took her patient's temperature. Then she straightened the chart.

Neither of them said anything.

There was fear in the room. There was shadow in the room. The present was no longer in the room. The future had taken its place.

Bringing fear, bringing shadow, bringing strangeness; worse than even the past could have brought.

The nurse held the thermometer toward the light and scanned it. Then her brows deepened. She put the thermometer down.

She asked the question carefully, as though she had gauged its tone and its tempo before allowing herself to ask it. She said, "What happened? Has something upset you? You're running a slight temperature."

The girl in the bed answered with a question of her own. Frightenedly, tautly. "What's that doing on my bed? Why is it there?"

"Everyone who's ill has to have one," the nurse answered soothingly. "It's nothing, just a—"

"But look—the name. It says—"

"Does the sight of your own name frighten you? You mustn't look at it. You're really not supposed to see it there. Sh, don't talk now any more."

"But there's something I—But you have to tell me, I don't understand—"

The nurse took her pulse.

And as she did so, the patient was suddenly looking at her own hand, in frozen, arrested horror. At the little circlet with diamonds, enfolding the third finger. At the weddingband. As though she'd never seen it before, as though she wondered what it was doing there.

The nurse saw her trying to take it off, with flurried little tugs. It wouldn't move easily.

The nurse's face changed. "Just a moment, I'll be right back," she said uneasily.

She brought the doctor in with her. Her whispering stopped as they crossed the threshold.

He came over to the bed, put his hand to her forehead.

He nodded to the nurse and said, "Slight."

He said, "Drink this."

It tasted salty.

They put the hand under the covers, out of sight. The hand with the ring on it.

They took the glass from her lips. She didn't want to ask any questions, any more. She did, but some other time, not right now. There was something they had to be told. She'd had it a minute ago, but now it had escaped her again.

She sighed. Some other time, but not right now. She didn't want to do anything right now but sleep.

She turned her face toward the pillow and slept.

9

IT CAME RIGHT back again. The first thing. With the first glimpse of the flowers, the first glimpse of the fruit, right as her eyelids first went up and the room came into being. It came right back again.

Something said to her: Tread softly, speak slow. Take care, take care. She didn't know what or why, but she knew it must be heeded.

The nurse said to her, "Drink your orange juice."

The nurse said to her, "You can have a little coffee in your milk, starting from today on. Each day a little more. Won't that be a pleasant change?"

Tread softly, speak with care.

She said, "What happened to—?"

She took another sip of beige-colored milk. Tread warily, speak slow.

"To whom?" the nurse finally completed it for her.

Oh, careful now, careful. "There was another girl in the train washroom with me. Is she all right?" She took another sip of milk for punctuation. Hold the glass steady, now; that's right. Don't let it shake. Down to the tray again, even and slow; that's it.

The nurse shook her head reticently. She said, "No."

"She's dead?"

The nurse wouldn't answer. She too was treading softly. She too felt her way, she too wouldn't rush in. She said, "Did you know her very well?"

"No."

"You'd only met her on the train?"

"Only on the train."

The nurse had paved her own way now. It was safe to proceed.

The nurse nodded. She was answering the question two sentences before, by delayed action. "She's gone," she said quietly.

The nurse watched her face expectantly. The pavement held; there was no cave-in.

The nurse ventured a step farther.

"Isn't there anyone else you want to ask about?"

"What happened to—?"

The nurse took the tray away, as if stripping the scene for a crisis. "To *him?*"

Those were the words. She adopted them. "What happened to him?"

The nurse said, "Just a moment." She went to the door, opened it, and motioned to someone unseen.

The doctor came in, and a second nurse. They stood waiting, as if prepared to meet an emergency.

The first nurse said, "Temperature normal." She said, "Pulse normal."

The second nurse was mixing something in a glass.

The first nurse, her own, stood close to the bed. She took her by the hand and held it tightly. Just held it like that, tight and unyielding.

The doctor nodded.

The first nurse moistened her lips. She said, "Your husband wasn't saved either, Mrs. Hazzard."

She could feel her face pale with shock. The skin pulled as though it were a size too small.

She said, "No, there's something wrong—No, you're making a mistake—"

The doctor motioned unobtrusively. He and the second nurse closed in on her swiftly.

Somebody put a cool hand on her forehead, held her pressed downward, kindly but firmly; she couldn't tell whose it was.

She said, "No, please let me tell you!"

The second nurse was holding something to her lips. The first one was holding her hand, tight and warm, as if to say, "I am here. Don't be frightened, I am here." The hand on her forehead was cool but competent. It was heavy, but not too heavy; just persuasive enough to make her head lie still.

"Please—" she said listlessly.

She didn't say anything more after that. They didn't either.

Finally she overheard the doctor murmur, as if in punctuation: "She stood that very well."

10

IT CAME BACK again. How could it fail to now? You cannot sleep at all times, only at small times. And with it came: Tread softly, speak with care.

The nurse's name was Miss Allmeyer, the one she knew best.

"Miss Allmeyer, does the hospital give everyone those flowers every day?"

"We'd like to, but we couldn't afford it. Those flowers cost five dollars each time you see them. They're just for you."

"Is it the hospital that supplies that fruit every day?"

The nurse smiled gently. "We'd like to do that too. We only wish we could. That fruit cost ten dollars a basket each time you see it. It's a standing order, just for you."

"Well, who—?" Speak softly.

The nurse smiled winningly. "Can't you guess, honey? That shouldn't be very hard."

"There's something I want to tell you. Something you must let me tell you." She turned her head restlessly on the pillows, first to one side, then the other, then back to the first.

"Now, honey, are we going to have a bad day? I thought we were going to have such a good day."

"Could you find out something for me?"

"I'll try."

"The handbag; the handbag that was in the train-washroom with me. How much was in it?"

"*Your* handbag?"

"The handbag. The one that was there when I was in there."

The nurse came back later and said, "It's safe; it's being held for you. About fifty dollars or so."

That wasn't hers, that was the other one.

"There were two."

"There is another," the nurse admitted. "It doesn't belong to anyone now." She looked down commiseratingly. "There was just seventeen cents in it," she breathed almost inaudibly.

She didn't have to be told that. She knew by heart. She remembered from before boarding the train. She remembered from the train itself. Seventeen cents. Two pennies, a nickel, a dime.

"Could you bring the seventeen cents here? Could I have it just to look at it? Could I have it here next to the bed?"

The nurse said, "I'm not sure it's good for you, to brood like that. I'll see what they say."

She brought it, though, inside a small envelope.

She was alone with it. She dumped the four little coins from the envelope into the palm of her hand. She closed her hand upon them tightly, held them gripped like that, fiercely, in a knot of dilemma.

Fifty dollars, symbolically. Symbol of an untold amount more.

Seventeen cents, literally. Symbol of nothing, for there wasn't any more. Seventeen cents and nothing else.

The nurse came back again and smiled at her. "Now, what was it you said you wanted to tell me?"

She returned the smile, wanly. "It can keep for awhile longer. I'll tell you some other time. Tomorrow, maybe, or the next day. Not—not right today."

11

THERE WAS A letter on the breakfast-tray.

The nurse said, "See? Now you're beginning to get mail, just like the well people do."

It was slanted toward her, leaning against the milk glass. On the envelope it said:

"Mrs. Patrice Hazzard"

She was frightened of it. She couldn't take her eyes off it. The glass of orange juice shook in her hand. The writing on it seemed to get bigger, and bigger, and bigger, as it stood there.

"MRS. PATRICE HAZZARD"

"Open it," the nurse encouraged her. "Don't just look at it like that. It won't bite you."

She tried to twice, and twice it fell. The third time she managed to rip one seam along its entire length.

> "Patrice, dear:
> "Though we've never seen you, you're our daughter now, dear. You're Hugh's legacy to us. You're all we have now, you and the little fellow. I can't come to you, where you are; doctor's orders. The shock was too much for me and he forbids my making the trip. You'll have to come to us, instead. Come soon, dear. Come home to us, in our loneliness and loss. It will make it that much easier to bear. It won't be long now, dear. We've been in constant touch with Dr. Brett, and he sends very encouraging reports of your progress—"

The rest didn't matter so much; she let it fade from her attention. It was like train-wheels going through her head.

Though we've never seen you.

Though we've never seen you.

Though we've never seen you.

The nurse eased it from her forgetful fingers after awhile, and put it back in its envelope. She watched the nurse fearfully as she moved about the room.

"If I weren't Mrs. Hazzard, would I be allowed to stay in this room?"

The nurse laughed cheerfully. "We'd put you out, we'd throw you right outside into one of the wards," she said, bending close toward her in mock threat.

The nurse said, "Here, take your young son."

She held him tightly, in fierce, almost convulsive protectiveness.

Seventeen cents. Seventeen cents last such a short time, goes such a short way.

The nurse felt in good humor. She tried to prolong their little joke of a moment ago. "Why? Are you trying to tell me you're not Mrs. Hazzard?" she asked banteringly.

She held him fiercely, protectively close.

Seventeen cents, seventeen cents.

"No," she said in a smothered voice, burying her face against him, "I'm not trying to tell you that. I'm not trying."

12

SHE WAS IN a dressing-robe, sitting by the window in the sun. It was quilted blue silk. She wore it every day when she got up out of bed. On the breast-pocket it had a monogram embroidered in white silk; the letters "P H" intertwined. There were slippers to match.

She was reading a book. On the flyleaf, though she was long past it, it was inscribed "To Patrice, with love from Mother H." There was a row of other books on the stand beside the bed. Ten or twelve of them; books with vivacious jackets, turquoise, magenta, vermilion, cobalt, and with vivacious, lighthearted contents to match. Not a shadow between their covers.

There was a scattering of orange peel, and two or three seeds, in a dish on a low stand beside her easy chair. There was a cigarette burning in another, smaller dish beside that one. It was custom-made, it had a straw tip, and the initials "P H" on it had not yet been consumed.

The sunlight, falling from behind and over her, made her hair seem hazily translucent, made it almost seem like golden foam about her head. It skipped the front of her, from there on down, due to the turn of the chair-back, and struck again in a little golden pool across one outthrust bare instep, lying on it like a warm, luminous kiss.

There was a light tap at the door and the doctor came in.

He drew out a chair and sat down facing her, leaving its straight back in front of him as an added note of genial informality.

"I hear you're leaving us soon."

The book fell and he had to pick it up for her. He offered it back to her, but when she seemed incapable of taking it, he put it aside on the stand.

"Don't look so frightened. Everything's arranged—"

She had a little difficulty with her breathing. "Where—? Where to?"

"Why, home, of course."

She put her hand to her hair and flattened it a little, but then it sprang up again, gaseous as before, in the sun.

"Here are your tickets." He took an envelope out of his pocket, tried to offer it to her. Her hands withdrew a little, each one around a side of the chair toward the back. He put the envelope between the pages of the discarded book finally, leaving it outthrust like a place-mark.

Her eyes were very large. Larger than they had seemed before he came into the room. "When?" she said with scarcely any breath at all.

"Wednesday, the early afternoon train."

Suddenly panic was licking all over her, like a shriveling, congealing, frigid flame.

"No, I can't! No! Doctor, you've got to listen—!" She tried to grab his hand with both of hers and hold onto it.

He spoke to her playfully, as if she were a child. "Now, now, here. What's all this? What *is* all this?"

"No, doctor, no—!" She shook her head insistently.

He sandwiched her hand between both of his, and held it that way, consolingly. "I understand," he said soothingly. "We're a little shaky yet, we've just finished getting used to things as they are— We're a little timid about giving up familiar surroundings for those that are strange to us. We all have it; it's a typical nervous reaction. Why, you'll be over it in no time."

"But I can't *do* it, doctor," she whispered passionately. "I can't *do* it."

He chucked her under the chin, to instill courage in her. "We'll put you on the train, and all you have to do is ride. Your family will be waiting to take you off at the other end."

"My family."

"Don't make such a face about it," he coaxed whimsically.

He glanced around at the crib.

"What about the young man here?"

He went over to it, and lifted the child out; brought him to her and put him in her arms.

"You want to take him home, don't you? You don't want him to grow up in a hospital?" He laughed at her teasingly. "You want him to *have* a home, don't you?"

She held him to her, lowered her head to him.

"Yes," she said at last, submissively. "Yes, I want him to have a home."

13

A TRAIN AGAIN. But how different it was now. No crowded aisles, no jostling figures, no flux of patient, swaying humanity. A compartment, a roomette all to herself. A little table on braces, that could go up, that could go down. A closet with a full-length mirrored door, just as in any ground-fast little dwelling. On the rack the neat luggage in recessive tiers, brand-new, in use now for the first time, glossy patent finish, hardware glistening, "P H" trimly stencilled in vermilion on the rounded corners. A little shaded lamp to read by when the countryside grew dark. Flowers in a holder, going-away flowers —no, coming-homeward flowers—presented by proxy at the point of departure; glazed fruit-candies in a box; a magazine or two.

And outside the two wide windows, that formed almost a single panel from wall to wall, trees sailing peacefully by, off a way in a single line, dappled with sunshine; dark green on one side, light apple-green on the other. Clouds sailing peacefully by, only a little more slowly than the trees, as if the two things worked on separate, yet almost-synchronized, belts of continuous motion. Meadows and fields, and the little ripples that hillocks made off in the distance every once in awhile. Going up a little, coming down again. The wavy line of the future.

And on the seat opposite her own, and more important by far than all this, snug in a little blue blanket, small face still, small eyes closed—something to cherish, something to love. All there was in the world to love. All there was to go on for, along that wavy line outside.

Yes, how different it was now. And—how infinitely preferable the first time had been to this one. Fear rode with her now.

There hadn't been fear then. There hadn't been a seat, there hadn't been a bite to eat, there had only been seventeen cents. And just ahead, unguessed, rushing ever nearer with the miles, there had been calamity, horror, the beating of the wings of death.

But there hadn't been fear. There hadn't been this gnawing inside. There hadn't been this strain and counterstrain, this pulling one way and pulling the other. There had been the calm, the certainty, of going along the right way, the only way there was to go.

The wheels chattered, as they always chatter, on every train that has ever run. But saying now, to her ear alone:

> *"You'd better go back, you'd better go back,*
> *Clicketty-clack, clicketty-clack,*
> *Stop while you can, you still can go back."*

A very small part of her moved, the least part of her moved. Her thumb unbracketed, and her four fingers opened slowly, and the tight white knot they'd made for hours past dissolved. There in its center, exposed now—

An Indian-head penny.

A Lincoln-head penny.

A buffalo nickel.

A Liberty-head dime.

Seventeen cents. She even knew the dates on them by heart, by now.

> *"Clicketty-clack,*
> *Stop and go back,*
> *You still have the time,*
> *Turn and go back."*

Slowly the fingers folded up and over again, the thumb crossed over and locked them in place.

Then she took the whole fist and struck it distractedly against her forehead and held it there for a moment where it had struck.

She stood up suddenly, and tugged at one of the pieces of luggage, and swivelled it around, so that its outermost corner was now inward. The "P H" disappeared. Then she did it to the piece below. The second "P H" disappeared.

The fear wouldn't disappear. It wasn't just stencilled on a corner of her, it was all over her.

There was a light knock outside the door, and she started as violently as though it had been a resounding crash.

"Who's there?" she gasped.

A porter's voice answered, "Five mo' minutes fo' Caulfield."

She reared from the seat, and ran to the door, flung it open. He was already going down the passage. "No, wait! It can't be—"

"It sho' enough is, though, ma'm."

"So quickly, though. I didn't think—"

He smiled back at her indulgently. "It always comes between Clarendon and Hastings. That's the right place fo' it. And we've had Clarendon already, and Hastings's comin' right after it. Ain't never change since I been on this railroad."

She closed the door, and swung around, and leaned her whole back against it, as if trying to keep out some catastrophic intrusion.

> *"Too late to go back,*
> *Too late to go back—"*

"I can still ride straight through, I can ride past without getting off," she thought. She ran to the windows and peered out ahead, at an acute angle, as if the oncoming sight of it in itself would resolve her difficulty in some way.

Nothing yet. It was coming on very gradually. A house, all by itself. Then another house, still all by itself. Then a third. They were beginning to come thicker now.

"Ride straight through, don't get off at all. They can't make you. Nobody can. Do this one last thing that's all there's time for now."

She ran back to the door and hurriedly turned the little finger-latch under the knob, locking it on the inside.

The houses were coming in more profusion, but they were coming slower too. They didn't sail any more, they dawdled. A school-building drifted by; you could tell what it was even from afar. Spotless, modern, brand-new looking, its concrete functionalism gleaming spic-and-span in the sun; copiously glassed. She could even make out small swings in motion, in the playground beside it. She glanced aside at the small blanketed bundle on the seat. That would be the kind of school she'd want—

She didn't speak, but her own voice was loud in her ears. "Help me, somebody; I don't know what to do!"

The wheels were dying, as though they'd run out of lubrication. Or like a phonograph record that runs down.

> *"Cli-ck, cla-ck,*
> *Cli-i-ck, cla-a-a-ck."*

Each revolution seemed about to be the last.

Suddenly a long shed started up, just outside the windows, running along parallel to them, and then a white sign suspended from it started to go by, letter by letter in reverse.

"D-L-E-I-"

It got to the F and it stuck. It wouldn't budge. She all but screamed. The train had stopped.

A knock sounded right behind her back, the vibration of it seeming to go through her chest.

"Caulfield, ma'm."

Then someone tried the knob.

"Help you with yo' things?"

Her clenched fist tightened around the seventeen cents, until the knuckles showed white and livid with the pressure.

She ran to the seat and picked up the blue blanket and what it held.

There were people out there, just on the other side of the window. Their heads were low, but she could see them, and they could see her. There was a woman looking right at her.

Their eyes met; their eyes locked, held fast. She couldn't turn her head away, she couldn't withdraw deeper into the compartment. It was as though those eyes riveted her where she stood.

The woman pointed to her. She called out in jubilation, for the benefit of someone else, unseen. "There she is! I've found her! Here, this car up here!"

She raised her hand and she waved. She waved to the little somnolent, blinking head coifed in the blue blanket, looking solemnly out the window. Made her fingers flutter in that special wave you give to very small babies.

The look on her face couldn't have been described. It was as when life begins all over again, after an interruption, a hiatus. It was as when the sun peers through again at the end, at the end of a bleak wintry day.

The girl holding the baby put her head down close to his, almost as if averting it from the window. Or as if they were communing together, exchanging some confidence in secret, to the exclusion of everyone else.

She was.

"For you," she breathed. "For you. And God forgive me."

Then she carried him over to the door with her, and turned the latch to let the harassed porter in.

14

SOMETIMES THERE IS a dividing-line running across life. Sharp, almost actual, like the black stroke of a paintbrush or the white gash of a chalk-mark. Sometimes, but not often.

For her there was. It lay somewhere along those few yards of car-passage, between the compartment-window and the car-steps, where for a moment or two she was out of sight of those standing waiting outside. One girl left the window. Another girl came down the steps. A world ended, and another world began.

She wasn't the girl who had been holding her baby by the compartment-window just now.

Patrice Hazzard came down those car-steps.

Frightened, tremulous, very white in the face, but Patrice Hazzard.

She was aware of things, but only indirectly; she only had eyes for those other eyes looking into hers from a distance of a few inches away. All else was background. Behind her back the train glided on. Bearing with it its hundreds of living passengers. And, all unknown, in an empty compartment, a ghost. Two ghosts, a large one and a very small one.

Forever homeless now, never to be retrieved.

The hazel eyes came in even closer to hers. They were kind; they smiled around the edges; they were gentle, tender. They hurt a little. *They were trustful.*

She was in her fifties, their owner. Her hair was softly graying, and only underneath had the process been delayed. She was as tall as Patrice, and as slim; and she shouldn't have been, for it wasn't the slimness of fashionable effort or artifice, and something about her clothes revealed it to be recent, only the past few months.

But even these details about her were background, and the man of her own age standing just past her shoulder was background too. It was only her face that was immediate, and the eyes in her face, so close now. Saying so much without a sound.

She placed her hands lightly upon Patrice's cheeks, one on each, framing her face between them in a sort of accolade, a sacramental benison.

Then she kissed her on the lips, in silence, and there was a lifetime in the kiss, the girl could sense it. The lifetime of a man. The many years it takes to raise a man, from childhood, through boyhood, into a grown son. There was bitter loss in the kiss, the loss of all that at a single blow. The end for a time of all hope, and weeks of cruel grief. But then too there was the reparation of loss, the finding of a daughter, the starting over with another, a smaller son. No, with the same son; the same blood, the same flesh. Only going back and starting again from the beginning, in sweeter sadder sponsorship this time, forewarned by loss. And there was the burgeoning of hope anew.

There were all those things in it. They were spoken in it, they were felt in it; and they were meant to be felt in it, they had been put into it for that purpose.

This was not a kiss under a railroad-station shed; it was a sacrament of adoption.

Then she kissed the child. And smiled as you do at your own. And a little crystal drop that hadn't been there before was resting on its small pink cheek.

The man came forward and kissed her on the forehead.

"I'm Father, Patrice."

He stooped and straightened, and said, "I'll take your things over to the car." A little glad to escape from an emotional moment, as men are apt to be.

The woman hadn't said a word. In all the moments she'd been standing before her, not a word had passed her lips. She saw, perhaps, the pallor in her face; could read the shrinking, the uncertainty, in her eyes.

She put her arms about her and drew her to her now, in a warmer, more mundane, more everyday greeting than the one that had passed before. Drew the girl's head to rest upon her own shoulder for a moment. And as she did so, she spoke for the first time, low in her ear, to give her courage, to give her peace.

"You're home, Patrice. Welcome home, dear."

And in those few words, so simply said, so inalterably meant, Patrice Hazzard knew she had found at last all the goodness there is or ever can be in this world.

15

AND SO THIS was what it was like to be home; to be in a home of your own, in a room of your own.

She had another dress on now, ready to go down to table. She sat there in a wing chair waiting, very straight, looking a little small against its outspread back. Her back was up against it very straight, her legs dropped down to the floor very straight and meticulously side by side. She had her hand out resting on the crib, the crib they'd bought for him and that she'd found already here waiting when she first entered the room. He was in it now. They'd even thought of that.

They'd left her alone; she would have had to be alone to savor it as fully as she was doing. Still drinking it in, hours after; basking in it, inhaling the essence of it; there was no word for what it did to her. Hours after; and her head every now and then would still give that slow, comprehensive, marvelling sweep around from side to side, taking in all four walls of it. And even up overhead, not forgetting the ceiling. A roof over your head. A roof to keep out rain and cold and loneliness—Not just the anonymous roof of a rented building, no; the roof of home. Guarding you, sheltering you, keeping you, watching over you.

And somewhere downstairs, dimly perceptible to her acutely attuned ears, the soothing bustle of an evening meal in preparation. Carried to her in faint snatches now and then at the opening of a door, stilled again at its closing. Footsteps busily crossing an uncarpeted strip of wooden floor, then coming back again. An occasional faint clash of crockery or china. Once even the voice of the colored housekeeper, for an instant of bugle-like clarity. "No, it ain't ready yet, Miz' Hazzard; need five mo' minutes."

And the laughingly protesting admonition that followed, miraculously audible as well: "Sh, Aunt Josie. We have a baby in the house now; he may be napping."

Someone was coming up the stairs now. They were coming up the stairs now to tell her. She shrank back a little in the chair. Now she

was a little frightened, a little nervous again. Now there would be
no quick escape from the moment's confrontation, as at the railroad
station. Now came the real meeting, the real blending, the real taking
into the fold. Now was the real test.

"Patrice dear, supper's ready whenever you are."

You take *supper* in the evening, when you're home, in your own
home. When you go out in public or to someone else's home, you
may take *dinner*. But in the evening, in your own home, it's *supper*
you take, and never anything else. Her heart was as fiercely glad as
though the trifling word were a talisman. She remembered when she
was a little girl, those few brief years that had ended so quickly—
The call to *supper*, only *supper*, never anything else.

She jumped from the chair and ran over and opened the door.
"Shall I—shall I bring him down with me, or leave him up here in
the crib till I come back?" she asked, half-eagerly, half-uncertainly.
"I fed him already at five, you know."

Mother Hazzard slanted her head coaxingly. "Ah, why don't you
bring him down with you just tonight, anyway? It's the first night.
Don't hurry, dear, take your time."

When she came out of the room holding him in her arms moments
later, she stopped a moment, fingered the edge of the door lingeringly.
Not where the knob was, but up and down the unbroken surface
where there was no knob.

Watch over my room for me, she breathed unheard. I'm coming
right back. Take care of it. Don't let anyone—Will you?

She would come down these same stairs many hundreds of times
to come, she knew, as she started down them now. She would come
down them fast, she would come down them slowly. She would come
down them blithely, in gayety. And perhaps she might come down
them in fear, in trouble. But now, tonight, this was the very first time
of all that she was coming down them.

She held him close to her and felt her way, for they were new to
her, she hadn't got the measure of them, the feel of them, yet, and
she didn't want to miss her step.

They were standing about in the dining-room waiting for her. Not
rigidly, formally, like drill-sergeants, but in unselfconscious ease, as
if unaware of the small tribute of consideration they were giving her.
Mother Hazzard was leaning forward, giving a last-minute touch to
the table, shifting something a little. Father Hazzard was looking up

toward the lights through the spectacles with which he'd just been reading, and polishing them off before returning them to their case. And there was a third person in the room, somebody with his back half to her at the moment of entrance, surreptitiously pilfering a salted peanut from a dish on the buffet.

He turned forward again and threw it away when he heard her come in. He was young and tall and friendly-looking, and his hair was— A camera-shutter clicked in her mind and the film rolled on.

"There's the young man!" Mother Hazzard revelled. "There's the young man himself! Here, give him to me. You know who this is, of course." And then she added, as though it were wholly unnecessary even to qualify it by so much, "Bill."

But who—? she wondered. They hadn't said anything until now.

He came forward, and she didn't know what to do, he was so close to her own age. She half-offered her hand, hoping that if it was too formal the gesture would remain unnoticed.

He took it, but he didn't shake it. Instead he pressed it between both of his, held it warmly buried like that for a moment or two.

"Welcome home, Patrice," he said quietly. And there was something about the straight, unwavering look in his eyes as he said it that made her think she'd never heard anything said so sincerely, so simply, so loyally, before.

And that was all. Mother Hazzard said, "You sit here, from now on."

Father Hazzard said unassumingly, "We're very happy, Patrice," and sat down at the head of the table.

Whoever Bill was, he sat down opposite her.

The colored housekeeper peeked through the door for a minute and beamed. "Now this look right! This what that table been needing. This just finish off that empty si—"

Then she quickly checked herself, clapping a catastrophic hand to her mouth, and whisked from sight again.

Mother Hazzard glanced down at her plate for a second, then immediately looked up again smiling, and the hurt was gone, had not been allowed to linger.

They didn't say anything memorable. You don't say anything memorable across the tables of home. Your heart speaks, and not your brain, to the other hearts around you. She forgot after awhile to notice what she was saying, to weigh, to reckon it. That's what home is, what home should be. It flowed from her as easily as it did from them. She knew that was what they were trying to do for her. And they were succeeding. Strangeness was already gone with the soup, never to return. Nothing could ever bring it back again. Other things could come—she hoped they wouldn't. But never strangeness, the unease of unfamiliarity, again. They had succeeded.

"I hope you don't mind the white collar on that dress, Patrice. I purposely saw to it there was a touch of color on everything I picked out; I didn't want you to be too—"

"Oh, some of those things are so lovely. I really hadn't seen half of them myself until I unpacked just now."

"The only thing that I was afraid of was the sizes, but that nurse of yours sent me a complete—"

"She took a tapemeasure all over me one day, I remember that now, but she wouldn't tell me what it was for—"

"Which kind for you, Patrice? Light or dark?"

"It really doesn't—"

"No, tell him just this once, dear; then after that he won't have to ask you."

"Dark, then, I guess."

"You and me both."

He spoke a little less frequently than the remaining three of them. Just a touch of shyness, she sensed. Not that he was strained or tonguetied or anything. Perhaps it was just his way; he had a quiet, unobtrusive way.

The thing was, who exactly was he? She couldn't ask outright now any longer. She'd omitted to at the first moment, and now it was twenty minutes too late for that. No last name had been given, so he must be—

I'll find out soon, she reassured herself. I'm bound to. She was no longer afraid.

Once she found he'd just been looking at her when her eyes went to him, and she wondered what he'd been thinking while doing so. And yet not to have admitted that she knew, that she could tell by the lingering traces of his expression, would have been to lie to herself. He'd been thinking that her face was pleasant, that he liked it.

And then after a little while he said, "Dad, pass the bread over this way, will you?"

And then she knew who he was.

16

EPISCOPAL CHURCH OF St. Bartholomew, social kingpin among all the churches of Caulfield, on a golden April Sunday morning.

She stood there by the font, child in her arms, immediate family and their close friends gathered beside her.

They had insisted upon this. She hadn't wanted it. Twice she had postponed it, for two Sundays in succession now, after all the arrangements had been made. First, by pleading a cold that she did not really have. Secondly, by pleading a slight one that the child actually did have. Today she hadn't been able to postpone it any longer. They would have finally sensed the deliberation underlying her excuses.

She kept her head down, hearing the ceremony rather than seeing it. As though afraid to look on openly at it. As though afraid of being struck down momentarily at the feet of all of them for her blasphemy.

She had on a broad-brimmed hat of semi-transparent horsehair and that helped her, veiling her eyes and the upper part of her face when she cast it down like that.

Mournful memories, they probably thought. Grief-stricken.

Guilty, in reality. Scandalized. Not brazen enough to gaze at this mockery unabashed.

Arms reached out toward her, to take the child from her. The godmother's arms. She gave him over, trailing the long lace ceremonial gown that—she had almost said "his father"—that a stranger named Hugh Hazzard had worn before him, and that *his* father, Donald, had worn before *him*.

Her arms felt strangely empty after that. She wanted to cross them protectively over her breast, as though she were unclad. She forced herself not to with an effort. It was not her form that was unclad, it was her conscience. She dropped them quietly, clasped them before her, looked down.

"Hugh Donald Hazzard, I baptize thee—"

They had gone through the parody of consulting her preferences in this. To her it was a parody; not to them. She wanted him named

after Hugh, of course? Yes, she had said demurely, after Hugh. Then
how about the middle name? After her own father? Or perhaps two
middle names, one for each grandfather? (She actually hadn't been
able to recall her own father's name at the moment; it came back to
her some time after, not without difficulty. Mike: a scarcely remembered figure of a looming longshoreman, killed in a drunken brawl
on the Embarcadero when she was ten.)

One middle name would do. After Hugh's father, she had said
demurely.

She could feel her face burning now, knew it must be flushed with
shame. They mustn't see that. She kept it steadily down.

"—in the name of the Father, and of the Son, and of the Holy
Ghost. Amen."

The minister sprinkled water on the child's head. She could see a
stray drop or two fall upon the floor, darken into coin dots. A dime,
a nickel, two pennies. Seventeen cents.

The infant began to wail in protest, as numberless infants before
it since time immemorial. The infant from a New York furnished
rooming house who had become heir to the first, the wealthiest family
in Caulfield, in all the county, maybe even in all that State.

"You have nothing to cry about," she thought morosely.

17

THERE WAS A cake for him, on his first birthday, with a single candle
standing defiantly in the middle of it, its flame like a yellow butterfly
hovering atop a fluted white column. They made great to-do and
ceremony about the little immemorial rites that went with it. The
first grandson. The first milestone.

"But if he can't make the wish," she demanded animatedly, "is it
all right if I make it for him? Or doesn't that count?"

Aunt Josie, the cake's creator, instinctively deferred to in all such matters of lore, nodded pontifically from the kitchen-doorway. "You make it for him, honey; he git it just the same," she promised.

Patrice dropped her eyes and her face sobered for a moment.

Peace, all your life, Safety, such as this. Your own around you always, such as now. And for myself—from you, someday—forgiveness.

"You got it? Now blow."

"Him or me?"

"It count just like for him."

She leaned down, pressed her cheek close to his, and blew softly. The yellow butterfly fluttered agitatedly, shrivelled into nothingness.

"Now cut," coached the self-imposed mistress of ceremonies.

She closed his chubby little hand around the knife-handle, enfolded it with her own, and tenderly guided it. The mystic incision made, she touched her finger to the sugary icing, scraped off a tiny crumb, and then placed it to his lips.

A great crowing and cooing went up, as though they had all just been witnesses to a prodigy of precocity.

A lot of people had come in, they hadn't had so many people all in the house at one time since she'd first been there. And long after the small honor-guest had been withdrawn from the scene and taken upstairs to bed, the festivities continued under their own momentum, even accelerated somewhat. In that way grown-ups have of appropriating a child's party, given the slightest encouragement.

She came down again, afterward, to the lighted, bustling rooms, and moved about among them, chatting, smiling, happier tonight than she ever remembered being before. A cup of punch in one hand, in the other a sandwich with one bite gone, that she never seemed to get around to taking a second bite out of. Every time she raised it toward her mouth somebody said something to her, or she said something to somebody. It didn't matter, it was more fun that way.

Bill brushed by her once, grinning. "How does it feel to be an *old* mother?"

"How does it feel to be an *old* uncle?" she rejoined pertly over her shoulder.

A year ago seemed a long time away; just a year ago tonight, with its horror and its darkness and its fright. That hadn't happened to her; it *couldn't* have. That had happened to a girl named—No, she

didn't want to remember that name, she didn't even want to sum-
mon it back for a fleeting instant. It had nothing to do with her.

"Aunt Josie's sitting up there with him. No, he'll be all right; he's
a very *good* baby about going to sleep."

"Coming from a detached observer."

"Well, I *am* detached at this minute, so I'm entitled to say so. He's
all the way upstairs and I'm down here."

She was in the brightly lighted living-room of her home, here, with
her friends, her family's friends, all gathered about her, laughing and
chatting. A year ago was more than a long time away. It had never
happened. No, it had never happened. Not to her, anyway.

A great many of the introductions were blurred. There were so
many firsts, on an occasion like this. She looked about, dutifully re-
capitulating the key-people, as befitted her role of assistant hostess.
Edna Harding and Marilyn Bryant, they were those two girls sitting
one on each side of Bill, and vying with one another for his attention.
She suppressed a mischievous grin. Look at him, sober-faced as a
totem pole. Why, it was enough to turn his head—if he hadn't happened to have a head that was unturnable by girls, as far as she'd
been able to observe. Guy Ennis was that dark-haired young man
over there getting someone a punch-cup; he was easy to memorize
because he'd come in alone. Some old friend of Bill's, evidently.
Funny that the honeybees didn't buzz around him more thickly, instead of unresponsive Bill. He looked far more the type.

Grace Henson, she was that stoutish, flaxen-haired girl over there,
waiting for the punch-cup. Or was she? No, she was the less stout
but still flaxen-haired one at the piano, softly playing for her own
entertainment, no one near her. One wore glasses and one didn't.
They must be sisters, there was too close a resemblance. It was the
first time either one of them had been to the house.

She moved over to the piano and stood beside her. She might
actually be enjoying doing that, for all Patrice knew, but she should
at least have somebody taking an appreciative interest.

The girl at the keyboard smiled at her. "Now this." She was an
accomplished player, keeping the music subdued, like an undertone
to the conversations going on all over the room.

But suddenly all the near-by ones had stopped. The music went
on alone for a note or two, sounding that much clearer than it had
before.

The second flaxen-haired girl quitted her companion for a moment, stepped up behind the player's back, touched her just once on the shoulder, as if in some kind of esoteric remonstrance or reminder. That was all she did. Then she went right back to where she'd been sitting. The whole little pantomime had been so deft and quick it was hardly noticeable at all.

The player had broken off, uncertainly. She apparently had understood the message of the tap, but not its meaning. The slightly bewildered shrug she gave Patrice was evidence of that.

"Oh, finish it," Patrice protested unguardedly. "It was lovely. What's it called? I don't think I've ever heard it before."

"It's the Barcarolle, from *Tales of Hoffman*," the other girl answered unassumingly.

The answer itself was in anticlimax. Standing there beside the player, she became conscious of the congealing silence immediately about her, and knew it wasn't due to that, but to something that must have been said just before. It had already ended as she detected it, but awareness of it lingered on—in her. Something had happened just then.

I've said something wrong. I said something that was wrong just now. But I don't know what it was, and I don't know what to do about it.

She touched her punch-cup to her lips, there was nothing else to do at the moment.

They only heard it near me. The music left my voice stranded, and that only made it all the more conspicuous. But who else in the room heard? Who else noticed? Maybe their faces will tell—

She turned slowly and glanced at them one by one, as if at random. Mother Hazzard was deep in conversation at the far end of the room, looking up over her chair at someone. She hadn't heard. The flaxen-haired girl who had delivered the cautioning tap had her back to her; she might have heard and she might not. But if she had, it had made no impression; she was not aware of her. Guy Ennis was holding a lighter to a cigarette. He had to click it twice to make it spark, and it had all his attention. He didn't look up at her when her glance strayed lightly past his face. The two girls with Bill, they hadn't heard, it was easy to see that. They were oblivious of everything else but the bone of contention between them.

No one was looking at her. No one's eyes met hers.

Only Bill. His head was slightly down, and his forehead was querulously ridged, and he was gazing up from under his brows at her with a strange sort of inscrutability. Everything they were saying to him seemed to be going over his head. She couldn't tell if his thoughts were on her, or a thousand miles away. But his eyes, at least, were.

She dropped her own.

And even after she did, she knew that his were still on her none the less.

18

AS THEY CLIMBED the stairs together, after, when everyone had gone, Mother Hazzard suddenly tightened an arm about her waist, protectively.

"You were so brave about it," she said. "You did just the right thing; to pretend not to know what it was she was playing. Oh, but my dear, my heart went out to you, for a moment, when I saw you standing there. That look on your face. I wanted to run to you and put my arms around you. But I took my cue from you, I pretended not to notice anything either. She didn't mean anything by it, she's just a thoughtless little fool."

Patrice moved slowly up the stairs at her side, didn't answer.

"But at the sound of the very first notes," Mother Hazzard went on ruefully, "he seemed to be right back there in the room with all of us again. So *present*, you could almost see him in front of your eyes. The Barcarolle. His favorite song. He never sat down to a piano but what he played it. Whenever and wherever you heard that being played, you knew Hugh was about someplace."

"The Barcarolle," Patrice murmured almost inaudibly, as if speaking to herself. "His favorite song."

19

"—DIFFERENT NOW," Mother Hazzard was musing comfortably. "I was there once, as a girl, you know. Oh, many years ago. Tell me, has it changed much since those days?"

Suddenly she was looking directly at Patrice, in innocent exclusive inquiry.

"How can she answer that, Mother?" Father Hazzard cut in drily. "She wasn't there when you were, so how would she know what it was like then?"

"Oh, you know what I mean," Mother Hazzard retorted indulgently. "Don't be so hanged precise."

"I suppose it has," Patrice answered feebly, turning the handle of her cup a little further toward her, as if about to lift it, and then not lifting it after all.

"You and Hugh were married there, weren't you, dear?" was the next desultory remark.

Again Father Hazzard interrupted before she could answer, this time with catastrophic rebuttal. "They were married in London, I thought. Don't you remember that letter he sent us at the time? I can still recall it: 'married here yesterday.' London letterhead."

"Paris," said Mother Hazzard firmly. "Wasn't it, dear? I still have it upstairs, I can get it and show you. It has a Paris postmark." Then she tossed her head at him arbitrarily. "Anyway, this is one question Patrice *can* answer for herself."

There was suddenly a sickening chasm yawning at her feet, where a moment before all had been security of footing, and she couldn't turn back, yet she didn't know how to get across.

She could feel their three pairs of eyes on her, Bill's were raised now too, waiting in trustful expectancy that in a moment, with the wrong answer, would change to something else.

"London," she said softly, touching the handle of her cup as if deriving some sort of mystic clairvoyance from it. "But then we left immediately for Paris, on our honeymoon. I think what happened was, he began the letter in London, didn't have time to finish it, and then posted it from Paris."

"You see," said Mother Hazzard pertly, "I was partly right, anyhow."

"Now isn't that just like a woman," Father Hazzard marvelled to his son.

Bill's eyes had remained on Patrice. There was something almost akin to grudging admiration in them; or did she imagine that?

"Excuse me," she said stifledly, thrusting her chair back. "I think I hear the baby crying."

20

AND THEN, A few weeks later, another pitfall. Or rather the same one, ever-present, ever lurking treacherously underfoot as she walked this path of her own choosing.

It had been raining, and it grew heavily misted out. A rare occurrence for Caulfield. They were all there in the room with her and she stopped by the window a moment in passing to glance out.

"Heavens," she exclaimed incautiously, "I haven't seen everything look so blurry since I was a child in San Fran. We used to get those fogs th—"

In the reflection on the lighted pane she saw Mother Hazzard's head go up, and knew before she had even turned back to face them she had said the wrong thing. Trodden incautiously again, where there was no support.

"In San Francisco, dear?" Mother Hazzard's voice was guilessly puzzled. "But I thought you were raised in—Hugh wrote us you were originally from—" And then she didn't finish it, withholding the clue; no helpful second choice was forthcoming this time. Instead a flat question followed. "Is that where you were born, dear?"

"No," Patrice said distinctly, and knew what the next question was sure to be. A question she could not have answered at the moment.

Bill raised his head suddenly, turned it inquiringly toward the stairs. "I think I hear the youngster crying, Patrice."

"I'll go up and take a look," she said gratefully, and left the room.

He was in a soundless sleep when she got to him. He wasn't making a whimper that anyone could possibly have heard. She stood there by him with a look of thoughtful scrutiny on her face.

Had he really thought he heard the baby crying?

21

THEN THERE WAS the day she was slowly sauntering along Congress Avenue, window-shopping. Congress Avenue was the main retail thoroughfare. Looking at this window-display, looking at that, not intending to buy anything, not needing to. But enjoying herself all the more in this untrammelled state. Enjoying the crowd of well-dressed shoppers thronging the sunlit sidewalk all about her, the great majority of them women at that forenoon hour of the day. Enjoying the bustle, the spruce activity, they conveyed. Enjoying this carefree moment, this brief respite (an errand for Mother Hazzard, a promise to pick something up for her, was what had brought her downtown), all the more for knowing that it was a legitimate absence, not a dereliction, and that the baby was safe, well taken care of while she was gone. And that she'd enjoy returning to it all the more, after this short diversion.

It was simply a matter of taking the bus at the next stop ahead, instead of at the nearer one behind her, and strolling the difference between the two.

And then from somewhere behind her she heard her name called. She recognized the voice at the first syllable. Cheerful, sunny. Bill. She had her smile of greeting ready before she had even turned her head.

Two of his long, energetic strides and he was beside her.

"Hello there. I thought I recognized you."

They stopped for a minute, face to face.

"What are you doing out of the office?"

"I was on my way back just now. Had to go over and see a man. And you?"

"I came down to get Mother some imported English yarn she had waiting for her at Bloom's. Before they send it out, I can be there and back with it."

"I'll walk with you," he offered. "Good excuse to loaf. As far as the next corner anyhow."

"That's where I'm taking my bus anyway," she told him.

They turned and resumed their course, but at the snail's pace she had been maintaining by herself before now.

He crinkled his nose and squinted upward appreciatively. "It does a fellow good to get out in the sun once in awhile."

"Poor abused man. I'd like to have a penny for every time you're out of that office during hours."

He chuckled unabashedly. "Can I help it if Dad sends me? Of course, I always happen to get right in front of him when he's looking around for someone to do the legwork."

They stopped.

"Those're nice," she said appraisingly.

"Yes," he agreed. "But what are they?"

"You know darned well they're hats. Don't try to be so superior."

They went on, stopped again.

"Is this what they call window-shopping?"

"This is what they call window-shopping. As if you didn't know."

"It's fun. You don't get anywhere. But you see a lot."

"You may like it now, because it's a novelty. Wait'll you're married and get a lot of it. You won't like it then."

The next window-display was an offering of fountain pens, a narrow little show-case not more than two or three yards in width.

She didn't offer to stop there. It was now he who did, halting her with him as a result.

"Wait a minute. That reminds me. I need a new pen. Will you come in with me a minute and help me pick one out?"

"I ought to be getting back," she said halfheartedly.

"It'll only take a minute. I'm a quick buyer."

"I don't know anything about pens," she demurred.

"I don't myself. That's just it. Two heads are better than one."
He'd taken her lightly by the arm by now, to try to induce her. "Ah,
come on. I'm the sort they sell anything to when I'm alone."

"I don't believe a word of it. You just want company," she
laughed, but she went inside with him nevertheless.

He offered her a chair facing the counter. A case of pens was
brought out and opened. They were discussed between him and the
salesman, she taking no active part. Several were uncapped, filled at
a waiting bottle of ink at hand on the counter, and tried out on a
pad of scratch-paper, also at hand for that purpose.

She looked on, trying to show an interest she did not really feel.

Suddenly he said to her, "How do you like the way this writes?"
and thrust one of them between her fingers and the block of paper
under her hand, before she quite knew what had happened.

Incautiously, her mind on the proportions and weight of the barrel
in her grasp, her attention fixed on what sort of a track the nib would
leave, whether a broad bold one or a thin wiry one, she put it to the
pad. Suddenly "Helen" stood there on the topmost leaf, almost as if
produced by automatic writing. Or rather, in the fullest sense of the
word, it was just that. She checked herself just in time to prevent
the second name from flowing out of the pen. It was already on the
preliminary upward stroke of a capital G, when she jerked it clear.

"Here, let me try it a minute myself." Without warning he'd taken
both pen and pad back again, before she could do anything to obliterate or alter what was on it.

Whether he saw it or not she couldn't tell. He gave no indication.
Yet it was right there under his eyes, he must have, how could he
have failed to?

He drew a cursory line or two, desisted.

"No," he said to the salesman. "Let me see that one."

While he was reaching into the case, she managed to deftly peel
off the topmost leaf with that damaging "Helen" on it. Crumpled it
surreptitiously in her hand, dropped it to the floor.

And then, belatedly, realized that perhaps this was even worse
than had she left it on there where it was. For surely he'd seen it
anyway, and now she'd only pointed up the fact that she did not
want him to. In other words, she'd doubly damned herself; first by
the error, then by taking such pains to try to efface it.

Meanwhile, his interest in the matter of pens had all at once flagged. He looked at the clerk, about to speak, and she could have almost predicted what he was about to say—had he said it—his expression conveyed it so well. "Never mind. I'll stop in again some other time." But then instead he gave her a look, and as though recalled to the necessity for maintaining some sort of plausibility, said hurriedly, almost indifferently, "All right, here, make it this one. Send it over to my office later on."

He scarcely looked at it. It didn't seem to matter to him which one he took.

And, she reminded herself, after making such to-do about her coming in with him to help him select one.

"Shall we go?" he said, a trifle reticently.

Their parting was strained. She didn't know whether it was due to him or due to herself. Or just due to her own imagining. But it seemed to her to lack the jaunty spontaneity of their meeting just a few minutes ago.

He didn't thank her for helping him select a pen, and she was grateful for that at least. But his eyes were suddenly remote, abstracted, where until now they had been wholly on her at every turn of speech. They seemed to be looking up this way toward the top of a building, looking down that way toward the far end of the street, looking everywhere but at her any more, even while he was saying "Here's your bus," and arming her into it, and reaching in from where he stood to pay the driver her fare. "Goodbye. Get home all right. See you tonight." And tipped his hat, and seemed to have already forgotten her even before he had completed the act of turning away and going about his business. And yet somehow she knew that just the reverse was true. That he was more conscious of her than ever, now that he seemed least so. Distance had intervened between them, that was all.

She looked down at her lap, while the bus swept her along past the crowded sidewalks. Funny how quickly a scene could change, the same scene; the sunlit pavements and the bustling shoppers weren't fun any more to watch.

If it had been a premeditated test, a trap— But no, it couldn't have been that. That much at least she was sure of, though it was no satisfaction. He *couldn't* have known that he was going to run into her just where he had, that they were going to walk along just as they had, toward that pen emporium. At the time he'd left the house this morning, she hadn't even known herself that she was coming downtown like this; that had come up later. So he couldn't have lain in wait for her there, to accost her. That much at least had been spontaneous, purely accidental.

But maybe as they were strolling along, and he first looked up and saw the store sign, that was when it had occurred to him, and he'd improvised it, on the spur of the moment. What was commonly said must have occurred to him then, as it only occurred to her now. That when people try out a new pen, they invariably write their real names. It's almost compulsory.

And yet, even for such an undeliberated, on-the-spot test as that, there must have been some formless suspicion of her already latent in his mind, in one way or another, or it wouldn't have suggested itself to him.

Little fool, she said to herself bitterly as she tugged at the overhead cord and prepared to alight, why didn't you think of that before you went in there with him? What good was hindsight now?

A night or two later his discarded coat was slung over a chair and he wasn't in the room with it at the moment. She needed a pencil for something for a moment anyhow, that was her excuse for it. She sought the pocket and took out the fountain pen she found clasped to it. It was gold and had his initials engraved on it; some valued, long-used birthday or Christmas present from one of his parents probably. Moreover, it was in perfect writing order, couldn't have been improved on, left a clear, deep, rich trace. And he wasn't the sort of man who went around displaying two fountain pens at a time.

It had been a test, all right. And she had given a positive reaction, as positive as he could have hoped for.

22

SHE'D HEARD THE doorbell ring some time before, and dim sounds of conglomerate greeting follow it in the hall below, and knew by that some visitor must have arrived, and must still be down there. She didn't think any more about it. She'd had Hughie in his little portable tub at the moment, and that, while it was going on, was a full-time job for anyone's attention. By the time she'd finished drying and talcuming and dressing him, putting him to bed for the night, and then lingering treacherously by him awhile longer, to watch her opportunity and worm the last celluloid bath-duck out of his tightly closed little fist, the better part of an hour had gone by. She felt sure the caller, whoever he was, must already be long gone by that time. That it had been a masculine visitor was something she could take for granted; anyone feminine from six to sixty would automatically have been ushered upstairs by the idolatrous Mother Hazzard to look in on the festive rite of her grandson's bath. In fact it was the first time she herself had missed attending one in weeks, if only to hold the towel, prattle in an unintelligible gibberish with the small person in the tub, and generally get in the uncomplaining mother's way. Only something of importance could have kept her away.

She thought they were being unusually quiet below, when she finally came out of her room and started down the stairs. There was a single, droning, low-pitched voice going on, as if somebody were reading aloud, and no one else was audible.

They were all in the library, she discovered a moment later; a room that was never used much in the evenings. And when it was, never by all of them together, at one time. She could see them in there twice over, the first time from the stairs themselves, as she came down them, and then in an afterglimpse, through the open doorway at nearer range, as she doubled back around the foot of the stairs and passed by in the hall just outside.

The three of them were in there, and there was a man with them whom she didn't know, although she realized she must have seen him at least one or more times before, as she had everyone who came to this house. He was at the table, the reading-lamp lit, droning aloud in a monotonous, singsong voice. It wasn't a book; it seemed more like a typed report. Every few moments a brittly crackling sheet would sweep back in reverse and go under the others.

No one else was saying a word. They were sitting at varying distances and at varying degrees of attention. Father Hazzard was drawn up to the table with the monologist, following every word closely, and nodding in benign accord from time to time. Mother Hazzard was in an easy chair, a basket on her lap, darning something and only occasionally looking up in sketchy aural participation. And Bill, strangely present, was off on the very outskirts of the conclave, a leg dangling over the arm of his chair, head tilted all the way back with a protruding pipe thrust ceilingward, and giving very little indication of listening at all. His eyes had a look of vacancy, as though his mind were elsewhere while his body was dutifully and filially in the room with them.

She tried to get by without being seen, but Mother Hazzard looked up at just the wrong time and caught the flicker of her figure past the door-gap. "There she is now," she said. A moment later her retarding call had overtaken and halted her. "Patrice, come in here a moment, dear. We want you."

She turned and went back, with a sudden constriction in her throat.

The droning voice had interrupted itself to wait. A private investigator? No, no, he couldn't be. She'd met him here in the house on a friendly basis, she was sure of it. But those voluminous briefs littered in front of him—

"Patrice, you know Ty Winthrop."

"Yes, I know we've met before." She went over and shook hands with him. She kept her eyes carefully off the table. And it wasn't easy.

"Ty is Father's lawyer," Mother Hazzard said indulgently. As though that were really no way to describe an old friend, but it was the shortest one for present purposes.

"And golf rival," supplied the man at the table.

"Rival?" Father Hazzard snorted disgustedly. "I don't call that rivalry, what you put up. A rival has to come up somewhere near you. Charity-tournament is more what I'd call it."

Bill's head and pipe had come down to the horizontal again. "Lick

him with one hand tied behind your back, eh Dad?" he egged
him on.

"Yeah, *my* hand," snapped the lawyer, with a private wink for
the son. "Especially last Sunday."

"Now, you three;" reproved Mother Hazzard beamingly. "I have
things to do. And so has Patrice. I can't sit in here all night."

They became serious again. Bill had risen and drawn up a chair
beside the table for her. "Sit down, Patrice, and join the party," he
invited.

"Yes, we want you to hear this, Patrice," Father Hazzard urged,
as she hesitated. "It concerns you."

Her hand tried to stray betrayingly toward her throat. She kept it
down by sheer will-power. She seated herself, a little uneasily.

The lawyer cleared his throat. "Well, I think that about takes care
of it, Donald. The rest of it remains as it was before."

Father Hazzard hitched his chair nearer. "All right. Ready for me
to sign now?"

Mother Hazzard bit off a thread with her teeth, having come to
the end of something or other. She began to put things away in her
basket, preparatory to departure. "You'd better tell Patrice what it
is first, dear. Don't you want her to know?"

"I'll tell her for you," Winthrop offered. "I can put it in fewer
words than you." He turned toward her and gazed friendlily over
the tops of his reading-glasses. "Donald's changing the provisions of
his will, by adding a codicil. You see, in the original, after Grace
here was provided for, there was an equal division of the residue
made between Bill and Hugh. Well now we're altering that to make
it one-quarter of the residue to Bill and the remainder to you."

She could feel her face beginning to flame, as though a burning
crimson light were focussed on it, and it alone, that they could all
see. An agonizing sensation of wanting to push away from the table
and make her escape, and of being held trapped there in her chair,
came over her.

She tried to speak quietly, quelling her voice by moistening her
lips twice over. "I don't want you to do that. I don't want to be
included."

"Don't look that way about it," Bill said with a genial laugh.
"You're not doing anybody out of anything. I have Dad's business—"

"It was Bill's own suggestion," Mother Hazzard let her know.

"I gave both the boys a lump sum in cash, to start them off, on the day they each reached their twenty-first—"

She was on her feet now, facing all of them in turn, almost panic-stricken. "No, please! Don't put my name down on it at all! I don't want my name to go down on it!" She all but wrung her clasped hands toward Father Hazzard. "Dad! Won't you listen to me?"

"It's on account of Hugh, dear," Mother Hazzard let him know in a tactful aside. "Can't you understand?"

"Well, I know; we all feel bad about Hugh. But she has to go on living just the same. She has a child to think of. And these things shouldn't be postponed on account of sentiment; they have to be taken care of at the right time."

She turned and fled from the room. They made no attempt to follow her.

She closed the door after her. She stormed back and forth, two, three times, holding her head locked in her upended arms. "Swindler!" burst from her muffledly. "Thief! It's just like someone climbing in through a window and—"

There was a low knock at the door about half an hour later. She went over and opened it, and Bill was standing there.

"Hello," he said diffidently.

"Hello," she said with equal diffidence.

It was as though they hadn't seen one another for two or three days past, instead of just half an hour before.

"He signed it," he said. "After you went up. Winthrop took it back with him. Witnessed and all. It's done now, whether you wanted it or not."

She didn't answer. The battle had been lost, downstairs, before, and this was just the final communiqué.

He was looking at her in a way she couldn't identify. It seemed to have equal parts of shrewd appraisal and blank incomprehension in it, and there was just a dash of admiration added.

"You know," he said, "I don't know why you acted like that about it. And I don't agree with you, I think you were wrong in acting like that about it." He lowered his voice a little in confidence. "But somehow or other I'm glad you acted like that about it. I like you better for acting like that about it." He shoved his hand out to her suddenly. "Want to shake goodnight?"

23

SHE WAS ALONE in the house. That is, alone just with Hughie, in his crib upstairs, and Aunt Josie, in her room all the way at the back. They'd gone out to visit the Michaelsons, old friends.

It was nice to be alone in the house once in awhile. Not too often, not all the time, that would have run over into loneliness. And she'd known what that was once, only too well, and didn't want to ever again.

But it was nice to be alone like this, alone *without* loneliness, just for an hour or two, just from nine until eleven, with the sure knowledge that they were coming back soon. With the whole house her own to roam about in; upstairs, down, into this room, into that. Not that she couldn't at other times—but this had a special feeling to it, doing it when no one else was about. It did something to her. It nourished her feeling of *belonging*, replenished it.

They'd asked her if she didn't want to come with them, but she'd begged off. Perhaps because she knew that if she stayed home alone she'd get this very feeling from it.

They didn't importune her. They never importuned, never repeated any invitation to the point of weariness. They respected you as an individual, she reflected, that was one of the nice things about them. Only one of the nice, there were so many others.

"Then next time, maybe," Mother had smiled in parting, from the door.

"Next time without fail," she promised. "They're very nice people."

She roamed about for awhile first, getting her "feel" of the place, saturating herself in that blessed sensation of "belonging." Touching a chair-back here, fingering the texture of a window-drape there.

Mine. My house. My parents' house and mine. Mine. Mine. My *home*. My chair. My window-drape. No, hang back like that, that's the way I want you to.

Silly? Childish? Fanciful? No doubt. But who is without childishness, fancies? What is life without them? Or, *is* there life without them?

She went into Aunt Josie's pantry, took the lid off the cookie-jar, took one out, took a big bite out of it.

She wasn't hungry. They'd all finished a big dinner only a couple of hours ago. But—

My house. I can do this. I'm entitled to them. They're waiting there for me, to help myself whenever I feel like it.

She put the lid on the jar, started to put the light out.

She changed her mind suddenly, went back, took out a second one.

My house. I can even take two if I want to. Well, I *will* take two.

And one in each hand, each with a big defiant bite taken out of it, she came out of there. They weren't food for the mouth, actually, they were food for the soul.

The last crumbs brushed off her fingers, she decided to read a book finally. Utter repose had come to her now, a sense of peace and well-being that was almost therapeutic in its depth. It was a sensation of *healing*; of becoming one, becoming whole again. As though the last vestiges of an old ache, from an old split in her personality (as indeed there was one in the fullest sense), had been effaced. A psychiatrist could have written a learned paper on this; that just roaming about a house, in utter security, in utter relaxation, for half an hour or so, could achieve such a result for her, beyond all capacity of cold-blooded science, in the clinic, to have done likewise. But, human beings are human beings, and science isn't what they need; it's a home, a house of their own, that no one can take away from them.

It was the right time, almost the only time, for reading a book. You could give it your full attention, you could lose yourself in it. You become one with it for awhile, selfless.

In the library, it took her some time to make a definitive selection. She did a considerable amount of leaf-fluttering along the shelves, made two false starts back to the chair for an opening paragraph or two, before she'd finally settled on something that gave an indication of suiting her.

Marie Antoinette, by Katharine Anthony.

She'd never cared much for fiction, somehow. Something about it made her slightly uncomfortable, perhaps a reminder of the drama in her own life. She liked things (her mind expressed it) *that had really happened.* Really happened, but long ago and far away, to someone entirely else, someone that never could be confused with herself. In the case of a fictional character, you soon, involuntarily, began identifying yourself with him or her. In the case of a character who had once been an actual living personage, you did not. You sympathized objectively, but it ended there. It was always, from first to last, someone else. Because it had once, in reality, *been* someone else. (Escape, they would have called this, though in her case it was the reverse of what it was for others. They escaped from humdrum reality into fictional drama. She escaped from too much personal drama into a reality of the past.)

For an hour, maybe more, she was one with a woman dead a hundred and fifty years; she lost track of time.

Dimly, with only a marginal part of her faculties, she heard brakes go on somewhere outside in the quiet night.

". . . Axel Fersen drove swiftly through the dark streets." (They're back. I'll finish this chapter first.) "An hour and a half later, the coach passed through the gate of Saint-Martin. . . ."

A key turned in the front door. It opened, then it closed. But no murmur of homecoming voices eddied in. Vocal silence, if not the total kind. Firm, energetic footsteps, a single pair, struck across the preliminary gap of bare flooring adjacent to the door, then blurred off along the hall carpeting.

". . . A little way beyond, they saw a large travelling-carriage drawn up at the side of the road." (No, that's Bill, not they. He's the one just came in. I forgot, they didn't take the car with them, the Michaelsons live just around the corner) "a large travelling-carriage drawn up at the side of the road. . . ."

The tread went to the back. Aunt Josie's pantry-light flashed on again. She couldn't have seen it from where she was, but she knew it by the click of its switch. She knew all the lights by the clicks of their switches. The direction from which the click came, and its sharpness or faintness of tone. You can learn those things about a house.

She heard water surge from a tap, and then an emptied glass go down. Then the lid of the cookie-jar went down, with its heavy, hollowed, ringing, porcelain thud. It stayed down for some time, too, was in no hurry to go back on again.

"I don't give a hang about gardens," he answered almost gruffly. "Nor walking in them. Nor the flowers in them. You know why I came down here. Do I have to tell you?"

He flung his cigarette down violently, backhand, with the same gesture as if something had angered him.

Suddenly she was acutely frightened. She'd stopped short.

"No, wait, Bill. Bill, wait— Don't—"

"Don't what? I haven't said anything yet. But you know already, don't you? I'm sorry, Patrice, I've got to tell you. You've got to listen. It's got to come out."

She was holding out her hand protestingly toward him, as if trying to ward off something. She took a backward step away, broke their proximity.

"*I* don't like it," he said rebelliously. "It does things to me that are new. I was never bothered before. I never even had the sweetheart-crushes that they all do. I guess that was my way to be. But this is it, Patrice. This is it now, all right."

"No, wait— Not now. Not yet. This isn't the time—"

"This is the time, and this is the night, and this is the place. There'll never be another night like this, not if we both live to be a hundred. Patrice, I love you, and I want you to ma—"

"Bill!" she pleaded, terrified.

"Now you've heard it, and now you're running away. Patrice," he asked forlornly, "what's so terrible about it?"

She'd gained the lower-porch step, was poised on it for a moment in arrested flight. He came after her slowly, in a sort of acquiescent frustration, rather than in importunate haste.

"I'm no lover," he said. "I can't say it right—"

"Bill," she said again, almost grief-strickenly.

"Patrice, I see you every day and—" He flung his arms apart helplessly, "What am I to do? I didn't ask for it. I think it's something good. I think it's something that should be."

She leaned her head for a moment against the porchpost, as if in distress. "Why did you have to say it yet? Why couldn't you have— Give me more time. Please, give me more time. Just a few months—"

"Do you want me to take it back, Patrice?" he asked ruefully. "How can I now? How could I, even if I hadn't spoken? Patrice, it's so long since, now. Is it Hugh, is it still Hugh?"

"I've never been in love bef—" she started to say, penitently. She stopped suddenly.

He looked at her strangely.

I've said too much, flashed through her mind. Too much, or not enough. And then in sorrowful confirmation: Not enough by far.

"I'm going in now." The shadow of the porch dropped between them like an indigo curtain.

He didn't try to follow. He stood there where she'd left him.

"You're afraid I'll kiss you."

"No, that isn't what I'm afraid of," she murmured almost inaudibly. "I'm afraid I'll want you to."

The door closed after her.

He stood out there in the full bleach of the moonlight, motionless, looking sadly downward.

25

IN THE MORNING the world was sweet just to look at from her window. The sense of peace, of safety, of belonging, was being woven about her stronger all the time. Soon nothing could tear its fabric apart again. To wake up in your own room, in your own home, your own roof over your head. To find your little son awake before you and peering expectantly out through his crib, and giving you that crowing smile of delight that was already something special he gave to no one but you. To lift him up and hold him to you, and have to curb yourself, you wanted to squeeze so tightly. Then to carry him over to the window with you, and hold the curtain back, and look out at the world. Show him the world you'd found for him, the world you'd made for him.

The early sunlight like goldenrod pollen lightly dusting the sidewalks and the roadway out front. The azure shadows under the trees and at the lee sides of all the houses. A man sprinkling a lawn a few doors down, the water fraying from the nozzle of his hose twinkling

like diamonds. He looked up and saw you, and he gave you a neigh-
borly wave of the hand, though you didn't know him very well. And
you took Hughie's little hand at the wrist, and waved it back to him
in answering greeting.

Yes, in the mornings the world was sweet all right.

Then to dress, to dress for two, and to go downstairs to the
pleasant room waiting for you below; to Mother Hazzard, and her
fresh-picked flowers, and her affectionate, sunny greeting, and the
mirror-like reflection of the coffee-percolator (that always delighted
him so) showing squat, pudgy images seated around it on its various
facets: an elderly lady, and a much younger lady, and a very young
young-man, the center of attraction in his high chair.

To be safe, to be at home, to be among your own.

Even mail for you, a letter of your own, waiting for you at your
place. She felt a pleased little sense of completion at sight of it. There
was no greater token of permanency, of belonging, than that. Mail
of your own, sent to your home.

"Mrs. Patrice Hazzard," and the address. Once that name had
frightened her. It didn't now. In a little while she would no longer
even remember that there had been another name, once, before it. A
lonely, frightened name, drifting ownerless, unclaimed, about the
world now—

"Now Hughie, not so fast, finish what you've got first."

She opened it, and there was nothing in it, Or rather, nothing
written on it. For a moment she thought there must have been a
mistake. Just blank paper. No, wait, the other way around—

Three small words, almost buried in the seam that folded the sheet
in two, almost overlooked in the snowy expanse that surrounded
them.

"Who are you?"

26

In the mornings the world was bitter-sweet to look at from her window. To wake up in a room that wasn't rightfully yours. That you knew—and you knew somebody else knew—you had no right to be in. The early sunlight was pale and bleak upon the ground, and under all the trees and on the lee side of all the houses, tatters of night lingered, diluted to blue but still gloomy and forbidding. A man sprinkling the lawn a few doors down was a stranger; a stranger you knew by sight. He looked up, and you hurriedly shrank back from the window, child and all, lest he see you. Then a moment later, you already wished you hadn't done that, but it was too late, it was done.

Was he the one? Was he?

It isn't as much fun any more to dress for two. And when you start down the stairs with Hughie, those stairs you've come down so many hundreds of times, now at last you've learned what it's like to come down them heavyhearted and troubled, as you said you might some day have to, that very first night of all. For that's how you're coming down them now.

Mother Hazzard at the table, beaming; and the flowers; and the gargoyle-like reflections on the percolator-panels. But you only have eyes for one thing, furtive, straining eyes, from as far back as the threshold of the doorway. From farther back than that, even; from the first moment the table has come into sight. Is there any white on it, over on your side of it? Is there any rectangular white patch showing there, by or near your place? It's easy to tell, for the cloth has a printed pattern, with dabs of red and green.

"Patrice, didn't you sleep well, dear?" Mother Hazzard asked solicitously. "You look a little peaked."

She hadn't looked peaked out on the stairs a moment ago. She'd only been heavyhearted and troubled then.

She settled Hughie in his chair, and took a little longer than was necessary. Keep your eyes away from it. Don't look at it. Don't think about it. Don't try to find out what's in it, you don't want to know what's in it; let it stay there until after the meal, then tear it up un—

"Patrice, you're spilling it on his chin. Here, let me."

She had nothing to do with her own hands, from that point on. And she felt as though she had so many of them; four or five at least. She reached for the coffee-pot, and a corner of it was in the way. She reached for the sugar-bowl, and another corner of it was in the way. She drew her napkin toward her, and it sidled two or three inches nearer her, riding on that. It was all about her, it was everywhere at once!

She wanted to scream, and she clenched her hand tightly, down beside her chair. I mustn't do that, I mustn't. Hughie's right here next to me, and Mother's just across the table—

Open it, open it fast. Quick, while you still have the courage.

The paper made a shredding sound, her finger was so thick and maladroit.

One word more this time.

"Where are you from?"

She clenched her hand again, down low beside her chair. White dissolved into it, disappearing through the finger-crevices.

27

IN THE MORNINGS the world was bitter to look at from the window. To wake up in a strange room, in a strange house. To pick up your baby—that was the only thing that was rightfully yours—and edge toward the window with him, creeping up slantwise and peering from the far side of it, barely lifting the curtain; not stepping forward to the middle of it and throwing the curtain widely back. That was for people in their own homes, not for you. And out there, nothing. Nothing that belonged to you or was for you. The hostile houses of a hostile town. An icy wash of sun upon a stony ground. Dark shadows like frowns under each tree and leeward of each house. The man watering the lawn didn't turn around to greet you today. He was more than a stranger now, he was a potential enemy.

She carried her boy with her downstairs, and every step was like a knell. She was holding her eyes closed when she first went into the dining-room. She couldn't help it; she couldn't bring herself to open them for a moment.

"Patrice, you don't look right to me at all. You ought to see your color against that child's."

She opened her eyes.

Nothing there.

But it would come. It would come again. It had came once, twice; it would come again. Tomorrow maybe. The day after. Or the day after that. It would surely come again. There was nothing to do but wait. To sit there, stricken, helpless, waiting. It was like holding your head bowed under a leaky faucet, waiting for the next icy drop to detach itself and fall.

In the mornings the world was bitter, and in the evenings it was full of shadows creeping formlessly about her, threatening from one moment to the next to close in and engulf her.

28

SHE HADN'T SLEPT well. That was the first thing she was conscious of on awakening. The cause, the reason for it, that came right with it. That was what really mattered; not the fact that she hadn't slept well, but knowing the cause, the reason for it. Only too well.

It wasn't new. It was occurring all the time lately, this not sleeping well. It was the rule rather than the exception.

The strain was beginning to tell on her. Her resistance was wearing away. Her nerves were slowly being drawn taut, a little more so each day. She was nearing a danger-point, she knew. She couldn't stand very much more of it. It wasn't when they came; it was in-between, waiting for the next one to come. The longer it took to come, the greater her tension, instead of the less. It was like that well-known simile of the second dropped shoe, prolonged ad infinitum.

She couldn't stand much more of it. "If there's another one," she told herself, "something will snap. Don't let there be another one. Don't."

She looked at herself in the glass. Not through vanity, conceit, to see whether damage had been done her looks. To confirm, objectively, the toll that was being taken. Her face was pale and worn. It was growing thinner again, losing its roundness, growing back toward that gauntness of cheek it had had in New York. Her eyes were a little too shadowed underneath, and just a little too bright. She looked tired and frightened. Not acutely so, but chronically. And that was what was being done to her by this.

She dressed herself, and then Hughie, and carried him down with her. It was so pleasant in the dining-room, in the early morning like this. The new-minted sun pouring in, the color of champagne; the crisp chintz curtains; the cheery colored ware on the table; the fragrant aroma of the coffee-pot; the savory odor of fresh-made toast seeping through the napkin thrown over it to keep it warm. Mother Hazzard's flowers in the center of the table, always less than an hour old, picked from her garden at the back. Mother Hazzard herself, spruce and gay in her printed morning-dress, beaming at her. Home. Peace.

"Leave me in peace," she pleaded inwardly. "Let me be. Let me have all this. Let me enjoy it, as it's meant to be enjoyed, as it's waiting around to be enjoyed. Don't take it from me, let me keep it."

She went around the table to her and kissed her, and held Hughie out to her to be kissed. Then she settled him in his highchair, between the two of them, and sat down herself.

Then she saw them, waiting for her.

The one on top was a department-store sales brochure, sealed in an envelope. She could identify it by the letterhead in the upper corner. But there was something under it, another one. Its corners stuck out a little past the top one.

She was afraid to bring it into fuller view, she postponed it.

She spooned Hughie's cereal to his mouth, took alternating sips of

her own fruit juice. It was poisoning the meal, it was tightening up
her nerves.

It mightn't be one of those, it might be something else. Her
hand moved with a jerk, and the department-store folder was out of
the way.

"Mrs. Patrice Hazzard."

It was addressed in pen and ink, a personal letter. She never got
letters like that from anyone; who wrote to her, whom did she know?
It must be, it was, one of those again. She felt a sick, cold feeling in
her stomach. She took in everything about it, with a sort of hypnotic
fascination. The three-cent purple stamp, with wavy cancellation-
lines running through it. Then the circular postmark itself, off to the
side. It had been posted late, after twelve last night. Where? She
wondered. By whom? She could see in her mind's eye an indistinct,
furtive figure slinking up to a street mail-box in the dark, a hand
hastily thrusting something into the chute, the clang as the slot fell
closed again.

She wanted to get it out of here, take it upstairs with her, close
the door. But if she carried it away with her unopened, wouldn't
that look secretive, wouldn't that call undue attention to it? It was
safe enough to open it here in the very room; they never pried in this
house, they never asked questions. She knew she could even have
left it lying around open after having read it herself, and it would
have been safe, nobody would have put a hand to it.

She ran her knife through the flap, slit it.

Mother Hazzard had taken over Hughie's feeding, she had eyes
for no one but him. Every mouthful brought forth a paean of praise.

She'd opened the once-folded inner sheet now. The flowers were
in the way, they screened the shaking of her hand. So blank it was,
so much waste space, so little writing. Just a line across the middle
of the paper, where the crease ran.

"What are you doing there?"

She could feel her chest constricting. She tried to quell the sudden
inordinate quickness of her breathing, lest it betray itself.

Mother Hazzard was showing Hughie his plate. "All gone. Hughie ate it all up! Where *is* it?"

She'd lowered it into her lap now. She managed to get it back into its envelope, and fold that over, singly and then doubly, until it fitted into the span of her hand.

"One more and something will snap." And here it was, the one more.

She could feel her self-control ebbing away, and didn't know what catastrophic form its loss might take. "I've got to get out of this room," she warned herself. "I've got to get away from this table—now—quickly!"

She stood up suddenly, stumbling a little over her chair. She turned and left the table without a word.

"Patrice, aren't you going to have your coffee?"

"I'll be right down," she said smotheredly, from the other side of the doorway. "I forgot something."

She got up there, into her room, and got the door closed.

It was like the bursting of a dam. She hadn't known what form it would take. Tears, she'd thought, or high-pitched hysterical laughter. It was neither. It was anger, a paroxysm of rage, blinded and baffled and helpless.

She went over to the wall and flailed with upraised fists against it, held high over her head. And then around to the next wall and the next and the next, like somebody seeking an outlet, crying out distractedly: "Who are you yourself? Where are you sending them from? Why don't you come out? Why don't you come out in the open? Why don't you come out where I can see you? Why don't you come out and give me a chance to fight back?"

Until at last she'd stopped, wilted and breathing fast with spent emotion. In its wake came sudden determination. There was only one way to fight back, only one way she had to rob the attacks of their power to harm—

She flung the door open. She started down the stairs again. Still as tearless as she'd gone up. She was going fast, she was rippling down them in a quick-step. She was still holding it in her hand. She opened it up, back to its full size, and started smoothing it out as she went.

She came back into the dining-room still at the same gait she'd used on the stairs.

"—drank all his milk like a good boy," Mother Hazzard was crooning.

Patrice moved swiftly around the table toward her, stopped short beside her.

"I want to show you something," she said tersely. "I want you to see this."

She put it down on the table squarely in front of her and stood there waiting.

"Just a moment, dear; let me find my glasses," Mother Hazzard purred acquiescently. She probed here and there among the breakfast things. "I know I had them with me when Father was here at the table; we were both reading the paper." She looked over toward the buffet on the other side of her.

Patrice stood there waiting. She looked over at Hughie. He was still holding his spoon, entire fist folded possessively around it. He flapped it at her joyously. Home. Peace.

Suddenly she'd reached over to her own place at the table, picked up the department-store circular still lying there, replaced the first letter with that.

"Here they are, under my napkin. Right in front of me the whole time." Mother Hazzard adjusted them, turned back to her. "Now what was it, dear?" She opened the folder and looked at it.

Patrice pointed. "This pattern, right here. The first one. Isn't it—attractive?"

Behind her back, held in one hand, the abducted missive slowly crumpled, deflated, was sucked between her fingers into compressed invisibility.

29

QUIETLY AND DEFTLY she moved about the dimly lighted room, passing back and forth, and forth and back, with armfuls of belongings from the drawers. Hughie lay sleeping in his crib, and the clock said almost one.

The valise stood open on a chair. Even that wasn't hers. It was the one she'd first used on the train-ride here, new-looking as ever, the one with "P H" on its rounded corner. She'd have to borrow it. Just as she was borrowing the articles she picked at random, to throw into it. Just as she was borrowing the very clothes she stood in. There were only two things in this whole room with her now that were rightfully hers. That little bundle sleeping quietly there in the crib. And that seventeen cents lying spread out on a scrap of paper on the dresser-top.

She took things for him, mostly. Things he needed, things to keep him warm. They wouldn't mind, they wouldn't begrudge that; they loved him almost as much as she did, she reasoned ruefully. She quickened her movements, as if the danger of faltering in purpose lay somewhere along this train of thought if she lingered on it too long.

For herself she took very little, only what was of absolute necessity. Underthings, an extra pair or two of stockings—

Things, things. What did things matter, when your whole world was breaking up and crumbling about you? *Your* world? It wasn't *your* world, it was a world you had no right to be in.

She dropped the lid of the valise, latched it impatiently on what it held, indifferent to whether it held enough, or too much, or too little. A little tongue of white stuff was trapped, left protruding through the seam, and she let it be.

She put on the hat and coat she'd left in readiness across the foot of the bed. The hat without consulting a mirror, though there was one right at her shoulder. She picked up her handbag, and probed into it with questing hand. She brought out a key, the key to this house, and put it down on the dresser. Then she brought out a small change-purse and shook it out. A cabbagy cluster of interfolded currency fell out soundlessly, and a sprinkling of coins, these last with a tinkling sound and some rolling about. She swept them all closer together, and then left them there on top of the dresser. Then she picked up the seventeen cents and dropped that into the change-purse instead, and replaced it in the handbag, and thrust that under her arm.

She went over beside the crib, then, and lowered its side. She crouched down on a level with the small sleeping face. She kissed it lightly on each eyelid. "I'll be back for you in a minute," she whispered. "I have to take the bag down first and stand it at the door. I can't manage you both on those stairs, I'm afraid." She straightened up, lingered a moment, looking down at him. "We're going for a ride, you and I; we don't know where, and we don't care. Straight out, along the way the trains go. We'll find someone along the road who'll let us in next to him—"

The clock said a little after one now.

She went over to the door, softly opened it, and carried the valise outside with her. She eased it closed behind her, and then she started down the stairs valise in hand, with infinite slowness, as though it weighed a lot. Yet it couldn't have been the valise alone that seemed to pull her arm down so, it must have been the leadenness of her heart.

Suddenly she'd stopped, and allowed the valise to come to rest on the step beside her. They were standing there without a sound, down below her by the front door, the two of them. Father Hazzard and Doctor Parker. She hadn't heard them until now, for they hadn't been saying anything. They must have been standing there in a sort of momentary mournful silence, just preceding leavetaking.

They broke it now, as she stood there unseen, above the bend of the stairs.

"Well, goodnight, Donald," the doctor said at last, and she saw him put his hand to Father Hazzard's shoulder in an attempt at consolation, then let it trail heavily off again. "Get some sleep. She'll be all right." He opened the door, then he added: "But no excitement, no stress of any kind from now on, you understand that, Donald? That'll be your job, to keep all that away from her. Can I count on you?"

"You can count on me," Father Hazzard said forlornly.

The door closed, and he turned away and started up the stairs, to where she stood riveted. She moved down a step or two around the turn to meet him, leaving the valise behind her, doffed hat and coat flung atop it now.

He looked up and he saw her, without much surprise, without much of anything except a sort of stony sadness.

"Oh, it's you, Patrice," he said dully. "Did you hear him? Did you hear what he just said?"

"Who is it—Mother?"

"She had another of those spells soon after we retired. He's been in there with her for over an hour and a half. It was touch and go, for a few minutes, at first—"

"But Father! Why didn't you—?"

He sat down heavily on the stair-step. She sat down beside him, slung one arm about his shoulders.

"Why should I bother you, dear? There wouldn't have been anything you could have— You have the baby on your hands all day long, you need your rest. Besides, this isn't anything new. Her heart's always been weak. Way back before the boys were born—"

"I never knew. You never told me— But *is* it getting worse?"

"Things like that don't improve as you get on in years," he said gently.

She let her head slant to rest against his shoulder, in compunction.

He patted her hand consolingly. "She'll be all right. We'll see that she is, you and I, between us, won't we?"

She shivered a little, involuntarily, at that.

"It's just that we've got to cushion her against all shocks and upsets," he said. "You and the young fellow, you're about the best medicine for her there is. Just having you around—"

And if in the morning she had asked for Patrice, asked for her grandchild, and he'd had to tell her—She fell strangely silent, looking down at the steps under their feet, but no longer seeing them. And if she'd come out of her room five minutes later, just missing the doctor as he left, she might have brought death into this house, in repayment for all the love that had been lavished on her. Killed the only mother she'd ever known.

He misunderstood her abstraction, pressed her chin with the cleft of his hand. "Now don't take it like that; she wouldn't want you to, you know. And Pat, don't let her know you've found out about it. Let her keep on thinking it's her secret and mine. I know she'll be happier that way."

She sighed deeply. It was a sigh of decision, of capitulation to the inevitable. She turned and kissed him briefly on the side of the head and stroked his hair a couple of times. Then she stood up.

"I'm going up," she said quietly. "Go down and put out the hall-light after us, a minute."

He retraced his steps momentarily. She picked up the valise, the coat, the hat, and quietly reopened the door of her own room.

"Goodnight, Patrice."

"Goodnight, Father; I'll see you in the morning."

She carried them in with her, and closed the door, and in the darkness on the other side she stood still a minute. A silent, choking prayer welled up in her.

"Give me strength, for there's no running away, I see that now. The battle must be fought out here where I stand, and I dare not even cry out."

30

THEN THEY STOPPED suddenly. There were no more. No more came. The days became a week, the week became a month. The month lengthened toward two. And no more came.

It was as though the battle had been won without striking a blow. No, she knew that wasn't so; it was as though the battle had been broken off, held in abeyance, at the whim of the crafty, shadowy adversary.

She clutched at straws—straws of attempted comprehension—and they all failed her.

Mother Hazzard said: "Edna Harding got back today; she's been visiting their folks in Philadelphia the past several weeks."

But no more came.

Bill remarked: "I ran into Tom Bryant today; he tells me his older sister Marilyn's been laid up with pleurisy; she only got out of bed for the first time today."

"I *thought* I hadn't seen her."

But no more came.

Caulfield: Population, 203,000, she thought. That was what the atlas in the library said. And a pair of hands to each living soul of them. One to hold down the flap of a letter-box, on some secret shadowy corner; the other to quickly, furtively slip an envelope through the slot.

No more came. Yet the enigma remained. What was it? Who was it? Or rather, what had it been? Who had it been?

Yet deep in her innermost heart she knew somehow the present tense still fitted it, none other would do. Things like that didn't just happen and then stop. They either never began at all, or else they ran on to their shattering, destructive conclusion.

But in spite of that, security crept back a little; frightened off once and not so bold now as before, but crept tentatively back toward her a little.

In the mornings the world was bitter-sweet to look at, seeming to hold its breath, waiting to see—

31

MOTHER HAZZARD KNOCKED on her door just as she'd finished tucking Hughie in. There wasn't anything exceptional about this, it was a nightly event, the filching of a last grandmotherly kiss just before the light went out. Tonight, however, she seemed to want to talk to Patrice herself. And not to know how to go about it.

She lingered on after she'd kissed him, and the side of the crib had been lifted into place. She stood there somewhat uncertainly, her continued presence preventing Patrice from switching out the light.

There was a moment's awkwardness.

"Patrice."

"Yes, Mother?"

Suddenly she'd blurted it out. "Bill wants to take you to the Country Club dance with him tonight. He's waiting down there now."

Patrice was so completely taken back she didn't answer for a moment, just stood there looking at her.

"He told me to come up and ask you if you'd go with him." Then she rushed on, as if trying to talk her into it by sheer profusion of wordage, "They have one about once each month, you know, and he's going himself, he usually does, and—why don't you get dressed and go with him?" she ended up on a coaxing note.

"But I—I" Patrice stammered.

"Patrice, you've got to begin sooner or later. It isn't good for you not to. You haven't been looking as well as you might lately. We're a little worried about you. If there's something troubling you— You do what Mother says, dear."

It was apparently an order. Or as close to an order as Mother Hazzard could ever have brought herself to come. She had opened Patrice's closet-door, meanwhile, and was peering helpfully inside. "How about this?" She took something down, held it up against herself to show her.

"I haven't very much—"

"It'll do nicely." It landed on the bed. "They're not very formal there. I'll have Bill buy you an orchid or gardenia on the way, that'll dress it up enough. You just go and get the *feel* of it tonight. It'll begin coming back to you little by little." She smiled reassuringly at her. "You'll be in good hands." She patted her on the shoulder as she turned to go outside. "Now that's a good girl. I'll tell Bill you're getting ready."

Patrice overheard her call down to him from above-stairs, a moment later, without any attempt at modulating her voice: "The answer is yes. I talked her into it. And you be very nice to her, young man, or you'll hear from me."

He was standing waiting for her just inside the door when she came downstairs.

"Am I all right?" she asked uncertainly.

He was suddenly overcome with some sort of awkwardness. "Gee, I—I didn't know how you could look in the evening," he said haltingly.

For the first few moments of the drive, there was a sort of shyness between them, almost as though they'd only just met tonight for the first time. It was very impalpable, but it rode with them. He turned on the radio in the car. Dance music rippled back into their faces. "To get you into the mood," he said.

He stopped, and got out, and came back with an orchid. "The

biggest one north of Venezuela," he said. "Or wherever they come from."

"Here, pin it on for me." She selected a place. "Right about here."

Abruptly, he balked at that, for some strange reason. All but shied away bodily. "Oh no, that you do yourself," he said, more forcefully than she could see any reason for.

"I might stick myself," he added lamely as an afterthought. A little too long after.

"Why, you great big coward."

The hand that would have held the pin was a trifle unsteady, she noticed, when he first put it back to the wheel. Then it quieted.

They drove the rest of the way. The rest of the way lay mostly through open country. There were stars overhead.

"I've never *seen* so many!" she marvelled.

"Maybe you haven't been looking up enough," he said gently.

Toward the end, just before they got there, a peculiar sort of tenderness seemed to overcome him for a minute. He even slowed the car a little, as he turned to her.

"I want you to be happy tonight, Patrice," he said earnestly. "I want you to be *very* happy."

There was a moment's silence between them, then they picked up speed again.

32

AND FOR THE next one, right after that, the tune they played was "Three Little Words." She remembered that afterward. That least of all things about it, the tune they had been playing at the time. She was dancing it with Bill. For that matter she'd been dancing them all with him, steadily, ever since they'd arrived. She wasn't watching, she wasn't looking around her, she wasn't thinking of anything but the two of them.

Smiling dreamily, she danced. Her thoughts were like a little brook running swiftly but smoothly over harmless pebbles, keeping time with the tinkling music.

I like dancing with him. He dances well, you don't have to keep thinking about your feet. He's turned his face toward me and is looking down at me; I can feel it. Well, I'll look up at him, and then he'll smile at me; but I won't smile back at him. Watch. There, I knew that was coming. I will *not* smile back. Oh, well, what if I did? It slipped out before I could stop it. Why shouldn't I smile at him, anyway? That's the way I feel about him; smilingly fond.

A hand touched Bill's shoulder from behind. She could see the fingers slanted downward for a second, on her side of it, without seeing the hand or arm or person it belonged to.

A voice said: "May I cut in on this one?"

And suddenly they'd stopped. Bill had stopped, so she had to, too.

His arms left her. A shuffling motion took place, Bill stepped aside, and there was someone else there in his place. It was like a double exposure, where one person dissolves into another.

Their eyes met, hers and the new pair. His had been waiting for hers, and hers had foolishly run into his. They couldn't move again.

The rest was horror, sheer and unadulterated. Horror such as she'd never known she could experience. Horror under the electric lights. Death on the dance floor. Her body stayed upright, but otherwise she had every feeling of death coursing through it.

"Georgesson's the name," he murmured unobtrusively to Bill. His lips hardly seemed to stir at all. His eyes didn't leave hers.

Bill completed the ghastly parody of an introduction. "Mrs. Hazzard, Mr. Georgesson."

"How do you do?" he said to her.

Somehow there was even worse horror in the trite phrase than there had been in the original confrontation. She was screaming in silent inward panic, her lips locked tight, unable even to speak Bill's name and prevent the transfer.

"May I?" Georgesson said, and Bill nodded, and the transfer had been completed; it was too late.

Then for a moment, blessed reprieve. She felt his arms close about her, and her face sank into the sheltering shadow of his shoulder, and she was dancing again. She no longer had to stand upright, unsupported. There, that was better. A minute to think in. A minute to get your breath in.

The music went on, their dancing went on. Bill's face faded away in the background.

"We've met before, haven't we?"

Keep me from fainting, she prayed, keep me from falling.

He was waiting for his answer.

Don't speak; don't answer him.

"*Who'd* he say you were?"

Her feet faltered, missed.

"Don't make me keep on doing this, I can't. Help me—outside someplace—or I'm—"

"Too warm for you?" he said politely.

She didn't answer. The music was dying. She was dying.

He said, "You went out of step, just then. My fault, I'm afraid."

"Don't—" she whimpered. "Don't—"

The music stopped. They stopped.

His arm left her back, but his hand stayed tight about her wrist, holding her there beside him for a moment.

He said, "There's a veranda outside. Over there, out that way. I'll go out there and wait for you, and we can—go ahead talking."

She hardly knew what she was saying. "I can't—You don't understand—" Her neck wouldn't hold firm; her head kept trying to lob over limply.

"I think I do. I think I understand perfectly. I understand you, and you understand me." Then he added with a grisly sort of emphasis that froze her to the marrow: "I bet we two understand one another better than any other two people in this whole ballroom at the moment."

Bill was coming back toward them from the sidelines.

"I'll be out there where I said. Don't keep me waiting too long, or—I'll simply have to come in and look you up again." His face didn't change. His voice didn't change. "Thanks for the dance," he said, as Bill arrived.

He didn't let go her wrist; he transferred it to Bill's keeping, as though she were something inanimate, a doll, and bowed, and turned, and left them.

"Seen him around a few times. Came here stag, I guess." Bill shrugged in dismissal. "Come on."

"Not this one. The one after."

"Are you all right? You look pale."

"It's the lights. I'm going in and powder. You go and dance with someone else."

He grinned at her. "I don't want to dance with someone else."

"Then you go and—and come back for me. The one after."

"The one after."

She watched him from just outside the doorway. He went out front toward the bar. She watched him go in there. She watched him sit down on one of the tall stools. Then she turned and went the other way.

She walked slowly over to the doors leading outside onto the veranda, and stood in one of them, looking out into the fountain-pen-ink blueness of the night. There were wicker chairs, in groups of twos and threes, spaced every few yards, encircling small tables.

The red sequin of a cigarette-coal had risen perpendicularly above one, all the way down at the end, imperiously summoning her. Then it shot over the balustrade laterally, cast away in impatient expectancy.

She walked slowly down that way, with the strange feeling of making a journey from which there was to be no return, ever. Her feet seemed to want to take root, hold her back of their own volition.

She came to a halt before him. He slung his hip onto the balustrade, and sat there askew, in insolent informality. He repeated what he'd said inside. "*Who*'d he say you were?"

The stars were moving. They were making peculiar eddying swirls like blurred pinwheels all over the sky.

"You abandoned me," she said with leashed fury. "You abandoned me, with five dollars. Now what do you want?"

"Oh, then we have met before. I *thought* we had. Glad you agree with me."

"Stop it. What do you want?"

"What do I want? I don't want anything. I'm a little confused, that's all. I'd like to be straightened out. The man introduced you under a mistaken name in there."

"What do you want? What are you doing down here?"

"Well, for that matter," he said with insolent urbanity, "what are you doing yourself down here?"

She repeated it a third time. "What do you want?"

"Can't a man show interest in his ex-protégée and child? There's no way of making children ex, you know."

"You're either insane or—"

"You know that isn't so. You wish it were," he said brutally.

She turned on her heel. His hand found her wrist again, flicked around it like a whip. Cutting just as deeply.

"Don't go inside yet. We haven't finished."

She stopped, her back to him now. "I think we have."

"The decision is mine."

He let go of her, but she stayed there where she was. She heard him light another cigarette, saw the momentary reflection from behind her own shoulder.

He spoke at last, voice thick with expelled smoke. "You still haven't cleared things up," he purred. "I'm as mixed-up as ever. This Hugh Hazzard married—er—let's say you, his wife, in Paris, a year ago last June fifteenth. I went to considerable expense and trouble to have the exact date on the records there verified. But a year ago last June fifteenth you and I were living in our little furnished room in New York. I have the receipted rent-bills to show for this. How could you have been in two such far-apart places at once?" He sighed philosophically. "Somebody's got their dates mixed. Either he had. Or I have." And then very slowly, "Or *you* have."

She winced unavoidably at that. Slowly her head came around, her body still remaining turned from him. Like one who listens hypnotized, against her will.

"It was you who's been sending those—?"

He nodded with mock affability, as if on being complimented on something praiseworthy. "I thought it would be kinder to break it to you gently."

She drew in her breath with an icy shudder of repugnance.

"I first happened on your name among the train-casualties, when I was up in New York," he said. He paused. "I went down there and 'identified' you, you know," he went on matter-of-factly. "You have that much to thank me for, at any rate."

He puffed thoughtfully on his cigarette.

"Then I heard one thing and another, and put two and two together. I went back for awhile first—got the rent-receipts together and one thing and another—and then finally I came on the rest of the way down here, out of curiosity. I became quite confused," he said ironically, "when I learned the rest of the story."

He waited. She didn't say anything. He seemed to take pity on her finally. "I know," he said indulgently, "this isn't the time nor place to—talk over old times. This is a party, and you're anxious to get back and enjoy yourself."

She shivered.

"Is there anywhere I can reach you?"

He took out a notebook, clicked a lighter. She mistakenly thought he was waiting to write at her dictate. Her lips remained frozen.

"Seneca 382," he read from the notebook. He put it away again. His hand made a lazy curve between them. In the stricken silence that followed he suggested after awhile, casually: "Lean up against that chair so you don't fall; you don't seem very steady on your feet, and I don't want to have to carry you bodily inside in front of all those people."

She put her hands to the top of the chair-back and stood quiet, head inclined.

The rose-amber haze in the open doorway down at the center of the terrace blotted out for a moment, and Bill was standing there looking for her.

"Patrice, this is our dance."

Georgesson rose for a second from the balustrade in sketchy etiquette, immediately sank back against it.

She made her way toward him, the blue pall of the terrace covering her uncertainty of step, and went inside with him. His arms took charge of her from that point on, so that she no longer had to be on her own.

"You were both standing there like statues," he said. "He can't be very good company."

She lurched against him in the tendril-like twists of the rumba, her head dropped to rest on his shoulder.

"He isn't very good company," she agreed sickly.

33

THE PHONE-CALL came at a fiendishly unpropitious moment.

He'd timed it well. He couldn't have timed it better if he'd been able to look through the walls of the house and watch their movements on the inside. The two men in the family were out. She'd just finished putting Hughie to sleep. She and Mother Hazzard were both up on the second floor, separately. Which meant that she was the only one fully eligible to answer.

She knew at the first instant of hearing it who it was, what it was. She knew too, that she'd been expecting it all day, that she'd known it was coming, it was surely coming.

She stood there rooted, unable to move. Maybe it would stop if she didn't go near it, maybe he would tire. But then it would ring again some other time.

Mother Hazzard opened the door of her room and looked out.

Patrice had swiftly opened her own door, was at the head of the stairs, before she'd fully emerged.

"I'll get it on this phone, dear, if you're busy."

"No, never mind, Mother, I was just going downstairs, anyway, so I'll answer it there."

She knew his voice right away. She hadn't heard it for over two years, until just last night, and yet it was again as familiar to her as if she'd been hearing it steadily for months past. Fear quickens the memory.

He was as pleasantly aloof at first as any casual caller on the telephone. "Is this the younger Mrs. Hazzard? Is this Patrice Hazzard?"

"This is she."

"I suppose you know, this is Georgesson."

She did know, but she didn't answer that.

"Are you—where you can be heard?"

"I'm not in the habit of answering questions like that. I'll hang up the receiver."

Nothing could seem to make him lose his equanimity. "Don't do that, Patrice," he said urbanely. "I'll ring back again. That'll make it worse. They'll begin wondering who it is keeps on calling so repeatedly. Or, eventually, someone else will answer—you can't stay there by the phone all evening—and I'll give my name if I have to and ask for you." He waited a minute for this to sink in. "Don't you see, it's better for you this way."

She sighed a little, in suppressed fury.

"We can't talk very much over the phone. I think it's better not to, anyway. I'm talking from McClellan's Drugstore, a few blocks from you. My car's just around the corner from there, where it can't be seen. On the left side of Pomeroy Street, just down from the crossing. Can you walk down that far for five or ten minutes? I won't keep you long."

She tried to match the brittle formality of his voice with her own. "I most certainly can not."

"Of course you can. You need cod-liver-oil capsules for your baby, from McClellan's. Or you feel like a soda, for yourself. I've seen you stop in there more than once, in the evening."

He waited.

"Shall I call back? Would you rather think it over awhile?"

He waited again.

"Don't do that," she said reluctantly, at last.

She could tell he understood: her meaning had been a positive and not a negative one.

She hung up.

She went upstairs again.

Mother Hazzard didn't ask her. They weren't inquisitive that way, in this house. But the door of her room was open. Patrice couldn't bring herself to reenter her own without at least a passing reference. Guilty conscience, this soon? she wondered bitingly.

"That was a Steve Georgesson, Mother," she called in. "Bill and I ran into him there last night. He wanted to know how we'd enjoyed ourselves."

"Well, that was real thoughtful of him, wasn't it?" Then she added, "He must be a decent sort, to do that."

Decent, Patrice thought dismally, easing the door closed after her.

She came out of her room again in about ten minutes' time. Mother Hazzard's door was closed now. She could have gone on down the stairs unquestioned. Again she couldn't do it.

She went over and knocked lightly, to attract attention.

"Mother, I'm going to take a walk down to the drugstore and back. Hughie's out of his talc. And I'd like a breath of air. I'll be back in five minutes."

"Go ahead, dear. I'll say goodnight to you now, in case I'm asleep by the time you're in again."

She rested her outstretched hand helplessly against the door for a minute. She felt like saying, Mother, don't let me go. Forbid me. Keep me here.

She turned away and went down the stairs. It was her own battle, and no proxies were allowed.

She stopped beside the car, on darkened Pomeroy Street.

"Sit in here, Patrice," he said amiably. He unlatched the door for her, from where he sat, and even palmed the leather cushion patronizingly.

She settled herself on the far side of the seat. Her eyes snapped refusal of the cigarette he was trying to offer her.

"We can be seen."

"Turn this way, toward me. No one'll notice you. Keep your back to the street."

"This can't go on. Now once and for all, for the first time and the last, what is it you want of me, what is this about?"

"Look, Patrice, there doesn't have to be anything unpleasant about this. You seem to be building it up to yourself that way, in your own mind. I have no such— It's all in the way you look at it. I don't see that there has to be any change in the way things were going along—before last night. You were the only one knew before. Now you and I are the only ones know. It ends there. That is, if you want it to."

"You didn't bring me out here to tell me that."

He went off at a tangent. Or what seemed to be a tangent. "I've never amounted to—as much as I'd hoped, I suppose. I mean, I've never gotten as far as I should. As I once expected to. There are lots of us like that. Every once in awhile I find myself in difficulties, every now and then I get into a tight squeeze. Little card-games with the boys. This and that. You know how it is." He laughed deprecatingly. "It's been going on for years. It's nothing new. But I was wondering if you'd care to do me a favor—this time."

"You're asking me for money."

She almost felt nauseated. She turned her face away.

"I didn't think there were people like you outside of—outside of penitentiaries."

He laughed in good-natured tolerance. "You're in unusual circumstances. That attracts 'people like me.' If you weren't, you *still* wouldn't think there were any, you wouldn't know any different."

"Suppose I go to them now and tell them of this conversation we've just been having, of my own accord. My brother-in-law would go looking for you and beat you within an inch of your life."

"We'll let the relationship stand unchallenged. I wonder why women put such undue faith in a beating-up? Maybe because they're not used to violence themselves. A beating doesn't mean much to a man. Half an hour after it's over, he's as good as he was before."

"You should know," she murmured.

He tapped a finger to the points of three others. "There are three alternatives. You go to them and tell them. Or I go to them and tell them. Or we remain in status quo. By which I mean, you do me a favor, and then we drop the whole thing, nothing further is said. But there isn't any fourth alternative."

He shook his head slightly, in patient disapproval. "You overdramatize everything so, Patrice. That's the unfailing hallmark of cheapness. You're a cheap girl. That's the basic difference between us. I may be, according to your lights, a rotter, but I have a certain tone. As you visualize it, I'd stride in there, throw my arms out wide in declamation, and blare, 'This girl is not your daughter-in-law!' Not at all. That wouldn't work with people like that. It would overreach itself. All I'd have to do would be to let you accuse yourself out of your own mouth. In their presence. You couldn't refuse the house to me. 'When you were in Paris with Hugh, Patrice, which bank did you live on, Left or Right?' 'What was the name of the boat you made the trip back on, again?' 'Well, when I ran into you over there that day with him—oh, you forgot to mention that we'd already met before, Pat?—why is it you looked so different from what you do today? You don't look like the same girl at all.' Until you crumpled and caved in."

He was capable of it. He was too cold about the whole thing, that was the dangerous feature. No heat, no impulse, no emotion to cloud the issue. Everything planned, plotted, graphed, ahead of time. Drafted. Charted. Every step. Even the notes. She knew their purpose now. Not poison-pen letters at all. They had been important to the long-term scheme of the thing. Psychological warfare, nerve warfare, breaking her down ahead of time, toppling her resistance before the main attack had even been made. The research-trip to New York in-between, to make sure of his own ground, to make sure there was no flaw, to leave her no loophole.

He skipped the edge of his hand off the wheel-rim, as if brushing off a particle of dust. "There's no villain in this. Let's get rid of the Victorian trappings. It's just a business transaction. It's no different from taking out insurance, really." He turned to her with an assumption of candor that was almost charming for a moment. "Don't you want to be practical about it?"

"I suppose so. I suppose I should meet you on your own ground." She didn't try to project her contempt; it would have failed to reach him, she knew.

"If you get rid of these stuffy fetishes of virtue and villainy, of black and white, the whole thing becomes so simple it's not even worth the quarter of an hour we're giving it here in the car."

"I have no money of my own, Georgesson." Capitulation. Submission.

"They're one of the wealthiest families in town, that's common knowledge. Why be technical about it? Get them to open an account for you. You're not a child."

"I couldn't *ask* them outright to do such a—"

"You don't *ask*. There are ways. You're a woman, aren't you? It's easy enough; a woman knows how to go about those things—"

"I'd like to go now," she said, reaching blindly for the door-handle.

"Do we understand one another?" He opened it for her. "I'll give you another ring after awhile."

He paused a moment. The threat was so impalpable there was not even a change of inflection in the lazy drawl.

"Don't neglect it, Patrice."

She got out. The crack of the door was the unfelt slap-in-the-face of loathing she gave him.

"Goodnight, Patrice," he drawled after her amiably.

34

"—PERFECTLY PLAIN," she was saying animatedly. "It had a belt of the same material, and then a row of buttons down to about here."

She was purposely addressing herself to Mother Hazzard, to the exclusion of the two men members of the family. Well, the topic in itself was excuse enough for that.

"Heaven sakes, why didn't you take it?" Mother Hazzard wanted to know.

"I couldn't do that," she said reluctantly. She stopped a moment, then she added: "Not right—then and there." And played a lot with her fork. And felt low.

They must have thought the expression on her face was wistful disappointment. It wasn't. It was self-disgust.

You don't have to ask openly. There are ways; it's easy enough. A woman knows how to go about those things.

This was one of them now.

How defenseless those who love you are against you, she thought bitterly. How vicious and how criminal it is to trade on that self-imposed defenselessness. As I am doing now. Tricks and traps and wiles, those are for strangers. Those should be used against such only. Not against those who love you; with their guard down, with their eyes trustfully closed. It made her skin crawl in revulsion. She felt indecent, unclean, obscene.

Father Hazzard cut into the conversation. "Why didn't you just charge it up and have it sent? You could have used Mother's account. She deals there a lot."

She let her eyes drop. "I wouldn't have wanted to do that," she said reticently.

"Nonsense—" He stopped suddenly. Almost as though someone had trodden briefly on his foot under the table.

She caught Bill glancing at her. He seemed to be holding the glance a moment longer than was necessary. But before she could verify this, it had stopped, and he resumed bringing the suspended forkful of pie-fill up to his mouth.

"I think I hear Hughie crying," she said, and flung her napkin down and ran out to the stairs to listen.

But in the act of listening upward, she couldn't avoid overhearing Mother Hazzard's guarded voice in the dining-room behind her, spacing each word with structural severity.

"Donald Hazzard, you ought to be ashamed of yourself. Do you men-folk have to be told *everything*? Haven't you got a grain of tact in your heads?"

35

IN THE MORNING Father Hazzard had lingered on at the table, she noticed when she came down, instead of leaving early with Bill. He sat quietly reading his newspaper while she finished her coffee. And there was just a touch of secretive self-satisfaction in his attitude, she thought.

He rose in company with her when she got up. "Get your hat and coat, Pat, I want you to come with me in the car. This young lady and I have business downtown," he announced to Mother Hazzard. The latter tried, not altogether successfully, to look blankly bewildered.

"But what about Hughie's feeding?"

"I'll give him his feeding," Mother Hazzard said serenely.

"You'll be back in time for that. I'm just borrowing you."

She got in next to him a moment later and they started off.

"Did poor Bill have to walk to the office this morning?" she asked.

"Poor Bill indeed!" he scoffed. "Do him good, the big lug. If I had those long legs of his, I'd walk it myself, every morning."

"Where are you taking me?"

"Now just never you mind. No questions. Just wait'll we get there, and you'll see."

They stopped in front of the bank. He motioned her out and led her inside with him. He said something to one of the guards in an aside, and he and she sat down to wait for a moment on a bench.

For the briefest moment only. Then the guard had come back with a noticeable deference. He led them toward a door marked "Manager, Private." Before they could reach it it had already opened and a pleasant-faced, slightly stout man wearing horn-rimmed spectacles was waiting to greet them.

"Come in and meet my old friend Harve Wheelock," Father Hazzard said to her.

They seated themselves in comfortable leather chairs in the private office, and the two men shared cigars.

"Harve, I've got a new customer for you. This is my boy Hugh's wife. Not that I think your mangy old bank is any good, but—well, you know how it is. Just habit, I reckon."

The manager shook appreciatively all over, as if this were some joke between them that had been going on for years. He winked for Patrice's benefit. "I agree with you there. Sell it to you real cheap."

"How cheap?"

"Quarter of a million." Meanwhile he was penning required entries on a filing-form, as though he had all the information called for at his fingers' tips, didn't need to ask anything about it.

Father Hazzard shook his head. "Too cheap. Can't be any good." He offhandedly palmed an oblong of light blue paper onto the desk, left it there face down.

"You think it over and let me know," the manager said drily. And to her, reversing his pen, "Sign here, honey."

Forger, she thought scathingly. She handed it back, her eyes downcast. The strip of light blue was clipped to it and it was sent out. A midget black book came back in its stead.

"Here you are, honey." The manager tendered it to her across his desk.

She opened it and looked at it, unnoticed, while the two resumed their friendly bickering hammer and tongs. It was so spotless, so unused yet. At the top it said "Mrs. Hugh Hazzard." And there was just one entry, under today's date. A deposit.

"5000.00"

36

SHE STOOD THERE holding the small round canister, staring frozenly at it as though she couldn't make out what was in it. She'd been holding it like that for long moments, without actually seeing it. She tilted it at last and dumped its contents into the washbowl. It had been better than half-full.

She went out, and closed the door, and went across the hall and knocked softly.

"I'm stepping out for just a moment, Mother. Hughie upset his whole can of talc in the bath just now, and I want to get another before I forget."

"All right, dear. The walk'll do you good. Oh—bring me back a bottle of that shampoo while you're in there, dear. I'm on the last of it now."

She got that slightly sickened feeling she was beginning to know so well. It was so easy to fool those who loved you. But who were you really fooling—them or yourself?

His arm was draped negligently atop the car-door, elbow out. The door fell open. He made way for her by shifting leisurely over on the seat, without offering to rise. His indolent taking of her for granted was more scathingly insulting than any overt rudeness would have been.

"I'm sorry I had to call. I thought you'd forgotten about our talk. It's been more than a week now."

"Forgotten?" she said drily. "I wish it were that easy."

"I see you've become a depositor of the Standard Trust since our last meeting."

She shot him an involuntary look of shock, without answering.

"Five thousand dollars."

She drew a quick breath.

"Tellers will chat for a quarter cigar." He smiled. "Well?"

"I haven't any money with me. I haven't used the account yet. I'll have to cash a check in the morning and—"

"They give a checkbook with each account, don't they? And you have that with you, most likely—"

She gave him a look of unfeigned surprise.

"I have a fountain pen right here in my pocket. I'll turn on the dashboard-lights a minute. Let's get it over and done with; the quickest way's the best. Now; I'll tell you what to write. To Stephen Georgesson. Not to Cash or Bearer. Five hundred."

"Five hundred?"

"That's academic."

She didn't understand what he meant, and was incautious enough to let him go on past that point without stopping him.

"That's all. And then your signature. The date, if you want."

She stopped short. "I can't do this."

"I'm sorry, you'll have to. I don't want it any other way. I won't accept cash."

"But this passes through the bank with both our names on it, mine as payer, yours as payee."

"There's such a flood of checks passing through the bank every month, it's not even likely to be noticed. It could be a debt of Hugh's, you know, that you're settling up for him."

"Why are you so anxious to have a check?" she asked irresolutely.

A crooked smile looped one corner of his mouth. "Why should you object, if I don't? It's to your advantage, isn't it? I'm playing right into your hands. It comes back into your possession after it clears the bank. After that you're holding tangible evidence of this—of blackmail—against me if you should ever care to prosecute. Which is something you haven't got so far. Remember, up to this point, it's just your word against mine, I can deny this whole thing happened. Once this check goes through, you've got living proof."

He said, a little more tartly than he'd yet spoken to her, "Shall we get through? You're anxious to get back. And I'm anxious to pull out of here."

She handed him the completed check and pen.

He was smiling again now. He waited until she'd stepped out and he'd turned on the ignition. He said above the low throb of the motor, "Your thinking isn't very clear, nor very quick, is it? This check is evidence against *me*, that *you*'re holding, if it clears the bank and returns to you. But if it doesn't—if it's kept out, and never comes

up for payment at all—then it's evidence against *you*, that *I'm*
holding."

The car glided off and left her standing behind looking after it in
her shattered consternation.

37

SHE ALL BUT ran toward the car along the night-shaded street, as if
fearful it might suddenly glide into motion and escape her, instead
of directing her steps toward it grudgingly as she had the two previous times. She clung to the top of the door with both hands when
she'd reached it, as if in quest of support.

"I can't stand this! What are you trying to do to me?"

He was smugly facetious. His brows went up. "Do? I haven't done
anything to you. I haven't been near you. I haven't seen you in the
last three weeks."

"The check wasn't debited."

"Oh, you've had your bank statement. That's right, yesterday was
the first of the month. I imagine you've had a bad twenty-four hours.
I must have overlooked it—"

"No," she said with fierce rancor, "you're not the kind would over-
look anything like that, you vicious leech! Haven't you done enough
to me? What are you trying to do, drive me completely out of my
mind—"

His manner changed abruptly, tightened. "Get in," he said crisply.
"I want to talk to you. I'll drive you around for a quarter of an hour
or so."

"I can't *ride* with you. How can you ask me to do that?"

"We can't just stand still in this one place, talking it over. That's
far worse. We've done that twice already. We can circle the lake
drive once or twice; there's no one on it at this hour and no stops.
Turn your collar up across your mouth."

"Why are you holding the check? What are you meaning to do?"

"Wait until we get there," he said. Then when they had, he answered her, coldly, dispassionately, as though there had been no interruption.

"I'm not interested in five hundred dollars."

She was beginning to lose her head. Her inability to fathom his motives was kindling her to panic. "Give it back to me, then, and I'll give you more. I'll give you a thousand. Only, give it back to me."

"I don't want to be *given* more. I don't want to be *given* any amount. Don't you understand? I want the money to belong to *me*, in my own right."

Her face was suddenly stricken white. "I don't understand. What are you trying to say to me?"

"I think you're beginning to, by the look on your face." He fumbled in his pocket, took something out. An envelope, already sealed and stamped for mailing. "You asked me where the check was. It's in here. Here, read what it says on it. No, don't take it out of my hand. Just read it from where you are."

> *"Mr. Donald Hazzard*
> *Hazzard and Loring*
> *Empire Building*
> *Caulfield."*

"No—" She couldn't articulate, could only shake her head convulsively.

"I'm mailing it to him at his office, where you can't intercept it." He returned it to his pocket. "The last mail-collection, here in Caulfield, is at nine each night. You may not know that, but I've been making a study of those things recently. There's a mail-box on Pomeroy Street, just a few feet from where I've been parking the last few times I've met you. It's dark and inconspicuous around there, and I'll use that one. It takes the carrier until nine-fifteen to reach it, however; I've timed him several nights in a row and taken the average."

He silenced her with his hand, went on: "Now, if you reach there before the carrier does, this envelope stays out of the chute. If you're not there yet when he arrives, I drop it in. You have a day's grace, until nine-fifteen tomorrow night."

"But what do you want me to be there for—? You said you didn't want more—"

"We're going to take a ride out to Hastings, that's the next town over. I'm taking you to a justice of the peace there, and he's going to make us man and wife."

He slowed the car as her head lurched soddenly back over the top of the seat for a moment.

"I didn't think they swooned any more—" he began. Then as he saw her straighten again with an effort and pass the back of her hand blurredly before her eyes, he added: "Oh, I see they don't; they just get a little dizzy, is that it?"

"Why are you doing this to me?" she said smotheredly.

"There are several good reasons I can think of. It's a good deal safer, from my point of view, than the basis we've been going on so far. There's no chance of anything backfiring. A wife, the law-books say, cannot testify against her husband. That means that any lawyer worth his fee can whisk you off the stand before you can so much as open your mouth. And then there are more practical considerations. The old couple aren't going to be around forever, you know. The old lady's life is hanging by a thread. And the old man won't last any time without her. Old Faithful, I know the type. When they go, you and Bill share unequally between you— Don't look so horrified; that lawyer of theirs hasn't exactly talked, but this is a small town, those things sort of seep around without even benefit of word-of-mouth. I can wait that year, or even two or three if I have to. The law gives a husband one-third of his wife's property. Three-quarters of—I may be underestimating, but roughly I'd say four hundred thousand, that's three hundred thousand. And then a third of that again— Don't cover your ears like that, Patrice; you look like someone out of a Marie Corelli novel."

He braked. "You can get out here, Patrice. This is close enough." And then he chuckled a little, watching her flounder to the pavement. "Are you sure you're able to walk steady? I wouldn't want to have them think I'd plied you with—"

The last thing he said was, "Make sure your clock isn't slow, Patrice. Because the United States Mail is always on time."

38

THE HEADLIGHT-BEAMS of his car kept slashing up the road ahead of them like ploughshares, seeming to cast aside its topsoil of darkness, reveal its borax-like white fill, and spill that out all over the roadway. Then behind them the livid furrows would heal again into immediate darkness.

It seemed hours they'd been driving like this, in silence yet acutely aware of one another. Trees went by, dimly lit up from below, along their trunks, by the passing reflection of their headlight-wash, into a sort of ghostly incandescence. Then at times there weren't any trees, they fell back, and a plushy black evenness took their place—fields or meadows, she supposed—that smelled sweeter. Clover. It was beautiful country around here; too beautiful for anyone to be in such a hell of suffering in the midst of it.

Roads branched off at times, too, but they never took them. They kept to this wide, straight one they were on.

They passed an indirectly lighted white sign, placed at right angles to the road so that it could be read as you came up to it. It said "Welcome to Hastings," and then underneath, "Population—" and some figures too small to catch before they had already gone by.

She glanced briefly after it, in a sort of fascinated horror.

He'd apparently seen her do it, without looking directly at her. "That's across the State line," he remarked drily. "Travel broadens one, they say." It was nine forty-five now according to her wristwatch. It had taken them only half an hour's drive to get here.

They passed through the town's nuclear main square. A drugstore was still open, two of the old-fashioned jars of colored water that all drugstore-windows featured once upon a time flashing emerald and mauve at them as they went by. A motion-picture theatre was still alive inside, but dying fast externally, its marquee already dark, its lobby dim.

He turned up one of the side streets, a tunnel under leafy shade trees, its houses all set back a lawn-spaced distance so that they were almost invisible in the night-shade from the roadway. A dim light peering through from under the recesses of an ivy-covered porch seemed to attract him. He shunted over to the walk suddenly, and back a little, and stopped opposite it.

They sat for awhile.

Then he got out on his side, came around to hers, and opened the door beside her.

"Come in," he said briefly.

She didn't move, she didn't answer.

"Come on in with me. They're waiting."

She didn't answer, didn't move.

"Don't just sit there like that. We had this all out before, back at Caulfield. Move. Say something, will you?"

"What do you want me to say?"

He gave the door an impatient slap-to again, as if in momentary reprieve. "Get yourself together. I'll go over and let them know we got here."

She watched him go, in a sort of stupor, as though this were happening to someone else; heard his tread go up the wooden plank-walk that led up to the house. She could even hear the ring of the bell, from within the house, all the way out here where she was. It was no wonder, it was so quiet. Just little winged things buzzing and humming in a tree overhead.

She wondered: How does he know I won't suddenly start the car and drive off? She answered that herself: He knows I won't. He knows it's too late for that. As I know it. The time for stopping, for drawing back, for dashing off, that was long ago. So long ago. Long before tonight. That was in the compartment on the train coming here, when the wheels tried to warn me. That was when the first note came. That was when the first phone-call came, the first walk down to the drugstore. I am as safely held fast here as though I were manacled to him.

She could hear their voices now. A woman saying, "No, not at all; you made very good time. Come right in."

The doorway remained open, lighted. Whoever had been standing in it had withdrawn into the house. He was coming back toward her now. The sound of his tread along the wooden walk. She gripped the edge of the car-seat with her hands, dug them in under the leather cushions.

He was up to her now, standing there.

"Come on, Patrice," he said casually.

That was the full horror of it, his casualness, his matter-of-factness. He wasn't acting the part.

She spoke quietly too, as quietly as he, but her voice was as thin and blurred as a thrumming wire.

"I can't do it. Georgesson, don't ask me to do this."

"Patrice, we've been all over this. I told you the other night, and it was all settled then."

She covered her face with cupped hands, quickly uncovered it again. She kept using the same four words; they were the only ones she could think of. "But I can't do it. Don't you understand? I can't *do* it."

"There's no impediment. You're not married to anyone. Even in your assumed character, you're not married to anyone, much less as yourself. I investigated all that in New York."

"Steve. Listen, I'm calling you Steve."

"That doesn't melt me," he assured her jocosely. "That's my name, I'm supposed to be called that." He lidded his eyes at her. "It's my *given* name, not one that I took for myself—*Patrice*."

"Steve, I've never pleaded with you before. In all these months, I've taken it like a woman. Steve, if there's anything human in you at all I can appeal to—"

"I'm only too human. That's why I like money as much as I do. But your wires are crossed. It's my very humanness, for that reason, that makes your appeal useless. Come on, Patrice. You're wasting time."

She cowered away edgewise along the seat. He drummed his fingers on the top of the door and laughed a little.

"Why this horror of marriage? Let me get to the bottom of your aversion. Maybe I can reassure you. There is no personal appeal involved; you haven't any for me. I've got only contempt for you, for being the cheap, tricky little fool you are. I'm leaving you on the doorstep of your ever-loving family again, just as soon as we get back to Caulfield. This is going to be a paper marriage, in every sense of the word. But it's going to stick, it's going to stick to the bitter end. Now does that take care of your mid-Victorian qualms?"

She cast the back of her hand across her eyes as though a blow had just blinded her.

He wrenched the door open.

"They're waiting for us in there. Come on, you're only making it worse."

He was beginning to harden against her. Her opposition was commencing to inflame him against her. It showed inversely, in a sort of lethal coldness.

"Look, my friend, I'm not going to drag you in there by the hair. The thing isn't worth it. I'm going inside a minute and call the Hazzard house from here, and tell them the whole story right now. Then I'll drive you back where I got you from. They can have you—if they want you any more." He leaned toward her slightly across the door. "Take a good look at me. Do I look like I was kidding?"

He meant it. It wasn't an empty bluff, with nothing behind it. It might be a threat that he would prefer not to have to carry out, but it wasn't an idle threat. She could see that in his eyes, in the cold sullenness in them, the dislike of herself she read in them.

He turned and left the car-side and went up the plank-walk again, more forcefully, more swiftly, than he'd trod it before.

"Excuse me, could I trouble you for a minute—" she heard him start to say as he entered the open doorway, then the rest was blurred as he went deeper within.

She struggled out, clinging to the flexing door like somebody walking in his sleep. Then she wavered up the plank-walk and onto the porch, and the ivy rustled for a minute as she teetered soddenly against it. Then she went on toward the oblong of light projected by the open doorway, and inside. It was like struggling through knee-deep water.

A middle-aged woman met her in the hallway.

"Good evening. Are you Mrs. Hazzard? He's in here."

She took her to a room on the left, parted an old-fashioned pair of sliding doors. He was standing in there, with his back to them, beside an old-fashioned telephone-box bracketed to the wall.

"Here's the young lady. You can both come into the study when you're ready."

Patrice drew the doors together behind her again. "Steve," she said.

He turned around and looked at her, then turned back again.

"Don't—you'll kill her," she pleaded.

"The old all die sooner or later."

"Has it gone through yet?"

"They're ringing Caulfield for me now."

It wasn't any sleight-of-hand trick. His finger wasn't anywhere near the receiver-hook, holding it shut down. He was in the act of carrying it out.

A choking sound broke in her throat.

He looked around again, less fully than before. "Have you decided once and for all?"

She didn't nod, she simply let her eyelids drop closed for a minute.

"Operator," he said, "cancel that call. It was a mistake." He replaced the receiver.

She felt a little sick and dizzy, as when you've just looked down from some great height and then drawn back again.

He went over to the sliding-doors and swung them vigorously back.

"We're ready," he called into the study across the hall.

He crooked his arm toward her, backhand, contemptuously tilting up his elbow for her to take, without even looking around at her as he did so.

She came forward and they went toward the study together, her arm linked in his. Into where the man was waiting to marry them.

39

IT WAS ON the way back that she knew she was going to kill him. Knew she must, knew it was the only thing left to be done now. She should have done it sooner, she told herself. Long before this; that first night as she sat with him in his car. It would have been that much better. Then this, tonight's ultimate horror and degradation, would at least have been avoided. She hadn't thought of it then; that was the one thing that had never occurred to her. It had always been flight, escape from him in some other way; never safety in this way—his removal.

But she knew she was going to do it, now. Tonight.

Not a word had passed between them, all this way, ever since leaving the justice's house. Why should one? What was there to say? What was there to do, now—except this one final thing, that came to her opposite a white-stockinged telegraph-pole, about four miles out of Hastings. Just like that it came: click, snap, and it was there. As though she had passed through some electric-eye beam stretched across the road, there from that particular telegraph-pole. On the one side of it, still, just passive despair, fatalism. On the other, full-grown decision, remorseless, irrevocable: I'm going to kill him. Tonight. Before this night ends, before the light comes again.

Neither of them said anything. He didn't, because he was content. He'd done what he'd set out to do. He did whistle lightly, once, for a short while, but then he stopped that again. She didn't say anything, because she was undone. Destroyed, in the fullest sense of the word. She'd never felt like this before. She didn't even feel pain of mind any more. Struggle was ended. She was numb now. She'd even had more feeling left in her after the train-crash than now.

She rode all the way with her eyes held shut. Like a woman returning from a funeral, at which everything worth keeping has been interred, and to whom nothing left above ground is worth looking at any longer.

She heard him speak at last. "There, was that so bad?" he said.

She answered him mechanically, without opening her eyes.

"Where are you—? What do you want me to do now?"

"Exactly nothing. You go on just as you were before. This is something between the two of us. And I want it to stay that way, understand? Not a word to the Family. Not until I'm ready. It'll be Our Little Secret, yours and mine."

He was afraid if he took her with him openly, they'd change the will, she supposed. And afraid if he left her with them, and they learned of it, they'd have it annulled for her.

How did you kill a man? There was nothing here, no way. The country was flat, the road level, straight. If she snatched at the wheel, tried to throw the car out of control, nothing much would happen. You needed steep places, hairbreadth turns. And the car was only trundling along, not going fast. It would only roll off into the dirt maybe, strike a telegraph-pole, shake them up a little.

Besides, even if that had been the feasible way, she didn't want to die with him. She only wanted him to die. She had a child she

was devoted to, a man she loved. She wanted to live. She'd always
had an unquenchable will to live, all her life; she still had it now.
Numbed as she was, it was still flickering stubbornly inside her.
Nothing could put it out, or—she would already have contemplated
another alternative, probably, before now.

Oh God, she cried out in her mind, if I only had a—

And in that instant, she knew how to do it. Knew how she was
going to do it. For the next word-symbol flashing before her senses
was "gun," and as it appeared it brought its own answer to the plea.

In the library, at home. There was one in there, somewhere.

A brief scene came back to mind, from many months ago. Buried
until now, to suddenly reappear, as clear as if it had just taken place
a moment ago. The reading-lamp, comfortably lit and casting its
cheerful glow. Father Hazzard, sitting there by it, lingering late over
a book. The others gone to bed, all but herself. She the last one to
leave him. A brief kiss on his forehead.

"Shall I lock up for you?"

"No, you run along. I will, in a moment."

"You won't forget, though?"

"No, I won't forget." And then he'd chuckled, in that dry way of
his: "Don't be nervous, I'm well-protected down here. There's a re-
volver in one of the drawers right by me here. We keep it specially
for burglars. That was Mother's idea, once, years ago—and there
hasn't been hide nor hair of one in all the time since."

She'd laughed at this melodramatic drollery, and told him quite
truthfully: "It wasn't prowlers I was thinking of, but a sudden rain-
storm in the middle of the night and Mother's best drapes."

She'd laughed. But now she didn't.

Now she knew where there was a gun.

You crooked your finger through. You pulled. And you had peace,
you had safety.

They stopped, and she heard the car-door beside her clack open.
She raised her eyes. They were in a leafy tunnel of the street trees.
She recognized the symmetrical formation of the trees, the lawn-
slopes on either side of them, the dim contours of the private homes
in the background. They were on her own street, but further over,
about a block away from the house. He was being tactful, letting her
out at a great enough distance from her own door to be inconspicuous.

He was sitting there, waiting for her to take the hint and get out. She looked at her watch, mechanically. Not even eleven yet. It must have been around ten when it happened. It had taken them forty minutes coming back; they'd driven slower than going out.

He'd seen her do it. He smiled satirically. "Doesn't take long to marry, does it?"

It doesn't take long to die, either, she thought smoulderingly.

"Don't you—don't you want me to come with you?" she whispered.

"What for?" he said insolently. "I don't want you. I just want what eventually—comes with you. You go upstairs to your unsullied little bed. (I trust it is, anyway. With this Bill in the house.)"

She could feel heat in her face. But nothing much mattered, nothing counted. Except that the gun was a block away, and he was here. And the two of them had to meet.

"Just stay put," he advised her. "No unexpected little trips out of town, now, Patrice. Unless you want me to suddenly step forward and claim paternity of the child. I have the law on my side, now, you know. I'll go straight to the police."

"Well—will you wait here a minute? I'll—I'll be right out. I'll get you some money. You'll need some—until—until we get together again."

"Your dowry?" he said ironically. "So soon? Well, as a matter of fact, I don't. Some of the men in this town play very poor cards. Anyway, why give me what's already mine? Piecemeal. I can wait. Don't do me any favors."

She stepped down, reluctantly.

"Where can I reach you, in case I have to?"

"I'll be around. You'll hear from me, every now and then. Don't be afraid of losing me."

No, it had to be tonight, tonight, she kept telling herself grimly. Before the darkness ended and the daybreak came. If she waited, she'd lose her courage. This surgery had to be performed at once, this cancer on her future removed.

No matter where he goes in this city tonight, she vowed, I'll track him down, I'll find him, and I'll put an end to him. Even if I have to destroy my own self doing it. Even if I have to do it in sight of a hundred people.

The car-door swung closed. He tipped his hat satirically.

"Good night, Mrs. Georgesson. Pleasant dreams to you. Try sleeping on a piece of wedding-cake. If you haven't wedding-cake, try a hunk of stale bread. You'll be just as crummy either way."

The car sidled past her. Her eyes fastened on the rear license-plate, clove to it, memorized it, even as it went skimming past. It dwindled. The red tail-light coursed around the next corner and disappeared. But it seemed to hang there before her eyes, like a ghost-plaque, suspended against the night, for long minutes after.

NY09231

Then that, too, dimmed and went out.

Somebody was walking along the quiet night sidewalk, very close by. She could hear the chip-chipping of the high heels. That was she. The trees were moving by her, slowly rearward. Somebody was climbing terraced flagstone steps. She could hear the gritty sound of the ascending tread. That was she. Somebody was standing before the door of the house now. She could see the darkling reflection in the glass opposite her. It moved as she moved. That was she.

She opened her handbag and felt inside it for her doorkey. Hers, was good. The key they'd given her. It was still there. For some reason this surprised her. Funny to come home like this, just as though nothing had happened to you, and feel for your key, and put it into the door, and—and go into the house. To *still* come home like this, and *still* go into the house.

I have to go in here, she defended herself. My baby's asleep in this house. He's asleep upstairs in it, right now. This is where I have to go; there isn't any other place for me to go.

She remembered how she'd had to lie, earlier tonight, asking Mother Hazzard to mind Hughie for her while she visited a new friend. Father had been at a business meeting and Bill had been out.

She put on the lights in the lower hall. She closed the door. Then she stood there a minute, her breath rising and falling, her back supine against the door. It was so quiet, so quiet in this house. People sleeping, people who trusted you. People who didn't expect you to bring home scandal and murder to them, in return for all their goodness to you.

She stood there immobile. So quiet, so still, there was no guessing what she had come back here for, what she had come back here to do.

Nothing left. Nothing. No home, no love, even no child any more. She'd even forfeited that prospective love, tarnished it for a later day. She'd lose him too, he'd turn against her, when he was old enough to know this about her.

He'd done all this to her, one man. It wasn't enough that he'd done it once, he'd done it twice now. He'd wrecked two lives for her. He'd smashed up the poor inoffensive seventeen-year-old simpleton from San Francisco who had had the bad luck to stray his way. Smashed her up, and wiped his feet all over her five-and-ten-cent-store dreams, and spit on them. And now he'd smashed up the cardboard lady they called Patrice.

He wouldn't smash up anybody more!

A tortured grimace disfigured her face for a moment. The back of her wrist went to her forehead, clung there. An inhalation of terrible softness, yet terrible resolve, shook her entire frame. Then she tottered on the bias toward the library entrance, like a comic drunk lacking in sufficient coordination to face squarely in the direction in which he is hastening.

She put on the big reading-lamp in there, center-table.

She went deliberately to the cellarette, and opened that, and poured some brandy and downed it. It seemed to blast its way down into her, but she quelled it with a resolute effort.

Ah, yes, you needed that when you were going to kill a man.

She went looking for the gun. She tried the table-drawers first, and it was not in there. Only papers and things, in the way. But he'd said there was one in here, that night, and there must be, somewhere in this room. They never told you anything that was untrue, even lightly; he, nor Mother, nor—nor Bill either for that matter. That was the big difference between them and her. That was why they had peace—and she had none.

She tried Father Hazzard's desk next. The number of drawers and cubicles was greater, but she sought them all out one by one. Something glinted, as she moved a heavy business-ledger aside, in the bottommost under-drawer, and there it lay, thrust in at the back.

She took it out. It's inoffensive look, at first, was almost a disappointment. So small, to do so great a thing. To take away a life.

Burnished nickel, and bone. And that fluted bulge in the middle, she
supposed, was where its hidden powers of death lay. In her unfamiliarity, she pounded at its back with the heel of her hand, and
strained at it, trying to get it open, risking a premature discharge,
hoping only that if she kept fingers clear of the trigger she would
avert one. Suddenly, with astonishing ease at the accidental right
touch, it had broken downward, it slanted open. Round black chambers, empty.

She rummaged in the drawer some more. She found the same small
cardboard box, half-noted in her previous search, that she had hastily
cast aside. Inside, cotton-wool, as if to hold some very perishable
medicinal capsule. But instead, steel-jacketed, snub-nosed, the cartridges. Only five of them.

She pressed them home, one by one, into the pits they were meant
for. One chamber remained empty.

She closed the gun.

She wondered if it would fit into her handbag. She tried it spade-
wise, the flat side up, and it went in.

She closed the handbag, and took it with her, and went out of the
room, went out to the back of the hall.

She took out the classified directory, looked under "Garages."

He might leave it out in the streets overnight. But she didn't think
he would. He was the kind who prized his cars and his hats and his
watches. He was the kind of man prized everything but his women.

The garages were alphabetized, and she began calling them
alphabetically.

"Have you a New York car there for the night, license 09231?"

At the third place the night attendant came back and said: "Yes,
we have. It was just brought in a few minutes ago."

"Mr. Georgesson?"

"Yeah, that's right. What about it, lady? Whaddya want from us?"

"I—I was out in it just now. The young man just brought me
home in it. And I find I left something with him. I have to get
hold of him. Please, it's important. Will you tell me where I can
reach him?"

"We ain't supposed to do that, lady."

"But I can't get in. He has my doorkey, don't you understand?"

"Whyn'tcha ring your doorbell?" the gruff voice answered.

"You fool!" she exploded, her fury lending her plausible eloquence.

"I wasn't supposed to be out with him in the first place! I don't want to attract any attention. I *can't* ring the doorbell!"

"I getcha, lady," the voice jeered, with that particular degree of greasiness she'd known it would have, "I getcha." And a double tongue-click was given for punctuation. "Wait'll I check up."

He left. He got on again, said: "He's been keeping his car with us for some time now. The address on our records is 110 Decatur Road. I don't know if that's still—"

But she'd hung up.

40

SHE USED HER own key to unlock the garage-door. The little roadster that Bill habitually used was out, but the big car, the sedan, was in there. She backed it out. Then she got out a moment, went back to refasten the garage-door.

There was the same feeling of unreality about this as before; a sort of dream-fantasy, a state of somnambulism, yet with over-all awareness. The chip-chip of footsteps along the cement garage-driveway that were someone else's, yet were her own—sounding from under her. It was as though she had experienced a violent personality split, and one of her selves, aghast and helpless, watched a phantom murderess issue from the cleavage and start out upon her deadly quest. She could only pace this dark thing, this other self, could not recapture nor reabsorb it, once loosed. Hence (perhaps) the detached objectivity of the footsteps, the mirror-like reproduction of her own movements.

Reentering the car, she backed it into the street, reversed it, and let it flow forward. Not violently, but with the suave pick-up of a perfectly possessed driver. Some other hand, not hers—so firm, so steady, so pure—remembered to reach for the door-latch and draw the door securely closed with a smart little clout.

Outside, the street-lights went spinning by like glowing bowls coming toward her down a bowling-alley. But each shot was a miss, they went alternately too far out to this side, too far out to that. With herself and the car, the kingpin in the middle that they never knocked down.

She thought: That must be Fate, bowling against me. But I don't care, let them come.

Then the car had stopped again. So easy it was to go forth to kill a man.

She didn't study it closely, to see what it was like. It didn't matter what it was like; she was going in there, it was going to happen there.

She pedalled the accelerator again, went on past the door and around the corner. There she made a turn, for the right-of-way was against her, pointed the car forward to the way from which she had just come, brought it over against the sidewalk, stopped it there, just out of sight.

She took up her bag from beside her on the seat, as a woman does who is about to leave a car, secured it under her arm.

She shut off the ignition and got out. She walked back around the corner, to where she'd just come from, with the quick, preoccupied gait of a woman returning home late at night, who hastens to get off the street. One has seen them that way many times; minding their own business with an added intentness, for they know they run a greater risk of being accosted then that during the daylight hours.

She found herself alone on a gloomy nocturnal strip of sidewalk in front of a long rambling two-story structure, hybrid, half commercial and half living quarters. The ground floor was a succession of unlighted store-fronts, the upper a long row of windows. The white shape of a milk bottle stood on the sill of one of these. One was lighted, but with the shade drawn. Not the one with the milk bottle.

Between two of the store-fronts, recessed, almost secretive in its inconspicuousness, there was a single-panel door, with a waffle-pattern of multiple small panes set into it. They could be detected because there was a dim hall-light somewhere beyond them, doing its best to overcome the darkness.

She went over to it and tried it, and it swung out without any demur, it had no lock, was simply a closure for appearances' sake. Inside there was a rusted radiator, and a cement stair going up, and at the side of this, just as it began, a row of letter boxes and push-buttons. His name was on the third she scanned, but not in its own right, superimposed on the card of the previous tenant, left behind. He had pencil-scratched the name off, and then put in his own underneath. "S. Georgesson." He didn't print very well.

He didn't do anything very well, except smash up people's lives. He did that very well, he was an expert.

She went on up the stairs and followed the hall. It was a jerry-built, makeshift sort of a place. During the war shortage they must have taken the attic or storage-space part of the stores below and rigged it up into these flats.

What a place to live, she thought dimly.

What a place to die, she thought remorselessly.

She could see the thin line the light made under his door. She knocked, and then she knocked again, softly like the first time. He had his radio on in there. She could hear that quite distinctly through the door.

She raised her hand and smoothed back her hair, while waiting. You smoothed your hair—if it needed it—just before you were going to see anyone, or anyone was going to see you. That was why she did it now.

They said you were frightened at a time like this. They said you were keyed-up to an ungovernable pitch. They said you were blinded by fuming emotion.

They said. What did they know? She felt nothing. Neither fear nor excitement nor blind anger. Only a dull, aching determination all over.

He didn't hear, or he wasn't coming to open. She tried the knob, and this door too, like the one below, was unlocked, it gave inward. Why shouldn't it be, she reasoned, what did he have to fear from others? They didn't take from him, he took from them.

She closed it behind her, to keep this just between the two of them.

He didn't meet her eyes. The room was reeking with his presence, but it was a double arrangement, bed- and living-quarters, and he must be in the one just beyond, must have just stepped in as she arrived outside. She could see offside light coming through the opening.

The coat and hat he'd worn in the car with her tonight were slung over a chair, the coat broadside across its seat, the hat atop that. A cigarette that he'd incompletely extinguished a few short moments ago was in a glass tray, stubbornly smouldering away. The drink that he'd started, then left, and was coming back to finish any second now—the drink with which he was celebrating tonight's successful enterprise—stood there on the edge of the table. The white block of its still-unmelted ice cube peered through the side of the glass, through the straw-colored whiskey it floated in.

The sight of it brought back a furnished room in New York. He took his drinks weak; he liked them strong, but he took them weak when it was his own whiskey he was using. "There's always another one coming up," he used to say to her.

There wasn't now. This was his last drink. (You should have made it stronger, she thought to herself wryly.)

Some sort of gritty noise was bothering her. A pulsation, a discord of some sort. It was meant for music, but no music could have reached her as music, as she was now. The hypertension of her senses filtered it into a sound somewhat like a scrubbing-brush being passed over a sheet of ribbed tin. Or maybe, it occurred to her, it was on the inside of her, and not outside anywhere.

No, there it was. He had a small battery-portable standing against the side wall. She went over to it.

"*Che gelida mannina—*" some far-off voice was singing; she didn't know what that meant. She only knew that this was no love-scene, this was a death-scene.

Her hand gave a brutal little wrench, like wringing the neck of a chicken, and there was a stupor of silence in his two shoddy rooms. This one out here, and that one in there.

Now he'd step out to see who had done that.

She turned to face the opening. She raised her handbag frontally to her chest. She undid it, and took out the gun, and fitted her hand around it, the way her hand was supposed to go. Without flurry, without a tremor, every move in perfect coordination.

She sighted the gun toward the opening.

"Steve," she said to him, at no more than room-to-room conversational pitch in the utter stillness. "Come out here a second. I want to see you."

No fear, no love, no hate, no anything at all.

He didn't come. Had he seen her in a mirror? Had he guessed? Was he that much of a coward, cringing away even from a woman?

The fractured cigarette continued to unravel into smoke-skeins. The ice cube continued to peer through the highball glass, foursquare and uneroded.

She went toward the opening.

"Steve," she rasped. "Your wife is here. Here to see you."

He didn't stir, he didn't answer.

She made the turn of the doorway, gun wheeling before her like some sort of foreshortened steering-gear. The second room was not parallel to the first; it was over at a right angle to it. It was very small, just an alcove for sleeping in. It had a bulb up above, as though a luminous blister had formed on the calcimined surface of the ceiling. There was also a lamp beside the iron cot, and that was lit as well, but it was upside-down. It was standing on its head on the floor, its extension-wire grotesquely looped in air.

She'd caught him in the act of getting ready for bed. His shirt was lying over the foot of the cot. That was all he'd taken off. And now he was trying to hide from her, down on the floor somewhere, below cot-level, on the far side of it. His hand peered over it—he'd forgotten that it showed—clutching at the bedding, pulling it into long, puckered lines. And the top of his head showed, burrowed against the cot—just a glimpse of it—bowed in attempt at concealment, but not inclined deeply enough. And then, just on the other side of that, though his second hand *didn't* show, more of those puckered wrinkles ran over the edge of the bedding at one place, as though it were down below there somewhere out of sight, but hanging on for dear life.

And when she looked at the floor, out beyond the far side of the cot, she could glimpse the lower part of one leg, extended out behind him in a long, lazy sprawl. The other one didn't show, must have been drawn up closer under his body.

"Get up," she sneered. "At least I thought I hated a man. Now I don't know what you are." She passed around the foot of the cot, and his back came into view. He didn't move, but every line of his body expressed the arrested impulse to get away.

Her handbag sprang open and she pulled something out, pitched it at him. "Here's the five dollars you gave me. Remember?" It fell between his shoulderblades, and lay there lengthwise across his spine, caught in the sharp upcurve his back made, oddly like a label or tag loosely pasted across him.

"You love money so," she said scathingly. "Now here's the interest. Turn around and get it."

She'd fired before she'd known she was going to. As though there were some cue in the words for the gun to take of its own accord, without waiting for her. The crash surprised her, she could feel it go up her whole arm, as though someone had stingingly slapped her wristbone, and the fiery spittle that gleamed for a moment at the muzzle made her blink her eyes and swerve her head aside involuntarily.

He didn't move. Even the five-dollar bill didn't flutter off him. There was a curious low moaning sound from the tubular rod forming the head of the cot, as when a vibration is slowly dimming, and there was a black pockmark in the plaster of the wall, sharply off to one side of it, that seemed to leap up into being for the first time only as her eyes discovered it.

Her hand was at his shoulder now, while her mind was trying to say "I didn't—I didn't—" He turned over lazily, and ebbed down to the floor, in a way that was almost playful, as if she had been threatening to tickle him and he was trying to avoid it.

Indolent dalliance, his attitude seemed to express. There was even a sort of gashed grin across his mouth.

His eyes seemed to be fixed on her, watching her, with that same detached mockery they'd always shown toward her. As if to say, "What are you going to do now?"

You could hardly tell anything was the matter. There was only a little dark streak by the outside corner of one eye, like a patch of patent leather used instead of court plaster; as though he'd hurt himself there and then covered it over. And where that side of his head had come to rest against the lateral thickness of the bedding, there was a peculiar sworled stain, its outer layers of a lighter discoloration than its core.

Somebody screamed in the confined little room. Not shrilly, but with a guttural wrench, almost like the bark of a terrified dog. It must have been she, for there was no one in there to scream but her. Her vocal chords hurt, as though they had been strained asunder.

"Oh, God!" she sobbed in an undertone. "I didn't need to come—"

She cowered away from him, step by faltering step. It wasn't that little glistening streak, that daub of tar, nor yet the way he lay there, relaxed and languid, as if they had had such fun he was exhausted, and it was too much trouble to get up off his back and see her out. It was his eyes that knifed her with fear, over and over, until panic had welled up in her, as though gushing through a sieve. The way they seemed fixed on her, the way they seemed to follow her back-ward, step by step. She went over a little to one side, and that didn't get her away from them. She went over a little to the other, and that didn't get her away from them either. Contemptuous, patronizing, mocking, to the end; with no real tenderness in them for her, ever. He looked on her in death as he'd looked on her in life.

She could almost hear the drawled words that went with that look. "Where d'you think you're going now? What's your hurry? Come back here, you!"

Her mind screamed back: "Away from here—! Out of here—! Before somebody comes—! Before anybody sees me!"

She turned and fled through the opening, and beat her way through the outside room, flailing with her arms, as though it were an endless treadmill going the other way, trying to carry her back in to him, instead of a space of a brief few yards.

She got to the door and collided against it. But then, after the first impact, after her body was stopped against it, instead of stilling, it kept on thumping, and kept on thumping, as though there were doz-ens of her hurling themselves against it in an endless succession.

Wood shouldn't knock so, wood shouldn't bang so— Her hands flew up to her ears and clutched them. She was going mad.

The blows didn't space themselves and wait between. They were aggressive, demanding, continuous. They were already angered, and they were feeding on their own anger with every second's added delay. They drowned out, in her own ears, her second, smothered scream of anguish. A scream that held more real fear in it than even the first one had, in the other room just now. Fear, not of the su-pernatural now, but of the personal; a fear more immediate, a fear more strong. Agonizing fear, trapped fear such as she'd never known existed before. *The fear of losing the thing you love.* The greatest fear there is.

For the voice that riddled the door, that welled through, bated but flinty with stern impatience, was Bill's.

Her heart knew it before the sound came, and then her ears knew it right as it came, and then its words told her after they had come.

"Patrice! Open. Open this door. Patrice! Do you hear me? I knew I'd find you here. Open this door and let me in, or I'll break it down!"

A moment too late she thought of the lock, and just a moment in time he thought of it too. That it had been unlocked the whole while, just as she had found it to be earlier. She crushed herself flat against it, with a whimper of despair, just too late, just as the knob gave its turn and the door-seam started to widen.

"No!" she ordered breathlessly. "No!" She tried to hold it closed with the full weight of her whole palpitating body.

She could almost feel the currents of his straining breath beating into her face. "Patrice, you've—got—to—let—me—in—there!"

And between each word she lost ground, her heels scraped futilely backward over the surface of the floor.

He could see her now, and she could see him, through the fluctuating gap their opposing pressures made, widening a little, then narrowing again, then widening more than ever. His eyes, so close to her own, were a terrible accusation, far worse than that dead man's had been inside. Don't look at me, don't look at me! she implored them despairingly in her mind. Oh, turn away from me, for I can't bear you!

Back she went, steadily and irresistibly, and still she tried to bar him, to the last, after his arm was in and his shoulder, straining her whole body insensately against him, flattening her hands till they showed bloodless against the door.

Then he gave one final heave to end the unequal contest, and she was swept back along the whole curved arc of the door's path, like a leaf or a piece of limp rag that got caught in the way. And he was in, and he was standing there next to her, his chest rising and falling a little with quickened breath.

"No, Bill, no!" she kept pleading mechanically, even after the cause of her plea was lost. "Don't come in. Not if you love me. Stay out."

"What're you doing here?" he said tersely. "What brought you?"

"I want you to love me," was all she could whimper, like a distracted child. "Don't come in. I want you to love me."

He took her suddenly, and shook her fiercely by the shoulder for a moment. "I saw you. What did you come here to do? What did you come here for, at this hour?" He released her again. "What's this?" He picked up the gun, which she had completely lost track of until now in her turmoil. It must have fallen, or she must have flung it to the floor, in her flight from the inner room.

"Did you bring it with you?" He came back toward her again. "Patrice, *answer* me!" he said with a flinty ferocity she hadn't known he possessed. "What did you come here for?"

Her voice kept backing and filling in her throat, as if unable to rise to the top. At last it overflowed. "To—to—to kill him." She toppled suddenly against him, and his arm had to go around her, tight and firm, to keep her up.

Her hands tried to crawl up his lapels, up his shirt-front, toward his face, like wriggling white beggars pleading for alms.

A swipe of his hand and they were down again.

"And did you?"

"Somebody—did. Somebody—has already. In there. He's dead." She shuddered and hid her face against him. There is a point beyond which you can't be alone any more. You have to have someone to cling to. You have to have someone to hold you, even if he is to reject you again in a moment of two and you know it.

Suddenly his arm dropped and he'd left her. It was terrible to be alone, even just for that minute. She wondered how she'd stood it all these months, all these years.

Life was such a crazy thing, life was such a freak. A man was dead. A love was blasted into nothingness. But a cigarette still sent up smoke in a dish. And an ice cube still hovered unmelted in a highball glass. The things you wanted to last, they didn't; the things it didn't matter about, they hung on forever.

Then he reappeared from the other room, stood in the opening looking at her again. Looking at her in such a funny way. A little too long, a little too silent—she couldn't quite make out what it was she didn't like about it, but she didn't like him to look at her that way. Others, it didn't matter. But not him.

Then he raised the gun, which he was still holding, and put it near his nose.

She saw his head give a grim nod.

"No. No. I didn't. Oh, please believe me—"

"It's just been fired," he said quietly.

There was something rueful about the expression of his eyes now, as if they were trying to say to her: Why don't you want to tell me? Why don't you get it out of the way by telling me, and then I'll understand. He didn't say that, but his eyes seemed to.

"No, I didn't. I fired it at him, but I didn't hit him."

"All right," he said quietly, with just that trace of weariness you show when you don't believe a thing, but try to gloss it over to spare someone.

Suddenly he'd thrust it into the side-pocket of his coat, as though it were no longer important, as though it were a past detail, as though there were things of far greater moment to be attended to now. He buttoned his coat determinedly, strode back to her; his movements had a sort of lithe intensity to them now that they'd lacked before.

An impetus, a drive.

He swept a sheltering arm around her again. (That sanctuary that she'd been trying to find all her life long. And only had now, too late.) But this time in hurried propulsion toward the door, and not just in support. "Get out of here, quick," he ordered grimly. "Get down to the street again fast as you can."

He was pulling her along, hurrying her with him, within the curve of his protective arm. "Come on. You can't be found here. You must have been out of your mind to come here like this!"

"I was," she sobbed. "I am."

She was struggling against him a little now, trying to keep herself from the door. She pried herself away from him suddenly, and stood back, facing him. Her hands kept rebuffing his arms each time they tried to reclaim her.

"No, wait. There's something you've got to hear first. Something you've got to know. I tried to keep you out, but now you're in here with me. I've come this far; I won't go any further." And then she added, "The way I was."

He reached out and shook her violently, in his exasperation. As if to get some sense into her. "Not now! Can't you understand? There's a man dead in the next room. Don't you know what it means if you're found here? Any minute somebody's apt to stick his head into this place—"

"Oh, you fool," she cried out to him piteously. "You're the one who doesn't understand. The damage has been done already. Can't *you* see that? I *have* been found here!" And she murmured half-audibly, "By the only one who matters to me. What's there to run away and hide from now?" She brushed the back of her hand wearily across her eyes. "Let them come. Bring them on now."

"If you won't think of yourself," he urged her savagely, "think of Mother. I thought you loved her, I thought she meant something to you. Don't you know what a thing like this will do to her? What are you trying to do, kill her?"

"Somebody used that argument before," she told him vaguely. "I can't remember who it was, or where it was."

He'd opened the door cautiously and looked out. Narrowed it again, came back to her. "No sign of anyone. I can't understand how that shot wasn't heard. I don't think these adjoining rooms are occupied."

She wouldn't budge. "No, this is the time, and this is the place. I've waited too long to tell you. I won't go a step further, I won't cross that door-sill—"

He clenched his jaw. "I'll pick you up and carry you out of here bodily, if I have to! Are you going to listen to me? Are you going to come to your senses?"

"Bill, I'm not entitled to your protection. I'm not—"

His hand suddenly clamped itself to her mouth, sealing it. He heaved her clear of the floor, held her cradled in his arms. Her eyes strained upward at him in muted helplessness, above his restraining hand.

Then they dropped closed. She didn't struggle against him.

He carried her that way out the door, and along the hall, and down those stairs she'd climbed so differently a little while ago. Just within the street-entrance he set her down upon her feet again.

"Stand here a minute, while I look out." He could tell by her passiveness now that her recalcitrance had ended.

He withdrew his head. "No one out there. You left the car around the corner, didn't you?" She didn't have time to wonder how he knew that. "Walk along close to me, I'm going to take you back to it."

She took his arm within a doublecoil of her own two, and clinging to him like that, they came out unobtrusively and hurried along together close in beside the building-front, where the shadow was deepest.

It seemed a long distance. No one saw them; better still, no one was there to see them. Once a cat scurried out of a basement-vent up ahead of them. She crushed herself tighter against him for a moment, but no sound escaped her. They went on, after the brief recoil.

They rounded the corner, and the car was there, only its own length back away from the corner.

They crossed on a swift diagonal to it, and he unlatched the door for her and armed her in. Then suddenly the door was closed again, between them, and he'd stayed on the outside.

"Here are the keys. Now take it home and—"

"No," she whispered fiercely. "No! Not without you! Where are you going? What are you going to do?"

"Don't you understand? I'm trying to keep you out of it. I'm going back up there again. I have to. To make sure there's nothing there linking you. You've got to help me. Patrice, what was he doing to you? I don't want to know why, there isn't time for that now, I only want to know *what*."

"Money," she said laconically.

She saw his clenched hand tighten on the rim of the door, until it seemed to be trying to cave it in. "How'd you give it to him, cash or check?"

"A check," she said fearfully. "Only once, about a month ago."

He was speaking more tautly now. "You destroyed it when it came back, of c—?"

"I never got it back. He purposely kept it out. He must still have it someplace."

She could tell by the way he stiffened and slowly breathed in, he was more frightened by that than he had been by anything else she had told him so far. "My God," he said batedly. "I've got to get that back, if it takes all night." He lowered his head again, leaned it in toward her. "What else? Any letters?"

"None. I never wrote him a line in my life. There's a five-dollar bill lying in there, by him, but I don't want it."

"I'd better pick it up anyway. Nothing else? You're sure? Now, think, Patrice. Think hard."

"Wait; that night at the dance—he seemed to have my telephone number. Ours. Jotted down in a little black notebook he carries around with him." She hesitated. "And one other thing."

"What? Don't be afraid; tell me. What?"

"Bill—he made me marry him tonight. Out at Hastings."

This time he brought his hand up, let it pound back on the door-rim like a mallet. "I'm glad he's—" he said balefully. He didn't finish it. "Did you sign your own name?"

"The family's. I had to. That was the whole purpose of it. The justice is mailing the certificate in to him, here at this address, in a day or two."

"There's still time enough to take care of that, then. I can drive out to-morrow and scotch it out there, at that end. Money works wonders."

Suddenly he seemed to have made up his mind what he intended doing. "Go home, Patrice," he ordered. "Go back to the house, Patrice."

She clung fearfully to his arm. "No— What are you going to do?"

"I'm going back up there. I have to."

She tried to hold him back. "No! Bill, no! Someone may come along. They'll find *you* there. Bill," she pleaded, "for *me*—don't go back up there again."

"Don't you understand, Patrice? Your name has to stay out of it. There's a man lying dead upstairs in that room. They mustn't find anything linking you to him. You never knew him, you never saw him. I have to get hold of those things—that check, that notebook. I have to get rid of them. Better still, if I could only move him out of there, leave him somewhere else, at a distance from here, he mightn't be identified so readily. He might never be identified at all. He's not from town here, there isn't anybody likely to inquire in case of his sudden disappearance. He came and he went again; bird of passage. If he's found in the room there, it'll be at once established who he is, and then that'll bring out of lot of other things."

She saw him glance speculatively along the length of the car, as if measuring its possibilities as a casket.

"I'll help you, Bill," she said with sudden decision. "I'll help you—do whatever you want to do." And then, as he looked at her dubiously, "Let me, Bill. Let me. It's a small way of—making amends for being the cause of the whole problem."

"All right," he said. "I can't do it without the car, anyway. I need that." He crowded in beside her. "Give me the wheel a minute. I'll show you what I want you to do."

He drove the car only a yard or two forward, stopped it again. It now stood so that only the hood projected beyond the corner building-line, the rest of it still remained sheltered behind that. The driver's seat was exactly aligned with the row of store-fronts around the turn.

"Look down that way, from where you sit," he instructed her. "Can you see that particular doorway from here?"

"No. I can see about where it is, though."

"That's what I mean. I'll stand in it, light up a cigarette. When you see that, bring the car on around in front of it. Until then, stay back here where you are. If you see anything else, if you see something go wrong, don't stay here. Drive straight out and away, without making the turn. Drive for home."

"No," she thought stubbornly, "no, I won't. I won't run off and leave you here." But she didn't tell him so.

He'd gotten out again, was standing there facing her, looking cautiously around on all sides of them, without turning his head too much, just holding his body still, glancing over his shoulders, first on this side, then on that.

"All right," he said finally. "It's all right now. I guess I can go now."

He touched the back of her hand consolingly for a minute.

"Don't be frightened, Patrice. Maybe we'll be lucky, at that. We're such novices at anything like this."

"Maybe we'll be lucky," she echoed, abysmally frightened.

She watched him turn and walk away from the car.

He walked as he always walked, that was one nice thing about him. He didn't slink or cringe. She wondered why that should have mattered to her, at such a time as this. But it made what he, what they, were about to attempt to do a little less horrible, somehow.

He'd turned and he'd gone inside the building where the man was lying dead.

41

IT SEEMED LIKE an eternity that he'd been up there. She'd never known time could be so long.

That cat came back again, the one that had frightened her before, and she watched its slow, cautious circuitous return to the place from which they had routed it. She could see it while it was still out in the roadway, but then as it closed in toward the building-line, the deeper shading swallowed it.

You can kill a rat, she found herself addressing it enviously in her mind, and they praise you for it. And your kind of rat only bites, they don't suck blood.

Something glinted there, then was gone again.

It was surprising how clearly she could see the match-flame. She hadn't expected to be able to. It was small, but extremely vivid for a moment. Like a luminous yellow butterfly held pinned for a second at full wing-spread against a black velvet backdrop, then allowed to escape again.

She promptly bore down on the starter, trundled around the corner, and brought the car down to him with facile stealth. No more than a soft whirr and sibilance of its tires.

He'd turned and gone in again before she'd reached him. The cigarette that he'd used to attract her lay there already cast down.

She didn't know where he wanted to—wanted to put what he was bringing out. Front or back. She reached out and opened the rear door on his side, left it that way, ready and waiting for him.

Then she stared straight ahead through the windshield, with a curious sort of rigidity, as though she were unable to move her neck.

She heard the building-door open, and still couldn't turn her neck. She strained, tugged at it, but it was locked in some sort of rigor of mortal terror, wouldn't carry her head around that way.

She heard a slow, weighted tread on the gritty sidewalk—his—and accompanying it a softer sound, a sort of scrape, as when two shoes are turned over on their softer topsides, or simply on their sides, and trail along that way, without full weight to press them down.

Suddenly his voice breathed urgently (almost in her ear, it seemed), "The front door. The front."

She couldn't turn her head. But she could move her arms at least. She extended them without looking, broke the latch open for him. She could hear her own breath singing in her throat, like the sound a teakettle-spout makes when it is simmering toward a catastrophic overflow.

Someone settled on the seat beside her. Just the way anyone does, with the same crunchy strain on the leather. He touched her side, he nudged her here and there.

The muscular block shattered, and her head swung around.

She was looking into his face. Not Bill's, not Bill's. The mocking eyes wide open in the dark. *His* head had had to swing toward her, just as hers had toward him—it couldn't have remained inert!—to make the grisly face-to-face confrontation complete. Even in death he wouldn't let her alone.

A strangled scream wrenched at her windpipe.

"Now, none of that," the voice of Bill said, from just on the other side of him. "Get in back. I want the wheel. I want him next to me."

The sound of his voice had a steadying effect on her. "I didn't mean it," she murmured blurredly. She got out, got in again, holding onto the car for support in the brief transit between the two places. She didn't know how she did it, but she did.

He must have known what she was going through, though he didn't look at her.

"I told you to go home," he reminded her quietly.

"I'm all right," she said. "I'm all right. Go ahead." It came out tinny, like something on a worn-out disk played by a feathered needle.

The door cracked shut, and they were in motion.

Bill kept the car down to a laggard crawl the first few moments, using only one hand to the wheel. She saw him reach over with the other and tilt down the hat-brim low over the face beside him.

He found time for a word of encouragement to her, conscious of her there behind him, though still he didn't turn to glance at her.

"Can you hear me?"

"Yes."

"Try not to be frightened. Try not to think of it. We've been lucky so far. The check and the notebook were on him. Either we make it or we don't. Look at it that way. It's the only way. You're helping me, too, that way. See, if you're too tense, then I'm too tense too. You react on me."

"I'm all right," she said with that same mechanical bleat as before. "I'll be quiet. I'll be controlled. Go ahead."

After that, they didn't talk. How could you, on such a ride?

She kept her eyes away. She'd look out the side as long as she

could; then when that became a strain, she'd look up at the car
ceiling for a moment to rest. Or down at the floor directly before her.
Anywhere but straight ahead, to where those two heads (she knew)
must be lightly quivering in synchronization to the same vibration.

She tried to do what he'd told her. She tried not to think of it.
"We're coming home from a dance," she said to herself. "He's bringing me home from the Country Club, that's all. I'm wearing that
black net with the gold disks. Look, see? I'm wearing that black
dress with the gold disks. We had words, so I'm—I'm sitting in the
back, and he's sitting alone up front."

Her forehead was a little cold and damp. She wiped it off.

"He's bringing me home from the movies," she said to herself. "We
saw—we saw—we saw—" Another of those blocks, this time of
the imagination, occurred; it wouldn't come. "We saw—we saw—
we saw—"

Suddenly she'd said to him, aloud, "What was the name of that
picture we just now came away from?"

"Good," he answered instantly. "That's it. That's a good idea. I'll
give you one. Keep going over it." It took him a moment to get one
himself. "Mark Stevens in *I Wonder Who's Kissing Her Now,*" he
said suddenly. They'd seen that together back in the sunlight, a thousand years ago (last Thursday). "Start in at the beginning, and run
through it. If you get stuck, I'll help you out."

She was breathing laboredly, and her forehead kept getting damp
again all the time. "He wrote songs," she said to herself, "and he
took his foster-sister to a—to a variety-show, and he heard one of
them sung from the stage—"

The car made a turn, and the two heads up front swung together,
one almost landed on the other's shoulder. Somebody pried them
apart.

She hurriedly squeezed her eyes shut. "When—when did the title-
song come into it?" she faltered. "Was that the opening number, they
heard from the gallery?"

He'd halted for a light, and a taxicab had halted beside him,
wheel-cap to wheel-cap. "No, that was—" He looked at the taxicab.
"That was—" He looked at the taxicab again, the way you look
vaguely at some external object when you're trying to remember
something that has nothing to do with it. "That was 'Hello, Ma
Baby.' Cakewalk number, don't you remember? The title-song

didn't come until the end. He couldn't get words for it, don't you remember?"

The light had changed. The taxicab had slipped on ahead, quicker to resume motion. She crushed the back of her hand against her mouth, sank her teeth into it. "I can't," she sighed to herself. "I can't." She wanted to scream to him, "Oh, open the door! Let me out! I'm not brave! I thought I could, but I can't—I don't care, only let me get out of here, now, right where we are!"

Panic, they called this panic.

She bit deeper into her own skin, and the hot frenzied gush subsided.

He was going a little faster now. But not too fast, not fast enough to attract suspicion or catch any roving eye. They were in the outskirts now, running along the turnpike that breasted the sunken railroad right-of-way. You were supposed to go a little faster along there.

It took her several moments to realize that the chief hazard was over. That they were already out of Caulfield, clear of it; or at least clear of its built-up heart. Nothing had happened. No untoward event. They hadn't grazed any other car. No policeman had come near them, to question them over some infraction, to look into the car. All those things that she had dreaded so, had failed to materialize. It had been a ride completely without incident. The two of them might have been alone in the car, for all the risk they'd run— outwardly. But inwardly—

She felt all shrivelled-up inside, and old; as though there were permanent wrinkles on her heart.

"He wasn't the only one that died tonight," she thought. "I died too, somewhere along the way, in this car. So it didn't work, it was all for nothing. Better to have stayed back there, still alive, and taken the blame and the punishment."

They were out in open country now. The last cardboard-box factory, kept at a civic-minded distance away from the city limits, the last disused-brewery stack, even those had long slipped by. The embankment that carried the turnpike had started a very gradual rise, the broad swath of railroad-tracks, by illusory contrast, seemed to depress still further. The neat, clean-cut concrete-facing that had been given the embankment further in toward town didn't extend this far out; here there was just a natural slope, extremely steep, but with weeds and bushes clinging to it.

He'd stopped all of a sudden, for no apparent reason. Run the two outside wheels off the road on the railroad's side, and stopped there. That was all the space that was allowed, just two wheels of the car; even that was an extremely precarious position to take. The down-slope began almost outside the car door.

"Why here?" she whispered.

He pointed. "Listen. Hear it?" It was a sound like the cracking of nuts. Like a vast layer of nuts, all rolling around and being cracked and shelled.

"I'd like to get him out of town," he said. He got out, and scrambled down the slope a way, until she could only see him from the waist up, and stood looking down. Then he picked up something— a stone, maybe, or something—and she saw him throw. Then he turned his head a little, and seemed to be listening.

Finally he fought his way back up to her again, digging his feet in sideways to gain leverage.

"It's a slow freight," he said. "Outbound. It's on the inside track, I mean the one right under us here. I could see a lantern go by on the roof of one of the cars. It's unearthly long—I think they're empties—and it's going very slow, almost at a crawl. I threw a stone, and I heard it hit one of the roofs."

She had already guessed, and could feel her skin crawling.

He was bending over the form on the front seat, going through its pockets. He ripped something out of the inside coat-pocket. A label or something.

"They don't always get right of way like the fast passengers do. It may have to stop for that big turnpike crossing not far up, you know the one I mean. The locomotive must be just about reaching it by now—"

She'd fought down her repulsion; she'd made up her mind once more, though this was going to be even worse than back there at the doorway. "Shall I— Do you want me to—?" And she got ready to get out with him.

"No," he said, "no. Just stay in it and watch the road. The slope is so steep, that when you get down below a certain point with— anything—it will plunge down the rest of the way by itself. It's been sheared off at the bottom, it's a sheer drop."

He'd swung the front door out as far as it would go, now.

"How's the road?" he asked.

She looked back first, all along it. Then forward. The way it rose ahead made it even easier to sight along.

"Empty," she said. "There's not a moving light on it anywhere."

He dipped down, did something with his arm, and then the two heads and the two pairs of shoulders rose together. A minute later the front seat was empty.

She turned away and looked at the road, looked at the road for all she was worth.

"I'll never be able to sit on the front seat of this car again," it occurred to her. "They'll wonder why, but I'll always balk, I'll always think of what was there tonight."

He had a hard time getting him down the slope, he had to be a brake on the two of them at once, and the weight was double. Once the two of them went down momentarily, in a stumble, and her heart shot up into her throat, as though there were a pulley, a counterweight, working between them and it.

Then he regained his balance again.

Then when she could only see him from the waist up, he bent over, as if laying something down before him, and when he'd straightened up again, he was alone, she could only see him by himself.

Then he just stood there waiting.

It was a gamble, a wild guess. A last car, a carboose, could have suddenly come along, and—no more train to carry their freight away. Just trackbed left below, to reveal what lay on it as soon as it got light.

But he'd guessed right. The sound of cracking nuts thinned, began to die out. A sort of rippling wooden shudder, starting way up ahead, ran past them and to the rear. Then a second one. Then silence.

He dipped again.

Her hands flew up to her ears, but she was too late. The sound beat her to it.

It was a sick, hollow thud. Like when a heavy sack is dropped. Only, a sack bursts from such a drop. This didn't.

She put her head down low over her lap, and held her hands pressed to her eyes.

When she looked up again, he was standing there beside her. He looked like a man who has himself in hand, but isn't sure that he isn't going to be sick before long.

"Stayed on," he said. "Caught on that catwalk, or whatever it is, that runs down the middle of each roof. I could see him even in the dark. But his hat didn't. That came off and went over."

She wanted to scream: "Don't! Don't *tell* me! Let me not know! I know too much already!" But she didn't. And by that time it was over with, anyway.

He got in again and took the wheel, without waiting for the train to recommence its run.

"It'll go on again," he said. "It has to. It was already on its way once. It won't just stand there the rest of the night."

He ran the car back onto the rim of the road again, and then he brought it around in a U-turn, facing back to Caulfield. And still nothing came along, nothing passed them. On no other night could this road have been so empty.

He let their headlight beams shoot out ahead of them now.

"Do you want to come up here and sit with me?" he asked her quietly.

"No!" she said in a choked voice. "I couldn't! Not on *that* seat."

He seemed to understand. "I just didn't want you to be all alone," he said compassionately.

"I'll be all alone from now on, anyway, no matter where I sit," she murmured. "And so will you. We'll both be all alone, even together."

42

SHE HEARD THE brakes go on, and felt the motion of the car stop. He got out and got into the back next to her. They stayed just the way they were for several long moments. She with her face pressed against the bosom of his shirt, buried against him as if trying to hide it from the night and all that had happened in the night. He with one hand to the back of her head, holding it there, supporting it.

They didn't move nor speak at first.

Now I have to tell him, she kept thinking with dread. Now the time is here. And how shall I be able to?

She raised her head at last, and opened her eyes. He'd stopped around the corner from their own house. (*His* own. How could it ever be hers again? How could she ever go in there, after what had happened tonight?) He'd stopped around the corner, out of sight of it, and not right at the door. He was giving her the chance to tell him; that must be why he had done it.

He took out a cigarette, and lit it for her in his mouth, and offered it to her inquiringly. She shook her head. So then he threw it out the side of the car.

His mouth was so close to hers, she could smell the aroma of the tobacco freshly on his breath. It'll never be this close again, she thought, never; not after I'm done with what I have to tell him now.

"Bill," she whispered.

It was too weak, too pleading. That feeble a voice would never carry her through. And it had such rocky words ahead of it.

"Yes, Patrice?" he answered quietly.

"Don't call me that." She turned toward him with desperate urgency, forcing her voice to be steady. "Bill there's something you've got to know. I don't know where to begin it, I don't know how— But, oh, you've got to listen, if you've never listened to me before!"

"Sh, Patrice," he said soothingly. "Sh, Patrice." As though she were a fretful child. And his hand gently stroked her hair; downward, and then downward again, and still downward.

She moaned, almost as though she were in pain. "No—don't—don't—don't."

"I know," he said almost absently. "I know what you're trying so hard, so brokenheartedly, to tell me. That you're not Patrice. That you're not Hugh's wife. Isn't that it?"

She sought his eyes, and he was gazing into the distance, through the windshield and out ahead of the car. There was something almost abstract about his look.

"I know that already. I've always known it. I think I've known it ever since the first few weeks you got here."

The side of his face came gently to rest against her head, and stayed there, in a sort of implicit caress.

"So you don't have to try so hard, Patrice. Don't break your heart over it. There isn't anything to tell."

She gave an exhausted sob. Shuddered a little with her own frustration. "Even the one last chance to redeem myself, you've taken away from me," she murmured hopelessly. "Even that little."

"You don't have to redeem yourself, Patrice."

"Every time you call me that, it's a lie. I can't go back to that house with you. I can't go in there ever again. It's too late now—two years too late, two years—but at least let me tell it to you. Oh God, let me get it out! Patrice Hazzard was killed on the train, right along with your brother. I was deserted by a man named—"

Again he placed his hand over her mouth, as he had at Georgesson's place. But more gently than he had then.

"I don't want to know," he told her. "I don't want to hear. Can't you understand, Patrice?" Then took his hand away, but now she was silent, for that was the way he wanted her to be. And that was the easier way to be. "*Won't* you understand how I feel?" He glanced about for an instant, this way and that, as if helplessly in search of some means of convincing her. Some means that wasn't there at hand. Then back to her again, to try once more; speaking low and from the heart.

"What difference does it make if there once was another Patrice, another Patrice than you, a girl I never knew, some other place and some other time? Suppose there *were* two? There are a thousand Marys, a thousand Janes; but each man that loves Mary, he loves only his Mary, and for him there are no others in the whole wide world. And that's with me too. A girl named Patrice came into my life one day. And that's the only Patrice there is for me in the world. I don't love the name, I love the girl. What kind of love do you think I have, anyway? That if she got the name from a clergyman, it's on; but if she helped herself to it, it's off?"

"But she *stole* the name, took it away from the dead. And she lay in someone else's arms first, and then came into your house with her child—"

"No, she didn't; no," he contradicted her with tender stubbornness. "You still don't see, you still won't see; because you're not the man who loves you. She couldn't have; because she *wasn't*, until I met her. She only began then, she only starts from then. She only came into existence, as my eyes first took her in, as my love first started in to start. Before then there wasn't any she. My love began her, and when my love ends, she ends with it. She has to, because she *is* my love. Before then, there was a blank. A vacant space. That's the way with any love. It can't go back before itself.

"And it's you I love. The you I made for myself. The you I hold in my arms right now in this car. The you I kiss like this, right now . . . right now . . . and now.

"Not a name on a birth-certificate. Not a name on a Paris wedding-license. Not a bunch of dead bones taken out of a railroad-car and buried somewhere by the tracks.

"The name of my love is Patrice to me. My love doesn't know any other name, my love doesn't want any."

He swept her close to him, this time with such quivering violence that she was almost stunned. And as his lips found hers, between each pledge he told her:

"You are Patrice. You'll always be Patrice. You'll *only* be Patrice. I give you that name. Keep it for me, forever."

They lay that way for a long while; one now, wholly one. Made one by love; made one by blood and violence.

Presently she murmured, "And you knew, and you never—?"

"Not right away, not all in a flash. Life never goes that way. It was a slow thing, gradual. I think I first suspected inside of a week or two after you got here. I don't know when I was first sure. I think that day I bought the fountain pen."

"You must have hated me that day."

"I didn't hate you that day. I hated myself, for stooping to such a trick. (And yet I couldn't have kept from doing it, I couldn't have, no matter how I tried!) And do you know what I got from it? Only fear. Instead of *you* being the frightened one, I was. I was afraid that you'd take fright from it, and that I'd lose you. I knew *I'd* never be the one to expose you; I was too afraid I'd lose you that way. A thousand times I wanted to tell you, 'I know; I know all about it,' and I was afraid you'd take flight and I'd lose you. The secret wasn't heavy on you; it was me it weighted down."

"But in the beginning. How is it you didn't say anything in the very beginning? Surely you didn't condone it from the very start?"

"No; no, I didn't. My first reaction was resentment, enmity; about what you'd expect. But for one thing, I wasn't sure enough. And the lives of too many others were involved. Mainly there was Mother. I couldn't risk doing that to her. Right after she'd lost Hugh. For all I knew it might have killed her. And even just to implant seeds of suspicion, that would have been just as bad, that would have wrecked her happiness. Then too, I wanted to see what the object was, the game. I thought if I gave you enough rope—Well, I gave you rope and rope, and there was no game. You were just you. Every day it became a little harder to be on guard against you. Every day it became a little easier to look at you, and think of you, and like you. Then that night of the will—"

"You knew what you did, and yet you let them go ahead and—"

"There was no real danger. Patrice Hazzard was the name they put down in black and white. If it became necessary, it would have been easy enough to break it; or rather restrict it to its literal application, I should say. Prove that you and Patrice Hazzard were not identically one and the same and, therefore, that you were not the one intended. The law isn't like a man in love; the law values names. I pumped our lawyer a little on the q.t., without of course letting on what I had on my mind, and what he told me reassured me. But what that incident did for me once and for all, was to show me there was no game, no ulterior motive. I mean, that it wasn't the money that was at the bottom of it. Patrice, the fright and honest aversion I read on your face that night, when I came to your door to tell you about it, couldn't have been faked by the most expert actress in creation. Your face got as white as a sheet, your eyes darted around as though you wanted to run out of the house for dear life then and there; I touched your hand, and it was icy-cold. There is a point at which acting stops, and the heart begins.

"And that gave me the answer. I knew from that night on what it was you really wanted, what it was that had made you do it: safety, security. It was on your face a hundred times a day, once I had the clue. I've seen it over and over. Every time you looked at your baby. Every time you said, 'I'm going up to my room.' The way you said '*my* room.' I've seen it in your eyes even when you were only looking at a pair of curtains on the window, straightening them out, caressing them. I could almost hear you say, 'They're mine, I belong here.' And every time I saw it, it did something to me. I loved you a little more than I had the time before. And I wanted you to have all that rightfully, permanently, beyond the power of anyone or anything to ever take it away from you again—"

He lowered his voice still further, till she could barely hear the message it breathed.

"At my side. As my wife. And I still do. Tonight more than ever, a hundred times more than before. Will you answer me now? Will you tell me if you'll let me?"

His face swam fluidly before her upturned eyes.

"Take me home, Bill," she said brokenly, happily. "Take Patrice home to your house with you, Bill."

43

FOR A MOMENT, as he braked and as she turned her face toward it, her overtired senses received a terrifying impression that it was on fire, that the whole interior was going up in flame. And then as she recoiled against him, she saw that bright as the light coming from it was, brazier-bright against the early-morning pall, it was a steady brightness, it did not quiver. It poured from every window, above and below, and spilled in gradations of intensity across the lawn, and even as far as the frontal walk and the roadway beyond, but it was the static brightness of lighted-up rooms. Rooms lighted up in emergency.

He nudged and pointed wordlessly, and on the rear plate of the car already there, that they had just drawn up behind, stood out the ominous "MD." Spotlighted, menacing, beetling, within the circular focus of their own headlights. Prominent as the skull and crossbones on a bottle label. And just as fear-inspiring.

"Doctor Parker," flashed through her mind.

He flung open the door and jumped down, and she was right behind him.

"And we sat talking back there all this time," she heard him exclaim.

They chased up the flagstone walk, she at his heels, outdistanced by his longer legs. He didn't have time to use his key. By the time he'd got it out and put it to where the keyhole had last been, the keyhole was already back out of reach and Aunt Josie was there instead, frightened in an old flowered bathrobe, face as gray as her hair.

They didn't ask her who it was; there was no need to.

"Ever since happass eleven," she said elliptically. "*He's* been with her from midnight straight on through."

She closed the door after them.

"If you'd only phoned up," she said accusingly. "If you'd only left word where I could reach you." And then she added, but more to him than to Patrice, "Daybreak. I hope the party was wuth it. It sure must have been a good one. I know one thing, it sure coss more than any party you ever went to in your life. Or ever likely to go to."

Patrice screamed out within herself, wincing: How right you are! It wasn't good, no, it wasn't—but oh, how costly!

Dr. Parker accosted them in the upper hall. There was a nurse there with him. They had thought he'd be in with her.

"Is she asleep?" Patrice breathed, more frightened than reassured at this.

"Ty Winthrop's been in there alone with her for the past half-hour. She insisted. And when people are quite ill, you overrule them; but when they're even more ill than that, you don't. I've been checking her pulse and respiration at ten-minute intervals."

"That bad?" she whispered in dismay. She caught the stricken look on Bill's face, and found time to feel parenthetically sorry for him even while she asked it.

"There's no immediate danger," Parker answered. "But I can't make you any promises beyond the next hour or two." And then he looked the two of them square in the eyes and said, "It's a bad one this time. It's the daddy of them all."

It's the last one, Patrice knew then with certainty.

She crumpled for a moment, and a scattered sob or two escaped from her, while he and Bill led her over to a hall-chair, there beside the sickroom-door, and sat her down.

"Don't do that," the doctor admonished her, with just a trace of detachment—perhaps professional, perhaps personal— "There's no call for it at this stage."

"It's just that I'm so worn-out," she explained blurredly.

She could almost read his answering thought. Then you should have come home a little earlier.

The nurse traced a whiff of ammonia past her nose, eased her hat from her head, smoothed her hair soothingly.

"Is my baby all right?" she asked in a moment, calmer.

It was Aunt Josie who answered that. "I know how to look after him," she said a trifle shortly. Patrice was out of favor right then.

The door opened and Ty Winthrop came out. He was putting away his glasses.

"They back yet—?" he started to say. Then he saw them. "She wants to see you."

They both started up at once.

"Not you," he said to Bill, warding him off. "Just Patrice. She wants to see her alone, without anyone else in the room. She repeated that several times."

Parker motioned her to wait. "Let me check her pulse first."

She looked over at Bill while they were standing there waiting, to see how he was taking it. He smiled untroubledly. "I understand," he murmured. "That's her way of seeing *me*. And a good way it is, too. Just about the best."

Parker had come out again.

"Not more than a minute or two," he said disapprovingly, with a side look at Winthrop. "And then maybe we'll all get together to see that she gets a little rest."

She went in there. Somebody closed the door after her.

"Patrice, dear," a quiet voice said.

She went over to the bed.

The face was still in shadow, because of the way they'd left the lamp.

"You can raise that a little, dear. I'm not in my coffin yet."

Her eyes looked up at Patrice in the same way they had that first day at the railroad station. They were kind. They smiled around the edges. They hurt a little, they were so *trustful*.

"I didn't dream—" she heard herself saying, "We drove out further than we'd intended to— It was such a beautiful night—"

Two hands were feebly extended for her to clasp.

She dropped suddenly to her knees and smothered them with kisses.

"I love you," she pleaded. "That much is true; oh, that much is true! If I could only make you believe it. My mother. You're my mother."

"You don't have to, dear. I know it already. I love you too, and my love has always known that you do. That's why you're my little girl. Remember that I told you this: *you're my little girl.*"

And then she said, very softly, "I forgive you, dear. I forgive my little girl."

She stroked Patrice's hand consolingly.

"Marry Bill. I give you both my blessing. Here—" She gestured feebly in the direction of her own shoulder. "Under my pillow. I had Ty put something there for you."

Patrice reached under, drew out a long envelope, sealed, unaddressed.

"Keep this," Mother Hazzard said, touching the edge for a moment. "Don't show it to anyone. It's just for you. Do not open until—after I'm not here. It's in case you need it. When you're in greatest need, remember I gave it to you—open it then."

She sighed deeply, as though the effort had tired her unendurably.

"Kiss me. It's late. So very late. I can feel it in every inch of my poor old body. *You* can't feel how late it is, Patrice, but *I* can."

Patrice bent low above her, touched her own lips to hers.

"Goodbye, my daughter," she whispered.

"Goodnight," Patrice amended.

"Goodbye," she insisted gently. There was a faint, prideful smile on her face, a smile of superior knowledge, as of one who knows herself to be the better informed of the two.

44

LONELY VIGIL BY the window, until long after it had grown light. Sitting there, staring, waiting, hoping, despairing, dying a little. Seeing the stars go out, and the dawn creep slowly toward her from the east, like an ugly gray pallor. She'd never wanted to see daybreak less, for at least the dark had covered her sorrows like a cloak but every moment of increasing light diluted it, until it had reached the vanishing-point, it was gone, there wasn't any more left.

Motionless as a statue in the blue-tinged window, forehead pressed forward against the glass, making a little white ripple of adhesion across it where it touched. Eyes staring at nothing, for nothing was all there was out there to see.

I've found my love at last, only to lose him; only to throw him away. Why did I find out tonight I loved him, why did I have to know? Couldn't I have been spared that at least?

The day wasn't just bitter now. The day was ashes, lying all around her, cold and crumbled and consumed. No use for pinks and blues and yellows to try to tint it, like watercolors lightly applied from some celestial palette; no use. It was dead. And she was sitting there beside its bier.

And if there was such a thing as penance, absolution, for mistakes that, once made, can never be wholly undone again, can only be regretted, she should have earned it on that long vigil. But maybe there is none.

Her chances were dead and her hopes were dead, and she couldn't atone any further.

She turned and slowly looked behind her. Her baby was awake, and smiling at her, and for once she had no answering smile ready to give him. She couldn't smile, it would have been too strange a thing to fit upon her mouth.

She turned her face away again, so that she wouldn't have to look at him too long. Because, what good did crying do? Crying to a little baby. Babies cried to their mothers, but mothers shouldn't cry to their babies.

Outside, the man came out on that lawn down there, pulling his garden-hose after him. Then when he had it all stretched out, he let it lie, and went back to the other end of it, and turned the spigot. The grass began to sparkle, up where the nozzle lay inert, even before he could return to it and take it up. You couldn't see the water actually coming out, because the nozzle was down too flat against the ground, but you could see a sort of irridescent rippling of the grass right there, that told there was something in motion under it.

Then he saw her at her window, and he raised his arm and waved to her, the way he had in the beginning, that first day. Not because she was she, but because his own world was all in order, and it was a beautiful morning, and he wanted to wave to someone to show them how he felt.

She turned her head away. Not to avoid his friendly little salutation, but because there was a knocking at her door. Someone was knocking at her door.

She got up stiffly and walked over toward it, and opened it.

A lonely, lost old man was standing out there, quietly, unassumingly. Bill's father was standing out there, very wilted, very spent. A stranger, mistaking her for a daughter.

"She just died," he whispered helplessly. "Your mother just died, dear. I didn't know whom to go to, to tell about it—so I came to your door." He seemed unable to do anything but just stand there, limp, baffled.

She stood there without moving either. That was all she was able to do too. That was all the help she could give him.

45

THE LEAVES WERE dying, as she had died. The season was dying. The old life was dying, was dead. They had buried it back there just now.

"How strange," Patrice thought. "To go on, before one can go on to something new, there has to be death first. Always, there has to be a kind of death, of one sort or another, first. Just as there has been with me."

The leaves were brightly dying. The misty black of her veil dimmed their apoplectic spasms of scarlet and orange and ochre, tempered them to a more bearable hue in the fiery sunset, as the funeral limousine coursed at stately speed homeward through the countryside.

She sat between Bill and his father.

"I am the Woman of the Family now," she thought. "The only woman of their house and in their house. That is why I sit between them like this, in place of prominence, and not to the outside."

And though she would not have known how to phrase it, even to herself, her own instincts told her that the country and the society she was a part of were basically matriarchal, that it was the woman who was essentially the focus of each home, the head of each little individual family-group. Not brazenly, aggressively so, not on the outside; but within the walls, where the home really was. She had succeeded to this primacy now. The gangling adolescent who had once stood outside a door that wouldn't open.

One she would marry and be his wife. One she would look after in filial devotion, and ease his loneliness and cushion his decline as best she could. There was no treachery, no deceit, in her plans; all that was over with and past.

She held Father Hazzard's hand gently clasped in her own, on the one side. And on the other, her hand curved gracefully up and around the turn of Bill's stalwart arm. To indicate: You are mine. And I am yours.

The limousine had halted. Bill got out and armed her down. Then they both helped his father and, one on each side of him, walked slowly with him up the familiar terraced flagstones to the familiar door.

Bill sounded the knocker, and Aunt Josie's deputy opened the door for them with all the alacrity of the novice. Aunt Josie herself, of course, a titular member of the family, had attended the services with them, was on her way back now in the lesser of the two limousines.

She closed the door in respectful silence, and they were home.

It was she who first saw them, Patrice. They were in the library.

Bill and his father, going on ahead, supporting arm about waist, had passed the open doorway obliviously. She had lingered behind for a moment, to give some muted necessary orders.

"Yes, Mrs. Hazzard," Aunt Josie's deputy said docilely.

Yes, Mrs. Hazzard. That was the first time she had heard it (Aunt Josie always called her "Miss Pat"), but she would have that now all her life, as her due. Her mind rolled it around on its tongue, savoring it. Yes, Mrs. Hazzard. Position. Security. Impregnability. The end of a journey.

Then she moved forward and, passing the doorway, saw them.

They were sitting in there, both facing it. Two men. The very way they held their heads—they were not apologetic, they were not disclaiming enough, for such a time and such a place and such a visit. Their faces, as she met them, did not say: "Whenever you are ready." Their faces said: "*We* are ready for you now. Come in to us."

Fear put out a long finger and touched her heart. She had stopped.

"Who are those two men?" she breathed to the girl who had let her in. "What are they doing in there?"

"Oh, I forgot. They came here about twenty minutes ago, asking to see Mr. Hazzard. I explained about the funeral, and suggested maybe they'd better come back later. But they said no, they said they'd wait. I couldn't do anything with them. So I just let them be."

She went on past the opening. "He's in no condition to speak to anyone now. You'll have to go in there and—"

"Oh, not old Mr. Hazzard. It's Mr. Hazzard his son they want."

She knew then. Their faces had already told her, the grim way they had both sized her up that fleeting second or two she had stood in the doorway. People didn't stare at you like that, just ordinary people. Punitive agents did. Those empowered by law to seek out, and identify, and question.

The finger had become a whole icy hand now, twisting and crushing her heart in its grip.

Detectives. Already. So soon, so relentlessly, so fatally soon. And today of all days, on this very day.

The copybooks were right, the texts that said the police were infallible.

She turned and hurried up the stairs, to overtake Bill and his father, nearing the top now, still linked in considerate, toiling ascent.

Bill turned his head inquiringly at sound of her hasty step behind them. Father Hazzard didn't. What was any step to him any more? The only one he wanted to hear would never sound again.

She made a little sign to Bill behind his father's back. A quick little quirk of the finger to show that this was something to be kept between the two of them alone. Then said, trying to keep her voice casual, "Bill, as soon as you take Father to his room, I want to see you for a minute. Will you come out?"

He came upon her in her own room, in the act of lowering an emptied brandy-jigger from her lips. He looked at her curiously.

"What'd you do, get a chill out there?"

"I did," she said. "But not out there. Here. Just now."

"You seem to be shaking."

"I am. Close the door." And when he had, "Is he sleeping?"

"He will be in another minute or two. Aunt Josie's giving him a little more of that sedative the doctor left."

She kneaded her hands together, as though she were trying to break each bone separately. "They're here, Bill. About the other night. They're here already."

He didn't have to ask, he knew what she meant by "the other night." There was only one other night for them, there would always be only one, from now on. As the nights multiplied, it would become "that night," perhaps; that was the only alteration.

"How do you know? Did they tell you?"

"They don't have to. I know." She snatched at his coat-lapels, as though she were trying to rip them off him. "What are we going to do?"

"*We* are not going to do anything," he said with meaning. "*I*'ll do whatever is to be done about it."

"Who's that?" she shuddered, and crushed herself close to him. Her teeth were almost chattering with nervous tension.

"Who is it?" he asked at full voice.

"Aunt Josie," came through the door.

"Let go of me," he cautioned in an undertone. "All right, Aunt Josie."

She put her head in and said, "Those two men that're down there, they said they can't wait for Mr. Hazzard any more."

For a moment a little hope wormed its way through her stricken heart.

"They said if he don't come down, they'll have to come up here."

"What do they want? Did they tell you?" he said to Aunt Josie.

"I asked 'em twice, and each time they said the same thing. 'Mr. Hazzard.' What kind of an answer is that? They're bold ones."

"All right," he said curtly. "You've told us."

She closed the door again.

He stood for awhile irresolute, his hand curled around the back of his neck. Then straightened with reluctant decision, squared off his shoulders, hitched down his cuffs, and turned to face the door. "Well," he said, "let's get it over with."

She ran to join him. "I'll go with you."

"You won't!" He took her hand and put it off his arm, in rough rejection. "Let's get that straight right now. You're staying up here, and you're staying out of it. Do you hear me? No matter what happens, you're staying out of it."

He'd never spoken to her like that before.

"Are you taking me to be your husband?" he demanded.

"Yes," she murmured. "I've already told you that."

"Then that's an order. The first and the last, I hope, that I'll ever have to give you. Now look, we can't tell two stories about this. We're only telling one: mine. And it's one that you're not supposed to know anything about. So you can't help me, you can only harm me."

She seized his hand and put her lips to it, as a sort of god-speed.

"What are you going to tell them?"

"The truth." The look he gave her was a little odd. "What did you expect me to tell them? *I* have nothing to lie about, as far as it involves me alone."

He closed the door and he went out.

46

AS SHE FOUND her hands leading the way down for her, one over the other, along the bannister-rail, while her feet followed them more slowly, a step behind all the way, she realized how impossible it would have been to follow his injunction, remain immured up there, without knowing, without listening; how futile of him to expect it of her. She couldn't have been involved as she was, she couldn't have been a woman at all, and obeyed him. This wasn't prying; you didn't pry into something that concerned you as closely as this did her. It was your right to know.

Hand over hand down the bannister, the rest of her creeping after, body held at a broken crouch. Like a cripple struggling down a staircase.

A quarter of the way down, the murmur became separate voices. Halfway down, the voices became words. She didn't go beyond there.

Their voices weren't raised. There was no blustering or angry contradiction. They were just men talking quietly, politely together. Somehow, it struck more fear into her that way.

They were repeating after him something he must have just now said.

"Then you do know someone named Harry Carter, Mr. Hazzard."

She didn't hear him say anything. As though he considered one affirmation on that point enough.

"Would you care to tell us what relationship—what connection—there is between you and this man Carter?"

He sounded slightly ironical, when he answered that. She had never heard him that way toward herself, but she caught a new inflection to his voice, and recognized it for irony. "Look, gentlemen, you already know. You must, or why would you be here? You want me to repeat it for you, is that it?"

"What we want is to hear it from you yourself, Mr. Hazzard."

"Very well, then. He is a private detective. As you already know. I selected and hired him. As you already know. And he was being paid a fee, he was being retained, to watch, to keep his eye on, this man Georgesson whom you're concerned with. As you already know."

"Very well, we do already know, Mr. Hazzard. But what we don't already know, what he couldn't tell us, because he didn't know himself, was what was the nature of your interest in Georgesson, why you were having him watched."

And the other one took up where the first had left off: "Would *you* care to tell us that, Mr. Hazzard? Why were you having him watched? What was your reason for doing that?"

Out on the stairs, her heart seemed to turn over and lie down flat on its face. "My God," went echoing sickly through her mind. "Now I come into it!"

"That's an extremely private matter," he said sturdily.

"I see; you don't care to tell us."

"I didn't say that."

"But still, you'd rather not tell us."

"You're putting words into my mouth."

"Because you don't seem to supply us with any of your own."

"It's essential for you to know this?"

"We wouldn't be here if it weren't, I can assure you. This man of yours, Carter, was the one who reported Georgesson's death to us."

"I see." She heard him take a deep breath. And she took one with him. Two breaths, one and the same fear.

"Georgesson was a gambler," he said.

"We know that."

"A crook, a confidence man, an all-around shady operator."

"We know that."

"Then here's the part you don't. Back about—it must be four years ago—three, anyway—my older brother Hugh was a senior at Dartmouth College. He started down here to spend the Christmas holidays at home, with us. He got as far as New York, and then he never got any further. He never showed up. He wasn't on the train that was to have brought him in the next day. We got a long-distance phone-call from him, and he was in trouble. He was practically being held there against his will. He'd gotten into a card-game, it seems, the night before with this Georgesson and a few of his friends—set-up, of course—and they'd taken him for I don't know how many thousands, which he didn't have, and they wanted a settlement before they'd let him go. They had him good, it had the makings of a first-class mess in it. Hugh was just a high-spirited kid, used to associating with decent people, gentlemen, not that kind of vermin, and he hadn't known how to handle himself. They'd built him up for it all evening long, liquored him up, thrown a couple of mangy chorus-girls at him in the various spots they'd dragged him around to first —well, anyway, because of my mother's health and the family's good name, there could be no question of calling the police into it, it would have been altogether too smelly. So my father went up there in person—I went along with him, incidentally—and squared the thing off for him. At about fifty cents to the dollar, or something like that. Got back the I.O.U.'s they'd extorted from the kid. And brought him home with us.

"That's about all there was to it. Not a very new story, it's happened over and over. But naturally, I wasn't likely to forget this Georgesson in a hurry. Well, when I learned he was down here in Caulfield a few weeks ago, showing his face around, I didn't know

if it was a coincidence or not, but I wasn't taking any chances. I got
in touch with a detective agency in New York and had them send
Carter down here, just to try to find out what he was up to.

"And there you have it. Now does that answer your question? Is
that satisfactory?"

They didn't say it was, she noticed. She waited, but she didn't
hear them say it was.

"He didn't approach you or your family in any way? He didn't
molest you?"

"He didn't come near us."

(Which was technically correct, she agreed wryly; she'd had to go
to him each time.)

"You would have heard about it before now, if he had," he assured
them. "I wouldn't have waited for you to look me up, I would have
looked you up."

With catastrophic casualness a non-sequitur followed. She suddenly heard one of them ask him, "Do you want to bring along a
hat, Mr. Hazzard?"

"It's right outside in the hall," he answered drily. "I'll pick it up
as we go by."

They were coming out of the room. With an infantile whimper,
that was almost like that of a little girl running away from goblins
in the dark, she turned and fled up the stairs again, back to her room.

"No—! No—! No—!" she kept moaning with feverish reiteration.
They were arresting him, they were accusing him, they were taking
him with them.

47

DISTRACTED, SHE FLUNG herself down on the bench before her
dressing-table. Her head rolled soddenly about on her shoulders, as
though she were drunk. Her hair was displaced, burying one eye.

"No—! No—!" she kept insisting. "They can't— It isn't fair—"

They wouldn't let him go— They'd never let him go again— He wouldn't come back— He'd never come back to her—

"Oh, for the love of God, help me! I can't take any more of this!"

And then, as in the fairy tales, as in the story-books of old, where everything always comes out all right, where good is good and bad is bad, and the magic spell is always broken just in time for the happy ending, there it was—right under her eyes—

Lying there, waiting. Only asking to be picked up. A white oblong, a sealed envelope. A letter from the dead.

A voice trapped in it seemed to whisper through the seams to her, faint, far away: "When you're in the most need, and I'm not here, open this. When your need is the greatest, and you're all alone. Good-bye, my daughter; my daughter, goodbye . . ."

"I, Grace Parmentier Hazzard, wife of Donald Sedgwick Hazzard, being on my death-bed, and in the presence of my attorney and lifelong counsellor Tyrus Winthrop, who will duly notarize my signature to this and bear witness to it if called upon to do so by the legally constituted authorities, hereby make the following statement, of my own free will and volition, and declare it to be the truth:

"That at approximately 10.30 P.M. on the evening of 24th September, being alone in the house with just my devoted friend and housekeeper, Josephine Walker, and my grandchild, I received a long-distance telephone-call from Hastings, in the neighboring State. That the caller was a certain Harry Carter, known to me as a private investigator and employed by my family and myself as such. That he informed me that just a few moments earlier my beloved daughter-in-law, Patrice, the widow of my late son, Hugh, had been driven against her will to Hastings by a man using the name of Stephen Georgesson, and had there been compelled to enter into a marriage-ceremony with him under duress. And that at that time, while he spoke to me, they were on their way back here, to this city, together.

"Upon receipt of this information, and having ob-

tained from this Mr. Carter the address of the afore-
mentioned Stephen Georgesson, I dressed myself,
called Josephine Walker to me, and told her I was going out, and would be away for only a short time. She
tried to dissuade me, and to prevail upon me to reveal
my purpose and where I was going, but I would not.
I instructed her to wait for me close beside the front
door, in order to admit me at once upon my return,
and under no circumstances, then or at any later time,
to reveal to anyone that I had left the house at that
time or under those circumstances. I caused her to take
an oath upon the Bible, and knowing the nature of her
religious beliefs and early upbringing knew she would
not break it afterward no matter what befell.

"I removed and carried with me a gun which habitually was kept in a desk in the library of my home,
having first inserted into it the cartridges. In order to
lessen recognition as much as possible, I put on the
heavy veil of mourning which I had worn at the time
of the death of my elder son.

"I walked a short distance from my own door, entirely alone and unaccompanied, and at the first opportunity engaged a public taxicab. In it I went to the
quarters of Stephen Georgesson, to seek him out. I
found he had not yet returned when I first arrived, and
I therefore waited, sitting in the taxi a short distance
from his door, until I saw him return and enter. As
soon as he had, I immediately entered in turn, right
after him, and was admitted by him. I raised my veil
in order to let him see my face, and I could see that he
guessed who I was, although he'd never seen me
before.

"I asked him if it was true that he had just now
forced my dead son's wife to enter a marriage-pact
with him, as had been reported to me.

"He readily admitted it, naming the place and time.

"Those were the only words that passed between
us. Nothing further was said. Nothing further needed
to be.

"I immediately took out the gun, held it close toward him, and fired it at him as he stood there before me.

"I fired it only once. I would have fired it more than once, if necessary, in order to kill him; it was my full intention to kill him. But having waited to see if he would move again, and seeing that he did not, but lay as he had fallen, then and only then I refrained from firing it any more and left the place.

"I had myself returned to my own home in the same taxi that had brought me. Within a short time after, I became extremely ill from the excitement and strain I had undergone. And now, knowing that I am dying, and being in full possession of my faculties and with full realization of what I am doing, I wish to make this statement before I pass away and have it, in the case of wrongful accusation of others, should that occur, brought to the attention of those duly constituted to deal with the matter. But only in such case, not otherwise.

> (*Signed*) Grace Parmentier Hazzard.

(*Witnessed and attested*)

Tyrus Winthrop, Att'y at Law."

She reached the downstairs doorway with it too late. The doorway was empty by the time she swayed that far, and clung there, all dazed and disheveled. They'd gone, and he'd gone with them.

She just stood there in the doorway. Empty in an empty doorway.

48

AND THEN, THERE he was at last.

He was so very real, so photographically real down there, that paradoxically, she couldn't quite believe she was seeing him. The very herringbone weave of his coat stood out, as if a magnifying glass were being held to the pattern, for her special inspection. The haggardness of his face, the faint trace of shadow where he needed a shave, she could see everything about him so clearly, as if he were much nearer than he was. Fatigue, maybe, did that, by some reverse process of concentration. Or eyes dilated from long straining to see him, so that now they saw him with abnormal clarity.

Anyway, there he was.

He turned, and came in toward the house. And just before he took the final step that would have carried him too far in under her to be in sight any more, his eyes went up to the window and he saw her.

"Bill," she said silently through the glass, and her two hands flattened to the pane, as if framing the unheard word into a benediction.

"Patrice," he said silently, from down below; and though she didn't hear him, didn't even see his lips move, she knew that was what he said. Just her name. So little, so much.

Suddenly she'd fled from the room as madly as though she'd just been scalded. The upflung curtain settled down again to true, and the backflung door ricocheted back again toward closure, and she was already gone. The baby's wondering head turned after her far too slowly to catch her in her flight.

Then she stopped short again, below the turn of the stairs, and waited for him there, unable to move any further. Stood waiting for him to come to her.

He left his hat, just as though this were any other time he was returning home, and came on up to where she was standing. And somehow her head, as if it were tired of being all alone, went down upon his shoulder and stayed there against his own.

They didn't speak at first. Just stood there pressed together, heads close. There was no message; there was only—being together.

"I'm back, Patrice," was all he said at last.

She shuddered a little and nestled closer. "Bill, now what will they—?"

"Nothing. It's over. It's already through. At least, as far as I'm concerned. That was just for purposes of identification. I had to go with them and look at him, that was all."

"Bill, I opened this. She says—"

She gave it to him. He read it.

"Did you show it to anyone else?"

"No."

"Don't." He tore it once across, and stuffed the remnants into his pocket.

"But suppose—?"

"It's not needed. His gambler-friends are already down on the books for it, by this time. They told me they found evidence to indicate that a big card-game had taken place up there earlier that night."

"I didn't see any."

He gave her an eloquent look. "They did. By the time they got there."

She widened her eyes a little at him.

"They're willing to let it go at that. So let us let it go at that too, Patrice." He sighed heavily. "I'm all-in. Feel like I've been on my feet for a week straight. I'd like to sleep forever."

"Not forever, Bill, not forever. Because I'll be waiting around, and that would be so long—"

His lips sought the side of her face, and he kissed her with a sort of blind stupefaction.

"Walk me up as far as the door of my room, Patrice. Like to take a look at the youngster, before I turn in."

His arm slipped wearily around her waist.

"*Our* youngster from now on," he added softly.

49

"MR. WILLIAM HAZZARD was married yesterday to Mrs. Patrice Hazzard, widow of the late Hugh Hazzard, at a quiet ceremony at St. Bartholomew's Episcopal Church, in this city, performed by the Reverend Francis Allgood. There were no attendants. Following their marriage Mr. and Mrs. Hazzard left immediately for a honeymoon trip through the Canadian Rockies."—*All Caulfield morning and evening newspapers.*

50

WHEN THE READING of the will had been concluded—that was on a Monday following their return, about a month later—Winthrop asked the two of them to remain behind a moment after the room had been cleared. He went over and closed the door after the others present had left. Then he went to the wall, opened a built-in safe, and took out an envelope. He sat down at his desk.

"Bill and Patrice," he said, "this is meant for you alone."

They exchanged a look.

"It is not part of the estate, so it concerns no one else but the two of you.

"It is from her, of course. It was transcribed on her death-bed, less than an hour before she died."

"But we already—" Bill tried to say.

Winthrop silenced him with upturned hand. "There were two of them. This is the second. Both dictated to me during the hours of that same night, or I should say, early morning. This follows the other. The first she gave you herself that same night, as you know. The other she turned over to me. I was to hold it until today, as I have done. Her instructions to me were: It is for the two of you alike. It is not to be delivered to the one without the other. When delivered, it is not to be opened by the one without the other. And finally, it is only to be delivered in the case of your marriage. If you were not married at this time, as she wanted you to be—and you know she did, very much—then it was to be destroyed by me, unopened. Singly, it is not for either one of you. United in marriage, it is a last gift to the two of you, from her.

"However. You need not read it if you do not want to. You can destroy it unopened. I am under pledge not to reveal what is in it, even though I naturally know, for I took her words down at the bedside, and witnessed and notarized her signature in my capacity as her attorney. You must, therefore, either read it or not read it for yourselves. And if you do read it, then when you have read it, you are to destroy it just the same."

He waited a moment.

"Now, do you want me to deliver it to you, or do you prefer that I destroy it?"

"We want it, of course," Patrice whispered.

"We want it," Bill echoed.

He extended it to them lengthwise. "You kindly place your fingers on this corner. You on this." He withdrew his own fingers, and they were left holding it.

"I hope it brings you the extra added happiness she wanted you both to have. I know that that is why she did it. She asked me to bless you both, for her, as I gave it to you. Which I do now. That concludes my stewardship in the matter."

They waited several hours, until they were alone together in their room that night. Then when he'd finished putting on his robe, and saw that she had doned a silken bridal something over her nightdress, he took it out of his coat-pocket and said:

"Now. Shall we? You do want to, don't you?"

"Of course. It's from her. We want to read it. I've been counting the minutes all evening long."

"I knew you'd want to. Come on over here. We'll read it together."

He sat down in an easy chair, adjusted the hood of the lamp over one shoulder. She perched beside him on the arm of the chair, slipped an arm about his shoulders.

The sealing-wax wafers crumbled and the flap shot upright, under his fingers.

In silent intensity, heads close together, they read:

> "My beloved children:
>
> You are married by now, by the time this reaches you. (For if you are not, it will not reach you; Mr. Winthrop will tell you all about that.) You are happy. I hope I have given you that happiness. I want to give you even a little more. And trust and pray that out of your plenty, you will spare a little of it for me, even though I am gone and no longer there with you. I do not want a shadow to cross your minds every time you recall me. I cannot bear to have you think ill of me.
>
> "I did not do that thing, of course. I did not take that young man's life. Perhaps you have already

guessed it. Perhaps you both know me well enough to know I could not have done such a thing.

"I knew that he was doing something to threaten Patrice's happiness, that was all. That was why we were having Mr. Carter investigate him. But I never actually set eyes on him, I never saw him.

"I was alone in the house last night (for as Mr. Winthrop writes this for me, it is still last night, though you will not read it for a long time to come). Even Father, who never goes out without me, had to attend an important emergency meeting at the plant. It meant settling the strike that much sooner, and I pleaded with him to go, though he did not want to. I was alone, just Aunt Josie and the child and I.

"Mr. Carter phoned around ten-thirty o'clock and told me he had bad news; that a marriage-service had just been performed joining the two of them at Hastings. I had taken the call on the downstairs phone. The shock brought on an attack. Not wishing to alarm Aunt Josie, I tried to get up the stairs to my room unaided. By the time I had reached the top, I became exhausted and could only lie there, unable to move any further or to call out.

"While I was lying there helpless like that, I heard the outside door open and recognized Bill's step below. I tried to attract his attention, but my voice was too weak, I couldn't reach him with it. I heard him go into the library, stay there several moments, then come out again. Afterward I remembered hearing something click between his hands right then, as he stood there by the door. And I knew he never uses a cigarette-lighter. Then he left the house.

"When Aunt Josie had come out some time later, found me there, and carried me to my bed, and while we were waiting for the doctor, I sent her to the library to see if that gun that belonged there was still there. She did not understand why I wanted her to do this, and I did not tell her. But when she came back and told me that the gun was missing, I was afraid what that might mean.

"I knew by then that I was dying. One does. I had time to think, lying there during those next long hours. I could think so clearly. I knew that there was a way in which either my Bill or my Patrice might need my protection, once I was no longer there to give it. I knew I had to give it none the less, as best I could. I wanted them to have their happiness. I wanted above all my little grandchild to have his security, his start in life without anything to mar it. I knew what the way was in which I could give this to them.

"So as soon as Dr. Parker would allow it, I had Ty Winthrop called to my bedside. To him, in privacy, I dictated the sworn statement which you have had by now.

"I hope, my dear ones, you have not had to use it. I pray you have not, and never will have to.

"But this is its retraction. This is the truth, just meant for you two alone. One tells the truth to one's loved ones, one does not have to swear to and notarize it. There is no guilt upon me. This is my wedding gift to you. To make your happiness even more complete than it is already.

"Burn it after you have read it. This is a dying woman's last wish. Bless you both.

Your devoted Mother."

The match made a tiny snap. Stripes of black crept up the paper, then ran together, before any flame could be seen. Then there was a little soundless puff, and suddenly yellow light glowed all around it.

And as it burned, over this yellow light, they turned their heads and looked at one another. With a strange, new sort of fright they'd never felt before. As when the world drops away, and there is nothing left underfoot to stand on.

"*She* didn't do it," he whispered, stricken.

"*She* didn't," she breathed, appalled.

"Then—?"

"Then—?"

And each pair of eyes answered, "You."

THE SUMMER NIGHTS are so pleasant in Caulfield. They smell of heliotrope, of jasmine, and of clover. The stars are warm and close above us. The breeze is gentle as a baby's kiss. The soothing whisper of the leafy trees, the lamplight falling on the lawns, the hush of perfect peace and security.

But not for us.

The house we live in is so pleasant here in Caulfield. Its blue-green lawn, always freshly watered; the dazzling whiteness of the porch-supports in the sun; the gracious symmetry of the bannister that curves down from above; the gloss of rich old floors; the lushness of pile carpeting; in every room some favorite chair that's an old friend. People come and say, "What more can there be? This is a home."

But not for us.

I love him so. More than ever before, not less. So bitterly I love him. And he loves me. And yet I know that on some day to come, maybe this year, maybe next, but surely to come, suddenly he'll pack and go away and leave me. Though he'll love me still, and never stop even after he's gone.

Or if he doesn't, I will. I'll take up my valise, and walk out through the door, and never return. I'll leave my heart behind, and leave my child behind, and leave my life behind, but I'll never come back.

It's certain, it's assured. The only uncertainty is: which one of us will be the first to break.

We've fought this thing. In every way we know, in every way there is. No good, no good at all. There's no way out. We're caught, we're trapped. For if he's innocent, then it has to be me. And if I am, it has to be he. But I *know* I'm innocent. (Yet he may know he is too.) We can't break through, there's no way out.

It's in the very kiss we give each other. Somehow we trap it right between our lips, each time. It's everywhere, it's all the time, it's *us*.

I don't know what the game was. I'm not sure how it should be played. No one ever tells you. I only know we must have played it wrong, somewhere along the way. I don't even know what the stakes are. I only know they're not for us.

We've lost. That's all I know. We've lost. And now the game is through.

THE END.

WALTZ
INTO
DARKNESS

"If one should love you with real love
(Such things have been,
Things your fair face knows nothing of
It seems, Faustine) . . . "

—SWINBURNE

CHARACTERS THAT APPEAR IN THE STORY

Louis Durand, the man in New Orleans
Tom, who works for him
Aunt Sarah, Tom's sister
Julia Russell, the woman who comes from St. Louis
   to marry him
Allan Jardine, his business partner
Simms, a bank manager
Commissioner of Police of New Orleans
Bertha Russell, sister of the woman who comes
   to marry Durand
Walter Downs, a private investigator of St. Louis
Colonel Harry Worth, late of the Confederate Army
Bonny, who once was Julia

CHARACTER THAT DOES NOT APPEAR
IN THE STORY

"Billy," a name on a burned scrap of letter, an unseen
figure watching a window, a stealthy knocking at a
door.

*The soundless music starts. The dancing figures appear,
slowly draw together. The waltz begins.*

1

THE SUN was bright, the sky was blue, the time was May; New Orleans was heaven, and heaven must have been only another New Orleans, it couldn't have been any better.

In his bachelor quarters on St. Charles Street, Louis Durand was getting dressed. Not for the first time that day, for the sun was already high and he'd been up and about for hours; but for the great event of that day. This wasn't just a day, this was *the* day of all days. A day that comes just once to a man, and now had come to him. It had come late, but it had come. It was now. It was today.

He wasn't young any more. Others didn't tell him this, he told himself this. He wasn't old, as men go. But for such a thing as this, he wasn't too young any more. Thirty-seven.

On the wall there was a calendar, the first four leaves peeled back to bare the fifth. At top, center, this was inscribed *May*. Then on each side of this, in slanted, shadow-casting, heavily curlicued numerals, the year-date was gratuitously given the beholder: 1880. Below, within their little boxed squares, the first nineteen numerals had been stroked off with lead pencil. About the twentieth, this time in red crayon, a heavy circle, a bull's-eye, had been traced. Around and around, as though it could not be emphasized enough. And from there on, the numbers were blank; in the future.

He had put on the shirt with starched ruffles that Maman Alphonsine had so lovingly laundered for him, every frill a work of art. It was fastened at the cuffs with garnet studs backed with silver. In the flowing ascot tie that spread downward fanwise from his chin was thrust the customary stickpin that no well-dressed man was ever without, in this case a crescent of diamond splinters tipped by a ruby chip at each end.

A ponderous gold fob hung from his waistcoat pocket on the right side. Linking this to the adjoining pocket on the left, bulky with a massive slab of watch, was a chain of thick gold links, conspicuous across his middle, and meant to be so. For what was a man without a watch? And what was a watch without there being an indication of one?

His flowing, generous shirt, above this tightly encompassing waist-coat, gave him a pouter-pigeon aspect. But there was enough pride in his chest right now to have done that unaided, anyway.

On the bureau, before which he stood using his hairbrush, lay a packet of letters and a daguerreotype.

He put down his brush, and, pausing for a moment in his preparations, took them up one by one and hurriedly glanced through each. The first bore the letter-head: "The Friendly Correspondence Society of St. Louis, Mo.—an Association for Ladies and Gentlemen of High Character," and began in a fine masculine hand:

> Dear Sir:
> In reply to your inquiry we are pleased to forward to you the name and address of one of our members, and if you will address yourself to her in person, we feel sure a mutually satisfactory correspondence may be engaged upon—

The next was in an even finer hand, this time feminine: "My dear Mr. Durand:—" And signed: "Y'rs most sincerely, Miss J. Russell."

The next: "Dear Mr. Durand: . . . Sincerely, Miss Julia Russell."

The next: "Dear Louis Durand: . . . Your sincere friend, Julia Russell."

And then: "Dear Louis: . . . Your sincere friend, Julia."

And then: "Dear Louis: . . . Your sincere Julia."

And then: "Louis, dear: . . . Your Julia."

And finally: "Louis, my beloved: . . . Your own impatient Julia." There was a postscript to this one: "Will Wednesday never come? I count the hours for the boat to sail!"

He put them in order again, patted them tenderly, fondly, into symmetry. He put them into his inside coat pocket, the one that went over his heart.

He took up, now, the small stiff-backed daguerreotype and looked at it long and raptly. The subject was not young. She was not an old woman, certainly, but she was equally certainly no longer a girl. Her features were sharply indented with the approaching emphases of alteration. There was an incisiveness to the mouth that was not yet, but would be presently, sharpness. There was a keen appearance to the eyes that heralded the onset of sunken creases and constrictions about them. Not yet, but presently. The groundwork was being laid. There was a curvature to the nose that presently would become a hook. There was a prominence to the chin that presently would become a jutting-out.

She was not beautiful. She could be called attractive, for she was attractive to him, and attractiveness lies in the eyes of the beholder.

Her dark hair was gathered at the back of the head in a psyche-knot, and a smattering of it, coaxed the other way, fell over her forehead in a fringe, as the fashion had been for some considerable time now. So long a time, in fact, that it was already unnoticeably ceasing to be the fashion.

The only article of apparel allowed to be visible by the limitations of the pose was a black velvet ribbon clasped tightly about her throat, for immediately below that the portrait ended in smouldering brown clouds of photographic nebulae.

So this was the bargain he had made with love, taking what he could get, in sudden desperate haste, for fear of getting nothing at all, of having waited too long, after waiting fifteen years, steadfastly turning his back on it.

That early love, that first love (that he had sworn would be the last) was only a shadowy memory now, a half-remembered name from the past. Marguerite; he could say it and it had no meaning now. As dry and flat as a flower pressed for years between the pages of a book.

A name from someone else's past, not even his. For every seven years we change completely, they say, and there is nothing left of what we were. And so twice over he had become somebody else since then.

Twice-removed he was now from the boy of twenty-two—called Louis Durand as he was, and that their only link—who had knocked upon the house door of his bride-to-be the night before their wedding, stars in his eyes, flowers in his hand. To stand there first with his summons unanswered. And then to see it swing slowly open and two men come out, bearing something dead on a covered litter.

"Stand back. Yellow jack."

He saw the ring on her finger, trailing the ground.

He didn't cry out. He made no sound. He reached down and placed his courtship flowers gently on the death-stretcher as it went by. Then he turned and went away.

Away from love, for fifteen years.

Marguerite, a name. That was all he had left.

He was faithful to that name until he died. For he died too, though more slowly than she had. The boy of twenty-two died into a young man of twenty-nine. Then *he* in turn was still faithful to the name his predecessor had been faithful to, until he too died. The young man of twenty-nine died into an older man of thirty-six.

And suddenly, one day, the cumulative loneliness of fifteen years, held back until now, overwhelmed him, all at one time, inundated him, and he turned this way and that, almost in panic.

Any love, from anywhere, on any terms. Quick, before it was too late! Only not to be alone any longer.

If he'd met someone in a restaurant just then—

Or even if he'd met someone passing on the street—

But he didn't.

His eye fell, instead, on an advertisement in a newspaper. A St. Louis advertisement in a New Orleans newspaper.

You cannot walk away from love.

His contemplation ended. The sound of carriage wheels stopping somewhere just outside caused him to insert the likeness into his money-fold, and pocket that. He went out to the second-story veranda and looked down. The sun suddenly whitened his back like flour as he leaned over the railing, pressing down the smouldering magenta bougainvillea that feathered its edges.

A colored man was coming into the inner courtyard or patio-well through the passageway from the street.

"What took you so long?" Durand called down to him. "Did you get my flowers?" The question was wholly rhetorical, for he could see the cone-shaped parcel, misty pink peering through its wax-wrappings at the top.

"Sure enough did."

"Did you get me a coach?"

"It's here waiting for you now."

"I thought you'd never get back," he went on. "You been gone all of—"

The Negro shook his head in philosophical good nature. "A man in love is a man in a hurry."

"Well, come on up, Tom," was the impatient suggestion. "Don't just stand down there all day."

Humorous grin still unbroken, Tom resumed his progress, passed from sight under the near side of the façade. Several moments later the outermost door of the apartment opened and he had entered behind the owner.

The latter turned, went over to him, seized the bouquet, and pared off its outer filmy trappings, with more nervous haste than painstaking care.

"You going give it to her, or you going tear it to pieces?" the colored man inquired drily.

"Well, I have to see, don't I? Do you think she'll like pink roses and sweet peas, Tom?" There was a plaintive helplessness to the last part of the question, as when one grasps at straws.

"Don't all ladies?"

"I don't know. The only girls I—" He didn't finish it.

"Oh, them," said Tom charitably. "The man said they do," he went on. "The man said that's what they all ask for." He fluffed the lace-paper collar encircling them with proprietary care, restoring its pertness.

Durand was hastily gathering together his remaining accoutrements, meanwhile, preparatory to departure.

"I want to go to the new house first," he said, on a somewhat breathless note.

"You was there only yesterday," Tom pointed out. "If you stay away only one day, you afraid it's going to fly away, I reckon."

"I know, but this is the last chance I'll have to make sure everything's— Did you tell your sister? I want her to be there when we arrive."

"She'll be there."

Durand stopped with his hand to the doorknob, looked around in a comprehensive sweep, and suddenly the tempo of his departure had slackened to almost a full halt.

"This'll be the last time for this place, Tom."

"It was nice and quiet here, Mr. Lou," the servant admitted. "Anyway, the last few years, since you started getting older."

There was a renewed flurry of departure, as if brought on by this implicit warning of the flight of time. "You finish up the packing, see that my things get over there. Don't forget to give the keys back to Madame Tellier before you leave."

He stopped again, doorknob at a full turn now but door still not open.

"What's the matter, Mr. Lou?"

"I'm scared now. I'm afraid she—" He swallowed down his rigid ear-high collar, backed a hand to his brow to blot imperceptible moisture, "—won't like me."

"You look all right to me."

"It's all been by letters so far. It's easy in letters."

"You sent her your picture. She knows what you look like," Tom tried to encourage him.

"A picture is a picture. A live man is a live man."

Tom went over to him where he stood, dejectedly sidewise now to the door, dusted off his coat at the back of his shoulder. "You're not the best-looking man in N'Orleans. But you're not the worst-looking man in N'Orleans either."

"Oh, I don't mean that kind of looks. Our dispositions—"

"Your ages suit each other. You told her yours."

"I took a year off it. I said I was thirty-six. It sounded better."

"You can make her right comfortable, Mr. Lou."

Durand nodded with alacrity at this, as though for the first time he felt himself on safe ground. "She won't be poor."

"Then I wouldn't worry too much about it. When a man's in love, he looks for looks. When a lady's in love, 'scusing me, Mr. Lou, she looks to see how well-off she's going to be."

Durand brightened. "She won't have to scrimp." He raised his head suddenly, as at a new discovery. "Even if I'm not all she might hope for, she'll get used to me."

"You want to—just make sure?" Tom fumbled in his own clothing, yanked at a concealed string somewhere about his chest, produced a rather worn and limp rabbit's foot, a small gilt band encircling it as a mounting. He offered it to him.

"Oh, I don't believe in—" Durand protested sheepishly.

"They ain't a white man willing to say he do," Tom chuckled. "They ain't a white man don't, just the same. Put it in your pocket anyway. Can't do no harm."

Durand stuffed it away guiltily. He consulted his watch, closed it again with a resounding clap.

"I'm late! I don't want to miss the boat!" This time he flung the symbolic door wide and crossed the threshold of his bachelorhood.

"You got the better part of an hour before her stack even climb up in sight 'long the river, I reckon."

But Louis Durand, bridegroom-to-be, hadn't even waited. He was clattering down Madame Tellier's tile-faced stairs outside at a resounding gait. A moment later an excited hail came up through the window from the courtyard below.

Tom strolled to the second-story veranda.

"My hat! Throw it down." Durand was jumping up and down in impatience.

Tom threw it down and retired.

A second later there was another hail, even more agonized.

"My stick! Throw that down too."

That dropped, was seized deftly on the fly. A little puff of sun-colored dust arose from Madame Tellier's none-too-immaculate flagstones.

Tom turned away, shaking his head resignedly.

"A man in love's a man in a hurry, sure enough."

2

THE COACH drove briskly down St. Louis Street. Durand sat straining forward on the edge of the seat, both hands topping his cane-head and the upper part of his body supported by it. Suddenly he leaned still further forward.

"That one," he exclaimed, pointing excitedly. "That one right there."

"The new one, cunnel?" the coachman marveled admiringly.

"I'm building it myself," Durand let him know with an atavistic burst of boyish pride, sixteen years late. Then he qualified it, "I mean, they're doing it according to my plans. I told them how I wanted it."

The coachman scratched his head. A gesture not meant to indicate perplexity in this instance, but of being overwhelmed by such grandeur. "Sure is pretty," he said.

The house was two stories in height. It was of buff brick, with white trim about the windows and the doorway. It was not large, but it occupied an extremely advantageous position. It sat on a corner plot, so that it faced both ways at once, without obstruction. Moreover, the ground-plot itself extended beyond the house, if not lavishly at least amply, so that it touched none of its neighbors. There was room left for strips of sod in the front, and for a garden in the back.

It was not, of course, strictly presentable yet. There were several small messy piles of broken, discarded bricks left out before it, the sod was not in place, and the window glass was smirched with streaks of paint. But something almost reverent came into the man's face as he looked at it. His lips parted slightly and his eyes softened. He hadn't known there could be such a beautiful house. It was the most beautiful house he had ever seen. It was his.

A questioning flicker from the coachman's whip stirred him from his revery.

"You'll have to wait for me. I'm going down to meet the boat from here, later on."

"Yessuh, take your time, cunnel," the coachman grinned understandingly. "A man got to look at his house."

Durand didn't go inside immediately. Instead he prolonged the rapture he was deriving from this by first walking slowly and completely around the two outermost faces of the house. He tested a bit of foundation stone with his cane. He put out his hand and tried one of the shutters, swinging it out, then flattening it back again. He fastidiously speared a small, messy puff-ball of straw with his stick and transported it offside of the walk, leaving a trail of scattered filaments that was worse than the original offender.

He returned at last to the door, his head proudly high. There was a place indicated by pencil marks on the white-painted pinewood where a wrought-iron knocker was to be affixed, but this was not yet in position. He had chosen it himself, making a special trip to the foundry to do so. No effort too great, no detail too small.

Scorning to raise hand to the portal himself, possibly under the conviction that it was not fitting for a man to have to knock at the door of his own house, he tried the knob, found it unlocked, and entered. There was on the inside the distinctive and not unpleasant —and in this case enchanting—aroma a new house has, of freshly planed wood, the astringent turpentine in paint, window putty, and several other less identifiable ingredients.

A virginal staircase, its newly applied maple varnish protected by a strip of brown wrapping paper running down its center, rose at the back of the hall to the floor above. Turning aside, he entered a skeletal parlor, its western window casting squared puddles of gold light upon the floor.

As he stood and looked at it, the room changed. A thick-napped flowered carpet spread over its ascetic floor boards. The lurid red of lazy wood-flames peered forth from the now-blank fireplace under the mantel. A rounded mirror glistened ghostly on the wall above it. A plush sofa, a plush chair, a parlor table, came to life where there was nothing standing now. On the table a lamp with a planet-like milky-white bowl topping its base began to glow softly, then stronger, and stronger. And with its aid, a dark-haired head appeared in one of the chairs, contentedly resting back against the white antimacassar that topped it. And on the table, under the kindly lamp, some sort of a workbasket. A sewing workbasket. A little vaguer than the other details, this.

Then a pail clanked somewhere upstairs, and a tide of effacement flowed across the room, the carpet thinned, the fire dimmed, the lamp went out and with it the dark-haired faceless head, and the room was just as gaunt as it had been before. Rolls of furled wallpaper, a bucket on a trestle, bare floor.

"Who's that down there?" a woman's voice called hollowly through the empty spaces.

He came out into the hall at the foot of the stairs.

"Oh, it you, Mr. Lou. 'Bout ready for you now, I reckon."

The gnarled face of an elderly colored woman, topped by a dust-kerchief tied bandana-style, was peering down over the upstairs guardrail.

"Where'd he go, this fellow down here?" he demanded testily. "He should be finishing."

"Went to get more paste, I 'spect. He be back."

"How is it up there?"

"Coming along."

He launched into an unexpected little run, that carried him at a sprightly pace up the stairs. "I want to see the bedroom, mainly," he announced, brushing by her.

"What bridegroom don't?" she chuckled.

He stopped in the doorway, looked back at her rebukingly. "On account of the wallpaper," he took pains to qualify.

"You don't have to 'splain to me, Mr. Lou. I was in this world 'fore you was even born."

He went over to the wall, traced his fingers along it, as though the flowers were tactile, instead of just visual.

"It looks even better up, don't you think?"

"Right pretty," she agreed.

"It was the closest I could get. They had to send all the way to New York for it. See I asked her what her favorite kind was, without telling her why I wanted to know." He fumbled in his pocket, took out a letter, and scanned it carefully. He finally located the passage he wanted, underscored it with his finger. "—and for a bedroom I like pink, but not too bright a pink, with small blue flowers like forget-me-nots." He refolded the letter triumphantly, cocked his head at the walls.

Aunt Sarah was giving only a perfunctory ear. "I got a passel of work to do yet. If you'll 'scuse me, Mr. Lou, I wish you'd get out the way. I got make this bed up first of all." She chuckled again.

"Why do you keep laughing all the time?" he protested. "Don't you do that once she gets here."

"Shucks, no. I got better sense than that, Mr. Lou. Don't you fret your head about it."

He left the room, only to return to the doorway again a moment later. "Think you can get the downstairs curtains up before she gets here? Windows look mighty bare the way they are."

"Just you fetch her, and I have the house ready," the bustling old woman promised, casting up a billowing white sheet like a sail in the wind.

He left again. He came back once more, this time from mid-stairs.

"Oh, and it'd be nice if you could find some flowers, arrange them here and there. Maybe in the parlor, to greet her when she comes in."

She muttered something that sounded suspiciously like: "She ain't going have much time spend smelling flowers."

"What?" he caught her up, horrified.

She prudently refrained from repetition.

He departed once more. Once more he returned. This time all the way from the foot of the stairs.

"And be sure to leave all the lamps on when you go. I want the place bright and cheery when she first sees it."

"You keep peggin' at me every secon' like that," she chided, but without undue resentment, "and I won't git nothing done. Now go on, scat," she ordered, shaking her apron at him with contemptuous familiarity as though he were seven or seventeen, not thirty-seven. "Ain't nothing git in your way more than a man when he think he helping you fix up a place for somebody."

He gave her a rather hurt look, but he went below again. This time, at last, he didn't come back.

Yet when she descended herself, some full five minutes later, he was still there.

His back was to her. He stood before a table, simply because it happened to be there in the way. His hands were planted flat upon it at each side, and he was leaning slightly forward over it. As if peering intently into vistas of the future, that no one but he could see. As if in contemplation of some small-sized figure coming toward him through its rotary swirls, coming nearer, nearer, growing larger as it neared him, growing toward life-size—

He didn't hear Aunt Sarah come down. He only tore himself away from the entranced prospect, turned, at the first sound of her voice.

"You still here, Mr. Lou? I might have knowed it." She planted her arms akimbo, and surveyed him indulgently. "Just look at that. You sure happy, ain't you? I ain't never seen such a look on nobody's face before."

He sheepishly passed his hand across the lower part of his face, as if it were something external she had reference to. "Does it show that much?" He looked around him uncertainly, as if he still couldn't fully believe that the surroundings were actually there as he saw them. "My own house—" he murmured half-audibly. "My own wife—"

"A man without a wife, he ain't a whole man at all, he's just a shadow walking around without no one to cast him."

His hand rose briefly to his shirt front, touched it questioningly, dropped again. "I keep hearing music. Is there a band playing on the streets somewhere around here?"

"There's a band playing, sure enough," she confirmed, unsmiling. "A special kind of band, for just one person at a time to hear. For just one day. I heard it once. Today's your day for hearing it."

"I'd better be on my way!" He bolted for the door, flung it open, chased down the walk and gave a vault into the waiting carriage that rocked it on its springs.

"To the Canal Street Pier," he sighed with blissful anticipation, "to meet the boat from St. Louis."

3

THE RIVER was empty, the sky was clear. Both were mirrored in his anxious, waiting eyes. Then a little twirl of smudge appeared, no bigger than if stroked by a man-sized finger against the God-sized sky. It came from where there seemed to be no river, only an embankment; it seemed to hover over dry land, for it was around a turn the river made, before straightening to flow toward New Orleans and the pier. And those assembled on it.

He stood there waiting, others like himself about him. Some so close their elbows all but grazed him. Strangers, men he did not know, had never seen before, would never see again, drawn together for a moment by the arrival of a boat.

He had picked for his standing place a pilehead that protruded above the pier-deck; that was his marker, he stood close beside that, and wouldn't let others preempt it from him, knowing it would play its part in securing the craft. For a while he stood with one leg raised, foot planted squarely upon it. Then he leaned bodily forward over it in anticipation, both hands flattened on it. At one time, briefly, he even sat upon it, but got up again fairly soon, as if with some idea that by remaining on his feet he would hasten the vessel's approach.

The smoke had climbed now, was high in the sky, like dingy black ostrich plumes massed together and struggling to escape from one another. Under its profusion a black that was solid substance, a slender cone, began to rise; a smokestack. Then a second.

"There she is," a roustabout shouted, and the needless, overdue declaration was immediately taken up and repeated by two or three of those about him.

"Yes sir, there she is," they echoed two or three times after him. "There she is, all right."

"There she is," Durand's heart told him softly. But it meant a different she.

The smokestack, like a blunted knife slicing through the earth, cleared the embankment and came out upon the open water bed. A tawny superstructure, that seemed to be indented with a myriad tiny niches in two long even rows, was beneath it, and beneath that, only a thin line at this distance, was the ungainly black hull. The paddles were going, slats turning over as they reached the top of the wheel and fell, shaking off spray into the turgid brown water below that they kept beating upon.

She made the turn and grew larger, prow forward. She was life-sized now, coursing down on the pier as if she meant to smash it asunder. A shrill falsetto wail, infinitely mournful, like the cry of a lost soul in torment, knifed from her, and a plume of white circled the smokestack and vanished to the rear. The *City of New Orleans*, out of St. Louis three days before, was back home again at its namesake-port, its mother-haven.

The sidewheels stopped, and it began to glide, like a paper boat, like a ghost over the water. It turned broadside to the pier, and ran along beside it, its speed seeming swifter now, that it was lengthwise, than it had been before, when it was coming head-on, though the reverse was the truth.

The notched indentations went by like a picket fence, then slower, slower; then stopped at last, then even reversed a little and seemed to lose ground. The water, caught between the hull and pier, went crazy with torment; squirmed and slashed and choked, trying to find its way out. Thinned at last to a crevicelike canal.

No more river, no more sky, nothing but towering superstructure

blotting them both out. Someone idling against the upper deck rail
waved desultorily. Not to Durand, for it was a man. Not to anyone
else in particular, either, most likely. Just a friendly wave of arrival.
One of them on the pier took it upon himself to answer it with a like
wave, proxying for the rest.

A rope was thrown, and several of the small crowd stepped back
to avoid being struck by it. Dockworkers came forward for their
brief moment of glory, claimed the rope, deftly lashed it about the
pile top directly before Durand. At the opposite end they were doing
the same thing. She was in, she was fast.

A trestled gangway was rolled forward, a brief section of lower-
deck rail was detached, leaving an opening. The gap between was
bridged. A ship's officer came down, almost before it was fixed in
place, took up position close at hand below, to supervise the discharge. The passengers were funnelling along the deck from both
directions into and down through the single-file descent-trough.

Durand moved up close beside it until he could rest his hand upon
it, as if in mute claim; peered up anxiously into each imminent face
as it coursed swiftly downward and past, only inches from his own.

The first passenger off was a man, striding, sample cases in both
his hands, some business traveler in haste to leave. A woman next, more
slowly, picking her way with care. Gray-haired and spectacled; not
she. Another woman next. Not she again; her husband a step behind
her, guiding her with hand to her elbow. An entire family next, in
hierarchal order of importance.

Then more men, two or three of them in succession this time.
Faces just pale ciphers to him, quickly passed over. Then a woman,
and for a moment— No, not she; different eyes, a different nose, a
different face. A stranger's curt glance, meeting his, then quickly
rebuffing it. Another man. Another woman. Red-haired and sandy-
browed; not she.

A space then, a pause, a wait.

His heart took premature fright, then recovered. A tapping run
along the deck planks, as some laggard made haste to overtake the
others. A woman by the small, quick sound of her feet. A flounce of
skirts, a face— Not she. A whiff of lilac water, a snub from eyes that
had no concern for him, as his had for them, no quest in them, no
knowledge. Not she.

And then no more. The gangplank empty. A lull, as when a thing is over.

He stared up, and his face died.

He was gripping the edges of the gangplank with both hands now. He released it at last, crossed around to the other side of it, accosted the officer loitering there, clutched at him anxiously by the sleeve. "No one else?"

The officer turned and relayed the question upward toward the deck in booming hand-cupped shout. "Anyone else?"

Another of the ship's company, perhaps the captain, came to the rail and peered down overside. "All ashore," he called down.

It was like a knell. Durand seemed to find himself alone, in a pool of sudden silence, following it; though all about him there was as much noise going on as ever. But for him, silence. Stunning finality.

"But there must be— There has to—"

"No one else," the captain answered jocularly. "Come up and see for yourself."

Then he turned and left the rail.

Baggage was coming down now.

He waited, hoping against hope.

No one else. Only baggage, the inanimate dregs of the cargo. And at last not even that.

He turned aside at last and drifted back along the pier-length and off it to the solid ground beyond, and on a little while. His face stiffly averted, as if there were greater pain to be found on one side of him than on the other, though that was not true, it was equal all around.

And when he stopped, he didn't know it, nor why he had just when he did. Nor what reason he had for lingering on there at all. The boat had nothing for him, the river had nothing for him. There was nothing there for him. There or anywhere else, now.

Tears filled his eyes, and though there was no one near him, no one to notice, he slowly lowered his head to keep them from being detected.

He stood thus, head lowered, somewhat like a muted mourner at a bier. A bier that no one but he could see.

The ground before his unseeing eyes was blank; biscuit-colored earth basking in the sun. As blank, perhaps, as his life would be from now on.

Then without a sound of approach, the rounded shadow of a small head advanced timorously across it; cast from somewhere behind him, rising upward from below. A neck, two shoulders, followed it. Then the graceful indentation of a waist. Then the whole pattern stopped flowing, stood still.

His dulled eyes took no note of the phenomenon. They were not seeing the ground, nor anything imprinted upon it; they were seeing the St. Louis Street house. They were saying farewell to it. He'd never enter it again, he'd never go back there. He'd turn it over to an agent, and have him sell—

There was the light touch of a hand upon his shoulder. No exacting weight, no compulsive stroke; velvety and gossamer as the alighting of a butterfly. The shadow on the ground had raised a shadow-arm to another shadow—his—linking them for a moment, then dropping it again.

His head came up slowly. Then equally slowly he turned it toward the side from which the touch had come.

A figure swept around before him, as on a turntable, pivoting to claim the center of his eyes; though it was he and not the background that had shifted.

It was diminutive, and yet so perfectly proportioned within its own lesser measurements that, but for the yardstick of comparison offered when the eye deliberately sought out others and placed them against it, it could have seemed of any height at all: of the grandeur of a classical statue or of the minuteness of an exquisite doll.

Her limpid brown eyes came up to the turn of Durand's shoulder. Her face held an exquisite beauty he had never before seen, the beauty of porcelain, but without its cold stillness, and a crumpled rose petal of a mouth.

She was no more than in her early twenties, and though her size might have lent her added youth, the illusion had very little to subtract from the reality. Her skin was that of a young girl, and her eyes were the innocent, trustful eyes of a child.

Tight-spun golden curls clung to her head like a field of daisies, rebelling all but successfully at the conventional coiffure she tried to impose upon them. They took to the ubiquitous psyche-knot at the back only with the aid of forceful pins, and at the front resisted the forehead-fringe altogether, fuming about like topaz sea spray.

She held herself in that forward-inclination that was *de rigueur*, known as the "Grecian bend." Her dress was of the fashion as it then was, and had been for some years. Fitting tightly as a sheath fits a furled umbrella, it had a center panel, drawn and gathered toward the back to give the appearance of an apron or a bib super-imposed upon the rest, and at the back puffed into a swollen pro-tuberance of bows and folds, artfully sustained by a wired founda-tion; this was the stylish bustle, without which a woman's posterior would have appeared indecently sleek. As soon expose the insteps or —reckless thought!—the ankles as allow the sitting-part to remain flat.

A small hat of heliotrope straw, as flat as and no bigger than a man's palm, perched atop the golden curls, roguishly trying to reach down toward one eyebrow, the left, without there being enough of it to do so and still stay atop her head.

Amethyst-splinters twinkled in the tiny holes pierced through the lobes of her miniature and completely uncovered ears, and a slender ribbon of heliotrope velvet girded her throat. A parasol of heliotrope organdy, of scarcely greater diameter than a soup plate and of the consistency of mist, hovered aloft at the end of an elongated stick, like an errant violet halo. Upon the ground to one side of her sat a small gilt birdcage, its lower portion swathed in a flannel cloth, the dome left open to expose its flitting bright-yellow occupant.

He looked at her hand, he looked at his own shoulder, so unsure was he the touch had come from her; so unsure was he as to the reason for such a touch. Slowly his hat came off, was held at questioning height above his scalp.

The compressed mouth curved in winsome smile. "You don't know me, do you, Mr. Durand?"

He shook his head slightly.

The smile notched a dimple; rose to her eyes. "I'm Julia, Louis. May I call you Louis?"

His hat fell from his fingers to the ground, and rolled once about, for the length of half its brim. He bent and retrieved it, but only with his arm and shoulder; his face never once quited hers, as though held to it by an unbreakable magnetic current.

"But no— How can—?"

"Julia Russell," she insisted, still smiling.

"But no— You can't—" he kept dismembering words.

Her brows arched. The smile expired compassionately. "It was unkind of me to do this, wasn't it?"

"But—the picture—dark hair—"

"That was my aunt's I sent instead." She shook her head in belated compunction. She lowered the parasol, closed it with a little plop. With the point of its stick she began to trace cabalistic designs in the dust. She dropped her eyes and watched what she was doing with an air of sadness. "Oh, I shouldn't have, I know that now. But at the time, it didn't seem to matter so much, we hadn't become serious yet. I thought it was just a correspondence. Then many times since, I wanted to send the right one in its place, to tell you— And the longer I waited, the less courage I had. Fearing I'd—I'd lose you altogether in that way. It preyed on my mind more and more, and yet, the closer the time drew— At the very last moment, I was already aboard the boat, and I wanted to turn around and go back. Bertha prevailed upon me to—to continue down here. My sister, you know."

"I know," he nodded, still dazed.

"The last thing she said to me, just before I left, was, 'He'll forgive you. He'll understand you meant no harm.' But during the entire trip down, how bitterly I repented my—my frivolity." Her head all but hung, and she caught at her mouth, gnawing at it with her small white teeth.

"I can't believe—I can't believe—" was all he could keep stammering.

She was an image of lovely penitence, tracing her parasol-stick about on the ground, shyly waiting for forgiveness.

"But so much younger—" he marveled. "So much lovelier even than—"

"That too entered into it," she murmured. "So many men become smitten with just a pretty face. I wanted our feeling to go deeper than that. To last longer. To be more secure. I wanted you to care for me, if you did care, because of—well, the things I wrote you, the sort of mind I displayed, the sort of person I really was, rather than because of a flibbertigibbet's photograph. I thought perhaps if I gave myself every possible disadvantage at the beginning, of appearance and age and so forth, then there would be that much less danger later, of its being just a passing fancy. In other words, I put the obstacles at the beginning, rather than have them at the end."

How sensible she was, he discovered to himself, how level-minded, in addition to all her external attractions. Why, there were the components here of a paragon.

"How many times I tried to write you the truth, you'll never know," she went on contritely. "And each time my courage would fail. I was afraid I would only succeed in alienating you entirely, from a person who, by her own admission, had been guilty of falsehood. I couldn't trust such a thing to cold paper." She gestured charmingly with one hand. "And now you see me, and now you know. The worst."

"The worst," he protested strenuously. "But you," he went on after a moment, still amazed, "but you, knowing all along what I did not know until now, that I was so much—well, considerably, older than you. And yet—"

She dropped her eyes, as if in additional confession. "Perhaps that may have been one of your principal attractions, who knows? I have, since as far back as I can remember, been capable of—shall I say, romantic feelings, the proper degree of emotion or admiration—only toward men older than myself. Boys of my own age have never interested me. I don't know what to attribute it to. All the women in my family have been like that. My mother was married at fifteen, and my father was at the time well over forty. The mere fact that you *were* thirty-six, was what first—" With maidenly seemliness, she forebore to finish it.

He kept devouring her with his eyes, still incredulous.

"Are you disappointed?" she asked timidly.

"How can you ask that?" he exclaimed.

"Am I forgiven?" was the next faltering question.

"It was a lovely deception," he said with warmth of feeling. "I don't think there's been a lovelier one ever committed."

He smiled, and her smile, still somewhat abashed, answered his own.

"But now I will have to get used to you all over again. Grow to know you all over again. That was a false start," he said cheerfully.

She turned her head aside and mutely half-hid it against her own shoulder. And yet even this gesture, which might have seemed maudlin or revoltingly saccharine in others, she managed to carry off successfully, making it appear no more than a playful parody while at the same time deftly conveying its original intent of rebuked coyness.

He grinned.

She turned her face toward him again. "Are your plans, your, er, intentions, altered?"

"Are yours?"

"I'm here," she said with the utmost simplicity, grave now.

He studied her a moment longer, absorbing her charm. Then suddenly, with new-found daring, he came to a decision. "Would it make you feel better, would it ease your mind of any lingering discomfort," he blurted out, "if I were to make a confession to you on my own part?"

"You?" she said surprised.

"I—I no more told you the entire truth than you told me," he rushed on.

"But—but I see you quite as you said you were, quite as your picture described you—"

"It isn't that, it's something else. I too perhaps felt just as you did, that I wanted you to like me, to accept my offer, solely on the strength of the sort of man I was in myself. For myself alone, in other words."

"But I see that, and I do," she said blankly. "I don't understand."

"You will in a moment," he promised her, almost eagerly. "Now I must confess to you that I'm not a clerk in a coffee-import house."

Her face betrayed no sign other than politely interested incomprehension.

"That I *haven't* a thousand dollars put aside, to—to start us off."

No sign. No sign of crestfall or of frustrated avarice. He was watching her intently. A slow smile of indulgence, of absolution granted, overspread her features before he had spoken next. *Well* before he had spoken next. He gave it time.

"No, I *own* a coffee-import house, instead."

No sign. Only that slightly forced smile, such as women give in listening to details of a man's business, when it doesn't interest them in the slightest but they are trying to be polite.

"No, I have closer to a hundred thousand dollars."

He waited for her to say something. She didn't. She, on the contrary, seemed to be waiting for him to continue. As if the subject had been so arid, and barren of import, to her, that she did not realize the climax had already been reached.

"Well, that's *my* confession," he said somewhat lamely.

"Oh," she said, as if brought up short. "Oh, was that it? You mean—" She fluttered her hand with vague helplessness. "—about your business, and money matters—" She brought two fingers to her mouth, and crossed it with their tips. Stifling a yawn that, without the gesture of concealment, he would not have detected in the first place. "There are two things I have no head for," she admitted. "One is politics, the other is business, money matters."

"But you do forgive me?" he persisted. Conscious at the same time of a fierce inward joy, that was almost exultation; as when one has encountered a perfection of attitude, at long last, and almost by chance, that was scarcely to be hoped for.

She laughed outright this time, with a glint of mischief, as if he were giving her more credit than was due her. "If you must be forgiven, you're forgiven," she relented. "But since I paid no attention whatever to the passages in your letters that dealt with that, in the first place, why, you're asking forgiveness for a fault I was not aware, until now, of your having committed. Take it, then, though I'm not sure what it's for."

He stared at her with a new intentness, that went deeper than before; as if finding her as utterly charming within as she was at first sight without.

Their shadows were growing longer, and they were all but alone now on the pier. He glanced around him as if reluctantly awakening to their surroundings. "It's getting late, and I'm keeping you standing here," he said in a reminder that was more dutiful than honest, for it might mean their separation, for all he knew.

"You make me forget the time," she admitted, her eyes never leaving his face. "Is that a bad omen or a good? You even make me forget my predicament: half ashore and half still on the boat. I must soon become the one or the other."

"That's soon taken care of," he said, leaning forward eagerly, "if I have your own consent."

"Isn't yours necessary too?" she said archly.

"It's given, it's given." He was almost breathless with haste to convince her.

She was in no hurry, now that he was. "I don't know," she said, lifting the point of her parasol, then dropping it again, then lifting it once more, in an uncertainty that he found excruciating. "If you had not seemed satisfied, if you had looked askance at the deceiver that you found me to be, I intended going back onto the boat and remaining aboard till she set out on the return trip to St. Louis. Don't you think that might still be the wiser—"

"No, don't say that," he urged, alarmed. "Satisfied? I'm the happiest man in New Orleans this evening—I'm the luckiest man in this town—"

She was not, it seemed, to be swayed so easily. "There is still time. Better now than later. Are you quite sure you wouldn't rather have me do that? I won't say a word, I won't complain. I'll understand your feelings perfectly—"

He was gripped by a sudden new fear of losing her. She, whom he hadn't had at all until scarcely half an hour ago.

"But those aren't my feelings! I beg you to believe me! My feelings are quite the opposite. What can I do to convince you? Do *you* want more time? Is it you? Is that what you are trying to say to me?" he insisted with growing anxiety.

She held him for a moment with her eyes, and they were kindly and candid and even, one might have said, somewhat tender. Then she shook her head, very slightly it is true, but with all the firmness of intention that a man might have given the gesture (if he could read it right), and not a girl's facile undependable negation.

"My mind has been made up," she told him, slowly and simply, "since I first stepped onto the boat at St. Louis. Since your letter of proposal came, as a matter of fact, and I wrote you my answer. And I do not lightly undo my mind, once it has been made up. You will find that once you know me better." Then she qualified it: "If you do," and let that find him out with a little unwelcome stab, as it promptly did.

"I'll let this be my answer, then," he said with tremulous impatience. "Here it is." He opened his cardcase, took out the daguerrotype, the one of the other, older woman—her aunt's—minced it with energetic fingers, then let it fall in trifling pieces downward all over the ground. Then showed her both his hands, empty.

"My mind is made up too."

She smiled her acceptance. "Then—?"

"Then let's be on our way. They're waiting for us at the church the past quarter-hour or more. We've delayed here too long."

He tilted his arm akimbo, offered it to her with a smile and a gallant inclination from the waist, that were perhaps, on the surface, meant to appear as badinage, merely a bantering parody, but were in reality more sincerely intended.

"Miss Julia?" he invited.

This was the moment of ultimate romance, its quintessence. The betrothal.

She shifted her parasol to the opposite shoulder. Her hand curled about his arm like a friendly sun-warmed tendril. She gathered up the bottom of her skirt to reticent walking-level.

"Mr. Durand," she accepted, addressing him by surname only, in keeping with the seemly propriety of the still-unmarried young woman that made her drop her eyes fetchingly at the same time.

4

THE INTERIOR of the Dryades German Methodist Church at sundown. Fulminating orange haze from without blurring its leaded windows into swollen shapelessness; its arched apse disappearing upward into cobwebby blue twilight. Grave, peaceful, empty but for five persons.

Five persons gathered in a solemn little conclave about the pulpit. Four facing it, the fifth occupying it. Four silent, the fifth speaking low. The first two of the four, side by side; the second two flanking them. Outside, barely audible, as if filtered through a heavy screen, the sounds of the city, muffled, dreamy, faraway. The occasional clop of a horse's hoof on cobbles, the creaking protest of a sharply curving wheel, the voice of an itinerant hawker crying his wares, the bark of a dog.

Inside, stately phrases of the marriage service, echoing serenely in the spacious stillness. The Reverend Edward A. Clay the officiant, Louis Durand and Julia Russell the principals. Allan Jardine and Sophie Tadoussac, housekeeper to the Reverend Clay, the witnesses.

"And do you, Julia Russell, take this man, Louis Durand, to be your lawful wedded husband—

"To cleave to, forsaking all others—

"To love, honor and obey—

"For better or for worse—

"For richer or for poorer—

"In sickness and in health—

"Until death do ye part?"

Silence.

Then like a tiny bell, no bigger than a thimble in all the vastness of that church, but clear and silver-pure—

"I do."

"Now the ring, please. Place it upon the bride's finger."

Durand reaches behind him. Jardine produces it, puts it in his blindly questing hand. Durand brings it to the tapered point of her finger.

There is a momentary awkwardness. Her finger measurement was taken by a string, knotted at the proper place and sent enclosed in a letter. But there must have been an error, either in the knotting or on the jeweler's part. It balks, won't go on.

He tried a second, a third time, clasping her hand tighter. Still it resists.

Quickly she flicks her finger past her lips, returns it to him, edge moistened. The ring goes on, ebbs down it now to base.

"I now pronounce you man and wife."

Then, with a professional smile to encourage the age-old shyness of lovers when on public view, for the greater the secret love, the greater the public shyness: "You may kiss the bride."

Their faces turn slowly toward one another. Their eyes meet. Their heads draw together. The lips of Louis Durand blend with those of Julia, his wife, in sacramental pledge.

ANTOINE'S, rushing all alight toward its nightly rendezvous with midnight; glittering, glowing, mirrored; crowded with celebrants, singing with laughter, sizzling with champagne; sparkling with half-a-thousand jeweled gas flames all over its ceilings and walls, in bowers of crystal; the gayest and best-known restaurant on this side of the ocean; the soul of Paris springing enchanted from the Delta mud.

The wedding table stretched lengthwise along one entire side of it, the guests occupying one side only, so that the outer side mignt be left clear for their view of the rest of the room—and the rest of the room's view of them.

It was by now eleven and after, a disheveled mass of tortured napkins, sprawled flowers, glassware tinged with repeated refills of red wines and white; champagne and kirsch and little upright thimbles of benedictine for the ladies, no two alike at the same level of consumption. And in the center, dominating the table, a miracle of a cake, snow-white, sugar-spun, rising tier upon tier; badly eaten away by erosion now, so that one entire side was gone. But atop its highest pinnacle, still preserved intact, a little bride and groom in doll form, he in a thumbnail suit of black broadcloth, she with a wisp of tulle streaming from her head.

And opposite them, the two originals, in life-size; sitting shoulder pressed to shoulder, hands secretively clasped below the table, listening to some long-winded speech of eulogy. His head still held upright in polite pretense at attention; her head nestled dreamy-eyed against his shoulder.

He was in suitable evening garb now, and a quick trip to a dress-shop (first at her mention, but then at his insistence) before coming on here had changed her from her costume of arrival to a glorious creation of shimmering white satin, gardenias in her hair and at her throat. On the third finger of her left hand the new gold wedding-band; on the fourth, a solitaire diamond, a husband's wedding gift to his wife, token of an engagement contract fulfilled rather than of one entered into before the event.

And her eyes, like any new wearer's, stray over and over to these new adornments. But whether they go more often to the third finger or to the fourth, who is to detect and who is to say?

Flowers, wine, friendly laughing faces, toasts and wishes of well-being. The beginning of two lives. Or rather, the ending of two, the beginning of one.

"Shall we slip away now?" he whispers to her. "It's getting on to twelve."

"Yes. One more dance together first. Ask them to play again. And then we'll lose ourselves, without coming back to the table."

"As soon as Allan finishes speaking," he assents. "If he's ever going to."

Allan Jardine, his business partner, has become so involved in the mazes of a congratulatory speech that he cannot seem to find his way out of it again. It has been going on for ten minutes; ten minutes that seem like forty.

Jardine's wife, sitting beside him, and present only because of an unguessed but very strenuous domestic tug-of-war, has a dour, disapproving look on her face. Disapproving something, but doing her best to seem amiable, for the sake of her own husband's business interests. Disapproving the good looks of the bride, or her youth, or perhaps the unorthodox circumstances of the preceding courtship. Or perhaps the fact that Durand has married at all, after having waited so many years already, without waiting a few years more for her own under-age daughter to grow up. A favorite project which even her own husband has had no inkling of so far. And now will never have.

Durand took out a small card, wrote on it "Play another waltz." Then he folded a currency note around it, motioned to a waiter, handed it to him to be taken to the musicians.

Jardine's wife was surreptitiously tugging at the hem of his coat now, to get him to bring his oration to a conclusion.

"Allan," she hissed. "Enough is enough. This is a wedding-supper, not a rally."

"I'm nearly through," he promised in an aside.

"You're through now," was the edict, delivered with a guillotine-like sweep of her hand.

"And so I give you the two newest apprentices to this great and happy profession of marriage. Julia (May I?" with a bow toward her) "and Louis."

Glasses went up, down again. Jardine at last sat down, mopping his brow. His wife, for her part, fanned herself by hand, holding her mouth open as she did so, as if to get rid of a bad taste.

A chord of music sounded.

Durand and Julia rose; their alacrity would have been highly uncomplimentary if it had not been so understandable.

"Excuse us, we want to dance this together."

And Durand solemnly winked at Jardine, to show him that he must not expect to see them back at their places again.

A fact which Jardine immediately imparted to his wife behind the back of his hand the moment they had left the table. Whereupon she seemed to disapprove that, too, in addition to everything else that she already disapproved about this affair, and took a prudish, astringent sip from her wineglass with a puckered mouth.

The bows of the violinists all rose together, fell together, and they swept into the waltz from *Romeo and Juliet*.

They stood facing one another for a moment, he and she, in the usual formal preliminary. Then she bent to pick up the loop of her furbelowed dress, he opened his arms, and she stepped into his embrace.

The waltz began, the swiftest of all paired dances. Around and around and around, then reversing, and around and around once more, the new way. The tables and the faces swept around them, as if they were standing still in the middle of a whirlpool, and the gaslights flashed by on the walls and ceilings like comets.

She held her neck arched, her head slightly back, looking straight upward into his eyes, as if to say "I am in your hands. Do with me as you will. Where you go, I will go. Where you turn, I will follow."

"Are you happy, Julia?"

"Doesn't my face tell you?"

"Do you regret coming down to New Orleans now?"

"*Is* there any other place but New Orleans now?" she asked with charming intensity.

Around and around and around; alone together, though there was a flurry of other skirts all around them.

"Our life together is going to be like this waltz, Julia. As sleek, as smooth, as harmonious. Never a wrong turn, never a jarring note. Together as close as this. One mind, one heart, one body."

"A waltz for life," she whispered raptly. "A waltz with wings. A waltz never ending. A waltz in the sunlight, a waltz in azure, in gold —and in spotless white."

She closed her eyes, as if in ecstasy.

"Here's the side way out. And no one's watching."

They came to a deft, toe-gliding halt, such as skaters use. They separated, and gave a quick look over at the oblivious wedding party table, half-screened from them by the dancers in between. Then he guided her before him, around palms, and a bronze statuette of a nymph, and a fluted column, out of the main dining room and into a scullery passage, redolent of steamy food and loud with unseen voices somewhere near at hand. She giggled as a small cat, coming their way, stopped to eye them amazed.

He took her by the hand now, and took the lead, and drew her after him, on quick-running joyous little steps, out to an outside alleyway that ran beside the building. And from here they emerged to the street at last. He threw up his arm at a carriage, and a moment later was sitting beside her in it, his arm protectively about her.

"St. Louis Street," he ordered proudly. "I'll show you where to stop."

And as the bells of St. Louis Cathedral near by began their slow tolling of midnight, Louis Durand and his bride drove rapidly away toward their new home.

6

THE HOUSE was empty, waiting. Waiting to begin its history, which, for a house, is that of its occupants. Oil lamps had been left lighted, one to a room, by someone, most likely Aunt Sarah, before leaving, their little beaded flames, safe within glass chimneys, winking just high enough to disperse the darkness and cast an amber glow. The same blend of wood shavings, paint, and putty, spiced with a dash of floor varnish, was still in evidence, but to a far lesser degree now, for carpets had been laid over the raw floors, drapes hung athwart the window casings.

Someone had brought flowers into the parlor, not costly store flowers but wildflowers, cheery, colorful, winning none the less; a generous spray of them smothering a widemouthed bowl set on the parlor center table, with spears of pussywillow sticking out all over like the quills of a hedgehog's back.

A clock had even been wound up and started on its course, a new clock on the mantelpiece, imported from France, its face set in a block of green onyx, a little bronze cupid with moth wings clambering up a chain of bronze roses at each side of its centerpiece. Its diligent, newly practised ticking added a note of reassuring, homely tranquility to what otherwise would have been a stony-cold silence.

Everything was ready, all that was lacking were the dwellers.

A house, waiting for a man and his wife to come and claim it.

The resonant, cuplike sound of a horse's hoofs drew near in the stillness outside, came to a halt on a double down-beat. Axles creaked with a shift of weight, then settled again. A human tongue clucked professionally, then the hoofs recommenced, thinned away into silence once more.

There was a slight scrape of leather on paving stone, a mischievous little whisper, like a secret told by one foot to another.

A moment afterward a key turned in the outside of the door.

They stood there revealed in the opening, Durand and she. Limned amber by the light before them in the house, framed by a panel of night sky sanded with stars behind them and over their heads. They were motionless, as oblivious of what lay before them as of what lay behind them. Face turned to meet face, his arms about her, her hands on his shoulders.

Nothing moved, neither they nor the stars at their back nor the open-doored house waiting to receive them. It was one of those moments never to be captured again. The kiss at the threshold of marriage.

It ended. A moment cannot last beyond itself. They stirred at last and drew apart, and he said softly: "Welcome to your new home, Mrs. Durand. May you find as much happiness here as you bring to it."

"Thank you," she murmured, eyes downcast for a second. "And may you as well."

He lifted her bodily in his arms. She came clear of the ground with a little foamy rustle of skirt bottoms. Moving sideward so that his shoulder might ward off the loose-swinging door, he carried her over the sill and in. Then dipped again and set her back on her feet, in a little froth of lacy hems.

He stepped aside, closed the door, and bolted it.

She was looking around, standing in one place but moving her body in a half-circle from there, to take in everything.

"Like it?" he asked.

He went to a lamp, turned the little wheel, heightening its flame to a yellow stalagmite. Then to another, and another, wherever they had been left. The walls brightened from dull ivory to purest white. The newness of everything became doubly conspicuous.

"Like it?" he beamed, as though the reward for it all lay in hearing her say that.

Her hands were clasped, and elevated upward to height of her face; held that way in a sort of stylized rhapsody.

"Oh, Louis," she breathed. "It's ideal. It's exquisite."

"It's yours," he said, and the way he dropped his voice showed the gratitude he felt at her appreciation.

She moved her hands out to one side of her face now, still clasped, and nestled her cheek against them slantwise. Then across to the other side, and repeated it there.

"Oh, Louis," was all she seemed capable of saying. "Oh, *Louis.*"

They moved around then on a brief tour, from room to room, and he showed her the parlor, the dining room, the others. And for each room she had an expiring "Oh, Louis," until at last, it seemed, breath had left her altogether, and she could only sigh "Oh."

They came back to the hall at last, and he said somewhat diffidently that he would lock up.

"Will you be able to find our room?" he added, as she turned toward the stairs. "Or shall I come up with you?"

She dropped her eyes for a moment before his. "I think I shall know it," she said chastely.

He placed one of the smaller lamps in her hands. "Better take this with you to make sure. She probably left lights up there, but she may not have."

With the light brought close to her like that, raying upward into her face from the glowing core held at about the height of her heart, there was to him something madonna-like about her countenance.

She was like some inexpressibly beautiful image in an old cathedral of Europe come to life before the eyes of a single devotee, rewarded for his faith. A miracle of love.

She rose a step. She rose another. An angel leaving the earthly plane, but turned backward in regretful farewell.

His hand even went out slightly, as if to trace her outline against the air on which he beheld it, and thus prolong her presence.

"Goodbye for a little while," he murmured softly.

"For a little while," she breathed.

Then she turned. The spell was broken. She was just a woman in an evening gown, going up a stair.

The graceful back-draperies of the most beautiful costume-style in a hundred years gently undulated with her climb. Her free hand trailed the banister.

"Keep an eye out for the wallpaper," he said. "That will tell you."

She turned inquiringly, with a look of incomprehension. "How's that?"

"I meant, you'll know it by the wallpaper, when you come to it."

"Oh," she said docilely, but as though she still didn't fully understand.

She reached the top of the stairs and went over their lip, shrinking down toward the floor now as she went on, until her shoulders, then her head, were gone. The ceiling-halo cast by her lamp receded past his ken, down that same illusory incline.

He went into the parlor, first, and then the other downstairs rooms, latching each window that had not already been latched, trying those that had, flinging out the drapes and drawing them sleekly together over each one. Night air was bad, the whole world knew that; it was best kept out of a sleeping house. Then at last blotting out each welcoming lamp, room by room.

In the kitchen Sarah had left a bunch of fine green grapes set out on a platter, as another token of welcome to the two of them. He plucked one off and put it in his mouth, with a half-smile for her thoughtfulness, then put out the light in there too.

The last lamp of all went out, and he moved slowly up the ghost-stairs in the dark, that was already a familiar dark to him though he'd been in this house less than half an hour. The dark of a man's own home is never strange and never fearful.

He found his way toward their own door, in the equal darkness of
the upper hall, but guided now by the thread of light stretched taut
across its sill.

He stopped a moment, and he stood there.

Then he knocked, in a sort of playful formality.

She must have sensed his mood, by the tenor of the knock alone.
There was an answering playful note in her own voice.

"Who knocks?" she inquired with mock gravity.

"Your husband."

"Oh? What does he say?"

" 'May I come in?' "

"Tell him he may."

"Who is it invites me to?"

The answer was almost inaudible, but low-voiced as it was, it
reached his heart.

"Your wife."

7

ARRIVING HOME from his office—this was about a week later, ten
days at most—he hastened up the stairs to greet her, not having found
her in any of the lower-floor rooms when he entered. He was cush-
ioning his tread, to surprise her, to come up unexpectedly behind
her and cover her eyes, have her guess who it was. Though how could
she fail to know it was he, for who else should it be? But homecoming was still an exquisite novelty, it had to be decked out with all
these flourishes and fancies; though it was repeated daily, it still held
all the delightful anticipation of a first meeting, each time.

The door of their room was open and she was seated in there,
docilely enough, in a fan-backed chair, only the top of her head
visible above it, for she was looking away from the entrance. He
stood for a moment at the threshold, still undiscovered, caressing

her with his eyes. As he watched he could see her hand move, limply turning over the page of some book that was occupying her.

He started over toward her, intent now on bending suddenly down over the back of the chair and pressing his lips to the top of her head, coppery-gilt in the waning sunlight. But as he advanced, and as her hidden form slowly came into view, lengthening into perspective with his own approach, something he saw made him stop again, amazed, almost incredulous.

He changed his purpose now. Moved openly, in a wide circle about the chair, to take it in from the side, and stopped at last before it, with a sort of pained puzzlement discernable on his face.

She had looked up at discovery of him, closed her book with a little throaty exclamation of pleasure.

"Here you are, dear? I didn't hear you come in below."

"Julia," he said, in a tone of blank incomprehension.

"What is it?"

He described her form with a sketchy lengthwise gesture of his hand, and still she didn't understand. He had to put it into words.

"Why, the way you're sitting—"

Her legs were crossed, as only men crossed theirs. One knee reared atop the other in unashamed prominence, the shank of her leg boldly thrust forth, the suspended foot had even been swinging a little, though that had stopped now.

The sheath of her skirt veiled the full rakishness of the position, but shadowy outlines and indentations outlined it only too distinctly even so.

She had been caught in a very real grossness, not to be understood by any later standard of manners, but only when set against its own contemporary code of universal conduct. For a woman to sit like that would have drawn stares anywhere, then, even ostracism and a request that she leave forthwith. No woman, not even the flightiest, sat but with the knees both level and the feet both flat upon the floor, though one might be drawn back behind the other for added grace. Immorality lies not in the nature of an act itself, but in the universality of the accepted tenet which it flouts. Thus a trifling variation of posture can be more shocking, to one era of strictly-maintained behavior, than a very real transgression would be to another and more lax one. The one cannot understand the other, and finds it only a laughable prissiness. Which it was not at the time.

Durand was no more prudish than the next, but he saw something which he had never seen any other woman do. Not even the "young ladies" of Madame Rachel's "Academy," when he visited there during his bachelor days. And this was the wife under his own roof.

"Do you sit that way at other times too?" he queried uneasily.

Subtly, with a sort of dissembling stealth, the offending knees uncoupled, the projecting leg descended beside its mate. Almost without the alteration being detected, she was once more sitting as all ladies sat. Even alone, even before only their own husbands.

"No," she protested virtuously, tipping horrified palms. "Of course not. How should I? I—I was alone in the room, and it must have come about without my thinking."

"But think if it should come about, some time, without your thinking, where others could see you."

"It shan't," she promised, tipping horrified palms at the very thought. "For it never did before, and it never will again."

She dismissed the subject by elevating her face toward him expectantly.

"You haven't kissed me yet."

The incident died out in his eyes, to match its extinction in his mind, in the finding of her lips with his.

8

ROSY-CHEEKED, dewy-eyed, winsome in the early morning sunlight, in a dressing sack of warm yellow whose hue matched the sunny glow falling about her, she quickly forestalled Aunt Sarah, took the coffee urn from her hand, insisting as she did every day on pouring his cupful herself.

He smiled, flattered, as he did every day when this same thing happened.

Next she took up the small silver tongs, fastened them on a lump of twinkling sugar, carefully carried it past the rim of his cup, and holding it low so that it might not splash, released it.

He beamed.

"So much the sweeter," he murmured confidentially.

She gave her fingertips a brisk little brushing-together, though they had not as a matter of fact touched anything at first hand, placed a kiss at the side of his head, hurried around to her side of the table, and seated herself with a crisp little rustling.

It was like a little girl, he couldn't help thinking, pressing a little boy into playing at house with her. You be the papa, and I'll be the mamma.

Settled in her own chair, she raised her cup, eyes smiling at him to the last over its very rim, until she must drop them to make sure of fitting it exactly to her still incredibly, always incredibly, tiny mouth.

"This is really excellent coffee," she remarked, after a sip.

"It's some of our own. One of the better grades, from the warehouse. I have a small sackful sent home every now and again for Aunt Sarah's use."

"I don't know what I should do without it. It is so invigorating, of a chilly morning. There is nothing I am quite so fond of."

"You mean since you have begun to sample Aunt Sarah's?"

"No, always. All my life I—"

She stopped, seeing him look at her with a sort of sudden, arrested attention. It was like a stone cast into the bubbling conversation, and sinking heavily to the bottom, stilling it.

There was some sort of contagion passed between them. Impossible to give it a name. She seemed to take it from him, seeing it appear on his face, and her own became strained and watchful. It was unease, a sudden chilling of assurance. It was the unpleasant sensation, or feeling of loss, that a worthless iron washer might convey, suddenly detected in a palmful of golden disks.

"But—" he said at last, and didn't go on.

"Yes?" She said with an effort. "Were you going to say something?" And the turn of one hand appeared over the edge of the table before her, almost as if in a bracing motion.

"No, I—" Then he gave himself the lie, went on to say it anyway. "But in your letter once you said the opposite. Telling me how you went down to a cup of tea in the morning. Nothing but tea would do. You could not abide coffee. 'Heavy, inky drink.' I can still remember your very words."

She lifted her cup again, took a sip. She was unable therefore to speak again until she had removed it out of the way.

"True," she said, speaking rather fast to make up for the restriction, once it had been removed. "But that was because of my sister."

"But your preferences are your own, how could your sister affect them?"

"I was in her house," she explained. "She was the one liked tea, I coffee. But out of consideration for her, in order not to be the means of causing her to drink something she did not like, I pretended I liked it too. I put it in my letter because I sometimes showed her my letters to you before I sent them, and I did not want her to discover my little deception."

"Oh," he grinned, almost with a breath of relief.

She began to laugh. She laughed almost too loudly for the small cause she had. As if in release of stress.

"I wish you could have seen your face just then," she told him. "I didn't know what ailed you for a moment."

She went on laughing.

He laughed with her.

They laughed together, in a burst of fatuous bridal merriment.

Aunt Sarah, coming into the room, joined their laughter, knowing as little as either of them what it was about.

9

HER COMPLEXION was a source of considerable wonderment to him. It seemed capable of the most rapid and unpredictable changes, almost within the twinkling of an eye. These flushes and pallors, if such they were, did not actually occur before his eyes, but within such short spans of time that, for all practical purposes, it amounted to the same thing.

They were not blushes in the ordinary sense, for they did not diminish again within a few moments of their onset, as those would have; once the change had occurred, once her coloring had heightened, it remained that way for hours after, with no immediate counteralteration ensuing.

It was most noticeable in the mornings. On first opening the shutters and turning to behold her, her coloring would be almost camelia-like. And yet, but a few moments later, as she followed in his wake down the stairs and rejoined him at the table, there would be the fresh hue of primroses, of pink carnations, in her cheeks, to set off the blue of her eyes all the more, the gold of her hair, to make her a vision of such loveliness that to look at her was almost past endurance.

In a theatre one night (they were seated in a box) the same transfiguration occurred, between two of the acts of the play, but on this occasion he ascribed it to illness, though if it were, she would not admit it to him. They had arrived late and had therefore entered in the darkness, or at least dimness relieved only by the stage lights. When the gas jets flared high, however, between the acts, she discovered (and seemed quite concerned by it, why he could not make out) that their loge was lined with a tufted damask of a particularly virulent apple-green shade. This, in conjunction with the blazing gas beating full upon her face, gave her a bilious, verdant look.

Many eyes (as always whenever she appeared anywhere with him) were turned upward upon her from the audience, both men and women alike, and more than one pair of opera glasses were centered upon her, as custom allowed them to be.

She shifted about impatiently in her chair for a moment or two, then suddenly rose and, touching him briefly on the wrist, excused herself. "Are you ill?" he asked, rising in the attempt to follow her, but she had already gone.

She returned before the lights had had time to be lowered again, and she was like a different person. The macabre tinge was gone from her countenance; her cheeks now burned with an apricot glow that fought through and mastered the combined efforts of the gaslights and the box-lining and made her beauty emerge triumphant.

The number of pairs of opera glasses tilted her way immediately doubled. Some unaccompanied men even half rose from their seats. A sibilant freshet of admiring comment could be sensed, rather than heard, running through the audience.

"What was it?" he asked anxiously. "Were you unwell? Something at supper, perhaps—?"

"I never felt better in my life!" she said confidently. She sat now, secure, at ease, and just before the lights went down again for the following act, turned to him with a smile, brushed a little nonexistent speck from his shoulder, as if proudly to show the whole world with whom she was, to whom she belonged.

One morning, however, his concern got the better of him. He rose from the table they were seated at, breakfasting, went over to her, and tested her forehead with the back of his hand.

"What do you do that for?" she asked, with unmarred composure, but casting her eyes upward to take in his overhanging hand.

"I wanted to see if you had a temperature."

The feel of her skin, however, was perfectly cool and normal. He returned to his chair.

"I am a little anxious about you, Julia. I'm wondering if I should not have a doctor examine you, just to ease my mind. I have heard of certain—" he hesitated, in order not to alarm her unduly, "—certain ailments of the lung that have no other indication, at an early stage, than these—er—intermittent flushes and high colorings that mount to the cheeks—"

He thought he saw her lips quiver treacherously, but they formed nothing but a small smile of reassurance.

"Oh no, I am in perfectly good health."

"You are as white as a ghost, at times. Then at others— A few moments ago, in our room, you were unduly pale. And now your cheeks are like apples."

She turned her fork over, then turned it back again the way it had been.

"It is the cold water, perhaps," she said. "I apply it to my face with strong pats, and that brings out the color. So you need not worry any longer, there's really nothing to be alarmed at."

"Oh," he exclaimed, vastly relieved. "Is *that* all that causes it? Who would have believed—!"

He turned his head suddenly. Aunt Sarah was standing there motionless, a plate she had forgotten to deliver held in her hand. Her eyes stared at Julia's face with a narrow-lidded scrutiny.

He thought, understandingly, that she too must feel concern for the state of her young mistress' health, just as he had, to fix upon her such a speculative stare of secretive appraisal.

10

COMFORTABLY ENGROSSED in his newspaper, he was vaguely aware of Aunt Sarah somewhere at his back, engaged in a household task known as "wiping." This consisted in running a dustcloth over certain surfaces (when they were equal to or lower than her own height) and flicking it at others (when they were higher). Presently he heard her come to a halt and cluck her tongue enticingly, and surmised by that she must have at last reached the point at which Julia's canary, Dicky Bird, hung suspended in its gilt cage from a bracket protruding close beside the window.

"How my pretty?" she wheedled. "Hunh? Tell Aunt Sarah. How my pretty bird?"

There was a feeble monosyllabic twit from the bird, no more.

"You can do better than that. Come on now, perk up. Lemme hear you sing."

There was a second faltering twit, little better than a squeak.

The old woman gingerly thrust her finger through, apparently with the idea of gently stroking its tiny feathers.

As though that slight impetus were all that were needed, the little yellow tenant promptly fell to the floor of the cage. He huddled there inert, head down, apparently unable to regain the perch he had just lost. He blinked repeatedly, otherwise gave no sign of life.

Aunt Sarah became vociferously alarmed. "Mr. Lou!" she brayed. "Come here, sir! Something the matter with Miss Julia's little old bird. See you can find out what ails her."

Durand, who had been watching her over his shoulder for several minutes past, promptly discarded his newspaper, got up and went over.

By the time he had reached her, Aunt Sarah had already opened the cage wicket, reached a hand in with elephantine caution, and brought the bird out. It made no attempt to flutter, lay there almost inanimately.

They both bent their heads over it, with an intentness that, unintentionally, had a touch of the ludicrous to it.

"Why, it starving. Why, 'pears like it ain't had nothing to eat in days. Nothing left of it under its feathers at all. *Feel* here. Look at that. Seed dish plumb empty. No water neither."

It continued to blink up at them, apparently clinging to its life by a thread.

"Come to think of it, I ain't heard it singing in two, three days now. Not singing right, anyhow."

Durant, reminded by her remark, now recalled that he hadn't either.

"Miss Julia's going to have a fit," the old lady predicted, with an ominous headshake.

"But who's been feeding it, you or she?"

She gave him a look of blank bewilderment. "Why, I—I 'spected she was. She never said nothing to me. She never *told* me to. It b'long to her, I thought maybe she don't want nobody but herself to feed it."

"She must have thought you *were*," he frowned, puzzled. "But funny she didn't *ask* if you were. I'll hold it in my hand. Go get it some water."

They had it back in the cage, somewhat revived, and were still busy watching it, when Julia came into the room, the long-winded toilette that had been occupying her, apparently at last concluded.

She came toward him, tilted up her face, and kissed him dutifully. "I'm going shopping, Lou dear. Can you spare me for an hour or so?" Then without waiting for the permission, she went on toward the opposite door.

"Oh, by the way, Julia—" he had to call after her, to halt her.

She stopped and turned, sweetly patient. "Yes, dear?"

"We found Dicky Bird nearly dead just now, Aunt Sarah and I."

He thought that would bring her back toward the cage at least, if only for a brief glance. She remained where she was, apparently begrudging the delay, though brooking it for his sake.

"He going to be all right, honey," Aunt Sarah quickly interjected. "They ain't nothing, man or beast or bird, Aunt Sarah can't nurse back to health. You just watch, he going to be all right."

"Is he?" she said somewhat shortly. There was almost a quirk of annoyance expressed in the way she said it, but that of course, he told himself, was wholly imaginary on his part.

She began to mould her glove to her hand with an air of hauteur. Unnoticeably the subject had changed. "I do hope I don't have a hard time finding a carriage. Always, just when you want them, there's not one to be had—"

Aunt Sarah, among other harmless idiosyncrasies, had a habit of being behindhand in changing subjects, of dwelling on a subject, once current, for several minutes after everyone else had quitted it.

"He be singing again just as good as ever in a day or two, honey."

Julia's eyes gave a flick of impatience. "Sometimes that singing of his can be too much of a good thing," she said tartly. "It's been a blessed relief to—" She moistened her lips correctively, turned her attention to Durand again. "There's a hat I saw in Ottley's window I simply must have. I hope somebody hasn't already taken it away from there. May I?"

He glowed at this flattering deference of seeking his permission. "Of course! Have it by all means, bless your heart."

She gave a gay little flounce toward the door, swept it open. "Ta ta, lovey mine." She blew him a kiss, up the tilted flat of her hand and over the top of it, from the open doorway.

The door closed, and the room dimmed again somewhat.

Aunt Sarah was still standing beside the cage. "I sure enough 'spected she'd come over and take a look at him," she said perplexedly. "Reckon she ain't so fond of him no more."

"She must be. She brought him all the way down from St. Louis with her," Durand answered inattentively, eyes buried in his newspaper once more.

"Maybe she done change, don't care 'bout him no more."

This monologue was for her own benefit, however, not her employer's. He just happened to be there to overhear it.

She left the room.

A moment passed. Several, in fact. Durand's attention remained focused on the printed sheet before him.

Then suddenly he stopped reading.

His eyes left the paper abruptly, stared over its top.

Not at anything in particular, just in abstract thought.

11

HER TRUNK was recalled to his mind one day by the very act of his own sitting on it. It was no longer recognizable at sight for a trunk, it had a gaily printed slip cover over it to disguise it, and stood there over against the wall.

It was a Sunday, and though they did not go to church, they never failed, in common with all other good citizens, to dress up in their Sunday finest and take their Sunday morning promenade; to see and be seen, to bow and nod and perhaps exchange a few amiable words with this one and that of their acquaintances in passing. It was an established custom, the Sunday morning promenade, in all the cities of the land.

He was waiting for her to be ready, and he had sat down upon this nondescript surface without looking to see what it was, satisfied merely that it was level and firm enough to take him.

She was slowed, at the last moment, by difficulties.

"I wore this last week, remember? They'll see it again."

She discarded it.

"And this—I don't know about this—" She curled her lip slightly. "I'm not very taken with it."

She discarded it as well.

"That looks attractive," he offered cheerfully, pointing at random. She shrugged off his ignorance. "But this is a weekday dress, not a *Sunday* one."

He wondered privately, and with a soundless little chuckle, how one told the first from the second, but refrained from asking her.

She sat down now, still further delaying their start. "I don't know what I'll do. I haven't a thing fit to be seen in." This, taken in conjunction with the fact that the room was already littered with dresses, struck him as so funny that he could no longer control himself, but burst out laughing, and as he did so, swung his arm down against the surface he was sitting on, in a clap of emphasis. He felt, through the covering, the unmistakable shape of a pear-shaped metal trunk lock. And at that moment, he first realized it was her trunk he was sitting upon. The one she had brought from St. Louis. She had never, it suddenly struck him as well, opened it since her arrival.

"What about this?" he asked. And stood up and stripped the cover off. The initialled "J.R.," just below the lock in blood-red paint, stood out conspicuously. "Haven't you anything in here? I should think you would, a trunk this size." And meaning only to be helpful to her, pasted his hand against the top of it in indication.

She was suddenly looking, with an almost taut scrutiny, at one of the dresses, holding it upraised before her. As closely, as arrestedly, as if she were nearsighted or were seeking to find some microscopic flaw in its texture.

"Oh no," she said. "Nothing. Only rags."

"How is it I've never seen you open it? You never have, have you?"

She continued to peer at this thing in her hands. "No," she said. "I never have."

"I should imagine you would unpack. You intend to stay, don't you?" He was trying to be humorous, nothing more.

She didn't answer this time. She blinked her eyes, at the second of the two phrases, but it might have had nothing to do with that; it might simply have occurred simultaneously to it.

"Why not?" he persisted. "Why haven't you?" But with no intent whatever, simply to have an answer.

This time she took note of the question. "I—I can't," she said, somewhat unsurely.

She seemed to intend no further explanation, at least unsolicited, so he asked her: "Why?"

She waited a moment. "It's the—key. It's—ah, missing. I haven't got it. I lost it on the boat."

She had come over to the trunk while she was speaking, and was rather hastily trying to rearrange the slip cover over it, almost as if nettled because it had been disarrayed. Though this might have been an illusion due simply to the nervous quickness of her hands.

"Why didn't you tell me?" he protested heartily, thinking merely he was doing her a service. "I'll have a locksmith come in and make you a new one. It won't take any time at all. Wait a minute, let me look at it—"

He drew the slip cover partly back again, while she almost seemed to be trying to hold it in place in opposition. Again the vivid "J.R." peered forth, but only momentarily.

He thumbed the pear-shaped brass plaque. "That should be easy enough. It's a fairly simple type of lock."

The slip cover, in her hands, swept across it like a curtain a moment later, blotting out lock and initials alike.

"I'll go out and fetch one in right now," he offered, and started forthwith for the door. "He can take the impression, and have the job done by the time we return from our—"

"You can't," she called after him with unexpected harshness of voice, that might simply have been due to the fact of her having to raise it slightly to reach him.

"Why not?" he asked, and stopped where he was.

She let her breath out audibly. "It's Sunday."

He turned in the doorway and came slowly back again, frustrated. "That's true," he admitted. "I forgot."

"I did too, for a moment," she said. And again exhaled deeply. In a way that, though it was probably no more than an expression of annoyance at the delay, might almost have been mistaken for un-utterable relief, so misleadingly like it did it sound.

12

THE RITE of the bath was in progress, or at least in preparation, somewhere in the background. He could tell by the sounds reaching him, though he was removed from any actual view of what was going on, being two rooms away, in the sitting room attached to their bedroom, engrossed in his newspaper. He could hear buckets of hot water, brought up in relays from the top of the kitchen stove down-stairs by Aunt Sarah, being emptied into the tub with a hollow drum-like sound. Then a great stirring-up, so that it would blend properly with the cold water allowed to flow into it in its natural state from the tap. Then the testing, which was done with one carefully pointed foot, and usually followed by abrupt withdrawals and squeals of "Too cold!" or "Too hot!" as well as loud contradictions on the part of the assistant, Aunt Sarah: "No it ain't! Don't be such a baby! Leave it in a minute, how you going to tell, you snatch it back like that? Your husban's sitting right out there; ain't you ashamed to have him know what a scairdy-cat you is?"

"Well, he doesn't have to get in it, I do," came the plaintive answer.

Over and above this watery commotion, and cued by its semi-musical tone, the canary, Dicky Bird, was singing jauntily, from the room midway between, the bedroom.

Aunt Sarah passed through the room where he sat, an empty water-bucket in each hand.

"She sure a pretty little thing," she commented. "White as milk and soft as honey. Got a fo'm like—*unh-umh!*"

His face suddenly suffused with color. It took quite some time for the heightened tide to descend again. He pretended the remark had not been addressed to himself, took no note of it.

She went down the stairs.

The canary's bravura efforts rose to a triumphant, sustained, almost earsplitting trill, then suddenly broke off short. That had been, even he had to admit to himself, quite a considerable amount of noise for so small a bird to emit, just then.

A strange, almost complete silence had succeeded it.

Then the rolling, somehow-undulating sound usually produced by total immersion in a body of water.

After that only an occasional watery ripple.

Aunt Sarah returned, stopped en route to shake out and inspect a fleecy towel, also warmed by courtesy of the kitchen stove, that she was taking in with her. She went on into the bedroom.

"Hullo there," he heard her say, from in there. "How my bird? How my yallo baby?" Suddenly her voice deepened to strident urgency. "Mr. Lou! Mr. Lou!"

He went in running.

"He dead."

"He can't be. He was singing only a minute ago."

"He dead, I tell you! Look here, see for yourself—" She had removed him from the cage, was holding him pillowed on the palm of her hand.

"Maybe he needs water and seed again, like that last—" But the two receptacles were filled; Aunt Sarah had made that her responsibility ever since then.

"It ain't that."

She gave the edge of her hand a slight dip.

Something dropped over the edge of it, hung there suspended, while the body of the bird remained in position.

"His neck's done been broken."

"Maybe he fell off the perch—" Durand tried to suggest inanely, for lack of any other explanation that came to mind.

She scowled at him belligerently.

"*They* don't fall! What they got wings for?"

He repeated: "But he was singing only a few minutes ago—"

"What he was a few minutes ago and what he is now is two different things!"

"—and no one's been in here. No one but you and Miss Julia—"

In the silence, and incredibly, Julia could be heard in the adjoining bathroom, lightly whistling a bar or two to herself.

Then, as though belatedly realizing how unladylike she was guilty of being, she checked herself, and the water gave a playful little splash for finale.

13

It was quite by chance that he happened to go through the street in which his former lodgings were. He had no concern with them, would have passed them by with no more than a glance of fond recollection; his errand and his destination lay elsewhere entirely, and it only happened that this was the shortest way to it.

And it was equally by chance that Madame Tellier, his erstwhile landlady, happened to come out and stand for a moment in the entrance just as he was in the act of walking by.

She greeted him effusively, with shrieks of delight that could be heard for doors away in either direction, flung her arms about him like a second mother, asked about his health, his happiness, his enjoyment of married life.

"Oh, but we miss you, Louis! Your old rooms are rented again—to a pair of cold Northerners (I charge them double)—but it's not the same." She creased her rather large nose distastefully. Suddenly she was all alight again, gave her fingers a crackling snap of self-reminder. "I just remembered! I have a letter waiting for you. It's been here several days now, and I haven't seen Tom since it came, to ask where your new address is, or I would have forwarded it. He still comes around now and then to work for me, you know. Wait here, I'll bring it out to you."

She patted him three times in rapid succession on the chest, as if cajoling him to stand patiently as he was for a moment, turned and whisked inside.

He had, he only now recalled rather ruefully, completely overlooked having his mailing address changed from here, his old quarters, to the new house on St. Louis Street, when he made the move. Not that it was vitally important; his business mail all continued to go to the office, as it always had, and of personal correspondence he had never had a great deal, only his courtship letters with Julia, now brought to a happy termination. He would stop by the post office, on his way home, and file the new delivery instructions, if only for the sake of an occasional stray missive such as this.

Meanwhile she had come back with it. "Here! Isn't it good you just happened to come by this way?"

He gave the inscription a brief glance, simply to confirm it, as he took it from her. "Mr. Louis Durand," in spidery penmanship; the three capitals, M, L, and D, standing out in black enlargement, the minuscule letters too finely traced and too diminished in size to make for legibility. However, it was his own name, there could be no mistaking that, so he questioned it no further; thrust it carelessly into the side pocket of his coat for later reference and promptly forgot about it.

Their leavetaking was as exclamatory and enthusiastic as their greeting had been. She kissed him on the forehead in a sort of maternal benediction, waved him steadily on his way for a distance of the first three or four succeeding house-lengths, even touched her apron to the corner of her eye before at last turning to go inside. She wept easily, this Madame Tellier; wept with only a single glassful of wine, or at sight of any once-familiar face. Even those she had once ruthlessly evicted for non-payment of rent.

He accomplished his errand, he returned to his office, he absorbed himself once more in the daily routine of his work.

He discovered the letter a second time only within the last quarter of an hour before leaving to go home, and as equally by accident as it had been thrust upon him in the first place by happening to thrust his hand blindly into his pocket, in search of a pocket handkerchief.

Reminded of its presence, he rested himself for a moment by taking it out, tearing it open, and leaning back to read it. No sooner had his eyes fallen on the introductory words than he stopped again, puzzled.

"My own dearest Julia:"

It was for her, not himself.

He turned to the envelope again, looked at it more closely than he had on the street in presence of Madame Tellier. He saw then what had misled him. The little curl, following the "Mr." so tiny as almost to escape detection, was meant for an "s."

He went back to the paper once more; turned this over, glanced at the bottom of its reverse side.

"Your ever-loving and distressed Bertha."

It was from her sister, in St. Louis.

"Distressed." The word seemed to cast itself up at him, like a barbed fishhook, catch onto and strain at his attention. He could not pry it off again.

He did not intend to read any further. It was her letter, after all. Somehow the opening words held him trapped, he could not stop once they had seized his eyes with their meaning.

My own dearest Julia:
I cannot understand why you treat me thus. Surely I deserve better than this of you. It is three weeks now since you have left me, and in all that time not a word from you. Not so much as the briefest line, to tell me of your safe arrival, whether you met Mr. Durand, whether the marriage has taken place or not. Julia, you were never like this before. What am I to think? Can you not imagine the distracted state of mind this leaves me in—

14

HE WAITED until after they were through their supper to speak of it, and then only in the mildest, least reproachful way.

He took it out and gave it to her, after they had entered the sitting room from the dining room, and settled themselves there, she across the lamplit table from him. "This came for you today. I opened it by mistake, not noticing. I hope you'll forgive me."

She took the whole envelope first, and studied it a second, this way and that. "Who's it from?" she said.

"Can't you tell?"

Just as he was about to wonder why the script in itself did not tell her that, she had already withdrawn its contents and opened them, and murmured "Oh," so the question never had a chance to form itself in his mind. But whether the "Oh" meant recognition of its sender or merely recognition of the nature of the letter, or even something else quite different, there was no way for him to distinguish.

She read it rather quickly, even hurriedly, her head moving with each line, then back again, in continuous serried little twitchings. Then reached the bottom and had done.

He thought he saw remorse on her face, in its sudden, still abstraction, that held for a moment after.

"She says—" She half-tendered it to him. "Did you read it?"

"Yes, I did," he said, slightly uncomfortable.

She put it back in the envelope, gave the latter two taps where its seam was broken.

He looked at her fondly, to soften the insistence of his appeal. "Write to her, Julia," he urged. "That is not like you at all."

"I will," she promised contritely. "Oh, I will, Louis, without fail." And twisted her hands a little, about themselves, and looked down at them as she did so.

"But why didn't you before now?" he continued gently. "I never asked you, because I felt sure you had."

"Oh, so much has happened—I meant to, time and again I meant to, and each time there was something to take my mind off it. You see, Louis, this has been the beginning of a whole new life for me, these past few weeks, and everything seemed to come at one time—"

"I know," he said. "But you *will* write?" And he took up and lost himself in his newspaper.

"The very first thing," she vowed.

Half an hour went by. She was, now, turning the leaves of a heavy ornamental album, regaling herself with the copperplate engravings, snubbing the text.

He watched her covertly from under lowered lids a moment. Presently he cleared his throat as a reminder.

She took no notice, went ahead, with childlike engrossment.

"You said you would write to your sister."

She looked slightly disconcerted. "I know. But must it be right tonight? Why won't tomorrow do as well?"

"Don't you *want* to write to her?"

"Of course I do, how can you ask that? But why must it be this instant? Will tomorrow make such a difference?"

He put his newspaper aside. "A great deal in time of arrival, I'm afraid. If you write it now, it can go off in the early morning post. If you wait until tomorrow, it will be held over a full day longer; she will have that much more anxiety to endure."

He rose, closed the album for her, since she gave no signs of intending to do this herself. Then he stopped momentarily, looked at her searchingly to ask: "There's no ill-feeling between you, is there? Some quarrel just before you left that you haven't told me about?" And before she could speak, if she had meant to, put the answer in her mouth. "She doesn't write as though there had been."

The lines of her throat, extended for an instant, dropped back again, as if he'd aborted what she'd been about to say.

"How you talk," she murmured. "We're devoted to one another."

"Well, then, come. Why be stubborn? There's no time like the present. And you have nothing to occupy yourself with, that I can see." He took her by both hands and had to draw her to her feet. And though she made no active sign of resistance, he could feel the weight of her body against the direction of his pull.

He had to go to the desk and lower the writing-slab. He had to draw out a sheet of fresh notepaper from the rack, and put it in place for her, slightly tilted of corner.

He had to go back and bring her over, from where she stood, by the hand. Then even when he had her seated, he had to dip the pen and place it in her very fingers. He gave her head a pat. "You are

like a stubborn child that doesn't want to do its lessons," he told
her humorously.

She tried to smile, but the effect was dubious at best.

"Let me see her letter a moment," she said at last.

He went back to the table, brought it to her. But she seemed only
to glance at the very top line of the page, almost as if referring to
the mode of address in order to be able to duplicate it. Though he told
himself this thought on his part must be purely fanciful. Many people
had to have the physical sight of a letter before them to be able to
answer it satisfactorily; she might be one of those.

Then turning from it immediately after that one quick look, she
wrote on her own blank sheet, "My own dear Bertha:" He could see
it form, from over her shoulder. Beyond that she seemed to have no
further use for the original, edged it slightly aside and didn't concern
herself with it any further.

He let her be. He returned to his own chair, took up his newspaper
once more. But the stream of her thoughts did not seem to flow easily.
He would hear the scratch of her pen for a few words, then it would
stop, die away, there would be a long wait. Then it would scratch for
a few jerky words more, then die away again. He glanced over at her
once just in time to see her clap her hand harassedly to her forehead
and hold it there briefly.

At length he heard her give a great sigh, but one more of short-
patienced aversion continuing even after a task has been completed
than of relief at its conclusion, and the scratching of the pen had
stopped for good. She flung it down, as if annoyed.

"I've done. Do you want to read it?"

"No," he said, "it's between sister and sister, not for a husband to
read."

"Very well," she said negligently. She passed her pink tongue
around the gummed edge of the envelope, sealed it in. She stood it
upright against the inside of the desk, prepared to close the slab over
it. "I'll have Aunt Sarah post it for me in the morning."

He had reached for it and picked it up before her hands could
forestall him, though they both flew out toward it just a moment too
late. She hadn't expected him to be standing there behind her.

He slid it into his inside breast pocket, buttoned his coat over
it. "I can do it for you myself," he said. "I leave the house earlier.
It'll be that much sooner on its way."

He saw a startled expression, almost of trapped fear, cause her eyes to dodge cornerwise for an instant, but then they evened again so quickly he told himself he must have been mistaken, he must not have seen it at all.

When next he looked she was stroking the edge of her fingers with a bit of chamois penwiper, against potential rather than actual spots, however, and that seemed to be her sole remaining concern at the moment, though she puckered her brows pensively over the task.

15

THE NEXT morning, he thought she never had looked lovelier, and never had been more loving. All her past gracious endearment was as a coldness compared to the warmth of her consideration now.

She was in lilac watered silk, which had a rippling sheen running down it from whichever side you looked at it. It sighed as she walked, as if itself overcome by her loveliness. She did not stay at table as on other days, she accompanied him to the front door to see him off, her arm linked to his waist, his arm to hers. And as the slanting morning sunlight caught her in its glint, then released her, then caught her again a step further on, playing its mottled game with her all along the hall, he thought he had never seen such a vision of angelic beauty, and was almost awed to think it was his, walking here in his house, here at his side. Had she asked him to lie down and die for her then and there, he would have been glad to do it, and glad of her having asked it, as well.

They stopped. She raised her face from the side of his arm, she took up his hat, she stroked it of dust, she handed it to him.

They kissed.

She prepared his coat, held it spread, helped him on with it.

They kissed.

He opened the door in readiness to go.

They kissed.

She sighed. "I hate to see you go. And now I'll be all alone the rest of the livelong day."

"What will you do with yourself?" he asked in compunction, with the sudden—and only mometary—realization of a male that she too had a day to get through somehow, that she continued to go on during his absence. "Go shopping, I suppose," he suggested indulgently.

Her face brightened for a moment, as though he had read her heart. "Yes—!" Then it dimmed again. "No—" she said, forlorn. Instantly his attention was held fast. "Why not? What's the matter?"

"Oh, nothing—" She turned her head away, she didn't want to tell him.

He took the point of her chin and turned it back again. "Julia, I want to know. Tell me. What is it?" He touched her shoulder.

She tried to smile, wanly. Her eyes looked out the door.

He had to guess finally.

"Is it money?"

He guessed right.

Not an eyelash moved, but somehow she told him. Certainly not with her tongue.

He gasped, half in laughter. "Oh, my poor foolish little Julia—!" Instantly his coat flew open, his hand reached within. "Why, you only have to ask, don't you know that—?"

This time there could be no mistaking the answer. "No—! No—! *No!*" She was almost vehement about it, albeit in a pouty, petulant child's sort of way. She even tapped her toe for emphasis. "I don't like to *ask* for it. It isn't nice. I don't care if you are my own husband. It still isn't nice. I was brought up that way, I can't change."

He was smiling at her. He found her adorable. But still he didn't understand her, which was no detraction to the first two factors. "Then what *do* you want?"

She gave him a typically feminine answer. "I don't know." And raised her eyes thoughtfully, as if trying to scan the problem in her own mind, find a solution somehow.

"But you do want to go shopping, don't you? I can see you do by your look. And yet you don't want me to give you the money for it."

"Isn't there some other way?" she appealed to him helplessly, as if willing to extricate herself from her own scruples, if only she could be shown how without foregoing them.

"I could slip it under your plate, unasked, for you to find at breakfast," he smirked.

She saw no humor in the suggestion, shook her head absently, still busy pondering the problem, finger to tooth edge. Suddenly she brightened, looked at him. "Couldn't I have a little account of my own—? Like you have, only— Oh, just a *little* one, tiny—small—"

Then she decided against that, before he could leap to give his consent, as he had been about to.

"No, that'd be too much bother, just for hats and gloves and things—" About to fall into disheartened perplexity again, she recovered, once more lighted up as a new variant occurred to her. "Or better still, couldn't I just share yours with you?" She spread out her hands in triumphant discovery. "That'd be simpler yet. Just call it ours instead. It's there already."

He crouched his shoulders down low. He slapped his thigh sharply. "By George! Will that make you happy? Is that all it will take? God bless your trusting little heart! We'll do it!"

She flew into his arms like a shot, with a squeal for a firing-report. "Oh, Lou, I'll feel so *big*, so important! Can I, really? And can I even write my own checks, like you do?"

To love someone, is to give, and to want to give more still, no questions asked. To stop and think, then that is not to love, any more.

"Your own checks, in your own handwriting, in your own purse. I'll meet you at the bank at eleven. Will that time suit you?"

She only pressed her cheek to his.

"Will you know how to find it?"

She only pressed her cheek to his again, around on the other side of his face.

She allowed him to precede her there, as was her womanly prerogative. But once he had arrived, she kept him waiting no more than the fractional part of a minute. In fact so precipitately did she enter, on his very heels, that it could almost have been thought she had been waiting at some nearby vantage point simply to allow him first entry before starting forward in turn.

She accosted him before he had little more than cleared the vestibule.

"Louis," she said, placing her hand confidentially atop his wrist to detain him a moment, and drawing him a step aside, "I have been thinking about this since you left the house. I am not sure I—I want

you to do this after all. You may think me one of these presuming
wives who— Had we not better let things be as they are—?"

He patted her arresting wrist. "Not another word, Julia," he said
with fine masculine authority. "I want it so."

He was now sure that the idea was his own, had been from its very
inception.

She deferred to his dictate as it was a wife's place to do, with a
seemly little obeisance of her head. She linked her arm in his and
accompanied him with slow-moving elegance across the bank floor
toward its farther end, where the bank manager had emerged and
stood waiting to greet them with courtly consideration behind a low
wooden partition banister set with amphora-shaped uprights erected
three-square about his private office door. He was a moonfaced gentleman, the roundness of his face emphasized by the circular fringe of
carefully waved iron-gray whiskers that surrounded it, the lips and
sides of the cheeks clean-shaven. The gold chain across his plaid vest
front must have been composed of the thickest links in all New
Orleans, a veritable anchor.

Even he, the establishment's head, visibly swelled like a pouter-
pigeon at sight of Julia advancing toward him. The pride she afforded
Durand, in escorting her, in itself, would have made the entire proceeding worth while had there been no other reason.

She had donned, for this unwonted invasion of the precincts of
commerce and finance, azure crinoline, that filled the arid air with
whispers, midget pink velvet buttons in symmetrical rows studding
its jerking, pink ruching sprouting at her throat and wrists; a crushed
bonnet of azure velvet low over one eye like a tinted compress to
relieve a headache, ribbons of pink tying it under her chin, a dwarf
veil sprinkled with pink dots like confetti hanging only as low as
the underlashes of her eyes. Her steps were as tiny and tapping as
though she were on stilts, and her spine was held in the forward-
curved bow of the Grecian bend almost to a point where it defied
Nature's plan that the human figure hold itself upright on the hip
sockets, without falling over forward out of sheer unbalance.

Never had a bustle floated so airily, swaying so languorously, over
a bank floor before. Her passage created a sensation behind the
tellers' cagelike windows lining both sides of the way. Pair upon pair
of eyes beneath their green eyeshades were lifted from dry, stuffy
figures and accounts to gaze dreamily after her. The personnel of

banking establishments at that time was exclusively male, the clientele almost equally so. Though a discreetly curtained-off little nook, as rigidly segregated as a harem anteroom, bearing over it the placard "Ladies' Window," was reserved for the use of the occasional females (widows and the like) who were forced to come in person to see to their money matters, having no one else to attend to these grubby transactions for them. At least they were spared the ignominy of having to rub elbows with men in the line, or stand exposed to all eyes while money was publicly handed to them. They could curtain themselves off and be dealt with by a special teller reserved for their use alone, and always a good deal gentler and older than the rest.

There was no definite stigma attached to banks, for women; unlike saloons, and certain types of theatrical performance where tights were worn, and almost all forms of athletic contest, such as boxing matches and ball games. It was just that they were to be spared the soilage implicit in the handling of money, which was still largely a masculine commodity and therefore an indelicate one for them.

Durand and his breath-taking (but properly escorted) wife stopped before the whiskered bank manager, and he swung open a little hinged gate in the banister-rail for their passage.

Durand said, "May I present Mr. Simms to you, my dear? A good friend of mine."

Mr. Simms said with a gallant inclination, "I am inclined to doubt that, or you would not have delayed this for so long."

She cast her eyes fetchingly at him, certainly not in flirtation, for that would have been discreditable to Durand, but at least in a sort of beguiling playfulness.

"I am surprised," she said, and allowed that to stand alone, the better to make her point with what followed.

"How so?" Simms asked uncertainly.

She gave the compliment to Durand, to be passed on by him, instead of directly, face to face. "I had thought until now all bank managers were old and rather forbidding looking."

Mr. Simms' vest buttons had never had a greater strain put upon them, not even after Sunday meals.

She said next, looking about her with ingenuous interest, "I have never been in a bank before. What a superb marble floor."

"We *are* rather proud of that," Mr. Simms conceded.

They entered the office. They seated themselves, Mr. Simms seeing to her chair himself.

They chatted for several moments on a purely social plane, business still having the grace to conceal itself behind a preliminary screen of sociability, even where men alone were involved. (Always providing they were of an equal level.) To come too bluntly to the point without a little pleasant garnishing first was considered bad mannered. But year by year the garnishing was growing less.

At last Durand remarked, "Well, we mustn't take too much of Mr. Simms' time, I know he's a busy man."

The point had now arrived.

"In what way can I be of service to you?" Simms inquired.

"I should like to arrange," said Durand, "for my wife to have full use of my account here, along with myself."

"Oh, really," she murmured disclaimingly, upping one hand. "He insists—"

"Quite simple," said Simms. "We merely change the account from a single one, as it now stands, to a joint account, to be participated in by both." He sought out papers on his desk, selected two. "And to do that all I have to do is ask you both for your signatures, just once each. You on this authorization form. And you, my dear, on this blank form card, just as a record of your signature, so that it will be known to us and we may honor it."

Durand was already signing, forehead inclined.

Simms edged forward another paper tentatively, asked him: "Did you wish this on both accounts, the savings as well as the checking, or merely the one?"

"It may as well be both alike, and have done with it, while we're about it," Durand answered unhesitatingly. He wasn't a grudging gift-giver, and any other answer, it seemed to him, would have been an ungracious one.

"Lou," she protested, but he silenced her with his hand.

Simms was already offering her the inked pen for her convenience. She hesitated, which at least robbed the act of seemingly undue precipitation. "How shall I sign? Do I use my own Christian name, or—?"

"Perhaps your full marriage name might be best. 'Mrs. Louis Durand.' And then you'll remember to repeat that exactly each time you draw a check."

"I shall try," she said obediently.

He blotted solicitously for her.

"Is that all?" she asked, wide-eyed.

"That's quite all there is to it, my dear."

"Oh, that wasn't so bad, was it?" She looked about her in delighted relief, almost like a child who has been dreading a visit to the dentist only to find nothing painful has befallen her.

The two men exchanged a look of condescending masculine superiority, in the face of such inexperience. Their instincts made them like women to be that way.

Simms saw them off from the door of his office with an amount of protocol equal to that with which he had greeted them.

Again the bustle floated in such airy elegance above that workaday bank floor as bustle never had before. Save this same one on its way in. Again the sentimental calflike eyes of cooped-up clerks and tellers and accountants rose from their work to follow her in escapist longings, and an unheard sigh of romantic dejection seemed to go up from all of them alike. It was like the sheen of a rainbow trailing its way through a murky bog, presently to fade out. But while it passed, it was a lovely thing.

"He was nice, wasn't he?" she confided to Durand.

"Not a bad sort," he agreed with more masculine restraint.

"May I ask him to dinner?" she suggested deferentially.

He turned and called back, "Mrs. Durand would like you to dine with us soon. I'll send you a note."

Simms bowed elaborately, from where he stood, with unconcealed gratification.

He stood for several moments after they had gone out into the street, thoughtfully cajoling his own whiskers and envying Durand for having such a paragon of a wife.

16

THE LETTER was on his desk when he returned to the office from his noonday meal. It must have come in late, therefore, been delayed somehow in delivery, for the rest of his mail for that day had already been on hand awaiting his attention when he first came in at nine.

It was already well on toward three by now. The noonday meal of a typical New Orleans businessman, then, was no hurried snack snatched on the run, there then back again. It was a leisurely affair with due regard for the amenities. He went to his favorite restaurant. He seated himself in state. He ordered with care and amplitude. Friends and acquaintances were greeted, or often joined him at table. Business was discussed, sometimes even transacted. He lingered over his coffee, his cigar, his brandy. Finally, in his own good time, refreshed, restored, ready for the second half of the day's efforts, he went back to his place of work. It was a process that consumed anywhere from two to three hours.

Thus it was midafternoon before, returning to his desk, he found the letter there lying on his blotting-pad.

Twice he started to open it, and twice was interrupted. He took it up, finally, and prepared to spare it a moment of his full attention.

The postmark was St. Louis again. Whether spurred by that or not, he recognized the handwriting, from the time before. From her sister again.

But this time there could be no mistake. It was addressed to him directly. Intentionally so. "Louis Durand, Esq." To be delivered here, at his place of business.

He slit it along the top with a letter opener and plucked it out of its covering, puzzled. He swung himself sideward in his chair and gave it his attention.

If dried ink on paper can be said to scream, it screamed up at him.

Mr. Durand!

I can stand this no longer! I demand that you give me an explanation! I demand that you give me word of my sister without delay!

I am writing to you direct as a last resource. If you do not inform me immediately of my sister's whereabouts, satisfy me that she is safe and sound, and have her communicate with me herself at once to confirm this, and to enlighten me as to the cause of this strange silence, I shall go to the police and seek redress of them.

I have in my hand a letter, in answer to the one I last sent her, purporting to be from her, and signed by her name. It is not from my sister. It is written by someone else. *It is in the handwriting of a stranger,—an unknown person—*

17

How LONG he sat and stared at it he did not know. Time lost its meaning. Reading over and over the same words. "The handwriting of an unknown person. Of an unknown person. An unknown person." Until they became like a whirring buzz saw slashing his brain in two.

Then suddenly hypnosis ended, panic began. He flung himself out of his swivel-backed chair, so that it fell over behind him with a loud clatter. He crushed the letter into his pocket, in such stabbing haste as if it were living fire and burned his fingers at touch.

He ran for the door, forgetting his hat. Then ran back for it, then ran for the door a second time. In it he collided with his office boy, drawn to the entryway just then by the sound the chair had made. He flung him almost bodily aside, gripping him by both shoulders at once; fled on, calling back "Tell Jardine to take over, I've gone home for the day!"

In the street, he slashed his upraised arm every which way at once, before, behind him, sideward, like a man combatting unseen gnats, hoping to draw a coach out of the surrounding emptiness. And when at last he had, after a moment that seemed an hour of agonized waiting, he had run along beside it, was in before it had stopped; standing upright in the middle of it like a latter-day charioteer, leaning over the driver's shoulder in the crazed intensity of giving him the address.

"St. Louis Street, and quickly! I must get there without delay!"

The wheel spokes blurred into solid disks of motion, New Orleans' streets began to stream backward around him, quivering, like scenes pictured on running water.

He struck his own flank, as if he were the horse. "Quicker, coachman! Will you never get there?"

"We're practically flying now, sir. We apt to run down somebody."

"Then run down somebody and be damned! Only get me there!"

He jumped from the carriage as he had entered it, slapped coins from his backward-reaching palm into the driver's forward-reaching one, ran for his own door as if he meant to hurl himself bodily against it and crash it down.

Aunt Sarah opened it with surprising immediacy. She must have been right there in the front hall, on the other side of it.

"Is she in?" he flung into her face. "Is she here in the house?"

"Who?" She drew back, frightened by the violence of the question. But then answered it, for it could refer to only one person. "Miss Julia? She been gone all afternoon. She tole me she going shopping, she be back in no time. That was 'bout one o'clock, I reckon. She ain't come back since."

"My God!" he intoned dismally. "I was afraid of that. Damn that letter for not coming an hour earlier!"

Then he saw that a young girl was huddled there waiting on a backless seat against the wall. Frugally dressed, a large boxed parcel held in her lap. She was shrinking timidly back, her wan face coloring painfully as a result of the recent expletive he had used.

"Who's this?" he demanded, lowering his voice.

"Young lady from the dressmaker's, sent over to have Miss Julia try on a dress they making for her. She say she tole her to be here at three. She been waiting a couple hours now."

Then she didn't intend to remain away today, in the ordinary course of events, flashed through his mind. And her doing so now proves—

"When was this appointment made?" he challenged the girl, causing her to cower still further.

"Some—some days ago," she faltered. "I believe last week, sir."

He ran up the stairs full tilt, oblivious of appearances, hearing behind him Aunt Sarah's tactful whisper, "You better go now, honey. Some kind of trouble coming up; you call back some other day."

He stood there in their bedroom, breathing hard from the violence of his ascent but otherwise immobile for a moment, looking about in mute helplessness. His eye fell on the trunk. The trunk that had never been opened. Draped deceptively, but he knew it now, since that Sunday, for what it was. He wrenched off the slip cover, and the initials came to view again. "J.R.," in paint the color of fresh blood.

He turned, bolted out again, ran down the stairs once more. Only part of the way this time, stopping halfway to the bottom.

The young apprentice was at the door now, in the act of departing; turning over to Aunt Sarah the boxed parcel. "Tell Mrs. Durand I'm—I'm sorry to have misunderstood, and I'll come back tomorrow afternoon at the same time, if that's convenient."

"Run out and fetch me a locksmith!" he called out from midstairs, shattering their low-voiced parting interview like an explosive shell. The timid emissary whisked from sight, and Aunt Sarah tried to close the door on her with one hand and at the same time come away from it in fulfilment of his order.

Then he changed his mind again before she could carry out the errand. "No, wait! That would take too long. Bring me a hammer and a chisel. Have we those?"

"I reckon so." She scurried for the back.

When she'd handed them to him, he sped upward from sight again. He dropped to his knees, launched himself at the trunk with vicious energy, his mouth a white scar; he inserted the chisel in the crevice about the lock, began to pound at it mercilessly. In a moment or two the lock had sprung open, dangled there half-severed from its recent mounting.

The fall of the hammer and chisel made a dull clank in the new stillness of the room, like a funereal knell.

He plucked down the side-latchpieces, unbuckled the ancient leather strap that had bound it about the middle, rose and heaved as he rose, and the slightly domed lid came up and swung rearward with a shudder.

There was an exhalation of mothballs, as if an active breath had blown in his face.

It was the trunk of a neat, a fastidious, a prissy person. Symmetrical stacks of belongings, each one not so much as a hairsbreadth out of line and the crevices between artfully stopped with handkerchiefs and such slighter articles, so that the various mounds could not become displaced in transit.

The top tray held only intimate undergarments, of both day- and night-wear; all of them utilitarian rather than beautiful. Yellow flannel nightrobes, flannel petticoats, thick woollen articles of covering with drawstrings whose nature he did not try to discover.

In a moment his hands had ravaged it beyond recognition.

He shifted the upper section aside, and found neatly spread layers of dresses beneath that. Of a more sober nature than any she had bought since coming here; browns and grays, with prim little rounded white collars, black alpacas, an occasional staid plaid of dark blue or green, no brighter hue.

He picked the topmost one out at random, then added a second one.

He stood there, full length like that, between them, helplessly holding one up in each hand, looking from one to the other.

Suddenly his gaze caught his own reflection, in the full-length mirrored panel facing her wardrobe door. He stepped out more fully from behind the trunk, looked again. Something struck his eye as being wrong. He couldn't tell what it was.

He drew a step back with the two trophies, to gain added perspective. Then suddenly, at the shift, it exploded into recognition. There was too much of each dress. He was holding his hands, the hands that held them, at his own shoulder level. They fell away straight to the floor, and, touching it, even folded over in excess.

In memory he saw her stand beside him again, in the mirror. She appeared there for a moment, in brief recapture. The top of her head just rising over the turn of his shoulder: when her hair was up.

He dropped the two wraithlike rags, almost in fright. Stepped to the wardrobe, flung both panels of it wide, with two hands at once. Empty; a naked wooden bar running barren across its upper part. A little puff of ghostly violet scent, and that was all.

This discovery was anticlimactic to the one that had just preceded it, somehow. His real fright lay in the dresses that were here, and not the dresses that were gone.

He ran out again to the stairs, and bending to be seen from below, called to Aunt Sarah, until she had come running in renewed terror. "Yes sir! Yes sir!"

"That girl. What did she leave here? Was that something of Mrs. Durand's?"

"New dress they running up for her."

"Bring it here. Hand it up to me, quick!"

He ran back to the room with it, burst the cardboard open, rifled it out. Gay, sprightly; heliotrope ribbons at its waist. His eye took no note of that.

He retrieved the one from the trunk he had dropped to the floor. He flattened it on the bed, smoothing it out like a paper pattern, spreading the sleeves, drawing down the skirt to its full length.

Then he superimposed the new one, the one just delivered, atop it. Then stood back and looked, already knowing.

At no point did the one match the other. The sleeves were longer, by a full cuff-length. The bosom was fuller, spilling out in an excess curve at either side when rendered two dimensional. The waist was almost half again as wide. The wearer of the one could not have entered the other. And most glaring of all the skirt of one reached in a wide band of continuation far below, broad inches below, where the other had ended.

There was only one length for all skirts, even he knew that; floor-length. There was no such thing as a skirt other than floor-length. Any variation in length was not due to fashion, it was due to the height of the wearer.

And in this undersized, topmost one there still twinkled the pins of her living measurements as he had known her, taken from her very body less than a week ago, waiting for the final sewing.

The clothes from St. Louis—

The color slowly drained from his face, and there was a strange sort of fear in his heart that he'd never known before. He'd already known when he came into this house, a while ago; but now, in this moment, he'd proved it, and there was no longer any escaping from the proof.

The clothes from St. Louis were the clothes of someone else.

18

It was dark now, the town had dropped into night. The town, the world, his mind, were hanging suspended in bottomless night. It was dark outside in the streets and it was dark in here in the room where he stood.

There was no eye to pierce the darkness where he stood; he was alone, unseen, unguessed-at. He was something motionless standing within a black-lined box. And if it breathed, that was a secret between God and itself. That, and the pain he felt in breathing, and a few other things.

Then at last pale light approached, rising from below, ascending the stairs outside. As it rose, it strengthened, until at last its focus came into view: a lighted lamp dancing restlessly from a wire hoop, held by Aunt Sarah as she climbed toward the upper floor. It paled her figure into a ghost. A ghost with a dark face, but with a sifting of flour outlining its seams.

She came up to the level at last, and turned toward his room; the lamp exploded into a permanent dazzle that filled the doorway, burgeoning in and finding him out.

She halted there and looked at him.

He was standing, utterly, devastatingly motionless. The light fell upon the pile of dresses strewed on the bed, tumbled to the floor. It flushed color into them as it revealed them, like a syringe filled with dye. Blue, green, maroon, dusty pink, they became. It flushed color into him too, the colors a waxen image has, dressed to the last detail like a live man. So clever it could almost fool you; the way those things are supposed to do in waxworks. Verisimilitude without animation.

He was like one struck dead. Upright on his feet, but dead. He could see her, for his eyes were on her face; gravely gazing on her face, that part of the body which the eye habitually seeks when it looks on someone. He could hear her, for when she whispered half-frightenedly: "Mr. Lou, what is it? What is it, Mr. Lou?"; he answered her, he spoke, his voice came.

"She's not coming back," he whispered in return.

"You been in here all this time like this, without a light?"

"She's not coming back."

"How much longer I'm going to have to wait for supper? I can't keep that chicken much more."

"She's not coming back."

"Mr. Lou, you're not hearing me, you're not heeding."

That was all he could keep saying. "She's not coming back." All the thousands of words were forgotten, the thousands it had taken him fifteen years to learn, and only four remained of his whole mother tongue: "She's not coming back."

She ventured into the room, bringing the lamp with her, and the light eddied and fluxed, before it had settled again. She set it down upon the table. She wrung her hands, and knotted parts of her dress in them, as if not knowing what to do with them.

At last she took a small part of her own skirt and wiped sadly at the edge of the table with it, from old habit, as if thinking she were dusting it. That was the only help she could give him, the only ease she could bring him: to dust an edge of the table in his room. But pity takes many forms, and it has no need of words.

And it was as though she had brought warmth into the room; warmth at least sufficient to thaw him, to melt the glacial casque that held him rigid. Just by being there, another human being, near him.

Then slowly he started to come back to life. The dead started to come back to life. It wasn't pleasurable to watch. Rebirth after death. The death of the heart.

Death-throes in reverse. Coming after the terminal blow, not before. When the heart dies, it should stay dead. It should be given the coup de grace, struck still once and for all, not allowed to agonize.

His knees broke their locked rigidity, and he dropped down at half-height beside the bed. His arms reached out across it, clawing in torment.

And one of the dresses stirred, as if under its own impulse; rippled in serpentine haste across the bed top, and was sucked up into the maelstrom of his grief; his head falling prone upon it, his face burrowing into it in ghastly parody of kisses once given, that could never be given again, for there was no one there to give them to. Only the empty cocoon he pleaded with now.

"Julia. Julia. Be merciful."

The old woman's hand started toward his palsied shoulder in solace, then held itself suspended barely clear of touch.

"Hush, Mr. Lou," she said with guttural intensity. "Hush, poor man."

She raised her outstretched hand then, held it poised at greater height, up over his oblivious, gnawing head.

"May the Lawd have mercy on you. May He take pity on you. You weeping, but you ain't got nothing to weep for. You mourning, but you mourning for something you never had."

He rolled his head sideward, and looked up at her with sudden frightened intentness.

As if kindled into anger now by sight of his wasted grief, as if vindictive with long-delayed revelation, she went to the bureau that had been Julia's. She threw open a drawer of it with such righteous violence that the whole cabinet shook and quivered.

She plunged her hand in, unerringly striking toward a hiding place she knew of from some past discovery. Then held it toward him in speechless portent. Within it was rimmed a dusty cake, a pastille, of cheek rouge.

She threw it down, anathema.

Again her hand burrowed into secretive recesses of the drawer. She held up, this time, a cluster of slender, spindly cigars.

She showed him, flung them from her.

Her hands went up overhead, quivered there aloft, vibrant with doom and malediction, calling the blind skies to witness.

She intoned in a blood-curdling voice, like some Old Testament prophetess calling down apocalyptic judgment.

"They's been a bad woman living in your house! They's been a stranger sleeping in your bed!"

19

HATLESS, COATLESS, hair awry, just as the discovery had found him in his room moments before, he was running like someone demented through the quiet, night-lidded streets now, unable to find a coach and too crazed to stand still and wait for one in any one given place. Onward, ever onward, toward an address that had fortuitously recurred to him just now, when he needed it most. The house of the banker Simms, halfway across New Orleans. He would have run the whole distance on foot, to get there, if necessary.

But luckily, as he came to a four-way crossing, a gaslit post brooding over it in sulphuric yellow-green, he spied a carriage just ahead, returning idle from some recent hire, screaming after it and without waiting for it to come back and get him, ran down the roadway after it full tilt; floundered into it and choked out Simms' address.

At the banker's house he rang the bell like fury.

A colored servant led him in, showing an offended mien at his impetuosity.

"He's at supper, sir," she said disapprovingly. "If you'll have the patience to seat yourself just a few minutes and wait till he gets through—"

"No matter," he panted. "This can't wait! Ask him to come out here a moment—"

The banker came out into the hall, brow beetling with annoyance, still chewing food and with a napkin still trussed about his collar. When he saw who it was his face cleared.

"Mr. Durand!" he said heartily. "What brings you here at such an hour? Will you come in and join us at table?" Then noting his distracted appearance more closely as he came nearer, "You're all upset— What's the matter, man? Bring him some brandy, Becky. A chair—"

Durand swept a curt hand offside in refusal of the offered restoratives. "My money—" he gasped out.

"What is it, Mr. Durand? What of your money?"

"Is it there—? Has it been touched—? When you closed at three, what was my balance on your ledgers—?"

"I don't understand you, Mr. Durand. No one can touch your money. It's safeguarded. No one but yourself and your wife—"

He caught an inkling of something from the agonized expression that had flitted across Durand's face just then.

"You mean—?" he breathed, appalled.

"I have to know— Now, tonight— For the love of God, Mr. Simms, do something for me, help me— Don't keep me waiting like this—"

The banker wrenched off his napkin, cast it from him, in sign his meal was ended for that evening at least. "My chief teller," he said in quick-formed decision. "My chief teller would know. That would be quicker than going to the bank; we'd have to open up and go over the day's transactions—"

"Where can I find him?" Durand was already on his way toward the door and out again.

"No, no, I'll go with you. Wait for me just a second—" Simms hurriedly snatched at his hat and a silken throat muffler. "What is it, what has happened, Mr. Durand?"

"I'm afraid to say, until I find out," Durand said desolately. "I'm afraid even to think—"

Simms had to stop first and secure his teller's home address; then they hurriedly left, climbed back into the same carriage that had brought Durand, and were driven to a frugal little squeezed-in house on Dumaine Street.

Simms got out, deterred Durand with a kindly intended gesture of his hand, evidently hoping to spare him as much as possible.

"Suppose you wait here. I'll go in and talk to him."

He went inside to be gone perhaps ten minutes at the most. To Durand it seemed he had been left out there the whole night.

At last the door opened and Simms had reappeared. Durand leaped, as though a spring had been released, to meet him, trying to read his face for the tidings as he went toward him. It looked none too sanguine.

"What is it? For God's sake, tell me!"

"Steady, Mr. Durand, steady." Simms put a supporting arm about him just below the turn of the shoulders. "You had thirty thousand, fifty-one dollars, forty cents in your check-cashing account and twenty thousand and ten in your savings account this morning when we opened for business—"

"I know that! I know that already! That isn't what I want to know—"

The teller had followed Simms out. The manager gestured to him surreptitiously, handing over to him the unwelcome responsibility of answering the question.

"Your wife appeared at five minutes of three to make a last-minute withdrawal," the teller said.

"Your balance at closing-time was fifty-one dollars, forty cents in the one account, ten dollars in the other. To have closed them both out entirely, your own signature would have been necessary."

20

THE ROOM was a still life. It might have been something painted on a canvas, that was then stood upright to dry; life-size, identical to life in every shading and every trifling detail, yet an artful simulation and not the original itself.

A window haloed by setting sunlight, as if there were a brush fire burning just outside of it, kindling, with its glare, the ceiling and the opposite wall. The carpeting on the floor undulant and ridged in places, as if misplaced by someone's lurching footsteps, or even an actual bodily fall or two, and then allowed to remain that way thereafter. A dark stain, crab-shaped, marring it in one spot, as if a considerable quantity of some heavy-bodied liquid had been overturned upon it.

Dank bed, that had once made a bridegroom blush; that would have made any fastidious person blush now, looking as if it had been untended for days. Graying linen receding from its skeleton on one side, overhanging it to trail the floor on the other. A single shoe, man's shoe, abandoned there beside it; as though the original impulse that had caused it to be removed, or else had caused its mate to be donned, had ebbed and faded before it could be carried to completion.

Forget-me-nots on pink wallpaper; wallpaper that had come from New York, wallpaper that had been asked for in a letter; "not too pink." There was a place where the plaster backing showed through in rabid scars; as if someone had taken a pair of shears and gouged at them in a rage, trying to obliterate as many as possible.

In the center of the still life a table. And on the table three immobile things. A reeking tumbler, mucous with endless refilling, and a bottle of brandy, and an inert head, crown-side up, matted hair bristling from it. Its nerveless body on an off-balance chair at tableside, one hand gripping the neck of the bottle in relentless possessiveness.

A tap at the door, but with no accompanying sound of approach, as though someone had been standing there for a long time, listening, trying to gain courage.

No answer, nothing moved.

Again a tap. A voice added to it this time.

"Mr. Lou. Mr. Lou, turn the key."

No answer. The head rolled a little, exposing a jawline pricked with bluish hair follicles.

Once more a tap.

"Mr. Lou, turn the key. It's been two days now."

The head broke contact with the table top, elevated itself a little, eyes still closed. "What are days?" it said blurredly. "I've forgotten. Oh—those things that come between the nights. Those empty things."

The knob on the door turned sterilely. "Lemme in. Lemme just fraishen up your bed."

"It's just for me alone now. Let it be."

"Don't you want a light, at least? It getting dark. Lemme change the lamp in there for you."

"What can it show me? What's there to see? There's only me in here now. Me, and—"

He tilted the brandy bottle over the tumbler. Nothing came out. He held it perpendicular. Nothing still.

He rose from his chair, swung the bottle back to launch it at the wall. Then he stayed his arm, lowered it, shuffled to the door on one shoe, turned the key at last.

He thrust the bottle at her.

"Get me another of these," he barked. "That's all I want. That's the best the world can do for me now. I don't want your lamps and your broths and your tidying of beds."

But she was brave in the cause of housekeeping cleanliness, this old, spare, colored woman. She sidled in past him before he could stop her, put down the fresh lamp beside the one that had exhausted its fuel, in a moment was pulling and tucking at the bedraggled bed linen, casting an occasional furtive glance toward him, to see if he meant to stop her or not.

She finished, made haste to get out of the room again, coursing the long way around, by the wall, in order not to come too close to him. The door safely in her hand again, she turned and looked at him, where he stood, bottle neck riveted to hand.

And he looked at her.

Suddenly a tremor of unutterable longing seemed to course through him. His rasping bitter voice of a moment ago became gentle. He put out his hand toward her, as if pleading with her to stay, now, to listen to him speak of *her,* the absent. To speak of *her* with him.

"Do you remember how she used to sit there cleaning her nails, with a stick tipped with cotton? I can see her now," he said brokenly. "And then she would hold her fingers up, like this, all spread out, and quirk her head, to one side and to the other, looking at them to see if they would do."

Aunt Sarah didn't answer.

"Do you remember her in that green dress, with stripes of lavender? I can see her now, with the sunlight coming from behind her, breeze stirring her gown, standing there on the Canal Street dock. A little wispy parasol open over her."

Aunt Sarah made no reply.

"Do you remember that way she had, of turning in the doorway, each time she was about to leave, and bending her fingers backward, as if she were calling you *to* her, and saying 'Ta ta!'?"

The old woman's taciturnity burst its floodgates at last, as if she were unable to endure hearing any more. The whites of her eyes dilated righteously and her withered lips drew back from her teeth. She flung up her hand at him, as if enjoining him to silence.

"God must have been angry with you the day He first let you look into that woman's face!"

He stumbled over to the wall, pressed his face against it, arms straight up over his head as if he were trying to claw his way upward toward the ceiling. His voice seemed to come from his stomach, through rolling drums of smothered agony—that were the weeping of a grown man.

"I want her back again. I want her back. I'll never rest until I find her."

"What you want her back again for?" she demanded.

He turned slowly.

"To kill her," he said through his clenched teeth.

He pushed away from the wall, and lurched soddenly to the bed. He overturned an edge of the mattress, and reached below it, and drew something out. Then he slowly raised it, held it in strangulated grip to show her; a bone-handled, steel-barreled pistol.

"With this," he whispered.

21

THE AUDIENCE was streaming out of the Tivoli Theatre, on Royal Street. Gas flames in the jets on the foyer walls and in the ceiling overhead flickered fitfully with the swirl of its crowded passage. The play had been most enjoyable, an adaptation from the French called *Papa's Little Mischief*, and every animated conversation bore evidence to that.

Once on the sidewalk, the solid mass of people began to disintegrate: the balcony-sitters to walk off in varying directions, the boxholders and orchestra occupants to clamber by twos, and sometimes fours, into successive carriages as they drew up in turn before the theatre entrance, summoned by the colored doorman.

The man lurking back from sight against the shadowy wall, where the brightness failed to reach, was unnoticed, though many passed close enough to touch him.

The crowd drained off at last. The brightness dimmed, as an attendant began to put out the gaslights one by one, with a long, upward-reaching stick that turned their keys.

Only a few laggards were left now, still awaiting their turn at carriage stop. There was no haste, and politeness and deference were the rule.

"After you."

"No, after you, sir. Yours is the next."

And then at last one final couple remain, and are about to enter their carriage. The woman short, and in a lace head-scarf that, drawn close against the insalubrious night air, effectively mists her head and mouth and chin.

Her escort leaves her side for a moment, to see what the delay is in locating their carriage, and suddenly, from out of nowhere, a man is beside her, peering at her closely. She turns her head away, draws the scarf even closer, and edges a step or two aside in trepidation.

He is bending forward now, craning openly, so that he is all but crouched under her lace-blurred face, staring intently up into it.

She gives a cry of alarm and cowers back.

"Julia?" he whispers questioningly.

She turns in fright the other way, giving him her back.

He comes around before her again.

"Madam, will you lower your scarf?"

"Let me be, or I'll call for help."

He reaches up and flings it aside.

A pair of terrified blue eyes, stranger's eyes, are staring taut at him, aghast.

Her escort comes back at a run, raises his stick threateningly. "Here, sir!" Brings it down once or twice, then discarding it as unsatisfactory, strikes out savagely with his unaided arm.

Durand goes staggering back and sprawls upon the sidewalk.

He makes no move to resist, nor to rise again and retaliate. He lies there extended, on the point of one elbow, passive, spent, dejected. The wild look dies out of his face.

"Forgive me," he sighs. "I thought you were—someone else."

"Come away, Dan. The man must be a little mad."

"No, I'm not mad, madam," he answers her with frigid dignity. "I'm perfectly sane. Too sane."

22

IN THE front parlor of Madame Jessica's house on Toulouse Street, there was a vivacious evening party going on. Madame Jessica's parlor was both expansive and expensively furnished. The furniture was ivory-white, touched with gold, in the Empire style; the upholstery was crimson damask brocade. Brussels carpeting covered the parquetry floor, and the flickering gas tongues above, in nests of crystal, were like an aurora borealis.

A glossy haired young man sat at the rosewood piano, running over Chopin's "Minute Waltz" with a light but competent touch. One couple were slowly pivoting about in the center of the room, but more absorbed in one another's conversation than in dancing.

Two others were on the sofa together, sipping champagne and engaged in sprightly chat. Still a third couple stood together, near the door, likewise lost to their surroundings. Always two by two. The young ladies were all in evening dress. The men were not, but at least all were well groomed and gentlemanly in aspect.

All was decorum, all was elegance and propriety. Madame was strict that way. No voices too loud, no laughter too blaring. None left the room without excusing themselves to the rest of the company.

A colored maid, whose duty it was to announce new arrivals, opened one of the two opposite pairs of parlor-doors and announced: "Mr. Smith." No one smiled, or appeared to pay any attention.

Durand came in, and Madame Jessica crossed the room to greet him cordially in person, arm extended, her sequins winking as she went.

"Good evening, sir. How nice of you to come to see us. May I introduce you to someone?"

"Yes," Durand said quietly.

Madame fluttered her willow fan, put a finger to the corner of her mouth, surveyed the room speculatively, like a good hostess seeking to pair off only those among her guests with the greatest affinity.

"Miss Margot is taken up for the moment—" she said, eying the sofa in passing. "How about Miss Fleurette? She's unescorted." She indicated the opposite pair of doors, leading deeper into the house, which had partially and unobtrusively drawn apart. A tall brunette was standing there, as if casually, in passing by.

"No."

Madame did something with her fan, and the brunette turned and disappeared. A more buxom, titian-haired young woman took her place in the opening.

"Miss Roseanne, then?" Madame suggested enticingly.

He shook his head.

Madame flickered her fan and the opening fell empty.

"You're difficult to please, sir," she said with an uncertain smile. "Is that—all? Is there—no one else?"

"Not quite. There's our Miss Juliette. I believe she's having a tête-à-tête. If you'd care to wait a few minutes—"

He sat down alone, in a large chair in the corner.

"May I send you over some refreshments?" Madame asked, bending attentively over him.

He opened his money-fold, passed some money to her.

"Champagne for everyone else. Don't send any over to me."

A colored butler moved among the guests, refilling glasses. The other young men turned, one by one, saluted with their glasses, and bowed an acknowledgement to him. He gravely bowed in return.

Madame must have been favorably impressed, she evidently decided to hasten Miss Juliette's arrival, in some unknown behind-the-scenes manner.

She came back presently to promise: "She'll be down directly. I've sent up word there's a young man down here asking for her."

She left him, then returned to say: "Here she is now. Isn't she just *lovely?* Everyone's simply mad about her, I declare!"

He saw her in the doorway. She stood for a moment, looking around, trying to identify him.

She was blonde.

She was beautiful.

She was about seventeen.

She was someone else.

Madame bustled over, led her forward through the room, an arm affectionately about her waist.

"Right this way, honey. May I present—"

She gasped. The beautiful creature's eyes opened wide, at the first rebuff she had ever received in her short but crowded life. A puzzled silence momentarily fell upon the animated room.

His chair was empty. The adjacent door, the door leading out, was just closing.

23

MARDI GRAS. A city gone mad. A fever that seizes the town every year, on the last Tuesday before Ash Wednesday. "Fat Tuesday." Over and over, for fifty-three years now, since 1827, when the first such celebration started spontaneously, no one knows how. A last fling before the austerities of Lent begin, as though the world of human frailty were ending, never to renew itself. Bacchanalia before recantation, as if to give penance a good hearty cause.

There is no night and there is no day. The lurid glare of flambeaux and of lanterns along Canal and Royal and the other downtown streets makes ruddy sunlight at midnight; and in the daytime the shops are closed, nothing is bought and nothing is sold. Nothing but joy, and that's to be had free. For eight years past, the day has already been a legal holiday, and since that same year, 1872, the Legislature has sanctioned the wearing of masks on the streets this one day.

There is always music sounding somewhere, near or far; as the strains of one street band fade away, in one direction, the strains of another approach, from somewhere else. There are always shouts and laughter to be heard, though they may be out of sight for a moment, around some corner or behind the open windows of some house. Though there may be a lull, along some given street, at some given moment, the Mardi Gras is going on just as surely somewhere else just then; it never stops.

It was during such a momentary lull that the motionless figure stood in a doorway sheltered beneath a gallery, along upper Canal Street. The air was still hazy and pungent with smoky pitch-fumes, the ground was littered with confetti, paper serpentines, shredded balloon skins looking like oddly colored fruit-peelings, a crushed tin horn or two; even a woman's slipper with the heel broken off. The feet of an inebriate protruded perpendicularly from a doorway, the rest of him hidden inside it. Someone had tossed a wreath of flowers, as a funereal offering is placed at the foot of a bier, and deftly looped it about his upturned toes.

But this other figure, in its own particular doorway, was sober, erect. It had donned a papier-mâché false face, out of concession to the carnival spirit; otherwise it was in ordinary men's suiting. The false face was grotesque, a frozen grimace of unholy glee, doubly grotesque in conjunction with the wearied, forlorn, spent posture of the figure beneath it.

A distant din that had been threatening for several moments suddenly burst into full volume, as it came around a corner, and a long chain, a snake dance, of celebrants came wriggling into view,

each member gripping waist or shoulders of the person before him.
The Mardi Gras was back; the pause, the breathing space, was
over.

Torches came with them, and kettle drums and cymbals. The
street lighted up again, as though it had caught fire. Wavering
giant-size shadows slithered across the orange faces of the buildings. At once people came back to the windows again on either side
of the way. Confetti once more began to snow down, turning rainbow-
hued as it drifted through varying zones of light; pink, lavender,
pale green.

The central procession, the backbone, of dancers was flanked
by detached auxiliaries on both sides, singly and in couples, trios,
quartettes, who went along with it without being integrated into
it. The chain was lengthening every moment, picking up strays,
though no one could tell where it was going, and no one cared. Its
head had already turned a second corner and passed from sight,
before its tail had finished coming around the first. The original
lockstep it had probably started with had long been discarded because of its unwieldy length, and now it was a potpourri. Some
were doing a cakewalk, prancing with knees raised high before them,
others simply shuffling along barely raising feet from the ground,
still others jigging, cavorting and kicking up their heels from side
to side, like jack-in-the-boxes.

The false face kept switching feverishly, to and fro, forward and
back, while the body beneath it remained fixed; centering its ogling
eyes on each second successive figure as it passed, following that a
moment or two, then dropping that to go back and take up the next
but one. The women only, skipping over the clowns, the pirates, the
Spanish smugglers, interspersed between.

Ogling, bulging, white-painted eyes, that promised buffoonery and
horseplay, ludicrous flirtation and comic impassionment. Anything,
but not latent death.

Many saw it, and some waved, and some called out in gay invitation, and one or two threw flowers that hit it on the nose. Roman
empresses, harem beauties, gypsies, Crusaders' ladies in dunce caps.
And a nursemaid in starched apron wheeling a full-grown man before
her in a baby's perambulator, his hairy legs dragging out at the
sides of it and occasionally taking steps of their own.

Then suddenly the comic popeyes remained fixed, the whole false face and the neck supporting it craned forward, unbearably intent, taut.

She wore a domino-suit, a shapeless bifurcated garb fastened only at the wrists, the ankles and the neck. A cowl covered her head. She wore an eye-mask of light blue silk, but beneath it her mouth was like an unopened bud.

She was no more than five feet two or three, and her step was dainty and graceful. She was not in the cavalcade, she was part of the footloose flotsam coursing along beside it. She was on the far side of it from him, it was between the two of them. She was passing from man to man, dancing a few steps in the arms of each, then quitting him and on to someone else. Thus progressing, with not a step, not a turn, wasted uncompanioned. She was a sprite of sheer gayety.

Just then her hood was dislodged, thrown back for a moment, and before she could recover and hastily return it, he had glimpsed the golden hair topping the blue mask.

He threw up his arm and shouted "Julia!" He launched himself from the door niche and three times dashed himself against the impeding chain, trying to get through to her side, and three times was thrown back by its unexpected resiliency.

"No one breaks through us," they told him mockingly. "Go all the way back to the end, and around, if you must cross over."

Suddenly she seemed to become aware of him. She halted for a moment and was looking straight across at him. Or seemed to be. He heard the high-pitched bleat of her laughter, in all that din, at sight of his comic face. She flung her arm out at him derisively. Then turned and went on again.

He plunged into the maelstrom, and like a drowning man trying to keep his head above water, was engulfed, swept every way but the way he wanted to go.

At last a Viking in a horned helmet, one of the links in the impeding chain, took pity on him.

"He sees someone he likes," he shouted jocularly. "It's Mardi Gras, after all. Let him through." And with brawny arms raised like a drawbridge for a moment, let him duck under them to the other side.

She was still intermittently in sight, but far down ahead. Like a light blue cork bobbing in a littered sea.

"Julia!"

She turned fully this time, but whether at sound of the name or simply because of the strength of his voice could not have been determined.

He saw her crouch slightly, as if taunting him to a mock chase. A chase in which there was no terror, only playfulness, coquetry, a deliberate incitement to pursuit. A moment later she had fled away deftly, slipping easily in and out because of her small size. But looking back every now and again.

It was obvious she didn't know who he was, but thought him simply an anonymous pursuer from out of the Mardi Gras, someone to have sport with. Once when he thought he had lost her altogether, and would have had she willed it so, for she purposely halted aside in a doorway and remained there waiting for him to single her out once more. Then when he had done so, and there could be no mistake, she drew out her clown-like suit wide at the sides, dipped him a mocking curtsey, and sped on again.

At last, with one more backward look at him, as if to say: "Enough of this. I've set a high enough price on your approaching me. Now have your way with me, whatever it is to be," she turned aside from the main stream of the revelers and darted down a dimly lighted alley.

He reached its mouth in turn moments later, and could still see the paleness of her light blue garb running ahead in the gloom. He turned and went in. There were no more obstacles here, nothing to keep him back. In a minute or two he had overtaken her, and had her back against the wall, his raised arms, planted against it, a barrier on either side of her.

She couldn't speak. She was too winded. She leaned back against the wall, in expectation of dalliance, the fruits of the chase now to be enjoyed alike by both of them. He could make out the pale blue mask shimmering there before him in the dark. The red and yellow glare of torches was kept to the mouth of this side street, this byway; it couldn't reach in to where they were. It was twilight dim. It was the very place for it—

He tried to lift the mask from her face and she warded him off, shunting her head aside. She tittered a little, and fanned herself limply with her own hand, to create additional air for breath.

"Julia," he panted full into her face. "Julia."

She tittered again.

"Now I've got you."

He looked around where the light was, where the crowd was still streaming by, as if in measurement.

Then his hand fumbled under his clothing and he took out the bone-handled pistol he'd carried with him throughout the Mardi Gras. She didn't see it for a moment, it was held low, below the level of their eyes.

Then he pulled at his own false face, and it fell to the ground.

"Now do you know me, Julia? Now do you see who I am?"

His elbow backed, and the gun went out away from her, to find room. It clicked as he thumbed back the hammerhead.

It came forward again. It found that empty place, where in others a heart was known to be.

Then he ripped ruthlessly at the eye-mask and pared it from her. The hood went back with it, and the blonde hair was revealed. She saw the gun at the same time that he saw her face fully.

"No, doan', mister, doan'—" she whimpered abjectly. "I din' mean no harm. I was jes foolin', jes foolin'—" She tried to grovel to the ground, but the taut closeness of his arms kept her up in spite of herself.

"Why, you're a—you're a—"

"Please, mister, I cain't help it if I doan' match up right—"

There was a sodden futile impact as the bone-handled gun fell beside him to the ground.

24

THE ROOM was a still life. Forget-me-nots on pink wallpaper in the background. In the foreground a table. On the table a reeking tumbler, an overturned bottle drained to its dregs, a prone head. Nothing moved. Nothing had feeling, or awareness.

A still life entitled "Despair."

25

THE COMMISSIONER OF POLICE of the city of New Orleans was the average man of his own métier, no more, no less. Fifty-seven years of age, weight two hundred and one pounds, height five feet ten, silver-black hair, now growing bald, caracul-like beard, parted in two, a poor dresser, high principled, but not beyond the point of normalcy, a hard worker, married, obliged to use spectacles only when reading, and subject to a mild form of kidney trouble. Not brilliant, but not dull; the former certainly more of a disqualification in a public civil servant than the latter.

His office, in the Police Headquarters Building, was not particularly prepossessing, but since it was not for social usage but strictly for work, this doubtless was of no great moment. It had a certain fustian atmosphere which was perhaps inescapable in an administrative business office of its type. Ivory wallpaper rapidly turning brown with age (and unevenly so) adhered to the walls, with pockets and bulges where it had warped; it dated at least from the Van Buren administration. A green carpet, faded sickly yellow, covered the floor. A gaslight chandelier of four burners within reversed tulip-shaped soapy-iridescent glass cups hung from the ceiling. The commissioner's desk, massed with papers, was placed so that he sat with his back to the window and those he interviewed had the disadvantage of the light in their faces.

His secretary opened the door, closed it at his back, and then announced: "There's a gentleman out here to see you, sir."

The commissioner looked up only briefly from a report he was considering. "About what? Have him state his business," he said in a rumbling deep-welled baritone.

The secretary retired, conferred, returned.

"It's a personal matter, for your ears alone, sir. I suggested he write, but he claims that cannot be done either. He begs you to give him just a moment of your time."

The commissioner sighed unwillingly. "All right. Interrupt us in five minutes, Harris. Make sure of that, now."

The secretary held the door back, motioned permission with two upraised fingers, and an old man entered. A haggard, dejected, beaten old man of thirty-seven.

The secretary withdrew to begin his five-minute count.

The commissioner put aside the report he had been consulting, nodded with impersonal civility. "Good day, sir. Will you be as brief as possible? I have a number of matters here—" He swept an arm rather vaguely past his own desk top.

"I'll try to, sir. I appreciate your giving me your time."

The commissioner liked that. He was favorably impressed so far. "Will you have a chair, sir?"

He would give him at least his allotted five minutes, if not more. He looked as if he had suffered greatly; yet behind that there was a certain surviving innate dignity visible, conducive to respect rather than mawkish pity.

The visitor sat down in a large black leather chair, lumpy with broken spring-coils.

"Now, sir," prodded the commissioner, to discourage any inclination toward dilatoriness.

"My name is Louis Durand. I was married on May the twentieth, last, to a woman who came from St. Louis and called herself Julia Russell. I had never seen her before. I have the certificate of marriage here with me. On the fifteenth of June last she withdrew fifty thousand dollars from my bank account and disappeared. I have not seen her since. I want a warrant issued for the arrest of this woman. I want her apprehended, brought to trial, and the money returned to me."

The commissioner said nothing for some time. It was obvious that this was not inattention or disinterest, but on the contrary a sudden excessive amount of both. It was equally obvious that he was re-phrasing the story, to himself, in his own mind; marshalling it into his own thought-symbols, so to speak; familiarizing himself with it, the better to have it at his command.

"May I see the certificate?" he said at last.

Durand produced, tendered it to him.

He read it carefully, but said nothing further in respect to it. In fact, he asked but two questions more, both widely spaced, but both highly pertinent.

One was: "You said you had never seen her before; how was that?"

Durand explained the nature of the courtship, and added, moreover, that he believed her not to be the woman he had proposed to,
but an impostor. He gave the reasons for that belief, but admitted
he had no proof.

The commissioner's second and final question, spoken through
steeple-joined fingers, was:

"Did she forge your name in order to withdraw the funds?"

Durand shook his head. "She signed her own. I had given her authorization with the bank to do so; given her access to the accounts."

The five minutes' grace had expired. The door opened and young
Harris wedged head and one shoulder through, said: "Excuse me,
Commissioner, but I have a report here for you to—"

Countermanding his former instructions, the commissioner silenced him with a sweep of his hand.

He addressed Durand with leisurely deliberation, showing that
the interview was not being terminated on that account, but for
reasons implicit in its own nature. "I would like to talk this matter
over with my associates first," he admitted, "before I take any action. It's a curious sort of case, quite unlike anything that's come
my way before. If you'll allow me to keep this marriage certificate
for the time being, I'll see that it's returned to you. Suppose you
come back tomorrow at this same time, Mr. Durand."

And turning, he enjoined his secretary with unmistakable emphasis: "Harris, I'm seeing Mr. Durand tomorrow morning at this
same hour. Make sure my appointments allow for it."

"Thank you, Mr. Commissioner," Durand said, rising.

"Don't thank me for anything yet. Let us wait and see first."

26

"HAVE A CHAIR, Mr. Durand," the commissioner said, after having
offered his hand.

Durand did so, waited.

The commissioner collected his words, ranged them in mind, and at last delivered them. "I'm sorry. I find that there's nothing we can do for you. Nothing whatever. And by we, I mean the police department of this city."

"What?" Durand was stunned. His head went back against the spongy black leather of the chair-back. His hat fell from his grasp and his lap, and it was the commissioner who retrieved it for him. He could hardly speak for a moment. "You—you mean a strange woman, a stray, can come along, perpetrate a mock marriage with a man, abscond with fifty thousand dollars of his money—and—and you say you can do nothing about it—?"

"Just a moment," the commissioner said, speaking with patient kindliness. "I understand how you feel, but just a moment." He offered him the certificate of marriage which he had retained from the previous day.

Durand crushed it in his hand, swept it aside in a disgusted fling. "This—this valueless forgery—!"

"The first point which must be made clear before we go any further is this," the commissioner told him. "This is not a counterfeit. That marriage is not a mock one." He underscored his words. *"That woman is legally your wife."*

Durand's stupefaction this time was even worse than before. He was aghast. "She is not Julia Russell! That is not her name! If I am married at all, I am married to Julia Russell, whoever and wherever she may be— This is a marriage by proxy, if you will call it that— *But this woman was someone else!"*

"There is where you are wrong." The commissioner told off each word with the heavy thump of a single fingerpad to the desk top. "I have consulted with the officials of the church where it was performed, and I have consulted as well with our own lay experts in jurisprudence. The woman who stood beside you in the church was married to you *in person,* and not by proxy for another. No matter what name she gave, false or true, no matter if she had said she was the daughter of the President of the United States, heaven forbid!—she is your lawfully wedded wife, in civil law and in religious canon; she and only she and she alone. And nothing can make her otherwise. You can have it annulled, of course, on the ground of misrepresentation, but that is another matter—"

"My God!" Durand groaned.

The commissioner rose, went to the water cooler, and drew him a cup of water. He ignored it.

"And the money?" he said at last, exhaustedly. "A woman can rob a man of his life savings, under your very noses, and you cannot help him, you cannot do anything for him? What kind of law is that, that punishes the honest and protects malefactors? A woman can walk into a man's house and—"

"No. Now hold on. That brings us back again to where we were. A woman cannot do that, and remain immune to reprisal. But a *woman*, just any woman at all, did *not* do that, in your case."

"But—"

"*Your wife* did that. And the law cannot touch her for it. You gave her signed permission to do just what she did. Mr. Simms at the bank has shown me the authorization card. Under such circumstances, where a joint account exists, a wife cannot steal from her husband, a husband from his wife."

He glanced sorrowfully around at the window behind him.

"She could pass by this building this very minute, out there in the street, and we could not detain her, we could not put a hand upon her."

Durand let his shoulders slump forward, crushed. "You don't believe me, then," was all he could think of to say. "That there's been some sort of foul play concealed in the background of this. That one woman started from St. Louis to be my wife, and another suddenly appeared here in her place—"

"We believe you, Mr. Durand. We believe you thoroughly. Let me put it this way. We agree with you thoroughly in theory; in practice we cannot lift a hand to help you. It is not that we are unwilling. If we were to make an arrest, we could not hold the person, let alone force restitution of the funds. The whole case is circumstantial. No crime has been proven committed as yet. You went to the dock to meet one woman, you met another in her stead. A substitution in itself is no crime. It may be, how shall I say it, a personal treachery, a form of trickerv, but it is no crime recognized by law. My advice to you is—"

Durand smiled witheringly. "Forget the whole thing."

"No, no. Not at all. Go to St. Louis and start working from that end. Get proof that a crime, either of abduction or even something worse, was committed against the true Julia Russell. Now listen to my words carefully. I said *get proof*. A letter in someone else's handwriting is proof only that—it is a letter in someone else's handwriting. Dresses that are too big are only—dresses that are too big. I said *get proof* that a crime was committed. Then take it—" He wagged his forefinger solemnly back and forth, like a pendulum— "not to us, but to whichever are the authorities within whose jurisdiction you have the proof to show it happened. That means, if on the river, to whichever onshore community lies closest to where it happened."

Durand brought his whole fist down despairingly on the commissioner's desk top, like a mallet. "I hadn't realized until now," he said furiously, "there were so many opportunities for a malefactor to commit an offense and escape scot-free! It seems to me it pays to flout the law! Why bother to observe it when—"

"The law as we apply it in this country," the commissioner said forebearingly, "leans backward to protect the innocent. In one or two rare cases, such as your own, it may work an injustice against an honest accuser. In a hundred times a hundred others, it has preserved an innocent person from unjust accusation, false arrest, wrongful trial, and maybe even capital punishment, which cannot be undone once it has taken place. The laws of the Romans, which govern many foreign countries, say a man is guilty until proven innocent. The Anglo-Saxon common law, which governs us here, says a man is innocent until he is proven guilty."

He sighed deeply. "Think that over, Mr. Durand."

"I understand," Durand said at last, raising his head from its wilted, downcast position. "I'm sorry I lost my temper."

"If I had been tricked into marriage," the commissioner told him, "and swindled out of fifty thousand dollars, I would have lost my own temper, and far worse than you just did yours. But that doesn't alter one whit of what I just told you. It still stands as I explained it to you."

Durand rose with wearied deliberation, ran two fingers down the outer sideward crease of each trouser leg to restore them. "I'll go up to St. Louis and start from there," he said with tight-lipped grimness. "Good day," he added briefly.

"Good day," the other echoed.

Durand crossed to the door, swung it inward to go out.

"Durand," the commissioner called out as an afterthought.

Durand turned his head to him.

"Don't take the law into your own hands."

Durand paused in the opening, held back his answer for a moment, as though he hadn't heard him.

"I'll try not to," he said finally, and went on out.

27

THE *City of Baton Rouge* reached the St. Louis dockside at 6 P. M., days later. That was Wednesday, the eleventh.

He'd never been in the town before, but where a year ago he would have relished and appreciated all its differences, its novelty: its brisker, more bustling air than languorous New Orleans, its faintly Germanic over-all aspect, impalpable but still very patent to one who came from the French-steeped city down-river; now his heart was too heavy to care or note anything about it, other than that his trip was at an end, and this was the place where it had ended; this was the place that was going to solve the riddle for him, decide his problem, settle his fate.

It was a cloudy day, but even in its cloudiness there was something spruce, tangy, lacking in New Orleans overcasts. There was energy in the air; less of graciousness, considerably more of ugliness.

It was, to him at any rate, the North; the farthest north he'd yet been.

He had Bertha Russell's address ready at hand, of course, but because of the advanced hour, and perhaps also without realizing it because of a latent cowardice, that strove to put off the climactic ordeal for as long as possible, he decided to find himself quarters in a hotel first before setting out to locate and interview this unknown woman upon whom all now depended.

He emerged cityward of the pier shed, was immediately accosted with upraised whips by a small bevy of coachmen gathered hopefully about, and climbed into one of their vehicles at random.

"Find me some kind of a hotel," he said glumly. "Nothing fancy. And not too far into the town."

"Yes sir. The Commercial Travelers' be about right, I reckon. Just a stone's throw from here."

Even the colored people spoke more rapidly up here than at home, he noted with dulled detachment.

The hotel was a dingy, beery, waterfront place, but it served his purpose well enough to be accepted. He was given key and directions and allowed to find his own way to a cheerless bedroom with an almost viewless window, triply blocked by a brick abutment, a film of congealed dust ground into its panes, and a dank curtain, its pores long-since sealed by soilage. But twilight was already blurring the air, and he wouldn't have looked forth even if he could. He hadn't come here to enjoy a view.

He dropped his bag and settled down with heavy despondency in a chair, to chafe his wrists and brood.

He pictured again the scene to come, as he had been doing all day on the boat, and the night before. Heard again the reassuring voice he hoped to hear. "She was always wild, Mr. Durand; our Julia was like that. This isn't the first time she has run away. She will come back to you again, never fear. When you least look for her, she will suddenly return and ask your forgiveness."

He must want it to be that way, he realized, always to shape it so in his imaginings. To be assured that she was the actual Julia; a cheat, a robber, an absconder, but still the person she had represented herself to be. Why, he wondered, why?

Because anonymity meant her loss would be even more complete, more irremediable. Anonymity meant she was gone forever, there was not even a she to hope to find some day, there was nothing left him.

Or was it because the alternative to her still being Julia was something still darker, even worse, the very thought of which sent a shudder coursing through him.

And then he remembered the letter, that Bertha had said was in a stranger's handwriting, and—all his hope was taken away.

He quitted his room presently and went down and tried to eat something in the wholly unprepossessing dining room connected with the hotel, a typical traveling salesman sort of eating place, filled with smoke, noisy with boastful voices, and with not a woman in the place; he ate out of sheer habit and without knowing what it was he ate. Then, sitting there with a cup of viscous, stone-cold coffee untouched before him, he suddenly noted that it was nearing nine on the large, yellowing clockface aloft on the wall, and decided to carry out his errand then and there and have done with it, without waiting for morning. To try to sleep on it would be agonizing, unbearable. He wanted it over, whether for best or worst; he wanted to know at once, he couldn't stand the uncertainty another half-hour.

He went back to his room for a moment, got the sister's two letters, his marriage certificate, and all the other pertinent memoranda of the matter, gathered them into one readily accessible pocket, came down, found a coach, and gave the address.

He couldn't tell much about the house from the outside in the gloom. It seemed large enough. The upper part of its silhouette sloped back, meaning it had a mansard roof. It was in a vicinity of eminent cleanliness and respectability. Trees lined the streets, and the streets were lifeless with the absence within doors, where law-abiding citizens belonged at this hour, of those who dwelt hereabout. An occasional gas lamppost twinkled like a lime-colored glowworm down the vista of trees. A church steeple sliced like a stubby black knife upward against the brickdust-tinted sky, paler than earth because of its luminous low-massed cloud banks.

As for the house itself, orange lamp shine showed through a pair of double windows on the lower floor, the rest were in darkness. Someone, at least, was within.

He got out and fumbled for money.

"Wait for you, sir?" the man asked.

"No," he said reluctantly, "no. I don't know how long I'm going to have to be." And yet he almost hated to see the coach turn about and go off and leave him there cut off, as it were, and helpless to retreat now at the last moment, as he felt sorely tempted to do.

He went over to the door and found a small bone pushbutton, and thumbed it flat.

There was a considerable wait, but he forebore from ringing again. Then presently, but very gradually, as if kindled by the approach of light from a distance, a fanlight that had been invisible to him until now slowly glowed into alternating bands of dark red and colorless glass.

A woman's voice called through the door, "Who is it, please? What did you wish?"

She lived alone, judging by these characteristic precautions.

"I'd like to speak to Miss Bertha Russell, please," he called back. "It's important."

"Just a moment, please."

He could hear a bolt forced out, then the catch of a finger lock being turned. Then the door opened, and she was standing there surveying him, kerosene lamp held somewhat raised in one hand so that its rays could reach out to and fall upon him for her own satisfaction.

She was about fifty, or very close upon it. She was a tall, large-built woman, but not stout withal; she gave an impression of angularity, rather. Her color was not good; it had a waxlike yellowishness, as of one who has worried and kept indoors for a considerable period. Her hair, coarse and glossy, was in the earlier stages of turning gray. Still dark at the back, it was above the forehead that the first slanting, upward wedges of white had appeared, and the way she wore it emphasized rather than attempted to conceal this: drawn severely back, so tight that it seemed to be pulled-at, and then carelessly wound into a knot. It gave her an aspect of sternness that might not have been wholly justified, though in truth there was little humor or tenderness to be read in her features even by themselves.

She wore a dress of stiff black alpaca, a stringy white crocheted collar closing its throat and fastened by a carnelian brooch.

"Yes" she said on a rising inflection. "I'm Bertha Russell. Do I know you?"

"I'm Louis Durand," he replied gravely. "I've just arrived from New Orleans."

He heard her draw a sharp breath. She stared for a long moment, as if familiarizing herself with him. Then abruptly slanted the door still further inward. "Come in, Mr. Durand," she said. "Come in the house."

She closed the street door behind him. He waited aside, then he once more let her take the lead.

"This way," she said. "The parlor's in here."

He followed her down a dark-floored, rag-carpeted hall, and in at one side. She must have been reading when he interrupted; as she set the lamp down on a center table, a massive, open, gilt-edged book swam into view, a pair of silver-edged spectacles discarded to one side. He recognized it as the Bible. A ribbon of crimson velvet protruded as a bookmark.

"Wait, I'll put on more light."

She lit a second lamp, evening the radius of brightness somewhat, so that it did not all come from one place. The room still remained anything but brilliant.

"Sit down, Mr. Durand."

She sat across the table from him, where she had originally been sitting while still alone. She drew the ribbon marker through the new place in the Bible, closed the heavy cubical volume, moved it slightly aside.

He could see her throbbing with a mixture of excitement and anticipatory fear. It was almost physical, it was so strong an agitation; and yet so strongly quelled.

She clasped her hands with an effort, and placed them against the edge of the table, where the Bible had been until now.

She moistened the bloodless outline of her lips.

"Now what can you tell me? What have you come here to say to me?"

"It's not what I can tell you," he replied. "It's what you can tell me."

She nodded somewhat dourly, as though, while disagreeing with the challenge, she was willing none the less to accept it, for the sake of progressing with the matter.

"Very well, then. I can tell you this much. My sister Julia received a proposal of marriage from you, by letter, on about the fifteenth of April of this year. Do you deny that?"

He brushed away the necessity of a direct answer to that; held silent to let her continue.

"My sister Julia left here on May the eighteenth, to join you in New Orleans." Her eyes bored into his. "That was the last I saw of her. *Since that date I have not heard from her again.*" She drew a long, tightly compressed breath. "I received an answer to one of my letters in a stranger's handwriting. And now you come here alone."

"There is no one down there any longer I could bring."

He saw her eyes widen, but she waited.

"Just a moment," he said. "I think it will save both of us time if we establish one thing before we go any—"

Then suddenly he stopped, without need of completing the sentence. He'd found the answer for himself, looking upward to the wall, past her shoulder. It was incredible that he had failed to see it until now, but his whole attention had been given to her and not to the surroundings, and it was subdued by the marginal shade beyond the lamps.

It was a large photographic portrait, set in a cherry-colored velour frame, of a head nearly life-size. The subject was not young, not a girl. There was an incisiveness to the mouth that promised sharpness. There was a keen appearance to the eyes that heralded creases. She was not beautiful. Dark hair, gathered at the back. . . .

Bertha had risen, was standing slightly aside from it, holding the lamp aloft and backward to it past her own shoulder, so that it was in fullest untramelled pathway of the upsurging glow.

"*That* is Julia. *That* is my sister. There. Before you. What you are looking at now. It's an enlargement taken only two or three years ago."

His voice was a whisper that barely reached her. "Then it was— not she I married."

She hastily put the lamp down, at what it showed her now in the opposite direction. "Mr. Durand!" She half started toward him, as if to support him. "Can I get you something?"

He warded her off with a vague lift of his hand. He could hear his labored breathing sounding in his own ears like a bellows. He sought the chair he had risen from and by his own efforts dropped back into it, half turned to clutch at it and hold it steady as he did so.

He extended his hand and pointed a finger; the finger switching up and down while it waited for his lips to gain speech and catch up to it. "That is the woman whose photograph I received from here. *But that is not the woman I was married to in New Orleans on last May the eighteenth.*"

Her own fright, which was ghastly on her face, was overruled, submerged, by the sight of his, which must have been that much greater to witness.

"I'll get you some wine," she offered hastily.

He raised his hand protestingly. Pulled at his collar to ease it.

"I'll get you some wine," she repeated helplessly.

"No, I'm all right. Don't take the time."

"Have you a photograph, any sort of likeness, of the other person you can show me?" she asked after a moment.

"I have nothing, not a scrap of anything. She somehow even postponed having our bridal photograph taken. It occurs to me now that this oversight may have been intentional."

He smiled bleakly. "I can tell you what she was like, if that will do. I don't need a photograph to remember that. She was blonde. She was small. She was a good deal—I should say somewhat younger than your sister." He faltered to a stop, as if realizing the uselessness of proceeding.

"But Julia?" she persisted, as though he were able to give her the answer. "Where's Julia, then? What's become of her? Where *is* she?" She planted her hands in flat despair on the tabletop, leaned over above them. "I saw her off on that boat."

"I met the boat. It came without her. She wasn't on it."

"You're sure, you're sure?" Her eyes were bright with questioning tears.

"I watched them get off it. All left it. She wasn't among them. She wasn't on it."

She sank back into the chair beyond the table. She planed the edge of her hand flat across the top of her forehead, held her head thus for a moment or two. She did not weep, but her mouth winced flickeringly once or twice.

They both had to face the thing. It was out in the open between them now. Not to be avoided, not to be shunned. It had come to this. It was a question of which of them would first put it into words.

She did.

She let her hand drop. "She was done away with!" she whispered hoarsely. "She met her end on that boat." She shuddered as though some insidious evil presence had come into the room, without need of door or window. "In some way, at someone's hands." She shuddered again, almost as if she had the ague. "Between the time I waved her goodbye that Wednesday afternoon—"

He let his head go down slowly in grim assent. Convinced now at last, understanding the whole thing finally for what it really was. He finished it for her.

"—and the time I stood by the gangplank to greet her that Friday afternoon."

28

HE FOUND Bertha Russell, coated, gloved and bonnetted, a spectral figure in the unrelieved black of full mourning, waiting for him in the open doorway of her house, early as it was, when he drove up shortly before nine the following morning to keep their appointment prearranged the night before. Whatever grief or bitterness had been hers during the unseen hours of the night just gone, she had mastered it now, there were only faint traces of it left behind. Her face was cold and stonelike in its fortitude; there were, however, bluish bruises under her eyes, and the transparent pallor of sleeplessness lay livid upon her features. It was the face of a woman bent upon retribution, who would show no more mercy than had been shown her, whatever the cost to herself.

"Have you breakfasted?" she asked him when he had alighted and come forward to join her.

"I have no wish to," he answered shortly.

She closed the door forthwith and made her way beside him to the carriage; the impression conveyed was that she would have served him food if obliged to, but would have begrudged the time it would have cost them.

"Have you anyone in mind?" he asked as they drove off. She had given an address, unfamiliar to him as all addresses up here were bound to be, on entering the carriage.

"I made inquiries after you left last evening. I have had someone recommended to me. He was well spoken of."

They were driven downtown into the bustling business section, the strange pair that they made, both so tight-lipped, both sitting so stark and straight, with not a word between them. The carriage stopped at last before a distinctly ugly-looking building, of beefy red brick, honeycombed with countless windows in four parallel rows, all with rounded tops. A veritable hive of small individual offices and businesses. Its appearance did not bespeak a very prosperous class of tenantry.

Durand paid off the carriage and accompanied her in. A rather chill musty air, far cooler than that outside on the street, immediately assailed them, as well as a considerable lessening of light, in no wise ameliorated by the bowls of gaslight bracketed at very sparing intervals along its corridors.

She consulted a populous directory-chart on the wall, but without tracing her finger down it, and had quitted it again before he could gain an inkling of whose name she sought.

They had to climb stairs, the building offered no lift. Following her up, first one flight, then a second, at last a third, he received the impression she would have climbed a mountain, Everest itself, to gain her objective. They were, she had told him, ancestrally of Holland-Dutch stock, she and her sister. He had never seen such silent stubbornness expressed in anyone as he did in every move of her hard-pressed laboring body on those stairs. She was more dreadfully inflexible in her stolid purpose than any passionate, quick-gesturing Creole of the Southland could have been. He couldn't help but admire her; and, for a moment, he couldn't help but wonder what sort of wife the other one, Julia, would have made him.

At the third landing stage they turned off down endless reaches of arterial passageway, even more poorly lighted than below, and in sections that were not of one level, some higher than others, some lower.

"It doesn't indicate very much prosperity in business, would you say?" he remarked idly, without thinking.

"It bespeaks honesty," she answered shortly, "and that is what I seek."

He regretted having made the observation.

She stopped at the very last door of all but one.

On a shield of blown glass set into its upper-half was painted in rounded formation, to make two matching arcs:

Walter Downs
Private Investigator.

Durand knocked for the two of them, and a rich baritone, throbbing with its own depth, vibrated "Come in." He opened the door, stood aside for Bertha Russell, and then entered behind her.

The light was greater on the inside, by virtue of the street beyond. It was a single room, and even less affluent in aspect than the building that housed it had promised it would be. A large but extremely worn desk divided it nearly in two, with the occupant on one side of it, the visitors—all visitors—on the other. On this other side there were two chairs, no more, one of them a negligible cane-bottomed affair. On the first side there was a small iron safe, its corners rusted, its face left ajar. Not accidentally, for several ledgers which protruded, and an unsorted mass of papers which topped them, seemed to have rendered it incapable of closing.

The man sitting in the midst of this rather unappetizing enclave was in his early forties, Durand's senior by no more than two or three years. His hair was sand colored, and still copious, save for an indented recession over each temple, which heightened his brow and gave his face somewhat of a leonine look. He was, uncommonly enough for his age in life, totally clean-shaven, even on the upper lip. And paradoxically, instead of lending an added youth, this idiosyncrasy on the contrary seemed to increase his look of maturity, so strong were the basic lines of his face and particularly of his mouth. His eyes were blue, and on the surface there was something kindly and humane about them. Yet deeper within there was an occasional glint of something to be caught at times, some tiny blue spark, that hinted at fanaticism. They were at any rate the steadiest Durand had ever met. They were sure of themselves and attentive as those of a judge.

"Am I speaking to Mr. Downs?" he heard Bertha say.

"You are, madam," he rumbled.

There was nothing ingratiating about his manner. Intentionally so, that is. It was as if he were withholding himself from commitment, to see whether the clients met with his approval, rather than he with theirs.

And so Durand was looking for the first time at Walter Downs. Out of a hundred lives that cross a particular one, during its single span, ninety-nine leave no trace, beyond the momentary swirl of their passing. And yet a hundredth may come that will turn it aside, deflect it from its course, alter it so, like a powerful cross-current, that where it was going before and where it goes thereafter are no longer recognizably the same direction.

"There is a chair, madam." He had not risen.

She sat down. Durand remained standing, breaking his posture with a shoulder occasionally against the wall to ease himself.

"I am Bertha Russell and this is Mr. Louis Durand."

He gave Durand a curt nod, no more.

"We have come to you about a matter that concerns both of us."

"Which one of you will speak, then?"

"You speak for the two of us, Mr. Durand. That will be easiest, I think."

Durand, looking down at the floor as if reading the words from it, took a moment to begin. But Downs, who had now altered the position of his head to direct his gaze upon him exclusively, showed no impatience.

The story seemed so old already, so often told. He kept his voice low, left all emphasis out of it.

"I corresponded with this lady's sister, from New Orleans, where I was, to here, where she was. I offered marriage, she accepted. She left here to join me, on May the eighteenth last. Her sister saw her off. She never arrived. Another person altogether joined me in New Orleans when the boat arrived, managed to convince me that she was Miss Russell's sister in spite of the difference in their appearances, and we were married. She stole upward of fifty thousand dollars from me, and disappeared in turn. The police down there inform me that they cannot do anything about it for lack of proof that the original person I proposed marriage to was done away with. The impersonation and the theft are not punishable by law."

Downs said only three words.

"And you want?"

"We want you to obtain proof that a murder was committed. We want you to obtain proof of *the* murder that we both know must have been committed. We want you to trace and apprehend this woman who was a chief participant in it." He took a deep, hot breath. "We want it punished."

Downs nodded dourly. He looked thoughtfully.

They waited. He remained silent for so long that at last Durand, almost feeling he had forgotten that they were present, cleared his throat as a reminder.

"Will you take this case?"

"I have taken it already," Downs answered with an impatient off-gesture of his hand, as if to say: Don't interrupt me.

Durand and Bertha Russell looked at one another.

"I made up my mind to take it while you were still telling me of it," he went on presently. "It is the kind of a case I like. You are both honest people. As far as you are concerned, sir—" He raised his eyes suddenly to Durand; "You must be. Only an honest man could have been such a fool as you appear to have been."

Durand flushed, but didn't answer.

"And I am a fool, too. I have not had a client in here for over a week before you came to me today. But if I had not liked the case, nevertheless I would not have taken it."

Something about him made Durand believe that.

"I cannot promise you I will succeed in solving it. I can promise you one thing and one only: I will never quit it again until I do solve it."

Durand reached for his money-fold. "If you will be good enough to tell me what the customary—"

"Pay me whatever you care to, to be put down against expenses," Downs said almost indifferently. "When they outrun whatever it is, if they should, I'll let you know."

"Just a moment." Bertha Russell interrupted Durand, opening her purse.

"No, please—I beg you— It's my obligation," he protested.

"This is no matter of parlor gentility!" she said to him almost fiercely. "She was my sister. I am entitled to the right of sharing the expense with you. I demand it. You shall not take that from me."

Downs looked at them both. "I see I was not mistaken," he murmured. "This is a fitting case."

He picked up a copy of that morning's newspaper, first shook it to spread it full, then narrowed it once more to the span of a single perpendicular column. He traced his finger down this, a row of paid commercial advertisements.

"This boat she sailed on from here," he said, "was which one?"

"The *City of New Orleans*," Durand and Bertha Russell said in unison.

"By a coincidence," he said, "here it is down again, for the company's next sailing. Its turn has come about once more, it leaves from here tomorrow, at nine o'clock in the forenoon."

He put the paper down.

"Do you propose remaining here, Mr. Durand?"

"I'm returning to New Orleans at once, now that I've put this matter in your hands," Durand said. Then he added wryly, "My business is there."

"Good," Downs remarked, rising and reaching for his hat. "Then we'll both be sailing together, for I'm going down there now and get my ticket. We will begin by retracing her steps, making the same journey she did, on the same boat, with the same captain and the same crew. Someone may have seen something, someone may remember. Someone must."

29

THE CABINS of the *City of New Orleans* were small, little better than shoeboxes ranged side by side along the shelves of a shop. The one they shared together seemed even smaller than the rest, perhaps because they were both in it at once. Even to move about and hang their things, they had continually to flatten themselves and swerve aside to avoid grazing and knocking into one another at every step.

Outside in the failing light two soiled ribbons, the lower gray, the upper tan, could be seen unrolling through the window; the Mississippi's bosom and its shore.

"I will help in any way I can," Durand offered. "Just tell me what to do and how to go about it."

"The passengers will not be the same on this trip as on that other," Downs told him. "That would be too much to hope for. Those who will be, are those whose job it is to run the boat and tend it. We will share them between us, from the captain down to the stokers. And if we find out nothing, we are no worse off than before. And if we find out something, no matter what, we are that much better off. So don't be discouraged. This may take months and years, and we are just at the very beginning of it."

"And what is it you—we—try to find out, now, for a beginning?"

"We try to find a witness who saw them *both together;* and by that I do not necessarily mean in one another's company: the true Julia and the false. I mean, both alive and on the boat during one and the same trip, at one and the same time. For the sister is a witness that the true one left on it, and you are a witness that the false one arrived on it. What I am trying to arrive at, by a process of elimination, is when was the true one last seen, when the false one first? I mark that off, as closely as I can get it, against that out there—" he gestured toward the two ribbons, "and that gives me, roughly, the point during the voyage at which it happened, the State whose jurisdiction it falls within, and the area in which to devote myself to searching for the only evidence, *if* any, there will ever be."

Durand didn't ask him what he meant by that last. Perhaps a chill sensation running down his back told him only too well.

The captain was named Fletcher. He was deliberate of speech; the type of man who thinks well before speaking, and thus later does not have to think ill of what he has spoken. His memory, by way of his hand, sought refreshment in his luxuriant black beard.

"Yes," he said at long last, after hearing Downs's exhaustive description. "Yes, I do recall a little lady such as you describe. The breeze caught up her skirt just as we were both coming along the deck from opposite directions. And she quickly held it down with her hands. But for a moment—" He didn't finish it; his eyes, however, were reminiscently kind. "Then as I passed, I tipped my cap. She dropped her eyes and would not see me—" he gave a little chuckle; "yet as she passed, she smiled, and I know the smile was for me, for there was no one else in sight."

"And now this one," Downs said.

He offered in assistance a small photograph of Julia, supplied them by Bertha, much similar to the one once owned by Durand.

The captain studied it at length, but with no great relish; and then after that ruminated a considerable while longer.

"No," he said at last. "No, I've never seen this old mai— this woman." He handed it back, as if glad to be rid of it.

"You're sure?"

The captain had no more interest in trying to recall, even if he could have.

"We carry many people, sir, trip after trip, and I cannot be expected to remember all their faces. I am only a man, after all."

"And strange," Downs repeated to Durand later, "are the ways of men; they see with their pulses and their blood. For the one whom I could only describe to him by word of mouth, and secondhand at that, he could recall instantly, and will go on recalling probably for the rest of his active life. But the one whose very photograph he had before him, he could not recall at all!"

Durand thumbed the pushbutton in their little cubbyhole, and after an in ordinate length of time, a shambling steward appeared.

"Not you," Durand told him. "Who takes care of the ladies' cabins?"

A stewardess appeared in dilatory turn. He gave her a coin.

"I want to ask you something. See if you can remember. Did you ever come to one of your ladies' cabins, of a morning, and find the bunk undisturbed, no one had been in it?"

She nodded readily. "Sho', lots times. We ain't full up every trip. Sometime' mo'n half my cabin' plumb empty."

"No, I'll have to ask it another way, then. Did you ever come to one of your ladies' cabins which had had someone in it *first,* and then find the bunk untouched?"

It seemed to present difficulties to her. "You mean nobody slep' in it, but somebody done tuk it just the same?"

"That's it; that's about it."

She wasn't sure; she scratched and strove, but she wasn't sure.

He tried to help her. "With somebody's clothes in it, perhaps. With somebody's belongings there for you to see. Surely you could tell by that. But no one had lain in the bunk."

She still wasn't sure.

He tried his trump card. "With a *birdcage* in it, perhaps."

She ignited into recollection, like tinder when the spark strikes it square. "Tha's right, tha's how it was! How you know that? Cab'n with a birdcage in it, and I didn't have to tech the bunk nohow—"

He nodded darkly. "No one had lain in it the night before."

She drew up short. "I di'n say that. The lady fix up her berth herseff befo' I get there; she kine of tidy that way, and used to doing things with her own han's 'thout waiting fo' nobody."

"Who told you that, how do you kn—?"

"She *in* there when I come in. The pretties' little lady I ever done see; blon' like an angel and li'l like a chile."

In the dining saloon, Durand saw, Downs had held back one of his plates even after he had finished with it. At the end of the meal, when all others but the two of them had left the single, long table, Downs called the waiter over and said to him simply: "Watch this. Watch me do this a minute."

Then he took out a pocket handkerchief, spread it flat on the table top. Into it he put a small scrap of lettuce that had decorated his plate as a garnish, folded the corners of the handkerchief over toward the center, like a magician about to cause something to disappear.

"Did you ever see anyone do that, at the end of a meal? Did you?"

"You mean fold up their napkin like—?"

"No, no." Downs had to reopen it to show him the lettuce, then start the process over. "Put a leaf of lettuce in first, to carry away. It's a handkerchief. Think of it as a smaller one, far smaller, a little wisp—"

The waiter nodded now. "I seen a lady do that, one trip. I wondered what she— It wasn't meat or nothin', just a little old—"

Downs held up his finger in admonition. "Now listen carefully. Think well. How many times can you remember seeing her do that? After how many meals?"

"Just once. On'y once. After on'y one meal. That was the on'y time I ever seen her, just at that one meal."

"I can't get the two of them together," Downs said to Durand under his breath afterward. "One ends before the other begins. But it happened sometime during the first night. At suppertime the waiter saw the real one filch a scrap of lettuce for her bird. At eight in the morning the stewardess found a blonde 'like an angel' had already made up her own bunk, in that cabin where the birdcage was."

The first stop, at eight the following morning, Durand found Downs already making his preparations for departure.

"You're getting off here?" he queried in surprise. "So soon? Already?"

Downs nodded. "That boat's first stop this time was the boat's first stop that time too. The same schedule is held to. She was already hours dead and hours in the water by this moment. To go on past here only carries me farther away at every turn of the paddles. Come, walk me to the landing plank."

"If she is anywhere," he said, lowering his voice as they went out on the misty early-morning deck together, "she is back there somewhere, along the stretch we have covered this past night. If she ever floats ashore—or has already, unrecognized or maybe even unseen—it will be back there somewhere. I will go back along the shoreline, hamlet by hamlet, yard by yard, inch by inch; on foot if necessary. First on this side, then on the opposite. And if she is not ashore already, I will wait until she comes ashore."

His face was that of a fanatic, with whom there is no reasoning.

"Back there she is, on the river bottom, in the great wide eddy below Cape Girardeau, and back there I will wait for her."

Durand's blood ran a little cold at the turn of speech.

Downs held out his hand.

"Good luck to you," Durand said, half frightened of the man now.

"And to you," Downs answered. "You will see me again some day, sooner or later. I can't say when, but you will surely see me again some day."

He went down the gangplank. Durand watched his head sink from sight. Then he turned away with an involuntary shiver, the last thing he had heard the other man say repeating itself strangely in his mind:

You will see me again some day. You will surely see me again some day.

30

THE DEATH of a man is a sad enough thing to watch, but he goes by himself, taking nothing else with him. The death of a house is a sadder thing by far to watch. For so much more goes with it.

On that last day, Durand moved slowly from room to room of the St. Louis Street house. It was already dying before his very eyes; the furniture dismantled, rugs stripped from its floor boards, curtains from its windows, closet doors left gapingly ajar with nothing behind them any more. Its skeleton was peering through. The skeleton that stays on after death, just as in a man's case.

And yet, he realized, he was not so much leaving this place as leaving a part of himself behind in a common grave with it. A part that he could never regain, never recall. He could never hope again as he'd once hoped here. There was nothing to hope for. He could never be as young again as he'd once been here, even though it was a youngness late in coming, at thirty-seven; late in coming and swift in going, just a few brief weeks. He could never love again— not only not as he'd once loved here, but to any degree at all. And that is a form of death in itself. His broken dreams were lying all around; he could almost hear them crunch, like spilled sugar, each time he moved his foot.

He was standing in the doorway of what-had been their bedroom, looking across at the wallpaper. The wallpaper that had come from New York—"pink, but not too bright a pink, with small blue flowers, like forget-me-nots"—put up for a bride to see, a bride who had never lived to see it, nor lived even to be a bride.

He closed the door. For no particular reason, for there was nothing to be kept in there any longer. Perhaps the more quickly to shut the room from sight.

And as it closed, a voice seemed to speak through it for a moment, with sudden lifelike clarity in his ears:

"*Who is it knocks? . . . Tell him he may.*"

Then was gone, stilled forever.

He went slowly down the stairs, his knees bending reluctantly over each step, as if they were rusted.

The front door was standing open, and there was a mule and

two-wheeled cart out before it, piled high with the effluvia he had donated to Aunt Sarah. She went hurrying past from the back just then, a dented-in gilt birdcage swinging from one hand, a bulky mantel clock hugged in her other. Then, seeing him, and still incredulous of his largesse, she stopped short to ask for additional assurance.

"This too? This yere clock?"

"I told you, everything," he answered impatiently. "Everything but the heavy pieces with four legs. Take it all! Get it out of my sight!"

"I'm sure going to have the grandest cabin in Shrevepo't when I gets back home there."

He looked at her grimly for a moment, but his grimness was not for her.

"That band's not playing today, I notice," he blurted out accusingly.

She understood the reference, remembered it with surprising immediacy.

"Hush, Mr. Lou. Anyone can make a mistake. That was the devil's music."

She went on out to the cart, where a gangling youth, a nephew by remote attribute, loitered in charge of the booty.

"Got everything you want now?" Durand called out after her. "Then I'll lock up."

"Yes sir! Yes *sir!* Couldn't ask for no more." And, apparently, secretly a little dubious, to the end, that Durand might yet change his mind and retract, added in a hasty aside: "Come on, boy! Get this mule started up. What you lingering for?" She clambered up beside him and the cart waddled off. "God bless you, Mr. Lou! God keep you safe!"

"It's a little late for that," thought Durand morosely.

He turned back to the hall for a moment, to retrieve his own hat from the pronged, high-backed rack where he had slung it. And as he detached it, something fell out sideward to the floor from behind it with a little clap. Something that must have been thrust out of sight behind there long ago, and forgotten.

He picked up the slender little stick, and withdrew it, and a little swath of bunched heliotrope came with it at the other end. Limp, bedraggled, but still giving a momentary splash of color to the denuded hall.

Her parasol.

He took it by both ends, and arched his knee to it, and splintered it explosively, not once but again and again, with an inordinate violence that its fragility didn't warrant. Then flung the wisps and splinters away from him with full arm's strength, as far as they would go.

"Get to hell, after your owner," he mumbled savagely. "She's waiting for you to shade her there!"

And slammed the door.

The house was dead. Love was dead. The story was through.

31

MAY AGAIN. May that keeps coming around, May that never gets any older, May that's just as fair each time. Men grow old and lose their loves, and have no further hope of any new love, but May keeps coming back again. There are always others waiting for it, whose turn is still to come.

May again. May of '81 now. A year since the marriage.

The train from New Orleans came into Biloxi late in the afternoon. The sky was porcelain fresh from the kiln; a little wisp of steam seeping from it here and there, those were clouds. The tree tops were shimmering with delicate new leaf. And in the distance, like a deposit of sapphires, the waters of the Gulf. It was a lovely place to come to, a lovely sight to behold. And he was old and bitter now, too old to care.

He was the last one down from the steps of the railroad coach. He climbed down leadenly, grudgingly, as though it were all one to him whether he alighted here or continued on to the next place. It was. To rest, to forget awhile, that was all he wanted. To let the healing process continue, the scars harden into their ugly crust. New Orleans still reminded him too much. It always would.

A romantic takes his losses hard, and he was a romantic. Only a romantic could have played the rôle he had, played the fool so letter-perfect. He was one of those men who are born to be the natural prey of women, he was beginning to realize it himself by now; if it hadn't been she, it would have been someone else. If it hadn't been a bad woman, then it would have been what they called a "good" woman. Even one of those would have had him in her power in no time at all. And though the results might have been less catastrophic, that was no consolation to his own innermost pride. His only defense was to stay away from them.

Now that the horse was stolen, the lock was on the stable door. The lock was on, and the key was thrown away, for good and all. But there was nothing it opened to any more.

Amidst all the bustle of holidaymakers down here from the hinterland for a week or two's sojourn, the prattle, the commotion as they formed into little groups, joining with the friends who had come to train side to meet them, he stood there solitary, apart, his bag at his feet.

The eyes of more than one marriageable young damsel in the groups near by were cast speculatively toward him over the shoulder of some relative or friend, probably wondering if he were eligible to be sketched into plans for the immediate future, for what is a holiday without a lot of beaux? Yet whenever they happened to meet his own eyes they hurriedly withdrew again, and not wholly for the sake of seemliness either. It left them with a rather disconcerting sensation, like looking at something you think to be alive and finding out it is inanimate after all. It was like flirting with a fence post or water pump until you found out your mistake.

The platform slowly cleared, and he still stood there. The train from New Orleans started on again, and he half turned, as if to reenter and ride on with it to wherever the next place was. But he faced forward again and let the cars go ticking off behind his back, on their way down the track.

32

HE SOON fell into the habit of dropping into the bar of one of the
adjacent hotels, the Belleview House, at or around seven each evening for a slowly drunk whiskey punch. Or at most two of them,
never more; for it wasn't the liquor that attracted him, but the
lack of anything to do until it was time for the evening meal. He
chose this particular place because his own hotel had no such establishment, and it was the nearest at hand and the largest of those
that had.

It was a cheery, bustling, buzzing place, this, characteristic of
its kind and of the period. A gentleman's drinking place. And like
all others of its nature, while it was strictly a male preserve, women
were never so pervasively present in thought, spirit, implication and
conversation, as here where they were physically absent. They
permeated the air; they were in every *double entendre,* and wink,
and toast, and bragging innuendo. And here they were as men wish-
fully wanted them to be, and as they so seldom were beyond these
portals: uncommonly accommodating. At all times and in every
reminiscence.

Even in allegory they presided. Upon the wall facing the horseshoe-
shaped mahogany counter, cheery lights blinking at either side of
it—like glass-belled altar lights at the shrine of woman incarnate—
extended a tremendous oil painting of a reclining feminine form,
presumably a goddess. Attended at its head by two winged cupids
flying in rotary course, at its feet a cornucopia spilling fruits and
flowers. Purple drapery was present, but more in discard than in
application; one skein straggling downward across the figure's shoulder, another wisp stretching across its middle. In the background,
and never noted by an onlooker since the canvas had first been hung,
was an azure sky with puffballs of cottony clouds.

Dominating the place as it did, and shrewdly intended to, it was
as a matter of fact the means of Durand's striking up his first
acquaintanceship since arriving in Biloxi. The man nearest to him,
on the occasion of his second successive visit to the place, alone as
he was, was standing there with his eyes raptly fixed on it, and
almost humid with a sort of silly, faraway greediness, when Durand

happened to idly glance that way and catch the expression.

Durand couldn't resist smiling slightly, but to himself and not the devotee; but the other man, catching the half-formed smile just as it was about to turn away, mistook it for one of esoteric kinship of thought, and promptly returned it, but with an increment of friendly gregariousness that had been lacking in the original.

"Bless 'em!" he remarked fervently, and hoisted his glass toward the composition for Durand to see.

Durand nodded in temperate accord.

Emboldened, the other man raised his voice and invited over the three or four yards that separated them: "Will you join me, sir?"

Durand had no desire to, but to have refused would have been unwarrantedly boorish, so he moved accommodatingly toward his neighbor, and the latter made up the difference from his side.

Their orders were renewed, they saluted one another with them, and swallowed: thus completing the preliminary little ritual.

The other man was in his mid-forties, as far as Durand could judge. He had a good-looking, but rather weak and dissipated face; lines of looseness, rather than age, printed on it, particularly across the forehead. His complexion was extremely pallid; his hair dark, but possibly kept so with the aid of a little shoeblacking here and there; this, however, could only be a matter of conjecture. He was of lesser height than Durand, but of greater girth, albeit in a pillowy, less compact way.

"You alone here, sir?" he demanded.

"Quite alone," Durand answered.

"Shame!" he said explosively. "First time here, then, I take it?"

It was, Durand admitted laconically.

"You'll like it, soon as you get to know the ropes," he promised. "Takes a man a few days, I don't care where it is."

It did, Durand agreed tepidly.

"You stopping at this hotel here?" He cast his thumb joint toward the inner doors leading into the building itself. "I am."

"No, I'm over at the Rogers."

"Should have come to this one. Best one in the place. Kind of slow over there where you are, isn't it?"

He hadn't noticed, Durand said. He didn't expect to remain for very long, anyway.

"Well, maybe you'll change your mind," the other suggested

breezily. "Maybe we can get you to change your mind about that," he added, as though vested with a proprietary interest in the resort.

"Maybe," Durand assented, without overmuch enthusiasm. "Now join me," he invited dutifully, noting that his companion's drink was near bottom.

"Honored," said the other man zestfully, making quick to complete its disappearance.

Just as Durand was about to give the order, one of the hotel page boys came through the blown-glass doors leading from the hotel proper, looked about for a moment, then, marking Durand's partner, came up to him, excused himself, and said a word in his ear which Durand failed to catch. Particularly since he did not try to.

"Oh, already?" the other man said. "Glad you told me," and handed the boy a coin. "Be right there."

He turned back to Durand. "I'm called," he said cheerfully. "We'll have to resume this where we left off, some other evening." He preened himself, touching at his tie, his hair, the fit of his coat shoulders. "Mustn't keep a lady waiting, you know," he added, unable to resist letting Durand know of what nature the summons was.

"By no means," Durand conceded.

"Good evening to you, sir."

"Good evening."

He watched him go. His face was anything but leisurely, even while still in full sight, and at the end he flung apart the doors quite violently, so anxious was he not to be delinquent.

Durand smiled a little to himself, half contemptuously, half in pity, and went back to his drink alone.

33

THE FOLLOWING evening they met again, he and the other man. The
other was already there when Durand entered from the street, so
Durand joined him without ceremony, since the etiquette of the bar
prescribed that he owed the other a drink, and to have shunned him
—as he would have preferred to do—might have seemed on his part
an attempt to avoid the obligation.

"Still alone, I see," he greeted Durand.

"Still," Durand said cryptically.

"Well, man, you're slow," he observed critically. "What's hinder-
ing you? I should think by this time you'd have any number of—"
He didn't complete the phrase, but allowed a soggy wink to do so
for him.

Durand smiled wanly and gave their order.

They saluted, they swallowed.

"By the way, let me introduce myself," the other said heartily.
"I'm Colonel Harry Worth, late of the Army." The way he said it
showed which army he meant; or rather that there was only one
to be meant.

"I'm Louis Durand," Durand said.

They gripped hands, at the other's initiative.

"Where you from, Durand?"

"New Orleans."

"Oh," nodded the colonel approvingly. "Good place. I've been
there some."

Durand didn't ask where he was from. He didn't, his own train
of thoughts phrased it to himself, give a damn.

They talked of this and that. Of business conditions (together).
Of a little girl in Natchez (the colonel). Of the current administration (together, and with bitterness, as if it were some sort of foreign yoke). Of a little girl in Louisville (the colonel). Of recipes
of drinks (together). Of horses, and their breeding and their racing
(together). Of a "yellow" girl in Memphis (the colonel, with a resounding slap against his own thigh).

Then just as Worth was about to reorder, again the page came in,
accosted him, said that word into his ear.

"Time's up," he said to Durand. He offered him his hand. "A pleasure, Mr. Randall. Be looking forward to the next time."

"Durand," Durand said.

The colonel recoiled with dramatic exaggeration, apologized profusely. "That's right; forgive me. There I go again. Got the worst-all head for names."

"No harm," said Durand indifferently. He had an idea the mistake would continue to repeat itself for as long as their acquaintanceship lasted; a name that is not got right the second time, is not likely to be got right the fourth or the tenth time either. But it mattered to him not the slightest whether this man miscalled him or not, for the man himself mattered even less.

Worth renewed their handclasp, this time under the authentic auspices. Then as he turned to go, he reached downward to the counter, popped a clove into his mouth.

"That's just in case," he said roguishly.

He left rearward, into the hotel. Durand, was standing near the outside of the café, toward the street. Several minutes later, turning his head disinterestedly, he was just in time to catch the colonel's passage across the thick, soapy greenish plate glass that fronted the place and bulged convexly somewhat like a bay window.

The thickness of the medium they passed through blurred his outlines somewhat, but Durand could tell it was he. On the far side of him three detached excrescences, over and above those pertaining to his own person, were all that revealed he was escorting a woman. At the height of his shoulder blades the tip of a glycerined feather projected, from a hidden woman's bonnet on the outside, as though a quill or bright-tipped dart were sticking into him.

Then at the small of his back, and extending far beyond his own modest contours, a bustle fluctuated both voluptuously and yet somehow genteelly, ballooning along as its hidden wearer walked at his side. And lastly, down at his heels, as though one of the colonel's socks had loosened and were dragging, a small triangular wedge of skirt hem, an evening train, fluttered along the ground, switching erratically from side to side as it went.

But Durand didn't even allow his tepid glance to linger, to follow them long enough until they had drawn away into perspective sufficient to separate into two persons, instead of the one composite one, superimposed, they now formed.

Again he gave that wearied smile as on the night before. This time his brows went up, much as to say: Each man to his taste.

34

THE PAGE was later tonight in putting in an appearance. The colonel, therefore, had had one drink more than on their former evenings. This showed itself only in the added warmth of his friendliness, and in a tendency to clap and grip Durand on the upper arm at frequent intervals, in punctuation of almost every second remark he made. Otherwise Worth's speech was clear enough and his train of thought coherent enough.

"My fiancée is a lovely girl, Randall, a lovely girl," he reiterated solemnly, as though unable to impress it sufficiently upon his hearer.

"I'm sure she is," Durand said, as he had twice already. "I'm sure." Having corrected the mistake in nomenclature once for the evening, he no longer took the trouble after that, let Worth have his way about it.

"I tell you, I'm the luckiest man. But you should see her. You don't have to believe *me;* you should just see her for yourself."

"Oh, I do believe you," Durand protested demurely.

"You should have a girl like that" (clap). "You should get yourself a girl like that" (clap, clap).

"We can't all be as lucky," Durand murmured, stropping the edge of one foot restlessly along the brass bar rail.

"Hate to see a fine figure of a man like you mooning around alone" (clap).

"I'm not complaining," Durand said, scouring the bottom of his glass disclaimingly around on the bar-top in interlocked circles, until he had brought it back again around to where it had started from.

"But, dammit, look at me. I have you bettered by ten years, I vow. I don't stand around waiting for them to come to me. You'll never get anyone that way. You have to go out and find one."

"That's right, you do," agreed Durand, with the air of a man pledging to himself: I'll keep up my end of this conversation if it kills me.

The colonel was suddenly assailed by belated misgivings of having transgressed good taste. This time he pinioned Durand fondly by the coat revere, in lieu of a clap. "I'm not being too personal, am I?" he besought. "If I am, just say so, and I'll back out. Wouldn't want you to think that for the world."

"No offense whatever," Durand assured him. Which was literally true. It was like discussing astrology or some other remote subject.

"Reason I take such an interest in you is, I like you. I find your company most enjoyable."

"I can reciprocate the feeling," said Durand gravely, with a brief inclination that seemed to be exerted by the top of his head alone.

"I'd like to have you meet my fiancée. There's a girl."

"I'd be honored," said Durand. He was beginning to wish the nightly page boy would put in an appearance.

"She'll be coming down in a minute or two for me to pick her up." The colonel was suddenly visited with an inspiration. Pride of possession very frequently being synonymous with pride of display. "Why don't you join us for tonight? Love to have you. Come on out with me and I'll introduce you."

"Not tonight," said Durand a little hastily. Grasping at any excuse he could find, he stroked his own jaw line tentatively. "I wasn't expecting— Afraid I'm not presentable."

The colonel cocked his head critically. "Nonsense. You look all right. You're clean shaven."

He bethought himself of a compromise. "Well, just step out the door with me a moment and let me have you meet her, as she comes down. Then we'll go on alone."

Durand was suddenly visited by scruples of delicacy, which came in handy to his purpose. "I don't think she'd thank you for bringing anyone straight out of *here* to be presented to her face to face. It mightn't look right; you know how the ladies are. After all, this is a men's drinking café."

"But I come in here every night myself," the colonel said uncertainly.

"But you know her; I'm a stranger to her. It's not the same thing."

Before Worth could make up his mind on this fine point of social etiquette, the habitual bellboy had come in and delivered his summons.

"Your lady's down, sir."

The colonel put a coin in his gloved hand, drained his drink.

"Tell you what. I have a better idea. Suppose we make it a foursome. I'll have my fiancée bring someone along for you. She must know some of the unattached young ladies around here by now. That'll make it more comfortable for you. How about tomorrow night? Nothing on for then, have you?"

"Not a thing," said Durand, satisfied with having gained his reprieve for the present at least, and toying with the thought of sending his excuses sometime during the course of the following day as the best way of getting out of it. Any further reluctance at the moment, he realized, would have veered over into offense, even where such a thick-skinned individual as Worth was concerned, and it was none of his intent to offend the man gratuitously.

"Fine!" said Worth, beaming. "That's an engagement, then. I'll tell you what's just the place for it. There's a little supper establishment called The Grotto. Open late. Not *fast*, you understand. Just good and lively. They have music there, and very good wine. We go there often, Miss Castle and I. Instead of meeting here at the hotel, where there are a lot of old fogies around ready to gossip, you join us there. I'll bring the two young ladies with me."

"Excellent," said Durand.

The colonel rubbed his hands together gleefully, evidently former facets of his life not having yet died out as completely as he himself might have wished to believe.

"I'll engage a private alcove. They have them there, curtained off from prying eyes. Look for us, you'll find us in one of them." He tapped Durand on the chest with his index finger. "And don't forget, the invitation's mine."

"I dispute you there," Durand said.

"We'll quarrel over that when the time comes. Tomorrow night, then. Understood?"

"Tomorrow night. Understood."

Worth went hurrying toward the page who stood waiting for him just within the doors, evidently having received literal instructions to *bring* him with him, on the part of one who knew the colonel well.

Suddenly he turned, came hastening back, rose on tiptoe, and whispered hoarsely into Durand's ear: "I forgot to ask you. Blonde or brunette?"

Her image crossed Durand's mind for a minute. "Brunette," he said succinctly, and a flicker of pain crinkled his eyes momentarily.

The colonel dug an elbow into his ribs with ribald camaraderie.

35

SOMEHOW, the next day, he was too lackadaisical about the engagement even to send his perfunctory regrets in time, and so before he knew it, it was evening, the appointment had become confirmed if only by default, and it was too late to extricate himself from it without being guilty of the grossest rudeness, which would not have been the case had he canceled it a few hours earlier.

He'd lain down on his bed, fully dressed, late in the afternoon for a short nap, and when he awoke the time set was already imminent, and there was nothing left to do now but fulfill the engagement.

He sighed and grimaced privately to his mirror, but then commenced the necessary preparations none the less, stirring his brush vigorously within his thick crockery mug until foam swelled up and beaded driblets of it ran down the sides. He could remain a half-hour, he promised himself, as a token of participation, then arrange to have himself called away by one of the waiters with a decoy message, and leave. Making sure to pay his share of the entertainment before he did, so they wouldn't think that the motive. They would be offended, he supposed, but less than if he were not to appear at all.

Fortified by this intention, shaved and cleanly shirted, he shrugged on his coat, thumbed open his money-fold to see that it was sufficiently well filled, and glumly set forth. No celebrant ever started out with poorer grace or longer face to join what was meant to be a pleasure party. He was swearing softly under his breath as he closed the door of his room behind him: at the overgregarious colonel for inveigling him into this; at the unknown he was expected to pay court to for the mere fact that she was a woman and so could force him into a position where he was obliged to; and at himself, first and foremost, for not having had the bluntness to refuse point-blank the night before when the invitation had first been put to him.

Some vapid, simpering heifer; everyone's leavings. He could imagine the colonel's taste in women, judging by the man himself.

A ten-minute walk, in this caustic frame of mind, and unmellowed to the very end by the spangled brocade of starred sky hanging over him, had brought him to his destination.

The Grotto was a long, narrow, cabinlike, single-story structure, flimsy and unprepossessing on the outside like many another ephemeral holiday resort catering-place. Gas and oil light rayed forth from every crack and seam of it, tinted rose and blue by some peculiarity of shading on the inside. The interior, due to some depression in the ground, was somewhat lower than the walks outside, so that he had to descend a short flight of entry steps once he had been bowed in by the colored door-flunkey. The main dining room itself, seen from their top, was a disordered litter of white-clothed table tops, heads studding them in circular formation, and each one set with a rose or blue-shaded table lamp, an innovàtion borrowed from Europe, which dimmed the glare, usual in such places, to a twilight softness and created a suggestion of illicit revelry and clandestine romance. It gave the place the appearance of a field of blinking fireflies.

A pompous dining steward, with wide-spreading frizzed sideburns, clasping a bill-of-fare slantwise like a painter holding a palette, greeted him at the foot of the stairs.

"Are you alone, sir? May I show you to a table?"

"No, I was to join a party," Durand said. "Colonel Worth and friends. In one of the private booths. Which way are they?"

"Oh, straight to the back, sir. At the far end of the room. You are expected. They are in the first one on the right."

He made his way down the long central lane of clearance to the rear, like someone wresting his way through a brawl, auditory and olfactory, if not combative. Through cellular entities or zones of disparate food odors, that remained isolated, each in its little nucleus, refusing to mingle; now lobster, now charcoaled steak, now soggy linen and spilled wine. Through dismembered snatches of conversation and laughter that likewise remained compartmentalized, each within its own little circular area.

"When he's with me he says one thing, and when he's with the next girl he says another. Oh, I've heard all about you, never you mind!"

"—an administration that's the ruination of this country! And I don't care who hears me, I'm entitled to my opinion!"

"—and now I come to the best part of the story. This is the part that will delight you—"

At the back, the room narrowed to a single serving passage leading to the kitchen. Lining each side of this, however, were openings leading into the little private alcoves or dining nooks Worth had mentioned. All alike discreetly curtained-off from view, although otherwise they were doorless. The nearest one on either side, however, was not strictly parallel to the passage but placed slantwise to it, cutting off the corner.

As he fixed his eyes upon the one to the right, marking that for his eventual destination, though still a little distance short of it, with the last bank of tables projecting somewhat between, the protective curtain gashed back at one side and a waiter came out backward, in the act of withdrawal but lingering a moment half-in half-out to allow the completion of some instruction being given him. He held the curtain, for that moment, away from the wall in a sort of diamond-shaped aperture, with one hand.

Durand's foot, striking ground, never moved on again, never took him a space nearer.

It was as if a cameo of purest line, of clearest design, were in that opening, held there for Durand to see, a cameo of dazzling clarity, presented against a dark velvet mounting.

On one side, fluctuating with utterance of orders to the waiter, was a slice of the lumpy profile of the colonel. At the other, facing back toward him, was a slice of the smooth-turned profile of an unknown, dark of hair and dark of eye.

Midway between the two, facing outward, bust-length, white as

alabaster, dazzling as marble, regal as a diminutive Juno, beautiful
as a blonde Venus or the Helen of the Trojans, were the face and
throat and bared shoulders and half-bared bosom that he would
never forget, that he could never forget, brought as if by magic
transmutation back from out his dreams into the living substance
again.

Julia.

He could even see the light on her hair, in moving golden sheen.
Even see the passing glint, as of crystal, as her eyes moved.

Julia, the killer. The destroyer of his heart.

That she failed to see him out there was incredible. All but the
pupils of her eyes alone were bearing straight toward him. They
must have been deflected, unnoticeable at that distance, toward one
or the other of her table companions, to miss striking him.

The waiter dropped his restraining hand, the curtainside swept
to the wall, the cameo was blotted out.

He stood there as stunned, as blasted, as robbed of his powers
of motion, as though that white, searing glimpse—there, then gone
again—had been a flash of lightning which had struck too close and
fused him to the ground. All its effects lacked was to cause him to
fall flat in front of everybody, then and there.

Then a waiter, hurrying obliviously by, jarred against him, and
that set him into motion at last; as one ball strikes another on a
billiard table, starting it off.

He was going back the other way, the way he'd come, now, unsteadily, jostling into tables and the backs of chairs that lined his
route, past momentarily upturned, questioning faces, past a blurred
succession of table lamps like worthless beacons that only confused
and failed to guide him straight through their midst.

He reached the other end of the raucous place, and the same
steward as before came solicitously to his side.

"Did you fail to find your party, sir?"

"I—I've changed my mind." He took out his money-fold, crushed
an incredible ten-dollar bill into the man's hand. "I haven't been
here asking for them. You didn't see me."

He stumbled up the steps and out, lurching as though he'd filled
himself with wine in those few minutes. Wine of hate, ferment of
the grapes of wrath.

36

HE HAD at first no very clear concept of what he meant to do. The black fog of hate that filled his mind clouded all plans and purposes. Instinct alone had kept him from rushing in through those curtains, not calculation.

Alone. Alone he must have her, where no onlookers could save her. He wanted no hot-mouthed denunciation, quickly over. What was one more denunciation to her? Her path must have been strewn with them already. He wanted no public wrangle, in which her coolness and composure would inevitably have the better of him. "I've never seen this man before. He must be mad!" One thing and one alone he wanted, one thing alone he'd have. He wanted her death. He wanted the few moments just ahead of it to be between the two of them alone.

He stood for a while outside their hotel, hers and Worth's, to calm himself, to compose himself. Stood with his back to it, looking out to seaward. And as he stood, motionless, inscrutable of attitude in all else, over and over and over again he brought his hand down upon the wooden railing. At stated intervals, like a pestle, pulverizing his intentions, grinding them fine.

Then it slackened, then it stopped. He was ready.

He turned abruptly and went into the brightly lighted lobby of the place, purposefully yet not too hurriedly. He went undeviatingly toward the desk, stopped before it, drummed his fingernails upon its white-veined black marble top to hasten the clerk's attention.

Then when he had it: "I'm a friend of Colonel Worth's. I've just left him and his party at the Grotto."

"Yes, sir. Can I be of service?"

"One of the young ladies with us—I believe she's stopping here—found the evening chillier than she expected it to be. She's sent me back for her scarf. She explained to me where it's to be found. May I be allowed to go up and fetch it for her?"

The clerk was professionally cautious. "Could you describe her to me?"

"She's blonde, and a rather small little person."

The clerk's doubts vanished. "Oh, that's the colonel's fiancée.

Miss Castle. In Room Two-six. I'll have a bellboy take you up immediately, sir."

He jarred a bell, handed over a key with the requisite instructions.

Durand was taken up to the second floor, in a ponderous latticework elevator, its shaft transparent on all sides. He noted that a staircase coiled around this on the outside, rising as it rose, attaining the same destination at last. He noted that, well and grimly.

They went down a hall. There was a brief delay as the bellboy fitted key to door and tried it. Then as the door opened, the most curious sensation that he had ever had swept over Durand. It was as though he were near her all over again. It was as though she had just this moment stepped out of the room on the far side as he entered it on the near. She was present to every faculty but vision. Her perfume still lay ghostly on the air. He could feel her at the ends of all his pores. A discarded taffeta garment flung over the back of a chair rustled again as she moved, in memory, in his ears.

It whipped his hate so, it steeled him to his purpose. He made no false step, wasted not a move. He went about it as one stalks an enemy.

The bellboy had remained deferentially beside the open door, allowing him to enter alone. He remained, however, in a position from which he could watch what Durand was about.

"She must be mistaken," Durand said plausibly, for the other's benefit but as if speaking to himself. "I don't see it over the chair." He raised the taffeta underslip, replaced it again. "It must be in one of these bureau drawers." He opened one, closed it again. Then a second.

The bellboy was watching him now with the slightly anxious air of a hen having its nest searched for eggs.

"Women never know where they leave things, did you ever notice?" Durand said to him in man-to-man confidence.

The boy grinned, flattered at being included into a stage of experience which he had not yet reached of his own efforts.

Durand, secretly desperate, at length discovered something in the third drawer, withdrew a length of flimsy heliotrope voile, sufficient at least for the purposes of his visit if nothing else.

"This, I guess," he said, concealing a relieved smile at his good fortune.

He closed the drawer, came back toward the door, stuffing it into his side pocket.

The boy's eyes, inevitably, were on his prodding hand. His were on the edge of the door, turned inward so that it faced him. It had, above the latch-tongue, a small rounded depression. A plunger, controlling the lock. Just as his own room door, in the other building, had. He had counted on that.

Before the boy was aware of it, Durand had relieved him of the duty of reclosing the door; grasping it by its edge, not its knob, directly over the plunger, and drawing it closed after the two of them.

He had, while doing so, changed the plunger, pressing it in, leaving the door off-lock and simply on-latch no matter whether a key was used or not.

He then allowed the boy to complete his appointed task of turning the key, extracting it and once that was done, distracted him from testing it further by having a silver half-dollar extended in his hand for him.

They went down together, the boy all smiles and congenitally unable to harbor suspicion of anyone who tipped so lavishly. Durand smiling a little too, a very little.

He nodded his thanks to the clerk as he went by, tapped his pocket to show him that he had secured what he'd come for.

There wasn't a glint of pity in the stars over him as he came out into the open night and his face dimmed to its secretive shade. There wasn't a breath of tenderness in the humid salt breeze that came in from the Gulf. He'd have her alone, and no one should save her. He'd have her death, and nothing else would do.

37

HE WENT from there to his own room, unlocked his traveling bag, and took out the pistol. The same pistol that one night in New Orleans he'd told Aunt Sarah he would kill her with. And now, it seemed, the time was near, was very near. He cracked it open, though he knew already it was fully charged; and found that it was. Then he sheathed it in the inside pocket of his coat, which was deep and took it up to the turn of the butt and held it securely.

He looked down and noted the heliotrope scarf dangling from his side pocket, and in a sudden access of hate he ripped it out and flung it on the floor. Then he ground his heel into the middle of it, and kicked it away from him, like something unclean, unfit to touch. His face was putrefied with the hate that reeks from an unburied love.

He tweaked out the gaslight, and the greenish-yellow cast of the room turned to moonlight tarnished with lampblack. He stood there in it for a moment, half-man, half-shadow, as if gathering purpose. Then he moved, the half of him that was man became shadow, the half that was shadow became man, as the window beams rippled at his passage. There was a flicker of citron from the lighted hall outside, as he opened the door, closed it after him.

He went up the stairs to the second floor without meeting anybody, and the hubbub of voices from the several public parlors on the main floor grew fainter the farther he ascended. Until at last there was silence. He quitted the staircase at the second, and followed the corridor along which the page had led him before, with its flower-scrolled red carpeting and walnut-dark doors. Here for the first time he nearly met mischance. A lady coming out of her room caught him midway along it, too far advanced to turn back. Her eyes rested on him for an instant only, then she passed him with discreetly downcast gaze, as befitted their distinction of gender, and the rustle of her multi-layered skirts sighed its way along the passage. He gave her time to turn and pass from sight at the far end, stopping for a moment opposite a door that was not his destination, as if about to go in there. Then swiftly going on and making for the door he had in mind, he cast a quick precautionary look about him, seized the knob, gave it a rapid turn, and was in. He closed it after him.

There were the same low night lights burning as before, and she wasn't back yet. Her presence was in the air, he thought, in faded sachet and in the warm, quilted voluptuousness the closed-for-hours room breathed. He couldn't have come any nearer to her than this; only her person itself was absent. Her aura was in here with him, and seeming to twine ghost-arms about his neck from behind. He squared his shoulders, as if to free them, and twisted his neck within his collar.

He stood at the window for a while, safely slantwise out of sight, staring ugly-faced at the moonlight, his face pitted like a smallpox victim's by the pores of the lacework curtain. Below him there was the sloping white shed of the veranda roof, like a tilted snowbank. Beyond that, the smooth black lawns of the hotel grounds. And off in the distance, coruscating like a swarm of fireflies, the waters of the inlet. Overhead the moon was round and hard as a medicinal lozenge. And, to him, as unpalatable.

Turning away abruptly at last, he retired deeper into the room, and selecting a chair at random, sank into it to wait. Shadow, the way he happened to be sitting, covered the upper part of his face, running across it in an even line, like a mask. A mask inscrutable and grim and without compunction.

He waited from then on without a move, and the night seemed to wait with him, like an abetting conspirator eager to see ill done.

Once toward the end he took out his watch and looked at it, dipping its face out into the moonlight. Nearly a quarter after twelve. He had been in here three full hours. They'd stayed the evening out without him at the supper pavilion. He clapped the watch closed, and it resounded bombastically there in the stillness.

Suddenly, as if in derisive answer, he heard her laugh, somewhere far in the distance. Perhaps coming up in the lift. He would have known it for hers even if he hadn't seen her in the alcove at the restaurant earlier tonight. He would, he felt sure, have known it for hers even if he hadn't known she was here in Biloxi at all. The heart remembers.

38

HE JUMPED up quickly and looked around. Strangely enough, for all the length of time he'd been in the room, he'd made no plans for concealment, he had to improvise them now. He saw the screen there, and chose that. It was the quickest and most obvious method of effacing himself, and she was already nearing the door, for he could hear her voice now, merrily saying something, close at hand in the hallway.

He spread the screen a little more, squaring its panels, so that it made a sort of hollow pilaster protruding from the wall, and got in behind there. He could maintain his own height, he found, and still not risk having the top of his head show. He could see through the perforated, lacelike, scrolled woodwork at the top, his eyes came up to there.

The door opened, and she had arrived.

Two figures came in, not one; and advancing only a step or two beyond the doorway, almost instantly blended into one, stood there locked in ravenous embrace in the semishadow of the little foyer. A gossamer piquancy of breath-borne champagne or brandy reached him, admixed with a little perfume. His heart drowned in it.

There was no motion, just the rustle of pressed garments.

Again her laugh sounded, but muffled, furtive, now; lower now that it was close at hand than it had been when at a distance outside.

He recognized the colonel's voice, in a thick whisper. "I've been waiting for this all evening. My li'l girl, you are, my li'l girl."

The rustling strengthened to active resistance.

"Harry, that's enough now. I must wear this dress again. Leave me at least a shred of it."

"I'll buy you another. I'll buy you ten."

She broke away at last, light from the hallway came between their figures; but the embrace was still locked about her like a barrel-hoop. Durand could see her pushing the colonel's arms perpendicularly downward, unable to pry them open in the usual direction. At last they severed.

"But I like this one. Don't be so destructive. I never saw such a man. Let me put the lights up. We mustn't stand here like this."

"I like it better as it is."

"I've no doubt!" she said pertly. "But up they go just the same."

She entered the room itself now, and went to the night light, and it flared from a spark to a sunburst at her touch. And as the light bathed her, washing away all indistinctness of outline and of feature, she glowed there before him in full life once more, after a year and a month and a day. No longer just a cameo glimpsed through a parted curtain, a disembodied laugh down a hallway, a silhouette

against an open door; she was whole, she was real, she was *she*.
She broke into bloom. In all her glory and her ignominy; in all her
beauty and all her treachery; in all her preciousness and all her
worthlessness.

And an old wound in Durand's heart opened and began to bleed
all over again.

She threw down her fan, she threw down her shoulder scarf; she
drew off the one glove she had retained and added that to the one
she had carried loose, and threw them both down. She was in garnet
satin, stiff and crisp as starch, and picked with scrolls and traceries
of twinkling jet. She took up a little powder-pad and touched it to
the tip of her nose, but in habit rather than in actual application.
And her courtier stood there and watched her every move, idolizing
her, beseeching her, with his greedy smoking eyes.

She turned to him at last, offhandedly, over one shoulder. "Wasn't
it too bad about poor Florrie? What do you suppose became of the
young man you arranged to have her meet?"

"Oh, blast him!" Worth said truculently. "Forgot, maybe. He's
no gentleman. If I run into him again, I'll cut him dead."

She was seeing to her hair now. Touching it a bit, without disturbing it too much. Gracefully crouching a trifle so that the top of
the mirror frame could encompass it comfortably. "What was he
like?" she asked idly. "Did he seem well-to-do? Would we—would
Florrie, I mean—have liked him, do you think?"

"I hardly know him. Name was Randall or something. I've never
seen him spend more than fifty cents at a time for a whiskey punch."

"Oh," she said on a dropping inflection, and stopped with her
hair, as if losing interest in it.

She turned and moved toward him suddenly, hand extended in
parting gesture. "Well, thank you for a congenial evening, Harry.
Like all your evenings it was most delectable."

He took the hand but kept it within his two.

"Mayn't I stay just a little while longer? I'll behave. I'll just sit
here and watch you."

"Watch me!" she exclaimed archly. "Watch me do what? Not what
you'd like to, I warn you." She pushed him slightly, at the shoulder,
to keep the distance between them even.

Then her smile faded, and she seemed to become thoughtful, ruefully sober for a moment.

"Wasn't it too bad about poor Florrie, though?" she repeated, as though discovering some remaining value in the remark that had not been fully extracted the first time.

"Yes, I suppose so," he agreed vaguely.

"She took such pains with her appearance. I had to lend her the money for the dress."

Instantly he released her. "Oh, here. Let me. Why didn't you tell me this sooner?" He busied himself within his coat, took out his money-fold, opened and busied himself with that.

She darted a quick glance down at it, then the rest of the time, until he had finished, looked dreamily past him to the rear of the room.

He put something in her hand.

"Oh, and while I think of it—" he said.

He fumbled additionally with the pocketbook, put something further into her uncoöperative, yet unresistant, hand.

"For the hotel bill," he said. "For the sake of appearance, it's better if you attend to it yourself."

She circled, swept her back toward him. Yet scarcely in offense or disdain, for she said to him teasingly: "Now don't look. At least, not over my left shoulder."

The folds of garnet satin swept up at her side for a moment, revealing the long shapely glint of smoky black silk. Worth, up on the toes of his feet to gain height, was peering hungrily over her right shoulder. She turned her face toward him for a moment, gave him a roguish look, winked one eye, and the folds of her dress cascaded to the floor again, with a soft little plop.

Worth made a sudden convulsive move, and they had blended into one again, this time in full light of mid-room, not in the shadow of the vestibule.

Durand felt something heavy in his hand. Looked down and saw that he'd taken the pistol out. "I'll kill both of them," stencilled itself in white-hot lettering across his mind.

"And now—?" Worth said, lips blurred against her neck and shoulder. "Are you going to be kind—?"

Durand could see her head avert itself from his; smiling benevolently, yet avert itself. She twisted to face the door, and in turning, managed to get him to turn likewise; then somehow succeeded in leading him toward it, her face and shoulders still caught in his endless kiss. "No—" she said temperately, at intervals. "No— No— I *am* kind to you, Harry. No more kind than I've always been to you, no less— Now that's a good boy—"

Durand gave a sigh of relief, put the gun away.

She was standing just within the gap of the door now, alone at last, her arm extended to the outside. Worth must have been kissing it repeatedly, the length of time she maintained it that way.

All he could hear was a subdued murmur of reluctant parting.

She withdrew her arm with effort, pressed the door closed.

He saw her face clearly as she came back into the full light. All the playfulness, coquetry, were wiped off it as with a sponge. It was shrewd and calculating, and a trifle pinched, as if with the long wearing of a mask.

"God Almighty!" he heard her groan wearily, and saw her strike herself a glancing blow against the temple.

She went first and looked out the window, as he had earlier; stood there motionless by it some time. Then when she'd had her fill of whatever thoughts the sight from there had managed to instill in her, she turned away suddenly, almost with abrupt impatience, causing her skirts to swirl and hiss out in the silence. She came back to the dresser, fetched out a drawer. No powdering at her nose, no primping at her hair, now. She had no look to spare for the mirror.

She withdrew the money from her stocking-top and flung it in, with a turn of the wrist that was almost derisive. But not of the money itself, possibly; of its source.

Reaching into some hiding place she had in there, she took out one of those same slender cigars Aunt Sarah had showed him in the St. Louis Street house in New Orleans.

To him there was something repugnant, almost obscene, in the sight of her bending to the lamp chimney with it until it had kindled, holding it tight-bitten, smoke sluicing from her miniature nostrils, as from a man's.

In a sickening phantasmagoric illusion, that lasted but a moment, she appeared to him as a fuming, horned devil, in her ruddy long-tailed dress.

She set the cigar down, presently, in a hairpin tray, and seated herself by the mirror. She unfastened her hair and it came tumbling down in a molasses-colored cascade to the small of her back. Then she opened a vent in her dress at the side, separating a number of hooks from their eyes, but without unfastening or removing it farther than that. Leaving a gap through which her tightly laced side swelled and subsided again at each breath.

She took out the money now she had cast in only a moment before, but took out far more than she had flung in, and counted it over with close attention. Then she put it into a small lacquered casket, of the type used to hold jewels, and locked that, and gave it a commending little thump on its lid with her knuckles, as if in pleased finality.

She reclosed the drawer, stood up, moved over to the desk, took down its lid and seated herself at it. She drew out a sheet of notepaper from the rack. Took up a pen and dipped it, and squaring her other arm above the surface to be written on, began to write.

Durand moved out from behind the screen and slowly walked across the carpet toward her. It gave his tread no sound, though he wasn't trying for silence. He advanced undetected, until he was standing behind her, and could look down over her shoulder.

"Dear Billy," the paper said. "I—"

The pen had stopped, and she was nibbling for a moment at its end.

He put out his hand and let it come lightly to rest on her shoulder. Left it there, but lightly, lightly, as she had once put her hand to *his* shoulder, lightly, on the quayside at New Orleans; lightly, but crushing his life.

Her fright was the fright of guilt, and not innocence. Even before she could have known who it was. For she didn't turn to look, as the innocent of heart would have. She held her head rigidly as it was, turned the other way, neck taut with suspense. She was *afraid* to look. There must have been such guilt strewn behind her in her life, that *anyone's* sudden touch, in the stillness of the night, in the solitude of her room, she must have known could bode no good.

Her one hand dropped the pen lifelessly. Her other clawed secretively at the sheet of notepaper, sucking it up, causing it to disappear. Then dropping it, crumpled, over the desk side.

Still she didn't move; the sleek taffy-colored head held still, like something an axe was about to fall on.

Her eyes had found him in the mirror by now. It was over to the left of her, and when he looked at it himself, he could see, in the reflection of her talcum-white face, the pupils darkening the far corners of her eyes, giving her an ugly unnatural appearance, as though she had black eyeballs.

"Don't be afraid to look around, Julia," he said ironically. "It's only me. No one important. Merely me."

Suddenly she turned, so swiftly that the transplacement of the silken back of her head by the plaster-white cast of her face was almost like that of an apparition.

"You act as though you don't remember me," he said softly. "Surely you haven't forgotten me, Julia. *Me* of all people."

"How'd you know I was here?" she demanded granularly.

"I didn't. I was the other man who was to have met you at the restaurant party tonight."

"How'd you get in here?"

"Through the door."

She had risen now, defensively, and was trying to reverse the desk chair to get it between them, reedy as it was, but there was no room to allow for its insertion.

He took it from her and set it to rest with his hand.

"How is it you don't order me from your room, Julia? How is it you don't threaten to scream for help? Or all those other things they usually do?"

She said, summoning up a sort of desperate tractability, that he couldn't help but admire for an instant, "This is a matter that has to be settled between us, without screams or ordering you from the room." She stroked one arm, shiveringly, all the way up to the top. "Let's get it over with as soon as we can."

"It's taken *me* better than a year," he said. "*You* won't grudge a few added minutes, I hope?"

She didn't answer.

"Were you going to marry the colonel, Julia? That would have been bigamous."

She shrugged irritably. "Oh, he's just a fool. I'm not accountable for him. The whole world is full of fools." And in this phrase, at least, there was unmistakable sincerity.

"And the biggest of them all is the one you're looking at right now, Julia."

He kicked the crumpled tossball of notepaper leniently with the toe of his foot, moving it a little. But gently, as if it held somebody else's wracked hopes.

"Who's Billy?"

"Oh, no one in particular. A chance acquaintance. A fellow I met somewhere." She flung out her hand, still with nervous irritability, as if causing the person to disappear from her ken in that way.

"The world must be full of Billys for you. Billys and Lous and Colonel Worths."

"Is it?" she said. "No, there was only one Lou. It may be a little late to say it now. But I didn't marry the Billys and the Colonel Worths. I married Lou."

"You acted it," he agreed mordantly.

"Well, it's late," she said. "What's the good now?"

"We agree on that, at least."

She went over to the lamp, and thoughtfully spanned her hand against it, so that her flesh glowed translucent brick-red, and watched that effect for a while. Then she turned toward him.

"What is it, Lou? What are your plans for me?"

His hand rose slowly to that part of his coat which covered where the gun was resting against him. Remained there a moment. Then crept around to the inside and found it, by the handle. Then drew it out, so slowly, so slowly, the bone handle, the nickelled chambers and fluted barrel seemed never to stop coming, like something pulled on an endless train.

"I came here to kill you, Julia."

A single glance was all she gave it. Just enough to identify it, to see that he had the means to do it on his person. Then after that, her eyes were for his alone, never left them from then on. Knowing where the signal would lie: in his eyes and not on the gun. Knowing where the only place to appeal lay: in his eyes.

She looked at him for a long time, as if measuring his ability to do it: what he'd said. What she saw there, only she could have told. Whether full purpose, hopeless to deflect, or half-purpose, waiting only to be crumbled.

He didn't point it, he didn't raise it to her; he simply held it, on the flat side, muzzle offside. But his face was white with the long pain she'd given him, and whatever she'd read in his look, still all that was needed was a turn of his hand.

Perhaps she was a gambler, and instinctively liked the odds, they appealed to her, whetted her; she hated to bet on a sure thing. Or perhaps the reverse: she was no gambler, she only banked upon a certainty, never anything else, in men or in cards; and this was a certainty now, though he didn't know it himself yet. Or perhaps, again it was solely vanity, self-esteem, that prompted her, and she must put her power over him to the test, even though to lose meant to die. Perhaps, even, if she were to lose, she would want to die, vanity being the thing it is.

She smiled at him. But in brittle challenge, not in anything else.

She suddenly wrenched at the shoulder of her dress, tore it down. Then pulled at it, farther down and still farther down, withdrawing her arm from the bedraggled loop it now made, until at last the whiteness of her side was revealed all but to the waist. On the left, the side of the heart. Moving toward him all the while, closer step by step. White as milk and pliable as China silk, flesh flexing as she walked.

Then halted as the cold gun touched her, holding her ravaged dress-bodice clear and looked deep into his eyes.

"All right, Lou," she whispered.

He withdrew the gun from between them.

She came a step closer with its removal.

"Don't hesitate, Lou," she breathed. "I'm waiting."

His heel edged backward, carrying him a hair's breadth off. He stuffed the gun into his side pocket, to be rid of it, hastily, fumblingly, careless how he did so, leaving the hilt projecting.

"Cover yourself up, Julia," he said. "You're all exposed."

And there was the answer. If she'd been a gambler, she'd won. If she'd been no gambler, she'd read his eyes right the first time. If it was vanity that had led her to the brink of destruction, it had triumphed, it was intact, undamaged.

She gave no sign. Not even of having triumphed; which is the way of the triumphant when they are clever as well. His face was bedewed with accumulated moisture, as though it were he who had taken the risk.

She drew her clothes upward again, never to where they had originally been but at least in partial restoration.

"Then if you won't kill me, what *do* you want of me?"

"To take you back to New Orleans and hand you over to the police." As if uneasy at their close confrontation, he sundered it, shifted aside. "Get yourself ready," he said over his shoulder.

Suddenly his head inclined, to stare downward at his own chest, as if in involuntary astonishment. Her arms had crept downward past his shoulders, soft as white ribbons, and were trying to join together before him in supplicating embrace. He could feel the softness of her hair as it came to rest against him just below the nape of his neck.

He parted them, flung them off, sending her backward from him. "Get yourself ready," he said grimly.

"If it's the money, wait—I have some here, I'll give it to you. And if it's not enough, I'll make it up—I swear I will—"

"Not for that. You were my wife, in law, and there was no crime committed, in law."

"Then for what?"

"To answer what became of Julia Russell. The real one. You're not Julia Russell and you never were. Do you pretend you are?"

She didn't answer. He thought he could detect more real fright now than at the time of the gun. Her eyes were wider, more strained, at any rate.

She quitted the drawer she had thrown open and been crouched beside, where the money was, and came toward him.

"To tell them what you did with her," he said. "And there's a name for that. Would you like to hear it?"

"No, no!" she protested, and even held her palms fronted toward him as she came close, but whether her protest was for the thought he had suggested, or for the very sound itself of the word he had threatened to utter, he could not tell. Almost, it seemed, the latter.

"Mur—" he began.

And then her palms had found his mouth and stopped it, terrifiedly. "No, no! Lou, don't say that! I had nothing to do with it. I don't *know* what became of her. Only listen to me, hear me; Lou, you must listen to me!"

He tried to cast her off as he had before, but this time she clung, she would not be rejected. Though his arms flung her, she came back upon them again, carried by them.

"Listen to what? More lies? Our whole marriage was a lie. Every word you spoke to me, every breath you drew, in all that time was a lie. You'll tell them to the police, not to me any longer. I want no more of them!"

That word, just as the one she'd stifled before, seemed to have a particular terror for her. She quailed, and gave a little inchoate moan, the first sound of weakness she'd made yet. Or if it was artifice, calculation pretending to be weakness for its effect upon him, it succeeded by that much, for he took it to be weakness, and thus its purpose was gained.

Still clinging in desperation to the wings of his coat, she dropped to her knees before him, grovelling in posture of utmost supplication the human figure is capable of.

"No, no, the truth this time!" she sobbed drily. "Only the truth, and nothing else! If you'll only listen to me, let me speak—"

He stopped trying to rid himself of her at last, and stood there stolid.

"Would you know it?" he said contemptuously.

But she'd gained her hearing.

Her arms dropped from him, and she turned her head away for a moment and backed her hand to her own mouth. Whether in hurried search of inspiration, or whether steeling herself for the honest unburdening about to come, he could not tell.

"There's no train a while yet," he said grudgingly. "And I can't take you to the railroad station as you are now and keep you dawdling about there with me half the night—so speak if you want to." He dropped back into a chair, pulled at his collar as if exhausted by the emotional stress they had both just been through. "It will do you no good. I warn you before you begin, the outcome will be the same. *You are coming back to New Orleans with me to face justice.* And all your tears and all your kneeling and all your pleas are thrown away!"

Without rising, she inched toward him, crept as it were, on her very knees, so that the distance between them was again lessened, and she was at his very feet, penitent, abject, her hands to the arm of the chair he was in.

"It wasn't I. I didn't do it. *He* must have done something to her, for I never saw her again. But what it was, I don't know. I didn't see it done. He only came to me afterward and said she'd had a mishap, and I was afraid to question him any further than—"

"*He?*" he said sardonically.

"The man I was with. The man on the boat I was with."

"Your paramour," he said tonelessly, and tried not to let her see him swallow the bitter lump that knobbed his throat.

"No!" she said strenuously. "No, he wasn't! You can believe it

if you choose, but from first to last he wasn't. It was purely a working arrangement. And no one else ever was either, before him. I've
learned to care for myself since I've been about in the world, and
whether I've done things that were right, or done things that were
wrong, I've been no man's but yours, Lou. No man's, until I married you."

He wondered why he felt so much lighter than a moment ago,
and warned himself sternly he mustn't; and in spite of that, did
anyway.

"Julia," he drawled reproachfully, as if in utter disbelief. "You
ask me to believe that? Julia, Julia."

"Don't call me Julia," she murmured remorsefully. "That isn't
my name."

"*Have* you a name?"

She moistened her lips. "Bonny," she admitted. "Bonny Castle."

He gave a nod of agreement that was a jeer in pantomime. "To
the colonel, Bonny. To me, Julia. To Billy, something else. To the
next man, something else again." He turned his face from her in
disgust, then looked back again. "Is that what you were christened?
Is that your baptismal name?"

"No," she said. "I was never christened. I never had a baptismal
name."

"Everyone has a name, I thought."

"I never had even that. You need a mother and father to give
you that. A wash basket on a doorstep can't give you that. Now do
you understand?"

"Then where is it from?"

"It's from a postal picture card," she said, and some old defiance
and rancor still alive in her made her head go up higher a moment.
"A postal picture card from Scotland that came to the foundling
home, one day when I was twelve. I picked it up and stole a look. And
on the face of it there was the prettiest scene I'd ever seen, of ivy-
covered walls and a blue lake. And it said 'Bonny Castle.' I didn't
know what it meant, but I took that for my name. They'd called
me Josie in the foundling home until then. I hated it. Anyway, it
was no more my rightful name than this was. I've kept to this one
ever since, so it's rightfully mine by length of usage if nothing
else. What difference do a few drops of holy water sprinkled on your
head make? Go on, laugh if you will," she consented bleakly.

"I no longer know how," he said in glum parenthesis. "You saw to that. How long were you there, at this institution?"

"Until I was fifteen, I think. Or close onto it. I've never had an exact birthday, you see. That's another thing I've done without. I made one up for myself, at one time; just as the name. I chose St. Valentine's Day, because it was so festive. But then I tired of it after a while, and no longer kept up with it."

He gazed at her without speaking.

She sighed weariedly, to draw fresh breath for continuation.

"Anyway, I ran away from there when I was fifteen. They accused me of stealing something, and they beat me for it. They'd accused me before, and they'd beaten me before. But at thirteen I knew no better than to endure it, at fifteen I no longer would. I climbed over the wall at night. Some of the other girls helped me, but they lacked the courage to come with me." And then she said with an odd, speculative sort of detachment, as though she were speaking of someone else: "That's one thing I've never been, at least: a coward."

"You've never been a coward," he assented, but as though finding small cause for satisfaction in the estimate.

"It was up in Pennsylvania," she went on. "It was bitterly cold. I remember trudging the roadside for hours, until at last a drayman gave me a ride in his wagon—"

"You're from the North?" he said. "I hadn't known. You don't speak as they do up there."

"North, South," she shrugged. "It's all one. I speak as they do wherever I've been last, until I come to a new place."

And always lies, he thought; never the truth.

"I came to Philadelphia. An old woman took me in for a while, an old witch. She found me ready to drop on the cobbles. I thought she was kind at first, but she wasn't. After she'd fed and rested me for a few days, she put me into the clothes of a younger child—I was small, you see—and took me with her to shop in the stores. She said 'Watch me,' and showed me how to filch things from the counters without being detected. I ran away from her too, finally."

"But not without having done it yourself, first." He watched her closely to see if she'd labor with the answer.

She didn't stop for breath. "Not without having done it myself, first. She would only give me food when I had."

"And then what happened?"

"I worked a little, as a scrub girl, a slavey; I worked in a bakery kitchen, helping to make the rolls; I even worked as a laundress' helper. I was homeless more often than I had a place to sleep." She averted her head for a moment, so that her neck drew into a taut line. "Mostly, I can no longer remember those days. What's more, I don't want to."

She probably sold herself on the streets, he thought, and his heart sickened at the suggestion, as though she were in actuality someone to cherish.

With an almost uncanny clairvoyance, she said just then: "There was one way I could have got along, but I wouldn't take it."

Lies, he vowed, lies; but his heart sang wildly.

"I ran in horror from a woman one night who had coaxed me into stopping in her house for a cup of tea."

"Admirable," he said drily.

"Oh, don't give me credit for goodness," she said, with a sudden little flare of candor. "Give me credit for perversity, rather. I hated every human being in the world, at times, in those days, for what I was going through; man, woman, and child. I would give no one what they wanted of me, because no one would give me what I wanted of them."

He looked downward mutely, trapped at last into credulity, however brief; this time even of the mind as well as the heart.

"Well, I'd best be brief. It's what happened on the river you want to know of, mainly. I fell in with a troupe of traveling actors, joined up with them. They didn't even play in regular theatres. They had no money to afford them. They went about and pitched tents. And from there I fell in with a man who was a professional gambler on the river boats. The girl who had been his partner before then had quitted him to marry a plantation owner—or so he told me— and he was looking for someone to take her place. He offered me a share of his profits, if I would join with him." She waved her hand. "And it was but a different form of acting, after all. With quarters preferable to the ones I'd been used to." She stopped.

"He was the one," she told him.

"What was his name, what was he called?" he said with a sudden access of interest.

"What does it matter? His name was false, like mine was. On

every trip it changed. It had to, as a precaution. Once it was Mc-Larnin. Once it was Rideau. I doubt that I ever knew his real one, in all the time we were together. I doubt that he did himself, any more. He's gone now. Don't ask me to remember."

She's trying to protect him, he thought. "You must have called him something."

She gave a smile of sour reminiscence. " 'Brother dear.' So that others could hear me. That was part of my rôle. We traveled as brother and sister. I insisted on that. We each had our own cabin."

"And he agreed." It wasn't a question, it was a statement of disbelief.

"At first he objected. His former partner, it seems—well, that's neither here nor there. I pointed out to him that it was better even for his own purposes that way, and when I had made him see that, he agreed readily enough. Business came first with him, always. He had a sweetheart in every river town, he could forego one more. You see, I acted as the—attraction, the magnet, for him. My part was to drop my handkerchief on the deck, or collide with someone in a narrow passageway, or even lose my bearings and have to seek directions of someone. There is no harm in gentlemen striking up a respectful acquaintance with a man's unmarried sister. Whereas had I been thought his wife—or something else—they would have been deterred. Then, as propriety dictated, I would introduce my brother to them at the earliest opportunity. And the game would take place soon afterward."

"You played?"

"Never. Only a shameless hussy would play cards with men."

"You were present, though."

"I replenished their drinks. Flirted a little, to keep them in good humor. I sided with them against my own brother when there was a dispute."

"You signalled."

Her shoulders tipped slightly, in philosophic resignation. "That's what I was there for."

His arms were folded, in the attitude of one passing grim judgment—or rather having already irrevocably passed it—whom none of the pleas, the importunities, of the suppliant could any longer sway. He tapped his fingers restlessly against the sides of his own arms.

"And what of Julia? The other Julia, the actual one?"

"I've come to that now," she murmured acquiescently. She drew deep breath to see her through the cumulative part of her recital. "We used to go down about once a month, never more often. It wouldn't have been prudent. Stop a while, and then go up again. We left St. Louis the eighteenth of May the last time, on the *City of New Orleans.*"

"As she did."

She nodded. "The first night out something went wrong. He met his match at last. I don't know how it came about. It could not have been sheer luck on the prospect's part, for he had too many sure ways of curing that. It must have been that he'd finally come across someone who had even better tricks than his own up his sleeve. I couldn't see the man's cards; he seemed to play from memory, keeping them turned inward to one another face to face. And all my messages to show the suits, by fondling necklace, bracelet, earring, finger ring, were worthless, I couldn't send them. The game kept on for half the night, and my partner lost steadily, until at last he had nothing left to play with any longer. And since, in these games, the players were always travelers and strangers to one another, nothing but actual money was ever used, so the loss was real."

"The cheaters cheated," he commented.

"But long before that, hours earlier, the man had already asked me to leave the two of them to themselves. Pointedly, but in such a polite way that there was nothing I could do but obey, or risk bringing to the point of open accusation the certainty that it was obvious he already felt about me. He pretended he was unused to playing in the presence of ladies, and wished to remove his coat and waistcoat, and the instant permission I gave him to do so, he rejected, so I had to go. My partner tried to forbid it by every urgent signal at his command, but there was no further use in my remaining there, so I went. We'd fallen into our own trap, I'm afraid.

"Loitering on deck, beside the rail, a woman, unaccompanied like myself, presently stopped beside me and struck up a conversation. I was not used to chatting with other women, there was no meat in it for my purpose, so at first I gave her only half an ear.

"She was a fool. Within the space of minutes she was telling me all her business, unsolicited. Who she was, where she was bound, what her purpose in going there was. She was too trustful, she had no experience of the outside world. Especially the world of the river boats, and the people you meet on them.

"I tried to shake her off at first, but without succeeding. She attached herself to me, followed me around. It was as though she were starving for a confidante, had to have someone to pour out her heart to, she was brimming so full of romantic anticipations. She gave me your name, and, stopping by a lighted doorway, insisted on taking out and showing me the picture you had sent her, and even reading passages from the last letter or two you had sent her, as though they were Holy Gospel.

"At last, just when I was beginning to feel I could bear no more of it without revealing my true feelings by a burst of temper that would have startled her into silence once and for all, she discovered the—for her—lateness of the hour and fled in the direction of her own cabin like a tardy child, turning all the way to wave back at me, she was so taken by me.

"We had a bitter quarrel later that night, he and I. He accused me of neglecting our 'business.' Unwisely, in self-defense, I told him about her. That she was on her way, sight unseen, to marry a man worth one hundred thousand dollars, who—"

He straightened alertly. "How could she know that?" he said sharply. "I only told the 'you' that was supposed to be she after you'd once arrived and were standing on the dock beside me."

She laughed humorlessly. "She'd investigated, long before she'd ever left St. Louis. I may have fooled you in the greater way, but she fooled you just as surely in the lesser."

He held silent for a long moment, almost as if finding in this new revelation of feminine guile some amelioration of her own.

Presently, unurged, as if gauging to a nicety the length of time he should be allowed for contemplation, of what she knew him to be contemplating, she proceeded.

"I saw him look at me when I told him that. He broke off our quarrel then and there, and left me, and paced the deck for a while. I can only tell you what happened as it happened. I did not know then its meaning as it was happening. Looking back, I can give it meaning now. I couldn't have then. You must believe me. You must, Lou."

She clasped her hands, and brought them close before his face, and wrung them supplicatingly.

"I must? By what compulsion?"

"This is the truth I'm telling tonight. Every word the truth, if never before, if never again."

If never before, if never again, he caught himself gullibly repeating after her, unheard in his own mind.

"I went out again to find him, to ask him if he intended to recoup his losses any more that night; if he'd have any further need of me, or if I could shut my door and go to sleep. I found him motionless, in deep thought, against the rail. The moon was down and the river was getting dark. We were still coasting the lower Missouri shore, I think we were to clear it before dawn. I scarcely knew him for sure until I was at his elbow, he was so indistinct in the gloom.

"He said to me in a whisper, 'Knock on her door and invite her out for a walk on deck with you.'

"I said, 'But it's late, she may have already retired. She's unused to hours such as we keep.'

"'Do as I tell you!' he ordered me fiercely. 'Or I'll put some compliance into you with my fists. Find some way of bringing her out here, you'll know how. Tell her you are lonely and want company. Or tell her there are some lights coming presently on the shore that are not to be missed, that she must see. If she is as innocent as you say, any excuse should do.'

"And he gave me a push that nearly sent me face down to the deck boards."

"You went?"

"I went. What could I do? Why should I suffer for a stranger? What stranger had ever suffered for me?"

He didn't answer that.

"I went to her door and I knocked, and when she called out, startled, to ask who it was, I remember answering in honeyed tones to reassure her, 'It's your new little friend, Miss Charlotte.'"

"You had that name upon the boat?"

"For that voyage. She opened at once, so great was her trust in me. She had not yet removed her clothes, but told me she had been about to do so. If only she already had!"

"You're merciful now in retrospect," he let her know. "You weren't at the time."

She didn't flinch. "I delivered my invitation. I complained of a headache, and refusing all the remedies she instantly put herself out to offer me, said I preferred to let the fresh air cure it, and would she walk with me a while, because of the lateness of the hour.

"I remember I was strangely uneasy, as to what his intentions might be—oh, I knew he boded her no good, but I didn't dare allow myself to believe he meant her any actual bodily harm; some intricate blackmailing scheme, at most, I thought, to be brought to bear on her later, once she was married to you—and even as I spoke, I kept hoping she would refuse me, and I could give him that for an excuse. But she seemed to have become inordinately fond of me. Before I could ask her twice she had already accepted, her face all alight with pleasure at my seeking her out. She hurriedly put a shawl about her for warmth, and closed the door after her, and came away with me."

His interest had been trapped in spite of himself. "You are telling the truth, Julia? You are telling the truth?" he said with bated breath.

"Bonny," she murmured deprecatingly.

"You are telling the truth? You did not know, actually, what the intent was?"

"Why do I kneel here at your feet like this? Why are there tears of regret in my eyes? Look at them well. What shall I say to you, what shall I do? Shall I take an oath on it? Fetch a Bible. Open it before me. Hold its pages to my heart as I speak."

He had never seen her cry before. He wondered if she ever had. She cried as one unused to crying, who leashes it, stifles it, not knowing what it is, rather than one who has many times before made use of it for her own ends, and hence knows it is an advantage and lets it flow untrammelled, even abets it.

He waved aside the suggestion that his own skepticism had produced. "And then? And then?" he pressed her.

"We walked the full length of the deck three times, in harmonious intimacy, as women will together." She stopped for a moment.

"What is it?"

"Something I just remembered. And wish I had not. *Her arm was about my waist* as we walked. Mine was not about hers, at least, but hers was about me. She chattered again about you, endlessly about you. It was always you, only you."

She drew a breath, as if again feeling the tension of that night, that promenade upon the lonely, darkened deck.

"Nothing happened. He did not accost us. At every shadow I had been ready to stifle a scream, but none of them was he. At last I had no further excuse to keep her out there with me. She asked me how my headache was, and I said it was gone. And she couldn't have dreamed the relief with which I told her so.

"I took her back to her door. She turned to me a moment, I remember, and even kissed my hand in fond good night, she was so taken with me. She said 'I'm so glad we've met, Charlotte. I've never really had a woman friend of my very own. You must come and see me and my—' and then she faltered prettily—'my new husband, visit with us, as soon as we're settled. I shall want new friends badly in my new life.' And then she opened her door and went in. Unharmed, untouched. I even heard her bolt it fast after her on the inside.

"And that was the last I ever saw of her."

She came to a full halt, as if knowing this was the time for it, to gain fullest the effect she wished to achieve.

"No more than that you participated?" he said slowly.

"No more than that I participated. No more than that I took part in it, whatever it was.

"I have thought of it since then," she resumed presently. "I see now what it was, what it must have been. I didn't at the time, or I would never have left her. I had thought he meant to accost her on the deck in some way; brutalize her into some predicament from which she could only extricate herself later by payment of money, or even steal some memento from her to be redeemed later in the same way, to preserve your trust in her and her own good name. It even occurred to me, as I made my way back to my own cabin alone, he might have changed his mind entirely, discarded the whole intention, whatever it had been. I'd known him to do that before, after a scheme was already under way, and without notifying me until afterward."

She shook her head sombrely. "No, he hadn't.

"He must have inserted himself in the cabin while she was gone from it with me, and lain in wait there on the inside. He wanted the opportunity, that was why he had me stroll the deck with her."

"But later—he never told you in so many words what happened in there, inside that cabin of hers?"

She shook her head firmly. "He never told me in so many words. Nor could I draw it out of him. He had no moments of confidence, no moments of weakness, especially not with women. The way in which he told me of it was not meant to be believed; I knew that, and he knew that as well. It was just a catch phrase, to gloss over a thing, to have done with it as quickly as possible. And yet that is the only way in which he would tell me of it, from first to last. And I must be content with that, that was all I got."

"And what was that?"

"This is the way in which he told me of it, word for word. He came and knocked surreptitiously upon my door, and woke me, about an hour before daylight, when the whole boat was still asleep. He was fully dressed, but whether newly so or still from the night before, I don't know. He had a single scratch on his forehead, over the eyebrow. A very small one, not more than a half-inch mark. And that was all.

"He came in, closed the door carefully, and said to me very business-like and terse in manner, 'Get dressed, I want you for something. Your lady friend of last night had an accident awhile ago and fell from the boat in the dark. She never came up again.' And then he flung my various things at me, stockings and such, one by one, to hurry me along. That was all he told me, then or ever again, that she'd had an accident and fallen from the boat in the dark."

"But you knew?"

"How could I help but know? I told him I knew. He even so much as agreed I might know, admitted I might know. But his answer for that was 'What are you going to do about it?'

"I told him that wasn't in our bargain. 'Card-games are one thing, this another.'

"He carefully took off his ring first, so it wouldn't mar my skin, and he gave me the back of his hand several times, until my head swam, and, as he put it, 'it had taken a little of the religion out of me.' He threatened me. He said if I accused him, he would accuse me in turn. That we would both be jailed for it alike. And I had been seen with her, and he hadn't. That it would serve neither one of us any good, and undo the two of us alike. He also threatened, finally, that he would kill me himself if necessary, as the quickest way of stopping my mouth, if I tried to get anyone's ear.

"Then when he saw he had me sufficiently cowed and intimidated to listen, he reasoned with me. 'She's gone now beyond recall,' he pointed out, 'nothing you can do will bring her back up over the side, and there's a hundred thousand dollars waiting for you when you step off this boat in New Orleans tomorrow.'

"He swung back the door for me, and I adjusted my clothing, and followed him out.

"He took my baggage, the little I had, into his cabin and blended it with his. And hers we removed, between us, from her cabin to mine, to take the place of my own. Not forgetting that caged bird of hers. He took from his pocket her letters from you, and the photograph you had sent her, and I put them in my own pocketbook. And then we bided our time and waited.

"In the confusion of docking and disembarking she was not missed. No passenger remembered her, they were all busy with their own concerns. And each baggage-handler, if he noted her empty cabin at all, must have thought some other baggage-handler had taken charge of her and her belongings. We left the boat separately, he at the very beginning, I almost at the last. And that was not noticed either.

"I saw you standing there, and knew you from your photograph, and when at last the dock had cleared, I approached and stopped there by you. And there's the story, Lou."

She stopped, and settled back upon her own upturned heels, and her hands fell lifeless to her lap, as if incapable of further gesture. She seemed to wait thus, inert, deflated, for the verdict, for his judgment to be passed upon her. Everything about her sloped downward, shoulders, head, and even the curve of her back; only one thing turned upward: her eyes, fixed beseechingly upon his graven face.

"Not quite," he said. "Not quite. And what of What's-his-name? What was the further plan?"

"He said he would send word to me when enough time had passed. And when I heard from him, I was to—"

"Do as you did."

She shook her head determinedly. "Not as I did. As it seemed to you I did, maybe. I met him once for a few moments, in secret, when I was out on one of my shopping tours without you—that part was by prearrangement—and I told him there was no need for him to count on me any longer, he must abandon the scheme, I could no longer prevail on myself to carry it out."

"Why did you have a change of heart?"

"Why must you be told that now?"

"Why shouldn't I be?"

"It would be breath wasted. It wouldn't be believed."

"Let me be the judge."

"Very well then, if you must be told," she said almost defiantly. "I told him I could no longer contemplate doing what it had been intended for me to do. I told him I'd fallen in love with my own husband."

It was like a rainbow suddenly glistening in all its striped glory across dismal gray skies. He told himself it was an illusion, just as surely as its counterpart, the actual rainbow, is an illusion in Nature. But it wouldn't dim, it wouldn't waver; there it beamed, the sign of hope, the sign heralding sunshine to come.

She had gone on without interruption, but the grateful shock of that previous remark, still flooding over him in benign warmth, had caused him to lose the sense of a part of her words.

"—laughed and said I no more knew what love was than the man in the moon. Then he turned vengeful and told me I was lying and simply trying to keep the whole of the stake for myself alone."

I'd fallen in love, kept going through his head, dimming the sound of her voice. It was like a counterpoint that intrudes upon the basic melody and all but effaces it.

"I tried to buy him off. I said he could have the money, all I could lay my hands on, almost as much as he might have expected in the first place, if he would only quit New Orleans, let me be. Yes, I offered to *rob* my own husband, endanger the very thing I was trying to hold onto, if he would only let me be, let me stay as I was, happy for the first time in my life."

Happy for the first time in her life, the paean swelled through his mind. She was really happy with me.

"If he would only have accepted the bribe, I had in mind some

desperate excuse to you—that my purse had been snatched in a
crowd, that I'd dropped the money in the street, after drawing it
from the bank; that my 'sister' had suddenly fallen ill and was
without means, and I'd sent it to her in St. Louis—oh, anything,
anything at all, no matter how thin, how paltry, so long as it was
less discreditable than the reality. Yes, I would have risked your
displeasure, your disapproval, even worse than that, your very real
suspicion, if only I was allowed to keep you for myself as I wanted
to, to go on with you."

To go on with you. He could remember the warmth of her kisses
now, the unbridled gaiety of her smiles. What actress could have
played such a part, morning, noon, and night? Even actresses play
but an hour or two of an evening, have a respite the rest of the
time. It must have been sincere reality. He could remember the
look in her eyes when he took leave of her that last day; a sort of
lingering, reluctant melancholy. (But had it been there then, or was
he putting it in now?)

"That wouldn't satisfy him, wouldn't do. He wanted *all* of it, not
part. And, I suppose, there was truly no solution. No matter how
large a sum I would have given him, he would still have thought I
was keeping far more than that myself. He trusted no one—I heard
it said of him, in a quarrel once—not even himself.

"Taking me at my word, that I loved you, he discovered he had
a more powerful threat to hold over me now. And no sooner had
he discovered it, than he brought it into play. That he would reveal
my imposture to you himself, anonymously, in a letter, if I refused
to carry out our deal. He wouldn't have his money, maybe, but
neither should I have what I wanted. We'd both be fugitives alike,
and back where we started from. 'And if you intercept my letter,'
he warned, 'that won't help you any. I'll go to him myself and make
the accusation to his face. Let him know you're not only not who you
claimed, but were my sweetheart all those years to boot.' Which
wasn't true," she added rather rapidly in an aside. " 'We'll see how
long he'll keep you with him then.'

"And as I left him that day," she went on. "I knew it was no
use, no matter what I did. I knew I was surely going to lose you, one
way or another.

"I passed a sleepless night. The letter came, all right. I'd known it would. He was as good as his word, in all things like that; and only in things like that. I seized it. I was waiting there by the door when the post came. I tore it open and read it. I can still remember how it went. 'The woman you have there in your house with you is not the woman you take her to be, but someone of another name, and another man's sweetheart as well. I am that man, and so I know what I am saying Keep a close watch upon your money, Mr. Durand. If you disbelieve me, watch her face closely when you say to her without warning, "Bonny, come here to me," and see how it pales.' And it was signed, 'A friend.'

"I destroyed it, but I knew the postponement I'd gained was only for a day or two. He'd send another. Or he'd come himself. Or he'd take me unaware sometime when I was out alone, and I'd be found lying there with a knife-hilt in my side. I knew him well; he never forgave anyone who crossed him." She tried to smile, and failed in the attempt. "My doll house had come tumbling down all about my ears.

"So I made my decision, and I fled."

"To him."

"No," she said dully, almost as if this detail were a matter of indifference, now, this long after. "I took the money, yes. But I fled from him just as surely as I deserted you. That small satisfaction was all I had out of it: he hadn't gained his way. The rest was ashes. All my happiness lay behind me. I remember thinking at the time, we formed a triangle, we three, a strange one. You were love, and he was death—and I was the mid-point between the two.

"I fled as far away as I could. I took the northbound boat and kept from sight until it had left New Orleans an hour behind. I went to Memphis first, and then to Louisville, and at last to Cincinnati, and stayed there hidden for some time. I was in fear for my life for a while. I knew he would have surely killed me had he found me. And then one day, in Cincy, I heard a report from someone who had once known us both slightly when we were together, that he had lost his life in a shooting affray in a gaming house in Cairo. So the danger was past. But it was too late by that time to undo what had been done. I couldn't return to you any more."

And the look she gave him was of a poignancy that would have melted stone.

"I made my way back South again, now that it was safe to do so, and only a few weeks ago met this Colonel Worth, and now I'm as you find me. And that's my story, Lou."

She waited, and the silence, now that she was through speaking, seemed to prolong itself into eternity.

He was looking at her steadfastly, but uttered not a word. But behind that calm, reflective, judicious front he maintained so stoically, there was an unguessed turmoil, raging, a chaos, of credulity and disbelief, accusation and refutation, pro and con, to and fro, and around and around and around like a whirlpool.

She took your money, none the less; why, if she "loved" you so? She was about to face the world alone for years to come, she knew only too well how hard it is for a woman alone to get along in the world, she'd had that lesson from before. Can you blame her?

How do you know she didn't cheat the two of you alike; that what it was, was nothing more than what he accused her of, of running off and keeping the entire booty for herself, without dividing it with him? A double betrayal, instead of a single.

At least she is innocent of Julia's death, you heard that. How do you know even that? The living, the survivor, is here to tell *her* side of the tale to you, but the dead, the victim, is not here to tell you hers. It might be a different story.

You loved her then, you do not question yourself on that. Why then do you doubt her when she says she loved you then? Is she not as capable of love as you? And who are you to say who is to feel love, and who is not? Love is like a magnet, that attracts its like. She must have loved you, for your love to be drawn to her. Just as you must have loved her—and you know you did—for her love to be drawn to you. Without one love, there cannot be another. There must be love on both sides, for the current to complete itself.

"Aren't you going to say something to me, Lou?"

"What is there to say?"

"I can't tell you that. It must come from you."

"Must it?" he said drily. "And if there is nothing there to give you, no answer?"

"Nothing, Lou?" Her voice took on a singsong timbre. "Nothing?" It became a lulling incantation. "Not even a word?" Her face rose subtly nearer to his. "Not even—this much?" He had seen pictures, once, somewhere, of India, of cobras rising from their huddles to the charmer's tune. And like one of those, so sleekly, so unguessably, she had crept upward upon him before he knew it; but this was the serpent charming the master, not the master the serpent. "Not even—this?"

Suddenly he was caught fast, entwined with her as with some treacherous tropic plant. Lips of fire were fused with his. He seemed to breathe flame, draw it down his windpipe into his breast, where the dry tinder of his loneliness, of his long lack of her, was kindled by it into raging flame, that pyred upward, sending back her kiss with insane fury.

He struggled to his feet, and she rose with him, they were so interlocked. He flung her off with all the violence he would have used against another man in full-bodied combat; it was needed, nothing less would have torn her off.

She staggered, toppled, fell down prone, one arm alone, thrust out behind her, keeping one shoulder and her head upward a little from the floor.

And lying there, all rumpled and abased, yet somehow she had on her face the glint of victory, on her lips a secretive smile of triumph. As though she knew who had won the contest, who had lost. She lolled there at her ease, too sure of herself even to take the trouble to rise. It was he who wallowed, from chair back to chair back, stifling, blinded, like something maimed; his ears pounding to his own blood, clawing at his collar, as if the ghosts of her arms were still there, strangling him.

He stood over her at last, clenched hand upraised above his head, as if in threat to strike her down a second time should she try to rise. "Get yourself ready!" he roared at her. "Get your things! Not that nor anything else will change it! I'm taking you back to New Orleans!"

She sidled away from him a little along the floor, as if to put herself beyond his reach, though her smirk denied her fear; then gathered herself together, rose with an innate grace that nothing could take from her, not even such violent downfall.

She seemed humbled, docile to his bidding, seemed resigned; all but that knowing smile, that gave it the lie. She made no further importunity. She swept back her hair, a lock of which had tumbled forward with her fall. Her shoulders hinted at a shrug. Her hands gave an empty slap at her sides, recoiled again, as if in fatalistic acceptance.

He turned his back on her abruptly, as he saw her hands go to the fastenings at the side of her waist, already partly sundered.

"I'll wait out here in this little entryway," he said tautly, and strode for it.

"Do so," she agreed ironically. "It *is* some time now that we have been apart."

He sat down on a little backless wall-bench that lined the place, just within the outer apartment door.

She came slowly over after him and slowly swung the second door around, the one between them, leaving it just short of closure.

"My windows are on the second floor," she reassured him, still with that overtone of irony. "And there is no ladder outside them. I am not likely to try to escape."

He bowed his head suddenly, as sharply as if his neck had fractured, and pressed his two clenched hands tight against his forehead, through the center of which a vein stood out like whipcord, pulsing and throbbing with a congestion of love battling hate and hate battling love, that he alone could have told was going on, so still he crouched.

So they remained, on opposite sides of a door that was not closed. The victor and the vanquished. But on which side was which?

A drawer ticked open, scraped closed again, behind the door. A whiff of fresh essence drifted out and found him, as if skimmed off the top of a field of the first flowers of spring. The light peering through from the other side dimmed somewhat, as if one or more of its contributing agents had been eliminated.

Suddenly he turned his head, finding the door had already been standing open a second or two before his discovery of it. She was standing there in the inviting new breadth of its opening, one arm to door, one arm to frame. The foaming laces that cascaded down her were transparent as haze against the light bearing directly on her from the room at her back. Her silhouette was that of a biped.

Her eyes were dreamy-lidded, her half-smile a recaptured memory of forgotten things.

"Come in, Lou," she murmured indulgently, as if to a stubborn little boy who has put himself beyond the pale. "Put out the light there by you and come into your wife's room."

39

A sound at the door awoke Durand. It was a delicate sort of tapping, a coaxing pit-pat, as if with one fingernail.

As his eyes opened he found himself in a room he had difficulty recalling from the night before. The cooling silvery-green of low-burning night lights was no longer there. Ladders of fuming Gulf Coast sunlight came slanting through the slits of the blinds, and formed a pattern of stripes across the bed and across the floor. And above this, there was a reflected brightness, as if everything had been newly whitewashed; a gleaming transparency.

It was simply that it was day in a place that he had last seen when it was night.

He thought he was alone at first. He backed a hand to his drugged eyes, to keep out some of the overacute brilliancy. "Where am I?"

Then he saw her. Her cloverleaf mouth smiled back at him, indirectly, via the surface of the mirror she sat before. Her hand sought her bosom, and she let it linger there a moment, one finger pointing upward, one inward as if toward her heart. "With me," she answered. "Where you belong."

There was something fragilely charming, he thought, in the evanescent little gesture while it lasted. And he watched it wistfully and hated to see it end, the hand drop back as it had been. It had been so unstudied. With me; finger unconsciously to her heart.

The stuttering little tap came again. There was something coy about it that irritated him. He turned his head and frowned over that way. "Who's that?" he asked sternly, but of her, not the door.

She shaped her mouth to a soundless symbol of laughter; then she stilled it further, though it hadn't come at all, by spoking her fingers over it, fanwise. "A suitor, I'm afraid. The colonel. I know him by his tap."

Durand, his face growing blacker by the minute, was at the bedside now, struggling into trousers with a sort of cavorting hop, to and fro.

The tapping had accosted them a third time.

He cut his thumb slashingly backhand toward the door, in pantomime to have her answer it temporizingly while he got ready.

"Yes?" she said sweetly.

"It's Harry, my dear," came through the door. "Good morning. Am I too early."

"No, too late," growled Durand surlily. "I'll attend to 'Harry, my dear' in a moment!" he vowed to her in an undertone.

She was in stitches by now, head prone on the dressing table, hands clasped across the back of her neck, palpitating with smothered laughter.

"In a minute," she said half-strangled.

"Don't hurry yourself, my dear," the cooing answer came back. "You know I'll wait all morning for you, if necessary. To wait outside your door for you to come out is the pleasantest thing I know of. There is only one thing pleasanter, and that would be—"

The door sliced back and he found himself confronted by Durand, feet unshod, hair awry, and in nothing but trousers and undershirt.

To make it worse, his face had been bearing down close against the door, to make himself the better heard. He found his nose almost pressed into Durand's coarse-spun barley-colored underwear, at about the height of Durand's chest.

His head went up a notch at a time, like something worked on a pulley, until it was level with Durand's own. And for each notch he had a strangulated exclamation, like a winded grunt. Followed by a convulsive swallowing. "Unh—? Anh—? Unh—?"

"Well, sir?" Durand rapped out.

Worth's hand executed helpless curlycues, little corkscrew waves, trying to point behind Durand but unable to do so.

"You're—in *there?* You're—not *dressed?*"

"Will you kindly mind your business, sir?" Durand said sternly.

The colonel raised both arms now overhead, fists clenched, in some sort of approaching denunciation. Then they faltered, froze that way, finally crumbled. His eyes were suddenly fixed on Durand's right shoulder. They dilated until they threatened to pop from his head.

Durand could feel her arm glide caressingly downward over his shoulder, and then her hand tipped up to fondle his chin, while she herself remained out of sight behind him. He looked down to where Worth was staring at it, and it was the one with the wedding band, their old wedding band, on it.

It rose, was stroking and petting Durand's cheek now, letting the puffy gold circlet flash and wink conspicuously. It gave the slack of his cheek a fond little pinch, then spread the two fingers that had just executed it wide apart, in what might have been construed as a jaunty salute.

"I—I—I didn't know!" Worth managed to gasp out asthmatically, as if with his last breath.

"You do now, sir!" Durand said severely. "And what brings you to my wife's door, may I ask?"

The colonel was backing away along the passage now, brushing the wall now at this side, now at that, but incapable apparently of turning around once and for all and tearing his eyes off the hypnotic spectacle of Durand and the affectionate straying hand.

"I—I beg your pardon!" he succeeded in panting at last, from a safe distance.

"I beg yours!" Durand rejoined with grim inflexibility.

The colonel turned at last and fled, or rather wallowed drunkenly, away.

The detached hand suddenly went up in air, bent its fingers inward, and flipped them once or twice.

"Ta ta," her voice called out gaily, "lovey mine!"

40

ARMS CLOSE-KNIT about one another's waists, leaning almost avidly from the open window of her room, shimmering in unison with laughter, they watched the streaming debacle of the colonel's luggage, poured forth from under the veranda shed, followed by its owner's hurried, trotting departure. The colonel could not seem to climb into his waiting coach quickly enough and be gone from this scene of ego-shrivelling discomfiture with enough haste; he all but hopped in on one leg, like an ungainly crane in waddling earthbound flight, and the whole buggy rocked with his plunge.

It was not his own private conscience that spurred him on, conjecturably, it was public ridicule. The story had obviously spread like wildfire about the establishment, in the inexplicable way of such things at seashore resorts, though neither Durand nor she had breathed a word to living soul. It was as though the tale were water and the hotel a sponge; it was as though the keyholes themselves had found tongues for their perpendicular slitted mouths and whispered it. Strollers entering or leaving, at this moment, as he was going, stopped and turned to stare at the spectacle he made in flight, with either outright smiles visible upon their faces, or tactfully sheltering hands to mouths, which betrayed the fact that there were smiles beneath them to conceal.

The colonel fled, within a sheltering turret of his own massed luggage piled high on the seat, the plumage of his male pride as badly frizzled as feathers in a flame. The yellow wheel spokes sluiced into solidified disks, a spurt of dust haze arose, the roadway was empty, the colonel was gone.

She had even wanted to wave, this time with her handkerchief, as she had waved at the door an hour or so before, but Durand, some remnants of masculine fellow-feeling stirring in him, held her hand back, quenched the gesture, though laughing all the same. They turned from the window, still chuckling, arms still tight about one another in new-found possession. They had been cruel just now, though they hadn't intended it, their only thought had been their own amusement. Yet what is cruelty but the giving of pain in the taking of pleasure?

"Oh, dear!" she exhaled, breathless. She parted from him, drooped exhausted over the back of a chair. "That man. He wasn't cut out to be a romantic lover. Yet always that is the type that tries hardest to play the rôle. I wonder why?"

"Am I?" he asked her, curious to hear what she would say.

She turned her eyes toward him, lidded them inexpressibly. "Oh, Louis," she said in bated whisper. "Can you ask *me* that? You're the perfect example. With the blushes of a boy—look at you now. The arms of a tiger. And a heart as easily broken as a woman's."

The tiger part was the only one that appealed to him; he decided the other two were wholly her own imaginings.

He exercised them once again, briefly but heartily, as any man would after such prompting.

"We'll have to go soon ourselves," he reminded her presently.

"Why?" she asked, as if willing enough but failing quite to understand the need to do so.

Then thinking she had found the answer for herself, gave it to him without waiting. "Oh, because of what's happened. Yes, it's true; I was seen with him constantly all these past—"

"No," he said, "that isn't what I meant. It's that—business on the boat. I told you last night, I went to a private investigator in St. Louis, and so far as I know he's still engaged upon it."

"There's no warrant out, is there?"

"No, but I think it's better for us to stay out of his way. I'd rather not have him accost us, or even learn where we are to be found."

"He has no police power, has he?" she asked with quick, brittle interest.

"Not so far as I know. I don't know what he can do or can't do, and I've no wish to find out. The police in New Orleans told me you were immune, but that was at that time, before he took hand in it. Your immunity may expire from one minute to the next, when least we expect it, while he's still around and about. It's safer for us not to place ourselves too close at hand, under their thumbs. Don't you see, we can't go back to New Orleans now."

"No," she agreed without emotion, "we can't."

"And it's better for us not to linger here too long either. Word travels quickly. You cannot help drawing the admiration of all eyes wherever you appear. You're no drab wallflower. Besides, my own presence here is well known; I made no secret I was coming here, and they'd know where to reach me—"

"Will you—be able to?"

He knew what she meant.

"I have enough for now. And I can get in touch with Jardine, if need should arise."

She raised her hand and snapped her fingers close before her face. "Very well, we'll go," she said gaily. "We'll be on our way before the sun goes down. Where shall it be? You name it."

He pocketed one hand, spread the other palm up. "How about one of the northern cities? They're large, they can swallow us whole, we'll never be noticed. Baltimore, Philadelphia, even New York—"

He saw her chew the corner of her underlip in sudden distaste.

"Not the North," she said, with a distant look in her eyes. "It's
cold and gray and ugly, and it snows—"

He wondered what Damoclean sword of retribution, from out of
the past, hung over her suspended there.

"We'll stay down here, then," he said, without hesitation. "It's
closer to them, and we'll have to keep moving about more often.
But I want to please you. What about Mobile or Birmingham, then;
those are large enough towns to lose ourselves in."

She made her choice with a pert little nod. "Mobile for now.
I'll begin to pack at once."

She stopped again in a moment, holding some article in her hands,
and drew close to him once more. "How different this is from last
night. Do you remember? Then it was an arrest. Now it is a honeymoon."

"The beginning of a new life. Everything new. New plans, new
hopes, new dreams. A new destination. A new you. A new I."

She crept into his arms, looked up at him, her very soul in her
eyes. "Do you forgive? Do you take me back?"

"I never met you before last night. There *is* no past. This is our
real wedding day."

The "tiger-arms" showed their stripes, went around her once more.

"My Lou," she sobbed ecstatically.

"My Jul—"

"Careful, there," she warned, with finger upright to his lips.

"My Bonny."

41

MOBILE, THEN.

They went to the finest hotel there, and like the bride and groom
they were in everything but count of time, they took its finest suite,
its bridal suite. Chamber and sitting room, height of luxury, lace
curtains over the windows, maroon drapes, Turkish carpeting thick

on the floors, and even that seldom-met-with innovation, a private bath of their own that no one else had access to, complete with claw-legged tub enamelled in light green.

Bellhops danced attendance on them from morning to night, and all eyes were on them every time they came and went through the public rooms below. The petite blonde, always so dainty, so exquisitely dressed, with the tall dark man beside her, eyes for no one else. "That romantic pair from—" Nobody knew just where, but everybody knew who was meant.

More than one sigh of benevolent regret swept after them.

"I declare, it makes me feel a little younger just to look at them."

"It makes *me* feel a little sad. Because we all know that it cain't last. They're bound to lose it 'fore long."

"But they've had it."

"Yes, they've had it."

Every sprightly supper resort in town knew them, every gay and brightly lighted gathering place, every theatre, public ball, entertainment, minstrelsy. Every time the violins played, somewhere, anywhere, she was in his arms there, turning in the endless, fevered spirals of the waltz. Every time the moon was full, she was in his arms there, somewhere, in a halted carriage, heads close together, sweetness of magnolia all around, gazing up at it with dreamy, wondering eyes.

But they were right, the musers and the sighers and the cast-asides in the hotel lobby. It lasts such a short time. It comes but once, and goes, and then it never comes again. Even to the upright, to the blessed, it never comes again. And how much less likely, to the hunted and the doomed.

But this was their moment of it now, this was their time for it, their share: Durand and his Julia. (Julia, for love's first thought is its lasting one, love's first name for itself, is its true one.) The sunburst of their happiness. The brief blaze of their noon.

Mobile, then, in the flood tide of their romance; and all was rapture, all was love.

42

WITHOUT RAISING her eyes, she smiled covertly, showing she was well aware that his gaze was lingering on her, there in the little sitting room outside their bedroom. Studying her like an elusive lesson; a lesson that seems simple enough at first glance, but is never to be fully learned, though the student goes back to it again and again.

"What are you thinking?" she teased, keeping her eyes still downcast.

"Of you."

She took that for granted. "I know. But what, of me?"

He sat down beside her, at the foot of the chaise longue, tilted his knee, hugged it, and cast his eyes upon her more speculatively than ever. Shaking his head a little, as if in wonderment himself, that this should be so.

"I used to want what they call a good wife. That was the only kind I ever thought I'd have. A proper little thing who'd sit demurely, working a needle through a hoop, both feet planted on the floor. Head submissively lowered to her task, who'd look up when I spoke and 'Aye' and 'Nay' me. But now I don't. Now I only want a wife like you. With yesterday's leftover dye still on her cheeks. With the tip of her bent knee poked brazenly through her dressing gown. With cigar ashes on the floor about her. Jeering at a man in their most private moments, egging him on, then ridiculing him, rather than swooning limp into his arms." He shook his head, more helplessly than ever. "Bonny, Bonny, what have you done to me? Though I still know you should be like that, like those others are, I don't want anyone like that any more. I've forgotten there are any. I only want you; bad as you are, heartless as you are, exactly as you are, I only want you."

Her tarnished golden laughter welled up, showered down upon the two of them like counterfeit coins.

"Lou, you're so gullible. There aren't two kinds of women; there never were, there never will be. Only one kind of woman, one kind of man— And both of them, alike, not much good." Her laughter had stopped; her face was tired and wise, and there was a little flicker of bitterness, as she said the last.

"Lou," she repeated, "you're so—unaware."

"Are you sure that's the word you had in mind?"

"Innocent," she agreed.

"Innocent?" he parried wryly.

"A woman's innocence is like snow on a hot stove; it's gone at the first touch. But when a man is innocent, he can have had ten wives, and he's as innocent at the end of them all as he was at the beginning. He never learns."

He shivered feverishly. "I know you drive me mad. At least I've learned that much."

She threw herself backward on the couch, her head hanging over so that she was looking behind her toward the ceiling, in a sort of floundering luxuriance. She extended her arms widely upward in a greedy, grasping, ecstatic V. Her voice was a dreamy chant of longing.

"Lou, buy me a new dress. All white satin and Chantilly lace. Lou, buy me a great big emerald for my pinkey. Buy me diamond drops for my ears. Take me out in a carriage to twelve o'clock supper at some lobster palace. I want to look at the chandelier lights through the layers of colored liqueurs in a pousse café. I want to feel champagne trickle down my throat while the violins play gypsy music. I want to live, I want to live, I want to live! The time is so short, and I won't get a second turn—"

Then, as her fear of infinity, her mistrust that Providence would look out for her if left to its own blind course—for it was that at bottom, that and nothing else—were caught by him in turn, and he was kindled into a like fear and defiance of their fate, he bent swiftly toward her, his lips found hers, and her litany of despair was stilled.

Until, presently, she sighed: "No, don't take me anywhere— You're here, I'm here— The champagne, the music are right here with us— Everything's here— No need to look elsewhere—"

And her arms dropped, closed over him like the trap they were.

43

Presently they quitted their suite in the hotel and rented a house. An entire house, for their own. A house with an upstairs and down.

It was at her suggestion. And it was she who engaged the agent, accompanied him to view the several prospects he had to offer, and made the final selection. An "elegant" (that was her word for it) though rather gingerbready affair on one of the quieter residential streets, tree flanked. Then all he had to do was sign the necessary papers, and with but a coaxing smile or two from her, he did so, with the air of a man fondly indulging a child in her latest whim. A whim that, he suspects, tomorrow she will have tired of; but that, while it remains valid, today, he has not the heart to refuse her.

It seemed to fill some long-felt, deep-seated, longing on her part: a house of one's own; to be—more than merely an expression of great wealth—an expression of *legitimate* great wealth; to be the ultimate in stability, in *belonging,* in caste. It was as if her catalogue of values ran thus: jewels and fine clothes, any fly-by-night may have them from her sweetheart; even a lawfully wedded husband, any sweetheart may be made into one if you cared to take the pains; but a house of your own, then indeed you had reached the summit, then indeed you were socially impregnable, then indeed you were a great lady. Or (pitiful parenthesis) as you fondly imagined one to be.

"It's so much grander," she said. She sighed wistfully. "It makes me feel like a really married woman."

He laughed indulgently. "What had you felt like until now, madame?"

"Oh, it is useless to tell this to a man!" she said with a little spurt of playful indignation.

And it was, in truth, for each of them had the instincts of their own kind.

Even when he tried, half-teasingly, and only when the arrangement had already been entered into, to warn her and point out the disadvantages, she would have none of it.

"But who'll cook for us? A house takes looking after. You're taking on a great many cares."

She threw up her hands. "Well, then I'll have servants, like the other ladies who have houses of their own. You'll see; leave that to me."

A colored woman appeared, and lasted five days. There was some question of a missing trinket. Then after her stormy discharge and departure, which filled the lower floor with noise for some fifteen minutes, Bonny came to him presently and admitted she had unearthed the valuable in a place she had forgotten having put it.

"Why didn't you search first, and then accuse her afterward?" he pointed out, as gently as he could. "That is what any other lady, mistress of her own house, would have done."

"Oh, would she?" She seemed at a loss. "I did not think of that."

"You must not tyrannize over them," he tried to instruct her. "You must be firm and gentle at the same time. Otherwise you show that you are not used to having servants of your own."

The second one lasted three days. There was less commotion, but there were tears this time. On Bonny's part.

"I tried being gentle," she came to him and reported, "and she paid no heed to any of my orders. I don't seem to know how to handle them. If I am severe, they walk out. If I am kind, they do not do their work."

"There is an art to it," he consoled her. "You will acquire it presently."

"No," she said. "There is something about me. They look at me and sneer. They do not *respect* me. They will take more from another woman, and be docile; they will take nothing from me, and still be impudent. Is this not my own house? Am I not your wife? What is it about me?"

He could not answer that, for he saw her with the eyes of love, and he could not tell what eyes they saw her with, nor see with theirs.

"No," she said in answer to his suggestion, "no more servants. I've had enough of them. Let me do it. I can try, I can manage."

A meal followed that was a complete fiasco. The eggs broke in the water meant to boil them, and a sort of milky stew resulted, neither to be eaten nor to be drunk. The coffee had the pallor of tea without any of its virtues, and on second try became a muddy abomination that filled their mouths with grit. The toast was tinctured with the cologne that she so liberally applied to her hands.

He uttered not a word of reproach. He stood up and discarded his napkin. "Come," he said, "we're going back to the hotel for our meals."

She hastened to get her things, as if overjoyed herself at this solution.

And on their way over he said, "Now aren't you sorry?" with a twinkle in his eye.

But on this point, at least, she was steadfast. "No," she said. "Even if we have to eat elsewhere, at least I still have my own house. I would not change that for anything." And she repeated what she'd said before. "I want to feel like a really married woman. I want to feel like all the rest do. I want to know what it feels like."

She couldn't, it seemed, quite get used to the idea that she was legally married to him, and all this was hers by right and not by conquest.

44

INCREASINGLY UNCOMFORTABLE, and extremely bored in addition, feeling that all eyes were on him, he paced back and forth in the modiste's anteroom, and at every turn seemed to come into collision with some hurrying young girl carrying fresh bolts of goods into a curtained recess behind which Bonny had disappeared an interminable length of time previously. These flying supernumeraries always came out again empty handed; judging by the quantity of material that he had already seen go in the alcove, with none ever taken out again, it should have been filled to ceiling height by this time.

He could hear her voice at intervals, topping the rustles of unwound fabric lengths and carefully chosen phrases of professional inducement.

"I cannot decide! The more you bring in to show me, the harder it becomes to settle on one. No, leave that, I may come back to it."

Suddenly the curtains parted, gripped by restraining hands just below the breach, so that it could not spread downward, and her head, no more, peered through.

"Lou, am I taking dreadfully long? I just remembered you, out there."

"Long, but not dreadfully," he answered gallantly.

"What are you doing with yourself?" she asked, as if he were a small boy left for a risky moment to his own devices.

"Getting in everyone's way, I'm afraid," he admitted.

There was a chorus of polite feminine laughter, both from before and behind the secretive curtain, as though he had said something very funny indeed.

"Poor thing," she said contritely. Her head turned to someone behind her. The grip on the curtain slit slid slightly downward for a moment, and the turn of an unclad shoulder was revealed, a tapelike strip of white ribbon its only covering. "Haven't you any magazines or something for him to look over, pass the time with?"

"Only pattern magazines, I'm afraid, madam."

"No, thank you," he said very definitely.

"It's so hard on *them*," she said patronizingly, still in conversation with someone behind her. Then back to him once more. "Why don't you leave and then call back for me again?" she suggested generously. "That way you needn't suffer so, and I can put my whole mind to this."

"How soon shall I come back?"

"I won't be through for another hour yet at the very least. We haven't even got past the choice of a material yet. Then will come the selection of a pattern, and the cutting, and the taking of the over-all measurements—"

"Unh," he groaned facetiously, and another courtier-like laugh went up.

"You had best give me a full hour and a half, I shall need that much. Or if you tire in the meantime, go straight back to the house, and I'll follow you there."

He took up his hat with alacrity, glad to make his escape.

Her bodyless face, formed its lips into a pout.

"Aren't you going to say goodbye to me?"

She touched her lips to show him what she meant, closed her eyes expectantly.

"In front of all these people?"

"Oh dear, how you talk! One would think you weren't my husband at all. I assure you it's perfectly proper, in such a case."

Again a chorus of flattery-forced laughter went up, almost as if on cue. She seemed to make quite an *opéra bouffe* entertainment of the making of a new dress, taking the part of main luminary surrounded by a doting, submissive chorus. There should have been music, he couldn't help reflecting, and a tiered audience surrounding her on three sides.

He stepped over to the curtains, coloring slightly, pecked at her lips, turned, and got out of the place.

Strangely, in spite of his embarrassment, he had a flattered, self-important feeling at the same time; he wondered how she had been able to give him that, and whether she had known she was doing it when she did. And secretly decided that she had.

She knew every cause, she knew every effect, she knew how to achieve them. Everything she did, she knew she did.

There must have been other times, in other modistes' fitting rooms, when the man waiting was not legally obligated to shoulder the expense she was incurring, that this glow of self-esteem had had an intrinsic value of its—

He put that thought hurriedly from mind, and set out to enjoy the afternoon sunlight, and the blue Gulf reaching to the horizon, and the crowd of strollers drifting along the shoreline promenade. He mingled with them for a while, taking his place in the leisurely moving outermost stream, then turned at the end of the structure and came back with them, but now a part of the inside stream going in the opposite direction.

The slow baking warmth of the sun was pleasant on his shoulders and his back, and occasionally a little salty breeze would come, just enough to temper it. Clouds that were thick and unshadowed as egg white broke the monotony of the sky, and on everyone's face there was a smile—as there must have been on his, he at last realized, for what he was seeing was the unthinking answer to his own smile, offered by face after face in passing; without purpose or premeditation, without knowing they were doing it, simply in shared contentment.

He had money enough now for a long while to come, and she loved him—she had shown it by inducing him to kiss her in front of a shopful of girls. What more was there to wish for?

The world was a good world.

A little boy's harlequin-sectioned ball glanced against his leg in rolling, and the child himself clung to it for a moment in the act of unsteady retrieval. Durand stopped where he was and reached down and tousled still further the already tousled cornsilk thatch.

"Does your mother let you take a penny from a strange man?"

The youngster looked up, open-mouthed with that infantile stupefaction that greets every act of the grown world. "I 'on't know."

"Well, take this to show her then and find out."

He went on again without waiting.

The world was a good world indeed.

After two complete circuits of the walking space provided, he stopped at last by the wooden rail flanking it, and rested his elbows on it, and stood in contemplation with his back to the slow-moving ambulators he had just been a member of.

He had been at rest that way for perhaps two or three minutes, no more, when he became conscious of that rather curiously compelling sensation that is received when someone's eyes are fixed on one steadfastly, from behind.

There was no time to be warned. The impulse was to turn and seek out the cause, and before he could check it he had done so.

He found himself staring full into the face of Downs, the St. Louis investigator, just as Downs was now staring full into his.

He was within two or three paces of Durand, almost close enough to have reached out and touched him had he willed. His whole body was still held in the act of an arrested footfall, the one at which recognition had struck; one leg out behind him, heel clear of ground. Shoulders still forward, the way in which he had been going; head alone oblique, frozen that way at first sight of Durand.

Durand had a sickening impression that had he kept his own place in the belt line of promenaders, they might have gone on circling after one another the rest of the afternoon, equidistant, never drawing any closer, they might have remained unaware of one another. For Downs must have been fairly close behind him, to come upon him this quickly after, and so they would both likely have been on the same side of the promenade at any given time. But by falling out of line and coming to a halt, he had allowed Downs to overtake him, single him out. Where everyone is at rest, a moving figure is quickly noted. But where everyone is moving, it is the motionless figure that is the more conspicuous.

"Durand," Downs said with a curious matter-of-factness.

Durand tried to match it: nodded temperately, said, "You, eh?" Try not to show any fear of him, he kept cautioning himself, try not to show any fear. Forget that she is in such terrible proximity at this very moment, or you will betray that to him by the very act of trying not to. Don't look over that way, where the shop is. Keep your eyes off it. Above all, move him around, circle him around the other way so that his back is to it. If she should happen suddenly to emerge—

"Are you alone here?" Downs asked. The question was idly turned, but following it, for a long moment, his eyes seemed to bore into Durand's, until the latter could scarcely endure it.

"Certainly," he said somewhat testily.

Downs lazily reared one palm in protest. "No offense," he drawled. "You seem to resent my asking."

"Can you give me any reason why I should take offense at such a question?" He realized he was speaking too quickly, almost on the verge of sputtering.

"If you cannot, then I cannot," Downs said with feigned amiability.

Durand gave the railing a slick smack of quittance, moved in away from it, drifted in an idle saunter past Downs and to the rear of him, closed up to the railing again, and came to rest against it on a negligent elbow. Downs automatically pivoted to face him where he now was.

"And what brings you here, in turn?" Durand said, when the adjustment had been completed.

Downs smiled with special meaning. Special meaning he, Durand, was intended to share, whether he would or not. "What brings me anywhere?" he countered. "Not a holiday, rest assured."

"Oh," was all Durand could think to say to that. A very small, limp "oh."

In the modiste shop entrance, in the middle distance, but still close enough at hand to be only too visible, a lengthwise streamer of color suddenly peered forth, as some woman, about to leave, lingered there half-in half-out in protracted farewell, probably talking to someone behind her. Durand's heart thrust hard against the cavern of his chest for a moment, like a pointed rock. Then the figure came out: tall, in blue; someone else.

His attention swerved back to Downs, to overtake what he had been about to miss. "I had heard reports," the latter was saying, "of a flashy blonde who has been creating a stir down here with some man. They even got back to New Orleans."

Durand shrugged, a little jerkily. The point of his elbow slipped a trifle on the rail top, and he had to readjust it. "There are blondes wherever there are women."

What fools we've been, he thought bitterly. Lingering on here week after week; we might have known—

"This was a flashy blonde, almost silver in her lightness," Downs took pains to elaborate, eyes on him intent and unmoving. "A fast woman, I understand."

"Someone has fooled you."

"I don't think anyone has fooled *me*," Downs emphasized, "because: this was not intended for *my* ears at all in the first place. They just happened to overhear it, to pick it up." He waited a moment. "Have you happened to note any such pair? You have been down here longer than I, I take it."

Durand looked down at the planks underfoot. "I have been cured of blondes," he murmured grudgingly.

"A relapse can occur," Downs said drily.

How did he mean that? thought Durand, startled. But—don't quarrel with it, or you will make it worse.

He took out his watch. "I must go."

"Where are you staying?"

Durand thumbed back across his shoulder, misleadingly. "Down that way."

"I'll walk back with you to your stopping place, wherever it is," Downs offered.

He wants to find out where it is; I'll never lose him! thought Durand, harassed.

"I'm a little pressed for time," he managed to get out.

Downs smiled calmingly. "I never force myself on a man." Then he added pointedly, "That is, in sociability."

"Which way are you going?" Durand asked suddenly, seeing that he was about to turn and go back the other way, toward and past the modiste's. She might emerge just as he neared there—

He took Downs by the arm all at once, pressing him. As insistent now as he had been reluctant a moment ago. "Come with me, anyway. Can I offer you a schooner of beer?"

Downs glanced overhead. "The sun *is* warm," he accepted. "Your own face, for instance, is quite moist." There was something faintly satiric in the way he said it, Durand thought.

They walked along side by side. At every pace Durand told himself: I've drawn him a step farther away from her. She is that much safer.

"Here's a place; let's try this," he said presently.

"I was just going to suggest it myself," Downs observed. Again there was that overtone of satire to be detected.

They went in and seated themselves at a small wicker table.

"Two Pilseners," Durand told the mustachioed, striped-shirted waiter. Then before he could withdraw again. "Where is the closet?"

"Straight back."

Durand rose. "Excuse me for a moment." Downs nodded, ironically it seemed to him.

Durand left him seated there, went out through the spring door. He found himself in a passage. Ignoring the intermediate door to the side, he followed it to the rear, let himself out at the back of the place. He began to run like one possessed. He *was* possessed; possessed with the thought of saving her.

45

HE RAN back and forth like mad between the gaping wardrobe and the uplidded trunk, empty-armed on each trip to, half-smothered under masses of her dresses on each trip fro. He dropped them into it in any old way, so that long before the potential capacity of trunk was exhausted, its actual capacity was filled and overflowing. This was no time for a painstaking job of packing. This was get out fast, run for their lives.

He heard her come in at the street door, and before she had even had time to quit the entryway, he called down to her sight-unseen from above, in wild urgency: "Bonny!" And then again, "Bonny! Come up here quick! Hurry! I have something to tell you!"

She delayed for some reason. Perhaps over the feminine trait of removing her bonnet or disposing of her parcels before doing anything further, even at a moment of crisis.

Half mad with his own haste, he rushed recklessly out of the room, ran down to get her. And then halfway to the bottom of the stairs he stopped short, as if his legs had been gripped by a brake; and stood still, stock still and yet trembling, and died a little.

The figure back to door, back to just-reclosed door, equally stock still, was Downs.

Neither of them moved. The discovery came, the discovery went, the discovery was long past. Just two icy still men endlessly looking at one another. From stairs to door. From door to stairs. One of them bleakly smiling now in ultimate vindication. One of them ashen-faced, stricken to death.

One of them sighed deeply at last. Then the other sighed too, as if in answer. Two sighs in the intense silence. Two different sighs. A sigh of despair, a sigh of completion.

"You called her just now," Downs said slowly. "You called her by name. Thinking it was her. So she *is* here with you."

Durand had turned partly sidewise, was gripping the rail with both hands and bent slightly over it, as if able to support himself by that means alone. He shook his head. First slowly. Then at each repetition, faster, faster; until he was beating the stubborn air with it. "No," he said. "No. No. No."

"Mr. Durand, I have good ears. I heard you."

Ostrichlike, terrified, craven, trying to hide his head in the sands of his own mesmeric denial. As though to keep saying No, if persisted in long enough, would ward off the danger. Using the word as a sort of talisman.

"No. No. *No!*"

"Mr. Durand, let's be men at least. You called her name, you hollered it down here."

"No. No." He took a toppling step, that brought him down a stair lower. Then another. But seeming to *slide* his body downward along the slanted rail rather than move his legs, so hard and fast did he cling to it. Like an inebriate; which he was. An inebriate of fright.

"Someone else. Woman that comes in to do my cleaning. Her name sounds like that—" He didn't know what he was saying any more.

"Very well," Downs said drily. "I'll take the woman that comes in to do your cleaning, the woman whose name sounds so much the same. I'm not hard to please."

They were suddenly wary, watchful of one another; both pairs of eyes slanting first far over to this side, then far over to that, in a sort of synchronization of wordless guile. Physical movement followed, also in complete unison.

Durand broke from the stairs, Downs broke from the door-back. Their two diagonal rushes brought them together before the mirrored, antlered hatrack cabinet against the wall, with its armed seat that was also the lid of a storage box. Durand tried to hold it down, Downs to pry it up. Downs' arm treacherously thrust in and out again, came up with the two long heliotrope streamers depending from a straw garden hat. The tip of one had been protruding, caught fast by the lid on its last closing; a fleck of color, a fingernail's worth of color, in all that vast ground-floor area of house.

("But why do you like it so?" he had once asked her.

"I don't know. It's my color, and anyone who knows me *knows* it's my color. Wherever I am, there's bound to be some of it around.")

Downs let it fall back again into the box. "The costume for the woman who comes here to do your work," he remarked. And then, looking his disgust and complete forfeiture of respect at Durand, he murmured something in a swallowed voice that sounded like, "God help you, in love with a—!"

"Downs, listen, I want to talk to you—!" The words tumbled over one another in their eagerness to be out. He was so breathless he could hardly articulate. He took him by the lapels, a hand to each, held him close in a sort of pleading stricture. "Come inside here, come in the next room, let me talk to you—!"

"You and I have nothing to talk about. All my talking is for—"

Durand moved insistently backward, drawing him after him by that close coat lock, until he had him in there past the threshold where he wanted him to be. Then let him go, and Downs stayed there where he'd brought him.

"Downs, listen— Wait a minute, there's some brandy here, let me pour you a drink."

"I keep my drinking for saloons."

"Downs, listen— She's not here, you're making a terrible mistake—" Then quickly stilling his presumed contradiction by a fanwise rotation of the hand; "—but that isn't what I want to talk to you about. It's simply this. I—I've changed my mind. I want to drop the matter. I want the proceedings to stop."

Downs repeated with ironic absence of inflection, "You want to drop the matter. You want the proceedings to stop."

"I have that right, I have that choice. It was my complaint originally."

"As a matter of fact, that's only partly true. You were cocomplainant along with Miss Bertha Russell. But let's say for the sake of argument, it *was* your sole complaint originally. Then what?" His brows went up. "*And* what?"

"But if I withdraw the complaint, if I cancel it—?"

"You have no control over me," Downs said stonily. He slung one hip astride the arm of a chair he was standing beside, settled himself as if to wait. "You can rescind your complaint. All well and good. You can cease payment of any further fees to me. And as a matter of fact, your original retainer to me expired months ago. But you can't compel me to quit the case. Is that plain enough to you? As the old saying goes, this is a free country. And I'm a free agent. If I happen to want to continue on my own account until I bring the assignment to a satisfactory conclusion—and it happens that I do—there's nothing you can do about it. I'm no longer working for you, I'm working for my own conscience."

Appalled, Durand began to tremble all over. "But that's persecution—" he quavered.

"That's being conscientious, I'd call it, though it's not for me to say so," Downs said with a frosty smile.

"But you're not a public police official— You have no right—"

"Fully as much right as I had in the first place, when I took up the assignment on *your* behalf. The only difference being that now I'll turn my findings over to them direct, when I'm ready, instead of through you."

Durand, his feet clogging, had stumbled around and to the far side of the large bulky table desk present in the room, pacing his way along its edge with both hands, as if in momentary danger of collapse.

"Now wait— Now listen to me—" he panted, and fumbled with

excruciating anxiety in the pockets of his waistcoat, one after the other, not finding the right one immediately. He brought out a key, turned it in the wood, pulled out a drawer. A moment later a compact ironbound box had appeared atop the desk, its lid standing up. He grubbed within it, came back toward Downs with both hands extended, paper money choking them.

"There's twenty thousand dollars here. Downs, open your hand. Downs, hold it a minute; just hold it a minute."

Downs' hands had retreated into his trouser pockets at his approach; there was nothing there to deposit the offering in.

Downs shook his head with indolent stubbornness. "Not a minute, not an hour, not for keeps." He switched his head commandingly. "Take it back where you got it, Durand."

"Just *hold* it for me," Durand persisted childishly. "Just hang onto it a moment, that's all I'm asking—"

Downs stared at him imperturbably. "You've got the wrong man, Durand. That's your misfortune. The one wrong man out of twenty. Or maybe even out of a hundred. I took the case professionally in the beginning, for a money payment. I'm on it for my own satisfaction now. I not only won't take any further money to stay on it, but no amount of money could make me quit it any more. And don't ask me why, because I can't answer you. I'm a curious johnny, that's all. You made a mistake, Durand, when you came to me in St. Louis. You should have gone to somebody else. You picked the one private investigator in the whole country, maybe, that once he starts out on something can't leave off again, not even if he wants to. Sometimes I wonder what it is myself, I wish I knew. Maybe I'm a fanatic. I want that woman, not for you any more, but for my own satisfaction." He drew his hands out of his pockets at last, but only to fold his arms flintily across his chest and lean back still farther against the chair he was propped against.

"I'm staying here until she comes in. And I'm taking her back with me."

Durand was back beside the money box again, hands bedded atop its replaced contents, pressing down on it in strained futility.

Downs must have seen him glance speculatively toward the doorway. He read his mind.

"And if you go out of here, to try to meet her on the outside and warn her off, I'm going right along with you."

"You can't forbid me to leave my own house," Durand said despairingly.

"I didn't say that. And you can't prevent me from walking along beside you. Or just a step or two behind you. The streets are public."

Durand pressed the back of his hand to his forehead, held it there a moment, as though there were some light overhead that was too strong in his eyes. "Downs, I can raise another thirty thousand in New Orleans. Inside twenty-four hours. Go with me there, keep me in sight every step of the way; you have my promise. Fifty thousand dollars, just to let us alone. Just to forget you ever heard of—"

"Save your breath, I made my speech on that," Downs said contemptuously.

Durand clenched a fist, shook it, not threateningly, but imploringly, at him. "Why do you have to blacken her name, ruin her life? What good—?"

Downs' mouth shaped a laugh, but no sound came. "Blacken the name of that wanton? Ruin the life of that murdering trollop?"

The impact left physical traces across Durand's face, blanching it in livid streaks across the mouth and eyes, yet he ignored it. "She didn't do anything. The whole thing's circumstantial. She just happened to be on the same boat, that's all. So were dozens of others. *You* can't say for certain what happened to Julia Russell. No one can, no one knows. She just disappeared. She may have met with an accident. People have. Or she may still be alive at this very hour. She may have run off with someone else she met on the boat. All Bonny is guilty of, was passing herself off on me under another name, in the very beginning. And if *I* forgive her for that, as I have long ago—"

Downs suddenly left his semirecumbent position on the chair arm. He was on his feet, facing him alertly, eyes glittering now.

"Here's something you don't seem to know yet, Mr. Durand. And I think you may as well know it now, as later. You're going to soon enough, anyway. There *isn't* just a disappearance involved any longer. And I *can* say for certain just what happened to Julia Russell! I can now, if I couldn't the last time you saw me!"

He was leaning slightly forward in his intensity, in his zeal; that zeal of which he had spoken himself a few minutes earlier.

"A body drifted ashore out of the eddies at Cape Girardeau on the tenth of this month. You can get white, Mr. Durand; you have reason. A body that had been murdered, thrown into the water dead. There was no water in the lungs. I took Bertha Russell down to look at it. And badly decomposed as it was, she identified it. As that of Julia Russell, her sister. Triply fortified, even though there was no face left any more. By twin moles high on the inner side of the left thigh. That no other human being ever saw since early childhood, practically. By the uncommon fact that both end-teeth on both jaws, all four in other words, bore gold crowns. And lastly by the fact that her side bore peculiar scars in a straight line, from the teeth of a garden rake; again from her childhood. The rake had been rusty and the punctures had had to be cauterized by a hot iron."

He stopped for lack of breath, and there was a moment of silence.

Durand was standing there, head bowed, looking downward before himself. Perhaps to the floor in implicit capitulation, perhaps to the outthrust drawer from which the strongbox had come. He was breathing with difficulty; his chest rose and fell with visible labor at each intake and expulsion.

"Do the official police know about this?" he asked finally, without raising his head.

"Not yet, but they will when I get her back there with me."

"You'll never get her back there with you, Downs. She's not going to leave this house. *And neither are you.*"

Now his head came up. And with it the pistol his hand had fallen upon, long ago, long before this.

Shock slashed across Downs's face; it mirrored fear, collapse, panic, for a moment each, in turn; all the usual and only-human reactions. But then he curbed them, and after that he bore himself well.

He spoke for his life, but his voice was steady and reasonable, and after the first abortive step back, he held his ground sturdily. Nor did he cringe and bunch his shoulders defensively, but held himself tautly erect. He did not try to disguise his fear, but he mastered it, which is the greater bravery of the two.

"Don't do anything like that. Keep your head, man. You're still not involved. There's nothing punishable as yet in your taking up with this woman. The crime was committed before you met her. You were not a party to it. You've been foolish but not criminal so far— Don't, Durand— Stop and think before it's too late. For your own sake, while there's still time, put that down. Put it back where you got it."

Durand, for the first time during the entire interview, seemed to be addressing, not the investigator, but someone else. But who it was, no one could have said. He didn't know himself. "It's already too late. It's been too late since I first met her. It's been too late since the day I was born. It's been too late since God first created this world!"

He looked down, to avoid seeing Downs's face. He looked down at his own finger, curled about the trigger. Watching it with a sort of detached curiosity, as though it were not a part of him. Watching as if to see what it would do.

"Bonny," he sobbed brokenly, as though pleading with her to let him go.

The detonation stunned him briefly, and smoke drew a transient merciful curtain between the two of them. But that thinned again and was wafted aside long before it could do any good.

Then he looked up and met the face he hadn't wanted to.

Downs was still up, strangely.

There was in his face such unutterable, poignant rebuke that, to have had to look at it a second time during a single lifetime would have cost Durand his reason, he had a feeling then.

A hushed word hovered about them in the sudden new stillness of the room, like a sigh of penitence. Somebody had breathed "Brother," and later Durand had the strange feeling it had been he.

Downs's legs gave abruptly, and he went with a crash. More violently, for the delay, than if he had fallen at once. And lay there dead. Dead beyond mistaking, with his eyes open but viscid opaque matter, with his lips rubbery and slightly unsealed.

The things he did then, Durand, he was slow in coming to, as though it were he and not Downs who was now in timeless eternity; and even as he did them, though he saw himself doing them, he was unaware of doing them. As though they were the acts of his hands and his body, and not of his brain.

He remembered sitting for a while on a chair, on the outermost edge of a chair, like someone uneasy, about to rise again at any moment, but yet who fails to do so. He only saw that he had been sitting when he finally did stand and quit the chair. He'd been holding the pistol in his hand the whole time, and tapping its muzzle against the cap of his knee.

He went over to the desk and returned it to where he'd taken it from. Then he noted the cash box still standing there on top the desk, with its lid up and some escaped bank notes lying about it. These he returned to it, and then closed and locked it, and then he put it away too. Then he locked the drawer and pocketed the key.

Yes, he thought dazedly, I can repair everything but one thing. There is one thing I cannot return to, what it was before. And he swayed, shuddering, for a moment against the corner of the desk, as if the thought were a strong cold wind assailing him and threatening to overbalance him.

The situation seemed timeless, as if he were going to stay in here forever with this dead man. This dead thing that had been a man; dressed like a man, but not a man any longer. He felt no immediate urge to get out of the room; instinct told him it was better to be here, behind its concealing walls, than elsewhere. But he wanted not to have to look at what lay on the floor any longer. He wanted his eyes not to have to keep returning to it every other moment.

Downs lay upon an oblong rug, and he lay transverse upon it, so that one upper corner protruded far out past his shoulder, one lower far down below his foot. There was in this violation of symmetry, too, an irritant that continually inflamed his nerves every time his gaze fell upon the high relief offered by the floor.

He went over at last and dropped down by the dead face, and, folding over the margin of rug, covered it, as with a thick, woolly winding sheet. Then noting in himself symptoms of relief or at least amelioration, shifted rapidly down by the feet of the corpse—without standing, by working his upended feet along under his body—and turned over that corner, swathing the feet and lower legs. All that lay revealed now was a truncated torso.

Suddenly, inspired, he turned the body over, and the rug with it. And then a second time, and the rug still with it. It was gone now, completely hidden, disappeared within a cocoon of roughspun rugback. But he did it still once more, and the rug had become a long, hollow cylinder. No more than a rolled rug; nothing about it to amaze or attest or accuse.

But it was in the way. It blocked passage in or out of the doorway.

He scrambled downward upon all fours and began to roll it across the room, toward the base of the opposite wall. It rolled lumpily and a little erratically, guided by the weight of its own fill rather than his manipulations. He had to stop and straighten, and move ahead of it to get a chair out of the way.

Then, tired, when he had returned to it, he no longer got down and used his hands to it. He remained erect and planted his foot against it and prodded it forward in that way, until at last he had it close up against the wall base, and as unobtrusive as it would ever be.

A small mother-of-pearl collar button had jumped out of it en route and lay there behind it on the floor. He picked that up, and returned to it, and tossed it in freehand at one of the openings; but no longer sure which one of the two it was, whether at head or at feet.

Exhausted now, he staggered back across the room, and found the wall nearest the door-opening, the farthest one from it, and sank back deflated against that, letting it support him at shoulders and at rump. And just remained that way, inert.

He was still there like that when she came in.

Her arrival now was anticlimax. He could give it no import any longer. He was drained of nervous energy. He turned listlessly at the sound of her entrance, back beyond sight in the hall. A moment later she had arrived abreast of him, was standing looking into the room, busied in taking a glove off one hand.

A little flirt of violet scent seemed to reach him; but perhaps more imagined by the sight of her, recalled to memory from former times, than actually inhaled now.

She turned her head and saw him there, propped upright, splayed hands at a loss.

Her puckered mouth ejaculated a note of laughter. "Lou! What are you doing there like that? Flat up against—"

He didn't speak.

Her gaze swept the room in general, seeking for the answer.

He saw her glance halt at the transverse dust patch coating the floor. The rug's ghost, so to speak.

"What happened to the rug?"

"There's someone in it. There's a man's body in it." Even as he said it, it struck him how curious that sounded. There's someone in it. As though there were some miniature living being dwelling in it.

But what other way was there to say it?

He turned his head to indicate it. She turned hers in accompaniment, and thus located it. A rounded shadow secretively nestling along the base of the wall; easy for the eye to miss, the legs of chairs distracting it.

"Don't go over—" he started to say. But she had already started swiftly for it. He didn't finish the injunction, more from lack of energy than because she had already disobeyed it.

He saw her crouch down by the oval, stovepipe-like opening, her skirts puddling about her. She put her face close and peered. Then she thrust her arm in, to feel blindly if there was indeed something in there. He saw her grasp it by its edges next, as if to partially unroll it, or at least stretch the aperture.

"Don't—" he said sickly. "Don't open it again."

She straightened and came back toward him again. There was an alertness in her face, a sort of wary shrewdness, but that was all; no horror and no fear, no pallor of shock. She even seemed to have gained vitality, as if this were—not a moral catastrophe—but a test to put her on her mettle.

"Who did it? You?" she demanded in a brisk whisper.

"It's Downs," he said.

Her eyes were on him with bright insistency; there was a single-minded intentness to them that almost amounted to avidity; insistency on knowing, on being told. Hard practicality. But no emotional dilution whatever.

"He came here to get you."

He wouldn't have gone ahead. His head dipped in conclusion. But she urged the continuation from him by putting hand to his chin and tipping it up again.

"He found out you were here."

She nodded now, rapidly. The explanation sufficed, that seemed to mean; she accepted it, she understood it. The act, the consequence stemming from it, was a normal one. None other could have been expected. None other could have been desired. A nod or two of her head spoke to him, saying these things.

She gripped his upper arm tight. He hadn't known she possessed so much strength, so much burning heat, in her fingers. He had the curious impression it was a form of commendation.

There was an intimacy tincturing her next remark, a rapport, none of their love passages had ever had before.

"What'd you do it with? What'd you take?"

"The gun there," he said. "The one in the desk."

She turned and looked at the rug. And while she stood turned thus, she struck him lightly on the chest with the back of her hand. And the only thing he could read in the gesture was rakish camaraderie, a sort of flippant, unspoken bond.

Then she looked back at him, and looked him in the face long and well. Lazily half smiling the while, as if discovering in the familiar outlines of his face, for the first time, some new qualities, to be appreciated, to be admired.

"You need a drink," she said with brittle decisiveness. "I do too. Wait a minute, I'll get us one."

He watched her go to it, and pour from the decanter twice, and put the glass stopper back in, and give it a little twist as if it were a knob.

He felt as if he were venturing into a strange new world. Which had had its well-established customs all along, but which he was only now encountering for the first time. That was what you did after you took a life; you took a drink next. He hadn't known that, it wouldn't have occurred to him, but for her. He felt like a novice in the presence of a practised hand.

She put one of the two glasses into his hand, and continuing to clasp that same hand about the wrist, as if in token of affection, poked her other hand wildly, vertically, up into the air.

"Now you're a man after my own heart," she said with glittering fervor. "Now you're worth taking up with. Now you're *my* kind of man."

She smote his uncertain glass with hers, and her head went back, and she pitched the liquor in through those demure lips, that scarcely seemed able to open at all.

"Here's to us," she said. "To you. To me. To the two of us. Drink up, my lovey. A short life and an exciting one."

She cast her drained glass against the wall and it sprayed into fragments.

He hesitated a moment, then, as if hurrying to overtake her, lest he be left all alone, drained his own and sent it after hers.

46

THE EYE, falling upon them unwarned half an hour later, would have mistaken them for a pretty picture of domesticity; discussing some problem of meeting household expense, perhaps, or of planning the refurnishing of a room.

He sat now, legs outspread, head lolling back, in a chair with arms, and she sat perched on one of the arms of it, close beside him, her hand occasionally straying absently to his hair, as they mulled and talked it over.

He had been holding a glass, a succeeding one, in his hand. She took it away from him at last and placed it on the table. "No more of that just now," she admonished, and patted him on the head. "You must keep your head clear for this."

"It's hopeless, Bonny," he said wanly.

"It's nothing of the sort." Again she patted him on the head. "I've been—"

She didn't finish it, but somehow he guessed what she'd been about to say. I've been in situations like this before. He wondered where, he wondered when. He wondered who had done it, who she'd been with at the time.

"To run flying out of here," she resumed, as if taking up a discussion that had been allowed to lapse some little time before, "would be the most foolhardy thing people in—our position—could do." As if hearing her from a great distance, he was amazed at how prim, how mincing, her words sounded; as if she were a pretty young schoolmistress patiently instructing a not-very-bright pupil in his lesson. She should have had some embroidery on her lap, and her eyes downcast to it as she spoke, to match her tone of voice.

"We can't *stay*, Bonny," he faltered. "What are we going to do? How can we *stay*?" And hid his eyes for a moment behind his own hand. "It's already an hour."

"How long was it before I came home?" she asked with an almost scientific detachment.

"I don't know. It seemed like a long time—" He started up rebelliously from the chair. "We could have been far from here, already. We should have been!"

She pressed him gently but firmly back.

"We're not staying," she calmed him. "But we're not rushing off helter-skelter either, at the drop of a hat. Don't you know what that would mean? In a few hours at most, someone would have found it out, be on our heels."

"Well, they will anyway!"

"No they won't. Not if we play our cards right. We'll go in our own good time. But that comes last of all, when we're good and ready for it. The first thing is—" she hooked her thumb negligently across the room, "—*that* has to be got out of the way."

"Taken outside the house?" he suggested dubiously.

She gnawed her lips reflectively. "Wait, let me think a minute." At last she shook her head, said slowly: "No, not outside— We'd be seen. Almost certainly."

"Then—?"

"Somewhere inside," she said, with a slight motion of her shoulders, as though that were to be understood, went without saying.

The idea horrified him. "Right here in the house—?"

"Of course. It's a lot safer. In fact, it's the only thing for us to do. We're here alone, just the two of us; no servants. We can take all the time we need—"

"Ugh," he groaned.

She was pondering again, worrying her lip; she seemed to have no time for emotion. She frightened him almost as much as the fact they were trying to conceal.

"One of the fireplaces?" he faltered. "There are two large ones down on this floor—"

She shook her head. "That would only be a matter of days."

"A closet?"

"Worse. A matter of hours." She stretched her foot out and tapped down her heel a couple of times. Then she nodded, as if she were at last nearing a satisfactory decision. "One of the floors."

"They're hardwood. It would be noticed the minute anyone came into the room."

"The cellar. What's the floor of that like?"

He couldn't recall having seen it; had never been down there, to his knowledge.

She quitted the chair abruptly. The period of incubation had ended, the period of action had begun. "Wait a minute. I'll go down take a look." From the doorway, without turning her head, she warned: "Don't take any more of those drinks while I'm gone."

She came running back, squinting shrewdly. "Hard dirt. That'll do."

She had to think for the two of them. She pulled at him briskly by the shoulder. "Come on, let's get it down there awhile. It's better than leaving it up here until we're ready. Someone may come to the door in the meantime."

He went over to it and stopped, trying to quell the nausea assailing his stomach.

She had to think of everything. "Hadn't you better take your coat off? It'll hamper you."

She took it from him and draped it carefully over a chair back, so that it would not wrinkle. She even brushed a little at one of the sleeves for a moment, before letting it be.

He wondered how such a commonplace, everyday act, her helping him off with his coat, could seem so grisly to him, making him quail to his marrow.

He took it up by its middle, the furled rug, packed it underarm, clasping it overarm with his other. One end, where the feet presumably were, of necessity slanted and dragged on the floor, of its own weight. The other end, where the head was, he managed to keep upward.

He advanced a few paces, draggingly. Suddenly the weight had eased, the lower end had lost its restraining drag on the floor. He looked, and she was holding that for him, helping him.

"No, for God's sake, no!" he said sickly. "Not you—"

"Oh, don't be a fool, Louis," she answered impatiently. "It's a lot quicker this way!" Then she added, with somewhat less asperity, "It's just a rug to me. I can't *see* anything."

They traveled with it out of the room, and along the cellarward passage to its back. Then had to stop and set it down, while he opened the door. Then in through there, and down the stairs, to cellar bottom. Then set it down once more, for good.

He was breathing hard. He passed his hand over his forehead.

"Heavy," she agreed. She blew out her breath, with a slight smile.

All the little things she did horrified him so. His blood almost turned cold at that.

They picked a place for it against the wall. She used the sharp toe of her shoe to test several, kicking and prodding at them, before settling on it. "I think this is about the best. It's a little less compact here."

He picked up a piece of rotting, discarded timber, broke it over his upthrust knee to obtain a sharp point.

"You're not going to do it with that, are you? It would take you the live-long night!" There was almost a hint of risibility in her voice, inconceivable as that was to him.

He drove it into the hard-packed floor, and it promptly broke a second time, proving its worthlessness.

"It'll take a shovel," she said. "Nothing else will do."

"There's none down here."

"There's none anywhere in the house. We'll have to bring one in." She started up the steps. He remained standing there. She turned at their top and beckoned him. "I'll go out and get it," she said. "You're kind of shaky yet, I can see that. Don't stay down there while I'm gone, it'll make you worse. Wait upstairs for me."

He followed her up, closed the cellar door after him.

She put on her poke bonnet, threw a shawl over her shoulders, as if it were the merest domestic errand she were going upon.

"Do you think it's prudent?" he said.

"People buy shovels, you know. There need be no harm in that. It's all in the way you carry it off."

She went toward the outside door, and he trailed behind her.

She turned to him there. "Keep your courage up, honey." She held his chin fast, kissed him on the lips.

He'd never known a kiss could be such a gruesome thing before.

"Stay up here, away from it," she counselled. "And don't go back to that liquor." She was like a conscientious mother giving a small boy last minute injunctions, putting him on his good behavior, before leaving him to himself.

The door closed, and he watched her for a moment through its pane. Saw her go down the front walk, just like any bustling little matron on a housewifely errand. She was even diligently stroking her mittens on as she turned up the road and went from sight.

He was left alone with his dead.

He sought the nearest room at hand, not the one in which it had happened, and collapsed into a chair, and huddled there inert, his face pressed inward against its back, and waited for her to return.

It seemed hours before she did. And it must, in truth, have been the better part of one.

She brought it in with her. She was carrying it openly—but then how else was she to have carried it? Its bit was wrapped in brown paper, tied with a string. The stick protruded unconcealed.

"Was I long?"

"Forever," he groaned.

"I deliberately went out of my way," she explained. "I didn't want to buy it too near here, where we're known by sight."

"It was a mistake to get it at all, don't you think?"

She gave him a confident smirk. "Not in the way I did it. I did not ask to buy a shovel at all. It was his advice that I buy one. What I asked was what implement he could suggest my using to cultivate in the space behind our house, whether a spade or a rake. I was dubious of a shovel; it took all his persuasion to convince me." She wagged her head cocksurely.

And she could stand there and dicker; he thought, incredulous.

He took it from her.

"Shall I come down with you?" she offered, carefully removing her bonnet with both hands, replacing the pins in it, and setting it down meticulously so that its shape would not suffer.

"No," he said in a stifled voice. To have had her watch him would have been an added horror, for some reason, that he could not have borne. "I'll let you know when—I've done."

She gave him helpful last minute instructions. "Mark it off first. You know, how long and how wide you'll want it. With the tip of the shovel. That'll keep you from doing more work than is needful."

His silent answer to this was the reflex of retching.

He closed the door after him, went down the steps.

The lamp was still burning where they'd left it before.

He turned it up higher. Then that was too bright, it showed him too much; he quickly moderated it a little.

He'd never dug a grave before.

He marked it off first, as she'd told him. He drove the shovel into the marked-off space and left it, standing upright of its own weight. He rolled his shirt sleeves up out of the way.

Then he took up the shovel and began.

The digging part was not so bad. *It* was behind him, out of sight, while he was at it. Horror, though it did not disappear altogether, was kept to a minimum. It might have been just a necessary trench or pit he was digging.

But then when he was through—

It took him some moments to work himself up to the necessary pitch of resoluteness. Then suddenly he walked rapidly over to it, from the far side of the cellar, where he'd withdrawn and kept his back to it in the interim.

He dragged the rug over, placed it even with the waiting cavity's edge. Then, taking a restraining hold along its exposed flap, he pushed the rounded part from him. It unrolled and emptied itself into the trough, with no more than a sodden thump. Then he drew it up. It came back to him again facilely unweighted. An arm flung up for a moment, but quickly dropped back again.

He avoided looking into it. He stepped around it to the other side, where the mound of disinterred fill was, and, holding his face averted, began to push and scrape that down into it with the back of the shovel.

Then when at last he had to look, to see how far he had progressed, the worst was over. There was no longer any face down there to confront him. There was just a fragmentary midsection seeming to float there on the surface, as it were; peering through the surrounding film of earth.

Then that went, presently.

"And all God's work has come to this," passed through his mind.

He had to tramp and stamp on it, at the end, to firm it down. That part was bad too.

He kept it up far longer than was needful. As if to keep what lay under from ever coming out again. He almost seemed to be doing a jig of fear and despair, unable to quit of his own volition.

He looked up suddenly.

She was standing there at head of the steps watching him.

"How did you know just when?" he panted, haggard.

"I came down twice to see how far along you were. I went back again without disturbing you. I thought perhaps you'd best be left alone." She looked at him inscrutably. "I didn't think you'd be able to go through with it to the finish. But you did, didn't you?"

Whether that was praise or not, he couldn't tell.

He kicked the shovel out of his path, tottered up the steps toward her.

He fell before he'd quite reached her. Or rather, let himself fall. He lay there, extended on the step, face buried in one arm, and sobbed a little.

She bent over toward him. Her hand came down upon his shoulder, consolingly.

"There, now. It's over. It's done. There's nothing more to worry about."

"I've killed a man," he said smotheredly. "I've killed a man. God has forbidden that."

She gave a curt, humorless snuff of laughter. "Soldiers in a battle kill them by the tens and never give it a second thought. They even give them medals for it."

She plucked at him by the arm, until he had found his feet again, stood beside her.

"Come, let's get out of here."

She stepped down there a moment to get the lamp, which he had forgotten, bring it with her, put it out. Then she closed the door after the two of them. She brushed her fingertips off fastidiously, against each other; no doubt from having touched the lamp. Or perhaps—

She put her arm comfortingly about his waist, as she rejoined him. "Come upstairs to bed. You're worn out. It's nearly ten o'clock, did you know that? You've been down there four full hours."

"You mean—?" He didn't think he'd heard her aright. "Sleep here in this same house tonight?"

She cast up her hand, as if at the nonsense of such a qualm. "It's late. What trains are there any more? And even if there were, people don't bolt out suddenly in the middle of the night. That *would* give them something to—"

"But *knowing,* as we do, Bonny. Knowing all the time, you and I both, what lies—"

"Don't be childish. Just put it from your mind. It's all the way down in the cellar. We're—all the way up in the bedroom."

She tugged at him until she got him to climb beside her.

"You're like a little boy who's afraid of the dark," she mocked.

He said nothing more.

In the lamplit bedroom he watched her covertly, while apatheti-
cally, with numbed motions, drawing off his own things. There was
no difference to be detected in the bustling routine with which she
prepared herself for retirement, from any other night. Again certain
under-layers of garments billowed up over her head in as much
armless commotion as ever. Again the petticoats dropped to the floor
and she stepped aside from them, one after the other. Again her unbound hair was trapped first on the inside of her high-collar flannel
gown, then freed and brought to the outside, with a little backward
shake. Every move was normal, unforced.

She even sat to the mirror and stroked her hair with the brush.

He lay back and closed his eyes, with a weazened sickish feeling.

They didn't say goodnight to one another. She perhaps thought he
was already asleep, or was a little offended at his excess of morality.
He was glad of that, at least. Glad she didn't try to kiss him. He had
a curious sensation for a moment or two, that if she had tried, he
would have, involuntarily, reared up, run for the window, and hurled
himself through it.

She turned their bedside lamp and the room dimmed indigo.

He lay there motionless, as rigid, as extended, as what he had
put into the trough down below in the cellar awhile ago.

Not only couldn't he sleep, he was afraid to sleep. He wouldn't
have let himself if he could have. He was fearful of meeting the
man he had just slain, should he drift across the border.

She too was sleepless, however, in spite of all her insouciance.
He heard her turning about a number of times. Presently she gave a
foreshortened sigh of impatience. Then he heard the bed frame jar
slightly as she propped herself up on her arm.

He could somehow tell, in another moment, that she was leaning
over toward him. The direction of her breath, perhaps, coming toward
him.

Her silken whisper reached him.

"Awake, Lou?"

He kept his eyes closed.

He heard her get up, the rustle as she put something over her.
Heard her take up the lamp, tread softly from the room with it, unlighted. Then outside the door, left ajar, the slowly burgeoning
glow as she lit it. Then this receded as she bore it down the stairs
with her.

His breath started to quicken. Was she leaving him? Was she about to commit some act of disloyalty, of betrayal, in the depths of night? Terrified, he suddenly burst the frozen mould that had encased him, started up himself, flung something on, crept cautiously out into the hall.

He could see the light from below peering wanly up the stairs. He could hear a faint sound now and again, as she moved softly about.

He felt his way down the stairs, step by step, his breath erratic, and rearward toward where the light was coming from. Then stepped up to the doorway at last and confronted her.

She was seated at the table, in the lamplight, holding a chicken-joint in her hand and busily gnawing at it.

"I was hungry, Lou," she said sheepishly. "I didn't have any supper." And then, putting her hand to the vacant chair beside her and swiveling it out invitingly, "Join me?"

47

THE GENTLE but insistently repeated pressure of her small hand on his shoulder, rubbed sleep threadbare, wore it away. He started upward spasmodically.

Then it came back. Then he remembered. Like a waiting knife it struck and found him.

"I'm going to get the tickets, Lou. Lou, wake up, it's after ten. I'm going to get the tickets. For us, at the station. I've done all the packing, while you were lying there. I've left out your one suit, everything else is put away—Lou, wake up, clear your eyes. Can't you understand me? I'm going to get the tickets. What about money?"

"Over there," he murmured vacantly, eyes turned inward on yesterday. "Back pocket, on the left side—"

She had it in a moment, as though she'd already known, but only wanted his cognizance to her taking it.

"Where will I get them for? Where do you want us to go?"

"I don't know—" he said blurredly, shading his eyes. "I can't tell you that—"

She gave her head a little toss of impatience at his sluggishness. "I'll go by the trains, then. Whichever one is leaving soonest, we'll take."

She came to him and, bending, gave him a hurried little peck of parting. The fragrance of her violet toilet water swirled about him.

"Be careful," he said dismally. "It may be dangerous."

"We have time. There's no danger yet. How can there be? It's not even known." She gave him a shrug of assurance. "If we go about it right, there may never be danger."

The froufrou of her skirts crossed the floor. She opened the door. She turned there. She bent the fingers of her hand as if beckoning him to her.

"Ta ta," she said. "Lovey mine."

48

SHE SEEMED to be gone the whole morning. How could it take that long just to buy tickets for a train? he asked himself over and over again, sweating agony. How? How? Even if you bought them twice over, three times over?

He was pacing endlessly back and forth, holding tightly clasped between his two hands, as if afraid to lose it, a cup of the coffee she had left for him warming on the stove. But the plume of steam that had at first, with a sort of rippling sluggishness, traced his course behind him on the air, had long since thinned and vanished. He took a hurried swallow every so often, but dipping his mouth nervously down into the cup, held low as it was, rather than raising it to his lips. He wasn't aware of its taste, or of its degree of warmth, or even what it was.

She wasn't coming back, that was it. She'd abandoned him, boarded a train by herself, left him to meet the consequences of his own act as best he might. Sweat would start out anew at the thought, sweat that hurt like blood, though it was only the dew of fear. Then he would remember that she had intentionally awakened him before leaving, that she would have carefully avoided that above all had desertion been her purpose, and he'd breathe again and his misgivings would abate somewhat. Only to return again presently, stronger than ever, as if on a wicked punishing spiral.

He was in the midst of this inner turmoil, when suddenly, on the outside, crisis confronted him, and he was alone to face it.

There was a knocking at the door that he knew could not possibly be hers, and when he peered from one of the sideward frontal windows, cloaking his face with the edge of the drape, there was a coach and coachman standing waiting empty out before the house for someone.

The rapping came again. And when he drew nearer, through the inside of the house, and stole a frightened look out from mid-hall toward the glass curtain veiling the upper part of the door, there were the filmy shadowed busts of a man and a woman imprinted on it, standing waiting on the threshold.

Side by side, in chiaroscuro; the cone of a man's tophat, the slanting line of a woman's bonnet brim.

The knocking repeated itself, and seemed to trap his voice into issuing forth, against every intent of his own to use it. "Who's there?" Too late he tried to stem it, to recall it, but it was already gone.

"Dollard," a man's voice answered, deeply resonant.

He didn't know the name, couldn't identify it.

Unmanned, he quailed there.

The voice came again. "May I speak with you a minute, Mr. Durand?"

So the voice knew him at least. It was no mistake, it was he that was wanted.

He would have been incapable of further movement, even after having revealed himself, had they let him be.

But his name came again. "Mr. Durand." And then the knocking, puzzled now and questioning. And then his name again. "Mr. Durand. Hello! Mr. Durand?"

He was drawn to it as if in a trancelike condition, and unbolted, and drew it back.

They flamed instantly into full color, from the pewter silhouettes they had been, and into full stature, from the shoulder busts.

The woman was dark haired, sallow skinned, rather thin of face but pretty none the less; wearing a costume of grape velveteen, adorned with black frogs across the bodice like a hussar's jacket. The man was florid of face, with a copper walrus mustache drooping over the corners of his mouth, a cane handle riding over the crook of his arm, and a shirt front with small blue forget-me-nots patterned all over it.

He raised his hat to Durand, in deference to his companion, and revealed the crown of his head to be somewhat bald, and also somewhat sunburned.

Durand didn't recognize him for a minute.

"I'm Dollard, the agent from whom you rented the house."

He waited, ready to smile at the expected acknowledgement, but there was none.

"Mrs. Durand tells me you are unexpectedly called away and the house will be available."

She had been there then. She had even thought of that.

"Oh," he said stupidly. "Oh. Oh, yes. Of course."

Dollard gave him a somewhat quizzical look, as if unable to understand his lack of immediate comprehension. "That *is* correct, isn't it?"

"Yes," he said, realizing he'd already blundered copiously in the moment or two since he'd appeared at the door.

"Have I your permission to show this possible client through the house?"

"*Now?*" he murmured aghast. He could almost feel his chest pucker, as if closing up for lack of oxygen.

Dollard seemed to miss the intonation, having suddenly remembered his best business manners. "Oh, forgive me. Mrs. Thayer, may I present Mr. Durand?"

He saw the young woman glance at the forgotten coffee cup his hand still clung to, as if it were some kind of a chalice with mystic powers to save him. "I'm afraid we may have come at an unfortunate time," she suggested deprecatingly. "We're disturbing Mr. Durand. Should we not perhaps come back at another time, Mr. Dollard?"

The agent had already deftly inserted himself on the inside, however, and since he refused to return to her, she had to follow somewhat hesitantly to where he was, even in the act of speaking.

"I know how upset everything is when a move is contemplated; the packing and all," she apologized.

"I'm sure Mr. Durand doesn't mind," Dollard said. "We won't be very long." And since he had unobtrusively managed to close the door after the three of them by this time, the fact was already an accomplished one.

They moved down the hall parallel to one another, the young woman in the middle; Dollard striding with heavy-footed assurance, Durand all but tottering.

"This is the hall. Notice how spacious it is." Dollard swept his arm up, like an opera tenor on a high note.

"The light is quite good too," agreed the young woman.

Dollard tapped his cane. "The finest hardwood parquetry. You don't always find it."

They advanced after the momentary halt.

"Now, in here is the parlor," Dollard proclaimed grandly, again with a sweep.

"Is the furniture yours, Mr. Durand?" she asked.

Dollard's answer overrode whatever one he might have brought himself to make, sparing him the necessity. "The furniture goes with the house," he stated flatly.

She nodded her head approvingly. "This is quite a nice room. Yes, it's quite nice."

She had already turned her shoulder to it, about to lead them on elsewhere, and Dollard had turned in accord with her. When suddenly, as if only now struck by something he had already observed a moment ago, he looked back, pointed unexpectedly with his cane.

"Shouldn't there be a rug here?"

The dust patch was suddenly the most conspicuous thing in the room. In the house, in the whole world. It glowed livid, as if limned with phosphorus. To Durand, at least, it almost appeared incandescent, and he felt sure they must see it that way too. He could feel his face bleaching and drawing taut over the cheekbones, as if the slack of his skin were being pulled at the back of his head by some cruel hand.

"Where?" he managed to utter.

Dollard's cane tapped down twice, for irritated emphasis. "Here. Here."

"Oh," Durand said pitifully, crumbling phrases in a play for time. "Oh, there—Oh, yes—I think you're—I'd have to ask my—" Then suddenly he'd regained command of himself, and his tone was firm, though still brittle. "It was removed to be beaten out. I remember now."

"Then it's outdoors?" Dollard queried, as though not wholly pleased. Without waiting to be answered, he crossed to one of the windows, lowered his head to avoid the interplay of the curtains, and swept his gaze about. "No, I fail to see it there." He turned his head back to Durand, as if uneasily asking reassurance.

The latter's eyelids, which had closed for a moment over some inner illness of his own, went up again in time to meet the agent's boring glance.

"It's safe," he said. "It's somewhere about the house. Just where, I couldn't exactly—"

"It was quite valuable," Dollard said. "I trust it hasn't been stolen. It will have to be accounted for, of course."

"It will be," Durand breathed almost inaudibly.

The young woman shifted her foot slightly, in forebearing reminder that she was being detained; this instantly succeeded in recalling his present duties to Dollard, and he dropped the topic.

He hastened back to her, and tipped two fingers to her elbow in courtly guidance. "Shall we continue, Mrs. Thayer? Next I would like you to see the upstairs."

They ascended in single file, she in the lead, Durand at the rear. They ascended slowly, and he seemed to feel each footfall imprinted on his heart, as though it were that they were treading upon. The rustle and hiss of her multiple skirts was like the sound of volatile water rushing down a wooden trough, though it flowed the other way, upward instead of down.

"You will notice the excellent light that is obtained throughout this house," Dollard preened himself, as soon as they were on level flooring once more. He hooked his thumbs to the armholes of his

waistcoat, allowed his fingers to trip contentedly against his chest.
"In here, an extra little sitting room for the lady of the house. To
do her sewing, perhaps." He smiled benevolently, winked at Durand
behind her back, as though to show him he knew women, knew what
pleased them.

He was in fine fettle today, apparently; enjoying every moment
of his often-performed duties. Durand remembered enjoyment, an
academic word from the vague past; remembered the word, but not
its sensation. His wrists felt as cold as though tight coils of wire
were cutting into their flesh, had long since stopped all circula-
tion.

At their bedroom door she balked, chastely withdrew the tentative
foot she had put forward, as soon as she had identified it for
what it was.

"And this room has a most desirable outlook," Dollard orated
heedlessly. "If you will be good enough to go in—"

Her eyes widened in dignified, gravely offered reproach. "Mr.
Dollard!" she reminded him firmly. "There is a *bed* in there. And
my husband is not accompanying me."

"Oh, your pardon! Of course!" he protested elaborately, with
recessive genuflections. "Mr. Durand?"

The two men delicately withdrew all the way up-hall to the stair-
head, to wait for her, and with the impurity of mixed company thus
removed, she proceeded to enter the room and inspect it at her
leisure.

"A real lady," Dollard commented admiringly under his breath,
punctiliously looking the other way so that even his eyes could not
seem to follow her on her unchaperoned expedition.

Durand's hand lay draggingly on his collar, forgotten there since
he had last tried to ease his throat some moments ago.

She came out again very shortly. Her color was a trifle higher than
when she had gone in, since the bed had not been made up, but
she had no comment to offer.

They descended again, in the same order in which they had gone
up. Her undulating hand left the railing at the bottom, and she
turned to Dollard.

"Have you shown me everything?"

"I believe so." Perhaps judging her to be not yet wholly convinced
of the house's desirability, he groped for additional inducements to

display to her, turned his head this way and that. "All but the cellar—"

Durand could feel a sharp contraction go through his middle, almost like a cramp. He resisted the instinctive urge to clutch at himself and bend forward .

Their eyes were not on him, fortunately; they were looking back there toward where its door was, Dollard's gaze having led her own to it.

"It is quite a large and commodious one. Let me show you. It will only take a moment—"

They turned and paced toward it.

Durand, clinging for a necessary moment to the newel post of the banister, released it again and took a faulty step after them.

His mind was suddenly spinning, casting off excuses for delaying them like sparks from a whirring whetstone. Rats, say there are rats; she will be afraid—Cobwebs, dust; she may harm her clothes—

"There is no light," he said hoarsely. "You will not be able to see anything. I'm afraid Mrs. Thayer may hurt herself—"

His tone was both too abrupt and too raucous for the intimate little elbow passage that now confined them all. Both turned their heads in surprise at the intensity of voice he had used, as though they were at a far greater distance. But then immediately, they seemed to take no further notice of the aberration, beyond that.

"No light in your cellar?" said Dollard with pouting dissatisfaction. "You should have a light in your cellar. What do you do when you wish to go down there yourself?" And glancing about him in mounting peevishness at thus being balked, his gaze suddenly struck the lamp which had been put down close by the doorframe by one of the two of them, Bonny or himself—Durand could no longer remember which it was—on coming up the night before.

Again he died inwardly, as he'd been dying at successive intervals for the past half-hour or more. He'd chosen the wrong preventative; it should have been rats or dust.

"No light, you said?" Dollard exclaimed, brows peaked. "Why, here's a lamp right here. What's this?"

All he could stammer in a smothered voice was: "My wife must have set it there— There was none last time— I remember complaining—"

Dollard had already picked it up, hoisted the chimney. He struck a match to it, recapped it, and it glowered yellow; to Durand like the fuming, imprisoned apparition of a baleful genie, called into being to destroy him.

He thought, Shall I turn and run from the house? Shall I turn and run out through the door? Why do I stand here like this, looking over their shoulders, waiting for them to—? And badly as he wanted to turn and flee, he found he couldn't; his feet seemed to have adhered to the floor, he found he couldn't lift them.

Dollard had opened the cellarway door. He stepped through onto the small stage that topped the stairs, and then downward a step or two. A pale yellow wash from the lamp, like something alive, lapped treacherously ahead of him, down the rest of the steps, and over the flooring, and even up the cellar walls, but growing fainter and dimmer the greater its distance from him, until it finally lost all power to reveal.

He went down a step or two more, and stretching out his arm straight before him, slowly circled it around, so that it kindled all sides of the place, even if only transiently.

"There are built-in tubs," he said, "for the family's washing, and a water boiler that can be heated by wood to supply you with—"

He descended farther. He was now all but at the foot of the stairs. Mrs. Thayer had come out onto the stage above, was holding her skirts tipped from the ground as a precaution. Durand, his own breath roaring and drumming in his ears, was gripping the doorframe with both hands, one above the other, head and shoulders thrust forward around it.

Dollard extended his hand upward in her direction. "Would you care to come down farther?"

"I believe I can see it from here," Mrs. Thayer said.

To accommodate her, he reversed the lamp, swinging it back again the other way. As its reflected gleam coursed past the place, an oblong darker than the rest of the flooring, a patch, a foursquare stain or shadow, seemed to shoot out into its path, then recede again as the heart of the glow swept past. It was as sudden as though it had moved of its own accord; as mobile, due to the coursing-past of the lamp, as a darkling mat suddenly whisked out, then snatched back again. There, then gone again.

It sent a shock through him that congested his heart and threatened to burst it. And yet they seemed not to have seen it, or if they had, not to have known it for what it was. Their eyes hadn't been seeking it as his had, perhaps.

Dollard suddenly hoisted the lamp upward, so that it evened with his head, and peered forward. A little over from the place, though, not quite at it.

"Why, isn't that the rug from the upstairs room we were just speaking of?" He quitted the bottom steps, crossed toward it.

Again that deeper-tinted strip sidled forward, this time under his very feet. He stopped directly atop it, both feet planted on it, bending forward slightly toward the other object nearby that had his attention. "How does it come to be down here? Do you beat out your rugs in the cellar, Mr. Durand?"

Durand didn't utter a sound. He couldn't recall if there had been any blood marks on the rug. All he could think of was that.

Mrs. Thayer tactfully came to his aid.

"I do that myself at times. When it's raining outdoors one has to. In any case I'm sure Mr. Durand doesn't attend to that *himself*, in person." She smiled pacifyingly from one to the other of them.

"One can wait until after it's stopped raining," Dollard grumbled thickly in his throat. "Besides, it hasn't rained all week long, that I can recall—" But he didn't pursue the stricture any further for the present.

A second later Durand was watching him stoop to recover the rug in his arms, lift it furled as it was, and turn toward the stairs bearing it with him crosswise in front of him, to return it to where it belonged. He perhaps wanted to avoid contaminating it further by spreading it open on the dusty cellar floor.

But the light would be better upstairs. And Durand's breath was hot against the roof of his mouth, like something issuing from a brick oven. He couldn't have formed words even if he'd had any to produce. They drew back one on each side to give Dollard passage, Mrs. Thayer with a graceful little retraction, Durand with a vertiginous stagger that fortunately seemed to escape their notice, or if not, to be ascribed to no more than a masculine maladroitness in maneuvering in confined spaces.

Then they turned and followed the rug-bearer back to the rear sitting room, Durand paying his way with hand to wall, unseen, like a lame man.

"That could have waited, Mr. Dollard," the young matron said.

"I know, but I wanted you to see this room at its best."

Dollard gave the unsecured edge of the rug a fine upward fling, let it fall, paid it out, shuffling backward to give it its full spread on the floor.

Something flew out as he did so. Something small, indeterminate. The eye could catch its leap, but not make out what it was. The wooden flooring offside clicked with its relapse.

Dollard stooped and pinched with two fingers at a place where there was nothing to be seen. At least not from where the other two people in the room stood. Then he straightened with it, whatever it was, came toward Durand with it.

"This is yours, I presume," he said, looking him straight in the eye. "One of your collar buttons, Mr. Durand."

He thrust it with a little peck, point first, into Durand's reluctantly receptive palm, and the latter closed his fingers over it. It was warm yet from Dollard's hand, but to Durand it seemed to be warm yet from Downs's throat. It felt like the nail of a crucifix going straight through the flesh of his palm, and he almost expected to see a drop of blood come stealing through the tight crevice of his fingers.

"Mr. Thayer is always dropping them about our house," put in the friendly Mrs. Thayer, in an effort to salve what she took to be his mortification at this public exposure, in her presence, of one of the necessary fastenings of his intimate apparel. Thinking that men were like women in that respect, and that if some safety pin or other similar clasp had been lost from her own undergarb, she too might very well have had that look of consternation on her face and confusedly sought support from the back of a chair, as she saw him do now.

"Hnh!" grunted Dollard, as if to say: *I* don't; only a sloven does

But he returned to the rug, smoothing out its ripples now with strokes of his foot.

Durand thrust the token deep into his pocket. A burning sensation, coming through his clothes, stayed with it. He beheld them swayingly through thick-lensed, fear-strained eyes. He wondered if, to them, he appeared to sway, as they did to him. Apparently not, for their expressions showed no sudden attention nor undue concern whenever they were momentarily cast his way.

"I think I've shown you everything," Dollard said at last.

"Yes, I think you have," his prospective client agreed.

They sauntered now toward the front door, Durand like a wraith faltering beside them. He had the door at last to cling to, and any see-saw vagary of balance could be ascribed to the flux of its hinges.

Mrs. Thayer turned toward him, smiled. "Thank you very much; I hope we haven't disturbed you."

"Good day," said Dollard, with an economy of urbanity that, from his point of view, it would have been a waste to use on people who were about to cease being lessees of the property.

He escorted her down to the carriage, helped her in, talking assiduously the while in an effort to persuade her into concluding the transaction. He was just about to step in after her and drive off with her—to Durand's unutterable relief—when suddenly Bonny appeared, walking rapidly along the sidewalk, and turned in toward the house, glancing back toward them as she did so.

Durand widened the door, to admit her and close it after her, but she stopped there, blocking it.

"For God's sake," he said exhaustedly, "get in here—I'm half-dead."

"Just a moment," she said, immovable. "He can't rent this place unless we sign a release. Did you give him the keys yet?"

"No."

"Good," she said crisply. To his horror, she raised her arm and beckoned Dollard back. She even called out his name. "Mr. Dollard! Just a moment, if you will!"

"Don't call him back," pleaded Durand. "Let him go, let him go. What are you thinking of?"

"I know what I'm doing," she said firmly.

Durand, aghast, saw the agent reluctantly descend, come back toward them again. He chafed his hands propitiously. "I think I have the transaction concluded," he confided. "And at a considerably better figure. Her mind is all but made up."

The remark brought a shrewd glint of calculation into Bonny's eyes, Durand saw.

"Yes?" she said dulcetly. "But there are a couple of things you've forgotten, aren't there? The keys, and the signed release."

Dollard fumbled hastily for his pocket. "Oh, so I have. But I have the form right here on me, and if you'll give me the keys now, that will save me a trip back for them later—" He glanced around at the waiting carriage. He was as anxious to be off, or nearly so, as Durand was anxious to have him be.

Bonny, however, seemed to be in no hurry. She intercepted the paper, which Dollard had been extending toward Durand, and consulted it herself. She studiously ignored the mute, frantic appeal in Durand's dilated eyes. He mopped furtively at his forehead.

She raised her head; then with no sign of returning the paper to Dollard, tapped it questioningly against her arched pulse.

"And what of the unused portion of our rental fee? I see no mention here—"

"The unused—? I don't understand you."

She retained the paper against his tentatively extended hand seeking to reclaim it. "The rental for this month has already been paid."

"Naturally."

"But today is only the tenth. What of the three weeks we relinquish?"

"You forfeit that. I cannot return it to you once it has been paid."

"Very well," she said waspishly. "But then neither can you rent it to anyone else until after the thirtieth of the month. You had best go and tell the lady that, and spare her a disappointment."

Dollard's mouth dropped slack, astounded. "But you are not going to be here! You leave today. It was you yourself who came to me this morning to tell me so." He glanced helplessly at the carriage, where the waiting Mrs. Thayer was beginning to show ladylike signs of impatience. She looked over at him inquiringly, she coughed pantomimically—unheard at that distance—into the hollow of her hand. "Come, be reasonable, madam. You said yourself—"

Bonny was adamant. There was even a small smile etched into the corner of her mouth. Her eyes, as if guessing the surreptitious, agonized signs Durand was trying to convey to her from behind the turn of the agent's shoulder, refused to look across at him. "You be reasonable, Mr. Dollard. My husband and I are not going to make you a present of the greater part of a month's rental. Our departure can very well be postponed in such a case. Either you return it to us, or we stay until the first of the new month."

She deliberately turned and entered the hallway. She stopped before the mirror. In full view of Dollard, she raised hands to her bonnet, removed it. She adjusted her hair, to make sure it was not disturbed.

"Close the door, dear," she said to Durand. "And then come upstairs and help me unpack our things. Good day, sir," she added pointedly to Dollard.

The agent looked apprehensively at the carriage, to gauge how much longer he might dare keep it waiting. Then to her; she was now moving toward the stairs, as if about to ascend them. Then, more quickly, to the carriage. Then, more quickly still, to her once more. The carriage, at least, was standing still, but she wasn't.

At last he blundered into the house after her, past the—by this time—almost audibly moaning Durand. "Just a moment!" he capitulated. "Very well; seventy-five dollars by the month. I will give you the amount for the last two weeks. Thirty-seven, fifty."

Bonny turned, gave him a granite smile, shook her head. Then she continued, put her foot to the bottommost step, her hand to the newel-post. "Today is not the fifteenth of the month. Today is the tenth. We have had the use of this house for only one third of the time paid for. Therefore there is two thirds coming to us. Fifty dollars."

"Madam!" said Dollard, striking hand to his scalp, forgetful that there was no longer hair there to ruffle.

"Sir!" she echoed ironically.

A shadow darkened the open doorway behind the three of them and the coachman had appeared in it. "Excuse me, sir, but the lady says she can't wait any longer—"

"Here," said Dollard bitterly, grubbing money from his billfold, "Fifty dollars. Let me get out of here before you demand payment for having *lived* in the house at all!"

"Sign the paper, dearest," she said sweetly. "And give Mr. Dollard his keys. We must not detain him any longer."

Durand got the door closed behind the fuming figure. Then he all but collapsed against it on the inside. "How could you do it, knowing all the time what's lying under the very floor we—?" he gagged, tearing at his collar. "What have you for nerves, what have you for heart?"

She was standing on the stairs, triumphantly counting over the cabbagehead of money she held bunched in her hand.

"Ah, but *he* didn't know; and that's where the difference lay. You never played poker, did you, Lou?"

49

SHE LED the way down the railroad car aisle, he following, the railroad porter struggling along in the rear with their hand baggage, three or four pieces on each arm. She had the jaunty little stride of one who has been on trains a great deal, enjoys traveling, and knows just how to go about getting the most out of it.

"No, not there," she called back, when Durand had stopped tentatively beside one of the padded green-plush double seats. "Down here, on this side. You'll get the sun on you, on that side."

They moved on obediently to her bidding.

She stood by, supervising with attentive look, piece by piece, the disposing of their luggage to the rack overhead. Intervening once to counsel: "Put that lighter one on top of the other; the other one will crush it if you don't."

Then when he had finished: "Draw up the shade a little higher."

Durand gave her a quickly cautioning glance over the porter's bent back, implying they should not make themselves too conspicuous.

"Nonsense," she answered it aloud. "Draw it up a little more, porter. There, that will do." Then gestured benevolently toward Durand, to have him tip the man for his trouble.

She sidled into the seat, when it had been sufficiently readied, drawing out her skirts sideward and settling them about her comfortably. Durand inserted himself beside her, his face pale and strained, as though he were sitting on spikes.

She turned her head and began to survey the scene outside the window with enjoyable interest, bending the back of her hand to support her chin.

"How soon do they start?" she asked presently.

He didn't answer.

She must have been able to view his reflection on the pane of glass. Without turning her head, she said slurringly out of the corner of her mouth: "Don't take on so. People will think you are ill."

"I am," he shuddered, blowing into his hands as if to warm them. "I am."

Her little lace-mittened hand suddenly reached across his body, below cover of the seat top before them. "Take my hand, hold it for a moment. We'll be out of here before you know."

"Merciful God," he whispered, with furtively downcast eyes, "why don't they start, what are they waiting for?"

"Read something," she suggested in a low voice, "take your mind off it."

Read something, he thought despairingly, read something! He could not have joined the letters of a single word together to make sense.

A locomotive bell began to peal, somewhere up front, and then a steam whistle blew in shrill warning.

"There," she said reassuringly. "Now!"

There was a sudden preliminary jar, that set aquiver the row of oil lamps dangling from the deep-set trough bisecting the car ceiling, then a secondary, lesser one; then the train stuttered into creaking motion. The fixed scene outside became fluid, began to slip slowly onward past the limits of their window pane, while a new one continually flowed into it, without a break, at the opposite side. She released his hand, turned her full attention to it, as enthralled as a child.

"I love to be on the go," she remarked. "Anywhere, I don't care where it is."

A butcher made his way slowly down the aisle, basket over arm, crying his wares to add to the noisy confusion of grinding wheels, creaking woodwork, and hum of blended voices that filled the car.

"Here you are, ladies and gentlemen. Mineral water, fresh fruit, all kinds of delicious sweets for yourselves or your children. Caramellos, gumdrops, licorice lozenges. It'll be a long, dusty ride. Here you are. Here you are."

She suddenly whisked her head around from the window that had absorbed her until now. "Lou," she said vivaciously, "buy me an orange, I'm thirsty. I love to suck an orange whenever I'm riding on a train."

The vendor stopped at his reluctant signal.

She leaned across him, pawing, rummaging, in the basket. "No, that one over there. It's plumper."

Durand hoisted himself sideward on the seat, to be able to reach into his pocket and draw up some coins.

The butcher took one and moved on.

Suddenly he stared, stricken, at the residue he had been left holding. Downs's collar button lay within the palm of his hand.

"Oh, God!" he moaned, and cast it furtively under the seat they were on.

50

ANOTHER HOTEL room, in another place. And yet the same. The hotel had a different name, that was all. The scene its windows looked out upon had a different name, that was all.

But they were the same two, in the same hotel room. The same two people, the same two runaways.

This, he realized, watching her broodingly, was what their life was going to be like from now on. Another hotel room, and then another, and still another. But always the same. Another town, and then another, and still another. Onward, and onward, and onward— to nowhere. Until some day they would come to their last hotel room, in their last town. And then—

A short life and an exciting one, she had toasted that night back in Mobile. She had it wrong. A short life and a dull one, she should have said. No pattern of security can ever be so wearyingly repetitious as the pattern of the refugee without a refuge. No monotony of law-abidance can ever compare to the monotony of crime. He had found that out by now.

She was sitting there in a square of orange-gold sunlight by the window, one leg crossed atop the other, head bent intently to her task. Which was that of tapering her nails with an emery board.

Her arms were bare to the shoulders, and the numerous all-white garments she wore were not meant to be seen by other eyes than his. The moulded cuirass of the corset was visible in its entirety, from underarms to well below the hips. And over this only the thinnest film of cambric, an in-between garment, neither under- nor over-, known as the "corset-cover" (he had learned), fell short at the unwonted height of her lower calf.

Her hair was unbound and fell loose, clothing her back in rippling finespun tawny-gold, but at the same time giving the top of her head an oddly flat aspect, ordinarily seen only on young schoolgirls. The bangs alone remained in evidence, of the customary coiffure.

One of the spikelike cigars was burning untouched on the dresser edge near her.

She felt his long-maintained, speculative look, and raised her eyes, and gave him that compressed, heart-shaped smile that was the only design her lips could fall into when expressing a smile.

"Cheer up, Lou," she said. "Cheer up, lovey."

She hitched her head pertly to indicate the scene beyond the sun-flooded window. "I like it here. It's pretty here. And they dress up to kill. I'm glad we came."

"Don't sit so close to the window. You can be seen."

She gave him an incredulous look. "Why, no one knows us here."

"I don't mean *that*. You're in your underthings."

"Oh," she said. Then, as if still not wholly able to comprehend his punctiliousness on this point, "But they can only see my back. Not one can see my face, tell *whose* back it is." She moved her chair a trifle, condescendingly, with a smile as if she were doing it simply to please him.

She went back to her nails for a complacent stroke or two.

"Don't you—think of it sometimes?" he couldn't resist blurting out. "Doesn't it weigh upon you?"

"What?" she said blankly, again looking up. "Oh—that, back there."

"That's what I mean," he said. "If I could only forget it, as you do."

"I don't forget it. It's just that I don't brood about it."

"But the very act of remembering at all, isn't that the same as brooding?"

"No," she said, flipping her hands outward in surprise. "Let me show you." She tapped the rim of her teeth, as if in search of an illustration. "Say I buy a new hat. Well, once it's bought, it's bought, and there's no more to it. I *remember* I bought the hat; it's not that I forget I've bought it. But I don't necessarily brood about it, dwell on it, every minute of the live-long day." She pounded one clenched hand into the hollow of the other. "I don't keep saying over and over: 'I've bought a hat,' 'I've bought a hat,' 'I've bought a hat.' Do you see?"

He was looking at her with a stunned expression. "You—you compare what happened that day at Mobile with buying a new hat?" he stammered.

She laughed. "No. Now you're twisting it around; making me out worse than I am. I know it's not punishable to buy a new hat, and the other thing is. I know you don't have to be afraid of anyone finding out you've bought a new hat, and you do of anyone finding out you've done the other thing. But that was just given for an example. You can remember a thing perfectly well, but you don't have to worry about it all the time, let it darken your life. That's all I mean."

But he was speechless; he still couldn't get past that horrendous illustration of hers.

She rose and moved over toward him slowly; stood at last, and looked down, and let her hand come to rest on his shoulder, with almost a patronizing air. Certainly not one of overweening admiration.

"Do you want to know what the trouble is, Lou? I'll tell you. The difference between you and me is *not* that I'm any less afraid than you of its being found out; I'm just as afraid. It's that you let your conscience bully you about it, and I don't. You make it a matter of good or bad, wrong or right; you know, like children's Sunday school lessons: going to heaven or going to hell. With me it's just something that happened, and there's no more to be said. You keep wishing you could go back and have it over again, so that you wouldn't have done it. That's where the trouble comes in. It's that your own conscience is nagging you. That's what's ailing you."

She saw that she'd shocked him. She shrugged a little, and turned away. She took up a muslin petticoat that lay in wait folded over the side of the bed, flung it out so that its folds opened circularly,

stepped into it, and fastened it about her waist. The grotesque short-
ness of her attire disappeared, and her extremities were once more
normally covered to the floor.

"Take my advice, and learn to look at it my way, Lou," she
went on. "You'll find it a lot simpler. It's not something good, and
it's not something bad; it's—" here she made him the concession of
dropping her voice a trifle, "—just something you have to be careful about, that's all."

She took up a second petticoat, this one of taffeta bordered with
lace, and donned that over the first.

He was appalled at the slow, frightening discovery he was in the
process of making: which was that she had no moral sense at all.
She was, in a very actual meaning of the word, a complete savage.

"Shall we go for a little stroll?" she suggested. "It's an ideal day
for it."

He nodded, lips parted, unable to articulate.

She was now turning this way and that before the glass, holding
up a succession of outer costumes at shoulder level to judge of their
desirability. "Which shall I wear? The blue? The fawn? Or this
plaid?" She made a little pouting grimace. "I've worn them all two
or three times now apiece. People will begin to know them. Lou,
fetch out that money box of yours before we go, that's a good boy.
I really think it's time you were buying me a new dress."

No moral sense at all.

51

THE DISCOVERY was catastrophically sudden, though it shouldn't have
been. One moment, they were affluent, he could afford to give her
anything she wanted. The next, they were destitute, they could
scarcely meet the cost of the immediate evening's pleasure they had
contemplated.

It shouldn't have been as unforeseen as all that, he had to admit to himself; shouldn't have taken them unaware like that. There had been no theft, save at his own hands; nothing like that. But there had been no replenishment either. A vanishing point was bound to be reached eventually. It had been imminent for some time, if he'd only taken the trouble to make inventory. But he hadn't; perhaps he'd been afraid to, afraid in his own mind of the too-exact knowledge that he would have derived from such a summing up: the certainty of termination. Afraid of the chill that would have been cast upon their feasting, the shadow that would have dimmed their wine. There was always tomorrow, tomorrow, to make reckoning. And tomorrow, there was always tomorrow still. And meanwhile the music swelled, and the waltz whirled ever faster, giving no pause for breath.

He'd delved in each time, in haste, in negligence, without counting what was over. So long as there was something left, that was all that mattered. Something that would take care of the next time. And now that next time was the last time, and there was no next time beyond.

They'd been about to go out for the evening, swirls of sachet fanning out behind her like an invisible white peacock's tail spread in flaunting gorgeousness, an electric tide of departure crackling about them, she stuffing frothy laced handkerchief within the collar of her gloves, he lingering behind a moment to pluck out gas jet after gas jet. She was sibilant in tangerine taffeta, flounced with bands of brown sealskin, orange willow plumes snaking like live tentacles upon her hat. She was already in the open doorway, thirsting to be gone, waiting a moment to allow him to overtake her and close the door after them, and grudging that moment's wait.

"Have you enough money with you, lovey?" she asked companionably. And somehow made it sound entrancingly domestic; a wife being solicitous of her husband's welfare, much as if she'd said "Are you warmly enough dressed?" or "Have you brought the latch key with you?"; though its ends were not domestic at all, but quite the reverse.

He consulted his money-fold.

"No, glad you reminded me," he said. "I'll have to get some more. I'll only be a moment, I won't keep you."

"I don't mind," she assented graciously. "When you enter late, everyone has a better chance to take in what you're wearing."

She was still there by the door, idly tapping the furled sticks of her small dress-fan, secured by silken loop about her wrist, upon the opposite recipient palm, when he returned from the bedroom where he had gone.

When she saw him coming, she dipped her knees a graceful trifle, caught higher the spreading bottom of her dress, and reached behind her to grasp the doorknob, prepared to go, this time offering to close the door for him instead of him for her.

Then she saw his gait had changed, was hesitant, expiring, not as it had been when he went briskly in.

"What is it? Something wrong?"

He was holding two single bank notes in his hand, half extending them before him, as though not knowing what to do with them.

"This is all that's left. This is all there is," he said stupidly.

"You mean it's missing, been taken?"

"No, we've used it all. We must have, but I didn't know it. I could see it growing slimmer, but—I should have looked more closely. Each time I'd just reach in and— There always seemed to be some over. I didn't know until this moment that—this was all it was—" He raised it helplessly, lowered it again.

He stood there without moving, looking at her now, not it, as if she could give him the answer he could not find for himself. She returned his look, but she said nothing. There was silence between them.

Her lips had parted, but in some sort of inward appraisal; they said no word. A little breath came through, in a soft, wordless "Oh" of understanding.

Her hand left the doorknob at last, and dropped down to its own level, against her side, with a little inert slap of frustration.

"What shall we do?" she said.

He didn't answer.

"Does that mean we—can't go now?"

He looked at her, still without answering. Surveyed her entire person, from head to toe. Saw how beautifully she'd arrayed herself, how perfect in every detail the finished artistic picture she was offering for presentation. Or rather, had intended to offer, if given opportunity.

Suddenly he swerved, reached purposefully—and defiantly—for his hat.

"I'll ask for credit. We've spent enough by now, wherever it is we've gone; they should give us that."

It was now she who didn't move, remained poised there by the door. She looked thoughtfully downward at nothing there was to be seen. At last she shook her head slightly, a smile without mirth influencing her lips. "No," she said. "It's not the same. It would cast a pall, now, just knowing. And then they treat you with less respect, when you ask them. Or they commence to hound you within a few days, and you're twice as badly off as before."

She came away from the door. She closed it at last, but now before, and not behind, her. And she gave it a sort of fling away from her, in doing so; let it carry itself to its proper junction. He tried to make out if there was ill temper lurking in the gesture, and couldn't tell for sure. It might have been nothing more than jaunty disregard, an attempt to show him she didn't care whether she stayed or went. But even if there *was* no ill temper in it, the thought of ill temper was in his mind. So it had already appeared on the scene, in a way.

He watched her return, with indolent gait, to the seat before the mirror that she had occupied for the better part of an hour only just now. But now she gave her back to the glass, not her face. Now the former process was reversed. Now she rid herself, one by one, with limp gesture, of the accessories she had so zestfully attached to herself only a brief while ago. Her gloves fell, stringy, over her shoulder on the dressing table. Her untried fan atop them a moment later, its stylized, beguiling usage never given a chance to go into effect. Off came the tiny hat with orange willow feathers, she pitched it from her broadside (but not with violence, with philosophic riddance), and it fell upon the seat of a nearby chair. The plume tendrils fluctuated above it for a moment, like ocean-bottom vegetation stirring in deep water, then settled down over it.

"You may as well turn up the gas jets again," she said dully, "as long as we're staying in."

She raised her feet, heels upward, one by one, and taking them from behind, plucked off the bronze satin slippers with their spool-shaped Louis XV heels, full three inches in length, a daring height but pardonable because of her own stature. And let them fall as they would, and set her stockinged soles back on the floor as they were.

And last of all, undoing some certain something behind her, she allowed her dress to widen and fall of its own looseness, but only down to her seated waist, and sat that way, half-in and half-out of it, in perfect disarray. Almost as if to make a point of it.

It did something to him, to watch her undo that completed work of art she had so deftly and so painstakingly achieved. More than any spoken reproaches could have, it implicitly rebuked him.

Hands grounded in pockets, he looked down at the floor and felt small and humbled.

She took off the string of pearls that had clasped her throat and, allowing them to drizzle together, tossed them in air as if weighing them and finding them wanting, caught them in her palm.

"Will these help? You can have them if they will."

His face whitened, as if with some deep inward incision. "Bonny!" he commanded her tautly. "Don't ever say anything like that to me again."

"I meant nothing by it," she said placatingly. "You paid better than a hundred for them, didn't you? I only thought—"

"When I buy you a thing, it's yours."

They were silent for a while, their lines of gaze in opposite directions. He looking toward the window, and the impersonal, aloof evening outside. She toward the door, and (perhaps) the beckoning evening outside that.

She lit a cigar after a while. Then said in immediate compunction, "Oh, I forgot. You don't like me to do that." And turned to discard it.

"Don't put it out," he said absently. "Finish it if you like."

She extinguished it nevertheless.

Turning back, she reared one knee high before her, clasped her hands about it, settled comfortably backward. Then instantly, and again with contrition, she dissolved the pose once more. "Oh, I forgot. You don't like me to do that either."

"That was before, when you were supposed to be Julia," he said. "It's different now."

Suddenly he looked at her with redoubled closeness, as if wondering belatedly if this was some new indirect way of chiding him: reminding him of his past criticism of *her* faults. Her face seemed plotless enough, however. She didn't even seem to see him looking at her. The edges of her trivial mouth were curved upward in placid contentment.

"I'm sorry, Bonny," he said at last.

She returned her attention to him, from wherever it had strayed. "I don't mind," she said evenly. "I've had this happen to me before. For you, it's your first time; that makes it hard."

"You haven't had any supper," he said presently. "And it's nearing eight."

"That's right," she agreed cheerfully. "We can still eat. Can't we?"

Again he wondered if that was an indirect jibe; again it seemed to be only in his mind. But at least it *was* there in his mind; it must have come from somewhere.

She got up and went over to the wall and took down the pneumatic speaking-tube. She blew through the orifice and a whistling sound went traveling far downward, to its destination below.

"Will you send up a waiter," she said. "We're in Suite 12."

When the man had arrived, she ordered, taking precedence over Durand.

"Bring us something *small*," she said. "We're not very hungry. A mutton chop apiece would do very nicely. No soup, no sweet—"

Again Durand's eyes sought out her face to see if that was meant for him, that ironic emphasis. But hers were not to be met.

"Will that be all, madam?"

"And, oh yes, one thing more. Bring us up a deck of cards, along with the tray. We're staying in this evening."

"What'd you want those for?" Durand asked, as soon as the door had closed.

She turned to him and smiled quite sweetly. "To play double solitaire," she said. "I'll teach you the game. There's nothing like it for passing the time."

His reaction didn't come at once. It was slow, it didn't materialize for some four or five minutes.

Then suddenly he picked up a bisque ornament from the center table and heaved it with all his strength, mouth knotted, and shattered it against the wall opposite him.

She must have been used to violence. She scarcely turned a hair, her eyelids barely rose enough to let her see what it had been.

"They'll charge us for that, Lou. We can't afford it now."

"I'm going to New Orleans tomorrow," he said, thick-voiced with truculence. "I'm taking the first train out. You wait for me here.

I'll have money for you again, you'll see. I'll raise it from Jardine."

Her eyes were wider open now, but whether any deeper with concern, could not have been told. "No!" she said aghast. "You can't go
near there. You mustn't. We're wanted. They'll catch you."

"Rather that than go on here this way, living like a dog."

Now she smiled a real smile, beaming-bright; no sweet pale copy
like a stencil on her lips. "That's my Lou," she purred, velvet smooth,
her voice velvet warm. "That was the right answer. I love a man
that takes chances."

52

JARDINE LIVED on Esplanade Avenue. Durand remembered the house
well. He'd had dinner with them there on many a Sunday night during his bachelor days, and been honorary "uncle" to Jardine's little
girl Marie.

The house had not changed. It was not houses that changed, he
reflected ruefully, it was men. It was still honest, amiable, open of
countenance. He might have been standing before it again back two
or three years ago, with a little bag of bonbons in his hand for Marie.
But he wasn't.

He stood there after he'd knocked, and kept holding his handkerchief to his nose, as if he were suffering from a bad head cold. It
was to hide as much of his features as possible, however. And even
while doing so, it occurred to him how futile such precautions were.
Anyone who knew him by sight at all, would know him as well from
the back, without seeing his face.

Before the door had opened he had already given up the attempt,
lowered and pocketed the handkerchief.

They still had the same colored woman he remembered, Nelly, to
open their door.

At sight of him her face lit up and her palms backed to shoulders.

"Well, lookit who's here! Well, I declare! Why, Mr. Lou! You *sure* a stranger!"

He smiled sheepishly, glanced uneasily down the street.

"Is Mr. Allan back from his office yet?"

"Why, no sir. But come in anyway. He'll be along right smart. Miss Gusta, she's home. And young Miss Marie. They'll both be mighty pleased to see you, I know."

He went in past the threshold, then faltered there. "Nelly, don't —don't tell them I'm calling—just yet; I have to see Mr. Allan on business first. Just let me wait down here somewhere until he comes home, without saying anything—" He caught himself winding the brim of his hat around in his hands, like a suppliant, and quickly stopped it.

Nelly's face dropped reproachfully.

"You don't want me to tell Miss Gusta you drap in?"

"Not just yet. I have to see Mr. Allan alone first."

"Well, come in the parlor, sir, and make yourself comf'table. I light the lamp." Her effusiveness was gone. She was a little cooler now. "Take your hat?"

"No, thanks; I'll keep it."

"You wants anything while you waiting, you just ring for me, Mr. Lou."

"I'll be all right."

She gave him a backward glance from the doorway, then she went out.

He was on thin ice, he realized. Any one of them, even Jardine himself, might have heard about it, could denounce his presence here, effect his immediate arrest. He was at their mercy; he was putting his trust where he had no certainty it could be put. Friendship? Yes, for an ordinary man, of their own kind. But friendship for a man branded a murderer? Those were two different matters, not the same thing at all.

He could hear a well-remembered woman's voice call down ringingly from somewhere above-stairs: "Who was that, Nelly?"

And at the momentary hesitation on Nelly's part, he involuntarily tightened his grip on his still nervously circling hat brim, held it arrested a moment.

"Gentleman to see Mr. Jardine on business."

"Did he wait?"

Nelly adroitly got around the problem of telling an outright lie. "I told him he not in yet."

The upstairs voice, still audible but no longer in as high a key, as if now pitched to someone else on the same floor with her, was heard to remark: "How strange to come here instead of to your papa's office." After which it withdrew, and there was no further colloquy.

Durand sat there in the glowing effulgence of the parlor, staring as if spellbound at a small handpainted periwinkle on the surface of the lamp globe, which seemed to hang suspended between himself and the white sheen that came translucently through all around it.

This is home, he thought. Nothing ever happens here, nothing bad. You come home to it with impunity, you go out again with immunity, you turn your face openly toward the world. And murder—human death brought about by the act of human hands—that is something in the Bible, in the history books, something done by the captains and the kings of old. In the passages that you perhaps skip over, when you are reading aloud to your children. Cortez and the Borgias and the Medici; poinards and poisons, long ago and faraway. But not in the full light of nineteenth-century day, in your own personal life.

This should be my home, he thought. I mean, my home should be like this man's. Why was I robbed of this? What did I do that was wrong?

Again the woman's voice came, upstairs, calling with pleasant firmness from one room to the next: "Marie. Your hair, dear, and your hands. It's getting near the time for Papa to come home."

And a younger, higher voice in answer: "Yes, Mamma. Shall I wear a ribbon in my hair tonight? Papa likes me to."

And below, sensuously drifting from the back somewhere, intermittent whiffs of rice and greens and savory frying fat.

This was all I wanted, he thought. Why have I lost it? Why was it taken from me? All other men have it. How did I offend? *Who* did I offend?

Jardine's key clicked in the door, and he swung around alertly in his chair, to face the open doorway, to be ready when he should appear beyond it, on his way through.

There was the tap of his stick going down to rest, and a little drumlike thump as his hat found a prong on the rack.

Then he appeared, facing stairward toward his family, unbuttoning the thigh-length mustard-colored coat he wore.

"Allan," Durand said in a circumspect voice, "I have to talk to you. Can you give me a few minutes? I mean before—before the family?"

Jardine turned abruptly, and saw him there for the first time. He came striding in, outstretched arm first, to shake his hand, but his face had already been sobered, made anxious, by Durand's opening remark.

"What are you *doing* here like this? When did you come back? Does Auguste know you're here? Why do they leave you sitting alone like this?"

"I asked Nelly not to say anything. I must talk to you alone first."

Jardine pulled a velour tape ending in a thin brass ring. Then went back to the open doorway, looked out, and when she had come in answer to the summons, said with a bruffness that betokened his uneasiness: "Hold supper a few minutes, Nelly."

"Yes sir. Only I hope you two gentlemen'll bear in mind it don't git no tastier with holding."

Jardine spread out his arms and drew together the two sliding doors that sealed off the parlor. Then he came back and stood looking at Durand questioningly.

"Look, Allan, I don't know how to begin—"

Jardine shook his head, as if in dissatisfaction at the condition he found him in. "Would a drink help, Lou?"

"Yes, I think it would."

Jardine poured them, and they each drank.

Again he stood there, looking down at him in the chair.

"There's something wrong, Lou."

"Very much so."

"Where did you go? Where've you been all this time? Not a word to me. I haven't known whether you're dead or alive—"

Durand stemmed the flow of questions with a half-hearted lift of his hand.

"I'm with her again," he said after a moment. "I can't come back to New Orleans. Don't ask me why. That isn't what I came here about." Then he added, "Haven't you seen anything in the papers, that would explain it to you?"

"No," Jardine said, mystified. "I don't know what you mean."

Hasn't he, Durand wondered. Doesn't he really know? Is he telling the truth? Or is he too delicate, too considerate, to tell me—

Jardine consulted his glass, drained the last drop, said: "I don't want to know anything you don't want to tell me, Lou. Each man's life is his own."

Downs's was his own too, passed through Durand's mind; until I—

"Well, then we'll come to the point that brings me here," he said, with a briskness he was far from feeling. He turned around in the chair to face him once more. "Allan, how much would the business bring as it stands today? I mean, what would be a fair price for it, if someone were to come along and—"

Jardine's face paled. "You're thinking of selling, Lou?"

"I'm thinking of selling, Allan, yes. To you, if you'll buy out my share from me. Will you? Can you?"

Jardine seemed incapable of answering immediately. He started walking slowly back and forth, on a short straight course beside the chair Durand sat in. He clasped his arms. Then presently he locked hands over his two rear pockets, and let the skirt of his coat flounce down over them.

"You may as well know this now, before we go any further," Durand added. "I can't sell to anyone else *but* you. I can't put in an appearance to do so. I can't approach anyone else. The lawyer will have to come here to your house. The whole thing will have to be done quietly."

"At least wait a day or two," Jardine urged. "Think it over—"

"I *haven't* a day or two in which to wait!" Durand slowly wagged his head from side to side in exasperated impatience. "Can't you understand? Must I tell you openly?"

In a moment more, he cautioned himself, it will be too late; once I have told him, I will be completely at his mercy. What I am asking him to buy from me, would go to him by default anyway; all he would have to do is step over to that bellpull over there—

But he went ahead and told him anyway, with scarcely the pause required by the warning thought to deliver its admonition.

"I'm a fugitive, Allan. I'm outside the law. I've lost all my rights of citizenship."

Jardine stopped his pacing, stunned. "Great God!" he breathed slowly.

Durand slapped at his own thigh, with a sort of angry despair. "It's got to be right tonight. Right now. It can't wait. *I* can't. I'm taking a risk even staying in the town that long—"

Jardine bent toward him, took him by the shoulders, gripped hard. "You're throwing away your whole future, your whole life's work—I can't let you—"

"I have no future, Allan. Not a very long one. And my life's work, I'm afraid, is behind me, anyway, whether I sell or not."

He let his wrists dangle limp, down between his legs, in a cowed attitude. "What are we going to do, Allan?" he murmured abjectly. "Are you going to help me?"

There was a tapping at the door. Then a childish voice: "Papa. Mamma wants to know if you're going to be much longer. The duck's getting awfully dry. Nelly can't do a thing with it."

"Soon, dear, soon," Jardine called over his shoulder.

"Go in to your family," Durand urged. "I'm spoiling your supper. I'll sit in here and wait."

"I couldn't eat with this on my mind," Jardine said. He bent to him once more, as if in renewed effort to extract the confidence from him that he sought. "Look, Lou. We've known each other since you were twenty-three and I was twenty-eight. Since we were clerks together in the shipping department of old man Morel, perched on adjoining stools, slaving away. We got our promotions together. When he wanted to promote you, you spoke for me. When he wanted to promote me, I spoke for you. Finally, when we were ready, we pooled our resources and entered into business together. Our own import house. On a shoestring at first, even with the help of the money Auguste had brought to me in marriage. And you remember those early days."

"I remember, Allan."

"But we didn't care. We said we'd rather work for ourselves, and fail, than work for another man, and prosper. And we worked for ourselves—and prospered. But there are things in this business of ours, today, that cannot be taken out again. There is sweat, and worry, and the high hopes of two young fellows, and the prime years of their lives. Now you come to me and want to *buy* these things from me, want me to *sell* them to you, as if they were sackfuls of our green beans from Colombia— How can I, even if I wanted to? How can I set a price?"

"You can tell what the business is worth, in cold cash, that is on our books. And give me half, in exchange for a quit-claim, a deed of sale, whatever the necessary paper is. Forget I am Durand. I am just anybody, I am a stranger who happens to have a fifty per cent interest. Give its approximate value back to me in money, that is all I ask you." He gestured violently. "Don't you see, Allan? I can no longer participate in the business, I can no longer play any part in it. I can't *be* here to do so, I can't *stay* here."

"But why? There isn't anything you can have done—"

"There is. There's one thing."

Jardine was waiting, looking at him fixedly.

"Once I tell you, Allan, I'm at your mercy. You needn't give me a cent, and my half of the business goes to you, eventually, anyway—by default."

But he was at his mercy anyway, he realized ruefully, whether he told him or not.

Jardine bridled a little, straightened up. "Lou, I don't take that kindly. We're friends—"

"Friendship stops short at what I'm about to tell you. There are no friends beyond a certain point. The law even forbids it, punishes it."

The tapping came again. "Mamma's getting put out. She says she's going to sit down without you, Papa. It was a special duck—"

And on that homespun domestic note, Durand blurted out, as if already past the point at which he could any longer stop himself:

"Allan, I've done murder. I can't stay here past tonight. I have to have money."

And dropped his head into his upturned, sheltering hands, as though the hangman's noose had already snapped his neck.

"Papa?" came questioningly through the door.

"Wait, child, wait," Jardine said sickly, his face white as a sheet. There was a ghastly silence.

"I knew it would come to this," Jardine said at last, dropping his voice. "She was bad for you from the first. Auguste sensed it on the very day of your marriage, she told me so herself; women are quicker that way—"

He was pouring himself a drink, as though it were his crime. "You met her— You found her— You lost your head—" He brought one to Durand. "But you're not to be blamed. Any man— Let me find you a good lawyer, Lou. There isn't a court in the state—"

Durand looked up at him and gave a pathetic smile.

"You don't understand, Allan. It isn't—she. It's the very man I engaged to find her and arrest her. He did find her, and to save her I—"

Jardine, doubly horrified now, for at least in his earlier concern there had been, noticeably, a glint of vengeful satisfaction, recoiled a step.

"I'm with her again," Durand admitted. And in an almost inaudible whisper, as if he were telling it to his conscience and not to the other man in the room with him, "I love her more than my life itself."

"Papa," accosted them with frightening proximity, in a piping treble, "Mamma said I shouldn't leave this door until you come out of there!" The doorknob twisted, then unwound.

Jardine stood for a long moment, looking not so much at his friend as at some scene he alone could see.

His arm reached out slowly at last and fell heavily, dejectedly, but with unspoken loyalty, upon Durand's shoulder.

"I'll see that you get your half of the business' assets, Lou," he said. "And now—we mustn't keep Auguste waiting any longer. Keep a stiff upper lip. Come in and have supper with us."

Durand rose and crushed Jardine's hand almost shatteringly for a moment, between both of his. Then, as if ashamed of this involuntary display of emotion, hastily released it again.

Jardine opened the door, bent down to kiss someone who remained unseen, through the guarded opening. "Run in, dear. We're coming."

Durand braced himself for the ordeal to come, straightened his shoulders, jerked at the wings of his coat, adjusted his collar. Then he moved after his host.

"You won't tell them, Allan?"

Jardine drew the door back and stood aside to let him go through first. "There are certain things a man doesn't take in to his supper-table with him, Lou." And he slung his arm about his friend's shoulder and walked beside him, loyally beside him, in to where his family waited.

53

AT DAWN he was already up, from a sleepless, worried bed, and dressed and pacing the floor of his shabby, hidden-away hotel room. Waiting for Jardine to come with the money—

("I can't get you the money before morning, Lou. I haven't it here in the house; I'll have to draw it from the bank. Can you wait?"

"I'll have to. I'm at the Palmetto Hotel. Under the name of Castle. Room Sixty. Bring it to me there. Or as much of it as you can, I cannot wait for a complete inventory.")

—fearing more and more with the passing of each wracking hour that he wouldn't. Until, as the hour for the banks to open came and went, and the morning drew on, fear had become certainty and certainty had become conviction. And he knew that to wait on was only to invite the inevitable betrayal to overtake him, trap him where he was.

A hundred times he unlocked the door and listened in the dingy corridor outside, then went back and locked himself in again. Nothing, no one. He wasn't coming. Only a quixotic fool would have expected him to.

Again it occurred to him how completely at the mercy of his former partner he had put himself. All he had to do was bring the police with him instead of the money, and there was an end to it. Why should he give up thousands of hard-earned dollars? And money, Durand reminded himself, did strange things to people. Turned them even against their own flesh and blood, why not an outsider?

Bonny's remark came back to him. "And we're none of us very much good, the best of us, men or women alike." She knew. She was wise in the ways of the world, wiser by far than he. She would never have put herself in such a false position.

No friend should be put to such a test. A man without the law no longer had a claim, no longer had a right to expect—

There was a subdued knock, and he shrank back against the wall. "Here they come now to arrest me," flashed through his mind. "He's put them onto me—"

He didn't move. The knock came again.

Then Jardine's whispered voice. "Lou. Are you in there? It's all right. It's me."

He'd brought them with him; he'd led them here in person.

With a sort of bitter defiance, because he could no longer escape, because he'd waited too long, he went to the door and unlocked it. Then took his hands from it and let it be.

There was a moment's wait, then it opened of itself, and Jardine came in, alone. He closed and relocked it behind him. He was holding a small satchel.

He carried it to the table, set it down.

All he said, matter of factly and with utter simplicity, was: "Here is the money, Lou. I'm sorry I'm so late."

Durand couldn't answer for a moment, turned away, overcome.

"What's the matter, Lou? Why, your eyes—!" Jardine looked at him as though he couldn't understand what was amiss with him.

Durand knuckled at them sheepishly. "Nothing. Only, you came as you said you would—You brought it as you said you would—" Something choked in his throat and he couldn't go ahead.

Jardine looked at him compassionately. "Once you would have taken such a thing for granted, you would have expected it of me. What has changed you, Lou? *Who* has changed you?" And softly, fiercely, through his clenched teeth, as his knotted hand came down implacably upon the table top, he exhaled: "And may God damn them for it! I hate to see a decent man dragged down into the gutter."

Durand stood there without answering.

"You know it's true, or else you wouldn't stand there and take it from me," Jardine growled. "But I'll say no more; each man's hell is his own."

(I know it's true, Durand thought wistfully; but I must follow my heart, how can I help where it leads me?) "No, don't say any more," he agreed tersely.

Jardine unstrapped and stripped open the bag. "The full amount is in here," he told him, brisk and businesslike now. "And that squares all accounts between us."

Durand nodded stonily.

"I cannot have you at my house again," Jardine told him. "For your own sake."

Durand gave a short, and somewhat ungracious, syllable of laughter. "I understand."

"No, you don't. I am trying to protect you. Auguste already suspects something, and I cannot vouch for her discretion if you return."

"Auguste hates me, doesn't she?" Durand said with detached curiosity, as though unable to account for it.

Jardine didn't answer, and by that confirmed the statement.

He gestured toward the contents of the satchel, still withholding it. "I turn this over to you under one condition, Lou. I ask it of you for your own good."

"What is it?"

"Don't turn this money over to anyone else, *no matter how close they are to you*. Keep it safe. Keep it by you. Don't let it out of your possession."

Durand laughed humorlessly. "Who am I likely to entrust it to? The very position I'm in ensures my not—"

Jardine repeated his emphasis, so that there could be no mistaking it. "I said, *no matter how close they are to you*."

Durand looked at him hard for a minute. "I'm in good hands, I see," he said bitterly at last. "Auguste hates me, and you hate— my wife."

"Your wife," Jardine said tonelessly.

Durand tightened his hands. "I said my wife."

"Don't let's quarrel, Lou. Your word."

"The word of a murderer?"

"The word of the man who was my best friend. The word of the man who was Louis Durand," Jardine said tautly. "That's good enough for me."

"Very well, I give it."

Jardine handed him the satchel. "I'll go now."

There was a constraint between them now. Jardine offered his hand in parting. Durand saw it waiting there, allowed a full moment to go by before taking it. Then when at last they shook, it was more under compulsion of past friendship than present cordiality.

"This is probably a final goodbye, Lou. I doubt we'll ever see one another again."

Durand dropped his eyes sullenly. "Let's not linger over it, then. Good luck, and thank you for having once been my friend."

"I am still your friend, Lou."

"But I am not the man whose friend you were."

Their hands uncoupled, fell away from one another.

Jardine moved toward the door.

"You know what I would do in your place, of course? I would go to the police, surrender myself, and have it over once and for all."

"And hang," Durand said sombrely.

"Yes, even to hang is better than what lies ahead of you. You could be helped, Lou. This way, no one can help you. If I were in your place—"

"You *couldn't* be in my place," Durand cut him short. "It wouldn't have happened to you, to start with. You are not the kind such things befall. I am. You repel them. I attract them. It happened to me. To no one but me. And so I must deal with it. I must do—as I must do."

"Yes, I guess you must," Jardine conceded sadly. "None of us can talk for the other man." He opened the door, looking up along its edge with a sort of melancholy curiosity, as if he had never seen the edge of an open door before. He even palmed it, in passing, as if to feel what it was.

The last thing he said was: "Take care of yourself, Lou."

"If I don't, who else will?" Durand answered from the depths of his aloneness. "Who is there in this whole wide world who will?"

54

HE ONLY breathed freely again when the train had pulled out, and only looked freely from the window again when the last vestiges of the town had fallen behind and the dreary coastal sand flats had begun. The town that he had once loved most of all places in this world.

The train was a rickety, caterpillar-like creeper, that stopped at every crossroads shed and water tank along the way, or so it seemed, and didn't deposit him at his destination until well onto one in the morning. He found the station vicinity deserted, and all but unlighted; carriageless as well, and had to walk back to their hotel bag in hand, under a panel of brittle (and somehow satiric) stars.

And though the thought of surprising her in some act of treachery had not been the motive for his arriving a half night sooner than he'd said he would, the realization of how fatally enlightening this unheralded return could very well prove to be, slowly grew on him as he walked along, until it had taken hold of him altogether. By the time he had reached the hotel and climbed to their floor and stood before their door, he was almost afraid to take his key to it and open it. Afraid of what he would find. Not afraid of conventional faithlessness so much as her own characteristic kind of faithlessness. Not afraid of finding her in other arms so much as not finding her there at all. Finding her fled and gone in his absence, as he had once before.

He opened softly, and he held his breath back. The room was dark, and the fragrance of violets that greeted him meant nothing, it could have been from yesterday as well as from today. Besides, it was in his heart rather than in his nostrils, so it was no true test.

He took out a little box of wax matches, that clicked and rattled with his trepidation, felt for the sandpaper tab fastened to the wall, and kindled the lamp wick. Then turned to look, as the slow-rising golden tide washed away night.

She was sleeping like a child, as innocent as one, as beautiful as one. (And only in sleep perhaps could she ever obtain such innocence any longer). And as gracefully, as artlessly disposed, as a child. Her hair flooded the pillow, as if her head were lying in the middle of a field of slanting sun-yellowed grass. One arm was hidden, the dimpled point of an elbow protruding from under the pillow all that could be seen of it. The other lay athwart her, to hang straight down over the side of the bed. Its thumb and forefinger were still touching together, making an irregular little loop that had once held something. Under it, on the carpet, lay two cards, the queen of diamonds and the knave of hearts.

The rest of the deck lay scattered about on the counterpane, some of them even on her own recumbent form.

He got down there beside her, at the bedside, on one knee, and took up her dangling hand, and found it softly, yet in a burning gratitude, with his lips. And though he didn't know it, had fallen into it without thought, his pose was that of the immemorial lover pleading his suit. Pleading his suit to a heart he cannot soften.

He swept off the cards onto the floor, replaced them with the money he had brought from New Orleans. Even raised his arms above her, holding it massed within them, letting it snow down upon her any which way it willed, in a green and orange leafy shower.

Her eyes opened, and following the undulant surface of the counterpane they were so close to, sighted at something, taking on a covetous expression with their whites uppermost, by the fact of their lying so low; but one that was perhaps closer to the truth than not.

"A hundred-dollar bill," she murmured sleepily.

"Lou's back," he whispered. "Look what he's brought you from New Orleans." And gathering up some of the fallen certificates, let them stream down all over again. One of them caught in her hair. And she reached up and felt for it there, with an expression of simpering satisfaction. Then having felt it was there, left it there, as though that was where she most wanted it to be.

She stretched out her hands to him, and traced his brows, and the turn of his face, and the point of his ear, in expression of lazy appreciation.

"What were those cards?"

"I was trying to tell our fortunes," she said. "And I fell asleep doing it. I got the queen of diamonds. The money card. And it came true. I'll never laugh at those things again."

"And what did I get?"

"The ace of spades."

He laughed. "What one's that?"

He felt her hand, which had been straying in his hair, stop for a moment. "I don't know."

He had an idea she did, but didn't want to tell him.

"What'd you do that for? Try reading them."

"I wanted to see if you were coming back or not."

"Didn't you know I would?"

"I did," she hedged. "But I wasn't sure."

"And I wasn't sure I'd find you here any longer," he confessed.

Suddenly she had one of those flashes of stark sincerity she was so capable of, and so seldom exercised. She swept her arms about his neck in a convulsive, despairing, knotted hug. "Oh, God!" she mourned bitterly. "What's wrong with the two of us anyway, Lou? Isn't it hell when you can't trust one another?"

He sighed for answer.

Presently she said, "I'm going back to sleep a little while more."

Her head came to rest against his, nestled there, in lieu of the pillow.

"Leave the money there," she purred blissfully. "It feels good lying all over me."

In a little while he could tell by her breathing she was sleeping again. Her head to his, her arms still twined collarlike about him. He could never get any closer to her than this, somehow he felt. He in her arms, she unconscious of him there.

His heart said a prayer. Not knowing to whom, but asking it of the nothingness around him, that he had plunged himself into of his own accord.

"Make her love me," he pleaded mutely, "as I love her. Open her heart to me, as mine is open to her. If she can't love me in a good way, let it be in a bad way. Only, in some way. *Any* way, at all. This is all I ask. For this I'll give up everything. For this I'll take whatever comes, even the ace of spades."

55

HE CAME upon it quite by accident. The merest chance of happening to go where he did, when he did. More than that even, of happening to do as he did, when he went where he did.

She had asked him to go out and get her some of the fledgling cigars she was addicted to, "La Favorita" was their name, while he waited about for her to catch up with him in her dressing, always a process from two to three times slower than his own. She smoked quite openly now, that is in front of him, at all times when they were alone together. Nothing he could do or say would make her desist, so it was he at last who desisted in his efforts to sway her, and let her be. And it was he, too, who emptied off and caused to disappear the ashes she recklessly left about behind her, or opened the windows to carry the aroma off, and even, once or twice when they had been intruded upon unexpectedly by a chambermaid or the like, caught up the cigar and drew upon it himself, as if it were his own, though he was a nonsmoker—all for the sake of her reputation and to keep gossip from being bruited about.

"What did you do—before?" he asked her, on the day of this present request.

He meant before she'd met him. Wondering if there'd been someone else, then, to go and fetch them for her.

"I had to go and get them for myself," she confessed.

"You?" he gasped. There seemed to be no end to the ways in which she could startle him.

"I usually told them it was for my brother, that he was ill and couldn't come for them himself, had sent me in his place. They always believed me implicitly, I could tell, but—" She shrugged with a nuance of aversion.

How could they have failed to, he reflected? How could anyone in his right senses have dreamed a woman would dare enter a tobacco shop on her own behalf?

"But I didn't like to do it much," she added. "Everyone always stared so. You'd think I were an ogre or something. If there were more than one in there, and there usually was, the most complete frozen silence would fall, as if I had cast a spell or something. And yet no matter how quickly it fell, it was never quickly enough to avoid my catching some word or other that I shouldn't, just as I first stepped in. Then they would stand there so guilty looking, wondering if I had heard, and if I had, if I understood its meaning." She laughed. "I could have told them that I did, and spared them their discomfort."

"Bonny!" he said in taut reproof.

"Well, I did," she insisted. "Why deny it?" Then she laughed once more, this time at the expression on his face, and pretended to fling something at him. "Oh, get along, old Prim and Proper!"

The tobacco shop he selected for the filling of her request, and his choice was quite at random, being in a resort town, sold other things as well with which to tempt its transient clientele. Picture cards on revolving panels, writing papers, glass jars of candy, souvenirs, even a few primary children's toys. There was in addition, just within the entrance where it could most readily catch the eye, an inclined wooden rack, holding newspapers from various other cities, an innovation calculated to appeal to homesick travelers.

He stopped by this as he was leaving and idly looked it over, hoping to find one from New Orleans. He had that slightly wistful feeling that the very name of the place alone was enough to cause him. Home. Word of home, in exile. Canal Street in the sunshine; Royal Street, Rampart Street, the Cabildo— He forgot where he was, and he felt lonely, and he ached somewhere so deep down inside that it must have been his very marrow. Love of another kind; the love every man has for the place he first came from, the place he first knew.

There were none to be found. He noticed one from Mobile, and withdrew that from the rack instead. It was not new; having remained unsold until now, he found it to be already dated two full weeks in the past.

Behind him meanwhile, disregarded, the storekeeper was urging helpfully: "Help you, sir? What town you from, mister? Got 'em all there. And if not, be glad to send for whichever one you want—"

He had opened it, meanwhile, casually. And from the inner page —it was only a single sheet, folded—this leaped up, searing him like a flash of gunpowder flame:

A Horrifying Discovery in This City.

The skeleton of a man has been unearthed in the cellar of a house on Decatur Street, in this city, within the last few days. At the time of the recent high water the occupants of the house quitted it, as did all their immediate neighbors. On their return the sunken outlines of a grave were revealed, its contents partly discernible. It is believed the flood washed away the loosely replaced soil, for there had been no sign until then of such an unlawful burial. Adding to the belief that foul play was committed, was the finding of a lead bullet imbedded in the remains. The present householders, who at once reported their grim find to the authorities, are absolved of all blame, since the condition of the remains prove the grave to have been in existence well before their occupancy began.

The authorities are at present engaged in compiling a record of all former occupants in order to trace them for questioning. More developments will be given later, as they are made known to us.

She turned from her mirror to stare, as he blasted the door in minutes later, breathing heavily, greenish of face. Her own cheeks were rosy as ripe peaches with the recent application of the rabbit's foot. "What is it? You're as white as though you'd seen a ghost."

I have, he thought; face to face. The ghost of the man we thought we'd buried forever.

"It's been found out," he said tersely.

She knew at once.

She read it through.

She took it with surprising matter-of-factness, he thought. No recoil, no paling; with an almost professional objectivity, as if her whole interest were in its accuracy and not in its context. She said nothing when she'd completed it. He was the one had to speak.

"Well?"

"That was something we had to expect some day." She gestured with the paper, cast it down. "And there it is. What more is there to say?" She shrugged philosophically. "We haven't done so badly. It could have been much quicker." She began to count on her fingers, the way gossiping housewives do over an impending childbirth. Or rather, its antecedents. "When was it? About the tenth of June, if I remember. It's a full three months now—"

"Bonny!" he retched, his eyes closing in horror.

"They won't know any more who it is. They won't be able to tell. That's one thing in our favor."

"But they *know*, they *know*," he choked, taking swift two-paced turns this way and that, like a bear seeking its way out through cage-bars.

She rose suddenly, flinging down something with a sort of angered impatience. Angered impatience with him, seeking to calm him, seeking to reason with him, for she went to him, took him by the two facings of his coat, and shook him once, quite violently, as if for his own good, to instill some sense in him.

"Will you listen to me?" she flared. "Will you use your head? They know *what*, now. Very well. But they still don't know *who*.

They don't know who caused it. And they never will." She gave a precautionary glance toward the closed door, lowered her voice. "There was no one in that room that day. No one in that house that day. No one who *saw* it happen. Never forget that. They can surmise, they can suspect, they can even feel sure, all they want, but they cannot *prove*. And the time is past, it is already too late; they will never be able to on the face of God's green earth. What was it they told you yourself when you went to them about me? You must have *proof*. And they have none. You threw the—you know what, away; it's lying rusted, buried in the sand, some-where along the beach at Mobile, being eaten away by the salt water. Can they tell that a certain bullet comes from a certain one, and no other?" She laughed derisively. "Not in any way that's ever been found yet!"

Half heeding her, he glanced around him at the walls, and even upward at the ceiling, as though he felt them closing in upon him.

"Let's get out of here," he said in a choked voice, pulling at his collar. "I can't stand it any more."

"It's not here it's been discovered. It's in Mobile. We're as safe here as we were before it was discovered. They didn't know we were here before. They still don't know we're here now."

He wanted to put an added move, an extra lap, even if a fruit-less unneeded one, between themselves and Nemesis, looming dark like a massing cloudbank on the horizon.

She sighed, giving him a look as if she found him hopeless. "There goes our evening, I suppose," she murmured, more to her-self than to him. "And I was counting on wearing the new wine-red taffeta."

She clapped him reassuringly on the arm. "Go down and get yourself a drink; make it a good stiff one. You need that now more than anything, I can see that. There's a good boy. Then come back, and we'll see how you feel by that time, and we'll figure it out then. There's a good boy." And she added, quite inconse-quentially, "I'll go ahead dressing in the meantime, anyway. I *did* want to show them that wine-red taffeta."

In the end they stayed for the time being. But it was not her reasoning that kept him, so much as a fascinating horror that held him in its grip now. He was waiting for the next Mobile news-paper to arrive at the tobacco shop, and knew no other way of obtaining it than by remaining close at hand, here where they were.

It took five days, though he prodded the shopkeeper almost continuously in between.

"Sometimes they send 'em, sometimes they don't," the latter told him. "I could write and hurry them up, if you'd want me to."

"No, don't do that," Durand said rather hastily. "It's just that— I find nothing to do with myself down here. I like to get the news of the old home town."

Then when it came, he didn't have the courage to examine it there in the store, he took it back to her and they searched for it together, she holding the sheets spread, his strained face low on her shoulder.

"There it is," she said crisply, and narrowed the expanse with a sharp, crackling fold, and they read it together.

. . . Bruce Dollard, a renting agent, who has had charge of the property for the past several years, has informed the authorities of one instance in which the occupants gave abrupt notice of departure, quitting the house within the space of a single morning, with no previous indication before that day of intending to do so.

The proprietor of a tool shop has identified a shovel found in the cellar of the house as one that he sold to an unidentified woman some time ago, and it is thought the purchase of this implement may well aid in fixing the approximate time of the misdeed.

Other than that, there have been no further developments, but the authorities are confident of bringing to light new . . .

"*Now* they know," he said bitterly. "*Now* there can be no denying it any longer. *Now* they know."

"No they don't," she said flatly. "Or it wouldn't be in here like this. They're guessing, as much as they ever were."

"The shovel—"

"The shovel was in the house, long after we left. Others could have used it, who came after us."

"It gets worse, all the time."

"It only seems to. They want to do the very thing to you they are doing: frighten you, cause you to blunder in some way. In actuality it's no whit worse than it was before it was found."

"How can you say that, when it stands there before you in black and white?"

She shook her head. "The barking dog can't bite you at the same time; he has to stop when he's ready to sink his teeth in. Don't

you know that when they *do* know, if they do, *we* will never know
they do? You are waiting for a message that will never reach us.
You are looking for news that will never come. Don't you know
that we're safe so long as they keep on mentioning it? When they
stop, that's the time to look out. When sudden silence falls, the
danger has really begun."

He wondered where she got her wisdom. From hard-won experience of her own? Or had it been born in her blood, as cats can
see in the dark and avoid pitfalls?

"Couldn't it mean that they've forgotten?"

She gave him another capsule of her bitter wisdom, sugared
with a hard, wearied smile.

"The police? They never forget, lovey. It's we who will have
to. If we want to live at all."

He brought in three papers the next time. Three successive ones,
each a day apart, but that had come in all together. They divided
them up, went to work separately, hastily ruffling them over page
by page, in search of what they were after.

He turned his head sharply, looked at her half frightened. "It's
stopped! There's not a word about it any more."

"Nor in these either." She nodded with sage foreboding. "Now
the real danger *is* beginning. Now it's under way."

He flung the sheets explosively aside, rose in instant readiness,
so much under her guidance had he fallen in these things. "Shall
we go?"

She considered, made their decision. "We'll wait for one more
newspaper. We can give ourselves that much leeway. They may
already know *who*, but I doubt that they still know *where*."

Another wait. Three days more this time. Then the next one
came. Again nothing. Dead silence. *Brooding* silence, it almost
seemed to him, as they pored over it together.

This time they just looked at one another. It was she who rose
at last, put hands to the shoulders of her cream satin dressing robe
to take it off. Coolly, unhurriedly, but purposefully.

"Now's the time to go," she said quietly. "They're on to us."

He was still baffled, even this late, at the almost sixth sense she
seemed to have developed. It frightened him. He knew, at least,
it was something he would never attain.

"I'll begin to pack," she said. "Don't go out any more. Stay up here where you are until we're ready."

He shuddered involuntarily. He sat on there, watching her, following her movements with his eyes as she moved about. It was like—observing an animated divining rod, that walked and talked like a woman.

"You went about it wrong," she remarked presently. "It's too late to mend now, but you may have even hastened it, for all we know. Singling out just the Mobile papers each time. Word of things like that can travel more swiftly than you know."

"But how else—?" he faltered.

"Each time you bought one, you should have bought one from some other place at the same time, even if you discarded it immediately afterward. In that way you divide suspicion."

She went on into the next room.

Even that there was a wrong and a right way to go about, he reflected helplessly. Ah, the wisdom of the lawless.

She came back to the door for a moment, pausing in mid-packing.

"Where shall it be now? Where shall we go from here?"

He looked at her, haunted. He couldn't answer that.

56

THEY CAME to a halt in Pensacola, at last, for a little while, to catch their breaths. They had now followed the great, slow, curve the Gulf Coast makes as far as they could go along it, heading eastward, always eastward. By fits and starts, by frightened spurts and equally frightened stops, some long, some short, they'd followed their destiny blindly. New Orleans, then Biloxi, then Mobile, then Pensacola. With many a little hidden-away place in between.

Now Pensacola. They couldn't go any farther than that, along their self-appointed trajectory, without leaving the littoral behind, and for some reason or other, probably fear of the unknown, they clung to the familiar coastline. From there the curve dropped sharply away, past the huddle of tin-roofed shacks that was Tampa, on down to the strange, other-language foreignness of Havana. And that would have meant cutting themselves off completely, exile irrevocable beyond power to return. (Returning ships were inspected, and they had no documents.) Nor did they want to cut inland and make for Atlanta, the next obvious step. She was afraid, for reasons of her own, of the North, and though that was not the North, it was a step toward it.

So, Pensacola. They took a house again in Pensacola. Not for grandeur now, not for style, not to feel "really" married, but for the sake of simple, elementary safety.

"They spot you much easier in a hotel," she whispered, in their rain-beaten, one-night hotel. "They nose into your business quicker. People come and go more, all around you, carrying tales away with them and spreading them all around."

He nodded, bending to peer from under the lowered window shade, then starting back as a flash of lightning limned it intolerably bright.

They took the most remote, hidden, inconspicuous house they could find, on a drowsing, tree-lined street well out from the center of town. Other houses not too near, neighbors not too many; they put heavy lace curtains in the windows, to be safer still from prying eyes. They engaged a woman out of sheer compulsion, but pared her presence to a minimum; only three days a week, and she must be gone by six, not sleep under their roof. They spoke guardedly in front of her, or not at all.

They were going to be very discreet, they were going to be very prudent this time.

The first week or two, every time Bonny came or went from the house in daylight, she held her parasol tipped low as she stepped to or from the carriage, so that it shielded her face. And he, without that advantage of concealment, kept his head down all he could. So that, almost, he always seemed to be looking for something along the ground each time he entered or left.

And when a neighbor came to offer a courtesy call, as the custom was, laden with homemade jellies and the like, Bonny held her fast at the door, and made voluble explanations that they were not settled yet and the house was not in order, as an excuse for not asking her in.

The woman went away, with affronted mien and taking her gifts back with her unpresented, and when next they sighted her on the walk she made no salutation and looked the other way.

"You should not have done that," he cautioned, stepping out from where he had listened, as the frustrated visitor departed. "That looks even more suspicious, to be so skittish."

"There was no other way," she said. "If I had once admitted her, then others would have come, and I would have been expected to return their calls, and there would have been no end to it."

After that once, no others came.

"They probably think we live together," she told him, once, jeeringly. "I always leave my left glove off, now, every time I go out, and hold my hand up high, to the parasol-stick, so that they cannot fail to see the wedding band." And punctuated it: "The filthy sows!"

Mr. and Mrs. Rogers had come to Pensacola. Mr. and Mrs. Rogers had taken a house in Pensacola. Mr. and Mrs. Rogers— from nowhere. On the way to—no one knows.

57

THIS TIME he did not tell her; she guessed it by his face. She saw him standing there by the window, staring out at nothing, gnawing at his lip. And when she spoke to him, said something to him, his answer, instead of being in kind, was to turn away, thrust hands in pockets, and begin to pace the room on a long, straight course, up and down.

She understood him so well by now, she knew it could be nothing but the thing it was.

She nodded finally, after watching him closely for some moments. "Again?" she said cryptically.

"Again," he answered, and came to a halt, and flung himself into a chair.

She flung from her irritably a stocking she had been donning upward over her arm in search of rents. "Why is it always that way with us?" she complained. "We no sooner can turn around and draw our breaths, than it's gone again, and the whole thing starts over!"

"It goes, with anyone," he said sombrely. "It's the one thing you can't hold and yet use at the same time."

"With us, it seems to dash!" she exclaimed bitterly. "I never saw the like." It was now she who had sought the window, was seeking out that distant, faltering star of their fortunes, up beyond somewhere, that he had been scanning earlier. There for only the two of them, and no one else, to see. "Does that mean New Orleans again?"

They had grown so, they could understand one another almost without words, certainly without the fully explicit rounded phrase.

"There's no more New Orleans; that's done. There's nothing left there any longer to go back for."

They had even grown alike in mannerisms. It was now she who gnawed at her underlip. "How much have we?"

"Two hundred and some," he answered without lifting his head.

She came close to him and put her hand to the outside of his arm, as if she wished to attract his attention; although she had it in full already.

"There are two things can be done," she said. "We can either sit and do nothing with it, until it is all gone. Or we can take it and set it to work for us."

He simply looked up at her; this time there was a flaw in their mutual understanding, a blind spot.

"I have known many men with less than two hundred for a stake to run it up to two or three thousand."

She kept her hand on his arm, as if the thought were entering by there in some way, and not by word of mouth. It still failed to.

"Do you know any card games?" she persisted.

"There was one I used to play with Jardine in our younger days, of an evening. Bezique, I think. I scarcely remem—"

"I mean real games," she interrupted impatiently.

He understood her, then.

"You mean gamble with it? Risk it?"

She shook her head, more impatient than ever. "Only fools *gamble* with it. Only fools *risk* it. I'll show you how to play so that you're *sure* of running up your two hundred."

He saw what she really meant, then.

"Cheat," he said tonelessly.

She flung her head away from him, then brought it back again. "Don't be so sanctimonious about it. Cheat is just a word. Why use that particular one? There are plenty of others just as good. 'Prepare' yourself. 'Insure' against losing. Why leave everything to chance? Chance is a harlot."

She stepped away, caught at the back of a chair, began dragging it temptingly after her, at a slant.

"Come, sit down. I'll teach you the game itself first."

She was a good teacher. In an hour he knew it sufficiently well.

"You now know faro," she said. "You know it as well as I or anyone else can show it to you. Now I'll teach you the really important part. I must put on some things first."

He sat there idly fingering the cards while she was gone. She came back decked with all her jewelry, as she would have worn it of any evening. It looked grotesque, overlaying the household deshabille she wore.

She sat down before him, and something made his hand shake a little. As does a hand that is about to commit something heinous.

"There are four suits, mark them well," she said briskly. "I will not be sitting in the game with you, they do not play with women, and everything depends upon the quick coördination between us, you and me. Yet on the river boats it never failed, and so it should not fail here. It is the simplest system of all, and the most easily discovered, but we must use it, for your own fingers are not yet deft enough at rigging a deal, and so you must rely on me and not yourself to see you through the tight places. We will use it sparingly, saving it each time for the moment that counts the most. Now, mark. When my hand strays to my bosom so, that's hearts. The pendant at my throat, that's diamonds. The eardrop on the left, spades. The one on the right, clubs. Then you watch my hand as it goes down again, that gives you the count. The fingers are numbered from one to ten, starting at the outside of the left hand. The little finger of the left hand is one, the little finger of the right, ten. Whichever one I fold back, or only shorten a little, gives the count."

"How does that tell me when he's holding jacks, queens or kings?"

"They follow in regular order, eleven, twelve, thirteen. A king would be a folding-back of the little finger on the left hand and of the third finger on the left hand. An ace is simply one."

"How can you hope to see every card he holds in his hand, and signal me?"

"I can't and I don't try. One or two of the top cards are all you need, and those are all I give you."

She thrust the deck toward him over the tabletop.

"Deal me a hand."

She arranged it.

"Now tell me what I am holding in my hand."

He watched her.

"Your top cards are the queen of diamonds, knave of hearts, ace of clubs."

He got no praise.

"You stared at me so, a blind man could have seen what you were about. You play this with your face, as well as with your fingers; learn that. Now again."

He told her again.

"Better, but you are too slow. They won't wait for you, while you sit there summing up in your mind. Now another."

Her only praise was a nod. "Once more."

This time, at last, she conceded: "You are not stupid, Louis."

He threw the cards aside suddenly.

"I can't do this, Bonny."

She gave him a scathing look.

"Why? Are you too good? Does it soil you?"

He dropped his eyes before hers, ran desperate fingers through his hair.

"You killed a man once in Mobile, if I remember!" she accused him. "But you cannot sharpen up a card game a little. No, you're too goody-goody."

"That was different somehow—" (And why do *you* throw that up to me, anyhow? he thought.)

"If there's anything that sickens me, it's a saintly man. You

should be wearing your collar back-to-front. Very well. We'll say
no more about it. Sit and nurse your two hundred until it is all
gone." She flung her chair angrily over to one side, while she rose
from it.

He watched her stride to the door, and pluck the knob, and
swing the door back to go out.

"You want me to do this very much?" he said. "*That* much?"

She stopped and turned to look at him. "It is to your advantage, not mine. I was only trying to help you. *I* gain nothing by
it. I can always make out. I have before, and I can again."

Louder than all the rest, he heard in it the one word she had
not spoken: *alone.*

"I'll do it for you, Bonny," he said limply. "I'll do it for you."

She dropped her eyes a moment complacently. She came back and
sat down. Her face slowly smoothed out. She bent to her tutoring
attentively. "Now what am I holding?"

58

How SHE found out about the place he never knew. He would
never have guessed it existed. She seemed to have a nose for
scenting such places from a mile off.

It was on the second floor, up a stair that occasionally someone
would come down but no one was ever seen to go up. Below it was
just a restaurant and wining place. They'd been there before once
or twice in their nightly rounds of pleasure, and not finding it
very entertaining, soon left again. If she'd detected anything then,
she'd said nothing about it to him at the time.

They came there now, the two hundred secreted on his person,
and first took seats below, just the two of them, close to the
stairs, over two glasses of Burgundy.

"Are you sure?" he kept asking her in a doubtful undertone.

She gave him a deft little frown of affirmation. "I know. I can tell. I saw the look on one or two faces as they came down those stairs the other night. I have seen those looks on faces before. The face too white, the eyes too bright and feverish." She patted his knee below the table. "Be patient. Do as I told you when the time comes."

They sat for a while, she inscrutable, he uneasy.

"Now," she said finally.

He beckoned the waiter. "The check, please." He took out the entire two hundred dollars, allowed him to see it, while he selected a bill for payment. She, meanwhile, elaborately stifled a yawn. He turned his head to the waiter. "It's dull here. Can't you offer anything—a little more interesting?"

The waiter went to the manager and spoke in a corner behind the back of his hand. The manager came over in turn, leaned confidentially across the back of Durand's chair.

"Anything I can do, sir?"

"Can't you offer us anything a little more exciting than this?"

"If you were alone, sir, I'd suggest—"

"Suggest it anyway," Durand encouraged him.

"There are some gentlemen upstairs— You understand me?"

"Perfectly," said Durand. "I wish I had known sooner. Come, my dear."

"The lady too?" the manager asked dubiously.

"I am very well behaved," she simpered. "I will be quiet as a mouse. No one will know that I am there."

"Tell them Mr. Bradford sent you from below. We do not like too much attention called to it. It is just for the diversion of a few of our steady customers."

They went up together at a propitious moment, when no one seemed to be watching. Durand knocked at a large double door, behind which a buzz of conversation sounded. A man opened it and looked out at them, holding it so that they could not see within.

"Mr. Bradford sent us from below."

"We don't allow ladies in here, sir."

She smiled her most dazzling smile. Her eyes looked into his. Her hand even came to rest upon his forearm for a moment. "There are exceptions to every rule. Surely you are not going to keep *me* out? I should be so lonely without him."

"But the gentlemen's conversation may—"

She pinched his chin playfully. "There, there. I have heard my husband swear before; it will not shock me."

"Just a moment."

He closed the door; reopened it in a moment to offer her a black velvet eye-mask. "Perhaps you would be more comfortable with this."

She gave Durand a satiric side look, as if to say "Isn't he naïve?" but put it on nevertheless.

The man stood aside, to hold back the door for them.

"Need you have been so coquettish?" Durand said to her in a rapid aside.

"It got me in, didn't it?"

Her entrance created a sensation. He had seen her attract attention wherever they went, but never anything comparable to this. The buzz of conversation stilled into a dead silence. The play even stopped short at several of the tables. One or two of the men reached falteringly behind them, as if to draw on their coats, though they did not complete the intention.

She said something behind her hand to their host, who announced in a clear voice: "The lady wishes you to forget that she is here, gentlemen. She simply enjoys watching card games."

She bowed her head demurely, in a feigned sort of modesty, and went on, her arm linked to Durand's.

Their guide introduced him at one of the tables, after having first obtained his name, and the willingness of the other players to accept him. "Mr. Castle—Mr. Anderson, Mr. Hoffman, Mr. Steeves."

Bonny was not introduced, propriety in this case dictating that she be omitted.

"Champagne for the gentlemen," Durand immediately ordered, as soon as he had taken seat.

A colored steward brought it, but she at once took over the task from him, remarking: "That shall be my pleasure, to see that the wants of the gentlemen at this table are attended to." And moved around from one to the next, filling their glasses, after the cards were already well in play. Then sat back some little distance removed, with the air of a little girl upon her best behavior, who has been allowed to sit up late in presence of her elders. If her legs did not actually dangle from her chair, that was the illusion she conveyed.

Durand took out the entire two hundred, with an indifferent gesture, as though it were simply a small fraction of what he had about him, and the game began.

Within minutes, it was no longer two hundred. And at no time after that did it ever again descend to two hundred, though sometimes it swelled and sometimes it shrank back again. It doubled itself in bulk, finally, and then when it had doubled itself again, he made two piles of it, so that he must have had a thousand dollars in winnings there on the table before him. He did not remove any of it from sight, as the etiquette of the game proscribed, the play still being in progress.

The room was warm and unaired, and the players were heated in addition by their own excitement. The champagne thoughtfully there beside them was gratefully downed in hectic gulps at every opportunity. And each time a glass fell empty, a fleeting shadow, less than a shadow, would tactfully withdraw it a short distance behind the player, in order not to interfere with his view of the table, and there refill it. With graceful, dainty, loving little gesture, hand to throat, or bosom, or toward ear, lest a drop be spilled, as the drink was returned to its place. Tapering fingers, one or the other folded shorter than the rest, clasped about its stem.

Occasionally she got an absent, murmured "Thank you," from the player, more often he was not even aware of her, so unobtrusively were his wants tended.

Once she motioned with her fan to the steward, and he brought another bottle, and when the cork popped, she gave a little start of alarm, as pretty as you please, so timorous a little thing was she, so unused to the ways of champagne corks.

But suddenly there was silence at the table. The game had halted, without a word. Each player continued to look at his cards, but no further move was made.

"Whenever you're ready, gentlemen," Durand said pleasantly.

No one answered, no one played.

"I'm waiting for the rest of you, gentlemen," Durand said.

No one looked up, even at sound of his voice. And the answer was given with the speaker's head still lowered to his cards.

"Will you ask the lady to retire, sir?" the man nearest him said.

"What do you mean?"

"Do you have to be told?" They were all looking at him now. Durand started to his feet with a fine surge of forced indignation. "I want to know what you meant by that!"

The other man rose in turn, a little less quickly. "This." He knocked his diffuse cards into a single block against the table, and slapped Durand in the face with them twice, first on one side, then the other.

"If there's one thing lower than a man that'll cheat at cards, it's a man that'll use a woman to do his cheating for him!" Durand tried to swing at him with his fist, the circumstances forgotten now, only the provocation remaining livid on his cheeks—for he had no past history of brooked insult to habituate him to this sort of thing. But the others had leaped up by now too, and they closed in on him and held his arms pinioned. He threshed about, trying to free himself, but all he could succeed in doing was swing their bodies a little too, along with his own; they were too many for him.

The table rocked, and one of the chairs went over. Her scream was faint and futile in the background, and tinny with horrified virtue.

The manager had appeared as if by magic. The struggle stopped, but they still held Durand fast, his marble-white face now cast limply downward as if to hide itself from their scorching stares.

"This man's a common, low-down cheat. We thought you ran a place for gentlemen. You should protect the good name of your establishment better than this."

He didn't try to deny it; at least that much he had left. That was all he had left. His shirt had come open at the chest, and his breast could be seen rising and falling hard. But scarcely from the brief physical stress just now, rather from humiliation. The whole room was crowded about them, every other game forgotten.

The manager signalled to two husky helpers. "Get him out of here. Quickly, now. I run an honest place. I won't have any of that."

He didn't struggle further. He was transferred to the paid attendants, with only the unvarying protest of the manhandled: "Take your hands off me," no more.

But then as he saw the manager clearing the disheveled table, sweeping up what was on it, he called out: "Two hundred of that money is mine, I brought it into the game."

The manager waved him on, but from a distance safely beyond his reach. "You've forfeited it to the house. That'll teach you not to try your tricks again! On your way, scoundrel!"

Her voice suddenly rang out in sharp stridency: "You robbers! Give him back his money!"

"The pot calling the kettle black," someone said, and a general laugh went up, drowning the two of them out.

He was hustled across the floor, and out through a back door, probably to avoid scandalizing the diners below at the front. There was an unpainted wooden slat-stair there, clinging sideward to the building. They threw him all the way down to the bottom, and he lay there in the muddy back-alley. Miraculously unhurt, but smarting with such shame as he'd never known before, so that he wanted to turn his face into the mud and hide it there.

His hat was flung down after him, and after doing so the thrower ostentatiously brushed his hands, as if to avoid contamination.

But that was not the full measure of humiliation, ignominy. The final degradation was to see the door reopen suddenly, and Bonny came staggering through. Impelled forth, *thrust* forth by the clumsy sweaty hands of men, like any common thing.

His wife. His love.

A knife went through his heart, and it seemed to shrivel and fold and close over upon the blade that pierced it.

Pushed forth into the night, so that she too all but overbalanced and threatened to topple down after him, but clung to the rail and managed to hold herself back just in time.

She stood there motionless for a moment, above him, but looking, not back at them but down below her at him.

Then she came on down and passed him by with a lift of her skirts to avoid him, as though he were some sort of refuse lying there.

"Get up," she said shortly. "Get up and come away. I never heard of a man that can't win either way; can't win honestly, and can't win by cheating either."

He had never known the human voice could express such corrosive contempt, before.

59

HE FORESAW the change in her that would surely follow this debacle before it had even come, so well did he know her now, so bitterly, so costly well. Know her by mood and know her by nature. And come it did, only a little less swiftly and surely than his apprehension of its coming.

The first day after, she was simply less communicative, perhaps; a shade less friendly. That was all. It was as if this was the period of germination, the seed at work but unseen as yet. Only a lover's eye could have detected it. And his was a lover's eye, though set in a husband's head.

But by that night, already, a chill was beginning. The temperature of her mood was going down steadily. Her remarks were civil, but in that alone was the gauge. Civility bespeaks distance. Husband and wife should never be civil. Sugared, or soured, but civil not.

By the second day dislike had begun to sprout like a noxious weed, overrunning everything in what was once a pleasant garden. Her eyes avoided him now. To bring them his way he had to make use of the question direct in addressing her, nothing less would do. And even then they refused to linger, as if finding it scarcely worth their while to waste their time on him.

Within but an additional day of that, the weeds had flowered into poisonous, rancid fruit. The cycle of the sowing was complete, all that was needful was the reaping; and who would the scythe wielder be? There was a sharp edge to her tongue now, the velvet was wearing thin in places. The least provocative remark of his might touch one of them, strike a flinty answer.

It was as though this had the better even of her herself; as though, at times, she tried to curb it, make an effort, at intervals, toward relenting, softening: only to find her own nature opposed to her intentions in the matter, and overcoming them in spite of the best she could do. She would smile and the blue ice in her eyes would warm, but only for fleeting minutes; the glacial cast that held her would close over her again and hide her from him.

He took refuge in long walks. They were a surcease, for when he took them he was not without her; when he took them he had her with him as she had been until only lately. He would restore, replenish the old she, until he had her whole again. Then coming back, with a smile and a lighter heart, the two would meet face to face, the old and the new, and in an instant he would have his work all for nothing, the new she had destroyed the old.

"I'll get a job, if this affects you so much," he blurted out at last. "I'm capable, there's no reason why I—"

He met with scant approval.

"I hate a man that works!" she said through tight-gripped teeth. "I could have married a dray horse if I'd wanted that. It'd be just about as dull." Then gave him a cutting look, as if he had no real wish to better their state, were purposely offering her alternatives that were useless, that were not to be seriously considered. "There must be *some* way besides that, that you could get your hands on some money for us."

He wondered uneasily what she meant by that, and yet was afraid to know, afraid to have it made any clearer.

"Only fools work," she added contemptuously. "Someone once told me that a long time ago, and I believe it now more than ever."

He wondered who, and wondered where he was now. What jail had closed around him long since, or what gallows had met him. Or perhaps he was still unscathed, his creed vindicated, waiting somewhere for word from her, in tacit admission that she had been wrong; knowing that some day, somehow, in his own good time, he would have it.

"He must have been a scalawag," was all he could think to say.

There was defiance in her cold blue eyes. "He was a scalawag," she granted, "but he was good company."

He left the room.

And now there was stone silence between them, following this;

not so much as a "By your leave," not so much as a "Good night."
It was hideous, it was unthinkable, but it had come about. Two
mutes moving about one another, two pantomimists, two sleepless silhouettes in the dimness of their chamber. He sought to
reach for her hand and clasp it, but she seemed to be asleep.
Yet in her sleep she guessed his intention, and withdrew her hand
before he could find it.

On the following day, coming from the back of the hall, he happened to pass by the sitting room, on his way out to take one of
his restorative walks, and caught sight of her in there, sitting at
the desk. He hadn't known her to be in there. She was not writing
a letter, by any evidence that was to be seen. She was sitting quite
aimless, quite unoccupied. The desk slab was out, but no paper was
in view. Yet for what other purpose do people sit at a desk, he
asked himself? There were more appropriate chairs in the room for
the purpose, in itself, of sitting.

He had an unhappy feeling that some action she had been engaged in had been hastily resumed as soon as he was gone. The
very cast of her countenance told him that; its resolute vacancy.
Not a natural vacancy, but a studied one, carefully maintained
just for so long as he was in the doorway watching. The pinkey of
her hand, which rested sideward along the desk slab, rose and
descended again, as he watched. The way the tip of a cat's tail
twitches, when all the rest of it is stilled; betraying a leashed,
lurking impatience.

There was nothing he could do. If he stopped her this time, she
would find another. If he accused, she would deny. If he proved,
then her smouldering resentment would burst into open flame, and
he didn't want that.

A letter to the past. A letter to that other, subterranean world
he thought she had left forever.

He went out and closed the door behind him, heavy hearted.

If there was an added quality to be detected in her, several
hours later, on his return, it was a glint of malicious satisfaction,
a sort of sneer within the eyes. The look of one who says to herself,
I have not been idle. Just wait, and you shall see.

Within another two days he could stand their estrangement no
longer, he had capitulated. He had capitulated in a lie; he had
prostituted the truth itself to his submission, than which there

can be no greater capitulation on the part of one to the desires of another. Making what is not so, so, for the sake of renewed amity.

"I lied to you, Bonny," he said without preamble.

She was stroking her hair in readiness for bed, her back was to him. Literally now, as it had been figuratively for days on end.

"There *is* more money. That was not the end of it."

She set down her brush smartly, turned to stare.

"Then why did you tell me that? What did you do it for?"

"I thought perhaps we might run through it too quickly. I thought perhaps we should put it by for a little while, for some later day."

Greed must have dulled her perceptions. He made a poor liar, at best. And now, because of the stake involved, he was at his worst. Yet she wanted to believe him, and so she wholeheartedly did. Instantly she had accepted for fact his faltering figment; that could be told by the swiftness with which she entered into argument over it. And you do not argue over something that is not a fact, you disregard it; you argue only over something that is.

"Later?" she said heatedly. "How much later? Will we be any younger when it comes, that precious day? Will a dress look as good on me then as it does now? Will my skin be as smooth, will your step be as firm?"

She picked up her brush again, but not for use; to fling it down in emphasis.

"No, I've never lived that way and I won't submit to it now! 'A rainy day.' I've heard that old fusty saying. I'll give you another, a truer one! 'Tomorrow never comes.' Let it rain tomorrow! Let it soak and drench me! If I'm dry and warm tonight, that's all I care about. Tomorrow's rain may never find me. I may be dead tomorrow, and so may you. And you can't spend money in a grave. I'll take on the bargain. I'll ask no odds. Bury me tomorrow, and welcome. In potter's field, if you want. Without even a shroud to cover me. If I can only have Tonight."

She was breathing fast with the heat and fury of her philosophy. The protest of the disinherited; the panic of the pagan, with no promise of ultramundane reward.

"How much is it?" she asked avidly. "How much, about?"

He wanted her happy. He couldn't give her heaven, so he gave her the only heaven she believed in, understood. "A great deal," he said. "A great deal."

"About?"

"A lot," was all he could keep saying. "A lot."

She had risen, ecstatic, was coming closer to him step by step. Each step a caress. Each step the promise of another caress still to come, beyond the last. She clasped hands over her bosom, as if to hold in the joy swelling it. "Oh, never mind, no need to tell me exactly. I never did like figures. A lot, that's all that matters. A bunch. A load. Where? Here, with us?"

"In New Orleans," he mumbled evasively. "But where I can put my hands on it easily." Anything to hold her. She wanted Tonight. Well, he wanted Tonight too.

She spun, suddenly, in a solo waltz step, as though unseen violins had struck a single chord. Then flung herself half onto the bed and into his waiting arms.

One again; love again. Whisperings, protestations, promises and vows: never another cold word, never another black silence, never another hurt. I forgive you, I adore you, I cannot live without you. "A new you, a new me."

Suddenly she alerted her head for a moment, almost as if an afterthought had assailed her. "Oh, I'm sorry," he heard her breathe, and whether it was to him or to herself, he could not even tell, it was so inward and subdued.

"It's over, it's forgotten," he murmured, "we've agreed on that." Her head dropped back again, solaced.

But the belatedness of the qualm, coming as it did *after* all the pardons had been asked and given, and not in their midst, made him think her compunction might have been for something else, and not their state of alienation itself, now happily ended. Some act he'd had no inkling of at the time, now rashly completed beyond recall.

She kept asking when he was going, and when he was going, with increasing frequency and increasing insistence, until at last he was face to face with the retraction he'd dreaded so; there was nothing left for him but to tell her. So tell her he did.

"I'm not."

"But—but how else can you obtain it?"

"There isn't any there to obtain. Not a penny. It's all gone long since, all been used. The money from the sale of the St. Louis Street house, that Jardine took care of for me; my share of the business. There's nothing more coming to me." He buried hands in pockets, drew a deep breath, looked down. "Very well, I lied. Don't ask me why; you should know. To see you smile at me a little longer, perhaps." And he murmured, half-inside his throat, "It was cheap at that price."

She said, still speaking quietly, "So you hoodwinked me."

She put aside her hand mirror. She stood. She moved about, with no settled destination. She clasped her own sides, in double embrace.

The storm brewed slowly, but it brewed sulphurous strong. She paced back and forth, her chest rising and falling with quickened breath, but not a word coming from her at first.

She seized her cut-glass flask of toilet water at last, and raising arm up overhead to full height, crashed it down upon the dresser top.

"So that's what you think of me. A good joke, wasn't it? A clever trick. Tell her you have money, tell her you haven't. The fool will believe anything you say. One minute yes, the next minute no." The talcum jar came down next, shattered into crystal shrapnel, some of which jumped almost to his feet, across the room. Then the hand mirror. "It isn't enough to lie to me once, you have to lie to me twice over!"

"The first time was the truth; the only lie was when I said I did have."

"You got what you wanted, though, didn't you? That was all you cared about, that was all that mattered to you!"

"Haven't you got any modesty at all? Isn't there anything you leave unsaid?"

"You'd better make it do, I warn you! It'll be a long long time—"

"You've got a filthy mouth for such a beautiful face," he let her know sternly. "A slut's tongue in a saint's face."

She threw a scent bottle, this time directly at him. He didn't swerve; it struck the wall just past his shoulder. A piece of glass nicked his cheek, and drops of sweet jasmine spattered his shoulder. She was not play-acting in some lovers' quarrel; her face was

maniacal with hate. She was beside herself. If there had been anything sharp at hand to use for weapon—

"You—" She called him a name that he'd thought only men
knew. "I'm not good enough for you, am I? I'm beneath you.
I'm just trash and you're a fine gentleman. Well, who told you
to come after me? Who wants you?"

He took a handkerchief to the tiny spot of blood on his cheek.
He held his peace, stood there steadfast against the sewage tor-
rents of her denunciation.

"What good are you to me? You're no good to me at all. You
and your romantic love. Faugh!" She wiped her hand insultingly
across her mouth, as though he had just kissed her.

"No, I suppose I'm not," he said, eyes hard now, face bitter.
"The wind has changed now. Now that I have nothing left. Now
that you've had everything out of me that's to be had. You greedy
little leech. Are you sure you haven't overlooked anything?" He
was trembling now with emotion. His hands sought into his pockets,
turning their linings out with the violence of their seeking. "Here."
He dragged some coins out, flung them full at her face. "Here's
something you missed. And here, have this too." He ripped the
jeweled stickpin from his tie, cast that at her. "And that's all there
is. An insurance policy among my papers somewhere, and maybe
you'd like me to cut my own throat to profit you—but unfortunately it's not in force."

She was pulling things out of the drawers now, dropping more
than she secured.

"I've left you once already, and I'll leave you again. And this
time for good, this time goodbye. I don't ever want to see the
sight of you again."

"I'm still your husband, and you're not leaving this house."

"Who's to stop me? *You?*" She threw back her head and
shrieked to the ceiling with wild laughter. "You're not man enough,
you haven't got the—"

They both ran suddenly for the door, from their two varying directions. He got there first, put his back to it, blocked it.

She raised diminutive fists, battered futilely at his chest, aimed
the points of her shoes at his insteps.

"Get out of my way. You can't stop me."

"Get back from this door, Bonny."

The blow, when it came, was as unexpected to him as it must have been to her. It was like a man swiping at a mosquito, before he stops to think. She staggered back, turned as she fell, and toppled sideward onto the bench that sat before her dressing table, the lower part of her body trailing the floor.

They looked at each other, stunned.

His heart, wrung, wanted to cry out "Oh, darling, did I hurt you?" but his stubborn lips would not relay the plea.

The room seemed deathly still, after the clamorous discord that had just filled it. She had become noticeably subdued. Her only reproach was characteristic. It was, rather, a grudging backhand compliment. As she picked herself stiffly up, she mouthed sullenly: "It's a wonder you were man enough to do that much. I didn't think you had it in you."

She came toward the door again, but this time with all antagonism drained from her.

He eyed her under narrowed, warning lids.

"Let me get to the bathroom," she said with sulky docility. "I need to put cold water on my face."

When he came up again later from below, she had dragged her bed things out of their room and into the spare bedroom at the back of the hall up there.

60

About four or five days later, he was returning toward the house from one of his walks—walks which had become habitual by now—when suddenly her figure came into view far ahead of him, some two or three road crossings in advance, but going the same way he was, down the same mottled tunnel made by the overhanging shade trees.

The distance was so great and the figure was so diminished by it, and above all the flickering effect given off by the alternating sun and shade falling over it made it so blurry in aspect, that he could not be altogether sure it was indeed she. Yet he thought he knew her gait, and when someone else had passed her he could tell by that yardstick she was small in proportion to others and not just because of the distance alone, and above all the coloring of the dress was the same as the one he had last seen her in when he'd left the house an hour before: plum serge. In short, there was too much over-all similarity; he felt sure it was Bonny.

It was useless to have hailed her; she would not have heard, she was too far ahead. The separation was too great even for him to have hoped to overtake her within a worthwhile time by breaking into a run; she would have been almost back at their own door by the time he had done so. Moreover, there was no reason for undue haste, no emergency, he would see her soon enough, and besides he was somewhat fatigued from his recent walk and disinclined to run just them.

She had not been in sight only a moment before, and the point at which she had suddenly appeared was midway between two of the intervening road crossings, so he surmised she must have emerged from some doorway or establishment at approximately that location just as he caught sight of her.

When he had gained the same general vicinity himself, in due course, he turned to look sideward, out of what was at first merely superficial curiosity, as he went past, to see where it was she had come from, what it was she had been about. Always presuming that it had been she.

Superficial curiosity became outright surprise at a glance, and halted him in his tracks. The building flanking him was the post office. Immediately adjoining it, it is true, was a rather shabby-looking general-purpose store, but since there were several others of the same kind, and far more prepossessing looking, closer at hand to where they lived, it seemed hardly likely she would have put her-self out to come all the way to this one. It must have been the post office she had quitted.

There was no reason for her to seek it out but one: subterfûge. There was a mailbox for the taking of their letters on the selfsame street with them; there was a carrier for the bringing of their letters who went past their very door. And what letters did they get any-way? Who knew they were here? Who knew who they were?

Uneasy now, and with the new-found sunlight dimming behind a scurrying of advance clouds, he had turned and gone in before even considering what he was about to do. And then once in, wished he hadn't, and tried to turn about and leave again. But uneasiness proved stronger than his reluctance to spy upon her, and forced him at last to approach the garter-sleeved clerk behind a wicket bearing the legend "General Delivery."

"I was looking for someone," he said shamefacedly. "I must have —missed her. Has there been a little blonde lady—oh, no higher than this—in here within the past few minutes?"

He remembered that day he had taken her to the bank with him in New Orleans. She must have had the same effect in here just now. She would be remembered, if she'd been in at all.

The clerk's eyes lit up, as with an afterglow. "Yes, sir," he said heartily. "She was at this very window just a few minutes ago." He spruced up one of his arm bands, then the other. "She was asking for a letter."

Durand's throat was dry, but he forced the obstructive question from it. "And did she— Did you have one for her?"

"Sure enough did." The clerk wagged his head in reflective admiration, made a popping sound with his tongue against some empty tooth-shell in his mouth. " 'Miss Mabel Greene,' " he reminisced. "She must be new around here, I don't recall ever—"

But Durand wasn't there anymore.

She was in the ground-floor sitting room. Bonnet and stole were gone, as if she had never had them on. She was standing before the center table frittering with some flowers that she had put there in a bowl the day before, some jonquils, withdrawing those that showed signs of wilting. There was a scorched, cindery odor in the air, as if something small had burned a few moments ago; his nostrils became aware of it the moment he entered.

"Back?" she said friendlily, turning her face over-shoulder to him, then back to the flowers once more.

He inhaled twice in rapid succession, in quite involuntary confirmation of the foreign odor.

Though she was not looking at him, she must have heard. Abruptly she quitted the flowers, went to the window, and raised it generously. "I was just smoking a cigar in here," she said, unasked. "It needs airing."

There was no trace of the remnants of one, on the usual salvers she used.

"I threw it out the window unfinished," she said. She had gone back to the flowers again. "It was quite unfit. They're making them more poorly all the time."

But the effluvia of her own cigars had never bothered her until now. And this was not the aromatic vestiges of tobacco, it was the more acrid pungency left behind by incinerated paper.

I'll know she lies now, I'll know, he thought mournfully. She cannot evade this. Ah, why do I ask her? Why must I seek my own punishment? But the question was already out and uttered, he could not have held it back had his tongue been torn from its roots a moment later.

"Was that you I saw on the street just now?"

She took a moment to answer; though how could she be uncertain, if she had just returned? She took out one more flower. She turned it about by its stem, studying it for faults. She put it down. Then she turned about and faced him, readily enough. She saw his eyes rest for a moment on her plum-serge costume. It was only then she answered.

"Yes."

"Where were you, to the post office?"

Again she took a moment. As though visualizing the topography of the vicinity she had recently been in, reminding herself of it.

"I had an errand," she said, steadily enough. "There was something I needed to buy."

"What?" he asked.

She looked down at the flowers. "A pair of garden shears, to clip the stems of flowers."

She had chosen well. They would sell those in a general store. And there had been a general store next to the post office.

"And did you?"

"They had none on hand. They offered to send away for some, but I told them it was not worth the trouble."

He waited. She intended to say nothing more.

"You didn't go to the post office?"

But in the repetition of the question itself, in fact in its first asking, lay by indirection her answer. He realized that himself. By the very fact of asking, he apprised her that he knew she had.

"I did step into the post office," she said negligently. "It comes to me now. I had forgotten about it. To buy stamps. They are in my purse now. Do you wish to see them?" She smiled, as one who is prepared for all eventualities.

"No," he said unhappily. "If you say you bought stamps, that ends it."

"I think I'd better show them to you." Her voice was neither injured nor hostile; rather, whimsical, amused. As one who patiently endures another's foibles, forgives them.

She opened the receptacle, took out its change purse, showed him two small crimson squares, adhering on a perforated line.

He scarcely looked. She could have bought those a half-hour ago. She could have had them for a month.

"The man said he had given you a letter."

"He did?" Her brows went up facetiously.

"I described you to him."

"He did," she said coolly.

"It was addressed to Mabel Greene."

"I know," she agreed. "That is why I returned it to him. He mistook me for somebody else. I stopped for a moment, close to his window, without noticing where I was, while I was putting the stamps away. My back was to him, you see. He suddenly called out: 'Oh, Miss Greene, I have a letter for you,' and thrust it out at me. He took me so by surprise that I took it in my hand for a moment without thinking. Then I said, 'I am not Miss Greene,' and handed it back to him. He apologized, and that ended it. Although on second thought, I don't think his mistake was an honest one. I think he was trying to—" she modulated her voice in reluctant delicacy "—flirt with me. He promptly tried to strike up a conversation with me, by starting to tell me how much I resembled this other person. I simply turned my head away and walked on."

"He didn't say you had returned it."

"But *I* say I did." There was no resentment in her voice, no emotion whatever. "And you have the choice there: which one of us to believe."

He hung his head. He'd lost the battle of wits, as he might have known he would. She was absolutely without consciousness of guilt. Which did not mean she was without guilt, but only without the fear that usually goes with it and helps unmask it. He could have brought her face to face with that clerk, and the situation would not have altered one whit. She would have flung back her denial into the very face of his affirmation, trusting that to weaken first of the two.

On her way out of the room, she let her hand trail, almost fondly, across the breadth of his back.

"You don't trust me, do you, Lou?" she said quite neutrally.

"I want to."

She shrugged, in the doorway, as she went out. "Then do so, that is all you have to do. It's simple enough."

She went up the stairs, in leisurely complacency. And though he couldn't see her face, he had never been surer of anything than that it bore on it a smile of the same leisurely complacency just then, to match her pace.

He flung himself down at a crouch before the fireplace, made rapid circling motions with his hands over its brick flooring. There was some brittle paper-ash lying on its otherwise scoured, blackened surface; very little, not enough to make a good-sized fistful. He turned up a piece that had not been consumed, perhaps because it had been held by the burner's fingers to the last. It was a lower corner, nothing more; two straight edges sheared off transversely by an undulant scorched line.

It bore a single word, in conclusion. "Billy." And even that was not wholly intact. The upper closure of the "B" had been opened, eaten into by the brown stain of flame.

61

Nothing more, then, for five days. No more visits to the post office. No more idle sittings beside a desk. No more letters sent, no more letters received. Whatever had been said was said, and only the inside of a fireplace knew what that had been.

For five days after that she did not even go out, she took no more walks. She loitered about the rooms, noncommunicative, self-assured. As if waiting for something. As if waiting for an appointed length of time to pass. Five days to pass.

Then on the fifth day, suddenly, without a word, the door of her room opened after long closure and he beheld her coming down the stairs arrayed for excursion. She was carefully dressed, far more carefully, far more exquisitely, than he had seen her for a long time past. She had taken a hot curling iron to her hair; ripples of artifice indented it. Her lips were frankly red, not merely covertly so. As if to meet a different standard than his own. Rouge that did not try to look like nature but tried to look like rouge. Her floral essence was strong to the point of headiness; again a different standard than his own.

She was going out. She made that plain, over and above his own powers of observation. As if she wanted no mistake about it, no hindrance. "I'm going out," she said. "I'll be back soon."

He did not ask her where.

That was about three in the afternoon.

At five she was not back yet. At six. At seven.

It was dark, and he lit the lamps, and they burned their way toward eight. She wasn't back yet.

He knew she hadn't left him; he knew she was coming back. Somehow that wasn't his fear. Something about the way she had departed, the open, ostentatious bearing she had maintained, was enough to tell him that. She would have gone off quietly, or he would not have seen her go off at all, if she were never coming back.

Once he went to her bureau drawer, and from far in the back of it took out the little case, the casket of burned wood, she kept her adornments in. Her wedding band was in there, momentarily discarded. But so was the solitaire diamond ring he had given her in New Orleans the first day of her arrival.

No, she hadn't left him; she was coming back. This was just an excursion without her wedding band.

On toward nine there was a sound at the door. Not so much an opening of it, as a fumbling incompletion of the matter of opening it.

He went out into the hall at last to see. To see why she did not finish coming in, for he knew already it was she.

She was half in, half out, and stopping there, her back sideward against the frame. Apparently resting. Or as if having given up the idea of entering the rest of the way as being too much trouble.

"Are you ill, Bonny?" he asked gravely, advancing toward her, but not hastily. Rather with a sort of reproachful dignity.

She laughed. A surreptitious, chuckling little sound, exchanged between herself and some alter ego, that excluded him. That was even at his expense.

"I knew you were going to ask me that."

He had come close to her now.

The floral essence had changed, as if from long exposure; fermented; there was an alcohol base to it now.

"No, I'm not ill," she said defiantly.

"Come away from the door. Shall I help you?"

She brushed his offered arm away from her, advanced past him without it. There was a stiffness to her gait. It was even enough, but there was a self-consciousness to it. As if she were saying: "See how well I can walk." She reminded him of a mechanical doll, wound up and striking out across the floor.

"I'm not drunk, either," she said suddenly.

He closed the door, first looking out. There was no one out there. "I didn't say you were."

"No, but that's what you're thinking."

She waited for him to reply to that, and he didn't. Either answer, he could tell, would have been an equal irritant; whether he contradicted or admitted it. She wanted to quarrel with him; her mood was one of hostility. Whether implanted or native, he could not tell.

"I never get drunk," she said, turning to face him from the sitting-room door. "I've never gotten drunk in my life."

He didn't answer. She went on into the sitting room.

When he entered it in turn, she was seated in the overstuffed chair, her head back a little, resting. Her eyes were open, but not on what she was doing; they were sighted remotely upward. She was stripping off her gloves, but not with the usual attentiveness he had seen her give to this. With an air of supine frivolity, allowing their empty fingers to dangle loosely and flutter about.

He stood and watched her for a moment.

"You're late," he said at last.

"I know I'm late. You don't have to tell me that."

She flung the gloves down on the table, jerked them from her with a little wrist-recoil of anger.

"Why don't you ask me where I've been?"

"Would you tell me?" he retorted.

"Would you believe me?" she flung back at him.

She took off her hat next. Regarded it intently, and unfavorably; circling its brim, the while, about one supporting hand.

Then unexpectedly, he saw her, with her other hand, hook two fingers together and snap them open against it, striking it a little spanking blow with her nail, so to speak, of slangy depreciation. A moment later she had cast it from her, so that it fell to the floor a considerable distance across the room from her.

He made no move to get it. It was her hat, after all. He merely looked after it, to where it had fallen. "I thought you liked it. I thought it was your fondest rage."

"Hoch," she said with throaty disgust. "In New York they're wearing bigger ones this season. These little things are out."

Who told you that? he said to her in bitter silence. Who told you that you're wasting yourself, buried down here, away from the big towns you used to know? He could hear the very words, almost as though he had been there when they were spoken.

"Can I get you anything?" he offered after awhile.

"You can't get me anything." She said it almost with a sneer. And he could read the unspoken remainder of the thought: I can get anything I want without you. Without your help.

He let her be. Some influence had turned her against him. Or rather had fanned to renewed heat the antagonism that was already latent there. It wasn't the liquor. It was more than that. The liquor was merely the lubricant.

He came back in a few minutes bringing her a cup of coffee he had boiled. It was a simple operation, and the only one he was capable of in that department. He had watched her do it, and thus he knew: pour water in, dribble coffee in, and stand it over the open scuttle hole.

And yet where some others—some others he had never known—might have recognized the wistful charm there was, unconsciously, in the effort, she rebelled and was disgusted almost to the point of nausea.

"Ah, you're so damned sweet it sickens me. Why don't you be a man? Why don't you give a woman a taste of your trouser belt once in a while? It might do the two of us a lot more good."

"Is that what they used to—?" he started to say coldly. He didn't finish it.

She drank the coffee down nevertheless. Nor thanked him for the trouble.

After a period of somnolent ingestion, it had its fortifying effect. She became voluble suddenly. As if seeking to undo whatever harmful impression her lack of inhibition had at first created. The antagonism disappeared, or at least submerged itself from sight.

"I had a drink," she admitted. "And I'm afraid it was too much for me. They insisted."

She waited to see if he would ask who "they" were. He didn't.

"I had started on my way home, this was at five, hours ago, and I think my mistake was in deciding to walk the entire way, instead of taking a carriage. I may have overtaxed myself. Or I may have been laced too tightly. I don't know. At any rate, as I was going along the street, I suddenly began to feel faint and everything swam before my eyes. I don't know what would have happened, I think I should have fallen to the ground. But fortunately a refined woman happened to be just a few steps behind me, on the same walk. She caught me in her arms and she held me up, kept me from falling. As soon as I was able to use my feet again, she insisted on taking me into her home, so that I might rest before going on. She lived only a few doors from there; we were almost in front of her house when it happened.

"Her husband came soon afterward, and they wouldn't hear of my leaving until they were sure I was fit. They gave me this drink, and it must have been stronger than I realized. They were really the kindest people. Their name is Jackson, I think she said. I'll point out the house to you sometime. They have a lovely home."

Warming to her recollection, she began describing it to him. "They took me into their front parlor and had me rest on the sofa. I wish you could see it. All kinds of money, you can tell. Oh, our place is nothing like it here. Louis XV furniture, gilded, you know, with mulberry upholstery. Full-length pier glasses on either side of the mantelpiece, and *gas* logs in the fireplace, iron logs that you can turn on or off—"

He could see in his mind's eye, as she spoke, the shabby, secretive hotel room, hidden away in one of the byways down around the railroad station; the shade drawn against discovery from the street; the clandestine rendezvous, unwittingly prolonged beyond the bounds of prudence in forgetfulness lent by liquor. She and the man, whoever he was—

The flame of an old love rekindled, with alcohol for fuel; the renewal of old ties, the whispers and the sniggered laughter, the reminiscences shared together— He could see it all, he was all but there, looking over their shoulders.

The factor of her physical unfaithfulness wasn't what shattered him the most. It was her mental treachery that desolated him; it was the far more irremediable of the two. She had betrayed him far more grievously with her mind and her heart, than she ever could have with her body. For he had always known he was not the first man to come into her life; but what he had always wanted, hoped and prayed for was to be the last.

It was easy, in retrospect, to trace the steps that had led to it. His lie about the money, a palliative that had only made things worse instead of bettering them. And then their bitter, brutal quarrel when he'd had to recant it at last, leaving her smarting and filled with spite and thirsting to requite the trick she felt he'd played on her. There must have been a letter North at about that time, and though he'd never seen it, he could guess what rancorous summons it contained: "Come get me; I can stand no more of this; take me out of it." And then, five days ago, the answer; the mysterious letter to "Mabel Greene."

She needn't go to the post office any more, stealthily to appropriate them. There would be no more sent. The sender was here with her now, right in the same town.

Yes, he thought with saddened understanding, I too would travel from a distance of five days away—or twenty times five days away— to be with a woman like Bonny. What man wouldn't? If the new love cannot provide for her, she has but to call back the old.

She saw by his face at last that he wasn't listening to her any more. "I'm chattering too much," she said lamely. "I'm afraid I'm palling on you."

"That you never do," he answered grimly. "You never pall on me, Bonny." And it was true.

She stifled a yawn, thrusting her elbows back. "I guess I may as well go up to bed."

"Yes," he agreed dully. "That might be best."

And as he heard her room door close upstairs, a moment after, his head sank slowly, inconsolably down into the refuge his bedded arms made for it upon the table top.

62

HE MADE no reference the following day to her liquored outing, much less the greater transgression that it had encased. He waited to see if she would attempt to repeat it (in his mind some half-formed intent of following her and killing the man when he found him), but she did not. If a succeeding appointment had been made, it was not for that next day.

She lay abed until late, leaving his needs to the tender care of the slovenly woman of all work who came in to clean and cook for them on alternate days, thrice a week. Even this disreputable malaise, which was purely and simply a "head," as they called it, the result of her over-indulgence, he did not tax her with.

When she came down at last to supper with him, she was amiable enough in all conscience. It was as if (he told himself) she had two selves. Her sober self did not know or recall the instinctive animosity her drunken self had unwittingly revealed the night before. Or, if it did, was trying to make amends.

"Did Amelia go?" she asked. It was a needless question, put for the sake of striking up conversation. The stillness in the kitchen and the fact that no one came in to wait at table, gave its own answer.

"At about six," he said. "She set our places, and left the food warming in there on the stove."

"I'll help you bring it in," she said, seeing him start out to fetch it.

"Are you up to it?" he asked.

She dropped her eyes at the rebuke, as if admitting she deserved it.

They waited on themselves. She shyly offered the bread plate to him across-table. He pretended not to see it for a moment, than relented, took a piece, grunted: "Thanks." Their eyes met.

"Are you very angry with me, Lou?" she purred.

"Have I reason to be? No one can answer that but yourself."

She gave him a startled look for a moment, as if to say "How much do you know?"

He thought to himself, What other man would sit here like this, meekly holding his peace, *knowing* what I do? Then he remembered what he himself had told Jardine on that visit to New Orleans: I must do as I must do. I can do no other.

"I was not very admirable," she said softly.

"You did nothing so terrible," he let her know, "once you were back here. You were a little sulky, that was all."

"And I did even less," she said instantly, *"before* I was back here. It was only here that I misbehaved."

How well we understand one another, he thought. We are indeed wedded together.

She jumped up and came around behind his chair, and leaning over his shoulder, had kissed him before he could thwart her.

His heart, like gunpowder, instantly went up, a flash of flame in his breast, though there was no outward sign to show it had been set off. How cheaply I am bought off, he thought. How easily appeased. Is this love, or is this a crumbling of my very manhood?

He sat there wooden, unmoving, hands to table, keeping them resolutely off her.

His lips betrayed him, though he tried to curb them. "Again," they said.

She lowered her face to his once more, and again she kissed him.

"Again," he said.

His lips were trembling now.

Again she kissed him.

Suddenly he came to life. He had seized her with such violence, it was almost an attack rather than an embrace. He pulled her bodily downward into his lap, and buried his face against hers, hungrily devoured her lips, her throat, her shoulders.

"You don't know what you do to me. You madden me. Oh, this is no love. This is a punishment, a curse. I'll kill any man who tries to take you from me—I'll kill you yourself. And I'll go with you. There shall be nothing left."

And as his lips repeatedly returned to find her, his only words of endearment, spaced each time with a kiss, were: "Damn you! . . . Damn you! . . . Damn you! No man should ever know you!"

When he released her at last, exhausted, she lay there limp, cradled in his arms. On her face the strangest, startled look. As though his very violence had done something to her she had not counted on.

She said, speaking trancelike, and slowly drawing her hand across her brow as if to restore some memory that was necessary to her, and that he had all but seared away, "Oh, Louis, you are not too safe to know yourself. Oh, darling, you almost make me forget—"

And then the crippled, staggering thought died unfinished.

"Forget whom?" he accused her. "Forget what?"

She looked at him dazed, as though not knowing she had spoken, herself. "Forget—myself," she concluded limply.

That is not whom she meant, he told himself with melancholy wisdom. But that word is the true one, none the less. I have no real rival, but in her. It is only herself that stands in the way of allowing her to love me.

She did not go out of the house the next day. Again he waited, again he held his breath, but she remained dutifully at hand. The appointment, if there was to be another, still hung fire.

Nor the next, either. The cleaning woman came, and coming down the stairs, he caught sight of them standing close together in the hall, as if they had been secretively conferring together. He thought he saw Bonny hastily fumble with her bodice, as if concealing something she had just received.

She would have carried it off, perhaps, but the Negress made a poor conspirator, she started theatrically back from her mistress, at sight of him, and thus put the thought in his head that something had passed between them.

There are other ways of communicating than by the rendezvous direct, he reminded himself. Perhaps the appointment I have been dreading so has already been kept, right before my eyes, on a mere scrap of paper.

Toward the latter part of their evening meal, that same day, she became noticeably pensive. Again the woman, the go-between of treachery, had gone, again they were alone together.

Her casual remarks, such as any meal shared by any two people is seasoned with, grew more and more infrequent. Soon she was making none at all of her own volition, only answering the ones he made. Presently even this proportion had begun to diminish, he was carrying the entire burden of speech for the two of them. All he got now was absent nods and vague affirmatives, while her thoughts were obviously elsewhere.

Finally it even affected her eating, began to slow and diminish it, so great was her own contemplation of whatever it was that her mind saw before it. And it must have seen something, for the mind by its very nature cannot contemplate vacancy. Her fork would remain in position to detach a portion of food, yet not complete the act for several minutes. Or it would halt in air, midway to her mouth, and again remain that way.

Then, quite as insolubly as it had begun, it had ended again, this abstraction. It was over. Whatever byways her train of thought had wandered down, were now closed off; or else it had arrived at its destination.

Her eyes now saw him when they rested on him.

"Do you recall that night we quarrelled?" she said, speaking softly. "You said something then about that old insurance policy you once took out when we were living on St. Louis Street. Was that true? Do you really still have it? Or did you just make that up, as you did about there still being money left?"

"I still have it," he said inattentively. "But it has lapsed, for lack of keeping up with the payments."

She was now busily eating, as if to make up for the time she had wasted loitering over her food before. "Is it completely worthless, then?"

"No, if the back payments were made up it would come into effect again. Not too much time has passed, I think."

"How much would be required?"

"Five hundred dollars," he answered impatiently. "Have we got that much?"

"No," she said docilely, "but is there any harm in asking?"

She pushed her plate back. She dropped her eyes, as if he had rebuffed her, and allowed them to rest on her clasped hands. Then

taking one finger in the others, she began slowly to twist and turn-
about the diamond ring that had once been his wedding gift to her.
She shifted it this way, that, speculatively, abstractedly.

Who could say whether she saw it or not, as she did so? Who
could say what she saw? Who could say what her thoughts were?
It told nothing. Just a woman's restless gesture with her ring.

"How would one go about it? I mean if we did have the money.
In what way is it done?"

"You simply send the money to New Orleans, to the insurance
company. They credit the payments against the policy."

"And then the policy comes into force again?"

"The policy comes into force again," he said somewhat testily,
annoyed by her persistence in clinging to the subject.

He had divined, of course, what her sudden interest was. She was
entertaining a vague hope that they could borrow against it in some
way, obtain money by that means.

"Could I see it?" she coaxed.

"Right now? It's upstairs somewhere, among my old papers.
But it's of no value, I warn you; the payments have not been maintained."

She did not press him further. She sat there meditatively fingering the diamond on her finger, shifting it a little bit this way, a little
bit that, so that it gave off sparks of brilliance in the lamplight.

She did not ask him for it nor about it again, but remembering
that she had, he set about looking for it on his own account. This
was not immediately, but some two or three days later.

He couldn't find it. He looked where he'd thought he had it, first,
and it wasn't there. Then he looked elsewhere, nor could he find it in
any of the other places he looked, either.

It must have been lost, during their many hurried moves from
place to place, in the course of hasty packing and unpacking. Or
else it would perhaps yet turn up, in some unlikely place he had
not yet thought of looking for it.

He desisted finally, with no great concern; with, if anything, a
mental shrug. Since it was worthless and could not have been borrowed against (which he thought had been the motive behind her
asking about it), there was no great loss, in any case.

He did not even mention to her that he could not locate it. There

was no reason to, for she too seemed to have forgotten her earlier
interest in it, as she sat there across the table from him, idly stroking
and contemplating her ringless hands.

Within the week, the cook and cleaning woman (one and the same)
whom they'd had until then, was suddenly gone, and they were
alone now in the house.

He asked her about this, after two successive days without her,
only noting her departure, man-like, after it had already taken place.
"What's become of Amelia?"

"I shipped her Tuesday," she said shortly.

"But I thought we owed her three or four weeks back wages. How
were you able to pay her?"

"I didn't."

"And she agreed to go none the less?"

"She had no choice, I ordered her to. She will get her money when
we have it ourselves, she knows that."

"Aren't you getting anyone else?"

"No," she said, "I can manage," and added something under her
breath that he didn't hear quite clearly.

"What?" he asked in involuntary surprise. He thought she had
said, "for the little time there is."

"I said, for a little time, that is," she repeated adroitly.

And manage she did, and far more successfully than in their Mobile
days, when she had first tried keeping her own house, and he had
had to take her back to the hotel for meals.

For one thing, she showed far more purpose than she had in those
far-off, light-hearted days; there was less of frivolity in her efforts
and a great deal more of determination. There was less laughter in
the preparations, maybe, but there was less dismay in the results.
She was not a child bride, now, playing at keeping house; she was
a woman, bent on acquiring new skills, and not sparing herself in
the endeavor.

For two full days she cooked, she washed the dishes, she swung a
broom all up and down the stairs. Then on the second night of this
apprenticeship—

He heard her scream out suddenly in the kitchen, and there was
the crash of a dropped dish as it slipped her hands. She had gone

in there to wash up after their meal, and he had remained behind browsing through the paper. Even the most enamored man did not offer to dry the dishes for a woman; it would have been as conventional as assisting at a childbirth.

He flung down his paper and darted in there. She was standing before the steaming washtub. "What is it, did you scald yourself?"

She was pointing, horrified.

"A rat," she choked. "It ran straight between my feet as I stood here. Into there." And with a sickened grimace, "Oh, the size of it! The horrid look!"

He took up a poker and tried to plunge it into the crevice at meeting-place of wall and floor that she had indicated. It balked. There was no depth to take it. It seemed a shallow rent in the plaster, no more.

"It could not have gone in there—"

Her fright turned to anger. "Do you call me a liar? Must it bite me and draw blood, for you to believe me?"

He dropped down now on all fours and began working the poker vigorously to and fro, in truth knocking out a hole if there had been none before.

She watched a moment. "What are you trying to do?" she said coldly.

"Why, kill it," he panted.

"That is not the way to be rid of them!" Her foot gave a clout of impatience against the floor. "You kill one, and there are a dozen left."

She flung down her apron, strode from the room and out to the front of the house. Sensing some purpose he could not divine, but disquieted by it, he put down the poker after a moment, struggled to his feet, and went after her. He found her in the hall, bonnetted and shawled, to his astonishment, in readiness to go out.

"Where are you going?"

"Since you don't know enough to, I am going to the pharmacist myself, to have him give me something that will exterminate them," she retorted ungraciously.

"Now? At this hour? Why, it's past nine; he'll be closed long ago."

"There is another, on the other side of town, that stays open until ten; you know that as well as I do." And she added with ill-humored decision, as though he were to blame for their presence in some way, "I will not go back into that kitchen and run the risk of being attacked. They will be running over our very bed, yet, while we sleep!"

"Very well, I'll go myself," he offered hastily. "No need for you to go, at this time of night."

She relented somewhat. She took off her shawl, though still frowning a trifle that he had not seen his duty sooner. She took him to the door.

"Don't go back in there," he cautioned, "until I come back."

"Nothing could prevail on me to," she agreed fearfully.

She closed the door after him.

She reopened it to call him back for an instant.

"Don't tell him who we are, what house it's for," she suggested in a lowered voice. "I would not like our neighbors to know we have rats in our house. It's a reflection on me, on my cleanliness as a housekeeper—"

He laughed at this typically feminine anxiety, but promised and went on.

When he came back he found that she had returned to her task in the kitchen none the less, in spite of his admonition and her own fear; a bit of conscientious courage which he could not help but secretly admire. She had, however, taken the precaution of bringing in the table lamp with her and placing it on the floor close by her feet, as a sort of blazing protection.

"Did you see any more since I was gone?"

"I thought I saw it come back to that hole, but I threw something at it, and it did not come out again."

He showed her what the druggist had given him. "This is to be spread around outside their holes and hiding places."

"Did he ask any questions?" she asked somewhat irrelevantly.

"No, only whether or not we had any children about the house."

"He did not ask which house it was?"

"No. He's rather elderly and doddering, you know; he seemed anxious to be rid of me and close for the night."

She half extended her hand.

"No, don't touch it. I'll do it for you."

He stripped off his coat, rolled up his shirt sleeves, and squatting on his haunches before the offending orifice, shook out a little powdery trail of the substance here and there. "Are there any others?"

"One over there, just a little back of the coal stove."

She watched, with housewifely approval.

"That will do. Not too much, or our feet will track it about."

"It has to be renewed every two or three days," he told her.

He put it on the shelf, at last, where the spice canisters were, but well over to the side.

"Make sure you wash your hands, now," she cautioned him. He had been about to neglect doing so, until her reminder. She held the huck-towel for him to dry them on, when he was through.

It was the following night that his illness really began. She discovered it first.

He found her looking at him intently as he closed his book at their retiring-time. It was a kindly scrutiny, but closely maintained. It seemed to have been going on for several moments before he discovered it.

"What is it?" he said cheerfully.

"Louis." She hesitated. "Are you sure you have been feeling well lately? I do not find you looking yourself. I do not like the way you—"

"I?" he exclaimed in astonishment. "Why, I never felt better in my life!"

She silenced him with tilt of hand. "That may well be, but your appearance belies it. More and more lately I have found you looking worn and haggard at times. I have not mentioned it before, because I didn't want to alarm you, but it has been on my mind for some time now to do so. It's very evident; I can see it quite plainly."

"Nonsense," he said, half laughing.

"I have an excellent remedy, if you will but let me give it to you. And I will join you in it myself, as an inducement."

"What?" he asked, amused.

She jumped up. "Starting tonight, we are to take an eggnog, the two of us, each night before retiring. It is an excellent tonic, they assure me, for fortifying the system."

"I am not an inval—" he tried to protest.

"Now, not another word, sir!" she ordered gaily. "I intend to prepare them right now, and you shall not hinder me. I have all the necessary ingredients right at hand, in there. Fresh-laid eggs, and the very best obtainable, at *twelve* cents a dozen, mind you! And the brandy we have in the house as well."

He couldn't help but smile indulgently at her, but he let her have her way. This was a new rôle for her; nursemaid to a nonexistent ailment. If it made her happy, why what was the harm?"

Her mood was amiable, sanguine, all gentleness and contrition now. She even bent to kiss him atop the head in passing.

"Was I cross to you before? Forgive me, Lou dear. You know I wouldn't want to be. A fright like that can make one into a harridan—" She went toward the kitchen, smiling back at him.

He could hear her cracking the eggs, somewhere beyond the open doorway, and crinkled his eyes appreciatively to himself.

Presently she. had even begun to hum lightly as she moved about in there, she was enjoying her self-imposed task so much.

Soon the humming gained words, had become a full song.

He had never heard her sing before. Laughter until now had always been her expression of contentment, never song. Her voice was light but true. Not very lyrical, metallic was the word that occurred to him instead, but she stayed adroitly on key.

> Just a song at twilight,
> When the lights are low—

Suddenly the song stopped, as if at something she were doing that required complete concentration. Measuring the brandy, perhaps. Be that as it might, it never resumed again.

She came in, holding one glass in each hand. Their contents pale gold in color, creamy in substance.

"Here. One for you, one for me." She offered them both. "Take whichever one you want." Then when he had, she tasted tentatively at the one that remained in her hand. "I hope I didn't put in too much sugar. Too much would sicken. May I try yours?"

"Of course."

She took it back from him, tasted at it in turn. It left a little white trace on her upper lip.

While she stood thus, holding both together, she turned her head toward the kitchen door.

"What was that?"

"What? I didn't hear anything."

She went back in again for a moment. She was gone a moment only. Then she returned to him.

"I thought I heard a sound in there. I wanted to make sure I had fastened the door."

She gave him back the one he had had in the first place, and which she had sampled.

"Since it has brandy in it," she said, "I suppose we should precede it with a toast." She nudged her glass to his. "To your better health."

She drained hers to the bottom.

He took a deep draught of his. He found it quite velvety and pleasurable. The liquor in it, with which she had been unsparing, gave a mellow warming effect to the stomach after it had lain there some moments.

"I wish all tonics were this palatable, don't you?" she remarked.

"It's quite satisfactory," he admitted, more to please her than because he saw any great virtue in it. It was after all, to his way of thinking, a bastard drink; neither honest liquor nor wholly medicine.

"You must drink it down to the bottom, that is the only way it will do you any good," she urged gently. "See, as I did mine."

To spare her feelings, after the trouble of having prepared it, he did so.

He tasted of his tongue, dubiously, after he had. "It is a little chalky, don't you find. A little—astringent. It puckers."

She took the glass from him. "That is because you are not used to milk. Have you never seen a baby's mouth after it feeds, all clotted and curdled?"

"No," he assured her with mock gravity, "you have not given me that pleasure."

They laughed together for a moment, in close-knit intimacy.

"I'll just rinse out the glasses," she said, "and then we can go up."

He slept soundly at first, feeling at the last the grateful glow the tonic had deposited in his stomach; albeit it seemed to confine itself to there, did not spread outward as in the case of unmixed liquor. But then after an hour or two he awakened into torment. The glow was no longer benign, it had a flaming bite to it. Sleep, once driven off, couldn't come near him again, held back by a fiery sword turning and turning in his vitals.

The rest of that night was an agony, a Calvary. He called out to her, more than once, but she was not near enough to hear him. Helpless and cut off from her, he sank his teeth into his own lip at last, and kept silent after that. In the morning there was dried blood all down his chin.

Across the room, over in the far corner, miles away, stood a chair with his clothes upon it. An ebony wood chair, with apricot-plush seat and apricot-plush back. Never heeded much before, but now a symbol.

Miles away it stood, and he looked longingly across the miles, the immeasurable distance from illness to health, from helplessness to ability, from death to life.

All the way across the room, many miles away.

He must get over there, to that chair. It was far away, but he must get over there to it somehow. He looked at it so intently, so longingly, that the rest of the room seemed to fog out, and narrowing concentric circles of clarity seemed just to focus on that chair alone, so that it stood as in the center of a bright disk, a bull's-eye, and all the rest was a blur.

He could not get out of bed legs upright, so he had to leave it head and shoulders first, in a slanting downward fall. Then there was a second, if less violent, fall as his hips and legs came down after the rest of him.

He began to sidle along the floor now, like some groveling thing, a worm or caterpillar, chin touching it at every other moment, hot striving breath stirring the nap of the carpet before him, like a wave spreading out from his face. Only, worms and caterpillars don't hope so, haven't such large hearts to agonize with.

Slowly, flowered pattern by flowered pattern. Each one like an island. And the plain-tinted background in between, each time like a channel or a chasm, leagues in width instead of inches. Some weaver somewhere, years ago, had never known his spaces would be counted so, with drops of human sweat and burning pain and tears of fortitude.

He was getting closer. The chair was no longer an entire chair; its top was too far up overhead now. The circle of vision, straight before him, level with the floor, showed its four legs, and the shoes under it, and part of the seat. The rest was lost in the blurred mists of height.

Then the seat went too, just the legs now remained, and he was getting very near. Perhaps near enough already to reach it with his arm, if he extended that full before him along the floor.

He tried it, and it just fell short. Not more than six inches remained between his straining fingertips and the one particular leg he was aiming them for. Six inches was so little to bridge.

He writhed, he wriggled. He gained an inch. The edge of the flower pattern told him that. But the chair, teasing him, tantalizing him, thefted the inch from him somehow. It still stood six inches away. He had gained one at one end, it had stolen it back at the other.

Again he gained an inch. Again the chair cheated him out of it, replaced it at the opposite end.

But this was madness, this was hallucination. It had begun to laugh at him, and chairs don't laugh.

He strained his arm down to its uttermost sinews, from finger-pad all the way back to socket. He swallowed up the six inches, at the price of years of his life. And this time it jerked back, abruptly. And there was another six inches, a new six inches, still between them.

Then through his blinding tears, he saw at last that there were one pair of shoes too many. Four instead of two. His own, under the chair, and hers, off to the side, unnoticed until now. She must have opened the door so deftly that he had not heard it.

She was arched over above him, from the side. One hand holding her skirts clear, to keep them from betraying her presence until the last possible moment. The other hand, to the back of the chair, had been keeping that from him, unnoticeably, each time he'd thought he'd reached it.

The jest must have been good. Her laughter came out, full-bodied, irrepressible, above him. Then she tried to check it, bite it back, for decency's sake, if nothing else.

"What did you want, your clothes? Why didn't you ask me?" she said mockingly. "You can have no possible use for them, my dear. You're not well enough."

And taking the chair in hand more fully this time, before his broken-hearted eyes swept it all the way back against the wall, a whole yard or two at once this time, hopeless of attainment ever.

But the trousers bedded on the seat fell off somehow, and in falling were kinder to him than she was, they fell upon his extended hand and let themselves be gripped, caught fast by it.

Now she bent to take them from him, and a brief, unequal contest of strength locked the two of them for a moment.

"They are no good to you, my dear," she said with the amusement one shows to a wilful child. "Come, let them be. What can you do with them?"

She drew them away from him little by little, plucked them from his bitterly clinging fingers by main strength at last.

Then when she had him back in bed again, she gave him a smile that burned, that seared, though it was only a sweet, harmless, solicitous thing, and the door closed after her.

Within its luminous halo the chair stood, ebony wood and apricot plush. All the way across the room, leagues away.

63

SHE CAME in later in the day and sat by him, cool and crisp of attire, pretty as a picture, a veritable Florence Nightingale, soothing, comforting him, ministering to his wants in every way. In every way but one.

"Poor Lou. Do you suffer much?"

He resolutely refused to admit it. "I'll be all right," he panted. "I've never been ill a day in my life. This will pass."

She dropped her eyes demurely. She sighed in comfortable agreement. "Yes, this will soon pass," she conceded with equanimity.

The image of a contented kitten that has just had a saucer of milk crossed his mind for a moment, for some strange reason; disappeared again into the oblivion from which it had come.

She fanned him with a palm-leaf fan. She brought a basin, and with a moist cloth gently laved and cooled his agonized brow and his heaving chest, each silken stroke lighter than a butterfly's wing.

"Would you like a cup of tea?"

He turned his head sharply aside, revolted.

"Would you like me to read to you? It may take your mind off your distress."

She went below and brought up a book they had there, of poems, and in dulcet, lulling cadences read to him from Keats.

> "O what can ail thee, knight-at-arms,
> So haggard and so woe-begone?"

And stopped to innocently inquire: "What does that mean, 'La Belle Dame Sans Merci'? The sound is beautiful but the words have no sense. Are all poems like that?"

He put hands over ears and turned his head away, excruciated.

"No more," he pleaded. "I can stand no more. I beg you."

She closed the book. She looked surprised. "I was only trying to entertain you."

When water alone would no longer quench his ravening, ever-increasing thirst, she went out and with great difficulty obtained a pail of cracked ice at a fishmonger's, and bringing it back, gave it to him piece by piece to chew and crunch between his teeth.

In every way she ministered to him. In every way but one.

"Get a doctor," he besought her at last. "I cannot fight this out alone. I must have help."

She kept her seat. "Shall we not wait another day? Is this my stout-hearted Lou? Tomorrow, perhaps, you will be so much better that—"

He clawed at her garments in mute appeal, until she drew back a little, to keep them from being disarranged. His face formed in weazened lines of weeping. "Tomorrow I shall be dead. Oh, Bonny, I cannot face the night. This fire in my vitals— If you love me, if you love me—a doctor."

She went at last. She was gone from the room a half-hour. She came back to it again, her shawl and bonnet on, and took them off. She was alone.

"You didn't—?" He died a little.

"He cannot come before tomorrow. He is coming then. I described to him what your symptoms were. He said there is no cause for alarm. It is a form of—of colic, and it must run its course. He prescribed what we are to do until he sees you— Come, now, be calm—"

His eyes were on her, bright with fever and despair.

He whispered at last: "I did not hear the front door close after you."

She gave him a quick look, but her answer flowed unimpeded.

"I left it ajar behind me, to save time when I returned. After all, I'd left you alone in the house. Surely—" Then she said, "You saw my bonnet on me just now, did you not?"

He didn't answer further. All his ravaged mind could keep repeating was:

I didn't hear the door close after her.

And then at last, slowly but at last, he knew.

Dawn, another dawn, a second one since this had begun, came creeping through the window, and with it a measure of tensile strength. Strength carefully hoarded a few grains at a time for this supreme effort that faced him now. Strength that was not as strength had used to be, of the body; strength that was of the spirit alone. The spirit, the will to live, to be saved; self-combustive, self-consuming, breathing purest oxygen of its own essence. And when that was gone, no more to replace it, ever.

Though nothing had moved yet but the lids of his eyes, this was the beginning of a journey. A long journey.

For a while he let his body lie inert, as it was. To begin it too soon would be to court interruption and discovery.

There; her step had sounded in the hall, she was coming out of her room. His lids dropped over his eyes, concealing them.

The door opened and he knew she was looking at him. His face wanted to cringe, but he held it steady.

What a long look. Would she never stop looking? What was she thinking? "You are such a long time dying?" Or, "My own love, are you not any better today?" Which was the true thought; which was the true she, and which his false dream of her?

She had entered the room. She was coming toward him.

She was bending over him now, in watchful attention. He could feel the warmth of her breath. He could smell the odor of the violet water she had sprinkled on herself only moments ago and which had scarcely yet dried. Above all, he could feel her eyes almost burning through his skin like a pair of sunray glasses held steady above shavings, to make them scorch and smoke and at last burst into flame. There was that concentration in their steady regard.

He must not stir, he must not flicker.

A sudden weight fell on his heart and nearly stopped it. It was her hand, coming to rest there, trying to see if it was still going. It fluttered like a bird caught under her outspread palm, and if she noted that, she must have thought it erratic and falteringly over-exerted. Suddenly her hand left him and he felt her fingers go instead to his eye, to try the reflex of that, perhaps. They gave him warning of their direction, for they brushed the skin there, just below it, a moment too soon. He rolled his pupils upward in their sockets, and a moment later when she had raised one lid and peered, only the sight-less white eyeball was revealed.

She took up his hand next and held it perpendicular, from elbow onward, her thumb pressed to its wrist. She was feeling his pulse.

She placed his hand back where she had drawn it from. And though she did not drop it, nor cast it down, yet to him there was somehow only too clearly expressed in the way she did it a fling of disappointment, a shortening of the gesture, as if in annoyance at finding him still alive, no matter by what test she applied.

Her garments whispered in withdrawal, fanned him softly in farewell. A moment later the door closed and she had gone from the room. The wooden stairs sounded off her descending tread, as if knuckles were lightly rapping on them step by step.

Now the flight back to life began.

Fortified by hoarded intensity, the earlier stages of it went well. He threw back the coverings, he forced his body slantingly sideward atop the bed, until it had dropped over the side.

He was now strewn prone on the floor at bedside; he had but to raise himself erect.

He rested a moment. Violent flickering pains, like low-burning log flames licking at the lining of his stomach, assailed him, went up his breathing passage as up a flue, and then died out again into the dull, aching torpor that was with him always and that was at least bearable.

He was on his feet now, and working his way alongside the bed down toward its foot. From there to the chair was an open space, with no support. He let go of the bed's footrail with a defiant backward fling, cast off into the unsupported area. Two untrammeled steps, a lurch. Two steps more, a third, he was hastening into a fall now. But if he could reach the chair first— He raced the distance to the chair against it, and the chair won. He reached it, gripped it, rocked it; but he stayed up.

He donned his coat, buttoning it over without any shirt below. That was comparatively easy. Trousers too; he managed them by sitting on the chair and drawing them from the floor up. But the shoes were an almost insuperable difficulty. To bend down to them in the ordinary way was an impossibility; the whole length of his body would have been excruciatingly curved.

He guided them, empty, first, by means of his feet, so that they stood perfectly straight, side by side. Then aimed each foot, one at a time, into the opening of its destined shoe, and wormed it in. But they gaped open, and it was impossible to proceed with them thus without imminent danger of being thrown from one step to the next.

He lay down on the floor, on his side. He scissored his legs, brought one up until he had caught his foot with both hands. There were five buttons on each shoe, but he chose only the topmost one, the most accessible, and forced it through its matching eyelet. Then changing legs, did it with the other.

Now he was erect again, accoutred to go, and there only remained lengthwise progress, over distance, to be accomplished. Only; he said the word over to himself with wistful irony.

Like a sleepwalker, taut at every joint; or like a mariner reeling across a storm-slanted deck, he crossed from chair to room door, and leaned inert there for a moment against its frame. Then softly took the knob in his grasp, and turned it, and held it after it was turned, so that it wouldn't click in recoil.

The door was open. He stepped through.

An oval window was let into the center of the hallway's frontal crosswall, to light the stairs and to give an outlook. A curtain of net was fastened taut across its pane.

He reached there, elbowing the wall for support, and put an eye to it, peering hungrily out into life. The curtain, brought so close to the eye's retina, acted like a filter screen; it dismembered the scene outside into small detached squares, separated by thick corded frames, which were the threads of the curtain, magnified at that short distance.

One square contained a segment of the front walk below, nothing else; all evenly slate-colored it was. The one above, again the walk, but at a greater outward distance now, a triangle of the turf bordering it beginning to cut in at the top, in green. The one still above that, turf and walk in equal proportions, with the white-painted base of one of the gate posts beginning to impinge off in the upper corner. And so on, in tantalizing fragments; but never the world whole, intact.

I want to live again, his heart pleaded; I want to live again out there.

He turned, and let the makeshift be, the quicker to be down below and at the original; and the stairs lay there before him, dropping away like a chasm, a serried cliff. His courage quailed at the sight for a minute, for he knew what they were going to cost. And the distant scrape of her chair in the kitchen below just then, added point to his dismay.

But he could only go onward. To go back was death in itself, death in bed.

He'd reached their tip now, and his eye went down them, all the cascading miles to their bottom. Vertigo assailed him, but he held his ground resolutely, clutching at the newel post with double grip as though it were the staff of life itself.

He knew that he would not be able to go down them upright, as the well did. He would overbalance, topple headfirst for sheer lack of leg support. He therefore lowered his own distance from the ground, first of all. He sat down upon the top step, feet and legs over to the second. He dropped them to the third, then lowered his rump to the second, like a child who cannot walk yet.

As he descended he was drawing nearer, ever nearer to her. For she was down there where he was going.

She sounded so close to him now. Almost, he could see before his very eyes everything she was doing, by the mere sound of it alone.

A busy little tinkering, ending with a tap against a cup rim: that meant she was stirring sugar into her coffee.

A creak from the frame of a chair: that meant that she was leaning forward to drink it.

A second creak: that meant that she had settled back after taking the first swallow.

He could hear bread crust crackle, as she tore apart a roll.

Crumbs lodged in her throat and she coughed. Then leaned forward to clear it with another swallow of her coffee.

And if he could hear her so minutely, how—he asked himself—could she fail to hear him; this stealthy rustling he must be making on the stairs?

He was afraid even to breathe, and he had never needed breath so badly.

At last the bottom, and he could only lie there a minute, rumpled as an empty sack that had fallen down from above, even if it had meant she would come out upon him any instant.

From where he was now there was only a straight line to travel, to the front door. But he knew he could not gain it upright. He had exhausted himself too much by now, spent himself too much on the way. How then gain support? How get there?

Struggling upright, it came to him of its own accord. He rotated his shoulders along the wall, turning now outward, next inward, then outward again, then inward—he *rolled* himself along beside the wall, and the wall supported him, and thus he did not fall, and yet progressed.

Midway there was an obstacle, to break his alliance with the wall. It was an antlered coatrack, its lower part a seat that extended far out, its upper part a tall thin panel of wood, set with a mirror. It was unsteady by its very nature, its proportions were untrue, he was afraid he would bring it down with him.

He circled his body awkwardly out and around it, holding it steady, so to speak, and got to the other side. But letting it go in safety was harder than claiming its support had been, and for a second or two he was held in a horrid trap there, afraid to take his hands off it, lest the sudden release of weight cause it to back and sway in revealing disturbance.

He took his near hand off it first, still held it on its far side, and that equalized the removal of pressure. Then cautiously he let go of it in the remaining place, and it did nothing but waver soundlessly for a moment or two, and then stilled again.

Safely free of it, he let himself down at last into a submerged huddle, sheltered now by its projection. Out of prostration, out of sheer inability to go on one additional step, and not out of caution, and yet it was that alone that saved him.

For suddenly, without any warning whatever, she had stepped to the kitchen doorway to the hall and was peering upward along the stairs. She even came forward, clambered up a few inquiring steps until she was in a position from which she could hear better, assure herself all was quiet. Then, satisfied, she came down again, turned about rearward, and went back to where she had been.

He removed the mangled length of shirting he had crushed into his mouth to stifle the hard breath that he would otherwise have been incapable of controlling, and it came away a watery pink.

Within moments after that, his lips were pressed flat against the seam of the outer door, in what was not meant for a kiss, but surely was one just the same.

So little was left to be done now, that he felt sure, even if his heart had already stopped beating and his body were already dead and cooling about him, he would still somehow have gone ahead and done it. Not even the laws of Nature could have stopped him now, so close to his goal.

The latch-tongue sucked back softly, and he waited, head still but held forward, to see if that little sound had reached her, would bring her out again. It didn't.

He pulled, and then, with a swimmingly uncertain motion, the door came away from its frame and an opening stood waiting.

He went through. He staggered forward and fell against the porch post outside, and stayed there inert, letting it hold him.

In a moment he had stumbled down the porch steps.

In another he had lurched the length of the walk, the gate post held him, as if he had fallen athwart it and been pierced through by it.

He was saved.

He was back in life again.

A curious odor filled his nostrils: open air.

A curious balm warmed his head, the nape of his neck: sunlight.

He was out on the public walk now. Swaying there in the white sunlight, his shadow on the ground swaying in accompaniment. Teetering master, teetering shadow. He marked for his own a tree growing at the roadside, a few short yards off.

He went toward it like an infant learning to walk; a grown infant. Short, stocky steps without bending the knees; kicking each foot up, in a stuttering prance; arms straight out before him to clasp the approaching objective. And then fell against its trunk, and embraced it, and clove there.

And then from there on to another tree.

And then another.

But there were no more trees after that. He was marooned.

Two women passed, market baskets over arms, and sodden there, he raised his hand to stay them, so that they might hear him long enough to give him help.

They swerved deftly to avoid him, tilted noses disdainfully in air, and swept on.

"Disgusting, at such an early hour!" he heard one say to the other.

"Time of day has no meaning for drunkards!" her companion replied sanctimoniously.

He fell down on one knee, but then got up again, circling about in one place like some sort of a broken-winged bird.

A man going by slowed momentarily, cast him a curious look, and Durand trapped his attention on that one look, took a tottering step toward him, again his hand raised in appeal.

"Will you help me, sir? I'm not well."

The man's slackening became a dead halt. "What is it, friend? What ails you?"

"Is there a doctor somewhere near here? I need to see one."

"There's one two blocks down that way, that I know of. I came past there just now myself."

"Will you lend me an arm just down that far? I don't think I can manage it alone—" The man split at times into two double outlines before his eyes, and then he would cohere again into just one.

The man consulted his pocket watch dubiously. "I'm late already," he grimaced. "But I can't refuse you on such a request." He turned toward him decisively. "Put your weight against me. I'll see that you get there."

They trudged painfully along together, Durand leaning angularly against his escort.

Once, Durand peered up overhead momentarily, at what everyone else saw every day.

"How wonderful the world is!" he sighed. "The sun on everything —and yet still enough left to spare."

The man looked at him strangely, but made no remark.

Presently he stopped, and they were there.

Out of all the houses in that town, or perhaps, out of all the doctors' houses in that town, it and it alone was not entered at ground level but had its entrance up at second-floor height. A flight of steps, a stoop, ran up to this. This was a new style in dwellings, mushrooming up in all the larger cities in whole blocks at a time, all of chocolate colored stone, and with their slighted first floors no longer called that, but known as "American basements."

Otherwise he could have been safely inside within a matter of moments after arriving before it.

But the good Samaritan, having brought him this far, at the cost of some ten minutes of his own time, drew a deep breath of private anxiety, took out his watch and scanned it once more, this time with every sign of furrowed apprehension. "I'd like to take you all the way up these," he confessed, "but I'm a quarter of an hour behind in an appointment I'm to keep, as it is. I don't suppose you can manage them by yourself— Wait, I'll run up and sound the bell a moment. Then whoever comes out can help you up the rest of the way—"

He scrambled up, dented the pushbutton, and was down again in an instant.

"Will you be all right," he said, "if I leave you now?"

"Thank you," Durand breathed heavily, clinging to the ornamental plinth at bottom of the steps. "Thank you. I'm just resting."

The man set off at a lumbering run down the street, back along the way they had just come, showing his lack of time to have been no idle excuse.

Durand, alone and helpless again, turned and looked upward toward the door. No one had yet come to open it. His eye traveled sideward to the nearest window, and in the lower corner of that was placed a placard both of them had neglected to read in its entirety.

Richard Fraser, M.D.
Consulting Hours: 11 to 1, Mornings—

The half-hour struck from some church belfry in the vicinity. The half-hour before eleven. Half-past ten.

Suddenly two white hands, two soft hands, cupped themselves gently, persuasively, to the slopes of his wasted shoulders, one on each side, from behind, and in a moment more she had insinuated herself around to the front of him, blocking him off from the house, blocking the house off from him.

"Lou! Lou, darling! What is it? What brings you here like this? What are you thinking of—I found the door standing open just now. I found you gone from your bed. I've been running through the streets—I saw you standing here, fortunately, from the block below—Lou, how could you do such a thing to me; how could you frighten me like this—?"

A door opened belatedly, somewhere near at hand, but her face was in the way, her face close to his blotted out the whole world.

"Yes?" a woman's voice said. "Did you wish something?"

She turned her head scarcely at all, the merest inch, to answer: "No, nothing. It was a mistake."

The door closed sharply, and life closed with it.

"Up," he breathed. "Up there. Someone—who can help me."

"Here," she answered softly. "Here, before you—the only one who can help you."

He moved weakly to one side to gain clearance, for an ascent he could never have made anyway.

She moved as he did, she stood before him yet.

He moved back again, waveringly.

She moved back again too, she stood before him always.

The waltz resumed, the slow and terrible waltz of death, there on those steps.

"Up," he pleaded. "Let me go up. The door. Have mercy."

Her voice was all compassion, she wept with honey. "Come back with me. My love. My poor dear. My husband." Her eyes too. Her hands, staying him so gently, so gently, he scarcely knew it.

"Be content," he wept weakly. "You've done enough. Give me this one last chance— Don't take it from me—"

"Do you think I would hurt you? Do you trust a stranger more than you would me? Don't you believe I love you, at *all?* Do you really doubt it that much?"

He shook his head bewilderedly. When the body's strength is spent, the mind's discernment dulls with it. Black is white and white is black, and the last voice that spoke is the true one.

"You do love me? You do, Bonny? In spite of all?"

"Can you ask that?" Her lips found his, there in broad daylight, in open street. Never was there a tenderer kiss, breathing such abnegation. Light as the wings of moths. "Ask your heart, now," she whispered. "Ask your heart."

"I've thought such terrible things. Bad dreams they must have been. But they seemed so real at the time. I thought you wanted me out of your way."

"You thought I was the cause of—your being ill like this?" Gambler to the end. She drew a step aside, the step that he had wanted her to take before. "My arms are here. The door is there above you. Now go to whichever one of us you want the most."

He took a swaying step toward her, where she now stood. His head fell upon her breast in ineffable surrender. "I am so tired, Bonny. Take me home with you."

Her breath stirred his hair. "Bonny will take you home."

She led him down the step, the one step toward salvation that was all he had been able to achieve.

Here and there, about them, the walks, the near one and the far, were dotted with a handful of curious passersby, halted in their tracks to watch the touching little scene, without knowing what it was about.

As he and she turned their way, these, their interest palling, set about resuming their various courses. But she called to one man, the nearest among them, before he could make good his departure.

"Sir! Would you try and find us a carriage? My husband is ill, I must get him home as soon as I can."

She would have moved a heart of stone. He tipped his hat, he hastened off on his quest. In a moment or two a carriage had come spanking around the lower turn, her envoy riding upright on the outside step.

It drew up and he helped her, supporting Durand on the one side while she, strong for all her diminutive height, sustained him bravely on the other. Between them they led him gently to the carriage, saw him comfortably to rest upon its seat; the stranger having to step up and into it backward, to do this, and then descend again from its opposite side after he had relinquished his hold on him.

She, settling down beside Durand, reached out and placed her own hand briefly atop the back of her anonymous helper's in accolade of tremulous gratitude. "Thank you, sir. Thank you. I do not know what I should have done without you."

"No one could do less, madam." He looked at her compassionately. "And may God be with the two of you."

"I pray He will," she answered devoutly as the carriage rolled off.

Behind it, on those same disputed steps, as it receded, a man now stood astraddle, a black bag in his hand, gazing after it with cursory interest, no more. He shrugged in incomprehension and completed his ascent, readying his key to put it to the door.

In the carriage on their brief run homeward no one could have been more solicitous.

"Lean down. Rest your head upon my lap, love. That will ease the jarring of the springs."

And in a moment, or so it seemed, they were back again at their own door; his long Calvary was undone, gone for nothing. He felt no pang; so complete, so narcoticizing, was the illusion of her love.

The driver, now, was the one to help her getting him down. And then she left him for a moment in his charge at their gate. "Stay here a moment, dear; hold to the post, until I find money to pay him. I came out without my purse, I was in such a fright over you." She ran in alone, the doorway stood empty for a brief while—(and he missed her, for that moment, he missed her)—then she came back again, still at full run, paid off the driver, took Durand into her sole charge.

Up onto the porch floor, a last receding flicker of the white sunlight draining off their backs, and in. A sweep of her arm, and the door was closed again behind him. Forever? For the last time?

Down the long dim hall, past the antlered hatrack, to the foot of the stairs. Every inch had once cost a drop of blood.

But love enfolded him, held him in its arms, and he didn't care. Or perhaps it was death already; and at onset of death you don't care either sometimes.

Then up the stairs a dragging step at a time. Her strength was superb, her will to help him indomitable.

At the landing, as the final turn began, he panted: "Stop here a moment."

"What is it?"

"Let me look back a moment at our sitting room, before we go up higher. I may never see it again. I want to say goodbye to it." He pointed with a wavering hand, out over the slanted rail. "See, there's the table that we sat by, so many evenings, before—this came upon me. See, there's the lamp, the very same lamp, that I always knew —when I was young and not yet married—would shine upon my wife's pretty face, just across from me. And it's shone on yours, Bonny. I thank it for that. Must it never shine on you for me again, Bonny?" His fingertips traced its outline, there against the empty distance that separated it from him. "The lamps of home, the lamps of love, are going out. For me they'll never shine again. Goodbye—"

"Come," she said faintly.

Back into the room again; the bier receiving back its dedicated dead.

She helped him to the bed, and eased him back upon it. Then drew up his feet after him. Took off his shoes, his coat, but nothing else. Then brought the covers slowly up and over him, sideward, like a winding sheet.

"Are you comfortable, Lou? Is your bed smooth enough?" She put hand to his brow. "This foolish foray of yours has cost you all your strength."

His eyes were fixed on her with a strange, melting softness. Like the eyes of a wounded dog, begging its release.

She turned hers away, then irresistibly they were drawn back again. "Why are you looking at me like that, my dear? What are you trying to say?"

He motioned to her with one finger to bend closer.

She inclined her head a little the better to hear what he had to say.

He reached up falteringly and stroked the fringe, the silken blonde bangs that curved before her cool smooth forehead.

Then he struggled higher, onto an elbow, as if cast upward by the ebb tide that was leaving him behind so rapidly.

"I love you, Bonny," he whispered fiercely. "No other one, no other love. From first to last, from start to finish. And beyond. Beyond, Bonny; do you hear me? Beyond. It will not end. *I* will, but it will not."

Her face came nearer still, slowly, uncertainly; like that of one dipping toward a new experience, feeling her way. Something had happened to it, was happening to it; he had never seen it so soft before. It was as if he were seeing another face, never born, peering shyly through the mask that had stifled it all these years; the face that should have been hers, that might have been—but that never had. The face of the soul, before the blasts of the world had altered it beyond recognition.

It came close to his, falteringly, through strange new latitudes of emotion, never traveled before.

There were tears in her eyes. It was no illusion; he saw them.

"Will a little love do, Lou?"

"Any amount."

"Then there *was* a moment in which I loved you. And this is it."

And the kiss, unforced, unsolicited, had all the bitter sweetness, the unattainable yearning, of a love that might have been. And he knew, his heart knew, it was the first she had ever really given him.

"That was enough," he smiled, content. "That was all I've ever wanted."

Claiming her hand, holding it in his, he fell into an uneasy sleep, a fever oblivion, for a while.

When he awoke, the dregs of daylight were settling in the west, like a fine white ash; the day was past. Her hand was still in his, and she was sitting there, her face toward him. She seemed not to have moved in all those hours, to have endured it, this thing new to her—pain for someone else's sake—without demur; to have kept her vigil with no company other than the sight of his deathbound face—and whatever thoughts that had brought her.

He released her hand. "Bonny," he sighed, agonized. "Get me another of those tonics, now. I am ready for it. It's better—that you do, I think—"

Involuntarily, she drew her head back sharply for a moment. Held her gaze to his. Then at last inclined it again to where it had been before.

"Why do you ask for it now? I haven't offered it."

"I'm in pain," he said simply. "I can't endure much more of it." And turned a little this way, then turned a little that. "If not in kindness, then in charity—"

"Later," she said evasively. "Don't talk that way, don't say such things."

Sweat started out on his face. His breath hissed through his nostrils. "When I did not want them, you urged them on me— Now that

I plead with you, you deny me—" He heaved his body upward, then allowed it to fall back again. "Now, Bonny, now; I can't bear any more. This is as good a time as any. Why wait for the night to be further advanced? Oh, spare me the night, Bonny, spare me the night! It is so long—so dark—so lonely—"

She stood slowly, absently rubbing her frozen hand. Then with even greater slowness moved toward the door. She opened it, then stopped there to look back at him. Then went out.

He heard her going down the stairs. And twice he heard her stop, as though impulse had flagged; and then go on again, as she fanned it back to life once more.

She was gone about ten minutes in all. Ten minutes of hell, while flames licked at him all over.

Then presently the door opened and she had returned. She was carrying it in her hand. She came to him and set it down upon the stand, a little to the side of him, beyond easy reach.

"Don't— Not yet—" she said in a stifled voice, when he tried to reach for it. "Let it wait a while. A little later will do."

She lit the lamp, and then went over by the fireplace to fling the match away. Then she remained there by it, looking down into it. He knew she was not looking at anything there was there before her to see; she was in a revery that saw nothing.

His revery, on its part, saw everything. Everything again. Again he waltzed with her at Antoine's on their wedding night—"A waltz in sunlight, love; in azure, white and gold." Again her playful query sounded through their marriage door— "Who knocks" "Your husband." Again she stood revealed against the lighted midnight entryway—"Come into your wife's bedroom, Louis." Again they walked the seafront promenade at Biloxi, arm in arm, and the breeze swept off his hat, and she laughed to see him chase it, herself a spinning cyclorama of windswept skirts. Again he raised his arms above her sleeping form to let hundred-dollar bills flutter down upon it. Again—

Again, again, again—for the last time.

The truly cruel part of death is not the end of the body; it is the expiration of all memories.

A bright light, like a hot, flickering, yellow star, burned through the ghostly mesh of his death dreams. He looked over and she was standing sideward to the fireplace, holding a burning brand outthrust toward it in her hand. Yet not a stick or twig; it was a scroll of tightly furled paper. And as the flame slowly slanted upward toward her hand, she deftly reversed it, taking it now by the charred end that had already been consumed and allowing the other to burn.

Then threw it down at last, and thrusting out her foot, trod upon its remnants here and there and the next place with little pats of finality.

"What are you doing, Bonny?" he whispered feebly.

She did not turn her head, as if it were of no consequence to her whether or not he had seen. "Burning a paper."

"What paper?"

Her voice had no tone. "A policy of insurance—upon your life—payable for twenty thousand dollars."

"It was not worth the trouble. It lacked force, I told you that."

"It was in force again just now. I pledged my ring and made up the payments."

Suddenly he saw her cover her face with the flats of her hands as if, even after having burned it, she still could not bear the remembered aftersight of it.

He sighed, but without much emotion. "Poor Bonny. Did you want the money that badly? I would have—" He didn't finish it.

He lay there for a moment or two after that, inert.

"I'd better drink this now," he said softly, at last.

He strained until his arm could reach the glass. He clasped it, took it up.

64

SUDDENLY SHE had turned, thrown herself toward him. He hadn't known the human form could move so quickly. But she was so deft, she was so small. Her hand flashed out, a white missile before his face. The tumbler was gone from his grasp. Glass riddled on the floor somewhere offside beyond his ken.

Her face seemed to melt into shapeless weeping lines, like a face seen through rain running down a pane. She caught him to her convulsively, crushing his face against her soft breast. He hadn't known her embrace could hold that much strength. She'd never loved him enough to exert it to the full before.

"Oh, merciful God," she cried out wildly. "Look down and forgive me! Stop this terrible thing, turn it back, undo it! Lou, my Lou! Only now I see it! Oh, my eyes are open, open now at last! What have I done?"

She dropped to her knees before him, as she had that night in Biloxi when they first came together again. But how different now; how false, how studied her pleas, her posture then, how inconsolable her passion of remorse now, a veritable paroxysm of penitence, that nothing, no word of his, could assuage.

Her sobbing had the wild, panting turbulence of a child's, strangling her words, rendering her almost incoherent. Perhaps this was a child crying now, a newborn self in her, a little girl held mute for twenty years, only now belatedly finding voice.

"I must have been mad— Out of my mind— How could I have listened to such a scheme? But when I was with him, I saw only him, never you— He brought out that old bad self in me— He made wrong things seem right, or just something to snicker at—"

Her fingers, pleading, traced the outlines of his face; trembling, felt of his lips, of his lidded eyes, as if seeking to restore them to what they had been. Nothing, no voracious kisses seeking him out everywhere, no splurge of teardrops falling all over him, could bring him back.

"I've killed you! I've killed you!"

And rebel to the end, fell prone and beat upon the floor with her fist, in helpless rebellion at the trickery fate had practised on her.

Then suddenly her weeping stopped. As suddenly as though a stroke of fear had been laid across her bowed head. Her pummelling hand stilled.

Her head came up. She was bated, she was watchful, she was crafty. Of what he could not tell. She turned and looked behind her at the window, in dreadful secretive apprehension.

"Nobody shall take you from me," she said through clenched teeth. "I'll not give you up. Not for anyone. It's *not* too late, it's *not*! I'm going to get you out of here, where you'll be safe— Hurry, get your things. We'll go together. I have the strength for the two of us. You're going to live. Do you hear me, Lou? You're going to live—yet."

She sidled up beside the window, creeping along the wall until she had gained an outer edge of it; then peered narrowly out, using the slit between curtain edge and wall. He saw her nod slightly to herself, as if in confirmation of something she had expected to see.

"What is it?" he whispered. "Who's out there?"

She didn't answer. Suddenly she drew her head back sharply, as if fearful she had been detected just then from the outside.

"Shall I put out the lamp?" he asked.

"No!" She motioned to him horrified. "For God's sake, no! *I* was to have done that. It will be taken for a signal that—it's over. Our only chance is to go now, and leave it still on, as if—as if we were here yet."

She came running back to him, yet not forgetting even as she did so to throw still another backward glance of dread at the window; she settled down beside him with a billowing-out of her dress, took hold of his untended foot, raised it, while he still strove valiantly with the first.

"Quickly, your other shoe! There, that's all— No time for more."

She helped him quit his sitting position on the edge of the bed, held him upright on his feet beside her, like some sort of an inanimate mannikin or rigid toy soldier that would fall over if her hands quitted him for just an instant and left him to himself.

"Lean on me, I'll help you. There! There! Move your feet, that's it! Oh, Lou, try this one time more. Just this one time more. You did it before. This time we're *together*, we're going together. This time it's our love itself that's running away—for its very life."

He smiled at her, as the floor slowly crept by beneath their tottering feet, inch by painful inch.

"Our love," he whispered bravely. "Our love, running away. Where are we going?"

"Any train, anywhere. Only let us get out of this house—"

She struggled heroically with him, as though she were the spirit of life itself, contesting with the spirit of death that sought to possess him. Now holding him back when he inclined too far forward, now drawing him on when he swayed too far backward. Out the room door and along the upper hall. But on the stairs once she nearly lost him. For a moment there was a terrible equipoise, while he hung forward, threatening to topple downward, all the way downward, head first, and she strained her small body backward to the last ounce of its strength, striving to regain the balance that had been incautiously lost.

Not a whimper came from her in that frightful moment, and surely had he gone downward to his own destruction, she would have clung to him to the end, gone down with him to her own, rather than release him. But a strength came into her arms that had never been in them before, and slowly her squeezing pull, her embrace of desperation, righted him, drew him back against her, and equilibrium was regained.

And then, as they rested half-recumbent against the rail a moment, she with her back to it, he with his head pillowed on her breast, she found time to stroke his hair back soothingly from his brow and whisper: "Courage, love. I will not let you fall. Is it very hard for you?"

"No," he murmured wanly, rolling his eyes upward toward her downturned face above him, "because you are with me."

Downward once more then, more cautiously this time, step by mincing step, like a pair of ballet dancers locked in one another's arms, pointed toe following pointed toe in a horrid, groping, blinded sort of pas de deux.

As they neared the bottom, were within one last step of it, she suddenly stopped, frozen. And in the silence, over the rise and fall of their two breaths, they both heard it.

There was a low, urgent tapping going on against the front door. Very stealthy it was, very secretive. Meant only to be caught by a single pair of ears, no other. A pair forewarned to expect it, to listen for it. Two fingers at the most, perhaps only one, kept striking at the woodwork; scratching at it, scraping at it, it might almost have been said, so softened was their impact.

A peculiar whistle sounded with it. Also modulated very low, very guardedly. Little more than a stirring of the breath against a wavering upper lip. Plaintive, melancholy, like the sound of a baby owl. Or a lost wisp of night wind trying to find its way in.

It was intermittent. It waited. Then sounded again. Waited. Sounded again.

"Sh, don't make any noise!" He could feel her arms tighten protectively about him. As if instinctively seeking to safeguard him against something. Something that she understood, knew the meaning of, he didn't. "The back way," she breathed. "We'll have to go out by there— Hold your breath, love. For the love of heaven, don't make a sound or—we'll both be dead in here where we stand."

Cautiously, straining against one another, as much now to insure their mutual silence as before now it had been to maintain his uprightness, they quitted the stairs, crept rearward on the lower floor, into the dining room. She halted him there for a preciously spared moment, to reach for a decanter of stimulant, give it a twisting shake, extract the glass stopper and moisten his lips with it, while she still continued to hold him within the curve of her other arm.

"I'm afraid to give you too much," she mourned. "You are so spent."

"My love's beside me," he promised, as if speaking to himself. "I won't fail."

They moved on into the unlighted kitchen beyond, swimming submerged in the blue tide of night, but with the curtained glass square of its door, the back way out, peering at them, distinguishable in the dimness.

He heard the bolt scrape softly back beneath her diligently groping fingers. Then the door moved inward, and the coolness of escape was grateful in their faces.

The last sound behind them, traveling through the whole length of the house from its front, was that low tapping, recommencing again after a grudging wait. A little more hurried now than before, a little more insistent. And with it the whistle, with its secretive message, that seemed to say: "Open to me. Open. You know who I am. You know me. Why do you delay?" A little sharper now, a little more importunate, as its patience shortened.

He did not ask her who it was. There were so many things in life it was too late now to ask, too late now to know. There was only one thing he wanted to know, he needed to know, and that at long last had been told him: she loved him.

They floundered out into the backyard of their house, and out through the gate that led into it, from the lane that ran behind the backs of all these houses; down that to its mouth, and from there onto the sideward street. Then along that, and around the turn,

and into the street that ran behind the one their house had faced
upon.

"The station," she kept saying. "The station— Oh, try, Lou. It's
just a few short streets ahead. We'll be safe, if we can only reach it.
There's always someone there, day or night— There are lights there,
no one can hurt us there. A train— Any train, to anywhere—"

Any train, his heart kept saying in time to its desperate pounding, to anywhere.

On and on and on, two lurching figures, breaths sobbing in their
throats; reeling drunken, yes, drunken with the will to live and
love, in peace. No eye to see them, no hand to help them.

It was in sight already, across the open square ahead, the station
square, the hub of the town,—or so she told him, he could no longer
see that far before him—when suddenly the combination of their
overtaxed strengths gave out, her arms, her will, could do no more,
and he fell flat there in the dust beside her.

She tried desperately to bring him up again, but she'd weakened
so that his inertness could only bring her down half recumbent beside him, instead, as if he were pulling at her, not she at him.

"Don't waste time," he sighed. "I can't— Not a step further."

She struggled upright again, drove fingers distractedly through
her hair, looked this way, that.

"I've got to get you in out of the open! Oh, my love, my love, we
may be caught yet if we stay here too long—"

Then bending to his face, to give him courage with a kiss, ran
on and left him there where he was. She disappeared into a building
fronting on the square, with a lighted gas bowl over its doorway and
the legend: "Furnished Rooms for Travelers."

In a moment she returned to view again, beckoning to someone
within to hasten out after her. She came running back toward him,
without waiting, holding her skirts with both hands at once, bunched
forward and aloft to give her feet the freedom they needed. Behind
her appeared a shirtsleeved man, struggling into his coat as he
emerged. He set out after her.

"Here," she cried. "Over this way. Here he is."

He joined her beside the loglike figure on the ground.

"Help me get him to one of your rooms."

The man, a beefy stalwart, lifted him bodily in both arms, turned
with him to face toward the lodging house. She ran around him from

one side to the next, trying to be of help, trying to take hold of Durand's feet.

"No, I can manage," the man said. "You go first and hold the door."

The black sky over the station square, pocked with stars, eddied about this way and that just over Durand's upturned eyes. He had a feeling of being very close to it. Then it changed to gaslight pallor on a plaster ceiling. Then this slanted off upward, gradually dimming, and he was being borne up stairs. He could hear the quick tap of her deft feet, pressing close behind them, in the spaces between his carrier's slower plod. And once he felt his dangling hand caught up swiftly for a moment by two small ones, and the fervent print of a pair of velvety lips placed on it.

"I'm sorry it's so high up," the man said, "but that's all I have."

"No matter," she answered. "Anything. Anything."

They passed through a doorway, the ceiling dark at first, then gradually brightening to tarnished silver following the soft, spongy fluff of an ignited gas flow. Their shadows swam about on it, then blended, faded.

"Shall I put him on the bed, madam?"

"No," Durand said weakly. "No more beds. Beds mean dying. Beds mean death." His eyes sought hers, as the man lowered him to a chair, and he smiled through them. "And I'm not going to die, am I, Bonny?" he whispered resolutely.

"Never!" she answered huskily. "I'll not let you!" She clenched her tiny fists, and set her jaw, and he could see sparks of defiance in her eyes, as if they were flint stones.

"Shall I get you a doctor, madam?" the man asked.

"Nothing more this minute. Leave us alone together. I'll let you know later. Here, take this for now." She thrust some money at him through the door. "I'll sign the registry book later."

She locked it, came running back to Durand. She dropped before him in an imploring attitude.

"Louis, Louis, did I once want money, did I once want fine clothes and jewels? I'd give them all at this minute to have you stand strong and upright on your legs before me. I'd give my very *looks* themselves—" she clawed at her own face, dragging its supple cheeks forward as if seeking to transfer it toward him, "—and what more have I to give?"

"Make your plea to God, dear, not to me," he said faintly, gently. "I want you as you are. I wouldn't change you even for life itself. I don't want a good woman, a noble woman. I want my vain, my selfish Bonny— It's you I love, the badness and the good alike, and not the qualities they tell us a woman should have. Be brave in this: don't change, ever. For I love you as I know you, and if God can love, then He can understand."

The tears were streaming in reckless profusion from her eyes, she who had never wept in all her life; the tears of a lifetime, stored up until now, and now splurging wildly forth all in one burst of regret.

His fingers reached tremulously to trace their course. "Don't weep any more. You've wept so much these past few minutes. I wanted to give you happiness, not tears."

She caught her breath and struggled with it, restraining it, quelling it. "I'm so new at love, Louis. It's only a half-day now. Only a half-day out of twenty-three years. Louis," she asked like a child in wonderment, "is this what it's like? Does it always hurt so?"

He remembered back along their story, spent now. "It hurts. But it's worth it. It's love."

A strange snorting sound came from the outside, somewhere near by, through the closed window, as if a great bull-like beast, hampered with clanking chains, were muzzling the ground.

"What was that?" he asked vaguely, raising his head a little.

"It's a train, out there somewhere in the dark. A train, coming into the station, or shuttling about in the yards—"

His arms stiffened on the chair rests, thrusting him higher.

"Bonny, it's for us, it's ours. Any train, to anywhere— Help me. Help me get out of here. I can do it, I can reach it—"

She had lived by violence all her life; by sudden change, and swift decision. She rose to it now on the instant, she was so used to it. She was ready at a word. Instantly her spirit flared up, kindled by his.

"Anywhere. Even New York. You'll stand by me there if they—"

She thrust her arm around behind him, helped him rise from the chair. Again the endless flight was about to recommence. Tight-armed together, they took a step forward, toward the door. A single one—

He fell. And this time there was a finality to it that could not be mistaken. It was the fall to earth of the dead. He lay there flat, unresisting, supine, waiting for it. He lay face up, looking at her with despairing eyes.

Her face swiftly dipped to his.

"No time," he whispered through immobile lips. "Don't speak. Put your lips to mine. Tell me goodbye with that."

Kiss of farewell. Their very souls seemed to flow together. To try to blend forever into one. Then, despairing, failed and were separated, and one slipped down into darkness and one remained in the light.

She drew her lips from his, for sheer necessity of breathing. There was a smile of ineffable contentment left on his, there where her lips had been.

"And that was my reward," he sighed.

His eyes closed, and there was death.

A shudder ran through her, as though the throes of dying were in her herself. She shook him, trying to bring back the motion that had only just left him, but left him forever. She pressed him to her, in desperate embrace that he was no longer within, only some dead thing he had left behind. She pleaded with him, called to him. She even tried to make a bargain with death itself, win a delay.

"No, wait! Oh, just one minute more! One minute give me, and then I'll let him go! Oh, God! Oh, Someone! Anyone at all! Just one more minute! I have something I want to tell him!"

No desolation equal to that of the pagan, suddenly bereft. For to the pagan, there is no hereafter.

She flung herself downward over him, and her hair, coming unbound, flowed over him, covering his face. The golden hair that he had loved so, made a shroud for him.

Her lips sought his ear, and she tried to whisper into it, for him alone to hear. "I love you. I love you. Can't you hear me? Where are you? That is what you always wanted. Don't you want it now?"

In the background of her grief, distant, dim, unheeded, echoes seemed to rise around her. A muffled pounding on the door, clamoring voices backing it, conjured there now, at just this place, this moment, who knows how? Perhaps by long-pent suspicions of neighbors overflowing at last into denunciation; perhaps that other crime in Mobile long, long ago, overtaking them at last—too late, too late. For she had escaped, just as surely as he had.

"Open, in there! This is a police order! Open this door, do you hear?"

Their meaning could not impress, their threat could not affright. For she was somebody else's prisoner now. She had escaped them.

Moaning anguished into a heedless ear: "Oh, Louis, Louis! I have loved you too late. Too late I have loved you."

The knocking and the clamor and the grief faded out, and there was nothing left.

"And this is my punishment."

The soundless music stops. The dancing figures wilt and drop. The Waltz is done.

THE END

FOR THE BEST IN PAPERBACKS, LOOK FOR THE

In every corner of the world, on every subject under the sun, Penguin represents quality and variety—the very best in publishing today.

For complete information about books available from Penguin—including Puffins, Penguin Classics, and Arkana—and how to order them, write to us at the appropriate address below. Please note that for copyright reasons the selection of books varies from country to country.

In the United Kingdom: Please write to *Dept. JC, Penguin Books Ltd, FREEPOST, West Drayton, Middlesex UB7 0BR.*

If you have any difficulty in obtaining a title, please send your order with the correct money, plus ten percent for postage and packaging, to *P.O. Box No. 11, West Drayton, Middlesex UB7 0BR*

In the United States: Please write to *Consumer Sales, Penguin USA, P.O. Box 999, Dept. 17109, Bergenfield, New Jersey 07621-0120.* VISA and MasterCard holders call 1-800-253-6476 to order all Penguin titles

In Canada: Please write to *Penguin Books Canada Ltd, 10 Alcorn Avenue, Suite 300, Toronto, Ontario M4V 3B2*

In Australia: Please write to *Penguin Books Australia Ltd, P.O. Box 257, Ringwood, Victoria 3134*

In New Zealand: Please write to *Penguin Books (NZ) Ltd, Private Bag 102902, North Shore Mail Centre, Auckland 10*

In India: Please write to *Penguin Books India Pvt Ltd, 706 Eros Apartments, 56 Nehru Place, New Delhi 110 019*

In the Netherlands: Please write to *Penguin Books Netherlands bv, Postbus 3507, NL-1001 AH Amsterdam*

In Germany: Please write to *Penguin Books Deutschland GmbH, Metzlerstrasse 26, 60594 Frankfurt am Main*

In Spain: Please write to *Penguin Books S. A., Bravo Murillo 19, 1° B, 28015 Madrid*

In Italy: Please write to *Penguin Italia s.r.l., Via Felice Casati 20, I-20124 Milano*

In France: Please write to *Penguin France S. A., 17 rue Lejeune, F–31000 Toulouse*

In Japan: Please write to *Penguin Books Japan, Ishikiribashi Building, 2–5–4, Suido, Bunkyo-ku, Tokyo 112*

In Greece: Please write to *Penguin Hellas Ltd, Dimocritou 3, GR–106 71 Athens*

In South Africa: Please write to *Longman Penguin Southern Africa (Pty) Ltd, Private Bag X08, Bertsham 2013*